CERTAIN PEOPLE OF IMPORTANCE

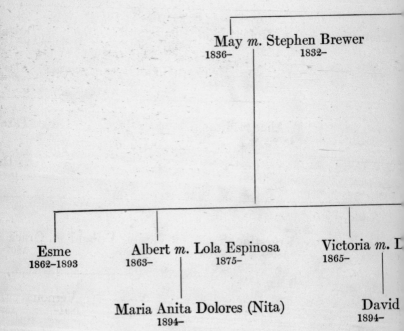

May *m.* Stephen Brewer
1836–   1832–

Esme
1862–1893

Albert *m.* Lola Espinosa
1863–   1875–

Maria Anita Dolores (Nita)
1894–

Victoria *m.* L
1865–

David
1894–

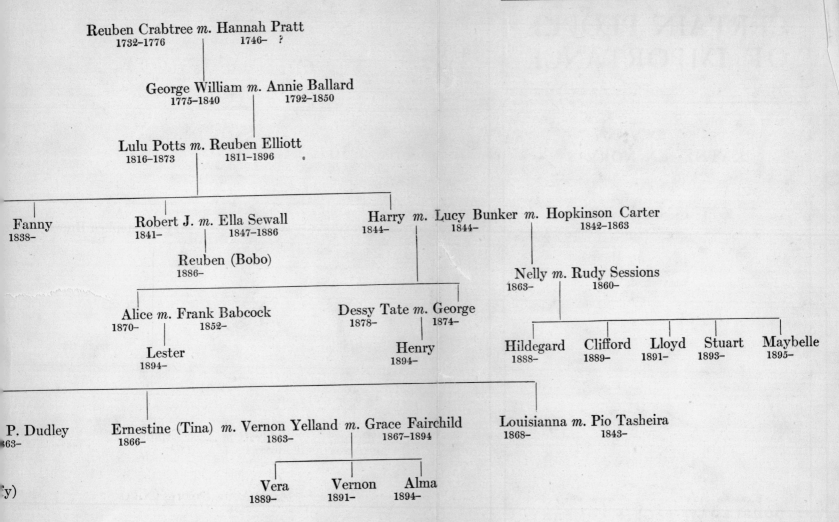

Reuben Crabtree *m.* Hannah Pratt
1732–1776   1746– ?

George William *m.* Annie Ballard
1775–1840   1792–1850

Lulu Potts *m.* Reuben Elliott
1816–1873   1811–1896

Fanny
1838–

Robert J. *m.* Ella Sewall
1841–   1847–1886

Harry *m.* Lucy Bunker *m.* Hopkinson Carter
1844–   1844–   1842–1863

Reuben (Bobo)
1886–

Nelly *m.* Rudy Sessions
1863–   1860–

Alice *m.* Frank Babcock
1870–   1852–

Dessy Tate *m.* George
1878–   1874–

Lester
1894–

Henry
1894–

Hildegard   Clifford   Lloyd   Stuart   Maybelle
1888–   1889–   1891–   1893–   1895–

P. Dudley
863–

Ernestine (Tina) *m.* Vernon Yelland *m.* Grace Fairchild
1866–   1863–   1867–1894

Louisianna *m.* Pio Tasheira
1868–   1843–

Vera   Vernon   Alma
1889– 1891–   1894–

y)

NEALOGY OF THE CRABTREE FAMILY

CERTAIN PEOPLE
OF IMPORTANCE

BY
KATHLEEN NORRIS, (Thompson) 1880-

GARDEN CITY   NEW YORK
DOUBLEDAY, PAGE & COMPANY
1922

TO

C I G I

1909–1922

If she is fair—the shining yacht that moves,
 Between the blue sky and the bluer bay,
 Erect and gallant on her virgin way
Into the unknown seas that yet she loves —

Then what is this more seasoned ship, who hails
 From the long cruise of years—hard years and bright,
 To find again the shining harbour light
In her old port, whence first she tried her sails?

CERTAIN PEOPLE
OF IMPORTANCE

Certain People of Importance

CHAPTER I

THE beginnings of the family in America are lost, unfortunately, in the obscurity that hangs over the old records and the older homestead of a few insignificant New England villages. That there were Crabtrees in America before the war of the Revolution is provable, but it has never been quite easy to connect the Charlestown and the Springfield families of that name with that of one Reuben Crabtree, a wheel-maker of Mendon, Massachusetts, whose marriage to Hannah Pratt of Bridgewater, Connecticut, took place in the year 1760.

Of Hannah Pratt we catch occasional glimpses in the mournful biography of her sister, Eliza, whose marriage to a missionary, whose heroic labours in the mission fields of darkest Sarawan, and whose edifying death, were made the subject matter of a small green cloth-bound volume printed in the year 1791. Eliza, whose life as the fourth wife of an extremely stern and orthodox clergyman was fraught with bodily miseries only partially mitigated by the tremendous spiritual benefits she enjoyed in his company, duly added three languishing babes to his family of thirteen motherless children, before further duly adding her name quietly and meekly to the other names on his family tombstone.

But before this, in her occasional letters, she frequently mentions her sister, the wife of Reuben Crabtree, the maker of wheels, who remained quietly in the little, plain-faced house under the magnificent elms behind the forge, and is never addressed by the missionary's wife except in connection with domestic calamities.

Eliza, writing courageously from Sarawan of fire, pestilence, and the attacks of head-hunters, does not fail to sympathize

1

with Hannah, upon the loss of her "fine boys." "Safer, ah, safer far, with the Comforter who *never faileth* than are the four left you!" says Eliza, passionately, perhaps thinking of her own lost darlings. She also commiserates her sister upon the failure of her husband's business hopes; the Reuben Crabtree family had migrated to Mendon again, after an unsuccessful experience in Bridgewater, and from Mendon they presently moved to Bedford, New Hampshire. Here a seventh child, George William, was born, and it was from Bedford that the father of the family, the first Reuben, went forth to battle in 1775.

He never returned, and it is probable that the widow married again, for there is no further record of her under the old name. The missionary aunt came back, but only to die patiently and agonizingly of cancer in her own old home: "so sweet to see Hannah and her beautiful children!" gasps Eliza, almost at the very end. She does not mention their names or ages, and we find no trace of George William for some years. But in 1808, say the Bedford records, there was the sale of a small section of land from George W. Crabtree to William Elder for $161.00, and shortly afterward G. W. Crabtree is married to Annie Ballard, of Binghamton, New York.

George William Crabtree, at the time of his marriage, was about thirty-three years old: it is possible that there was an earlier marriage, for those were lonely days for a bachelor whose business of store-keeper brought him in contact with all the youth and beauty of his neighbourhood. But of an earlier marriage there is no traceable record, and George apparently became a settled and self-respecting citizen rather late in life.

He moved his Annie to the far west, almost to Chicago, and in Lawrence County chopped out a clearing before his first little cross-roads store. Annie knew bitter cold in the endless winters, and dangers from animals, Indians, blizzards, and famines. Her nine children were born in a rough log cabin, and five of them perished there. Annie became a lean, silent, watchful woman, with no words at all, much less any hopes or ambitions. She wore dark shapeless homespun clothes, and made her own soap, her own rough shoes, and her children's shoes. By the flickering light of a home-made lamp, she taught her children to read and write, in the winter evenings, she heated great pails of water and washed them, she read them her mother's Bible.

If she ever remembered lovely Binghamton, with the lilacs in bloom on a May morning, and church bells clanging in the sunny air, she never said so. If she looked out at the muddy loop of the road between dark pines, the rough roofs of the few neighbouring cabins, and remembered the sunrise that was shining down upon elms and maples, upon green roofs and old white houses, upon roses and trim fences, more than a thousand miles away, she gave no sign. People called the place "Crabtree's Crossing," and for twenty-two years Annie Crabtree knew no other home.

Her son Reuben, her second child, was born in April, 1811. Mrs. Crabtree had been three days in labour with the older child fourteen months before, bearing successive convulsions of agony and intervening periods of exhaustion with only her husband's company for comfort. The first child had not lived, and the mother, only nineteen at the time of this second ordeal, had experienced some terrors of anticipation.

However, it proved mercifully brief and comfortable, and in the exquisite relief of being well again, with the hard hour safely over, and this splendid sturdy child to show for it, Annie perhaps knew the first real joy of her married life. She idolized her little "Rube"; she had before this ceased to have any particular feeling for his father. Wifehood in Annie's class and day meant cooking, washing, hurrying, apologizing, pacifying; it meant pleading for money for schooling and shoes; it meant terrified defence of whimpering babyhood. It meant physical weakness and helplessness, and under it, always and forever, ran the burdens and agonies of incessant child-bearing.

If she had had any feeling at all for George William it might well have been hate, as for the task-master who drove her too hard, who piled load after cruel load upon her, and who never spared her. Not once in twenty-two years did George William lend her the least comfort or service, not once was he tender, understanding, kind. Not once did he give a son or daughter anything that was fatherly or loving. When he thrashed the children Annie writhed in silence, and when he drove into Wabash occasionally on what she innocently supposed to be important business of the store, she rejoiced in a breathing-spell, a time when she might get the work on little Annie's dress a trifle forward, or give her girls and boys a candy-pull, which they called a "molasses stew."

Mercifully, childhood is inexacting, and the young Crabtrees extracted more pleasure from life than seems believable. They swam in the river, trapped and hunted, rode almost wild horses, ate heartily of the food their flushed and weary mother could hardly touch, and when the time came they wooed or were wooed and were married in turn.

Faded, silent, crushed Mrs. Crabtree developed an unsuspected feeling when her Rube selected for his wife one Lulu Potts; Rube was then but twenty-three, and the despised Lulu six years younger. The "Pottses of Lower Town" were disreputable people, and it was said of them that the girls "run round the place without much more on 'em than the Injuns!" Certainly Lulu's lean, oily-faced, drinking father was not a particularly desirable relative-to-be, and her whimpering, tremulous mother was not much better. The smells, the dirt, the tin cans and ashes and prowling cats of Lower Town were a stench in the nostrils of Crabtree's Crossing, and the Pottses were about the worst of Lower Town's degraded denizens. But the girls, Jenny and Lulu, were undeniably beautiful, and at about the time that Jenny, fifteen years old, was telling a crying and vituperative and hysterical story to "Sherf" Calhoun about one of the Crooker boys, Lulu stepped triumphantly into the limelight with young Reuben Crabtree for her mate.

All this made Annie Crabtree furious. Her darling, the oldest living child of her heart, wedded to this blowsy, handsome, noisy girl, whose sister was subsequently married to Lem Crooker at the point of a gun, was horrible to her; and everything that was clean and austere and of New England rose in Annie and revolted. She denounced her son Reuben, and they never spoke to each other again.

By this time the railroad had come to Crabtree's Crossing, and George William, at sixty, might have become a rich man. But George William had developed into a sort of genial, garrulous town idol, stout, lazy, good-natured with strangers, and always glad to sit near the stove in one of the new stores that lined the downtown streets and tell people of the day that he and his young wife—"the finest woman God ever made, gentlemen!" he would interpolate, with watering eyes—had come to Crabtree's Crossing when it "warn't no more'n a strip of virgin forest."

Old Crabtree was one of the "characters" of the place, harmless enough as far as the world went. But, after her bitter disappointment about her son, his wife became somewhat sickly and complaining and their home life was one of trial and discomfort.

She never knew that he gambled, that in one night the fruit of all their slaving years was thrown away. She never heard the men telling of the night Rube, after all his money was gone, and when his I. O. U.'s had assumed an enormous size, put up his railroad property on Everett's roulette wheel. First the lots down by the warehouse, and then the block next to Havens, and then the forest strip, up above town.

The red came seventeen times running, there was a roar from the group of flushed and excited and close-packed men about the wheel at the twelfth—and thirteenth—and fourteenth time. After that there was stillness, except for Reuben's hoarse, cracked voice, barking out fresh hazards. Everett's smooth, thin, shaven face did not change, except that his eyes shifted. The room was heavy with blue smoke; it billowed against the rafters; and the thick air smelled of strong drink and men's dirty hair and dirty bodies.

Dawn was breaking over the raw streets when George William Crabtree stumbled silently into the cool outer air; men said that he would kill himself. But instead of that he wavered home heavily to Annie and went to bed, and said that he was ill. Annie gave him "physic" and hot tea and hot rolls and "bonny clabber," and some weeks later he told her that the railroad had done him out of his rights, but to keep her mouth shut, because he wasn't done with those fellers yet.

Annie kept her mouth shut and worked and grieved and cooked and swept as she always had. Sometimes she saw her son Rube in the village; a year after his marriage she heard that he had moved west, with his wife. Her daughter Lizzie married, and had children, and her son Willy was killed on the railroads, and presently George William died, "of the rapidly passing type of our fine old pioneers," the paper said, and then Annie died, too, and the always ready press had it that friends of this devoted pioneer couple had foreseen that the wife would not long survive the partner to whom she had given her first young love many years before. To the end, Annie was ignorant of the dissipation of what should have been a comfortable fortune. She said that the railroads had "done poor Pa; he had owned them lots down by the warehouse, and that big place next to Havens that sold the other day for nineteen thousand dollars, and the forest strip that he and she had first settled on, before her first baby was born!" And Lizzie, her daughter, and Lizzie's children, of the now important town of Crabtree, tell the story so to this day.

Reuben and his Lulu, and her sister Jenny and Lem Crooker, had long before this moved westward, rejoicing in youth and love and health and high-spirits. They stopped when their off-horse died, in what was one day to be Polo, Illinois, and here several children were born to Reuben and his wife, Lulu, and one child to Jenny, a little girl also named Jenny. Lulu had a daughter in 1836, two years after she was married, a plump, good-natured little girl, May, who was a great favourite with everyone in the growing village, and two years later another daughter, Fanny. In 1841 the group of little girls was joined by a brother, Robert Potts, and more than two years later a fourth and last child, Harry. Both Lulu and Fanny bore other children, but none survived, and in 1848, when she was thirteen years old, Jenny's only child, little Jenny, died, to the mother's undying grief.

By this time Jenny had been widowed for several years, and the family of two women and five children was entirely supported by Reuben, in the old-fashioned way. Little Jenny's death prostrated both her mother and her aunt; she had been the oldest of all the children, beautiful and gentle and gifted in a most uncommon way, and they sickened of life in the raw little frontier town without her. Lulu's May was a fat, good-natured little dumpling, and Fanny the younger child promised to be a spirited and interesting girl later on, when she got her second teeth, but life in Polo had grown suddenly unendurable to both women, and it was because of their importunities that Reuben good-naturedly disposed of his thriving general store, with its calicoes, sardines, and Mexican saddles, and joined the army of emigration toward the fabled west, in 1849.

The women and children accompanied him to "Saint Jo," and with a pleasant flutter of novelty and excitement they watched the purchase of an outfit. The straggling town was filled with other thrilled and hopeful adventurers, and Jenny Crooker, a comely widow at thirty-two, might have married a dozen times in the first dozen days.

The sisters, with the quartette of ecstatic children swarming after them, wandered pleasantly about the curious and disorganized town, watching caravans arrive, dusty and weary, and unpack in the shade and sunshine under the cottonwoods, and other caravans depart in a sort of buoyant solemnity to the mysterious west. Reuben had some money; Jenny several hundreds from the late Lem Crooker. They bought a wagon, hooped in clean canvas, bought oxen, barrels of flour and hard-tack and pickled pork, bags of salt and sugar and coffee, whiskey, and wheat for planting, axes and guns and ropes; the town was wild with an orgy of buying.

Reuben "tied up" with a much larger party; there would be twenty-two caravans and thirty-seven sturdy men, in all. It was not safe to travel with less, and the late "Potts girls" of Crabtree's Crossing found themselves not the least educated and refined of the group. Little May, thirteen years old, amused and delighted her elders with a sudden assumption of elegance and exclusiveness.

There were plenty of friendly women in the twenty-two caravans, and some sixty children. It was a village in movement, when, upon the sweet and open plains, in the warm May weather, cattle grazed, campfires sent blue smoke into the twilight, and children and dogs and babies frolicked about after the weariness and the restrictions of the day. During the fifty-seven days of the trip there were constant rumours, alarms, and excitements, but no real suffering. Six or seven infants were born *en route*; scouts came back with reports of Indians ahead, and guns were loaded, and the scampering children sternly confined. But there was no real danger and no real fear; plump little May Crabtree well remembered, in later years, an evening when she and Fanny were surreptitiously scraping sugar from the hard lump in the wagon-body, under the driver's seat, sugar always faintly seasoned by tarred paper and sacking. Her father had glanced back, over his tightened reins, and had rebuked them.

"Git out of that, girls! I'll sugar ye if the Injuns git a mile nearer!"

It was thrilling, it was delightful, to scramble up beside him on the front seat, and to realize that the oxen were really moving along pretty steadily. Their mother, trying to get five-year-old Harry to sleep, had called out fretfully:

"Land sakes, Rube! Don't rattle a body's bones loose, if the Injuns *are* coming!"

Dirty, weary, but undaunted, the Crabtree party arrived in San Francisco late on a brilliant August afternoon, in 1849. Reuben had sold his outfit in Marysville, and bought a box wagon and a team: the trip down took him two days, but the family was in high spirits, and nobody resented the leisurely miles. Tales of murder, death on the plains, and Indian outrage, met them on every side, and they felt themselves not only fortunate, but wise, in all their moves and decisions.

San Francisco, lying upon her seven sandy hills, looked civilized to Jenny and Lulu. There were few women to be seen among the jumble of cheap wooden buildings, the Chinese "cook-houses" and "wash-houses," the saloons and gambling hells, the quarters where Mexicans and Indians and half-breeds of every type were housed together. There was a "Frenchman's" and a "Dutchman's" and a "Swede's"; the startled eyes of the two women, and of little May, Fanny, Bob, and Baby Harry, saw dark-skinned Indian women, stolidly watching them, over pipes, bold Mexican girls with exposed brown bosoms and black loose coils of hair, eyeing them curiously, and cowboys loping past them in a magnificent whirl of embossed and fringed leather and flying satiny ponies.

Reuben was in great spirits; every boyish longing for adventure, hidden in all men, was roused and satisfied at once. He and his women took possession of an empty, doorless, one-roomed shack, and the roof and walls seemed to give them a delicious sense of privacy, after the open plains. And the next day, with the extra barrels of sugar and flour, Reuben opened a grocery store.

Jenny, for two hundred dollars, bought two lots and an empty barn. The barn she floored and divided; it was one of the first houses in San Francisco to boast an indoor flight of stairs. The Mexican haciendas had stairs, to be sure, but they were flimsy outdoor affairs. Jenny developed an unexpected strength of character: no man could tempt her from her proud widowhood. But she and a derelict young coloured woman named Carra, whom Lulu had annexed, boarded half the men that were later to be the railroad and the gold-mine kings of the infant territory. Crooker's Hotel was famous as early as 1853, and in 1865

Jenny retired, comfortably wealthy, and went east for a year, and to Europe, taking with her Lulu's Fanny, then a sprightly, handsome girl of twenty-seven.

By this time Reuben was rich, too. The sugar and flour that had crossed the plains safely in 1849 had made a trail for tons of sugar and flour, for teas and coffees and other luxuries. Reuben Crabtree brought the first pepper and cinnamon and ginger into the new state, and his children grew up with the town.

They saw wealth come into it, and with wealth came schools and a library, "cable cars," theatres, shops. Magnificent homes went up like mushrooms on Nob Hill, the Vigilantes flourished at Fort Gunnybags, the Mexicans and miners vanished, and with them the murders and the riots. The railroad came, and there were regular side-wheel ferries plying across the ruffled blue bay, and gradually the distant faubourgs of "Mission Dolores" and "Tuckertown" melted into the greater city, and a drive was laid straight through miles of sandhills to the beach, and bull pines and pioneer peppers and eucalyptus were planted in what some day would be Golden Gate Park.

May and Fanny Crabtree had a glorious girlhood, with more admirers than a dozen girls usually can boast, and May was actually exhausted with conquests when, at twenty-four, she chose young Stephen Brewer, an "eastern" man, and a trusted clerk in her father's firm, for her life partner. May was a beauty and a belle, then, and there was no door on Nob Hill through which her tilting hoops had not triumphantly sailed. She and her Stephen rented a small house in Powell Street, at O'Farrell; her father had offered to buy them this house as a wedding gift, but the price seemed to the young couple exorbitant—seventeen hundred dollars for a home that was not new!—and May very sensibly preferred a seal-skin coat and cap, in which she looked bewitching.

Reuben, just before his oldest girl's marriage, had built himself a magnificent home, across the bay. It was really a farm then, two hundred gracious acres on the slopes above San Rafael, and the house was so pretentious, with its bay windows and its upstairs porches, that actual expeditions were sometimes made, by interested San Franciscans, to view it. San Rafael was a little country town behind Tamalpais Mountain; it was reached by a ferry trip to Saucelito, and a rattling half hour in the train.

The Potts girls of long ago, Lulu Crabtree and the still resolutely unmarried Jenny Crooker, planted peppers and palms about the mansion, with fuchsias and marigolds and roses, and the balmy western airs fanned them into miraculous beauty and growth. There were riding horses in the big stable, and the young people could extend a splendid hospitality in the matter of rooms, meals, rides, drives, picnics, and dances.

When young Fanny and her aunt Jenny went abroad, May and Stephen Brewer and their five children left the Powell Street house and came to live in her parents' beautiful home. Old Reuben's sons were not as definite, nor quite so satisfactory as his daughters. Bob, the older, was a somewhat indifferent member of the family firm; the business was known as "R. E. Crabtree and Company—Spices, Teas and Coffees," now.

Harry, the five-year-old baby who had been brought across the plains, was a gentle, negative youth, somewhat silent and diffident. In 1868 Harry, quite unexpectedly to his family, and perhaps to himself, married a strong-minded and vigorous widow named Lucy Carter, with one beautiful little girl, and after that he did not live at home or see much of his own people. He worked with an insurance firm, was presently sent to England in the interests of the business, returned with his wife and his step-daughter, and another little daughter and son really his own, and again dropped quietly from sight.

Thus May, as Mrs. Brewer, really became the representative of the family. May was an emotional, warm-hearted, not too brilliant woman, and during the last years of her happy girlhood she had developed a certain charming pride in herself and her family. She was a Crabtree, of Crabtree's Crossing, Illinois. Papa and Mama had come west, from the old home, because of Mama's health. The Crabtrees were—well, of course everyone knew *them*, back east. Carra, Jenny's old coloured assistant, who had now become a sort of general factotem, was "one of the family servants." May taught her daughters that they must respect themselves; "I suppose there is no older or finer family in America than ours," she used to say thoughtfully. And she was not generous with other San Francisco families who began to assert similar claims. The Murchisons and the Persons and the de Pinnas and the Barkers and the McIntyres—ha! These people setting up social affectations— well, perhaps it was all right. But it was very amusing, to May.

These were serene days for the entire family, after the stress and strain of the preceding years. Jenny was a square, squat, somewhat mustachioed woman, in middle life, determined, energetic, and spirited. Lulu was a somewhat quieter type, rather limp and gentle, dominated by her husband and her five children. She and Jenny wore bonnets and mantles, at fifty, when, which was rarely, they left the house. Jenny managed all household affairs; the sisters sat talking, for endless hours, over the "air-tight" stove in winter, and by the open dining-room windows in summer.

May's marriage and May's children supplied a tremendous interest for them. Sundays became extraordinarily pleasant, with Reuben puttering about the garden, a small grand-daughter's hand in his, and Harry, Bob, and Fanny still young enough to supply the house with excitement and life. May's husband, the handsome and dignified Stephen Brewer, was an ideal son-in-law, and when he and May arrived, with the caped and bonneted babies, a certain feeling of well-being and prosperity came with them.

When Aunt Jenny suddenly decided to go abroad and to take her niece Fanny with her, May was pained, for as an absorbed young wife and mother, who had no time for such enjoyments and rather despised them, she had previously felt her own life to be the ideal one. But May immediately decided that her parents would be too lonely with Aunt Jenny and Fan both gone, and she and Stephen moved to the San Rafael house and remained there. This proved a satisfactory arrangement, even when the travellers came back with glass tubes of bright ribboned sand from the Jordan and cuckoo clocks from Switzerland. The silent old grandmother clung to the little children, and May's children knew Grandpa's house well, and they loved it. Stephen made the trip back and forth, by train to Saucelito, by boat to San Francisco, daily, for something like thirty-five years.

There were five Brewer children, born between 1860 and 1868. First came Esme, and then the only boy, Albert. After Albert were three girls, Victoria, Ernestine, who was called Tina, and one who was named for her somewhat surprised grandmother, Louisianna. For May had long ago discovered that the rightful name of the one-time Lulu Potts of Crabtree's Crossing was Louisianna.

May had wanted sons, had seen herself as the proud possessor of "the Brewer boys." She would always have spoiled sons; having but one she spoiled him all the more heartily. She told the bewildered and indifferent little boy in his fifth summer, that he was the "only Brewer boy; in England he would have inherited everything." She playfully introduced Bertie, at seven, as "our son and heir." There was a quaver of honest emotion in her voice as she drew him forward. "This is our boy—he and his mama are chums already!"

Bertie had the riding-pony, and his sisters had to ask him for rides: if but one child could go on any expedition it was always the son. Bertie had his own room long before nursery days were outgrown for Esme, Vick, Tina, and Lou.

But May loved her daughters, too, and would always soften these decisions with motherly tact.

"Mama and Papa have decided to take Bertie, girlies. You see a boy gets into mischief, at home. And Mama knows that she can trust her girls!"

Presently both the grizzled and elderly women who had been the Potts girls died. Mrs. Crabtree died first, when her namesake grand-daughter was only five. May was undisputed mistress of the big San Rafael house then, for Aunt Jenny loved her and trusted her in everything, as did old Reuben. May's sister, Fanny Crabtree, found herself somewhat in the position of a superfluous old maid, in the full household, until Aunt Jenny Crooker suddenly had "her shock," too, and died as her sister had done, and left all her money to Fanny.

CHAPTER II

REUBEN CRABTREE was a grizzled old man of sixty-two when his wife died; the two years that her sister survived her were the hardest business years of his entire career. The entire country was experiencing a money panic; Crabtree and Company got the heavy outer washes of the wave of depression.

He missed his lean, silent wife, and her square, mustachioed sister, the two women who had accompanied him upon all his adventures since actual youth, whose opinions and personalities had formed his character and made his home world. Their heavy forms, in scalloped percale sacques, had moved about his house for years; they had given him his cue for action where his children were concerned. He missed them both, and shed hard, unaccustomed tears at their graves.

May managed his house now, and persistently and playfully May made "Grandpa" the centre of it. She and Fanny quarrelled over questions that they tearfully assured him were "only for his good," and Stephen consulted him on business matters and, when the old man kept regular office hours, made the daily trip with him on the boat.

But Reuben was not important in their lives, and he was shrewd enough to see it, and wise enough not to resent it. He became a silent, dry, chuckling old man only really animated when, by chance, the conversation was carried back some thirty or forty years. Pioneer days, old property fights between sheep-raising Spaniards and the encroaching *gringos*, the discovery of "out-croppings" and "quartz," roused him to sudden interest. He would drop his bloodless, bald little head to one side, shove his hands deep in his trouser pockets, chew rotatingly upon an unlighted cigar, and fix his swimming old gray eyes upon space, his small crossed foot waggling agitatedly, as with many a sharp "heh!" he contributed what an amazing memory had stored of California's youth.

13

For the rest, as years went by, his grandchildren were more and more his companions. They puttered with him in the garden, and shrieked to him to see them on the horses, to see them on the windmill, to see the big hole they had dug. He would leave them in mid-morning, and May would accompany him to the gate.

"Going into town to that horrid office, Pa?"

"Thought I would, May."

Reuben, in his office, or at Directors' meetings, chewed, looked sharply from face to face, chuckled and agreed, or—rarely—broke out into protest. Stephen had begun of late years to treat him with long-suffering, kindly contempt. But some of the other members of the firm, Yeasley and both the Fendersons, felt that the old president was still the real head of the concern by right of wisdom and experience.

His sons the old man rarely saw. Robert, the elder, handsome, bluff, always oddly unconvincing, had sold back to his father his stock in the family firm in 1872, had gone to Boston, married there, and so removed himself from the family group. Harry, always a sweet, vague, affectionate boy, had been, the old man thought, influenced by his wife—"that damn' widow," as the old man called the active Lucy—to withdraw his interest from Crabtree and Company, also, and at a most inconvenient time. This was in 1874, Lucy and Harry had just returned from England, their two little girls with them and a third baby expected, and Lucy had been persuaded by a train acquaintance, during the six days' train trip between Chicago and San Francisco, that there was a fortune to be made in Placer County gold mines. Their thousands might easily be made as many millions; such miracles were going on about them every day. The Harry Crabtrees put all their money into stock in a gold-mine on the American River, and might quite as well have put it into the river itself.

Reuben did not much mind buying back Harry's interest, although he was hard-pressed at the time and had secretly to place a mortgage upon the San Rafael homestead to meet his obligations, and borrow on other securities to weather the storm.

But he was sorry to have his youngest child and favourite so completely under his wife's thumb; Reuben disliked Harry's frog-eyed, garrulous, complacent wife, and he found himself unable to defend Harry, when May and Stephen and Fanny discussed him. He saw less and less of Harry, who was struggling with a small position with the Atlas Rubber people, and hardly knew the three children, Nelly, Alice, and baby Georgie, even by sight, for several years.

Fanny, at this time the family's unconsidered old maid, did not appear to great advantage during the financial panic, either. She could merely worry and wring her hands. Nobody cared what she did. But May and Stephen had shone in this trial. True, they lived with Pa, his home was theirs, and their entire income came from Crabtree and Company; they had no choice.

But May did not remember this lack of alternative. She only remembered that she had never, never, not for one instant, lost faith in Steve and Pa. Steve had "slaved," Steve had "not slept," for months. He and Pa had plodded to the office every day, and things had happened, and times had gotten better, and prosperity had returned. May cried with love and gratitude whenever she thought of it. If she and Steve had had money, every penny of it would have been Pa's! They hadn't had money, but they *had* given love, and courage, and devotion, hadn't they, Pa? May made herself obnoxious to her sister, and to Harry's wife, with her warm air of all-embracing perfection.

After awhile, however, time worked its usual restoring changes. Aunt Jenny died, and Fanny, who inherited a comfortable fortune, became an extremely important person. Reuben grew older, and began to be tired by the bay-trip; he and Fanny rented a house in the city, and moved away from the old home.

May watched this change uneasily. It left her mistress of the San Rafael house, as she had always dreamed she might be, but then she had always dreamed of Pa's dying, instead of being extremely lively, and wasting his money upon town rents and town expenses. He had always paid certain bills for May and Steve, water and gas and the hired man and for the horses' keep. Now this stopped, and Fanny's occasional erratic contributions stopped, too. Fanny had sometimes bought ferry-tickets, treated the "girlies" to a town lunch, had her room papered, or taken the whole family to a charity entertainment. May felt easier with Fanny's fortune in the house, as it were. May had her family to think for.

Pa would leave to Harry's children—not necessarily Lucy's

child by her first marriage, no—but to the two younger children, Alice and Georgie, Pa would leave *something*. But Bob and his Boston wife had no children, and Fanny was unmarried. Calculate as she would, May could not see how the bulk of Pa's fortune, and all of Fanny's, could fall otherwise than to her children. Bertie would go into the business, and inherit the lion's share. But dear Esme and Vick and Tina and Lou would have handsome marriage portions as well.

Nothing to worry about; time must bring it all to pass. But May, as her father aged, indulged sometimes in a dream of what must take place the *instant* "anything happened to Pa." Steve would be supreme at the office then, and she and the children "the heirs." If Rob or Harry put in any claim, Steve must be firm with them; they had lost their chance! As for Fanny, with all Aunt Jenny's money—May would like to hear her make any comment upon what Steve did or didn't do! The memory of Fan's airs, when Aunt Jenny died, and when Fanny had to see lawyers and take over responsibilities, galled May whenever she thought of it. The India shawl and the Spanish scarves, indeed! It was hard for May to accept these meekly for her girls, highly as she had always prized them, with Fanny being consulted about "securities" and "cash balances" in the Bank.

And as the years went by, and Fanny became a prosperous and highly respected maiden lady, and May's girls more and more of a responsibility, the position of the sisters seemed oddly reversed. May was harassed and pitied; Fanny blithe and care-free. May resented it bitterly; her Esme was twenty—was twenty-two—and Vicky and Tina coming along steadily, and there must be some entertaining, some social brilliance, some engagements. And still nothing "happened" to Pa, and Fanny saved her ridiculous hundreds jealously, and Lucy's Nelly, a girl absolutely without advantages, raised in a little Mission house without even a bathroom in it, was turning out a beauty and a belle and a heart-breaker, while Esme sat out dance after dance looking all sagging shoulders and discouraged eyes and stiff elbows.

May had a party for Pa on his seventieth birthday, and on his seventy-first, and on his seventy-second. On his seventy-third he was ill, and they were all very serious. Lucy came from the Mission, Harry and Steve, meeting for the first time in months, talked gravely in the halls. But Pa rallied, and was progressing cacklingly toward his seventy-fourth anniversary, one windy, warm August morning in 1885, when he received an unexpected letter from Robert, in Boston. Robert and his wife hoped Pa was well; they were coming to California for a visit. Reuben had not seen his son for more than ten years. He did not tell Fanny, who was fluttering about as a preparation for going to Market, but he did tell old Carra, who was a sort of body servant of his in these days.

"'At so?" said Carra, showing purple, smiling gums. "Mist' Rob ain' got no children, I raik'n?"

"No," the old man agreed. "Wish he had."

"He ain' been married so long," Carra suggested consolingly.

The old man went down to his office, on the day after the letter came, and took his place at his own desk, in the room that also contained the desk of his son-in-law and partner. He did not often go to the office, especially in this dry month of August, unless there was a special meeting of directors, and to-day, as he walked in from the hot street to the shadowy building, with its glassed offices and its oiled floor, the shirt-sleeved men from the packing-house, and the clerks, with their green eye-shades, all wondered, as they went busily about their business, just what had brought him.

Stephen Brewer was downstairs, inspecting some sample labels in the office of the cashier, when the word went round, that the "old man was down." But he at once mounted the stairs to the formal apartment that bore his own name as vice-president, under the name of Reuben Crabtree, President, and came in upon his wife's father with respectful haste and solicitude. The room faced the south, and upon the green window-blinds hot sunlight was mercilessly beating. But in the perfect bare order of the office the air was not too hot.

"Well—here you are!" Stephen, a large, loosely built bearded man with a smile that showed his smooth full lower lip, said somewhat expectantly. The old president of the firm, like any other man of his age, was an unmitigated nuisance about the place, but it was not for his partner and son-in-law to antagonize him. Stephen was helpless under his interference. He thought apprehensively now of half-a-dozen ways in which old Reuben could complicate and delay matters in the packing-room at this exact moment.

"How's everything, Steve?" Reuben said, with a dry cackle.

He pushed back his dusty derby hat, and Stephen saw the deep red mark it left on the papery, bloodless skin. "How's May and the girls?"

"They are very well—very well," Stephen said judicially. He knew that something else was coming, and he was a trifle concerned as to its nature.

"Find ye still need Bertie here?" Reuben chuckled. Stephen smiled, flushing as he smiled. This facetious allusion was to Stephen's remark, thrown out as a sort of feeler, some weeks ago, as to the advisability of his taking his one son, Bertie, into the business.

"I certainly did not mean that I—that we need Bertie *now*," he said, with comfortable dignity. "My remark was merely that—building for the future, it might be wise to have the boy with us. As a member of the family, his place is here. He may have his sisters to provide for, some day, and when the time comes for me to lay down——"

"Well, speaking of the family," old Reuben said, with a noticeable lack of sympathy, and fumbling in his pocket for a letter, "looks like you're goin' to get your wish as regards your wife's brother Robbit. He and his wife are leavin' for California in a few days, now."

"Bob!" Stephen said, much surprised. "Why—I haven't seen Bob Crabtree for—it must be ten years. What on earth is bringing him home?"

"I don't know!" The old man eyed his son-in-law with a shrewd grin. "P'raps he feels that if we need Bertie, we need *him!*"

Stephen laughed his comfortable laugh.

"Well, I can see that I certainly put my foot in it when I made that suggestion about Bertie!" he said good-naturedly. "I suppose what I meant was that we could develop and educate the boy to be useful to us. As to Bob, he left us of his own free will and accord——"

"And there hasn't been a day since that you haven't said that he ought to be here to carry his share of the responsibility," the old man interpolated mischievously.

"No—no, I hardly think that you can say that," Stephen said heavily, beginning to be a trifle annoyed. "I do think— or I did think—that Bob left us rather in the lurch, but things are different now. We know where we stand now; we've weathered a good deal since Bob went east. I—I resent the idea that I've ever grudged Bob his right to do what he pleased in the matter. He has chosen a different work—he is a cotton merchant now, and what's past is past. He doesn't—I suppose he doesn't intend to settle here?"

"I don't know." Bob's father took out a quill tooth-pick and began to chew it idly, as he swung about in his swivel chair. "The boy's place is here," he said musingly.

"I don't quite know what he would do," Stephen said lightly, yet sharply. "Woolcock and Fenderson——"

"Oh, I don't mean in the firm, Steve," his father-in-law said with his diabolic air of amusement. "I mean here in San Francisco."

"I see!" Stephen's ruffled spirit almost visibly quieted. There was a short pause. "How's Fanny?" he asked.

"Fine. Vicky runnin' things as usual?"

Stephen smiled. Victoria was not only his own but her grandfather's favourite, among his four girls.

"She's a great girl," he said. "She'll be excited to hear that her Uncle Bob is coming west. By the way, do you know anything of Bob's wife?"

"Boston woman—she was a Sewall—she ain't young, either," the old man summarized. "I gather that her folks are well-to-do. We'll hear"— his old eyes twinkled—"we'll hear considerable of Plymouth Rock and the *Mayflower*, you mark my words!" he grinned.

"That ought to please May," Stephen said, of his wife.

There was another short silence. It was about two o'clock. Stephen thought with relief that the old man would shortly be going out to his late lunch, and would not return. A hot wind had sprung up, and was whining outside the windows. Both men swung lazily in their chairs, Stephen's desk was open, but there was no reason why Reuben Crabtree should roll back the jointed top of his own.

Stephen said to himself that the old fellow was certainly failing. He surely could not keep on much longer. He visualized the immediate changes that he would make in the office, and in the administration downstairs, when the old head of the firm died.

"Hot over your way, hey?" Reuben asked. "Rob'll want to see the old place," he added thoughtfully.

"May'll ask them to San Rafael," Stephen said.

Reuben told his daughter the news that night, and the next day Fanny went all the way across the bay to San Rafael, to discuss it with her sister. It was a great event in the family.

"Do you think we ought to let Harry know?" May Brewer asked, hesitatingly.

"Harry doesn't care two cents about family affairs!" Fanny said decidedly, beating the tip of her nose with her hand. Everything she said was decided, often satirical or even bitter.

"No, but Lucy does," May offered hesitatingly. It was decided simply to notify Lucy, and let her act toward the unknown sister-in-law, and the brother-in-law she hardly knew, as she saw fit.

"Well, that was all, May," Fanny said, when they had reached this point. Mrs. Brewer immediately released a ballooning call toward unseen members of the family:

"Oh, girlies! You can come back now!"

They were in the sewing-room, which smelled of machine-oil and new woolens. The girls had been dismissed until the cream of the news had been skimmed by their elders. But now they streamed back to hear it.

CHAPTER III

THE Robert Crabtrees reached San Francisco on a Friday afternoon late in the same month and registered at the Occidental Hotel. They had a large room that gave on Montgomery Street, and between it and the hall a totally dark bathroom where a bead of gas burned in a round white globe. Ella Crabtree, Robert's Bostonian wife, was tired from her seven days in the rocking train, and to her the strange city, the blowing, gritty dust of the summer sunset, looked ugly and cheap.

But Bob was in good spirits. He breathed his native air again and he liked it. Various men on the train or in the hotel had recognized him, and he was elated and excited at getting home. His business experience in Boston had not been very successful, and he half-hoped now that some chance would prevent the necessity of his returning there, but no one knew that. He could say with perfect truth that he was "representing Sewall, Scott and Forster," the Boston cotton merchants, for his wife's elderly brother had intimated that a commission business modestly established on the coast might be a good thing for the old cotton firm. Bob was a big man, with an expansive, genial manner, and a hearty, often affected, laugh. His own family had alternated between thinking him a remarkably clever and an amazingly simple person. He had an air of being intimately acquainted with big affairs and important persons, yet he actually held only an underling's position.

After the dinner, selected from a list written in a flowing hand with green ink upon a gilt-edged card, Robert and his wife walked about the streets for awhile, and Robert showed Ella the old cable cars on Sutter Street, with their rattling "dummies" attached, and the more modern type of cable cars that filed up Market Street, with yellow lights for McAlister, blue for Valencia, and green for Eddy Street. These cars were built in one solid piece with their dummies; the "gripman" stood out of doors in all weathers. Each car bore its street name in a long board that stretched almost its entire length and was hooked to the clerestory. Like all San Franciscans, Robert was proud of this Californian invention.

But Ella felt far more pride and interest when, after some of his ready laughter, and some confused repetitions of "Here— let me see—where are we? It ought to be right here—let me see!" he led her to the corner of Sansome and Clay Streets, where, in the gloom, she could see the dusty façade of an old two-story building, with three windows in the upper floor, and on the street floor one wide office window, bearing the words "R. E. Crabtree and Company" in large letters, and on the dingy wooden sign above, "Spices, Teas and Coffees."

The building was crowded between two higher ones, and the whole neighbourhood exhaled an odour of dried pepper and roped onions, for the wholesale grocery trade had its quarters hereabouts. Ella liked it. She walked back to the hotel with Rob, feeling that she in a sense belonged to this odd, shabby-looking town of wooden buildings. She blinked smilingly as she followed him across the hotel foyer, where black-and-white tiles tipped and gave under her feet, and where the great calcium lights, in their white globes, flung an unearthly white light upon the smoking and spitting men, and hissed and flickered spasmodically at intervals.

"Bob, if they asked you, would you stay?" she asked later, braiding her hair into one thin, smooth braid. She had taken off her glasses, and washed her face with hot water and soap, and if she looked plain, she also looked younger so.

"Yes, I think so," Bob said thoughtfully. "I'll sound old Steve on Sunday. He ought to offer me something!"

"Oh, I wish he would!" Ella said fervently. And she went to sleep thinking that it would be a satisfaction to write George and Lizzie that Rob could only give the matter of cotton a little time now and then, as he had "decided to enter the family firm."

The next day at eleven o'clock the card of Mrs. Stephen Brewer, with one corner turned down and two cards of Mr. Brewer, were brought to Mrs. Robert Crabtree, who immediately gave herself and her brown cashmere dress a glance in the mirror, and went along the hotel corridors to the enormous parlours to meet her sister-in-law.

The parlour's draped high windows, reaching from the ceiling almost to the floor, let in a flood of pleasant summer sunshine through clean lace curtains, and Ella could only see, against the brightness, that it was a tall, well-made woman who rose to greet her.

Her cool, clean hand clasped the other's smooth kid glove: the ladies sat down, and Mrs. Brewer said, "Well!" lightly and laughingly.

Ella had been murmuring something: now it was heard.

"I'm so *sorry* Rob's out!"

She could see May Brewer now plainly: a smiling, rosy woman, with a bonnet covered with glinting and jingling paillettes, and with clusters and clusters of little bunches of tawny grapes. This was fastened under her chin with ribbons of tan velvet, and neatly veiled. Her thick brown hair, beginning to turn gray, showed in a smooth coil at the back of her head, and almost all her forehead was covered with a richly curled "front." Her bosom was high, and the fringe that trimmed her dress of purple cloth rose and fell on a plateau as she laughed and talked.

On her side May Brewer saw a rather pale, dark woman, older than she had expected, with eyeglasses, and with a rather cold and composed, and yet simple manner. The women eyed each other with primitive hostility and fear, yet both were anxious to be won into liking and friendship.

"But you must meet my daughter," said Mrs. Brewer, after a few minutes, and she nodded to a tall young woman who had been sitting near. "This is our second girl," the mother said. "Victoria—you know who this is!"

Victoria Brewer, shaking hands, said with unexpected animation:

"How are you, Aunt Ella?"

Ella thought her handsome, in a rather bold, savage way. Victoria was dark and rosy, with flashing eyes and vivacious, almost nervous manner. She wore a dress of dark blue cloth trimmed about the high collar and wide cuffs and about the thick panniers of the skirt with scallops of gray silk, and a high straw turban turned back sharply from the face with two triangles of brim and massed with roses. This somewhat elaborate dress was snugly fitted into a narrow waist line; Victoria wore tan kid gloves, and high scalloped boots of tan kid. Her forehead, like her mother's, was covered with curled hair, and bangles jangled on her wrists; about her neck was a long gold chain that held the little watch that was thrust into her bosom. She was twenty-one.

"We all wanted to come in to meet you, there was a regular fight," said Victoria, "but I had to come in for my singing lesson anyway, and Mother chose me!"

"Oh, no, Vicky, you mustn't say *that!*" began her mother, but Victoria did not hear her. She smiled her bright and animated smile, and looked down—she was unusually tall—in a most friendly fashion at her uncle's wife. She was brimming with enthusiasms, in love with life and with herself; and so joyously imaginative that this mere circumstance of having relatives from Boston visiting her parents, was enough to turn the fringed head with delightful schemes. Suppose that Uncle Rob invited her to visit them in Boston——

"What is your voice?" Ella asked.

"Contralto!" Victoria supplied, as her mother hesitated.

"It's more *like* a contralto!" said Mrs. Brewer.

"And what is his method?" the Bostonian pursued; not in the least knowing of what she spoke, but quoting some half-remembered conversation with a musical friend.

"Well——" Victoria laughed, a little at a loss. "I know he's very *thorough*," she stated presently. "His name is Signor Maroni, he's really—internationally known!" Victoria added eagerly. "He's taught for years in New York—but his health was bad. He's quite old—his son was there, to-day, from New York, too! and the *son* must be thirty! And I imagine," the girl ran on, "that those terrible, snowy winters, you know . . . ! Of course you know what *those* are!" she finished, sympathetically.

Ella was bewildered with the rapidity of it.

"For of course you have snow in Boston?" Victoria encouraged her.

"Oh, yes—we have terrible winters!" Ella agreed.

"I have never seen snow!" Victoria said, joyously. "And Bertie—my brother, who has been east, never saw it either, for of course he was there in July—and you never have it then, do you?"

Ella dissented somewhat dazedly, and Victoria went on:

"Of course we haven't *been* east, but we do get the illustrated magazines, and the snow must be simply fascinating!—Except for the poor people in the slums, of course—we don't have any real poverty here. Signor Maroni says that in Paris—why what a Californian household throws away would feed a whole family! Isn't it terrible? But I confess that since it *is* that way I'd like to see it. Mrs. Train—who teaches my sisters delsarte—laughs at me. She says I'll rush into something *once too often*, and even my sisters think I'm insane—but of course only time will tell what Fate has in store for us all!"

It was said with such a pleasant, youthful rush of health, egotism, beauty, and good spirits that both the older women smiled in sympathy. Mrs. Brewer indeed was entirely familiar with this phase of Victoria's somewhat complex temperament. Moody, silent, discontented, the girl might be at times; at other times she was only a particularly joyous child. Then there was this eager, pretentious, ambitious aspect, where her little French, her half-invented, half-inferred knowledge of distant things and people, her sense of her own potentiality, bubbled over in this radiant rush of absurdities, and she chattered with a magnetism that captivated herself as well as her listeners.

"Come, chatterbox!" said her mother. "You know we are country folks, Ella," she said, with some manner; "we want to show you the dear old San Rafael home—not pretentious, but *homey!*" Before they went away she received Ella's promise to spend the next day with them in the country.

Ella and Rob went down to the ferry, at eleven o'clock on Sunday morning on their way to San Rafael. A dense white fog enveloped the city, and through it the fog horns on the bay boomed steadily. But by the time the little steamer reached Saucelito the veil was lifting and spokes of sunlight were piercing it. In the old wooden ferry building that they crossed to their train at Saucelito a thousand sparrows wheeled and twittered; the smoke from the puffing engine spread and thinned against the roof. Ella looked out with interest at the old boat houses and the marshes: the train was hot, her velvet seat uncomfortable, but the trip was not long. Spurred to her best by the sight of Victoria's fineries, she wore a figured lavender foulard, pleated and flounced over the small bustle, its skirts sweeping the ground, its tight sleeve ending below the elbow, some inches above her "one-button" gloves of gray kid. Her bonnet was covered with pansies, her intelligent, spectacled face concealed by a dotted veil, and she carried a small parasol of ruffled black silk with a collapsible handle.

In sunshiny, quiet San Rafael, they walked past a little street of shops, and another street of small residences, whose picketed gardens were crowded with roses and fuchsias and marguerites, and showed the need of water. Then, toward the gentle rise of the hills that encircled the sleepy little town, they came to the more pretentious houses, big wooden mansions set in acres of garden, and protected from the road by long stretches of wooden fences, inside of which showed dusty pepper, willow and evergreen trees, and great bushes of silvery pampas.

One of the largest and most attractive of these homes Rob recognized as his father's. The house stood well back from the quiet, dusty road, in a plantation of great trees. Rob and Ella looked at it from the front gate, a great double carriage gate of slender rounded pickets, painted gray, set in deep scallops between the posts and flanked on either side by a narrow foot gate of the same design. All the gates were open, upon a curving drive, beside which the yellow grass of the dry western summer pushed its way between great overgrown bushes of syringa and fuchsias and lauristine. There were masses of smaller growth, irregular lines of pungent marigolds, wallflowers and stock, crowding ranks of shaggy sweet William, roses bent with bloom, widespread periwinkle, with the blue flowers peeping between the dark rich leaves, and dusty clumps of that close-wrapped shrub whose tightly coiled leaves children love to peel open. Between and about them all grew the shaggy yellow grass. Among the white of the marguerites were brown blossoms dead on the bushes, and over the whole dry, fragrant mass, white butterflies and scores of tiny yellow butterflies flickered and looped.

To the eye of the eastern woman it all looked untidy and fulsome. Yet there was something splendid and wasteful about it, too, very unlike the trim, orderly gardens of Brookline, Massachusetts, and not without charm.

The house was large, with three floors amply bay-windowed, tree-shadows and sunshine falling upon open sashes, and the white bedroom curtains hardly stirring in the summer air. The day was extremely hot, for that latitude, and the family had transferred rugs, chairs, and newspapers to the shade of the big trees near the house.

It was long before the day when the hostess's responsibility for her guests embraced tickets and meeting at trains; and Mrs. Brewer, rising from the centre of the group on the lawn, felt only an unclouded pleasure in seeing her guests. She wore today a flowing skirt of blue cashmere and a scalloped sacque of white percale; an obvious bridge between church-wear and formal afternoon attire. She and her daughter were unashamedly shelling peas.

She introduced them, Esme, the oldest, with fair hair in a fashionable "French twist," and a much-pleated challis gown, was twenty-three years old—a slender girl, with a rather colourless and anxious face and a studiedly gracious manner. Bertie, the one son, next in point of years, was away—riding with his father. Victoria, flushed from a walk home from church, smilingly recalled herself. Tina, the girl next in order was twenty, stout, quiet, and fair, with shrewd, inscrutable eyes. Louisianna, the youngest of all, a little beauty of seventeen, was most like the handsome Victoria, and like Tina, wore girlish white muslin and no bustle. Their broad, uncorseted waists were indicated by sashes of satin ribbon.

They all sat down under the trees. Ella was still in her bonnet and gloves; she felt that she did not know them well enough to offer to help with the peas. She said, in her crisp, pleasantly incisive Bostonian voice:

"I shall get them all mixed, of course! What big creatures they are! You know we have Brewers in Charlestown; or *Milton* I think the original family came from. But is that *your* Brewer?"

"Papa's father came from Rochester, New York," Victoria supplied brightly. "He was an auctioneer, wasn't he, Mama?"

"I believe so," May said reluctantly and disapprovingly. She felt that there was no reason to flaunt these truths. Ella's interest instantly waned.

"I don't know the New York family at all," she said disapprovingly. "The Milton Brewers are real colonial stock—Winship colony. But none of them ever lived in New York, I'm sure of *that*. In fact," Ella went on, with a wintry smile, "we feel—we miserable Bostonians who are just foolish enough to be proud of our record, as the finest in America—we feel that New York is—well, you mustn't ever mention New York to *us!*"

Clearly and smilingly delivered, this speech had a crushing effect upon the group: Victoria felt snubbed, the first beginning of the pitiful arrogance and snobbery of the well-born began to dawn in her mind. She never again would mention the auctioneer of Rochester, as long as she lived.

Fortunately there was an immediate interruption: Stephen Brewer and his son Albert came wheeling in, on high-wheel bicycles, from which they descended with graceful, flying leaps. They came across the yellow grass and the sickle-shaped fallen eucalyptus leaves to meet Ella and Rob. Bertie, the son, was a rosy handsome young man, with a laughing manner, bright thick hair inclined to curl, and a tiny patch of close-clipped hair under each ear, matching his wisp of moustache. Stephen Brewer was as usual kindly and grave in manner, pleasant in speech, and with a householder's alert affectionate interest in wife, daughters, and guests. Where his well-trimmed beard and moustache met, his smooth lower lip showed a trifle when he smiled; he was beginning to be a little gray, but his eyes were youthfully blue.

"We got out of that job well, Bert," he said indicating the now shelled peas, as he sat squarely down beside his wife. Bertie swooped down to kiss the back of Victoria's neck, and the vivacious Victoria, quite aware of the effect, said lightly:

"You may be fond of me, Bertie, but remember others are looking on!"

As a matter of fact, Bertie was not especially fond of her, he was simply in a mood that made a little ostentation of some sort necessary to him, as the one gallant admired son of the house. Victoria flushed as her mother and sisters exchanged glances over her gushing little speech, but her father drew all eyes to himself as he said:

"Well, here is the junior member, Mama!"

Bertie's sheepish grin and his mother's ecstatic exclamation told the tale. The fortunate Bertie was to be taken into the family firm, as an employee, at least.

"Yes," said Stephen thoughtfully, almost solemnly, "I spoke to the directors about it yesterday, and Bertie is to have a chance to see what he can do. He is to come in to-morrow, and old Mason will start him in the packing-room. Start him as low—just exactly as we'd start any little unknown Johnny Jones or Sammy Smith," he added, with a smiling look of warning for his son. "If he expects to rise, it must be as his father did—by his own efforts!"

Bertie was heard to murmur appreciatively and gruffly at this point that that was the way he expected to rise, and his mother kissed him fondly and eagerly. The return of the gentlemen of the family caused a scattering: May was to carry the peas to the kitchen, and Stephen hospitably wished to show his brother-in-law the place after Robert's years of absence. Victoria animatedly suggested that she walk about the grounds with her father and brother and Uncle Rob, but her father smilingly shook his head.

"Not just now, my dear! Some other time you may walk with your uncle and me," said Stephen, good-naturedly. "But I think your mother wants help in the kitchen now!"

"Tina and Lou are going to help, to-day!" Victoria persisted eagerly. Her father looked at her mildly and said:

"Vicky." And with a hot blush she subsided, slipping away with Lou in abashed silence.

"As for Tina," May said archly, "she has a very important message to take to Mr. Yelland, at the rectory. Mr. Yelland is our very handsome young minister, Aunt Ella," she explained smilingly, addressing Ella as if for the happily blushing Tina, "and several of our prettiest young ladies have become quite religious since he came!"

Tina's complacent expression changed somewhat as her mother spoke. The reference to Mr. Yelland was thrilling, but to be classed with several other impressionable girls was humiliating, and Tina's pride was touched.

"I *always* went to church, Mama!" she said, seriously reproachful.

"Yes, I know you did, ducky dear!" May said merrily, "so run along with your message, and have your little happy time!"

Ella presently found herself alone on the lawn among the scattered chairs, with the oldest of these strange, vivacious creatures.

"Esme?" she ventured.

"Yes, Esme!" the rather sallow, somewhat large-featured girl answered, with bright, hard, unnecessary laughter. "And by no means a very satisfactory niece, as I'm afraid you'll find, Aunt Ella! You'll fall in love with Vicky, she's the popular one, and she would do anything in the world to *be* popular! Poor Vick—but I'd give anything in the *world* to be able to drift along on the surface of life as she does!"

This rush of frankness rather amazed Ella, who made a vague sound in her throat and smiled aimlessly.

"Your brother seems quite devoted to—to Victoria," she said presently, to say something. Esme laughed again, heartily.

"Just one of Vick's little by-plays!" she said indulgently. "Dear old Vicky—she's *rich*. No, Bertie isn't especially fond of her," she added, musically and slowly; "he's had the very queer taste to select his oldest sister for his chum. Dear old Bertie! He and I have had some wonderful good times together," Esme mused—"unknown to the rest!" she added, after thought. For it occurred to her that if Aunt Ella mentioned this statement to the atrociously frank and heartless family, it might be denied.

She fell into a dream in which she married somebody unknown and had Bertie a great deal at her lovely home in San Francisco. The day was dreamy and the air hotly aromatic under the peppers and poplars and eucalyptus. At the house, wire doors slammed and indistinct voices laughed and called. A white horse, as he grazed with other horses in Sunday idleness in the paddock, neighed shrilly; the windmill creaked and splashed in the silence.

"You have a lovely home here," Ella offered.

"Isn't it? Ideal!" Esme responded lifelessly. Presently Lou came out, flushed from the kitchen, and silently sank into a chair. Esme glanced at her resentfully; it had just occurred to the older girl that she might gracefully apologize to Aunt Ella for not having called upon her at the hotel, but Lou might break into a disrespectful snicker at this remark.

Lou, after Vicky, was the prettiest of the sisters, in delicious early bloom at seventeen. Esme, Vick, and Tina were all secretly convinced that Lou was going to be a great belle, and probably eclipse them all where love-affairs were concerned. Already there was something almost sinister in Lou's silences, her calm knowledge of her own charm. It was known that the Talbot boy had walked home with her from a village concert, and that she had received a birthday gift of moss roses from him; but Lou was maddeningly secretive about her own affairs.

She never chattered, as did the older three; she never talked much, under any circumstances. Indeed, even upon the men that she was destined to enslave, it would be eyes and dimples and soft little confiding hands that would stamp Louisianna's likeness; she was not a reader, not a thinker; she neither sang like Victoria, nor practised delsarte, and painted on mirrors, like Esme, nor would she attend three hot church services a day, like Tina. She was lazy, and she thought too much of her clothes, and too much of that vague class of creatures known to her mother and Carra, the old coloured nurse, as "the boys."

Ella went upstairs, to big airy rooms furnished in walnut, and comfortably shabby, and laid aside her wraps before lunch. The beds were big and flat, the pillow-slips had mottoes—"Good Night" and "Good Morning"— embroidered on them in red cotton. All the floors were completely carpeted in dark colours, and the deep windows had draperies of dull reps; the effect was of space and darkness. There was only one bathroom, far down the hall past bedroom doors, but several of the bedrooms were joined by little passageways where there were "stationary wash-stands" of brown marble. Ella turned up her cuffs and washed her hands, combed back her hair, and readjusted her glasses; the girls' blooming faces emerged from the rough towel as fragrantly fresh as creams and powders, lip-stick and rouge would ever make their daughters' faces, and they all went downstairs together, hungry and good-natured, at two o'clock.

They were eleven at table, for just before lunch old Reuben Crabtree and Miss Fanny came in. The old man was carefully escorted to a place of honour at the table and lowered tenderly into it. He was feeble, rosy, talkative, with his fair skin showing through the sparse white hair on his head and face. He had a certain tremulousness of speech, continually combatted by the masterful upward swing of a deep old jaw; his eyes did not flit about the company as his grandchildren's did, but he looked earnestly at the person he happened to be addressing, like a very young child. He embraced his long-absent-son with a little emotion, telling him that now he was where he belonged, and repeating slowly to Mrs. Brewer more than once that he had told Robbit that now he was where he belonged.

Miss Fanny was keen, sharp, and talkative, beginning to be grizzled, rustling in black silk, a self-conscious fun-maker. All the girls fluttered about her, they were afraid of her satire, but they laughed when she said that the clothing of some unknown woman on the boat must have "come out of the ark!" They laughed when she called Bertie a "dude" too, for the word was new. "'But for goodness sake don't say I told you!'" she quoted gaily. The phrase, from a popular song, was the very latest thing. Fanny could be pugnacious when her face got red and she beat the end of her nose; but she was in great good humour to-day.

The meal was served by Addie, a sloppy, cheerful maid, and by Carra, the tall, deep-bosomed old negress, with coarse gray wool showing under a handkerchief turban. This gaunt old soul had come over with Reuben from San Francisco. But she was evidently comfortably at home in the Brewer house, too, addressing the young people readily by name, and directing Addie.

The family immediately sat down to luncheon, or dinner, as they called it then. The meal was lavish. Of course Mrs. Brewer knew that for a dinner-party she should have had oyster patties, and then soup, served by herself from the Canton tureen, and then formal courses to follow, but this, as she explained, was only a family party. So there were already soda crackers and pickles and jelly and preserved peaches scattered up and down the table, and great pyramids of delicious sliced bread, coloured flat glass plates holding thick circular slices of butter, teaspoons upright in a pink glass jar, and a blistered blue glass pitcher full of creamy milk.

The young people started briskly in on bread and milk and sweets, and their father carved a great ham, while the mother served fried chicken. Ella, at first almost appalled by the quantity of food, found herself ravenous and everything good. There were hot biscuits but no vegetables, except two kinds of potatoes and a great platter of fresh lettuce and sliced tomatoes; the table speedily became disordered, the conversation was almost entirely of food. It was the fashion to stuff, to come back for more, to protest almost breathlessly against the third helping. But as everyone was in a sympathetic mood, no harm was done, and presently Carra and Addie carried away the main platters and plates, leaving the bread and butter, and the little mussy butter dishes, and the wine glasses and gravy-boat, and the pickles and crackers, and all the odds and ends of biscuit and bread, into which confusion the melting pyramid of ice-cream was triumphantly set, and hastily helped. Then there was cake, and strong tea, and a general loitering and nibbling until four o'clock.

Bertie and Victoria and the cheerful Aunt Fanny rather monopolized the conversation; Stephen Brewer was given only to hospitable monosyllables regarding the food at the table, and Mrs. Brewer devoted herself to her old father, who, very happy in the general pleasant confusion, ate heartily, removing from his mouth chewed particles of food too hard for him, with his fingers, to the edge of his plate. Bertie talked of the fascinating novelty, the telephone: in New York there was a hotel, he said, that was going to have a telephone on every floor. Miss Fanny turned this to absurdity by suggesting that persons on the fifth floor, say, would some day be telephoning to friends on some other floor in the same building, and they all laughed. But Stephen, while admitting that the new invention would always be chiefly for business use, electrified the family by announcing that Crabtree and Company would probably have a telephone installed, were talking about it.

The sound of the doorbell clattered through the house, from the shaking big bell that was aligned with other bells high up on the kitchen wall, and Addie was heard to say, "Botheration!"

"The door, Addie. It's probably Mr. and Mrs. Harry Crabtree," May said, to the maid. "My brother Harry and his wife," she explained smilingly to Ella; "and when you know them you know us all!"

"I haven't seen old Harry for years!" Robert said, expanded and breathless from food. "They have kids, May?"

"Very nice kids!" Esme began, laughing at the slang. But May interrupted her.

"Esme—darling—does Mama like that word?"

"Children," Esme murmured, chilled.

"Harry and Lucy have a lovely girl, Alice, sixteen," May expanded, after a tender, smiling look at the shamed Esme, "and a boy, Georgie, who is twelve. He is rather delicate, but Alice is a dear child."

"Don't forget Nelly, Mama!" Bertie suggested.

"Well, Nelly isn't a Crabtree," May said, flushing a little. "That's Lucy's child by a first marriage—a pretty, nice girl," she explained.

"The sort of prettiness that fades!" Esme added quickly.

"You wish it did!" her brother said, pleasantly.

Esme gave him a withering glance, her lips set tightly.

"You wish Dave Dudley was half as crazy about you!" the boy pursued gaily.

This seemed to break Esme's lately erected barriers. Tears sprang to her eyes.

"Mama——" she began impetuously. But Mrs. Brewer was looking expectantly at the door.

"That can't have been your aunt Lucy," she said vaguely. But Tina, who had returned from a little trip of discovery, said, rather discontentedly:

"Aunt Lucy is coming, though, with Nelly and Alice; they're just at the gate. Davy Dudley is with them."

"Well, who rang then?" demanded her mother.

Tina looked with resentment at Victoria.

"It was Signor Maroni and his son," she said impatiently. "I wish Victoria wouldn't ask such freaks to break into our Sundays!"

Victoria, to whom this announcement was likewise embarrassing, gave her mother a panicky glance.

"Oh, heavens, what'll I do with them? I just casually said that some day they ought to come over! He'll expect to be asked to play, Mama! What shall I do?"

"Well, you'll have to ask them to stroll or something," said Mrs. Brewer, in annoyance. Like everyone else she was feeling the uncomfortable heat of the hottest hour and the full meal. "You'll have to get them out of the way. As far as sitting down and listening to music goes, I don't think any of us feel quite up to that!" she finished, with her cheerful laugh.

"We can play some tennis—doubles, hey, Lou?" Bertie said, adding one more drop of misery to Victoria's cup, as she went unhappily out to find her music master. Ordinarily Bertie always asked Victoria to play with him, and although the somewhat passionate and jealous young creature ofttimes resented Bertie's magnificent supremacy, still she liked to be his favourite.

Signor Maroni, an oily, thin old man, with a lined face the

colour of leather, and gray locks falling each side of his ears, nevertheless had a charming smile and a courteous manner, as he rose to greet his pupil. He and his big, square, black-looking son were sitting on the front porch, seeming warm from their walk, and somewhat dusty as to clothing. Sigismund Maroni showed his Jewish blood—his mother was a Hebrew, broadly and largely built, intense and energetic, and he was like her. He towered, coarse, moustached, smiling, above his little father.

Victoria had a truer sense of hospitality than she knew, truer even than that of her effusive mother, and her first thought was that these guests had surely breakfasted late, missed their lunch, and so acquired an appetite for some sort of tea. And if she might have taken them in to the disordered table, brought in bread and ham and tea, and gathered up the cake, she would have done so delightedly; she was neither critical nor discriminating; she would have bloomed into her happiest and most attractive self in ministering to them.

But at twenty-two Victoria was not out of the nursery. She knew she would be actually punished for such daring, and she knew that even as it was she would be reproved for her share in this awkward episode. Suddenly it seemed to her that the Sunday was disappointing and dull, the light glaring, and the whole sorry scheme of things a failure.

Uncomfortably smiling, she asked brief questions. The family had streamed out a side door, and was gathering again under the trees, she could see Alice Crabtree's long braids, and caught a glimpse of Nelly's blonde head, and the echoes of Nelly's giddy laughter. Conversation on the porch lagged.

"Pop, you and I are expected at Aunt Elsa's," Sigismund Maroni said, suddenly. Victoria could almost imagine this odious man, with his black moustache, to be laughing at her.

"But are we to have no music?" the old man asked, getting up obediently like a good but disappointed child. Victoria's wild imagination suddenly visualized her leading them into the parlour, opening the grand piano. The strains of exquisite music would lure the elders in, to admire, and then there might be tea, laughter, the remains of the cocoanut layer cake. . . .

But even in this dream she was too late, Addie and Lotta, who was the cook, at this moment walked across the side lawn; they would go to the graveyard, and then to seven o'clock

Benediction, and come home at nine, to wash the dishes the family would leave from a pick-up supper. This would be ended at about eleven; then Lotta and Addie would soak the laundry for a large family of women, which they would be hanging out when Victoria loitered downstairs at nine o'clock Monday morning. To be sure she would wait on herself at breakfast, her mother insisted on that, she said it was one of the things that kept "help" contented. Only the master and Bertie got any sort of service on Mondays, and even that was apt to be from mother and sisters.

"Look me up if you come to New York, Miss Brewer," said Sigismund Maroni. They were going, and she felt sick and ashamed. For weeks the memory of her helpless inhospitality would bring the blood to Victoria's sensitive face. She had a last impulse toward easy warmth, remembered that her grandfather, in the room directly over the piano, was taking his afternoon nap, stifled the impulse, and walked slowly and uncomfortably with her guests to the gate.

"Are you going back to New York?" she asked.

"Sure. And I want to take the old folks with me," Sigismund said. "There are people there," he added, "who are glad nough to pay my father to hear him play the piano!"

She remembered it when she walked back. And she told herself that she hated him! Yet the memory of his big figure swaggering along beside the little bent one was vaguely admirable, too.

"Pa tell you that Bertie's going into the firm?" Esme asked her, in the doorway. Esme had watched the tennis until she could bear being baked and ignored no longer, and was going upstairs to read "Strathmore," a contraband article, now hidden under her mattress, and eat a delicacy then known as "French candy."

"Into the firm!" Victoria said scornfully. "He'll be only a clerk! Did Pa say anything about me?" She added.

"Why should he?" Esme asked.

"Why, you know very well that I talked him and Mama—almost!—into letting me go and study to be a nurse," Victoria said eagerly, and not quite truthfully. "At the Children's Hospital, where you don't have anything but women and children anyway—and he said he'd see!"

There was an element of self-protection in the eager rush with which the subject had been changed. Victoria suffered with agonizing jealousy of Bertie—or rather, of Bertie's life. His ready pocket-money, years ago, his airs when he had escorted her to the dentist, his independence in college days, interesting his sisters and mother with the mere accounts of dinners at the Palace, and of bills at the Orpheum, and lately, his miraculous and enchanting visit of two months in the fabled eastern states had all made her almost writhe with envy. And now, he was to go in with Pa, and would put on goodness knows what airs on that account, while she, burning to share all this glorious youth and life with him, must go on listening, watching, admiring, envying——

"He's going to get seventy-five dollars to start with," Esme tossed off, in conclusion, as she went upon her way.

Victoria never forgot the moment. It was one of the most unpalatable of her life. This was too much.

She stood still, in the doorway of the dark, square hallway, and life was unendurably bitter in her mouth. Seventy-five dollars a month! To waste, to spend, to fling about royally. Bertie might ask his friends to lunch, he might buy himself a new tennis racket——! While she, cleverer and better read than Bertie, would go on teasing Pa for a dollar, or two dollars——!

Slow angry tears came to her eyes. She looked at herself in the hatrack mirror; the ugly glare of the afternoon sunlight cast an unbecoming shine upon her face, and her hair was mussed. Slowly she dragged herself upstairs, and slowly washed her face and brushed her hair.

But here, at her own better-lighted mirror, she suddenly perceived herself to be looking unusually pretty and serious, and this was enough to restore her to a melancholy but exquisite pleasure in life. She descended the stairs dramatically and joined the group of elders under the trees with the air of a leading lady.

As she quietly, and with a deep sigh, took a chair, her Aunt Lucy, Mrs. Harry Crabtree, gave her a shrewd but welcoming glance. Lucy was an alert, stout, dark woman, with heavy eyebrows and prominent frog-like eyes. She wore glasses on a chain and had a great many definite opinions. One of them was that she had thrown away far more brilliant prospects in life to marry the gentle, unsuccessful younger son of Reuben Crabtree, some sixteen years ago, and another that she herself was a tremendously capable woman, a pattern among the wives and mothers of her day. Lucy was always ready with promising schemes, and when other women mildly marvelled at them, she had a crisp and satisfied way of implying that it was only because she did not permit herself to be engulfed and buried in petty household drudgeries as they did that she had time for these glorious plans. She was one of those fortunate persons who can make listeners believe that they have achieved something by merely talking about it; Lucy could somehow make an overdue bill seem more creditable to her than many a woman could a bank-account. She was amazingly glib; and essentially an egotist. All their circle, May and Fanny included, were convinced that Lucy was a marvellous manager, and that the financial difficulties of the family were entirely Harry's fault, and would have been infinitely worse with any other wife than Lucy to handle them. When she boasted of the economical arrangement she had made to have the children's pictures taken, or to have the stove moved, nobody thought to ask her simply why these things need be done at all. Lucy had always anticipated any such possibility. She was one of the few women of her generation who would admit quite openly to poverty, and this made all other women feel that she was exceptionally practical.

"Three years old! May Brewer gave it to me. Cleaned 'em myself with Spanish bark!" said Lucy, when kindly comment was made upon her hats, frocks, or gloves. Twenty years later all women would be saying these things. But in the inarticulate days of Cleveland's first administration, Lucy's honesty was unique.

"Well, Vick, who are you in love with now?" she asked the girl to-day, with her brisk manner, after she had repeated for the tenth time the news that Uncle Harry and Georgie couldn't come. "Oh, Aunt Lucy, aren't you awful!" Vick protested, smiling. "I'm going to be a trained nurse—ask Papa," she countered, smiling.

"We'll see about that!" Stephen smiled, allowing her to play with the fantastic notion.

"Vick would soon get tired of wiping up bathroom floors and taking orders from a disagreeable head-nurse!" May said teasingly. "It's not all flirting with a handsome young doctor, I assure you, Vick!"

"Oh, Mama, I know it's not!" the girl defended herself uncomfortably.

"You haven't the faintest idea what you're talking about!" her father said, faintly annoyed. "I don't want any one of my daughters to get the idea she's strong-minded!" he added firmly. Victoria subsided, impressed, but Stephen did not leave her long in discomfort. Good-naturedly he invited her to walk with him to see how the tennis was going, and the girl eagerly sprang to her feet, hugging his arm as they sauntered away.

Now, his wife thought anxiously, was the moment in which Mrs. Bob and Mrs. Harry might naturally be expected to talk of farewells. But Ella and Lucy sat on comfortably;—they had missed the five-forty train, she reflected, or at least they could only catch it now by a scramble. The next was at seven-eight, and there was a later train at ten-ten.

Lucy knew this, if Ella did not, May reflected in exasperation. Ten minutes more—five minutes more—and the Robert Crabtrees and the three Harry Crabtrees would have to be asked to supper. She could have slapped Lucy when Lucy said idly:

"Wonderful here, under the trees. I always think the late afternoon is the pleasantest time of all, in summer. Look at the light there through the willow—wonderful red colour. You were a Miss Sewall, weren't you?" she said to Ella, to whom they were all speaking pointedly rather than risking the use of her name.

"I—yes, I was!" Ella answered nervously, blinking. "My mother was a Wade—Sayrah Wade."

"We were Southerners—Bunkers," Lucy claimed, elegantly.

Ella merely looked anxiously polite at this, but May felt a little resentful.

"Crabtree's Crossing, Illinois, was named for Pa's father," she stated. "I suppose Bob has told you that?"

"We have no branch of the Daughters of the Revolution here, yet," Lucy said; "I should like it so much! I was wondering, May," she added animatedly, "if it wouldn't pay me to get in touch with the national headquarters! I believe I could manage a western branch, going to Benecia and Marysville, you know—"

"Pa's grandfather fought in the Revolution," May answered

nervously. In her mind she said, "The cake—the cold meat—maybe Vick would make chocolate——"

"I believe I'll do that very thing," Lucy was murmuring interestedly. "They must have to have a secretary, somebody to manage a branch! And it's exactly the sort of work I could do. You see," she said aloud to Ella, "my Georgie's the only Crabtree grandson, after all!"

"Oh, come—come!" May protested laughingly. "Where does Bertie come in?"

"My dear, your Bertie doesn't count at all!" Lucy assured her lightly. "A daughter's child, you see. It's the *name!*"

This was a new and humiliating point, to May. She saw its force, and subsided into resentful silence.

"I wish Rob and I had had a boy," Ella said, with her crisp definiteness. "Too bad! Not only for the Crabtree name," she added, "but there's a great deal of furniture and silver that my sister has, but that my grandmother said was to be divided among our children. My sister has three children: Grace, Kate, and Tom!" finished Ella, shooting the names at them like projectiles.

"The Bunkers—that is the direct line from my uncle, Colonel Condé Bunker, have all the old things of the family, of course, at the homestead in Asheville," Lucy added. May felt the colour come into her face. Idiotic fashion for Lucy Crabtree to talk, May fumed. Lucy, who did her own work in a shabby little cottage in the Mission! In their fifteen years' acquaintance May had never heard such rubbish before!

Nettled, she was casting about for a fresh subject, when Lucy said graciously to Bob's wife:

"One feels a barbarian here! It is like hearing from home to realize that the east is still the east. How long shall you be here, Ella—I must call you Ella!"

Instantly May's attention was diverted, and she leaned forward eagerly to hear the reply.

For May Brewer, who, as happy wife, mother, sister, and daughter, was naturally the centre of this large group, had been secretly fretting ever since she had had a few minutes private conversation with her husband, just before the late mid-day dinner.

It had taken place upstairs, in their large, orderly bedroom, while Mrs. Brewer was changing her percale sacque for a flowered satine gown, and her husband was brushing up for dinner at the stationary wash-stand. He had rubbed his fine full head of hair about, rumpled his beard, splashed his face, and towelled vigorously. Now he was combing his thick hair into place and bending over to eye himself closely in the great mirror of the marble-topped bureau.

"May," said he, "have you any idea what brings Bob home?"

May Brewer instantly had come to attention. Her husband loved her, and trusted her with every possible domestic responsibility; but this was a tone she rarely heard, a tone he reserved for business.

"No, dear—why?" she fluttered.

"Just wondering!" And Stephen Brewer's soft red mouth, visible in his thick beard, formed for whistling. "Of course, it would be somewhat complicated for me if he has come west with any idea of entering the firm," he presently added.

"Why should he?" the woman said, promptly on the defensive. "*You've* made it what it is—you've worried and borrowed money and slaved over it! I fail to see"—May was getting heated—"I fail to see what earthly claim Robert has! He withdrew, just as Harry did——"

"Well, well, well!" Stephen soothed her. "It was just a notion——"

"What did he say?" his wife demanded. For where her man's happiness, or her children's welfare, were concerned, she was always alert and apprehensive.

"Nothing much. But he asked your father how old Rossi was getting along, and—as luck would have it!—your father said that the old man was retiring pretty soon. My taking Bertie in might make it awkward to refuse Bob."

"But Pa didn't say anything about the mail-order department?"

"Oh, no—no! It was just a notion. What has Mrs. Robert done with her Boston house?"

"Rented it." Mrs. Brewer's eyes had widened with sudden alarm. "She had inherited some money, you know. They spoke as if they might be here for some weeks."

"Bob," his brother-in-law had predicted firmly, "would be absolutely no good to me, in the firm! None whatever!"

And on this dark note the conversation had ended.

But it was her memory of this conversation, with its first thin wedge of fear, that May Brewer had in mind when Lucy quite innocently asked Ella how long her western visit was to be, and Ella quite innocently carried the subject nearest her thoughts a little further.

"We don't know," Ella had said. And then, "Is—is your husband—Harry, I mean, in the firm?"

Lucy said briskly, without looking at May:

"Ought to be, of course! For Father Crabtree is getting on—wonderful old man that he is, and naturally, with the business growing—as everyone says it is!—Stephen can't be expected——"

"Stephen has been very fortunate in getting splendid men to work with him," May said, quickly. She and Lucy were out in the lists now, and steel was ringing on steel, but Ella was quite unconscious of it.

"Still, the business is Father Crabtree's!" Lucy said. "Of course, he has made a place for Bertie, which is quite right," she pursued silkily, "but Bertie won't be worth that very generous salary for some time—and Harry's place is in the firm, and I think Harry—with his knowledge of human nature, would be quite invaluable to the house!"

"We'll see!" was all Mrs. Brewer could say, trembling nervously. She managed a shaken smile, but she was almost sick with shock. Lucy had never taken this tone with her before; the affairs of the firm had always been sacredly vested in Stephen. She realized that Lucy, always shameless in self-interest, had already tacitly engaged the sympathies of Mrs. Bob, whose own interests were naturally identical. She was wishing frantically that Stephen was here, when Lucy spoke again.

"What is Harry's business now? Why, we ran away to England when we were first married, and he had a position with an insurance company there. Afterward the same company sent him here with the agency, but they were English, of course, and we are—well, it was just a case of our *utter* provincialism!" said Lucy, warmly. "So that didn't do. So then Harry went in with the Atlas rubber people—hot water bags and gossamers, you know—and he's been there twelve years. But of course the desire of his heart is to be with his father—he's *devoted* to his father——"

"He wasn't so devoted, twelve years ago, but what he——"

May was beginning, tremblingly, when Lucy, whose eyes had wandered, rose with a sudden smile.

"Why, bless his heart, there he is!" she said, in her richest voice, fluttering maternally toward old Reuben, who was coming steadily, if shakily, from the house. May rose, and somewhat resentfully helped the capable Lucy to lower him into his seat.

"You had your hot milk, Pa?" the daughter asked, conscientiously.

The old man was smiling fatuously at Lucy.

"Where's your pretty girl, Lucy?" he cackled, the tremulous face muscles steadied by the upward sweep of the determined old jaw.

"Which one?" Lucy laughed. "Both my girls are pretty! But I'm afraid you mean Nelly, you bad old man!"

"Nelly—that's the one. I'm in love with little Nelly!" said Reuben Crabtree, in great spirits.

"Oh, then, you're like all the other boys!" Lucy scolded him, beating playfully upon the wrinkled, bloodless old hand. And a moment later she added: "Here they all come!"

They were streaming back, hot and tumbled and laughing, from the tennis-court and the croquet-ground. First came Miss Fanny, with Lou and Tina and Vick hanging upon her arms, and little Alice Crabtree also in the group, watching their animated faces in quiet pleasure. Then came three young men, Bertie, Davy Dudley, a gawky, loosely built big, shabbily dressed youth who had come to San Rafael with Lucy and her girls that morning, and lastly, a certain Rudy Sessions, introduced to his family by Bertie as an acquaintance of the ferryboat.

All three of these were crowding about Nelly and fighting for place beside her, laughing loudly and boyishly at her least little saucy remark, and leaning eagerly over her fairylike little face. She gave them pouts, little pushes, she widened her blue eyes and pursed her delicious mouth, she shook her flyaway curls. Fanny and the Brewer girls were rather ostentatiously unaware of her and her companions, but Lucy smiled knowingly: wherever young men and Nelly were, it was always like this.

Alice, Lucy considered was the family beauty—a tall, madonna-faced little girl, with wide-open, fine, conscientious blue eyes, and dark hair, flat straight shoulders like a boy's, and a

wide beautifully shaped mouth that showed big white teeth
when she smiled.   But Nelly possessed an undeniable and irresistible charm.   She was six years older than her half-sister,
slender, beautifully made, with a white dimpled hand and a
heart-shaped face that was as wistful as an upturned flower.
There was something flower-like about Nelly; in spite of her
perfectly healthy rosiness and her joyous laugh, her skin was too
fair, her lips too red, and her flyaway pale gold hair too soft and
bright for any human standard.

She was that perfectly normal product of the day, a born
flirt, as innocent as a butterfly, and as ignorant of life at twenty-
two years as she had been at twenty-two minutes.   Nelly's
daughters might never do what their mother did, without the
honest consciousness of wrong-doing.   So much they would
pay for a more independent and more enlightened heritage.

But Nelly could flirt with a perfectly free conscience.   Her
entire education, along certain much-discussed lines, was that
she must marry some day, and meanwhile might have as many
beaux and good times as she could.   So she dimpled, and rolled
her blue eyes, placed artless touches of her soft little hand upon
susceptible masculine wrists just when they would do the most
mischief, made engagements only to break them, wore one man's
flowers while she was out with another man, nibbled this one's
candy and clipped the stems of that one's roses, divided her
dances, sat out decorous measures like minuets and reels, and
wore out more slippers than she did shoes, in the course of a
year.

The Brewer girls, who called her cousin, were secretly envious and admiring of this brilliant creature.   But outwardly,
when they discussed her, they took their key from their mother
and Aunt Fanny, who said regretfully that it was not quite nice.
Aunt Fanny always admitted, in this connection, that she herself had done a good deal too much of that sort of thing years ago,
although in her younger days the men were somehow different,
much more in earnest, and much more respectful.   It was
generally conceded that Aunt Fanny had been a "terror" with
the men, and now and then, late at night, when her sister had
gone to bed and she was alone with her older nieces, Fanny
would confess delightful indiscretions—the time she had told
Mr. Runyon—who was married now, and a Judge at that!—
that she had a headache and must retire, and then had gone to

ride with Mr. Treat, who was also married, years ago, and had named his fourth daughter Frances. And the time that the French boy made her an offer of marriage after knowing her exactly one day——! And had taken out a pistol, too, and threatened to kill himself if she didn't accept him——! But when pressed, Fanny always became facetious. Men——! she would say. Wouldn't have any one of 'em bothering about! As for children, well, her young ones would have to have tin ears and copper bottoms, declared this daring and delightful aunt. The girls always laughed wickedly at this, and May, if she were present, would say, "My *land*, Fanny!"

Esme and Victoria, hugging their knees, getting chillier and chillier in their nightgowns, would listen in rapt excitement. Oh, to have men languishing at their feet! To have "offers"! Aunt Fanny had had her first at fifteen, when she came up from the San Jose Convent a very accomplished and desirable young lady indeed, in that womanless west. She played the piano, danced like a fairy, and had the prettiest dresses in the city, then.

But that was long ago. Aunt Fanny was religious now, and kept house for her old father, and had inherited Aunt Jenny's money. The dancing was over, and the pretty gowns were dark and decorous. And the bright young beauty was a lean, talkative woman nearing fifty, whose complexion was light brown under darker brown freckles, and whose two prominent upper front teeth had worn themselves two faint grooves in her full under lip.

Between herself and her sister there was real affection, tempered still sometimes by a little natural jealousy. May had the lovely family and the devoted husband, and May lived in the old home, although not without constant twinges of apprehension lest Pa in a moment of weakness leave it to Fanny. But Fanny had freedom, and had Aunt Jenny's money, and she also had what might have been described as the bodily possession of Pa. Pa adored Fanny, and just how influential she was with him both May and Stephen sometimes wondered. While they had all lived together here in San Rafael there had been nothing to fear. But suddenly Pa and Fanny had announced that they thought they would like to try the city, and furniture long in storage had been unpacked, and new furniture had been added, and now they had a little house in California Street, which was beginning to be very fashionable, just above Van Mess Avenue. There was an extra bedroom there, to be sure, for any one of the "darling girlies" who might want to spend a night away from home, and there were many Sundays, like to-night, when Pa and Fanny came back to the old home to stay; but still, May felt that she had somehow lost touch with her father, and as he was old, and as he was often unreasonable, she regretted that his last years should be influenced against what might be "his better judgment."

May was rasped now, as Fanny had been, by little Nelly Crabtree's—Nelly used her step-father's name—cool appropriation of all the young men. Bertie, too! May had no intention of encouraging any preposterous hopes on Nelly's part in *that* direction. What Davy Dudley did was a matter of supreme unimportance to May; he was a neighbour of Lucy's in the city, a country nobody, penniless and inconsiderable. But this new young man, this Rudy Sessions, who had turned up from nowhere about an hour ago, was worthy of consideration. All young men were potential husbands now, for Esme, Vicky, Tina, and Lou, and this youth had an unusual appearance and a good name. May looked keenly at Rudy Sessions.

She saw a slender, nicely built boy of perhaps twenty-four, so fair that his face would have looked almost babyish, but for the gold-rimmed glasses that were attached to a gold chain that was looped over his ear. His voice had a faintly feminine strain, but he was quick and definite in speech, and he spoke unusually well. His fair hair was smoothly brushed into a pompadour, his light summer suit was buttoned up to within a few inches of the chin, where the wide square folds of an ascot tie showed. He wore a straw hat with a blue band and elastic. There was something that faintly suggested boredom, superiority, sophistication, in young Mr. Sessions, and May felt quite a flutter of gratification when Victoria's nonsense suddenly made him laugh quite heartily.

"You are staying in our lovely San Rafael, Mr. Sessions?" asked May. She liked his quick, respectful, sobered look.

"A college friend and I have a little camp at San Anselmo, Mrs. Brewer," he said.

"Oh, you've been to college?" May said eagerly.

"Well, I didn't finish," he admitted readily. "Bert and I have exchanged momentous opinions on the boat several times, and he asked me to drop in and see his family sometime," he added, pleasantly.

"Well, now that you've found the way, you must come again," May said, delighted.

"Are you working—that is, do you do something—you know what I mean, Mr. Rudy?" Victoria fumbled.

Everyone laughed at the slip, and Vicky turned crimson, but the ready Rudy said, in his friendly way:

"That's all right—I wish you *would* call me Rudy. Yes," he answered, "I'm temporarily working with Furman, the piano house. My folks wanted me to finish college, but I only had a year. My mother says I'm a rolling stone. She and my sister live in Portland."

"And your father, too?" May asked.

"My father died twenty years ago," Rudy said, gravely. "But I've an uncle, my mother's brother, who's got a ranch in Contra Costa County; he wants me to farm with him. And I may—someday." May murmured sympathetically; she was immensely drawn to this romantic boy, and felt quite motherly toward him. Everything he had told her was right and fitting for a prospective son-in-law, and she mentally gave him to Esme, even as they sat there dreaming on the fallen dry scimitars of the eucalyptus.

But Vicky had already appropriated him to herself: she sat in a pleasant dream, his friendly "I wish you *would* call me Rudy," still sounding in her ears.

It was still broad daylight at six o'clock of the long Sunday afternoon when Stephen Brewer came very quietly in at the side door of the house. He and Robert had had a stroll, up toward the wooded hills that so loosely enfolded the sprawling country town, and Robert had seemed amenable to advice, which was, in this case, that he, Robert, would undoubtedly do very well with a cotton agency in the city. Now Robert had turned toward the invisible, but audible, group on the lawn, and Stephen was going upstairs for what was his usual custom: the kindly awakening of his old father-in-law, and a genial talk with the old man, while they both brushed and straightened themselves for supper.

Carra, the impassive old negress, met him in the upper hall.

"Mist' Steve," said she, clutching his arm. "Raik'n yo' pa ill!"

"Mr. Crabtree ill!" Stephen repeated, in a sharp whisper. "What makes you say so!"

"I ben knockin' and knockin' at he do'," Carra said, in the same unearthly undertone, "and he ain' answer. En I open d' do, and he all hunch' up on he baid, and he ain' move nor cry——"

"My God——!" Stephen said, horrified. And quickly and quietly they moved through the twilighted dimness of the bare upper hall to the old man's room. "The poor old fellow has dropped off—I knew it would come so!" Stephen thought. And he thought that Robert had come too late, all the threads were in his own hands now. He had been anticipating this moment for years.

The hall was dim, but streaming sunset light shone redly into the bedroom, as Stephen, followed by the whimpering old coloured woman, came swiftly in. He moved, with a quick exclamation, to the bed. But it was only the blue silk comforter and the old man's discarded dressing-gown, that had united to form the semblance of a twisted body, and Stephen started back with a great exclamation of reaction from shock.

"He simply waked early, Carra, and has gone downstairs!" he said. And with a hearty laugh at their scare he left her and went downstairs in his turn.

But so deep had been the sudden conviction of change, that he found himself recalling the abandoned phrases that had half formed themselves in his mind: the little dream of dignity and tenderness with which he would have taken his place as the head of the family, quieting May, reassuring Fanny, directing his children. And to-morrow—at the office!——

"Well, it was merely a scare!" Stephen said, shaking himself.

Sure enough, there was the old man, quite as hale and hearty as he had been for ten years, enjoying the homage of the big group. Stephen smiled at him, took a daughter's chair, and slipped a fatherly arm about the young waist. It was Tina who had given him her place, lazily hoping, as she kissed his forehead and smoothed his hair, that her mother would not shortly summon her to service for supper.

Victoria was on her mother's chair, and they were murmuring.

"Plenty of bread and butter, dear, and fruit, and the cream

cheese, and the cake—all the cake you can find.   And put on piles of plates, and make chocolate—use yesterday's milk. There may be corned beef and there may be sardines.   Just use your own judgment."

Victoria rose with a spring; she was healthily hungry, but Esme was headachy from chocolates, and Tina had had thrilling tea—weak tea and stale biscuits, with the rector.   She and Rose Pendergast had worked so late with the children at the Guild Room, that the young man had somewhat timidly suggested it, and with much merry investigation of his bachelor cupboard, Tina and the grim and angular and deeply devout Miss Pendergast had managed it.   So neither sister had any enthusiasm for supper, and Victoria, abandoning the possibility of Alice and Louisianna, who had disappeared, went kitchenward alone.

The kitchen in the old Crabtree house had not been built with the convenience of its occupants in mind.   It was some twenty by thirty feet, with a quite considerable walk between the large, well-equipped sink, and the enormous brick-based range.   To the china pantry was another long distance, and the table, under two splendid windows, was some twelve feet away from both range and sink.   It had been much admired, some years ago, when the big, pretentious house was new, and women visitors, peeping in at its spacious order, had exclaimed in envy. Mrs. Brewer could always say honestly that it was a lovely kitchen, and Victoria loved it.   What Addie and Lotta, who had it to sweep and scrub and walk over, thought of it, nobody ever thought or cared to ask.

Spotlessly clean, in the late Sunday afternoon, it smelled pleasantly of stored foods, apples and bread, and of scrubbed wood, and of sunshine captured and shut in.   The range winked one red eye, and the shining zinc of the sink was spattered by just a few drops of water falling into a handleless cup.   Lotta had washed and piled and rinsed and scrubbed vigorously, and had combed her own hair at this sink, and then had dressed, and, passing through the kitchen on her way to the cemetery, had stopped for a last cupful of cold water.   This cup was the only article out of place when Victoria bore down upon the scene and began to snap open pot-closets and bring forth half-consumed foods.

"Heavens—how you frightened me!" she said, as a young man stepped quietly behind her.   It was Davy Dudley, Nelly's admitted admirer for some months now, a tall, silent boy, with a bashful manner.

"I think I shall have to get the seven-ten," said this young man seriously, to Victoria, "I wonder if you will say good-bye to them all—and to Mrs. Harry Crabtree—and your mother—I should be so much obliged!"

"Oh, but why are you going?" Victoria said, eagerly. Here was a delightful and mysterious occurrence! "How did you happen to come through this way?"

"I was—I was reading in the dining-room," he said, embarrassed, "and I heard voices—Alice and your younger sister—and I thought I'd just—slip away!"

"Oh, but now listen," Victoria protested cheerfully, "we're just going to have supper! And I know Nelly will expect you to go back with them——"

"No, that's exactly what she won't," he said nervously; "she—she says she may stay all night, and that—that Mr. Sessions wants her to go riding with him to-morrow morning!"

"Rudy Sessions!" Victoria exclaimed. "Why, she hardly knows him!"

"That's what I thought," Davy Dudley said, not looking at her.

"In the first place," Victoria began, "in the first place, we none of us know him!—Thank you," she interrupted herself to say, as Davy Dudley quite simply helped her to lift out several great crusty home-made loaves from the big tin. "In the second place," pursued Victoria, conscious that she was romantically placed, and revelling in romance, "he'll have to hire horses from the livery stable—and they're awful! And then I don't see how she can stay all night, for I have to double up with Esme, anyway, when Grandpa's here.—Two peaches," she said, in reference to preserves, "and some of that marked 'Currant Pickle' for the meat. Thank you, Davy." She had never called him by his name before.

"She isn't the sort of woman that would ever care for a fellow like me," said Davy, casually, cutting ham sombrely, and unconscious of Victoria's little overture.

"I think she is!" Victoria assured him, thrilling. This was the next best thing to having a beau of one's own, and as she had never had that, it was a great occasion just as it stood. "Why, why don't you tell her how you feel, Davy?" she said.

"I *have* told her," said Davy desperately. "I told her to-day!"

The girl looked at his honest, unhappy young face, and her whole being was flooded with joy.

"Davy, I'm so sorry!" she breathed, over the spicy richness of pickled currants and the sliced fresh cheese.

Nelly, the recipient of these unbelievable attentions and honours, was only a year older than Victoria, to be sure, but Victoria always felt much the younger. This was perhaps because she was quite unconsciously affected by the fact that she, Victoria, was a rich man's protected daughter, her education was not complete, she was still watched and guided like a child. Whereas Nelly, whose circumstances were humble, had gone boldly into training, at seventeen, and was now a kindergarten teacher, and was accustomed to holding her own in the world. Victoria had simple faith that in a few years her own popularity would equal Nelly's; meanwhile the somewhat precocious career of Nelly was a thing to envy and admire.

Yet it was a very youthful Nelly who presently drifted into the kitchen, having parted affectionately from the obnoxious Sessions, and sent the equally devoted Bertie upstairs to wash and change. She joined Davy, at the side-door of the passage, and they pulled honeysuckle buds, and sucked them, while they murmured. Victoria, who had half a dozen appreciative assistants now—Louisianna and Alice, Aunt Lucy and Aunt Fanny—could hear some of their words as she came and went. "Well, you were a goose to think so, Davy. . . . Well, perhaps I am a goose. . . . You certainly are! . . . Well, perhaps I certainly am! . . . No, I was going to tell you, but now I won't! . . . Because I won't. . . ."

Not eloquent, yet with Nelly's bright, flyaway golden head close to the infatuated boy's face, and Nelly's wholly intoxicating penitence all for him, perhaps Davy Dudley found it sufficient. When they strolled to the gate, unnoticed, he could not resist the temptation to try it once again, wouldn't she—couldn't she—let him hope?

No, she definitely wouldn't, and he was a foolish boy. But she would sit next to him at the crowded happy supper table, and later, on the boat going home, he and she managed to slip away from her mother and Alice, and the Robert Crabtree's, and find seats downstairs on the narrowest little deck in the world, close above the tumbling dark water. And there, upon

Davy's complaining that Bertie had accompanied them half way, and she had talked to no one else, Nelly let him kiss her, more than once, under the twinkling summer stars.

Grandpa Crabtree and Aunt Fanny stayed at the big San Rafael homestead overnight, and in the evening after the guests had gone, as always, rushing for the train, the family sat on about the dinner table, and went on with microscopic helpings of jam and crackers and cheese and more cocoa, until almost nine o'clock. Bertie's perfectly unprecedented action, in accompanying Nelly as far as Saucelito on the homeward trip, seriously upset his mother. Nelly was no blood-kin, after all, and she was not inclined to welcome a future daughter-in-law in Nelly!

"How serious is Nelly's affair with David?" Fanny asked. Victoria looked important.

"It's very serious—for him!" she said. "Nelly doesn't like him. She's much crazier about Bertie."

"Now, how can you say that, dear?" her mother asked nervously. Victoria told all she knew, and much more. Quoted, Davy's confidences assumed great importance.

"But, Mama, wouldn't you like to have her marry Bertie?" she ended simply. Her mother flushed with annoyance.

"Ridiculous!" she said.

"Leetle Nelly's mighty pooty," said the old man, suddenly. Then he turned to his son-in-law. "Looks to me like Robbit is beginning to feel an interest in the old shop?" he ventured.

Stephen Brewer, now smoking a big cigar, and very genial and comfortable in the bosom of his family, smiled and nodded thoughtfully. He had not been attending Directors' Meetings with his father-in-law for twenty years without learning some caution.

"Shouldn't wonder!" he answered, noncommittally.

"Robert has shown no particular interest in all these bad years," May said, lightly. "Didn't——" She saw when she glanced at her husband that she was making a mistake, but she couldn't help it, and went on. "Didn't Robert sell his stock years ago, when he wanted cash, and leave you and Pa to carry the whole responsibility?"

"I thought he did!" Fanny assisted her, nervously beating her own nose.

"Well, we've got to pay salaries to someone!" cackled the old president and owner of the business. The old man had been delighted to see his son, and was quite innocently eager to keep him. But more than that, he was amazingly shrewd at seventy-five, and he was not quite pleased with the fashion in which young Bertie had been insinuated into a comfortable position with the firm. It had been managed very quickly and quietly. Stephen's offhand, "I suppose we must take the boy in?" had been the only question addressed to him on the subject, and the point of Bertie's salary had been passed through at the directors' meeting, in a list of more important details. Perhaps old Reuben had promised Bertie a start in the family business, but he did not remember doing so even once, much less the "hundred times" of which his daughter spoke. And if the Brewers could do a little manipulating for their son, then so might Reuben do a little for his; it was, after all, all in the family.

"I don't see why he couldn't try Rossi's work," the old man persisted, and May almost audibly gasped. But Stephen only went on smoking placidly, and smiled at his father-in-law.

"I doubt if he could do Rossi's work, but if you want to make work for Bob, we'll manage it!" said Stephen.

"I could step in to-morrow——" old Reuben Brewer Crabtree said. But for various reasons Stephen did not favour this, and he said hastily that he would talk to Yeasley and Woolcock, and they would "see."

The half-hour after nine struck, and such members of the family as were not heavy with food and idleness, bestirred themselves to clear the table. The dining room was a large, bay-windowed room, papered in reddish brown, and with a wainscot and woodwork painted yellowish brown, with a burl carefully brushed in in clear yellow. On the kitchen side of the room, beside the large heavy kitchen door, was a shelf, about waist-high, and behind it a sliding panel. Through this panel hot dishes were passed from the kitchen, from Lotta to Addie; now the dishes and plates were scrambled through again to the two maids, who had returned from church and were straightening the kitchen between raw heart-rending yawns.

Bertie came in late, and Victoria goodnaturedly brought him a second supper; his mother sat opposite him and watched him eat. He said he "had to see a fellow in Saucelito anyway, about a boat," but both mother and sister knew it was not true. Victoria to annoy Bertie said that she thought Rudy Sessions was crazy about Nelly, but maybe Nelly liked Davy Dudley best.

"She likes Davy merely because he is a neighbour—doesn't his mother keep boarders, next to Aunt Lucy's house?" Mrs. Brewer said, her heart yearning over her son.

"His aunt," Victoria said, yawning, and laying her head on the table.

"If you had better manners, and acted as nicely as Nelly does, maybe some day you'd have a man after you!" Bertie said, goaded quite out of his usual sweetness by the awful thought that Davy and Nelly were still together.

"I don't see any men about here anyway," Victoria said. "I only see a few kids that get sea-sick on a perfectly calm sea—when even the girls on the yacht don't get ill—and have to lie down——"

"Victoria!" said her mother. The girl laughed shame-facedly and took her departure with a great assumption of an airy manner, humming as she went. She was really fond of Bertie; she was really rather generous to her sisters and brother; but the thought of that preposterous salary, that dizzying financial independence that would soon be Bertie's, had been biting into her like an acid all day. She was almost as old as Bertie. If they would only take her own ambitions seriously—only help her to her own work!

In the hall she ran into Tina and her Aunt Fanny, who linked affectionate arms about her.

"Glad to have old Fanny back for a night?" asked the older woman archly. "Come out and get a breath of fresh air—it is delicious out!"

They stepped into the quiet dooryard. But Victoria declined. Two was company in this case. Aunt Fanny liked confidences, liked little tête-à-têtes. Victoria thought she could find her father, smoking beside her grandfather in the soft gloom of the porch, and coax him to let her consider the nursing possibility.

Miss Fanny and Tina blundered with some quiet laughter in the warm darkness between the berry bushes, down past a drying green, and through a long grape-arbour that was beginning to be silvered magically by the rising moon. The dry yellow grass under their feet gave up a sharp pungent scent in the dew, and all the dimly outlined bushes and trees looked softened and mysterious. Two or three hundred feet from the house there was the railing of a paddock, and the two women could see the horses, in the moonlight, the big outline of the hay barn, and the rising slopes of wood and field that led into the surrounding hills

". . . just Miss Pendergast and I. And so we had tea, *imagine!*" said Tina, leaning on the upper rail.

"Now—Tina, Tina! Am I mistaken or isn't that rather— rather something new?" Fanny asked, in the dark. The younger woman laughed a little consciously.

"Oh, it wasn't anything, Aunt Fanny! Truly. Why, you know I know men, we've always had such lots of 'em about— and this was just the most natural thing in the world—truly."

"I suppose he has the Hardisty girls and the Munheimer girls there, all the time?" Fanny suggested demurely.

"Oh, aren't you terrible, Aunt Fanny!" And Tina gave her a little push in the dark. "No, he said he hadn't had ladies there since his sister was here, but please don't go putting any significance on *that*—you bad thing!"

"Oh, I shan't do anything," Fanny said virtuously. The rest of the sentence was lost, until Tina said, "What did you say?" Then Fanny repeated innocently, "I said that I would leave the rest to *him!*"

Tina answered nothing to this, except an ecstatic little giggle and another little push. But presently she added: "I liked his sister so much—Mrs. Keating."

"That's good, that'll make things easier!" said the irrepressible Fanny. Tina turned to her shining eyes suddenly serious.

"You truly mustn't make so much of it, Aunt Fanny; you truly mustn't! It was just that we were late, and we had been working hard."

"And Miss Pendergast has such pretty golden hair!" Fanny suggested, and Tina laughed again, a little guiltily.

"We had to fumble and fuss about dreadfully, to get hold of the tea things, *imagine*," she confided, "and I gave him a good scolding for his untidiness! He *is* untidy, but personally I think he's the cleanest man I ever saw! I went into the bathroom to fill the kettle—and you ought to see the big sponges and towels!—of course I didn't really look about much, I knew Mama wouldn't wish me to. Miss Pendergast said that I mustn't dare scold him, but Mr. Yelland sat there smoking and smiling and saying that it did him good, it reminded him of home."

"Now, look here, dear, you mustn't play with him," Fanny said, after a fragrant, moon-flooded silence. Tina gave an exultant laugh and caught her aunt about the shoulders for a hug and a kiss.

"Not just the least tiny bit, Aunt Fanny?" she laughed naughtily. "Well, I'll promise you I'll be good!"

"Begin now, then," gasped Miss Fanny, straightening hair and collar and laughing breathlessly. "He made a very nice impression on me," she added, in an elder's judicial tone. Tina was glad only to talk of him, to keep the subject alive, in the enchanted moonlight.

"Mind you, Aunt Fanny, the girls laugh at him because he isn't—well, he isn't the sort of man who chatters with every lady he meets!" she said eagerly. Aunt Fanny, far from laughing at this, approved it very heartily, and was led to remember other young men, a quarter of a century ago, who had been similarly reserved. They hung on the fence of the corral, and talked on and on, coming blinking into the house at ten minutes past ten, amazed at the stuffy heat indoors and the lateness of the hour.

Esme, in pleading a headache, had merely been seeking privacy. All yesterday and to-day she had been busy, away from the prying eyes of mother and sisters, with a letter. A dozen times, in a panic, she had swept it into her table drawer. Now it was finished; she had only to watch for an opportunity to mail it unobserved, to-morrow. The letter was addressed to her chum, Miss Jenny Pembroke, in San Francisco, and covered thirty-seven closely written pages. The eighth, ninth, and tenth pages were typical of them all, and read: ". . . because rather than have him think that I could be guilty of even *dreaming* of that, I would gladly die. What I said, and what your brother and his friend must have heard, although I never *dreamed* that they were listening, was that I felt that it was hardly my place to explain it, because in the first place, it was Ada who made that most fatal and unfortunate remark, which really has changed my life for me, for I have never been placed in so terribly embarrassing a position before, and of course I will never get over it. I will never speak to Ada Lackey again, not if she was to implore me, but that is really not what I meant to write about. I thought if you could just casually mention to your brother, without even *hinting* that you had heard from me. . . ."

Esme had written and rewritten this twenty times—she hoped it was right now—she had been thinking about it all day. It was simply insufferable to her to have Frank Pembroke and that nice-looking friend of his think, for one instant, that she could say to Jenny that she, Esme Crabtree, didn't see anything so frightful about Ada Lackey's losing her petticoat at the Salisford picnic, "especially as she was engaged to be married." On the contrary, it was Ada who had said that, and Esme had said, as she felt, that if she had been Ada she would have died. And—whether the two young men had really heard the subject discussed or not, they had laughed suddenly, and had excused themselves from the breakfast room in the Pembroke house, where Jenny and Esme had been breakfasting and murmuring on the morning after the picnic—and Esme had hardly had a happy moment since, wondering what they thought of her. They might have been laughing at something else, of course, for she and Jenny had been at the far end of the table, and Frank and this Mr. Moran had been at the fire. But Esme's face grew scarlet every time she remembered how they had glanced her way, just as she had offered Ada's preposterous excuse of having been engaged to the man, and how they had laughingly retreated to the hall, and thence downtown. Yes, they must have heard. She went upstairs, and placed the letter conspicuously on her bureau, where she could not fail to see it in the morning, and already the phrases of another long letter began to shape itself in her head, upon the same subject.

"Of course they didn't!" she said, undressing. But getting into bed her face flamed again, and she said aloud, "I'll bet they did!"

Silence gradually established itself in the old Crabtree house, and the lights went out one by one. Fanny loitered long with her older nieces, before they turned out the gas; Louisianna was youthfully and beautifully asleep. Mrs. Brewer came in, plain and stout in her tucked long-sleeved nightgown, with her hair in a pigtail, and worriedly reminded them that it was eleven o'clock. She secretly felt sadly the burden of life—

Papa's worry about Robert, coming just now, did seem such a shame, and Bertie's being so unlike himself, when gently questioned about Nelly, had filled her with apprehension. Lucy Crabtree would put on most insufferable airs if her penniless girl captured the only son of May Brewer! And how the glory of having Bertie taken into the firm, suffered by this cloud of having Robert and his real or imaginary claims in the background!

Altogether it had been a long, full, hot Sunday, with some pleasant phases, as when she introduced her blooming girls to the childless Ella, and her glowing boy rode in on his bicycle, as when the obviously less prosperous Lucy and her rather shabbily dressed children joined in the happy confusion of Sunday supper getting—but then it had had its unfortunate side, too!

On the whole, the latter element predominated, and she lay awake for awhile in her big, plain room, with moonlight wheeling slowly over the worn "body Brussels" carpet that was so neatly pieced and nailed up against every baseboard, and with Stephen audibly and deeply slumbering beside her. They had been married more than twenty-five years and had never been one night apart.

CHAPTER IV

THE Harry Crabtrees lived in a little cottage in Shotwell Street, near Seventeenth, which was almost like living in a suburb in those days. To reach their neighbourhood, they took a Market Street car, left it at a crossing where a bearded old man had for many years called faithfully "Transfares fur the Mission!" and moved into a little horse car, whose driver would turn to look through the glass door behind him to see if his passengers were safely inside, and then shut the platform door with a rope and pulley. The passengers might not emerge from the car until they had deposited a five-cent piece in a bell box, but if they chanced not to have correct change, it was always possible to pass "two bits" or "four bits" through a flap in the front door to the driver, who stopped his horse, and groped in a leather-lined pocket for his change. Passengers, stumbling in and out, and stumbling to the door for change, made the interior of the car always diverting to onlookers, and to-night Davy and Alice and Nelly and their mother were interested in an old fisherman, with silvery scales on his rough coat, gold rings in his ears, and a curly beard, "like an apostle," Alice whispered, watching him in awe.

Leaving the car, the Crabtrees—for Nelly had been a mere baby at the time of her mother's second marriage, and always used her stepfather's name—walked two blocks south, passed a little shop, and two other two-story wooden houses with gardens, before coming to their own old-fashioned cottage, which stood well back in a space of almost vacant lots. There were a few fruit trees, gnarled old survivors of Spanish ownership. A little fence of wood, once painted red, but now with the faded colour peeling from its clumsy wheels and angles, ran across the front of the garden, but the side fences were plain planks, with here and there a board missing, and wild bushes, mallow and acacia and mustard, pushing themselves through, and the tracks of tag-playing children running under them.

In the garden were all the Californian garden flowers, with
a few truant poppies creeping in from the neighbouring lots,
and a few eastern blooms that Mrs. Crabtree, with other homesick eastern women, had somewhat unsuccessfully tried to
encourage there. She was an unusually energetic and restless woman, with real imagination, but she could never face
facts. Lucy indulged in dreams, and dish water cooled and
time passed while she elaborated them. She never went to
San Rafael without telling May what could be done with
that big house. She would sit down in her own disorderly
home, with beds unmade and dishes unwashed, three times a
week, from breakfast until almost noon, working out to the
last penny the profits that she would undoubtedly make from
some scheme or another.

There was never an empty house in the neighbourhood into
which Lucy did not, in imagination, move, taking boarders,
opening a girls' school, teaching music, cooking for other house-
wives.

"Biscuits——" she would say thoughtfully. "Nelly!"

"Yes, Mama!" Nelly would stop washing her face, in
the adjoining room, the better to hear.

"Nelly, what ought I get for my biscuits? Ten cents a
dozen?"

"Oh, fifteen." Nelly, hungry for lunch, would emerge.
"Mama, did you remember tea?"

"Oh, my dear, I didn't! And I don't know that we have
any butter. You might step round into Mission Street——"

No use to be angry: it was just Mama. Nelly would return,
nervously hungry and tired after her kindergarten day, to
find the stove still cold, and Lucy still tranced, at the table.

"Nelly, don't you marvel that people don't board out small
children, say from eight to six—or half-past-eight to half-past
five, say? Think of the convenience! A woman wants to go
downtown, she can't afford a regular nurse——"

"Move your arm just a little, Mama, I want the bread
knife," poor Nelly might say patiently. She knew that her
mother was mentally shepherding a score of small pensioners,
and would hear no reproach.

Harry had long ago learned to humour her; he was not clever
enough to realize just how difficult she made life for him.
Bills were never paid, there was neither system nor logic about

the way in which Lucy kept house. She forgot economies, and so had to turn, at the last moment, to extravagances. She bought ridiculous things, because they fitted into some one of her fantastic dreams. Her air was always that of the economist. It was economy, she said, to buy Georgie three pairs of shoes at a time, it was economy to pick up this large, almost new sail, at an auction, because if she ever carried out her idea of having a tea garden in the backyard, she would need it.

The Harry Crabtrees were always moving, because Lucy had always good reasons for the move. They must be near this street in case she opened her jelly shop, they must be near some other or she could not find a market for her hand-painted place cards. She bought boxes of oil paints, pyrographic outfits, straw for weaving, glass bottles to paint for bureau sets. She had a passion for walking into offices and information bureaus, and filling out blanks.

Lucy would take out a pencil and make notes, the delighted agent positive as he answered her question that he had gotten hold of a splendid woman at last.

"Now, if I lectured for this medicine," she would say, "how many small towns would you expect me to cover in a week?" And when he answered she would frown thoughtfully and nod. "I see. And I would always have Sunday with my husband and children? I see."

Walking home, elated and enthusiastic, she would buy herself a sensible hand-bag for travelling. And she would tell Fanny and May her plans quite definitely.

"Yes, I am to travel for the Mason's Magic Salve," she would assert positively. But a few weeks, or even days later, when Nelly spoke of it, she would answer with a vigorous, "Nelly, do you suppose, if I went into chicken farming, they would rent me that vacant lot next door?"

Her dreams, of recent years, included brilliant prospects, matrimonially, for Nelly and Alice. Nelly, in her kindergarten, would meet some wealthy philanthropist, preferably from New York. Alice should do something wonderful, too. For Georgie his mother had no plans; boys did not interest her, she quite frankly admitted.

Nelly was pretty and had undeniable charm, and Alice was one of those wonder-children who walk in an aura of sweetness.

beauty, goodness, and fairness of their own. Nelly often fretted against the ugliness and monotony of poverty and work; the necessity for self-denial was before her eyes, but she turned her head away, and would not admit it. With Nelly there were moods in which it was "*darn* these old dishes!" and "I don't see *why* we never have any money!"

And when these times came, Alice would come to her sister's side, and raising the blue eyes that shone like flowers in her angelic little face, would coax Nelly into a better mood.

"Ah, Nelly, darling, don't! Some day we'll have everything, you see if we don't! Everybody does, sooner or later. Mama, doesn't everybody's luck change sooner or later?"

"Changes for the worse, certainly!" Lucy might reply, with her brisk laugh. "No, my dears," she sometimes said, "in this world it's the people who grasp and cheat and steal that get everywhere."

"Mama!" gentle little Alice would say, shocked.

"Well, look about you. Your father and I have always been honest and hard-working," some contrary little gnawing devil within would prompt Lucy to continue, half idly and half mischievously. Her daughters' uncomfortable faces would satisfy some deep craving for revenge upon an unfair world.

"Mama!" Alice's lovely little earnest face would be wet with passionate tears at this point. "Can't we—can't we pray?"

"Certainly we can *pray!*" And Lucy would laugh carelessly again. Nelly usually laughed in response, her own gay light laugh, but the pained and responsible look would linger upon the little sister's face for hours afterward.

To-night, when they reached the house, Harry Crabtree came padding to the door, to welcome them. He had been reading under the kerosene lamp in the dining room, his fair lined face was blotched with heat, and his thin silky hair in disorder. Georgie, the twelve-year-old son of the house, was of course long asleep: his father spoke cautiously, not to awaken him.

Harry was, of old Reuben's four children, the one most like him. He had, at forty-three, the same deep eye-sockets and twinkling smile. But power and success had given Reuben a firmer jaw and a readier twinkle, and years of indecision and gentleness and failure had stamped Harry with a certain anxious timidity.

Like all the family, he looked first at Lucy; her mood would set the key for the conversation. To his infinite surprise and relief, he found her pleasantly inclined. Lucy was vicariously warmed by the attentions of Bertie, and Davy, and above all of Rudy Sessions to Nelly.

"Harry," she said by way of greeting, nodding as she passed him in the little hallway. "Well, here we are. You've cleaned up?"

"Georgie and I thought we would," Harry offered mildly. In the lamplight, the odd dome-shape of his head showed through his thin, silky hair. Alice fell, rather than sat, against his arm, perched on his old chair, her young body an agony of weariness. Nelly, smiling mysteriously, still thrilling to those stolen kisses above the waters of the bay, stood wearily stretching, yawning, shrugging, blinking, as she rolled the limp veil that had held her sugar-loaf hat in place.

"Cleaning the house," Lucy said, good-naturedly, "has never been a job that I would resent giving up, for once!"

Harry's face was radiant; he felt all a child's pleasure in seeing the faces it loves return.

"We had a real good time, slopping round with buckets and brooms," he said. "And then we went out to the Park, and—we had a real good time."

"You're welcome!" Lucy said drily, with her effect of wit; and the girls wearily laughed.

The dining room, especially to-night, in its cleaned and ordered state, was a pleasant, shabby little place; Georgie's schoolbooks, of an indeterminate brownish-black, were on a side-table, Alice's, neatly stitched into covers of blue silicia, beside them. And also there was the odorous little straw lunch box that Nelly carried to the kindergarten every wet day. This was Nelly's first job; she had eleven pupils and received fifteen dollars a month.

Harry and his wife had found this little cottage almost six years ago, when a plan for raising pigeons had been uppermost in Lucy's mind. It had been reached by wandering plank walks, then, and surrounded by open fields where cows and goats were pastured on ropes. Now it was less isolated; there was a sidewalk. Lucy hated it. It seemed to her that she had never lived anywhere else: she knew every knothole in the sidewalk, where Alice played "buttons" with neighbouring children, and every defect and limitation and stain and odour of the five stuffy rooms.

They seemed unusually odorous to-night, after the fresh country and the airy bay trip. The carpets smelled, and the old walls smelled, there was a suggestion of mice, of apples, of Georgie's carbolic liniment. Lucy sank into a chair and loosened her bonnet-strings, and launched into an account of the day.

"Rob's improved, I think. He still has that insincere laugh of his. But she's awful—his wife. A regular married old maid—it was nothing but family—family—family. One would think we were barbarians!"

"That's the Boston of it!" Harry said, mildly.

"Mama," Nelly asked animatedly, "her family's no better than ours, is it? Don't *we* come of a very good family?"

"Well, I should say so! I like her style!" Lucy said, vexedly. "I don't know what *she's* got to boast about, anyway, with her Copleys and her family silver!"

Nelly breathed relievedly; she had been uneasy. But Alice continued to study her mother with troubled eyes.

"Mama!" she burst out, "I thought you *liked* Aunt Ella and Uncle Rob!"

"Did you?" Lucy asked, amusedly and satirically. "Well, my dear, they are very probably going to have just what they want out of your grandfather, so don't write them a sonnet to tell them that I really think they're a pair of absolute snobs!"

This would not have hurt her feelings, which were indeed of the toughest, but Alice had recently attempted her first verse-making, and had bashfully and confidentially shown it to her mother. There were shamed tears in the little girl's eyes as she kissed her father good-night. Harry never got used to the miracle of it: this adorable creature his. In kissing any one of the three children he always made a little appreciative humming noise: "M-m-m-m! God bless her beautiful little heart and soul. . . ."

Alice shared with Nelly a little bedroom that opened off the kitchen. It had another door, leading into her mother's room, and from Lucy's room one might step in turn into the dining room again. These four rooms, square-set, were the entire cottage, except the little central hall they had entered, and the parlour opening from it, in front. A small oblong porch, roofed, ran along the side of the parlour, to the hall.

The parlour was bay-windowed and had, besides a bed lounge, an upright piano, on which the girls practised faithfully. There were fine inside wooden shutters in the bay, but no roller shades. In Mrs. Crabtree's room, and the girls' room behind it, were plain walnut wardrobes; there was no closet in the house, and no running water except at the kitchen sink. The family performed its ablutions at large china basins set on wooden stands.

Harry Crabtree paid fifteen dollars a month for the cottage, a sum that represented about one seventh of his income. He was employed in an eastern rubber firm that had been established for about ten years, on Market Street, and liked his home and his work with the unquestioning simplicity that was part of his nature.

He told his wife now that he and Georgie had had a fine day. They had cleaned the house thoroughly, and watered the garden, and then had gone out to Golden Gate Park. There was a special hill there, down which children were permitted to roll, and Georgie had watched the children while his father watched the astonishing number of fine-looking teams that were driven by, phaetons and surreys, and even a brougham or two. There was a bicycle club out too, and Harry and a man sitting near him had commented upon the new bicycles, "safety bicycles," that were beginning to be discussed. And finally, they had listened to the band. Harry was never particularly articulate, but his wife knew that in all his life there were no moments happier than those he spent every Sunday on the benches under the trees in the Park, reading the newspaper, watching the crowds and listening to the fresh, spirited strains of the band in its shell-shaped stand.

Every Sunday he hunted up the programme for the day in his breakfast newspaper, and cut it out carefully and placed it in his pocketbook. If one of his favourite selections was included, he was always delighted. Selections from "Faust," "The Lost Chord," and certain marches were his choice, but he liked everything. Sometimes Alice, sometimes Nelly and a young man, sometimes Georgie went with him, and sometimes they all went. But his wife never accompanied him; she could not bear idle and aimless wandering about, she had always some object in view when she left home.

To-day her expedition had given her food for thought. She announced herself as about to retire, but first she went into the parlour, where little George was asleep upon the bed lounge. The boy, picturesque in his sleep, was as fair almost as Nelly, a long, thin boy of twelve, who did not look strong, although he had never been ill. Lucy straightened the sprawling body and arranged the pillow; then she went into the kitchen to heat a kettle of water.

When the water, placed over a few sticks of blazing wood, was hot, she carried it into the bedroom and proceeded to wash her hands and face thoroughly with plenty of odorous soap that was streaked with pink, yellow, green, and blue. Harry was in bed, the lamp lighted at his elbow, a green shade over his eyes, and the Sunday paper in his hands.

"I declare I feel dusty into the marrow!" said Lucy. "You did the dishes?"

Her husband knew that she was pleased with him. She and the girls had hurried off after a late breakfast and had left the kitchen in great confusion. Harry had not only given the small boy a carefully cooked supper of poached eggs and stewed apricots, but he had washed every spoon and cup, wiped out the sink, and hung the ragged dish-towels neatly on the porch railing.

"I shouldn't be one bit surprised if Rob Crabtree had come back here expecting to go in with your father!" Lucy said presently. "I think May suspects it—and of course she is scared to death!"

"I don't see why she should be," Harry said, his finger holding a line; "Pa lets Stephen run everything and always will!"

"Yes, but that doesn't make the business Stephen's, Harry," his wife answered quickly. "And I don't think Stephen would welcome Rob one bit!"

"How's everyone over there?" Harry yawned.

"Oh—the whole crowd bores me almost to death," Lucy answered, sharply; "lots to eat, of course! Nelly had three beaux, and Alice got hold of a book, so they had a nice time! They're going to start Bertie in at the store."

She did not quite want to tell him; yet the fact had been angering her all day, and to impart it was to ease it. "Stephen, by some hocus-pocus, has managed to start him off at seventy-five dollars a month," she said.

That stirred him, as she knew it would. His own salary was not much more, and he had been faithfully and honestly and soberly clerking in one office or another for twenty-three years. Had he heard that Stephen Brewer had made ten thousand dollars in the past year—had he heard that Rob's wife wore the Cullinan diamond, it would have cut him less deep. But his nephew, the gay and handsome boy who had just returned from such a joyous holiday in the east as Harry had never had in his life, this ignorant Bertie was to waste on his pleasures almost as much as his uncle could earn to hold a family of five together. But Harry Crabtree had eaten the bread of mildness and humility for a long time now, and he could smile, after a minute, with a philosophical shake of his head.

"Well, I suppose I'd do it for Georgie, if I happened to be in Steve's shoes!"

"You ought to be in Steve's shoes," Lucy said. "You're a Crabtree. He's not!"

She had placed the big china basin of still warm water on the floor, and now put both her dusty, tired feet into it.

"My, that feels good!" she said, giving her silent husband, who was looking thoughtfully off his paper, a somewhat questioning glance.

"I suppose if I'd been the kind of fellow Steve is, Looce," he said, a little sadly, "I *would* be there! I—I kinder hope Bob will. I must run into the Occidental to-morrow and see Bob. Steve—Steve is going to pay Bertie—pay him all that money, eh? Well, money isn't happiness, after all. It'll give the boy queer ideas—I should think."

Mrs. Crabtree had brushed her fine, thick hair, washed face and hands and feet, and now stood up, refreshed and at peace. She carried out a tin pail of water, and stepping gingerly on the plank walks of the garden, in her ravelling, discoloured old worsted bedroom slippers, she splashed the unexpected drink upon the sweet peas, standing up like little gallant spears on their supported vines.

It was a balmy night, no hint of autumn yet in the air. There was a light in the two-story house next door—Miss Clay's room. Miss Clay was Davy Dudley's depressed and shabby aunt, who had kept boarders for years. Lucy Crabtree, peering sharply at the lighted window, under the mild arch of the Milky Way, wondered if Nelly was going to be fool enough to marry the lad, and turn sheets and peel vegetables for the rest of her life.

She went in, locked the kitchen door, and climbed into bed, immediately hooping herself, plunging her head into the pillow, and shutting her eyes. Her husband asked, as he had asked five thousand times, whether the light disturbed her, and she murmured, already half asleep, an emphatic "No!"

"Funny that this very night I should be reading—I mean funny in connection with what you told me about Bertie——" Harry began. But she did not answer even with the sleepy grunt he half expected, and realizing that she was exhausted, he smiled at her, and made no further attempt to disturb her.

If any one had told Lucy, the vivacious widow of seventeen years ago, that she would marry again, on the strength of a lead pencil, she would have laughed in utter disbelief. Yet she had done something very like that, and had made for herself a bed in which she sometimes found it hard to lie. Her first husband, Hopkinson Carter, had been a man of some little means, who had drifted to California immediately after the Civil War, eager to invest his capital in some one of the marvellous new enterprises that were beginning to interest the Golden State. In the hotel to which he went, a comfortable big place on Bush and Stockton Streets, whose spirited manager was a squarely built Irishwoman with silvery curls falling on each side of her rosy, smooth cheeks, he had met pretty Lucy Bunker, an eastern girl, whose uncle, a clergyman in Hawaii, was bringing the girl to his South Sea parish because he did not know what else to do with her. Lucy was seventeen.

Five weeks later she was married to Hopkinson Carter, and it was while they were animatedly discussing the investment of his seven thousand dollars that he suddenly fell ill. Mrs. Thompson, the kindly manager of the hotel, who pronounced every letter in her own name, and went to Mass every morning at old Saint Mary's, and to market afterward, with her Irish egg-ring in her shopping bag, was extremely tender with the frantic bride. She converted Hopkinson Carter to her own religion, in the last few hours of his life, superintended his obsequies, and insisted that the weeping Lucy remain with her and her daughter, at least until "the young boy" was born. The young boy proved to be a young girl, the beautiful and beloved Nelly of to-day, and with Mrs. Thompson's help, the seven thousand dollars lasted a long time. Lucy recovered her spirits and her interest in life.

However, when Nelly was four years old, the roving frog-like eyes fell upon young Harry Crabtree, and Harry was quickly enslaved. Lucy would not have married him for himself. She felt entirely independent, with her good old friend behind her, her thousands in the bank, and her beautiful child.

But one day Harry escorted her over to luncheon with his father and his married sister, at the very San Rafael mansion that she had visited to-day. It was still impressive: it had been an absolute landmark then. People went to visit it, pointed it out, asked permission to walk through the grounds. May, with her lovely nursery, had made a deep impression on Lucy, and little Nelly had shrieked with ecstasy over ducks and chickens.

Coming back on the boat, Harry had chanced to offer the weary, blissful Nelly a long pencil. Lucy, whose arms were full of flowers, had protested that Baby must not lose it.

"Plenty more!" Harry had said, and had shown her that the pencil was marked with the name, "E. R. Crabtree and Co. Spices, Teas, and Coffees."

Lucy had sat silent, struck.

"Who's the Co., Mr. Crabtree?"

"My brother Bob, and I, and Stephen—May's husband," he had answered simply. "Two or three years ago my father gave us all some stock!"

Lucy was not hard, not all system and ambition and calculation. But she felt that first pang, that first fear of losing her man, that is the sure forerunner of marriage.

So they were married, and lived delightfully on Harry's salary from Crabtree and Company, and Lucy's money, and occasional dividends from the firm, until Nelly was eight. They had a house in Stockton Street near Bush, with a picket fence, and bay-windows that came down to the floor, and with mill-work embroidery about the peaked roof. Lucy theorized and dreamed. At one time she had a blue-glass window put in for "health-rays," and at another studied mesmerism. She had been Harry's wife for almost four years and Alice was a tiny baby, when Harry was persuaded, largely by her eagerness, to resign from his father's employ and accept a most flattering offer to go to England for an insurance firm.

Lucy had had for months an uneasy feeling that justice was not being done Harry by Crabtree and Company. Stephen, she maintained, was running everything; Harry was a fool to stand it. His father would die, and then where would he be? One of Stephen's employees, practically, in spite of the fact that Harry had some stock in the business.

Meanwhile, she had been kept quiet with a small baby. Harry had warmly befriended an old Englishman, sent by the head of an insurance firm from London to investigate certain discrepancies in the accounts of the San Francisco office. Lionel Braithwaite had reached California sick and weary, and had gone to bed in Mrs. Thompson's boarding house with small idea of leaving it again. The San Francisco agent had fled, everything was in desperate confusion.

Harry, coming and going in the Thompson house almost like a son, had played cribbage with old Braithwaite, had won his confidence, had worked over troublesome columns of pounds and shillings, had interpreted such terms as "two bits" and a "fifty vara lot." When Braithwaite was pronounced too ill for anything but convalescense in the sunny south, he wrote of Harry, to London, and London wrote promptly for Harry. Would Mr. Crabtree consider the trip, bringing his figures and affidavits? The San Francisco agency was to be discontinued; perhaps Mr. Crabtree would consider a position in the London office?

Mr. Crabtree had laughed heartily at the mere idea. But Mrs. Crabtree's frog-like eyes had gleamed with excitement and determination. Of course they would go, and she would like to be present when Harry told Stephen and his father! She would like to hear what May said to the news!

Harry felt none of her satisfaction. His father's surprise hurt him; he loved his silent mother and was sorry to kiss her good-bye. It was a big salary, it seemed like a big chance, but it meant exile to him.

However, he got real happiness from Lucy's joy. They found a homesick little Devonshire girl who would travel with them as the children's nurse, just for the trip; Lucy's heart was bursting with a sense of importance as they went off, with new coats and new trunks, pretty little interested Nelly, and the lovely, white-caped baby.

They were gone more than two years; Harry never saw his mother again. He disliked London, the Pimlico apartment was small and dark, Lucy was unhappy, and the children did not flourish. A sheer mischance, beginning with a death, and ending with an entire change of management in the English insurance firm, altered his position from the beginning and handicapped him. The pleasant surface customs of the new life Lucy adopted fast enough, but there was a fundamental difference between her and the women she met that she never even vaguely grasped. Lucy could broaden her a's and drop her g's, she could serve tea and gabble about "haypnies," but her very adaptability antagonized her solid new neighbours they distrusted a woman so eager to accept the new, and so ready to despise her own country's ways. Loyalty was the backbone of their own creed.

So presently it seemed wise to Lucy, for a hundred glibly expressed reasons, for them to return to California. They came at the darkest hour the city had ever seen, from a business standpoint: the firm of Crabtree and Company was facing real danger for the first time in its flourishing existence, with a thousand other firms. But Lucy was buoyed by the thrilling discussions she had had on the train with a mining man from Placer County, and she urged Harry to sell his stock to his father, and put his money instantly into a mine.

Meanwhile, pending gratifying developments from the mine, Lucy took a comfortable house in which to await the birth of the child who was Georgie, and Harry accepted a position with the Atlas Rubber concern. She annoyed May and Fanny considerably at this time, and made them uneasy, by talk of the enormous fortune that was coming. Harry could not make less than a million, probably would make more. Look at the money the Fairs and the Crockers and the Hopkins had made! And what had they put in? Practically nothing.

Fanny's fortune and May's comfortable income seemed nothing beside these dreams. Harry's sisters were alternately incredulous and jealous as they listened.

But when months went by, and the mine remained passive, Lucy comforted herself with plans for a boarding house somewhat like Mrs. Thompson's. If Mrs. Thompson and Miss

Kitty went abroad, perhaps Lucy would take over the house,
"until the mine was paying." Lucy estimated what she must
charge her boarders, and how she would mark her linen. If
May and Stephen and the children came over for a winter stay
in the city, her rates would be this and this.

"I shall tuck Bertie into a hall bedroom," said Lucy; "he's a
boy—boys don't mind. A large room for you and Stephen, two
small ones, possibly alcoved, for the girls. Every Tuesday night
I shall talk things over frankly with my servants. They can express their grievances, and I will mine, so don't hesitate to tell
me if anything goes wrong; but tell me before Tuesday, if you
can. Now, at what time does Stephen come down to breakfast?"

May and Fanny thought that Lucy was really admirable to
take this splendid stand, even while lying in bed with her little
boy. They agreed reluctantly that it was just Lucy's luck,
capable and energetic as she was, to have the mine make her
a fortune after all.

Meanwhile, Harry got his job with the rubber company, and
the Harry Crabtrees moved "temporarily" into a small house.
Lucy, as the children grew older, read for an hour daily to old
Mrs. Lemmon; she planned a sort of old ladies' club meanwhile,
where a score, instead of one, might be amused. She took
charge of poor little Pidgie Reed, when Carrie Reed went to
New York for a month, and actually cured Pidgie of stuttering,
to her enduring credit and pride. And she came over to May,
in San Rafael, when Aunt Jenny died, and was extremely articulate and busy. May and Fanny appreciated this, and agreed
that they could not be under obligations to Lucy, and on the
very day of the funeral May came prettily to her sister-in-law,
with one of the old lady's scarfs in her hand, and a twenty-
dollar gold piece wrapped in the scarf.

"Please, Lucy! Steve and I know that you have good use
for it!" May had stammered. Tears were in both their
eyes as they kissed each other. And Lucy, with this precious
money, had bought a stock of liquid clothes-mender at three
cents a bottle to be retailed for ten, and later, a steamer that
cooked the seven articles of a dinner at once.

The former did not retail as she had expected, and was stored
in the cellar closet, where the next tenant found it—some one
hundred and thirty-five flat little inky bottles with saturated
labels. The latter cooked well enough, if a roaring fire was

under it, but it always got so hot and whistled so loudly, and its sections stuck so tightly together, that Lucy got furious at it and put it away.

At forty-four, she felt for her husband only a certain abstracted appreciation. He was her best audience. To his timid criticisms she paid not the faintest attention, but she liked him to listen to her schemes. And whenever he was ten minutes late to dinner, her insatiable imagination was off upon a favourite exercise. Harry had been instantly killed by a car; he had collapsed in the office. An accident had widowed her, and slowly and solemnly, they were bringing him home.

With what dignity she would meet them at the door; show them his room and his bed! Widowed! She must face life now courageously; the children looked to her; Fanny, May, all her world was watching. "May, will you take my boy for a little while? Stephen, will you go over my accounts? I must be a business woman now. . . ."

It was usually at about this time that the persistently living Harry would return, apologetic for the stopped car or the office delay. Lucy always welcomed him philosophically.

"Harry, my dear, I've been thinking about that scheme for school boy's lunches. If we were nearer the school—if we took that big place opposite the Horace Mann—I wonder if you would step out and get us some milk, Harry? You've got your hat on. I meant to ask Nelly. . . ."

To Nelly, who was far from being the sophisticated woman of the world that her San Rafael cousins thought her, had come a strange experience, on that Sunday night. She had been kissed before, in a haphazard youthful way, but she had never before known kisses like Davy Dudley's. The scene on the narrow lower deck of the ferry-boat, just above the dark backward streaming of the black water flecked with white foam, recurred and recurred to her, as she taught her little kindergarten class in the dreamy stillness of the warm Monday morning. Davy had been silent and resentful at first, because Rudy Sessions had monopolized her all afternoon, and Bertie Brewer had accompanied her to Saucelito on the way home. But Nelly had tucked her little person close beside him on the bench, and had slipped her boneless, soft little hand into his, and had murmured and apologized enchantingly, and then he

had kissed her, harshly and passionately, and with his arm
like a vise about her shoulders.

She thought of it, tired, dreamy, half-bewildered, during
the school hours of Monday, and she thought of it walking
home in the soft afternoon. The summer winds were over, and
the shabby Mission looked homelike, if not beautiful, to the
girl's changed eyes. She was conscious of a warm thrill throughout all her being, and a little sense of laughter behind that—
a little sense of marvelling that it was Davy Dudley who had
so stirred her! At one moment she thought that she would
like to see him again, and at another she decided that he must
be avoided.

The cottage was empty when she entered it by the kitchen
door, and on the kitchen table was a note in her mother's
beautiful clear handwriting.

"Your father has been injured—they say not seriously—and
taken to the hospital. Mr. Crane came for me. Give the
children their supper—Geordie has gone to Ollie's house.
Don't worry—we must all be brave. Muddy."

This—the most thrilling summons that had stirred Lucy
Crabtree's blood in many years—merely roused in Nelly a
gentle and shocked pity. Papa hurt! it didn't seem true. She
went vaguely about the supper preparations; she had little of
her mother's or even Alice's cleverness in the kitchen, and began
to remember Davy again.

Alice came in, breathless from running, and with the news
that Miss Polk of the Seventh was dead at last. She received
the intelligence of her father with round-eyed excitement.

"Oh, Nelly—I should rather hear that he was instantly
killed, than that he should have to linger and suffer!" Alice
said, awed. "Poor papa—and poor Muddy! I hope," she
added solemnly, "that the shock won't kill her! We should
just have to face the world ourselves, wouldn't we? Let me
do that, Nelly. Listen—I'm going to fry the cold beets right
in with the potatoes—I should think that would be good,
shouldn't you? It doesn't seem as if we ought to be going on
just as usual, does it? But I suppose we ought to. Nelly,
what could I do, if I had to work? Because if—if anything
happens—I *will* have to. What are we going to have? The
fried potatoes and sliced tomatoes and apple sauce. You
can have tea. There is some of that meat pie there——"

"I thought we might leave that in case Muddy came back," Nelly said, carelessly setting an end of the kitchen table, as was customary for the less formal meals. "Here's Georgie," she said, as a slender boy came smiling in, with a book under his arm. "Georgie——"

Both sisters kissed him as they told him the startling news, and Nelly smoothed back the fair, fine hair from his moist forehead. All three young people were almost pleasantly shaken by the unexpected event, and the unusualness of their eating alone in the kitchen, which was lighted by the streaming, straight rays of the sunset. They scraped their plates, which was usual in that house, while they discussed the possibilities, and had finished the last of the apple sauce when, with his usual little nervous clearing of the throat and his cheerful greeting, their father came in.

With great shrieks of laughter and surprise, the three gathered about him, and Harry Crabtree had no reason to complain of his welcome. He explained, sitting down rosy and rumpled in their midst, that he had indeed been knocked down by a Market Street cable car, had been rushed to a hospital, and had there recovered enough to protest that he was perfectly well. However, they had thumped and poked him a little, he said, before letting him come home.

"Well, you don't seem to like the idea of the old man getting killed!" he said, in great feather. "Where's your mother?"

"Gone after you—she'll be right back again," said Alice, as they finished, "so you go wash, and Nelly and I will get you some dinner!"

Nelly nodded and sighed. She secretly hated the kitchen. But as Harry turned to go he brought an odd little unexpected thrill to her heart by adding: "I meet Davy Dudley at the corner almost every night, Nelly. What's he doing now?"

"Oh, he's still with the Mission Hardware people. But he teaches night school, too, you know!"

"He said please to——" Harry rubbed his head. "He sent you some message—I think he said his aunt wanted to see you!" he said, and turned into the dim little bedroom. Here he laid his derby hat and coat on the bed and carefully unbuttoned his collar. It would do for to-morrow, he decided, hanging it on the little knob that regulated the mirror. He washed his face, and wet and brushed his thin hair, took his newspaper out of his coat, and went refreshed into the dining-room, where Nelly had already set the simple table for two and was moving about with final touches.

Harry drew her to him, and she kissed him lovingly. Alice came in with filled glasses, and kissed him, too, and his adored boy came and sat beside him, reading his book with avidity, but keeping one hand on his father's.

Upon this scene came Lucy, tired and hungry, and exasperated because she had wasted five carfares and three hours for nothing. She kissed her husband too, and had self-control enough to express relief before she said that that lying little alarmist of a clerk, who had seen the accident and given the alarm, should have been spanked, dragging people all over the city and scaring them to death.

However, the heated meat pie and freshly boiled potatoes appeared, and Alice had brewed delicious tea and toasted the bread, and under the soothing influence of supper, Lucy regained her usual good-nature and loitered in her usual fashion, after the lamp was lit and the food-supply reduced to the last mentioned article.

It was almost nine when she went into the kitchen with the last cup, to find that her daughters had finished all the other dishes and reduced the hot little region to perfect order. Altogether, life was just a little changed by Harry's near escape; a little glamour clung about it that was new.

Harry followed her to the kitchen, to read some article concerning the Mechanics Library, and Nelly, who had been watching her chance with a hammering heart, went to the yard door.

"Dearest child," her mother said, fussing about, "isn't there an egg?"

"Not one, Muddy—Papa and Georgie had fried egg sandwiches last night."

"Oh, I see!" Mrs. Crabtree stood irresolute. If there had been an egg, the absence of bread might have been made up with "johnny cake" for breakfast. With no eggs and no bread, still she might have quick biscuit. But the lard was out, too. Lucy was annoyed; she sighed. She had no eyes for the thrilling and glowing Nelly.

"Muddy—I wanted to stop and speak to Miss Clay. She asked me to. And I'll get some eggs——"

"Borrow six," Lucy decided, slowly. "And don't be long, dear." And she began to mix the cereal that would steep on the back of the warm stove all night.

Nelly, still irresolute, fluttered through the warm soft darkness of the yard and hesitated at the gate. The house next door showed a light at the kitchen and dining-room windows. She longed for Davy, and she was afraid of her longing. She wanted to add something new to last night's half amusing, half frightening facts, just to have more of that thrilling and novel emotion!

Miss Lillian Clay was a desolate, whining, down-at-heels woman, who dragged out a precarious existence next door to the Crabtrees, with a boarding and rooming house. She was a dark, lean, oily-skinned woman of fifty, with stringy gray hair. Sometimes she had roomers, sometimes boarders, sometimes what she called "tablers," families who came in simply for meals, from the neighbourhood. Her rooms were dirty and shabby, papered in depressing browns and grays; her meals were always bad. She generally kept a dirty and untrained Japanese school-boy to help her, but in particularly bad times gave up even this weekly expenditure of two dollars.

The Clays had settled in Napa about the middle of the century, when Lillian was a young girl. Her sister Della had married a prosperous young man, Jim Dudley, who operated the first small trucking business in the town. The Clays had a languishing farm. Lillian had had a comfortable childhood, and had drifted into one of those endless engagements so common in country towns. During the fourteen years of her "keeping company" with a consumptive young express agent, Lillian had chafed and fretted incessantly; when he died she had come at once to San Francisco, which seemed to her a great city. Meanwhile her mother and father had died of obscure and slow diseases, the farm was sold for the mortgage, and her sister Della Dudley had been widowed by the accidental discharge of a duck-hunter's gun; all the men in town went duck-hunting, and every season had its toll.

Della was left with an old mansarded house, and with three children, Mary, 'Lizabeth, and David. 'Lizabeth worked in the post-office, Mary had ambitions to graduate from Normal school; and Davy sent his money, every cent he could spare. Lilly didn't know how Della got along, she sometimes said irritably, and didn't want to know. Dell had probably got something for Jim's teams and trucks, and she could rent all them upstairs rooms. But Lilly personally would not concern herself; she said bitterly that the family seemed "God gifted with trouble. Let 'em work it out without her; she was foundered on hard times!"

She had no sympathy with Davy's ambition to become a doctor; but she was glad enough to house him and grumble at him and to him. She said he was a real "sweet feller," and she trusted him, if he *was* "sort of innocent."

David was a big, loosely jointed youth, with large hands and feet and a pleasant, bashful smile. His face was heavily freckled and his hair somewhat rough. He felt himself an outsider with young persons who were educated, refined, and rich, and stared at such girls as the Brewers in uncomfortable admiration and surprise. They were "young ladies"; with them he had nothing in common.

David had failed in his examinations to enter medical school; he felt himself a failure in every way. He worked now in a hardware store, taught mathematics and chemistry in a night school, waited on tables in a cheap restaurant for his lunch, studied his physiologies whenever he had a free half-hour, and prayed every night on his knees that everything would go all right with Mother and the girls, and that he would be a doctor, and that Nelly Crabtree would wait for him.

He had fallen in love with her by such slow degrees that he had not had time to be afraid of her. She was such a sweet little friendly creature that perhaps he never would have feared her anyway. When he was with her, Davy forgot how cold he was, all winter long, and how little money he had, and that his big arms were sticking out of his sleeves. He forgot the grim realities of his aunt's boarding house, and the sharp need in his mother's home; forgot his mother sweeping down the stairs, and 'Lizabeth crying over a lost postal-order, and Mary with her thin little jacket patched at the elbow. When he was with Nelly, the world held only Nelly.

To-night Nelly came into Miss Clay's kitchen somewhat timidly; it was just nine o'clock; Davy would be back from school in a few minutes now. Miss Clay, with her draggled black alpaca sleeves turned up at the wrists, was seated at the stained and scarred kitchen table, manipulating a blackened saucepan and a small disk of tin.

"Come in, Nelly, do!" she said.   "I was just settin' here wondering about you folks. How's Mama?—that's good. Look what I'm doin' here—some smarty alec sold me this at the door for two bits to-day. He and I got talking—I guess I was standing there half an hour in the hot sun—with my lunch fire goin' out! He says y' can mend anything that's got a hole in it with this here—but I showed it to Davy, and he said they had better than that in the store. 'S'e, 'just reeve round the hole, mam,' —well, I lay I'd make that feller travel if I could come up with him!" finished Miss Clay disgustedly, bundling the reever and the patches together into a small brown envelope and abandoning her efforts, "Take it over to your Mama, Nelly, and see what she can do!"

"How's your hand?" Nelly said. Miss Clay flexed the fingers, with a dubious eye.

"It hurt me some this morning," she admitted, and she added grimly, "That feller in the hall bedroom is going. Says he's got to get a room nearer where he works. I says, I hope you can get it for six dollars a week. That's all he pays—and his food's worth that, let alone the rent!"

"The man with all the fans up on the wall," Nelly identified him. "Then that leaves you only the Nugents and Davy?" she questioned, sympathetically.

"That's all! And Joe Nugent is afraid his firm is going to be bought up right over his head," Miss Clay admitted. "I tell you, Nelly, I can't keep the house!"

Nelly could only look her sympathy. She had nothing to suggest, since the last advertisement of "sunny rooms in the warm belt of the Mission," had failed to bring even a nibble. She glanced about the kitchen, a large, dark, dirty room, the stove greasy and rusted, the sink filled with miscellaneous soiled pots and china, a huddle of odds and ends threatening any minute to coast off the sink shelf, the table littered and old. Everything looked forlorn and poor; there was neither the effect of new furnishing in enamel ware and oilcloth nor of the homely comfortable disorder of the kitchen next door. Nelly was too young to analyze the difference; she simply felt that Miss Clay was dreadfully unfortunate, and that the atmosphere of their house, if equally poor, was much pleasanter.

Suddenly, Davy came in, and when his eyes met Nelly's, tired, dirty, discouraged as he was, a great smile broadened on his face. He dropped wearily into a chair and reached for the plates that had recently been removed from the dinner-table. There was a slice of bread in the wicker bread tray, and he buttered it and talked quite simply to Nelly and his aunt, as he ate it in great bites.

"Lord, sometimes I think we're fools not to go back to Napa, Aunt Lil!" he said, lazily. "I get thinking of old times and the teams, and the way the steam rises up at the stable, winter mornings, just as the sun comes up. . . ."

"It'd be jest starvation to me!" Miss Clay said firmly. "I don't propose to cook for my sister Della"—this was Davy's mother—"the rest of my life—if I *would* get my board out of it! I come away with my eyes open, and I've got my living here, and my seat in church, and my Sunday silk, and that's more than a lot up there has got. Your mother's a good woman, but there's a lot of women up there that would be well pleased to see Lilly Clay come sneaking home with her tail between her legs—and I ain't going to tickle them that far!"

Nelly murmured something soothing, and Miss Clay, who was now at the sink, throwing things about audibly, pounced upon her with a swift, "What say, dear?"

But Nelly, whatever she had said, decided not to repeat it, and brought up the subject of the eggs. This soothed Miss Clay quickly by distracting her. She hadn't an egg in the house. She had meant to ask Davy to bring her home some. Davy, rising, said he would go for eggs, and Nelly said she would go with him.

They walked down to the corner and into Mission Street silently, Nelly somewhat puzzled. His mood of last night was as absent as if it had never been.

She went with him, bareheaded, into the little corner store that was lamp-lighted, and that smelled of onions and dry grains and stale beer. Nelly knew this shop through and through; she could have found the spongy "baker's bread" as quickly as old man Cummings did, she knew with just what a gesture he would lift the thin light wooden covers from the cheeses, and just how thick a slice he would press off the "mild eastern" for a dime. There was a row of tea and coffee boxes neatly fitted in on the lowest shelf—pale-green tin boxes with dim paintings of pagodas and Japanese gardens on them above the words "Oolong," "Java," "Souchong," and "Mixed." The sugar stood out on the floor, in great barrels lined with dark blue paper, and the string hung in an iron filigree ball over old Cummings' head. Bluish milk was in a great can with a tight cup-top, and bread was loose on the counter. There was an odour of staleness, a certain universal fly-speckiness over it all, despite the great loops of scalloped and pinked yellow and green paper that were draped from the centre of the ceiling for the especial distraction of flies. Spiders had webbed the high corners with a dozen dark, filmy folds; there were rat-holes in the old wooden floor, and the sharp smell of rats and mice in some of the darker corners.

Nelly watched, with untiring interest, the whirl of a great red-and-black wheel on the big coffee-grinder, while Davy took a dozen eggs from the pyramid on the counter and put them in two bags. Sugar and cheese old Cummings twirled into cornucopias, as he wrapped them, but eggs demanded the luxury of paper bags. He jerked open a belled drawer to make change for Davy, and nodded good-night to the young pair as they went out under the stars again.

Again, Davy was silent, and after a few tentative remarks, and a troubled side-glance, Nelly fell silent, too. She was troubled, in the dark. What did he want to be so glum for? Nelly hated cross people.

At the cottage gate they stopped.

"Davy, that was fifteen cents, wasn't it? I'll give it to your aunt to-morrow."

"No, you won't!" he said, quickly, but with the new reticence, too.

"Please, Davy——" She was close to him in the starlight, her eyes showing their marvellous light in the soft gloom.

"Oh, my—my Gosh," he said bitterly and suddenly. "I should think I could treat you to half-a-dozen eggs!"

Nelly was bewildered, but glad to be talking at last.

"Why, of course you can if you want to!" she said, gently.

David gave a sort of groan. Then, quite deliberately, he gathered her bag of eggs and his together, and set them down on the dry yellow grass and tarweed that had sprung up outside the gate, and put his arm about her. And suddenly Nelly was satisfied, after all the bewilderment and longing of that sweet, weary, silent day.

"Oh, Nelly, I love you so—I love you so," half sobbed, half gritted Davy, with his hungry, great kisses, "and—my God! I'll never be able to marry you—I've not got a dollar in the world—my mother's got nothing! She and my aunt would starve to death if it wasn't for me! It's just cruel and mean to talk about it—when you're so sweet—and so little— and everyone is in love with you——!"

"But Davy—but Davy——" whispered Nelly, who was crying, "if I—if I like you——!"

Then their wet cheeks and their young lips were together, and they were stammering madness and sweetness. "I love you!" David said, over and over. Nelly kept her soft little head upon his shoulder.

"Davy—Davy——" she whispered.

The summer stars wheeled solemnly in their courses, and a late, pale moon arose and shone wearily over the humble little scattered roofs of the Mission and the silent, bare slopes of the surrounding hills. With the moonlight, an optimistic cock crowed, and a distant dog barked and was still. The wheel of the Silvas' windmill turned slowly, creaked; there was a splash of water.

But Nelly and Davy murmured on, uncaring, reiterating again and again the most amazing thing that had ever been said since the moon was made. They loved each other.

"No, but you *can't*—you angel! Nelly, you don't know what you're saying. You know so many men—and I've been next door to you for ten years!"

"But Davy—if I *do?*" There was a honey sweetness in the soft voice, it made him want to laugh, it made him want to cry, he flung back his head, flung out his arms, almost shouted in his ecstasy.

"Why, but you're so silly, Davy," she murmured, with her two hands holding his coat lapels and his two locked behind her and the light weight of her soft young body against his. "Did you remember to-day—about last night?"

"As if I could think of anything else, you darling!"

"Didn't you—didn't you think it was sweet?"

"Sweet! It was the sweetest thing that ever happened to me in my life! All day long——"

There was no end to it, no beginning. It was carried along on the current of his passionate young kisses.

CHAPTER V

OLD Reuben Crabtree and his eldest daughter, Fanny, had rented a small, bay-windowed house in California Street, with a narrow side-garden, full of calla lilies, standard roses, and fuchsias. Indoors was the usual narrow hall, the double parlours to the right, the dining room behind them, crossing the house, with a bay-window on the side garden. Upstairs was the old man's alcoved front room, Fanny's room over the dining room, a sewing room between, in which Carra slept in eternal vigilance for her master's call, and, at the end of the hall, a sky-lighted bathroom with a tin tub. The furniture was upholstered walnut, with a dreadful old horsehair set still lingering in inconspicuous corners and a square piano with a defective rack.

It was the day of conserving: furniture was patched, recovered, curtains were mended, dresses were turned. In the closet in the dining room, Fanny had half her mother's Canton china set, almost complete, rarely seen or used. In trunks in her little attic she had old clothes, rolled into balls, heavy old garments of her mother and Aunt Jenny, and of her own youth, old hats and linen collars. On the walls were dim prints, widely framed: "Welsh Peasants," and "Franklin at the Court of France," and many smaller coloured pictures, of dimpled little girls showing bare arms and shoulders and holding lambs or fruit. There were also dim, framed photographs in Fanny's orderly, dark, ugly bedroom: one of May's children, disposed artistically about a swing, in scallopped high-buttoned boots, plaid dresses, and saucer hats tipped over their flowing ringlets, and another of Fanny's mother, a pallid, flat-breasted big woman whose likeness had been enlarged from a daguerreotype The late Mrs. Crabtree was represented in a flowing gown of striped and scalloped silk, a mass of looped braids fell on her neck, her arms were crossed upon a small marble pillar.

Fanny rarely noticed anything in her room, unless it was out

83

of place. The rooms had a perpetual effect of neatness, barren order, close air. She had a sharp eye for dust and disarrangement, and prided herself on her housekeeping. Carra, to be sure, was a little out of Fanny's province, because she was absolutely necessary to the old man; even Fanny's curiosity stopped short at the delicate line that was drawn somewhere between Carra's sex and her father's dependence. Did she entirely dress and undress him? Did she decide when he was to take his medicine, and what weight of flannels were desirable?

She and May did not know. They knew that Carra's wrinkled, pink-lined hand rubbed the bloodless, dry old back; they knew that Carra ruled him to a degree that they would have resented had they dared.

"No, you ain't gwine get up now, eever!" they would hear the coloured woman say, firmly if good-naturedly, when old Reuben whined. "You lay there and read you' paper. What dat President you got now doin' wiv hisse'f? My lan', he's a stepper! Stick you' laigs in dere, Mist' Crabtree; you sneeze once and I'm comin' after you like you's no size at all!"

This shocking familiarity and disrespect would make May flush and Fanny dilate her nostrils and breathe deep; but what could they do? Pa had to have someone to care for him, and Carra certainly understood him, and he liked her. Perhaps while they were tip-toeing quietly away from the hallways to which the distressing sounds of her voice had penetrated, his door would open suddenly, and Carra would go by them, with one of the endless pitchers, buckets, or trays of her charge's room. But Carra, if invincible, was discreet, or perhaps she was just indifferent to the younger women. Carra was well past seventy herself.

Sometimes Fanny, beating the flexible top of her long nose back and forth, a sure sign of nervousness, could permit herself the luxury of saying lightly and briefly, in reference to Carra's influence in her carefully ordered house:

"Well, it won't be forever, you know!"

To which May's real answer was an alert widening of the space about the eyes, although she thought she answered in the spoken words:

"Dearest Papa—God forbid!"

Neither wished him a minute's pain or harm, and they truly loved him, as healthy persons in the prime of life may love the aged and infirm, whose going will simplify their problems. They knew he must go, and they all hovered solicitously about him, determining, each in her way, that nothing should fail Pa because of her.

Fanny never had to speak to Carra about the bedroom floor, of which the mulatto woman took complete charge. She listed the laundry for the Chinese laundryman and put away the clean linen when it came home. But she never volunteered for service below stairs, and had a habit, perfectly maddening to Fanny, of disappearing into her room when it might naturally have been asked of her. Fanny was a capable and even a hard mistress, and she fretted over this one great stumbling-block in the way of perfect housekeeping. However, she and May had decided that the matter was too delicate for them to touch, and Fanny soothed herself with an extra acerbity where other housekeeping details were concerned.

She had a blowsy, rosy, great peasant of a girl named Maggie in the kitchen, and Maggie's waking hours were entirely at Fanny's disposal. Fanny went to market in Polk Street every morning, and came back with her rather long, red face paled by summer heat, or bitten by winter chill, for a whole hour of earnest direction to Maggie. Fannie had nothing else to do, and Maggie must needs delay all her pressing affairs to listen to the mistress. There was nothing too small to escape the older woman's eye.

"You weren't using that broom on the parlour carpet, Maggie?" Fanny might interrupt herself to say. "And that reminds me, try to get your steps and sidewalk swept before seven— I looked out to-day, and you were practically the only servant on the block who was so late. Now, about the mock pigeons, my sister says they are quite simple. Try them, anyway, to-night, and bake Mr. Crabtree some cup-cakes. You have a cleaner apron than that, I think."

"Carra says that cake'll be the deat' of him, and him pushin' eighty!" Maggie might remark in her fresh, rushing Irish voice. "Me uncle, that wint on the parish——"

Fanny was always pleasant.

"Never mind, Maggie, or we will be forgetting that I am the mistress here and you the maid! Now get to your sweeping and then you can dust before lunch. Start a good fire now, for your baked potatoes, and get your soup-meat on. Then immediately after lunch rub out those towels, and you can rest nicely while you're doing your silver. Be sure to scatter wet paper before you sweep. And by the way, brush down the stairs again, that will only take you a few minutes. What do you say, Maggie?"

"Yes, Miss Fanny." Maggie would watch the thin, nervous form, the flushed face, the bonneted gray hair, with a scornful eye. She knew that Fanny was not done, although Fanny did not, and could turn with quite natural spontaneity to say:

"Wash the statuettes some time to-day or to-morrow, Maggie. And don't leave your bed unmade until after lunch. I glanced into your room yesterday and opened the window. It's just a question of habit, Maggie—get the right habit, and then you'll be happier all your life."

And she would move a few feet more, with bonnet-strings loosened, and gloves taken off, to be gathered with her shopping-bag and parasol or umbrella in her lean hand. But there was generally more to come.

"Oh—and Maggie. Eat what you wish at meal-times, as the rest of us do, and don't let me come into the kitchen to find you tasting this and bolting that. That's not necessary. Maggie, are you watching the time?—it's almost eleven.—Brush with the nap—that's right."

And Fanny would sail upstairs, to wrap her bonnet in tissue-paper, to lay her gloves in a painted silk box that Esme had made her, lettered "Gloves" in a running script.

She was religious and interested herself deeply in church and parish affairs. Fanny belonged to a charitable sewing-society that met every week, and her friends were almost all members of this little group of devoted women. It was a very active fear in her life that her father might die without a return to his old boyhood belief, and she was courageous in approaching the old man on the subject, and always met any religious argument with quick scorn and contemptuous dismissal.

With church charities, and marketing, her mornings went rapidly, but she found afternoons long, and then would sometimes indulge in "blues," especially if she found an interested listener. She altered her dresses, called downstairs to Maggie for a hot iron and the pressing-board, and washed woolens with sudsy "Spanish bark." Like almost all unmarried women of means, Fanny was suspicious of the sincerity of the friendships she made, and almost fanatically anxious that the world should not overestimate her fortune. She never told any one just what it was; it was partly invested in the family firm, partly in gilt-edged securities, and Fanny spent only the interest of it. She knew that there would be a little more "some day," and until that time she contented herself with what she had for pocket-money, and felt herself rich. To be sure, there were expenses here in the city that she had not foreseen when she so cheerfully transplanted her old father from San Rafael. Previously, there had been one family account at the "White House," the city's best dry-goods establishment, on Kearney Street, and she and May had charged their purchases there, Stephen comfortably paying the whole, or their father paying it, they did not know which. But now Fanny perforce had a separate account, and to her annoyed surprise her father good-naturedly tossed her the bills with the observation, "That's yours, Fanny."

This had gone on for three years now, and Fanny had often wondered uneasily what May was doing. Who paid her "White House" bill, the firm or Stephen, and how could Fanny find out?

Certainly neither from May nor her father; May was as discreetly close-mouthed as the old man was wary.

"I don't know the half that Stephen does," her father would say, irritatingly. "Better put on a pair of pants, Fanny, and come down and run things awhile, that's the notion!" and May, smiling encouragingly, would say earnestly, "Fanny, I leave all that to Stephen. I think he admires that quality in me more than any other—just minding my own business, as the children say."

"I know, May, but it just struck me that if Crabtree and Company is paying *your* bills," Fanny might counter, with thin lips firm, "it might as well pay *mine!*"

"Why, Fan—look at Aunt Jenny's money!"

"Yes, I know—but there wouldn't *be* any money to look at, if things went at this rate!" Fanny would always answer, nervously, beating the tip of her nose.

"Oh, nonsense—when the paper said a comfortable fortune!"

"May, that makes me *wild*.—What wicked nonsense! I wish people would mind their own business! Doctor Jerome came here yesterday, for a window in the church. 'Why, Doctor,' I said, 'you have been misinformed. I am *far* from being a rich woman—far from it!'"

"Well, Papa draws just what he pleases, anyway!" It was a favourite grievance of May's, for Stephen was on a fixed salary.

"Well, but that doesn't help me—I tell you I pay my own bills now!"

May never rose to real sympathy.

"I guess you can afford it, Fanny. Dear me—when I think of myself, with four girls to settle!" And the matron's high breast would rise with a great sigh that was half complacent, as she thought of Esme, Vicky, Tina, and Louisianna.

Ten days after the summer Sunday upon which Robert and his wife had been formally welcomed back into the family, Mrs. Brewer came over to the city, this time bringing Esme and Louisanna. She usually lunched with her sister on shopping days, and sometimes brought a great sheaf of country flowers to brighten the California Street house. She and her girls would stream past Maggie with a call of greeting, to Fanny upstairs, perhaps letting Maggie draw her own conclusion from their arrival, or perhaps granting her a kindly: "How do, Maggie! Be sure you have something nice for us; we're all hungry!"

On this occasion, while Maggie poured coal on her fire, tore off her apron, and flew to the grocery, the Brewers went upstairs, and there was kissing. Then Esme drifted downstairs to the piano, and Louisianna stood silently watching the street from her aunt's bedroom window. The older women chattered.

"And how does Bertie like his job?"

"Oh, my dear, he's so conscientious! Unless he gets his breakfast on the stroke of seven, poor Lottie gets into trouble! But"—and Mrs. Brewer fixed her sister with an anxious eye—"but hasn't Pa said anything about him?"

"Pa spoke of that dreadful oversight of the letter to China," Fanny remembered. "*Wasn't* that too bad!"

This was Bertie's first mistake, and his mother winced. He had been given an invoice to deliver to an outbound ship, in person, but upon leaving the office had met a friend, had drifted down to his own ferry-boat, and had been half-way home before he remembered the important document in his pocket. Then it had seemed good to the rather sobered Bertie to mail the letter at Saucelito hoping that, in its twelve hours of grace, it would still reach the vessel. But the envelope he so hastily jammed into the mail was unstamped and turned up at the office of Crabtree and Company late the following after-noon, when the oriental vessel was some hundred miles out to sea.

Bertie had been only ashamed and frightened at this slip, but his mother had suffered acutely. It was to her a personal matter, and to have Bertie's father sore over the delayed in-voice and the stupidity, and angry at the boy, caused her real pain. She was now trying to dwell upon wiser things that Bertie had done, trying to win the silent Stephen to recognition of Bertie's penitence and amendment.

"Fanny," she said, changing the subject suddenly, "did Tina say anything to you about this young clergyman—this Mr. Yelland?"

Fanny glanced at Louisianna's slender back, elevated her eye-brows.

"Of the wonderful work he has been doing with the Sunday-school class, I mean!" Mrs. Brewer corrected herself hastily, attempting to recover lost ground. Louisianna's back did not move, but could her elders have seen her face, they would have noted upon it an expression of calm scorn.

"No, I didn't hear of that!" Fanny said lightly. "Go down and tell Esme to play 'White Wings,' Baby," she inter-rupted herself to say carelessly. Louisianna, with her inscrut-able innocent smile, departed, and the sisters upstairs went comfortably into confidences.

"My dear, he's really a delightful young fellow, in spite of the glasses," said May, "and truly—I think the child's touched!"

Fanny, ripping the body seams of a thickly lined velvet waist, snapped the settled dust from them with thin red fingers.

"I thought it was just nonsense, May," she said, doubtfully.

"Well, yesterday he stopped at the house with some hymn-books, and he did certainly look foolish when I said that Tina was walking—which she and Esme most unfortunately were!"

"I suppose I feel it a pity—on account of the small salary," Fanny said, slowly. "I suppose there's no question that he's interested?"

"Not the slightest!" Mrs. Brewer said eagerly. "Why he said to Mrs. Ayers only a few days ago that he believed in celibacy for the clergy—poor lamb! You know they never say that until they're in love. It seemed to me an indication of what is in his mind. I wish—oh, I do wish we could have a garden wedding!"

CHAPTER VI

"VICKY love," said her mother, entering the family dining room on a sober silent morning in early November, "do you want to do Mama a real favour?"

Victoria, who was flushed from the performance of a weekly duty—the roasting of some five pounds of green coffee over a kerosene stove—closed her book, Miss Carey's innocuous "Uncle Max," and eyed her mother with a mixture of amiability and distrust.

"I want somebody to go up and call on the Tasheiras," Mrs. Brewer said pathetically, "really it should be done! I know your father feels so. We turn our cows out there in their range whenever they go dry, and they've been so obliging about buying the calves——"

Victoria's brow clouded, as indeed her mother had known it would. The Misses Tasheira, four elderly Spanish spinsters, lived on the remains of a great Spanish crown grant, which was some six miles away. Their parents, sheep-farmers in the early part of the century, had bequeathed them half the county, and by judicious sales of strips of woodland here and pasture there, they had lived in extreme comfort ever since. They still carried on a somewhat mismanaged dairy and cattle-raising business, which supported a small colony of Spanish, Mexican, Portuguese, and Indian half- and quarter-breeds, in an inconspicuous corner of the estate, and had been most amiable in permitting the Crabtree and Brewer families to turn in their own Jersey cows with the Tasheira half-wild Durham stock, whenever it was convenient.

The sisters lived, almost without moving, in the cool lower rooms of their big wooden hacienda, embroidering, cooking rich little eggy cakes and delicious rich meat sauces, playing a little on their old piano, and quarrelling and laughing with their Spanish women servants, who provided a human element by their constant marrying, child-bearing, and fighting, and by their rising families. The Brewer girls hated the occasional necessity of civilities, and Victoria, on this dull and dreamy Saturday, instinctively sought escape.

"But why to-day, Mama?" she began, looking out at the calm, sunless garden, yellowed and thinned, and at the blue mountains that were steeped in mournful quiet. Dampness glistened on the shabby cosmos and chrysanthemums outside the dining-room windows, the trees were motionless, chickens clucked in tentative undertone, pigeons walked busily along the stable yard fence. The sky was gray and low.

"Well, dearie, I suppose Mama need not give reasons!" her mother began briskly. "I really think the walk would do you good," she added, invitingly.

"Didn't you want us to drive?" Victoria asked, still unyielding.

"Just as you like, dear! Esme is in town with Aunt Fanny, so Lou would go with you. And you may either walk, in which case I know the Señoritas will send you home with the team, or you may have either of the horses!"

"We could take both horses and ride?" Victoria said, brightening. But her mother hesitated.

"Well, dearie—this is Bertie's only day home, you know. He'll be home about three, and he does so like a gallop, dear boy!"

"You don't make Bertie go with us," Victoria observed resentfully.

"Certainly not—the ladies bore him to death!" his mother said quickly. "You are not very generous to your brother, now that he is working so hard," she said, warmly. Victoria laughed and kissed her mother, even while she kept revolving the little barrel that held the now rapidly roasting and extremely odorous coffee. The dining room was very warm, and suddenly it seemed to Victoria that it would be good to get out into the cool air and tramp over the damp roads and the matted yellow leaves.

"All right, Mama!" she said good-naturedly. "We'll go, and have port wine and cake, and bring home more junk in the way of sweet apples and drawn-work and butter and stuff than you can shake a stick at!"

"You're such a good child, Vicky!" said her mother. Victoria did not understand why she looked just a trifle confused as Tina came in from the kitchen. Tina's face was flushed, too, and she looked a little self-conscious. She had a blue plate in her hand, and on the plate was smoking a small raisin cake. Mrs. Brewer took the cake, tasted it, and put the remainder against Victoria's willing mouth. "That's delicious, dear!" the older woman said, proudly.

"The first lot were a little too thin," Tina said. "They baked beautifully, but they didn't come out of the pans. So Lottie suggested that I put in a little more flour, and that made them perfect, *imagine*."

"We'll eat the broken ones for lunch, and save the good ones for somebody—at tea!" Mrs. Brewer settled it merrily, as she and her third daughter returned to the kitchen; Victoria's eyes widened intelligently; Vernon Yelland was going to call, and the coast must be clear for Tina.

Left alone again, with the sweet, sickening smell of the hot coffee, and her own thoughts, she thought that she would wear her old blue dress this afternoon, she thought of Davy Dudley, who might be coming to San Rafael with Nelly, if the day was pleasant. Victoria had pondered much upon Davy, during these weeks in which she had not seen him, and an audacious—almost an awful—resolve was forming in her heart. She was wondering if there had ever been such a thing in the world as a girl—a young lady—proposing marriage to a young man? But Vicky did not put it as marriage; her thoughts did not go so far. She thought merely of an engagement, and the young man of whom she thought in this connection was Davy Dudley.

Victoria was one of four sisters, all marriageable now, and there was no future for her except marriage. She had talked idly of nursing, and she had often dreamed shocking dreams of the stage, but the innocent first had been discouraged as firmly as the reprehensible second would have been, and now she knew that she must follow the usual course. Esme would soon be twenty-five, a hopeless age, Victoria secretly thought, and she herself was almost twenty-three. Tina might or might not marry Vernon Yelland. Louisianna was of course still very much in the background.

Victoria Brewer naturally thought of herself as a desirable wife for a poor man. She was the daughter of prosperous parents, whose home was one of the most hospitable in the county, and she was pretty, clever, well-educated, and talented. David Dudley was poor, a country boy, shy, ambitious, and obscure. He liked Victoria, and he was almost awed at the grandeur of Victoria's environment, she knew that. Then he was big, kind, handsome, and above all—if her little plan succeeded—she would be *married*, she would have money troubles, perhaps, but Papa would help out, and she would have the exquisite pleasure of coming to Sunday lunch in the old home, "our married daughter."

Since the Sunday upon which she had more or less gained his confidence, Victoria had thought so much of Davy that she was by this time quite convinced that he had also been thinking of her. Aunt Lucy was of course desperately opposed to his courtship of Nelly, and Victoria had no reason to suppose that he had continued in it.

"He may not be good enough for Nelly," Victoria mused, laughing to herself, "but he is good enough for me!" And she thought, with a proud humility, of a good man's surprise when a woman far above him stoops to give him more than he dares ask. He had a mother, she reflected, a good countrywoman who would raise her hands in amazement at Davy's prize——!

All this did not prevent Victoria from finishing the coffee roasting and from carrying the ungainly roaster into the kitchen, where the hot, rich brown grains were poured into their tin. It did not prevent the girl from making herself very pretty in the old blue dress and fresh frills before she and Louisianna started forth, at about two o'clock, for their distant call. The day was still soft and sunless, but the yellow leaves lent their own odd metallic light to the wide, little used roadway, and the girls locked hands and chattered for sheer lightness of heart, as they got into a good, steady stride.

Just as they were about to turn out of the village and up toward the hills, they encountered Nelly with Davy Dudley. The two explained that they had just arrived on the train and were bound for the Brewer mansion.

As a matter of fact they were a trifle off the direct road, but then it was a sweet afternoon, silent and fragrant, and neither Victoria nor Louisianna suspected the truth: that Davy had been begging Nelly, since they were so little alone, to walk with him before paying their call. He was sorry to have their solitude ended, but he smiled pleasantly at the grave Louisianna and the suddenly flushed Victoria, and they all went gaily on together.

"If you want to *walk*," urged Victoria, "why it's a perfectly wonderful walk! And the old Señoritas always give us oodles to eat, and its more fun—poking about the ranch! Come on, Davy, it's right along the beach part of the way, perfectly lovely, and there's nothing to do at home! Do, Nelly, and then we'll go back to our house for supper, and you stay overnight. Davy can take the ten o'clock!"

Davy now began to urge this celestial plan, too, and Lou, a girl of few words, linked her arm in Nelly's and began, slowly:

"Listen, Nelly——"

"Oh, say, *listen!*" burst in Victoria excitedly, linking herself on her cousin's free arm, and bubbling with the news, "Tina was making cup-cakes this morning, and my dear—yes! dressed in the new challis this afternoon, and when I went into the parlour she was putting the music she plays best on top—yes! and what do you s'pose—of course, our dearly beloved brother Yelland is coming to tea—if you please! and Mama shunting poor Lou and me out of the way—isn't it simply killing!"

"No!" exclaimed Nelly, in full delicious enjoyment of the gossip. "Did you *ever!* Does she like him?"

"I don't know whether she likes him or not," said Victoria, with a casual air intended to impress Davy, and saying what she would have liked to believe, "but he likes *her!*"

This was wonderful. Their arms locked, the three girls took the rising grade bravely, giggling, stumbling, and chattering delightedly over this new idea. The exercise brought all their spirits to the highest pitch, and when they reached a fence and needed Davy's help, he looked at the maddeningly dear little figure in the shabby blue velvet dress, with fair hair curling itself up against the blue velvet toque, and told himself that after all she had tacitly promised herself to him, she had let him kiss her—and became suddenly the gayest of them all. They descended a slope to a line of shore, and now they could see the Tasheira ranch, still far away, under a broad band of eucalyptus trees that crossed the bare hill.

"Ah, there, my size!" shouted a cheerful voice suddenly, and Rudy Sessions rose suddenly up before them. The girls screamed, and Davy Dudley's simple heart went down—down—down, as they greeted him. He had a camera in his hands, and confessed himself devoted to the new fad. Victoria's spirits rose almost to hysteria as he posed her for a trial picture. This was life! She had never had her picture taken by an amateur before. Then he took Nelly looking bashfully down, with Davy leaning at her ear, and said he should call that "The Proposal," and then he took the Brewer girls on a stile, making them laugh as he said he was going to write under this picture, "The Toll Gate." Finally they used the last plate on a picture of Victoria tying her handkerchief about Rudy's arm, in the immortal attitude of "The Huguenots." Victoria was by now at her gayest and best, her tongue out-flying them all, her laughter irresistible. She invited Rudy to join them on their pious mission, and Davy knew, from the instant he saw the other man, that Rudy would accept. Presently they were all swinging along the road again, Rudy beside Victoria, Louisianna following with Davy and Nelly. They stopped like children, to comment on ducks, on a crane, or turtles and frogs by the road. Cottontails sprang up and fled before them, and Davy told them that once on these hills he had started a little red fox, who kept the road gallantly ahead of him for a mile or two.

"You ride, Dudley?" young Sessions asked, with a worldly air. But Davy said no, he had been sent down by his father to drive two draft horses up from San Francisco to Marysville, some three years ago. Louisianna glanced quickly at Rudy, to see what effect this would have on him; Nelly flushed but Victoria gave her chosen knight a proud glance.

The Tasheira ranch house was almost as hideous as human hands could make it—a big, square, barn-like dwelling, with windows and doors set geometrically across its cheaply painted white façade. About the house stood the towering eucalyptus trees, peppers, masses of silvery-white pampas grass, and several weeping-willows, draping, at this season, shabby and bared whips in the sober air. Under the trees was an over-grown garden, and hundreds of white chickens pecked between the great bushes of the roses and the rank masses of bridal-wreath, syringa, and lemon verbena. What the Señoritas called their "Japanese wistaria" climbed over a trellis, and other great trellises and arbours bore passion-vines and grapevines, the withered and yellowed foliage of the latter thinned now to show black and greenish-yellow bunches of fruit. No foliage softened the ugly outlines of the house, and there was hardly an attempt at a path among the scattered shrubs and bushes of the garden. Yet there was a certain curious effect of spaciousness and even elegance in the forlorn bigness of the bare house and wide garden, and of this the Señoritas were all still conscious. These qualities were entirely lacking in the old *casa*, which stood, like a shy old mother, behind the pretentious new house, and was quite buried in old woody vines. Under the pink, pipe-tiled roof, and between the thick adobe walls of the *casa*, all the Señoritas, and a troop of little sisters and brothers, long dead, had been born, but now the building was used for servants, and the storage of kitchen grain, and the ripening of fruit, with an occasional bitch, with appealing eyes, littering on the odorous heaps of empty sacks, or a half-wild cat glaring down from some lofty hand-hewn rafter where she had precariously brought kittens into the world. In earlier days, Vicky and Bertie Brewer had sometimes found a limp, damp, panting lamb here, fighting with closed eyes for the unknown thing called life, and Victoria at least would never forget the ecstatic day in which an old shoe rendered up half a dozen tiny, blind, pink mice, couched in a litter of warm soft nibbled paper.

Cows were filing down from the ridged hillsides to-day, although it was but three o'clock, and milking was not until four. But the herbage was poor, and the day cool, and there was always bran mash slopped into the mangers of the milking shed, and hence the silent red herd gathered and stood waiting in the churned deep mud of the barnyard, with only an occasional brazen protest against delay.

The young people eyed this barnyard dubiously; it lay straight across the short cut they had chosen to take, and it seemed impassable. To Nelly the red cattle were a menace, but the boys took these quite for granted, and were far more concerned for the fate of the ladies' boots. Finally, they skirted the yard safely by climbing on the first rung of the fence and edging their way along clinging to the top rail with weakening interruptions of helpless laughter. On one side were the watching cows and the pitted black mud; on the other, a rising meadow, suspiciously green in all the burned brown land,

and apt to be marshy. Davy went first, then Victoria, then Rudy, with a gallant backward-held hand for Nelly. Louisianna, who had dainty little notions of her own, preferred to make a long detour by the field, and was to be seen serenely waving back a puzzled, but amiable, red bull, as she came along.

Presently they were all laughing and shaking themselves into shape, in the garden, and a few minutes later the delighted Señoritas were welcoming them into the large hall that smelled of plaster and damp on this sunless day. It was a bare hall, running straight through the house, extremely high, and furnished only by a stairway, which was reversed and began far back. The hall was flanked by large, bare rooms, in which the old pieces of horsehair and walnut furniture had an oddly unaccustomed effect, even after forty years. The pictures were almost all religious, and there were little shells filled with sponges soaked with holy-water at all the doors. Large wooden mantels, painted white, symmetrically broke the walls opposite the entrance doors, the iron grates were small, but the visitors to-day were delighted to find, in the large back room that matched the dining-room, a comfortably warmed atmosphere and a coal fire.

The four oily-faced, stout, brown old women were more than ordinarily delighted with their callers. Miss Refugio kissed Victoria, who was a favourite, and Miss 'Ception poured out a hospitable flood of Spanish to a maid, which resulted in immediate refreshments. To be sure, they caused the light-hearted girls a spasm of laughter by confusing Rudy with Bertie, and Davy with some mythical husband, but their hostess' own manner and the undercurrent of Spanish chatter remained equable and good-natured.

They were all in the sixties, but there was not a thread of gray in the heavy, plainly dressed hair. Miss Lupita, the youngest, indeed retained some of the vivacity of youth, her thin lips were red, in a parchment-brown face, and her eyebrows were cut from black court-plaster each morning, and pasted neatly over her bright black eyes. Miss Lupita drove them all to church on Sunday, and drove the meanest and the most "bronco" horses ever seen in those regions, she also rode spirited ponies, and the Brewer girls had seen her thrown, and seen her spring up with the reins still in her hands, her old habit muddy, her eyes blazing with fury, and herself more than a match for her mount or for ten horses. There was reason to believe that when the Señoritas quarrelled, their old servants locked themselves in the *casa* and lighted candles before the statue of Our Lady of Guadalupe. On the thick, leathery throat of Miss Yolanda, now the fattest and most stolid of them all, under the greasy twist of coral beads, might still be glimpsed an old white weal, the scar, almost half a century old, of a terrible day of love that was choked with jealousy and passion, and laughed at, and left alone.

But Miss Yolanda laughed more than any of them now, and enjoyed her meals with twice the gusto of those old days. 'Ception, the oldest, was the only one of the sisters who showed any real Castilian formality, but even 'Ception unbent to-day.

It appeared that a great-niece was visiting them from Buenos Aires.—"It must be delicious there! I've always wanted to go there!" Victoria interpolated enthusiastically. The speaker, Señorita 'Ception, was disconcerted for a second, smiled politely and inquiringly, and interrupted herself to say, "You 'ave be there?"

"Oh, no!" said Victoria encouragingly, "I haven't *been* there, but I hope to *go!*" She thought vaguely of Buenos Aires as an island off the south coast of Spain—or maybe it was Central America——? "Papa corresponds with a firm in Java——" she remembered brilliantly. But Miss 'Ception did not grasp this and went back to her original theme.

It appeared that the Señoritas had had a brother, now dead, who had left a son and daughter in Buenos Aires. The daughter had married and died, too, leaving a daughter in her place. This orphan girl, the Señoritas' nephew had sent to them in California, for schooling in the Mission Dolores Convent.

"She 'ave thirteen year hold, and she will be very rich, from her mama's brother, my nephew, and she take a—she take a lover—oh, she pretty girl, dance and sing, and her papa don' like that!" explained the eldest of her great-aunts, smiling. A moment later Miss Lola Espinosa came in.

The little Argentinian was extremely small, and rather too sharp and lean for beauty. Her thick straight braid was very black, her oval eyes black, her mouth too big, and her colour high on dark cheeks. She had a great deal of eager, precocious manner, and amused them all with her quick overtures of friendship, her broken English, her indiscreet confidences.

They were going to shut her up like a bad man that had killed some other man, she said, because she had eyes in her head and could not help but see the young men, but she didn't care, she was going to practise the scales, and learn to embroider the strawberries so beautifully that her Tia Refugia, to whose smiling face she here gave a passionate kiss, would eat them!

"She's cute, but she knows it!" was Victoria's dark thought. But there was a great deal of laughing and an immediate understanding among the young persons, and presently the cheering suggestion that they all stay to supper. This was rather a surprise to the visitors, and they eyed each other dubiously. Nelly's first polite impulse to imply that perhaps there wasn't *enough* never got so far as words, and a vague confidence that Victoria meditated to the effect that Rudy Sessions was almost a stranger, and that Davy needn't necessarily be included, also was obviously unsuitable. So the callers swiftly allowed themselves to be persuaded, and, feeling a little stiff and strange, heard Tony, who drove the milk wagon, directed in an avalanche of Spanish to inform the Señora Brewer of her daughters' whereabouts.

"Mama can't possibly object," thought Victoria, feeling a pleasurable excitement stir within her, a delicious thrill that she only felt when twilight found her away from home.

"Isn't this nobby?" said young Sessions to Victoria, evidently sharing the emotion, as Lola danced joyfully, and put her arm about Louisianna's waist, with the suggestion that they all make a little *pasear*.

"And we ought to make all these bad, smelling dogs go walking, too, for they are so fat!" said naughty little Lola. But her aunts protested; their little dogs—there were six in the sitting-room—were delicate, and the old mistresses were used to the laziness and the smell. Two of the dogs were mere dirty gray-brown masses of tangled hair, out of which rheumy red eyes looked suspiciously and pettishly; one was Señorita Refugio's lean spaniel, with two puppies dragging at her misshapen body, and the other was Señorita 'Ception's big hairless Mexican dog, who had some dry and hideous skin affliction upon his steel blue hide.

There were other dogs outside, however, who leaped joyfully to join the walk: ragged, half-savage dogs, who rolled and snapped at each other, and scrambled up the banks that rose on each side of the rough roads. The two youngest girls walked ahead, then came Rudy with Nelly, and lastly Victoria and David.

Victoria's colour was high, and her eyes sparkling; the dull duty call had turned out delightfully, all this was so much waste time, perhaps, inasmuch as both the young men were in love with Nelly, and the Tasheiras sufficiently unlike the people one knew to be negligible factors in her life, yet it was diverting. And then to-morrow was Sunday, and she was to go home with Nelly on Monday to spend the night, a rare event and an exciting one, for they would undoubtedly be sent into Mission Street for bread or chops, and they would stop at all the shop windows and have adventures.

So this was all sheer gain, and especially was it unexpectedly interesting to have Davy beside her.

"I should think every man who saw her would fall in love with her!" said Victoria, of Lola, as a feeler.

"Well, as near as I can see, they do!" Davy returned gloomily, of Nelly.

"Do you think so?" Victoria felt a pang of jealousy of the Argentinian heiress.

"Evidently Sessions is!" Davy said, briefly and bitterly.

"Oh, you mean Nelly!"

He smiled.

"Did you think I meant that affected little Spanish kid!" he exclaimed good-naturedly. Victoria laughed gaily and felt that she loved stupid, blundering old David.

"I don't think Sessions is in a position to marry," Victoria said wisely. This hit close to the ache in the boy's heart—he liked Victoria and he needed womanly sympathy.

"Neither am I!" he said, suddenly. Victoria saw an opening.

"It's too bad Uncle Harry isn't in Papa's position," she said. "Papa could always help out any one of us who married anybody who couldn't give us all they wished——"

Perhaps Davy did not understand this somewhat obscure sentence: he made no comment. They were still within the confines of the Tasheira ranch, and the group ahead had now reached a great gate, and had halted for Davy and Victoria. When they started walking again, Davy and Nelly led, and Victoria found herself with Rudy. Their talk was one shout of nonsense and laughter, and presently they all decided to go back straight over the shoulder of the hillside, a scrambling, screaming, slipping performance that left no time for breath, much less confidences.

But Rudy had said to Nelly, in the ten minutes in which he sauntered by her side, words that would have made Victoria feel that she did not know him, and words that lingered in Nelly's gay little heart for a long time.

There was an air about this eye-glassed, fair-headed youth, something at once poised, amused, superior, and yet friendly, that always had the effect of taking away Nelly's breath. She was half frightened at the things he said, and wondered, in her own heart, how any mere boy could know so much about girls. With Davy one merely talked, but with Rudy, Nelly was always making daring answers, only to find that he was ahead of her, ready to lead her into fresh boldness. He had said to her, on the Sunday they met, that he did not like her because she was simply trying to attract him out of vanity, and Nelly, although she pretended to scorn him, knew in her heart that it was true. He had confused her, and excited her, that first Sunday; she did not like him; he was "fresh"; but she had not forgotten him; perhaps, although she did not know it, it was something in her that Rudy had roused that had made Davy know, on the boat, that he might kiss her. Perhaps Rudy's easy audacities and half-insolent compliments had awakened her as Davy's shy, respectful overtures never could have done.

To-day she met Rudy boldly, her laughter ready for his, her crisp little saucy rebuffs meeting his familiarities wherever they struck. But he was exciting her, troubling her, again; she was breathing quickly, flushed and nervous, even while she laughed. Davy looked on in sullen puzzlement; it was not like Nelly to say daring and cutting and reckless things to a man she scarcely knew.

Then came the moment when Rudy, sauntering carelessly, was beside her and they were out of earshot of the rest.

"He's in love with you, isn't he?" he asked, with a shrug in Davy's direction. Nelly's heart leaped.

She could not answer; her eyes met his and the blood flew to her face. This assured familiarity was very different from Davy's husky stammering, and it made her uneasy.

"I thought his people were—hard up?" Rudy said.

"Well——?" Nelly managed to drag the word out into a challenge. Her companion smiled mysteriously, and did not immediately speak.

"So you're going up there to have a pack of barefooted children?" he asked, shrugging. "All right. *Chacun à son goût!*"

Nelly knew nothing of French: it impressed her in spite of herself. She knew she should rebuke him for his freedom; she knew that in any group of self-respecting women Rudy would have been condemned as coarse and rude. But Nelly was not a group of self-respecting women; she was only a girl, thrilled by this tremendous subject of the hunt and the surrender as by no other; feeling, for the first time in her life, the throbbing currents of love and passion stir within her. An actual physical weakness smote her, like a scented, languorous breeze from some dear and newly discovered country. His voice, and every word he said, seemed to be running in her veins like wine. The sweetness, the strangeness, the peril of it lifted her far above the things of earth.

"Nelly," he said, very low. "I don't want to hate him; he's decent enough, as far as he goes! Do I have to hate him?"

Nelly glanced at him timidly; he was striding along beside her with a dark look on his face. Now was the time to strike, *now*. But she could not strike—she was a living, breathing woman for the first time in her twenty-two years; there was no going back. This man loved her.

"You—you don't know Davy well enough to judge him," she said, with a pleading smile. For answer Rudy leaned close beside her, and his breath was in her face as he said:

"But you know I could get you away from him—if I tried, don't you? I'm not going to try—don't worry. But I could do it, and you know it!"

Strange mystery of a girl's heart that, trembling, uneasy, repelled as well as attracted, her one instinct—and she conquered it—was to falter: "Try!"

The girls went upstairs in a group to freshen their costumes a little for supper. Nelly was quiet, her face pale, her lips burning scarlet, and her eyes smouldering like blue fires. Lola and Lou were somewhat bashfully entering into friendship, and Victoria sparkled like a star. It was all such *fun*, this being away from home for dinner, the big, damp, plaster-scented bedroom, the mirror lighted warmly by a glass lamp. Victoria saw herself in this mirror, glowing and lovely, and her spirits rose to fever pitch. Señorita Refugio offered her an ivory comb, and the girl stuck it into her dark masses of hair with a conscious coquetry; she was wild with excitement and pleasure. The Spanish woman showed her the cunning hooks where the lace scarf fastened itself to the comb, and presently Victoria went laughing and confident to Señorita 'Ception's room, the delicate white lace of a *rebosa* falling about her bright face.

Señorita 'Ception kissed her, and simple affection and gaiety warmed them all; Victoria felt that she loved these kindly, sweet women, and she knew that they loved her. They offered her mellow old sherry, before dinner, and she drank it, as all the others did, but with a spontaneous grace and pleasure that astonished Nelly and Lou. She drew out the Señoritas' chairs with daughterly concern, and learned from the giggling Lupita a Spanish sentence: "A pretty girl has no choice but to marry a rich man." They said her accent was perfection.

They were ten at dinner: a great, gawky Spanish boy, who smelled of cow-barns, joining them at the last minute, with his sloe-black hair sleek and wet with oil, and his big red hands evidently just washed. Victoria sat between Tia 'Ception—the Señoritas by this time had insisted that all the girls call them "aunt"—and this newcomer: he was not introduced, but she knew that he was a reputed nephew, one Ruy da Sã, and she talked to him, and turned upon his agonized bashfulness the whole battery of her friendly beauty.

There were two high lamps on the table, one clear glass, one blue. The tablecloth was extremely handsome, but the cutlery was steel. The meal was served by five or six half-breed girls, who shuffled in in loose slippers, bare-legged, muttering to each other and giggling as they came and went, but it was both delicious and varied, and there was plenty of wine.

A sweet soup, like a sort of tapioca custard, *tortillas*, then a splendid salmon, with *frijoles*, then eggs scalloped with spinach, *enchiladas*, and a sort of sweet dumpling, with bananas and apples in it. Then an immense trencher of *chile con carne* was set before Señorita 'Ception, and another of stewed pigeons before Señorita Lupita, and side dishes of rice and vegetables and more beans and long loaves of crusty fresh sour bread appeared.

The sisters were enchanted with their guests' enthusiasm, and filled plates again and again. Everyone drank the red wine, and the conversation grew loud and gay; Victoria was quite the centre of attention, with her flashing eyes and her adventures in the Spanish tongue, and Nelly was quite unlike herself—excited and flushed and full of coquettish side-glances calculated to render Davy half-mad, and not lost upon Rudy Sessions. Altogether it was a most delightful meal, the girls as divertingly new to their hosts as the whole situation was to them.

Señorita 'Ception remembered a little song that she had sung years ago, and quite simply the old lady sang it, in a high, broken voice, with her fat elbows resting upon the table that was now littered with fruit skins, with rich little cakes, with tall glasses half full of wine, and broken shells of their own walnuts. Victoria, flashing, said that the sentiment was the same as in the new song, "Marguerite" and, after some urging, and a little panic, she rested her elbows on the table in turn, and sang it with such feeling that tears were in more eyes than her own. Then to make them laugh, she and Rudy and Davy sang the popular "Tit-willow" song from the "Mikado," and Señorita Yolanda laughed herself almost into hysterics at the meaning of the words, which she could easily grasp. Then somebody started "Juanita" and they all sang it, and it was at this felicitous moment that Stephen Brewer entered in search of his daughters.

Victoria gave him one frightened glance; for the moment she had almost forgotten where she was or what she was doing. But his good look of surprised fatherly pleasure in her beauty reassured her; Stephen loved feminine beauty. They made him sit down, and he had a glass of wine, and a fig, and a cake, while the girls ran upstairs for their hats.

And then they piled into the Brewer surrey, refusing all protests of offers of additional vehicles from the Tasheiras, the girls kissed each other and the old women, dogs barked, lights flashed, voices rang back and forth under the mackerel sky that showed gray patches near the hidden moon, and the horses were off with a great jerk. The three girls were wedged into the back seat, Rudy in front on Davy's lap; they swept in a gale of laughter down the sunken road into the dark. The night air was sharply cold.

"Vicky, wasn't it fun?" said Louisianna, who was only silent among strangers. "I was afraid it was going to be kind of—well, silly, when they asked you to sing, with no accompaniment, you know, and all that! But it wasn't."

"Wasn't it?" Victoria asked, eager for praise.

"It was perfectly charming!" said Nelly, in her pleasant voice. "Wasn't it, Mr. Sessions?"

"You are always charming, Miss Crabtree!" said Rudy over his shoulder.

Everyone laughed, but Nelly flushed too in the dark. He had not called her Miss Crabtree up at the gate, this afternoon. She fell to thinking about him.

When they reached the Tasheira's lower farm gate there was a holloa in the dark, and the gate wheeled slowly open before them, the shaking carriage lanterns picking up the grinning face of Ruy da Sã and his rough, long-haired, mud-spattered pony.

"It was very decent of the old Señoritas to send someone ahead to do that," Stephen Brewer said, after his shout of thanks. Victoria felt a special little thrill of thanks on her own account. It seemed improbable now that her father would scold her for the escapade. He seemed entirely good-natured, warmed with wine and cheer. And anyway, she reasoned, there had been five in the party, and Mama had wished her to show some civility to the Señoritas——

However, she was not to escape entirely, even though her mother had sent her to make the ungrateful duty call, and her father had temporarily overlooked the high-handed business of accepting, unadvised, an invitation *en masse* for supper. Just why it occurred to both her mother and father to snub her on this occasion, Victoria would never know. As a matter of fact her brilliant disorder, her bright eyes and loud voice irritated her mother, who suspected that Victoria had had the real experience of the day instead of poor disappointed Tina!

For Mr. Yelland had failed to come to tea, sending no warning of his change of plan, and no excuse. Tina had looked her prettiest, and the kettle had boiled and boiled, and Tina's music

had rested untouched on the piano. It was all extremely morti-
fying and stupid, and Mrs. Brewer felt an unreasonable inclination to vent her vexation on someone. So she met Victoria in
the close, cool, dark upper hall, and said:

"*Please* don't be so noisy! You all seem to be alive, at any
rate! Perhaps you will kindly give me some reason for the
extraordinary message that the Tasheira's milk-boys shouted
out at five o'clock. I don't like this, Vic, and you know very
well why! What on earth——" Mrs. Brewer had led the way
into her own bedroom now and turned to face her daughter in
the lamplight. "What *was* it? What happened?"

"Why, nothing, Mama!" Victoria, still under the spell
of the adventure, said lightly. "The Señoritas begged and
begged us to stay—and said that you and Papa never came near
them, and I really didn't know *what* you'd want me to do——"

"Another time do nothing unless your brother is with you!"
her father said kindly but reprovingly. Victoria scowled,
dropped her head, and bit her lip, standing before them, awkward and angry, for a minute, before she made her escape. Her
brother! She ventured a parthian shot. "I suppose Bertie
is over at Kitty Barbees!" she said, departing.

"I don't think that girl always tells the truth," said her father,
sighing. Victoria's indifference to accurate speech was indeed
more or less a recognized thing. "She doesn't get that from
the Brewers," Stephen commented. Mrs. Brewer instantly
bridled.

"Well, allow me to state, Steve, that it isn't a Crabtree trait!"
she said warmly. "Pa is almost a fanatic, when it comes to the
truth. Oh, we have our faults, I know —we're a hot-tempered
lot, and we're apt to be a little dictatorial—'uppity,' as Carra
says. But—why, they even tell of a Crabtree at the time of the
Revolution—colonial days!—who——"

"Your father has kind of rasped me—with Robert," said
Stephen, heavily.

Mrs. Brewer's eyes contracted.

"In what way?" she asked apprehensively.

"Robert say anything to you about going back?" her husband
demanded, instead of answering her.

"To Boston, you mean?"

Stephen Brewer, who had taken off collar and shirt, and was
washing himself, stood in the doorway that led to that stationary

wash-stand, and looked at her over the red-banded towel. Mrs. Brewer had removed her dress, and appeared in a neat garment that served both as petticoat and corset-cover, and was edged with scalloped tape. She was seated on the edge of her bed, thoughtfully embracing herself, and rubbing her full big arms.

"What else could I mean, Mama?" Stephen demanded. His wife, who had fallen into a muse, gave a sudden start.

"No," she said hastily and apologetically, "he didn't say anything when I met him at Fanny's yesterday."

"I have a notion your father has asked him to stay!" said Stephen.

"I think it's disgraceful!" May said. "What are they living on?"

Stephen, in his nightgown, a decorous, widely cut garment decently piped with red, now mounted with dignity into his bed. He drew the lamp a little nearer, and slipped the *Argonaut* from its cover. He wondered whether or not to further exasperate his wife, or to magnificently ignore the hated topic, as of small consequence.

"Rob is helping us with stock-taking," he said.

Mrs. Brewer stood transfixed. So Rob was worming his way in—Rob was worming his way in!

"Rob Crabtree is!" she said quietly.

"Unfortunately, yes," Stephen said. "I say unfortunately because I do not consider your brother as suited to our sort of business. Yes, your father suggested it. Or rather—we had to have someone, and Woolcock asked me my opinion. 'Let Bob in, let us see how he takes to it!' your father said."

"Let us see how he *takes* to it!" May repeated, ominously. And immediately she was all wife. "Stephen, that isn't fair! You've put the best years of your life into the firm, just to—just to——"

"Just to feather a nest for Harry and Rob!" Stephen said.

May mused, helpless and fuming.

"Oh, I think that is outrageous!" she sputtered. "Can't you go to Pa flatly, and say that you'll resign?"

For a moment Stephen had a mad vision of this dazzling step. But he knew firstly, that the old man would accept his resignation, even if it meant ruin, which it probably would not, and secondly, that his standing in the business would be weakened by a quarrel with his father-in-law, Bertie's future jeopardized, and his chance of securing an equally dignified position rendered very slim.

So he said, with his comfortable air of soothing an unreasonable woman:

"No, dear, I hardly see myself giving up six thousand a year just because your father takes his own son in temporarily for the stock-taking. I shall take good care that there isn't a berth handy by the time he's done! It's annoying—for I couldn't well suggest a smaller salary than what we pay Bertie. Bertie," his father added, reasonably, "promises to work into a valuable man, and I am paying him for the future, as well as the present. That's a perfectly sound business principle, perfectly reasonable."

"And Pa," May said thoughtfully, "of course Pa simply can't go on—go on going down to business—forever!"

"Is Bertie home to-night?" the man of the house suddenly asked.

"No, but he will be any moment now! He's with Neil Powers —they wanted to try some little Italian restaurant, and I saw no harm in it!" Mrs. Brewer hastened to say.

"Then what did Vic mean about—the Barbee girl?"

"Oh, nothing, dear—that's just Vic! Bertie has never mentioned her, himself. Neil rather admires the girl—she's a common sort of little creature, Kitty Barbee. Why, you know the Barbee crowd, Steve, the plumber, down near the station?— *his* daughter."

Stephen looked thoughtful, but said nothing. He wondered if Neil and Bertie were quite open in the matter. He himself had come home from the city on the six o'clock boat, and an acquaintance had said casually to him, "Just saw Bertie on board!"

Well, perhaps the little Italian restaurant was on this side of the bay. There were one or two in Saucelito, hanging shabbily over the water, and rather pleasant at high tide.

"I wonder that Bertie doesn't fancy Nelly—she's after all no blood kin!" he said presently. His wife flushed angrily.

"I devoutly hope he'll never be attracted *there!*" she said firmly.

For Mrs. Brewer, while not what was known as "in society," knew of no good reason why her children should not achieve that distinction and marry well. She knew a great many of the leading San Francisco families, called upon the city's richest and most fashionable women, and as the inchoate social mass of ten years before began definitely to shape itself into something exclusive and desirable, she was pleased to find herself, if not prominent, at least nominally on the right side of the wall. Slowly San Francisco's more prosperous matrons began to weed and readjust the available material, and there were certain hints given to the hosts at the bachelor dances, and there were certain calling cards steadily ignored. The fortunes that had been dragged from mines and rails, or even more rapidly gained in the stock-market, felt themselves stable at last, invested themselves in city property, displayed themselves in handsome homes. The shops began to show Paris fashions, and words forgotten, or never known on the last frontier, words like "governess" and "finish" and "genteel" began to float through refined conversations. The immediate business of bread-getting being solved for the moment, San Francisco turned herself to dances and dinners, and certain persons were acceptable and certain others not. Twenty years before a handsome French woman, a Spanish beauty, or any woman presentable and amusing, might be mistress of a man's house, and there were no questions asked by men only too eager to see a woman at all. But now this family discovered Plymouth Rock ancestors, and that referred affectionately to Lord Baltimore as cousin, and San Francisco became severely critical of lineage; none-the-less because even the most impeccable families found it somewhat difficult to reconcile with the enviable history of wealth, distinction, and birth, in Massachusetts or Virginia, their being there in California at all.

"I am afraid there is a sad streak of adventure in our blood!" the Brewer girls heard their mother say, to explain the first venturing westward. "My father was extremely delicate, and the family thought the trip across the plains would be wonderfully advantageous!" and "My dear husband's coming here was just the freak of a rich man's son!" the other women might reply.

Even the Brewer girls knew that their Grandfather Crabtree's early Californian days had been strange and rough, to say the least of it. He had opened a—yes, it was a grocery store, and Mama's Aunt Jenny had had a boarding house. There had been mention of fights, the early justice of the Vigilante Committee, and there had also been the scurvy—the odious-sounding affliction—which had destroyed his teeth, and a venture in the stock market which had made money for him, in some rather debatable fashion.

But from this long-ago beginning had been built the impeccable business of Crabtree and Company. Nobody could find any fault with *that*. And Mama had been one of the most popular and beautiful girls in society; she said so herself.

May Crabtree, as this admired belle of the long ago, and as young Mrs. Brewer, had thought little of her associates in the city. But now that these old friends were forming themselves into a definite and exclusive social circle, she was often heard to emphasize the familiarity with which she knew them all; she had danced many a dance with the de Pinnas and the Jordans, and she and Fan had been with the Holley girls when their father committed suicide in the stock market. She knew things about them all, the murders and bigamies and thefts and lies upon which a new society is built; she knew which family had a streak of Indian blood, and which proud name sheltered the identity of a jail-bird.

One never mentioned these things, of course, and one scorned the shameless press that occasionally aired them. But May saw the daughters of all these persons growing up fine and pretty, dancing and chattering French, and she followed suit as best she might. The united Crabtree and Brewer fortunes were not great fortunes, but there were the dozen teaspoons that Ma had bought, and the silver platter Pa and her children had given her on her twenty-fifth wedding anniversary. And then they *were* the Crabtrees of Crabtree, Illinois, and that could be inadvertently mentioned, now and then.

So May put up a bold fight, discovering, with a creeping little misgiving in her heart, that she was rather late. She had been too long absorbed in her nursery; life was moving too fast. The charmed circle was closing tighter and tighter, and she was not always sure that she was inside. For several years she had been nibbling about anxiously, seeing that Esme had a card to this, and that Vicky was not overlooked for that, without ever quite feeling that she belonged there. Esme, unfortunately, was distinctly hopeless material; pretty enough when one analyzed her features, but somewhat lifeless and colourless, too quickly jealous and critical to form warm friendships or attract lovers. She had selected for her bosom friend one Jenny Pembroke, a heavy, big, unpopular girl some years older, who would have resented Esme's successes, if Esme had been independent enough to make them, and the two looked on at dances, murmured scornfully, and congratulated themselves that they were not empty-headed fools like other girls.

Victoria's social experience was necessarily affected by Esme; the older sister had not made herself especially liked, and invitations were consequently a little less ready for the younger. More than that, the Brewers' fortunes did not quite keep pace with the demand. The ostentatious building of the handsome country home twenty years ago had indeed had its effect, but there were hundreds of such homes now, and scores much finer, and, after the war, different southern families had come to the coast, and those that had succeeded in rebuilding shattered fortunes, were beginning to rule the old mining and pioneering group. Indeed, for many years the San Francisco ideal was formed somewhere below the Mason and Dixon line, many a doubtful social standing was steadied by imaginary ties in the denuded south, and all the world—forgetting the blue uniforms that were even now packed away in western attics—clapped when the band played "Dixie."

So while their mother could laugh with Aunt Fanny at upstarts and parvenus, the Brewer girls knew that they were vaguely outside the ring, invited to subscription dances only, garden parties, weddings, and wedding-receptions, but not included in those madly exciting and exhilarating smaller affairs that went on continually among what the newspapers called the "jeunesse dorée."

Victoria's closest friend was also badly chosen, although the girl could have had no possible means of knowing that. Lily and Daisy Baker were among the seven children of "Baked Potato Baker," whose finding of a famous nugget had won him his nickname years before. His wife was a Spanish woman who died young, leaving her family to the care of a handsome, dashing housekeeper called "Mrs. Pringle," whose position in the Baker family was rather puzzling to all interested onlookers. Lily and Daisy were the oldest children and the only girls, and as Tom and Younger were quite out of leading strings—indeed were sowing desperate crops of wild oats by this time—and Bernardo, Charley, and Pio had been sent to the Jesuits' school in San Jose, Mrs. Pringle's comfortable settlement in the big house in Eddy Street was something of a superfluity. This was the more marked because Victoria's friend, Lily, had recently married a rich, handsome, dissipated young man named Elmer Duvalette, and was living in splendid style at the Palace Hotel, and because Daisy was almost as wild and reckless as her brothers.

The Bakers had spent their summers in Blithedale for many years, riding across the ridge once a week, like a troop of Indians, to call on the Brewers in San Rafael; they had seen each other constantly in the winters, and the old man's fabulous wealth had reconciled Mrs. Brewer to certain irregularities in his domestic affairs. There seemed to be no question of the money; Mrs. Pringle sent to Paris for the boys' ridiculous little suits, Tom and Younger opened champagne every day at the family luncheon, and drove the fastest and finest horses in the city, and the girls wore diamonds about their thin little throats and upon their unformed hands. Daisy was only twenty-one now, and Lily's marriage had been made at nineteen. Victoria secretly envied her friend. Lily had had several admirers, had laughed and flirted with them and struck them with her fan, and had told Victoria what they said to her. And now, suddenly, she was married, still so much younger even than Tina, and there was a barrier between her and her maiden friends. Perhaps it seemed none-the-less a barrier to Victoria because Lily was so complacently conscious of it; there were certain things one mightn't say to dear old Vicky any more; there was a married attitude too delicious not to be tasted to its last drop.

Lily, with Victoria silently and observantly following her, would flash gaily into the hotel, stop at the desk to ask if there was any mail for "Mrs. Duvalette," dimple distractingly at the clerk when she said that she wanted to know the very minute of "my husband's" coming in, not to keep him waiting for his lunch. She would lead Victoria to the great luxurious bedroom with its tumbled bed, and with perhaps the eggy and cooling remains of a lavish breakfast tray, and while she prettily scolded the chambermaid for dilatoriness she knew, and Victoria knew that she knew, exactly the effect of this intimate glimpse upon her friend. To be married, and to live at the Palace——! Life held nothing more intoxicatingly complete. But to be married, anyway——

Victoria felt it, Esme and Tina writhed over the unattainable necessity, perhaps even little Lou felt it, in her silent way. But most of all their mother longed to see them all settled well, to speak of "my daughters, all married now—alas!" and to have Bertie, if he married at all, marry securely. This little Kitty Barbee was a nice enough little nonentity—but Bertie's must be a brilliant wedding, with a Wesley, a Murchison, a Persons, a Jordan or a de Pinna. Tina might wed her parson, perhaps, and for Esme her mother already began to form the protective phrase "Mama's home girl," but Vicky and Louisianna must make brilliant matches. She always remembered in this connection that the little Cunningham boy, whose mother was a Murchison, had made violent love to Victoria, one sleepy afternoon at Blithedale, when he was fifteen and the girl a year younger, and that all the ladies, laughing at the infatuated youth, had augured Victoria's enormous popularity.

"After all," Mrs. Brewer thought sleepily, as the various troublesome thoughts about Vicky, and the disappointing Mr. Yelland, and Bob Crabtree, and Lottie's latest impudence, began to drift through her head, "after all, serious affairs come up very quickly—two months from now one or two of the girls will be engaged, and I shall have all this fretting for nothing!"

CHAPTER VII

LIFE moved on to Christmas time, slowly enough for the Brewer family, who filled it with embroidery, music-lessons, painting, and idle reading; rapidly for Lucy's household, which was always busy. Nelly, freed for a few weeks from the kindergarten, and frantically attempting to finish before the inexorably advancing twenty-fifth various effects in tissue paper, satin ribbon, and orris-root, known as her "Christmas presents," felt panic even early in December. Alice and Georgie cuddled together in their father's slippery great arm-chair in the evenings and whispered secrets, and Lucy bought, and domesticated in her back yard, a scrawny turkey. As for Harry, always happy, he was especially happy at these times, tramping home through the early and earlier dark, catching a great breath of homely warmth and comfort from the kitchen as he entered it.

One day in January, 1886, when sheets of rain were sweeping over the city, and the little Crabtree house was warm and smelled of wet woolens, he told his wife that Rob had been offered the management of the mail order department of Crabtree and Company. Lucy continued to strain her tomato soup, her eye speculative where it might once have been angry. The months had subtly changed the relationship between all four branches of the family, as introducing the element of Ella and Rob was bound to do. Fanny had naturally aligned herself with her father in giving the Robert Crabtrees every favour on their return. Of herself, Fanny might have done no such thing, but she could not very well do otherwise because of the determined stand of the old man. May Brewer had unwisely shown feeling over this, and Lucy had come in for the heated confidences of the older sister. Fanny immediately turned to Ella, discovering in Ella unsuspected charms, and guiding her on shopping and sightseeing tours. So that Lucy found her position with the Brewers stronger than it had ever been, the girls exchanged over-night visits with a frequency they had not enjoyed since childhood, and the ideal match, between Nelly and Bertie, of which Lucy had dreamed for years, did not seem as utterly unattainable as it had formerly.

Nelly had indeed confided to her mother her half promise to Davy Dudley, but Lucy, with a worldly wisdom that made Nelly but a baby again, was working against it with every means in her power. She saw Davy, and told him frankly and kindly that the arrangement was a great injustice to Nelly. When did he expect to be able to care for her? In five years? The five best and happiest and sweetest years of her life, Lucy reminded him.

"All very easy for you, Davy, you get a cook and a house-keeper," Lucy said, in her pleasant friendly voice that so masked the unfriendly words. "But what about her?"

Davy could only stammer huskily that of course he realized that, but he didn't expect that times would always be so hard.

"Oh, I know all about *times*," Lucy laughed ruefully, with her favourite air of being witty, "and they're *always* hard for some people!"

With Nelly she took a different attitude: she was extremely sympathetic, but with a manner of veiled amusement and sage tolerance, that routed the girl over and over again.

"Davy—you mention Davy," Lucy would say cozily, over the darning on a Saturday afternoon, "tell me about him. How are our wedding plans going on?"

"Mama—" Nelly would protest, uncomfortably. "As if we could talk of weddings, yet!"

"Oh, can't we?" Lucy was extremely innocent.

"Well, you *know* we can't! Davy has no money."

"I suppose not. But I didn't know that that was a barrier!"

"Mama," Nelly would plead, looking appealingly at the demure mouth that was smiling down at a worn heel, "*please* don't tease!"

"Was I teasing? Well, she shouldn't be teased. Go on, dear, tell me more of these wonderful schemes."

"There's nothing to tell, Mama—especially with you laughing at me. But Davy is saving——"

"Ah-h! This looks serious. We have a bank-account, have we?"

"Well, he has nearly a hundred—at least he has about sixty-two dollars!"

"Gracious! But go on. What are we to do with this wonderful sixty-two dollars?"

"Mama, *please*——"

"Please what, dear?"

"*Please* don't laugh at us!"

"My dear, if you want to marry into drudgery and hard work and poverty and sickness of all sorts, do you think your mother is going to find it a laughing matter?"

This would crush Nelly: the stocking she was darning would blur before tears of pain, and her throat would thicken and her face flush.

"It doesn't *have* to be that, Mama!"

"Doesn't it?" Lucy was brisk and self-controlled. "I think it *does*. I want you to promise me one thing, Nelly. There's to be no definite engagement between you and Davy, and no talk of marriage, until things are in a very different state!"

Nelly made no special protest against this; she loved to have Davy kiss her and tell her how wonderful she was, but she definitely disliked the idea of marrying a poor man. It made her impatient and tearful; she told Davy that she didn't know why he always wanted to talk so "crazy."

"There's nothing crazy about a man wanting to marry the woman he loves, Nell."

"I'm not a woman!"

"Well, the girl, then."

"But it is crazy, Davy, with your mother having that doctor bill to pay, and her roof leaking and everything! And you haven't had a suit since you came to the city——"

"I'm going to get myself some new clothes, after a while. Doc Hughes gave me this suit, and I'm twice his size," David explained laughing uncomfortably. "I drive his horse back to the barn for him, nights, and sometimes he takes me with him to the hospital. Maybe, some day, if I graduate, he'll take me in with him, but I don't know. You see, my aunt's in kind of trouble, Nelly, and things at home are going kind of bad. . . ."

Thus Davy, eager to enlist her sympathy and interest. But Nelly was irritated. It was always money—money—money; she hated money.

They were walking in winter sunlight, and she thought Davy

looked conspicuously shabby; she fancied other girls and men, also walking, looked as if they thought so, too. His hands were bare and his hat was old.

That was money again; it would be a long time before he could get a new suit and new shoes. She supposed that all her life long she was destined to worry about money, so hard to get, and so necessary to happiness! When he left her at her gate that night and saw the blue hat go up the path, and the three steps, and along the little oblong porch to the door, Davy knew that he had lost her, for a while at least. He carried to his aunt's depressing kitchen the heaviest heart that he had ever known. Everything hurt him: Miss Clay's casual reference to Nelly's mother; the snapshot of Nelly taken by Rudy Sessions on the Tasheira walk, weeks before; even the blonde smiling girl on the Hood's Sarsaparilla Calendar who looked a little like her. But he loved her so that he could not think but that she must come back to him, in the end.

Meanwhile his aunt's boarders had gone, rent was overdue, bills and interest on an old loan were pressing. And Miss Clay had developed a mysterious ailment, and consumed bottle after bottle of a black, odorous medicine. Through the black stains soaking the label Davy could read the dosage: "A tablespoonful three times daily," but Aunt Lilly took it much more often, every hour—every half-hour. She cried constantly, and it began to appear that their only escape was in a return to Napa.

Next door, affairs were not much better. Georgie Crabtree had a heavy bronchial cough all through November and December, and just after Christmas Harry was kept at home four days with a severe case of tonsillitis. Cold rains were falling over the city; amiable and sympathetic little Alice had to go downtown twice to explain at his office that her father was ill. He would try to be down to-morrow morning.

Harry, convalescent, was moved to the kitchen on the fourth day, where he sat weakly and contentedly watching his women-folk. The day was bleak and raw; Nelly was ironing a cross-barred muslin dress; Lucy lamenting over some jam that had coated over thickly with plushy green mould.

"Disgusting stuff!" she said, sticky and heated, and rubbing the end of her nose with a bent wrist. "Why women can't manage to do all their work through community kitchens is more than I know! This morning," said Lucy, smiling, "I got possessed of an idea for a kitchen costume, I couldn't do anything else until I sat down and wrote it all out! I do *think* the way we let ourselves suffer all sorts of discomforts, year after year . . ."

Nelly thumped an iron; a sheet of rain blew against the window. Georgie, reading a magazine, looked up from the floor upon which he was comfortably stretched.

"Pa, do you believe they'll ever have horseless carriages?"

"How do they propose to keep 'em going, son?" Harry asked, interested.

"Workless meals are a good deal more interesting to me!" Lucy, who was vigorously washing her hands at the sink, and at the same time sluicing mould, jam, and dust down the drain, said, crossly. Everyone laughed. Nelly, going to the door, stopped to give her father a kiss.

"Who's that?" Lucy said curiously, as the rotary bell on the front door sounded again.

"I'll see!" Nelly was gone only a moment; she came swiftly back from the icy front hall with a wet cardboard box in her hand. "It's for me," she said, bewildered and shyly expectant. "It was from Anderson's, in Mission Street. I guess it's flowers!"

"Who from, for the land's sake!" Lucy exclaimed.

"I guess Davy," Nelly said, breaking the string. But a minute later she looked up from the wet, sweet violets with shining eyes. "Mama! It's Mr. Sessions—isn't that nice of him! He says—" She read the card aloud, "'Saw you on the Polk Street dummy, but you wouldn't bow to me!' Mama," cried Nelly, with flaming cheeks, "don't you think that's sweet of him!"

"Yes, I do," Lucy said thoughtfully, taking the card daintily in damp fingers. Nelly was frankly radiant as she went back to her ironing; the event as it stood was enough to make her heart sing. Lucy was looking beyond it into a future that only she could see, and her eyes were contented, too.

Alice came in, breathless, wet, bringing a rush of cool air into the warm kitchen. Her father looked at her in painful expectation.

"Mr. Barrell was there—whoo! I'm blown to pieces," gasped Alice, in her fresh, laughing voice. "Mr. Barrell was there, Papa, and then Mr. Casey came out."

"And what did they tell you, dear?" Harry asked nervously.

"Well—not much," Alice said vaguely. "Mr. Barrell said that he had expected you yesterday——"

"Yes, I know he did!" Harry said quickly, with a glance at his wife. Lucy interpolated immediately, in a patient, monotonous tone.

"You couldn't have gone out yesterday with that throat in that rain!"

"But Mr. Casey said he was sorry, and that Mr. Lippey was helping with your bills!" Alice said, catching the drift of the conversation and anxious to please.

"Casey did?—he's fine old fellow," Harry said, brightening. "Did—did Barrell say anything then?"

"No, he just turned away," Alice answered conscientiously. "And then Mr. Casey said to me, 'Ask your father to get down to-morrow if he can,' because they were very busy!"

"Yes, I know—and I certainly will be back to-morrow!" Harry decided quickly. He did not speak of Mr. Barrell again, but two or three times, as the wet afternoon hours wore quietly on, he alluded gratefully to old Casey. He said he hoped some day to do something for old Casey. Alice sat down with her arithmetic; presently Miss Clay came in. She was a little damp too, and pleased to sit between Nelly's busy iron and the glowing stove, and contribute such news as she could to the listening circle.

"Johnson come round to see would I renew my lease," Miss Clay said, wiping her nose on a man's crumpled handkerchief, "but I don't know's I can. There's so much *to* it, Mr. Crabtree! I pay eighteen, and it's the least of my expenses! When you've got to pay for your milk, and every mouthful of vegetables you eat—it's terrible. Del wrote me—that's Davy's mother, and s'she, 'Lil, there's no place like the country, these times!' but I don't know that Del's having it any too easy. Ask me if I knew of a couple teachers who would like to board up there, this vacation——!"

"I should think that would be lovely," Alice said ardently.

"What say, dear?" Miss Clay said, suddenly turning a somewhat troubled smile upon the child. "You don't know nothin' about it," she assured her, not unkindly. "It's work—work—work. Well, that's life! I says to Davy this morning that I didn't know where we was going to end up at. But I guess we'll git through—folks generally does!"

Nelly listened thoughtfully; her eyes full of pain caused by some thought that tied these dismal reflections to her own bright and radiant dreams.

"Davy's mother is all wore out," pursued the visitor morosely. "Del ain't but forty-five, and she looks sixty! I don't know as she's ever had ten dollars to spend on herself in her life. Seen a beau of yours this afternoon, Nelly," she added, good-naturedly.

"Who's that?" Nelly wet her thumb, drew it over the cuff she was ironing, and pressed the iron on the damp muslin.

"Doc Hughes. He was clippin' along in that little buggy of his—I's way out past Fletcher's—went out to git some lettuce and cabbages off the Chinamen. It was rainin' to beat all, and he stopped and give me a lift. He's a real nice feller; Davy takes care of his horse, you know. He asked for you—says you was sweet-lookin', or something like that!"

"Well, forever!" Nelly said, pleased. "I hardly know him. Mama used to know his wife, before she died. Did you ever!"

"I've always felt that Nelly was going to marry a man older than she is!" Lucy said, struck. Both Alice and Nelly laughed joyously, and Alice said seriously:

"He's an awfully nice man, isn't he, Mama?"

But Lucy was thinking.

"I don't know why you don't get boarders, Lil," she said to her neighbour. "I know there's money in it. I've often thought I could make a small fortune at it. That Mrs. Thompson—where Harry and I were married—retired with a pile of money, they said!"

"I guess she didn't retire one minute before she had to!" Miss Clay opined, with grim enjoyment, as one who knew. "It's dredgery and debt, that's what it is! I borrowed four hundred dollars two years ago, and three hundred two years before that, and what with rent and interest, and gas—I wish I'd never had it turned on, but we had that fire, when my blue alpaca was burned, and two blankets, five years ago. . . ."

There was a most pleasant and welcome interruption: Victoria Brewer, with her hair curled up by the rain, and in her old suit and last winter's hat, opened the kitchen's outside door, and was suddenly being delightedly kissed and laughed over by everyone.

"I've only got about half an hour—I'm regularly running away!" she said, breezily. "I'm supposed to be at Aunt Fanny's, but she wasn't there, and it was so dismal and bleak! Carra has a toothache, and Maggie was crying about something, and I just thought I'd rush over here and rush back before it is quite dark! Mama sent me over to go to Quade and Strauts, and Michel Wand's for her."

Everyone was splendid, said the heartening visitor gaily. Mama was terrified because Bertie was beginning to like Kitty Barbee, but Bertie insisted that he wasn't ever going to marry any one!

"That's all your doing, Nelly," said Victoria, with vivacity, "you mean girl—you! I bet it's Davy Dudley! Oh, and my dear, who do you think is the latest? Esme! Yes—actually, or at least we think so. She met a man named Roscoe Beale—isn't it a perfectly stunning name?—at Mrs. Murchison's tea. It was a perfectly gorgeous tea, and I must say that Esme looked wonderful. And if he didn't come way over to call, with his mother—yesterday! Mama was helping Addie with the parlour and had her head tied up, but we flew round, and Esme did look so nice! Well, there may be nothing in it, but anyway I thought I'd tell you."

Nelly was watching her with very bright eyes, but now she smiled suddenly and said, quickly:

"Well, I'm sure I hope it'll happen. Esme is the sort of person that ought to marry a rich man!"

"Anybody is the sort of person who ought to marry a rich man!" Lucy said, with her sharp little air of being witty.

"Oh, don't say that, Aunt Lucy!" Victoria said, vivaciously. "The man I've picked out is as poor as Job's turkey!"

"Vicky——?" Nelly questioned, significantly. And as they exchanged a look Victoria flushed delightedly and confusedly and said, "Oh, you big goose! I'll never tell you anything again! No, of course it's not *him*. He's got piles of money, anyway. Aren't you awful!"

"Look here, are you setting up a lover of your own?" Lucy asked curiously, but Victoria, still rosy, only looked guiltily at Nelly and laughed again as she said:

"No. No—it's just—just nonsense. The—this—man—I've never even spoken to him!"

"But just the same——" Nelly was beginning. But Victoria put her hand over her cousin's mouth, and laughter interrupted them both.

"No, you hush, Nelly!" said Victoria, when she could speak. "You awful girl, you—Aunt Lucy, don't let her say it!"

"All right," Nelly gurgled, half-strangled. "But go on, tell us more news, Vicky! How's Tina's parson?"

"Oh, they are slower than death!" Victoria said gaily, and everybody laughed. "I don't believe she's seen him since Christmas—he came to dinner with us and told Bertie that Mama was so motherly. I said mother-in-lawly is what we're after. However, Tina seems perfectly contented to have it go so slowly, and now of course we're all wondering about Esme!"

"It would be awfully nice if she married first——" Nelly mused.

"It would be awfully nice if *somebody* got married!" Victoria said, half seriously, with a great sigh, and again the easily amused company found her amusing.

"Oh, we'll all get married, if that's all!" Nelly said, discontentedly, with sudden, inexplicable tears in her eyes.

"Stay and have supper, Vicky," her aunt said, affectionately. But the girl was suddenly reminded that she must go.

"You know Uncle Rob is in old Rossi's place," she said, reviewing the news. "He and Aunt Ella are probably going to have a flat in Jones Street, and Aunt Ella has sent east for some silver and things, and a Copley painting of her grandfather, if you please——"

"A flat—that's just having your kitchen and everything on one floor, isn't it?" Harry asked, deeply interested. "I shouldn't think that would be comfortable!"

"Nothing like this cottage, with ten floors!" Nelly said mischievously.

"Ah, well, but we have the yard and the garden here, Bootsy!" he said quickly. Nelly and Victoria, who had resumed her wraps, went into the girls' cold bedroom, and Nelly locking her arms about the other girl, and with eyes misting again, said, a little aimlessly:

"Don't go, Vicky! Stay and we can talk!"

"Oh, I'd love to! But I hadn't even planned for this, darling!" Victoria suddenly felt that she dearly loved pretty, troubled Nelly, and she longed to stay.

Nelly, looking downward, buttoned and unbuttoned the uppermost buttons of Victoria's shabby old coat.

"Anything wrong?" Victoria said. Nelly threw back her head, blinked, and said lightly: "Oh, no!"

"Is it somebody bothering you?" Victoria asked. Nelly violently shook her head. "Is it Davy?" questioned Victoria. But for some reason Nelly would not admit that it was Davy. She denied Davy.

"Vicky," she said, "tell me something. You know what I mean—is that—that Piute—Ruy da Sā—still following you about?"

"My dear—yesterday morning at the door, the side door, Addie found a basket—an Indian basket—with about two dozen fresh eggs in it!" Victoria said laughing. "Mama questioned her, and it appears that Lotta saw our young friend—she didn't know his name, of course, but she said, 'that wild-looking boy from the Señorita Tasheiras'—saw him riding away."

"Vicky! And haven't you told your mother?"

"Why, what can I tell her, Nelly? I've met the man twice, hanging about, but I never spoke to him, and how do I know that it's me he's—courting, if you call it courting!"

"Because you *do* know, perfectly well!" Nelly said delightfully stern. "Didn't he give you the heart—and the glass cross?"

"A plush heart pincushion and a little glass cross! No card, and no message, just shoved them into my hand, coming out of the station!" Victoria said, with exhilaration.

"Well, I suppose they were the best things he had, and perhaps he doesn't know how to write a card," Nelly said reflectively. But Victoria bridled a little at this.

"Doesn't know how to write a card! Why, Ruy da Sā went through grammar school, and one year of high!" she protested.

"He *did?*" Nelly marvelled.

"Certainly he did!"

"But he always looks so rough, scrambling over the ranch," Nelly protested. "Vicky, you—you wouldn't really consider him?" she stammered.

"No, I don't see how I could do *that*," Victoria said slowly. "Of course, I'd perfectly adore to live up there on the ranch, with all the pigs and cows and dogs and chickens, and Portuguese babies," she admitted.

"Oh, Vicky, you wouldn't! Why, the very smell of the

kitchens is enough for me!" Nelly said. "If you feel that way, you'd much better marry Davy Dudley, who is at least white!" she added, perversely. Victoria gave her an illuminated look.

"Nelly, what made you say that?" she asked.

"Nothing!" Nelly laughed, guiltily.

"But something did!" Victoria persisted.

"No, truly!" And now Nelly was curious. "Why?"

Victoria gave a cautious glance toward the closed kitchen door and then said quickly:

"Because I admire and like Davy Dudley—yes, I do. I like him—awfully!"

Suddenly inexplicable tears were in her eyes, and she fingered the collar of Nelly's little kitchen dress with meticulous care. Nelly was stupefied.

"But Vicky—but Vicky—has he ever—in any way——" she began.

"No, he hasn't!" laughed Victoria, angrily flashing away the one tear that had fallen. "Once he did me the honour to tell me that he liked *you*—but that was ever so long ago, and I never could be jealous of *you*, Nelly. But I've fancied sometimes that he liked me—of course I almost never see him—and of course Papa wouldn't care how poor the man was, if he was a man we all liked, like Davy—But I'm a fool to speak about it, of course," Victoria floundered on, thrilled to the marrow at this unexpected confidence, "and swear—*swear*——"

Nelly, bewildered, was duly swearing, when her mother's voice was heard.

"Girls—Vicky! It's nearly five, dear. Come, girls—stop chattering in that cold room!"

Out they came, and Victoria was embraced in farewells. Her grandfather was well?—That was good. And Aunt Fanny was well, and very busy about the big Charity Bazaar? That was good. Love to everyone at home, and perhaps if Uncle Harry was better, Aunt Lucy and Georgie might come over to San Rafael on Sunday.

"And Alice and I will take this old man out to the sunshine in the Park," Nelly said, kissing the thinning hair that was beginning to give Harry's forehead a somewhat spiritual look. He brightened at once. This was Thursday; he certainly would be quite well by Sunday.

Lucy said vigorously that he surely would be well if he would only spend to-morrow and Saturday in the house. But Harry shook his head.

"If Barrell had been willing to have me do that, he would have suggested it," he said. "Isn't she pretty, Lucy?"

This was said of Victoria, who went out radiant into the gathering dark.

She was out so little alone, especially after dusk, that the two street-car rides seemed a great adventure. She had to change cars at Tenth Street, and joggled comfortably along Larkin, past the monstrous failure of the new City Hall, and the Mechanics' Pavilion, where there were annual fairs. Every one of her wet and crowding neighbours interested Victoria, and at Sutter Street she almost gasped with pleasure at the brightly coloured lights in the windows of Wakelee's Pharmacy. Her uncle's compliment, her confidence regarding Davy—the very spoken words of which seemed to give the matter body—Nelly's questions about the ridiculous Ruy, Esme's affair and Tina's affair combined to make her feel that life was romantic and thrilling, and even the unwelcome, languorous glances of a moustached young man in the corner of the car, sent straight into her innocent and offended eyes, helped her mood of adventure and excitement.

She had had time to fling off her outer garments before her aunt returned from an exhausting committee meeting, in reference to the Charity Bazaar, and presently both women went harmoniously down to dinner, Victoria's arm about her Aunt Fanny's waist, Victoria's dark rich hair still curling into damp rings, and her face still glowing, from her escapade.

Aunt Fanny's house was always close; it had certain smells of its own; clothy, carpety smells that her nieces always associated with the sleepy, decorous evenings they spent with her. The marble-topped tables, with their tidies and their lamps, were always in the same places, the chairs stood squarely upon the padded carpets, clocks ticked steadily in the dusted, peaceful order of the long parlours. To be sure, there was a compensating sense of adventure in being so far from home after dark, but even to Victoria's bounding senses visiting Aunt Fanny was dull. The coke fire burned in a small grate heavily rodded with steel bars; between the richly draped lace curtains morning sunlight fell brightly upon the quiet breakfast table; there were un-familiar noises of street cries, and of Saint Brigid's bells; there was unfamiliar silence within, where Fanny went noiselessly about. Maggie was bullied into creaking consideration, and Carra was always a shadow.

There was a velvet box in the parlour, with a stereoscope, and a score of little double photographs for it—one of Fanny and May in the Yosemite Valley, with the Bridal Veil Falls for a background. And there was the piano, to be touched only when Grandfather was awake, and a massive heavy Inferno of Dante, with Doré plates, and a smaller, oblong book, Schiller's Bell, with illustrations in the lovely, flowing outlines of Flaxman. The Brewer girls had looked through both a thousand times, and looked through Aunt Fanny's heavy, big bound books of music, with "Fanny Crabtree" in gold on the covers, and with what that lady herself frankly admitted was "utter rubbish" bound in with the better selections—"Potpourris" from "Faust" and "Ernani." "Brother's Fainting at the Door," was an old Civil War song; "Please Save Me, Kind Sir, I Don't Want to be Drowned!" another favourite of about the same date. And Fanny's nieces could still find, pencilled on margins, faint re-minders of that giddy and girlish past of which she told them: "Isn't he a bore?" some youthful hand had rebelliously written on "The Brave Newfoundland Dog," and "I bet he pops the question to Minny to-night" still adorned "Bright Things Can Never Die." When Fanny saw these youthful indiscretions, she coloured and laughed uncomfortably, erasing them vigorously.

She had all a single woman's nervous apprehension of censure, a sort of eager sensitiveness. No husband or children ever hav-ing dispossessed her, she was still the centre of her own universe, still flaunting girlhood's bright and ignorant complacencies, and as positive and swift in her judgment of wife and matron as she was of the state of life she knew. One of Fanny's firmest convictions was that she was never deceived or outwitted by any one—friend, relative, or servant. Her apt answers to car-conductors, policemen, and the sales-persons in shops were a source of great satisfaction to her. The light brown, freckled skin would redden, and Fanny might beat her nose agitatedly, but she was rarely worsted.

"I turned very quietly to this man—I'd never seen him be-fore," she would say, "'Are you an inspector?' I said. 'Yes, madam,' he said. 'Then you saw *exactly* what occurred here,' I said. 'I wish you would take this man's number and report him! And——' I said, 'I shall stop at the car-company's office in a day or two and see what they have done!' Of course the conductor *then* was all apologies—he hadn't understood—he thought this and thought that!——"

"Of course," the listening Esme or Tina would say triumphantly.

"Ah, but you can't do that!" Fanny would say, flushing and bridling. "For the sake of other passengers it would be perfectly idiotic to allow such goings on!"

Or perhaps it would be Maggie who aroused her wrath.

"'Maggie,' I said," the report would run, "'to prove to you that I know what I am talking about, I just went to the dirty-clothes-basket and *took out* this apron. You say that I made you change a perfectly clean apron. *Look* at this apron! Tell me honestly if you think it is perfectly clean—honestly, I want your opinion! Look at that spot—look at this soot. Is that perfectly clean? Tell me frankly——'"

And so on and on, perhaps lowering her voice when the self-conscious and vanquished Maggie entered the room. Often Fanny, upon whom this peculiarity naturally grew with years, would vent upon Maggie the exasperation she felt toward the silently ubiquitous Carra. Always she was on the alert for offence, watching ticket-sellers shrewdly, quick to question butchers and bakers, and ready to answer them. She never gave to street beggars, remarking invariably that they were always persons of property, and to any friend who solicited alms from her, Fanny usually answered nervously and cheerfully that she had her own charities—which indeed she did, for she could be open-handed when she chose. It was one of Fanny's luxuries to be among the first to subscribe to a Fair, a new theological magazine, or what she called the deserving poor.

Her aunt's legacy had come at the critical time when she was passing from a spoiled and admired girlhood into dull middle age; and the Fanny whose saucy beauty and charm had won her great consideration, had that consideration still, on other terms. If she had had to look to her father for every penny, she would now have become simply the superfluous aunt in a sister's family, but Aunt Jenny's timely thousands had re-established her, or rather continued her establishment, in her own esteem. A rich maiden lady held a very different position from that of a penniless old maid. Fanny had always been happily assured and self-confident; she never had any reason to consider any other mental attitude.

To-night the little coke fire burned on, Fanny rocked noiselessly, Victoria turned page after page of "The Sister's Story," which lugubrious yet compelling history of tears, changes, consumption, and death, she had found on her aunt's table. The old man, sunk in his leather chair, was pushed up close under the bright light of a gas drop-lamp, slowly and deliberately playing solitaire. Now and then he interrupted the silence with a shifting of his body and a sharp "hem!" and sometimes, when he was pleased with the fall of the cards, he hummed gaily, with his lips set as if for whistling, "Too—too—too!"

Victoria interrupted her reading for a tearing but noiseless yawn, and looked over at her aunt. Miss Fanny had her glasses on, her lips were set firmly together, but she moved them occasionally as she read. She was reading a religious work by Phillips Brooks. Victoria knew that her aunt had travelled with the older Aunt Jenny years ago; she thought of the remembered offers of marriage Miss Fanny had received, of the excitement of learning that one had fallen heir to a fortune, of going up a steamer gang-plank, and of seeing Rome and Paris. Victoria resolved that if she herself ever had half such opportunities, she would feel herself fortunate. Certainly if any man at all eligible ever asked her to marry him, she would do it, and as for travel——!

The girl's longest journey had been to Sacramento, a hundred miles away. That was eight years ago now, and Victoria felt a pang as she recalled it: the exciting start, with her father and mother, her packed satchel, and the overnight stay with an affectionate elderly family friend called "Aunt Tally," by all the world. Why her heart should ache remembering the eager fifteen years' old Victoria she hardly knew; perhaps she had felt more sure, in that very morning of adventure, that the next eight years would bring her nearer her dreams.

She fell into a dream now, in which her grandfather suddenly died and was laid away, and her Aunt Fanny enthusiastically selected herself, Victoria, for a few years of travel. As a matter of fact she did not admire Aunt Fanny as she once had, and as Esme and Tina still did. Sometimes Aunt Fanny's manner, in public places, made Victoria flush apologetically and uncomfortably, and sometimes she was guilty of a secret utterance of the phrase "crank!" in reference to her relative. But still she dreamed—she was in Italy, tilting a parasol like Lily Duvalette's; and a handsome and boyish young man, a "steamer acquaintance," was beside her—Aunt Fanny would have to write Mama that apparently our Vicky had given her heart away——

"Aunt Fanny . . ."

"Vick . . ."

"Did you ever think you would like to run a bakery?"

Fanny eyed her humorously, ready to laugh.

"Why, my dear? Are your ambitions running that way?"

"Well," Victoria said, with a warm yawn. "I think it would be fun! At least, when I stopped on Polk Street for the rolls, to-night, everything was in such awful disorder at Muller's. And I couldn't help thinking that I'd love to straighten it all out, the rolls and cookies and biscuits—it looked sort of fun!"

"What a delightful surprise for society!" Fanny said, satirically, "Miss Victoria Brewer in a bakery!"

"I wouldn't mind society," Victoria countered, suddenly antagonized. "I'd like to do something!"

There was a pause, which Fanny filled with a superior smile. The hint of opposition annoyed her.

"I advise you to confine your cooking to your mother's kitchen," she said, significantly. "It seems to me that I haven't noticed any *particular* enthusiasm in Miss Vicky Brewer, there! When Addie's out, I don't remember any *particular* willingness on your part to take Tina's or Lou's share of the work, eh, Vicky? That comes a little nearer home, doesn't it?" And Fanny laughed heartily, and sent a sly look at her discomfited niece. "Maggie!" she called, an instant later, as a lumbering noise was heard in the dining room. Maggie came to the door. "Maggie, have you been out?" she asked, in displeased surprise. For a light rain was again falling, and Maggie breathed of the fresh, wet out-of-doors.

"I wint to the corner wid Lizzie," said Maggie, breathing hard.

"Oh, has Lizzie been here?"

"She run in," Maggie admitted, after thought.

Fanny continued to look at her steadily through her glasses; there was a brief silence.

"Does Mrs. de Paulo let Lizzie have a night off whenever Lizzie wishes it?" she asked, quietly. Maggie was unequal to the question, and after an awkward pause, tittered uncomfortably.

"She just run in," she submitted.

"Because if Mrs. de Paulo *does*," Fanny pursued, "she is proving herself a very poor friend to Lizzie, as Lizzie will find out. That simply spoils a girl; and when she gets another place, what happens? Oh, she has to be running over to see Maggie—and Bessy—and this one and that one, and she is unhappy when she can't. Then she neglects her work, and mopes, and is discharged!"

"Yes'm," Maggie said, when Fanny paused.

"Bring us some more coal, please," Fanny said, after another brief silence, and they could follow Maggie's thumping progress down the basement stairs, her heavy shovel in the coal, and her returning steps. Victoria, who had not enjoyed the little scene, took the opportunity, when Maggie's rough head was close to her, over the scuttle, to ask, in a low tone,

"How's your little brother that has the hip disease?"

"They're goin' to take him to the hospital, the way maybe they'll have a right to cut it," Maggie said, with ready gratitude. But when Victoria followed her question with another, she was horrified to see that the rosy face was running with tears and the big mouth was too unsteady for an answer.

"I wouldn't talk to Maggie when she's in here, darling," said Miss Fanny, when Maggie was gone. "You see it upsets her—she's going on Sunday to see poor little Hugh, and until then it's only cruelty to remind her of him. More than that—like all of them!—she's only too ready to take advantage of any familiarity!"

"I know——" Victoria murmured.

Silence fell again. It seemed to the visitor that these evenings had no beginning and no end. The tick of the fire, the measured punctual clicking of the clock, the purr of the lamp, and the far sounds of cable cars in the streets and boat whistles on the bay made her feel actually stupid.

At home there were a hundred activities that never entered here. Supper was later, less formal, and more drawn-out, afterward sometimes the girls sang for an hour or two, played Old Maid or Casino, or sat about the dining table laughing over "writing games." Then Victoria loved to copy, and loved to work out various diagrams, sometimes a plan of the village, or the drawing of an ideal house. Sometimes she would get a volume of the Encyclopædia, and drift along from Samoa to Sewing machine, occasionally coming upon some article that might be skimmed with guilty haste, her finger meanwhile keeping track of the innocuous essay near by that would be shown her mother in case of a surprise. Then Bertie sometimes brought friends in, and there was candy-pulling, or walking, if the night was fine, or there was a horse or cow sick, and a visitation to the stables, or the girls trooped up to the attic and dressed themselves up for charades. Tina's musical education had reached the point now where she could play duets with Victoria, and they loved to rush through the "Poet and Peasant" and "Die Schone Melusine," their father applauding them with the same amiability with which he applauded charades, sampled their candy, and even joined in their writing games.

But at Aunt Fanny's time went slowly. Yet somehow all the girls felt a thrill when their mother said, thoughtfully:

"You might stay in town that night, if Aunt Fanny asks you," and they all packed satchels for this experience with a real sense of adventure.

To-night, as the clock struck the half-hour after nine, Victoria yawned again, shut her book, and loitered to the table, to watch her grandfather's cards. He was playing a difficult game called "Napoleon," the laying out of which took far more time than the play. Yet he delayed over the play, sometimes laying his veined old ivory hand upon a card to remind him of the possible shifting.

"You can't put that King underneath," Victoria presently objected.

"Well, sometimes I—I move a card," the old man confessed.

"Cheating!" the girl reproached him, relentlessly.

For answer he fixed his amused eyes upon her, and winked one mischievously.

"Why, you bad old man!" Victoria said, "you ought to be in San Quentin!"

"Noo—Vicky, noo—Vicky!" he pleaded absently, absorbed

in his game. But when even his illicit manipulation failed, and he was shuffling again he said:

"How's Baker's little girl coming along?"

"Lily? Oh, she's fine," Victoria said. "She and her husband are living at the Palace, and Mr. Duvalette is just coining money! She's awfully happy."

"His boys are spending it as fast as he's making it," said Reuben Crabtree.

"You mean her brothers," Victoria adjusted him gently. "Tom and Younger are terrors! But isn't there lots and lots of money there, Grandpa?" she asked. She would have been glad of a denial, but her grandfather muttered "Tons of it!" as he went on playing.

"Did Uncle Rob get the Foster contract?" she asked presently. She was under the impression that Uncle Rob had not distinguished himself in this matter, and loyalty to her father made her willing to enlarge upon the subject. But somewhat to her confusion her grandfather chuckled an affirmative.

"Landed it at about four o'clock this afternoon!" he said.

"I thought Foster—" Victoria hesitated. "I thought Foster—" she began again, and stopped. "H'm!" she said, discontentedly.

"Bob is a good man—a very good man," his father said. "Fanny," he asked, "been to see Mrs. Bob in the new quarters?"

Fanny looked with her expression of ready self-justification at her father.

"You would have me walk in upon the poor woman before her beds were up!" she laughed. "I'm afraid I wouldn't be very welcome if I did! But I am going to-morrow, and I thought I'd take Victoria with me!"

"Music lesson at eleven," Victoria reminded her.

"Oh, is that so, my dear, and I suppose your poor stupid aunt had forgotten all about that!" Fanny, who did not like even so faint a suggestion of advice, said teasingly. "Well, if your royal highness can manage to get up for an eight o'clock breakfast, perhaps we can manage both!" she ended lightly.

"Possibly I can!" Victoria said, in the same vein, sitting on the arm of Fanny's chair, and resting her head against her aunt's well-arranged, graying hair. They both turned as Carra came in, and rose to go up to bed themselves, as she gently but firmly assisted the stiff old man to his feet. Victoria glanced into his room as they passed it; the bed was neatly turned down, the pillows waiting. There was a coke fire up here, too, medicine bottles stood in a row on the table. The girl felt herself almost sick with sleepiness and boredom, but when she and Fanny were undressed, she sat on the edge of her bed, while Fanny stood leaning against the door jamb, and they talked for a long time. Victoria, in a mood of confidence and expansion, told the older woman of her hopes of travel, or being a nurse, even of marriage.

"It's just that I—I feel I want to live!" Victoria said.

"Well, when I was your age I wouldn't have had any trouble about *that!*" Miss Fanny said, of marriage. But of other prospects she warned her niece as Victoria's mother had so often warned her. "Don't be strong-minded, dear. Men don't like women who are self-assertive and independent, Vicky; truly they don't. A man always likes to feel the superior!"

If the evening had been dull, yet it was very pleasant, in the spring-like February morning, to loiter along Polk Street marketing with Aunt Fanny. Vicky liked the clean little grocery, the tea shop where they chose a Japanese teacup for their long saved twenty certificates, and the butcher who chopped meat so expertly on a block that was the slice of a great tree, worn spongy at the top from long use. All butchers gave away soup vegetables with the soup meat at five cents a pound, and Fanny picked out her carrots and celery as sternly as if she were paying full price for them. The air was soft and sweet; last traces of fog were rising into the blue, and if there was still a trace of winter chill in the shade, in the sun they found a delicious warmth. The hilly city of homes looked cheerful and charming; there were flowers already in the gardens, and the people who came and went on cars and crossings waved their furled umbrellas gaily at each other, as they picked their way on the drying pavements.

Mrs. Robert Crabtree had selected a five-room flat for her first experience in western housekeeping, and Victoria was enchanted with the novelty of living on one compact floor. They laughed as they climbed the long flight of enclosed stairs that led up to the flat, and both the visitors exclaimed with pleasure at the wonderful view that lay beneath the windows. The street was so hilly here that they seemed far higher than they were, and could look down on near roofs and far shipping, all steaming in the heartening sunshine. Victoria identified the Palace Hotel and the "shot tower," and said that she saw the "ten-ten" boat for Saucelito, bravely setting forth from its slip, with a ribbon of foam following it.

Ella had furnished the place charmingly, with some new and many old things, and Victoria saw here for the first time a "treasure" picked up from the old second-hand shops in Mission Street.

"But second-hand, Aunt Ella!" she ejaculated.

"Oh, my dear, you can often get delightful things second-hand! This tray—now. I don't know who ever brought it round the Horn, but I was so delighted to find it!" Ella was sure of her ground here, for her sister's sister-in-law had recently impressed her with Pembroke chairs and Old Blue cups, just as she was now impressing Victoria. She blinked, and settled her glasses, and while Fanny experienced a sort of combined discomfort and contempt at this new domestic fad, Victoria secretly determined to enlist Esme for some second-hand prowlings of their own.

But besides these acquisitions, Ella had very nice upholstered mahogany chairs, and quite an imposing amount of silver spoons, two or three old paintings, and a framed Family Tree, done in delicate ink outline, with all the names written in clearly and finely. And from this document it would seem that Ella came of splendid stock indeed. Victoria pored over it, fascinated.

"Aunt Ella, were your ancestors really on the *Mayflower?*"

"That one was!" Ella said, briskly incisive, looking interestedly at the chart. "And my mother's uncle, the head of our family in America, was too. And you see here, where Jabez Cutter married Thomasine Herriet—her grandfather was a Baldwin, who was the ward of Captain John Smith."

It was fascinating to the ardent, eager girl. She decided she would work out a family chart of her own. Mama was always so sure of the family's distinction.

"If you write to—there is a society, and I'll remember the name of it presently!—they'll tell you at once just what branch you belong to, and what the collateral lines are," Ella said, looking from the family tree to Victoria and settling her glasses.

"Victoria has great ambitions, you must know," said Fanny, not very kindly, for she felt a trifle out of all this. "What were you telling me last night Vicky—that you want to *live*, wasn't that it?"

Victoria coloured, but more in embarrassment than resentment. Whenever she said anything in confidence to any one, even to her mother, it was usually betrayed, and she had come to feel herself rather stupidly outspoken. However, Aunt Ella, as was half the time the case, merely looked rather vaguely from one to the other, and then resumed her usual calm air of reserve. And just then Aunt Lucy came in.

Aunt Lucy, broad and square and cheerful looking, was breathless from the stairs, and she looked, as usual, somewhat shabby as to attire, but her frog-like eyes smiled even before she got her breath. She had great confidence in her own taste in dress, and turned and sponged and altered her garments interminably, piecing them with bits of oriental embroidery, vari-coloured silks or laces, in a manner considered by her family slightly bizarre. But she always looked comfortable, and enjoyed so much her own manipulation of odd bits of fur and brocade that nothing could be further from the onlookers' minds than either pity or doubt.

She in turn exclaimed at the view and approved of the flat. Ella was not going to have a maidservant at present, which her sisters-in-law approved, not until Rob's plans were more settled; still she managed to impress them with a certain sureness and poise, a certain almost wordless and perfectly pleasant superiority. Victoria had never seen finger-bowls or carver-rests before, and was delighted with them both; a silver teaball quite enchanted her.

"That was a Christmas present from my sister Lizzie's children, last year," Ella said. And she showed them a picture of Lizzie Stewart's three children, Grace, Kate, and Tom, wrapped and capped warmly, on a dim background of snowy street.

Immediately afterward Vick and Fanny went off for Victoria's music-lesson, and Ella and Lucy went into Ella's spotless kitchen, where they began preparations for a pot of tea, sliced bread and butter, and currant jelly, the usual luncheon for ladies alone in those days. The two had become quite friendly, although Ella felt more at ease with Fanny still. But to-day she wanted to speak to a married woman.

So delicate were the paths by which she led to her subject
that Lucy found herself staring at her keenly for some moments,
wondering if she could believe her own inferences. She asked
some questions, to which Ella answered briefly, and with a
blush. They had been married nearly six years and she was
almost thirty-nine. Yes. No. Yes, that was it. She hadn't
—dear me, no!—written her sister, yet, she hadn't even hinted
it to Rob. It seemed to frighten her even to discuss it openly,
having started the subject she gave every evidence of wishing
immediately to change it. Lucy, amazed, experienced, ad-
visory, counted on the lightly drumming fingers of one hand
on the table, and said mid-August.

CHAPTER VIII

KITTY BARBEE was twenty years old, bold, pretty, ambitious, and quick-tempered. She showed the quick temper whenever she felt inclined, and often went into long harangues, with tremendous gusto. The Barbees were described by all refined persons as "common," but there was nothing vicious about them. They worked hard, paid their bills, went to church, and were loyal to one another against the world. They also fought, ate, drank, and lived hard, their voices were high, the girls had rosy but coarse complexions, the boys were "tough." There was always a young Barbee boy in the neighbourhood gang, always a young Barbee girl laughing noisily at night under the street lamp on the corner with a beau, and on almost every summer Sunday there was a rumour that one of the Barbee boys had been drowned in their crazy old boat on the bay.

Sam Barbee, the father, was a San Francisco plumber, with a small home among the already decaying residences south of Market Street, and a large country house—really a sort of cabin—in San Rafael, for summer use. Here his wife, an enormously fat woman, cooked, scolded, swore, perspired, and shouted all summer long, screaming almost as loudly with felicity when an unexpected contingent of guests arrived from the city as she did with grief when the dark rumour of her son's drowning took form. She was a woman to slap an arriving guest heartily between the shoulders, to cry with emotion when the red wine had gone round, to call upon the Deity to witness that she was a good friend—that she never had cheated a soul in her life—that she couldn't love this one or that one more if he had been her son!

Kitty was the only girl now at home; Tenny had married a young feller with an elegant butcher business in Santa Rosa, Joe Boyle, to quote his mother-in-law exactly, and Ruby was dead. Ruby's mother never mentioned her without a burst of tears, and a great crayon enlargement of a photograph of Ruby, with a sheaf of wheat from Ruby's funeral floral piece, stood in the city parlour. But Tenny was a great joy, enriching the Fourth of July celebration less than a year ago by opportunely giving birth to her first child, in the very centre of a large mixed luncheon party in the country house. What with the company, the heat, the laughter, and excitement, the young mother had gotten through her ordeal splendidly, and had slept all through the broiling afternoon with her pretty head only a few actual feet away from the revellers, although there was a wall between. The Barbee house was really only a few boxes set together, pieced with burlap awnings, tents, and platforms, and set in a waste of crushed dry grass and odorous tar-weed. Most of the living was done in the open air.

Kitty was far more socially ambitious than the satisfactory Tenny, and when Kitty met the attractive Neil Powers she quite consciously set her cap for him. She did not invite him to the mixed entertainments of her mother's home, but met him for strolls, and by appointment for the hour's trip to the city. Neil was "in society" and bowed "to swells," and that was enough for Kitty. Neil was also handsome Bertie Brewer's chum, and that was an asset. Sometimes Kitty sat on the boat between Neil and Bertie, in the delicious consciousness that also travelling on that same boat, unattended by even one squire, was one or more of the Brewer girls.

But she was not satisfied with that; she wanted to marry well; she was astonished and delighted that she could hold her own with these educated and travelled boys, and she had no fears for the future. Neil had been her first choice, and when Neil told her that Bertie was in love with his pretty cousin, Nelly Crabtree, Kitty had no thought of using him other than as a satisfactory supernumerary. She questioned him about his cousin, and Bertie thought she was in the argot of the day, a daisy.

One suddenly warm March day Mrs. Brewer, unexpectedly returning home on an early afternoon train, was surprised in the car to recognize the head of her only son. Bertie was several seats ahead of her, and her first sensation was a puzzled fear at seeing him free from the toils of Crabtree and Company at three o'clock in the afternoon. But secondarily she noticed, and with a pang, that the pretty, frizzled head of Kitty Barbee was beside his, and that they were laughing, elbowing each other, pushing and talking in a manner decidedly rowdyish. Evidently Kitty had some small object in her hand that Bertie desired——

It was toward the end of the trip that this truly dreadful sight burst upon Mrs. Brewer's eyes. For a few minutes she felt almost sick. No course of action occurring to her, she sat still, wondering, as good mothers have wondered since time began, whether it would be wiser to ignore this episode entirely, or to say a few words of guidance and warning to Bertie.

Distracted, she mused, within hearing of the gay "Bertie, you behave!" and "No, sir, you don't!" of the unconscious pair; and while she mused, Miss Barbee, glancing from the window, chanced to see a tipsy-looking buckboard, manned by two of her three brothers, awaiting her at a station two miles south of the home station. With appreciative shrieks, she and Bertie streamed out, and decent neighbours heaved sighs of relief. May sat with flushed cheeks and downcast eyes for the rest of the trip.

To her increasing uneasiness, Bertie did not come home until after the regular dinner-hour; he said that he had had to go to Oakland, after lunch, for Papa. The man was out, darn it, further embroidered Bertie, innocently eating his boiled lamb.

When the table was cleared, and the girls and Stephen playing cribbage, May came beside her son, who was still sitting in his place, finishing his tea, and laid a soft, fat hand upon his.

"Bertie dear, may Mama speak to you honestly?"

He looked uneasy; she had a way of making him extremely uncomfortable.

"You are my only boy," May said gently, "and I think you never remember Mama as unkind or severe with you. I am not scolding you, dear. But I want you to give up your friendship with Kitty Barbee."

Bertie turned red; his blue eyes glinted dangerously.

"Is that too much for Mama to ask?" May asked, trembling.

"What's the matter with her?" Bertie muttered.

"What's the matter with her?" May began smoothly. "Why, the matter is that she is not a lady, dear. She doesn't belong to our class, Bertie. Your grandfather is one of the prominent men of San Francisco—Papa's people were prominent in the east. Kitty is very pretty—but is she the type I want for my daughter-in-law—the girls' sister—the mother of your children?"

"She's just as good as anybody else!" Bertie persisted after a pause.

"No, dear, she's not," May said firmly, but a little frightened, turning away. There was a silence. She dared not say more. And as she went toward the hall, and the library where Stephen and the girls were, she hoped that he would call her back. Bertie made no sound.

Everything was worrisome; life was too burdensome, May thought. Bertie infatuated with this little commoner; Ella going to have a baby. As if the Robert's hadn't done enough to make themselves popular with Pa, now they were going to have a child—it would be a son, of course. And Ella had already said, with her Bostonian firmness, that Robert must name his child for his father, Reuben Elliott Crabtree. Pa had been cacklingly delighted with the mere prospect! Of course he would leave Ma's silver to this namesake, and dear knew what else! The audacity of Ella!

And then a clerk in the office, Linton, with whom Bob had trusted an important bit of business, just as Stephen had expressed himself of the conviction that Linton would never be seen again, had absconded—had proved to be extremely capable and entirely honourable. That was another feather in Bob's cap.

Stephen's attitude to Bob, at first contemptuous, then hostile, had changed. He professed himself now as merely bored by all this talk of Robert—Robert—Robert! All this nonsense about phenomenal changes, sales, absconders, was profoundly dull. Robert was a good man, nothing sensational—just a good salary man.

"He hasn't had much experience in our particular line of business," Stephen would say, "but he is interested. I don't see him much—he's in Woolcock's department. If any one else but your father was at the head, Bob wouldn't last a week! And if—anything—happens, I don't know that I can conscientiously keep him. I would discuss that with the directors. Your father has asked him to step in to some of the meetings. Personally, I think he makes a mistake. But this can't last forever!"

May turned from these troublesome matters, to contemplate with satisfaction the affair between Tina and young Mr. Yelland. The clergyman was constantly at the house, with his pleasant little throaty laugh, and his academic interest in books and theories; he played tennis and croquet with Tina, and dined occasionally with the Brewers, and had long ago proved to them, as he himself expressed it, "that some of us preacher fellows are men as well as ministers!"

Tina was naturally very happy; she fluttered through her days in a pleasant glow of laughter and planning and being teased and considered. She had taken a stern position in the affair of Vicky's ridiculous lover, the calf-like nephew of the Señoritas Tasheira—Ruy da Sã. As a clergyman's bride—or almost that—Tina could countenance no such prospect of an unworthy alliance.

The clumsy, half-civilized nephew of the Señoritas Tasheira had paid assiduous court to Victoria, after his own fashion, all through the winter. Victoria, outwardly amused and annoyed with the rest of the family, secretly found something almost touching in his awkward attentions. He did not call, he was far too shy; but he hung about the Brewer homestead frequently, at night, and he was to be seen, in the late afternoons, walking briskly by the gate. He had bought himself two new suits, one a brilliant blue, the other a check in bright yellow and brown, both cut, Bertie Brewer suggested, by a butcher. Offerings of eggs, calla lilies, cream, and ducks appeared regularly, once a brace of stiff and dirty rabbits was left at the door, once a humming-bird's beautiful nest, and once a rough purse made from the fitted skins of two chipmunks.

Victoria laughed at him, but she really did not like to have other persons find him only funny. She experienced an odd thrill, half shame, half pride, wholly reluctant, when she caught a glimpse of the red, grinning face and the shambling figure. From October to April they exchanged only an occasional self-conscious bow, but one heavenly April Sunday, the Brewers, who were walking with Davy and Nelly, encountered him, in a little sheltered bit of wood, handling a lamb that had been prematurely born. Victoria, confused, bent over the limp body with him, manipulated the blind, meek little head. Ruy, with a great calf laugh, asked her if she had had the bird's nest, and if she didn't think "those leetl' bird was miracle!" and presently, followed by the anxious ewe, went striding, in his odorous muddy boots and with many a backward, sheepish grin of his own, across the hill.

The things he had said about the lamb, and about everything, afforded the young people exquisite mirth as they walked on. But Victoria, who was tramping beside her father to-day, scarcely heard them. She was thinking of the lamb, and of how interesting it would be to establish the little weakling in the old adobe *casa*. And from this dream she went on to another, in which she married Ruy—who was magically refined into Victoria's favourite sort of harsh and manly yet utterly generous and lovable hero—and in which she was the darling of the Señoritas and of the whole ranch, and went about, young, adored, busy, and beautiful——

"That boy," her father said presently, of Ruy, "has had an odd history. His mother was the oldest daughter of the Tasheiras—and she ran away with the head sheepman they had, who was an Indian, or half an Indian—I forget. Now, whether —look where you're stepping, Vicky!—whether she killed him, and then herself, or he killed her, and then himself, I can't remember. No, no, of course not! He killed himself, and she tried to kill herself—that was it. But she lingered a few weeks."

"But why *should* she kill herself?"

"Well, it was some religious question. Da Sã who was half Portuguese, I believe, never had been baptized, and Señorita Aña couldn't be married in church to him for that reason. They were married by a sea-captain, on the way to Honolulu, a sailing vessel, of course. There was a wreck, and they say that Da Sã, who was a giant, swam a mile with his wife in his arms. Anyway, a year later she told him she would have to leave him—she didn't want to continue living with a man to whom, in the eyes of God, she wasn't married, and—that was it!—he killed himself, and she slashed her own throat. Much later, two or three years later, her servant turned up here with this boy, asserting that it was the Señora's. I don't believe the old aunts know quite how to regard him. For awhile he lived with the servants entirely; now I understand that he's called nephew and calls them aunt, and is destined to marry that pretty little Argentinian cousin you girls met."

"Really, Papa!" Victoria said, feeling suddenly rather flat. "I don't—I don't—believe he loves her!"

"Why not?" her father said sharply. "He'd better," he added indifferently. "I understand that her uncle is one of the richest cattlemen in the Argentine. I don't know that anything's settled;—I believe the family wishes it."

Victoria walked on, over the fresh deep grass, under a mottled sky of dazzling white on dazzling blue. It was full springtime now, and the air was honey-sweet between the rains. The girl noted that the days were getting longer, her shadow lay ahead of her across the field.

"Well, he's always leaving flowers and things for me!" her hurt pride made her say aloud, almost resentfully.

"Who is?" her father asked quickly.

"Well, Ruy is—at least, we *suppose* he is!"

"You suppose a great deal of nonsense, Vicky!" her father said, good-naturedly. He gave the matter no further thought, but Victoria remembered the conversation later, and felt a certain resentment that this shadowy lover should be calmly snatched from her by the youthful Argentinian, still in her convent.

The next time she saw Ruy lingering about near the house, she managed to speak to him, and although they both were embarrassed and awkward for a few minutes, Victoria brought the conversation about to his horse, and horses in general, and so put him at his ease. She did not for one second lose sight of the loutish manner, the red face, the checked suit, while she was with him. But afterward she remembered with a sense of triumph that he was certainly desperately in love.

One July night, when she was staying in the city with Nelly, she told Nelly all about it. Nelly, in return, confided to Victoria that she was—well, in a sort of way—engaged to Davy, but Mummy disapproved, and nobody else knew about it, and—and—well, Davy was sort of funny about it, too——

And she began to cry. Victoria comforted her as best she could, feeling herself akin to Nelly in that Ruy, however ridiculous, was a genuine lover.

"It makes me so sick!" said Nelly, vigorously washing dishes with a rag and eyeing each one keenly before she placed it in the heap that Victoria was drying. "Davy slaves and slaves at that rotten old hardware story for sixty dollars a month—and teaching night-school, too, and taking care of Doctor Hughes' horse—I don't know!" Nelly said, in her little angry, helpless manner, "I don't know why I have to be the one to fall in love with a man who hasn't a penny—and that horrible aunt—I suppose it's a good joke on *me!*"

"Ah, Nelly—don't!" Victoria said, sympathetically. The two girls were alone in the kitchen; Alice and Georgie in San Rafael; Lucy and Harry at a church concert. The little kitchen was hot and odorous on an unusually sultry July night, and the girls were lingering over the dishpan more to prolong the hour of confidences than because they were detained there, when Davy came in at eight o'clock.

Davy, announcing that it was an exquisite night, invited them to walk into Mission Street with him, and they sauntered together through that fascinating thoroughfare. The bakery was open, the baker's wife and children perspiring as they snatched the hot loaves of milk-bread and the sheets of buns, and snapped the pink string, and the baker himself panting, coatless, vestless, and in a dirty apron, at the side door. The grocery was open, too, and the coffee machine grinding in the lamp-light, groups of people were sauntering back and forth in the street. The girls lingered at the windows of the stationer, and at the candy store, where little plaster pigs were scattered among the filled boxes of "French candy." A great coil of pale taffy with a little hatchet lying upon it elicited an exclamation from Nelly.

"Um—m! *doesn't* that look good!"

Victoria could not resist a side glance at David. He assumed an unbecoming jocularity.

"What'll you have, ladies? Two bits a pound—have a couple of tons?"

Nelly, who had been looking at him hopefully, shrugged her shoulders with a sudden expression of disappointment and hurt. David showed them a few coins on his big palm.

"Laundry and carfare!" he said whimsically. But the girls were unappreciative of his humour.

"Well, I'm going to have some, anyway!" Victoria said decidedly, and she went in and bought ten cents worth, which they munched as they strolled. Nelly's face was rosy, her voice a little strained. David was silent.

But presently they met Rudy Sessions, who seemed to have nothing to do, and he delightfully suggested ice-cream. They were a balanced party now, always a secret delight to Victoria, who hated a preponderance of girls, and she was in wild spirits as they gathered about a little iron table, and ordered four "bisques." Bisque meant nothing to any one of them, but it was the new and correct thing to order, and Postag made a specialty of it.

Small, eye-glassed, pleasantly self-confident in manner, Rudy led the conversation. He had a position in the Mission now, and unless he left in a few weeks to visit a farmer uncle in Contra Costa County, he would certainly look Miss Nelly up, and hope that they would all get together again for lots of these little parties. Victoria and Nelly talked about him half the night. It was almost two o'clock when, agreeing that they would not marry him if he was the last man in the world, they went to sleep.

It was at about this time that Esme Brewer began to find herself treated to the consideration that is given a girl who is engaged, or almost engaged. Afterward she used to feast upon the memory of Roscoe Beale's attentions—such definite, such unmistakable attentions!—and feel herself rich in just their shadowy memory.

Everyone supposed the existence of that satisfactory condition known as "an understanding," and Mrs. Brewer may be said to have been on tiptoe, posed like a hair-trigger, ready to spread the tidings the instant there was the first positive word on the subject. Nobody knew much about the Beales, but they lived at the Palace Hotel, which was in itself a patent of respectability, and Roscoe was handsome, outspoken, young, and doing well in a broker's office. Mrs. Brewer was not critical and allowed no one else to be; poor Esme was far from critical, she merely wanted a husband.

One day later in August Esme and her mother went to the city together, and chanced, in the happiest fashion imaginable, to meet Roscoe at the ferry. He said that he had nothing to do and had been planning a call upon Miss Brewer in San Rafael; Esme glowed at this statement with a radiance that made her rather lifeless face positively pretty, and there were a few minutes of laughter and teasing before it was decided that she had better not turn back with him because it was almost lunchtime now.

"I'll tell you what I wish you'd do, Mrs. Brewer," said Roscoe, "can't you and Miss Brewer have luncheon with me at the

Spa, and then we'll go round the bay on the *McDowell*—it's a great trip, and I've never taken it."

"Oh, you have to have a pass for that!" Esme exclaimed, The little tug visited all the government posts about the bay. Alcatraz, Fort Baker, the quarantine station, and Goat Island, and the trip was considered a delightfully privileged one by all mere civilians.

"But I have a pass!" smiled the resourceful Roscoe.

Suddenly Esme wanted to go on the *McDowell* more than she had ever wanted to go anywhere in her life. She almost danced up and down childishly as she importuned her mother.

"Oh, Mama—couldn't we? I've never been on the tug! Vick went once with Bertie—but I never have! Please— please——"

Mrs. Brewer hesitated. She wanted to further Esme's affair. And the man's eager, smiling face, and his youthful masculinity quite thrilled her. She had planned to see Mrs. Robert Crabtree—she could have let that go, to be sure. Any other day would do as well. But then she was going to get Vicky, after her music lesson; it was the last lesson, and there was seventeen dollars to pay for half a month. Mrs. Brewer had asked her husband for this money, as was her custom with all the money she handled, immediately after breakfast this morning, but he had not had it and had comfortably directed her to come into the office for it.

She could not disappoint the old Signor and perhaps embarrass and humiliate Vicky. May Brewer wished, with a shadow of irritation, that Stephen had given it to his daughter direct; but then he did not like his girls to handle money, and she supposed, with a wifely sigh, that he was wise. So Esme must make up her mind to give up the treat with Roscoe. That the twenty-five-year-old Esme might spend these few hours unchaperoned was not to be considered.

Tears came into Esme's eyes—it was too hard. She was gulping them down, and trying to smile, when suddenly an embracing arm went about her waist, and here, laughing and dimpling and quite distractingly pretty in her young wifely finery, was Lily Duvalette.

She was instantly cognizant of the situation and instantly enlisted in Esme's cause. She'd lunch with them, of course, and go round the bay with them, she'd love nothing better, and she was an old married woman, the best chaperone in the world.

Lily was younger than Esme and looked about sixteen, but Esme was only appreciative of the miraculously saved day. The three went off together, Lily and Roscoe discussing the Palace Hotel, and various friends there, Esme promising her mother that she would not miss the quarter past five boat. Mrs. Brewer could comfortably beam, in her long talk with her sister-in-law, that it was all but settled now.

Robert's wife listened only anxiously and absently. Her ordeal was very near, and she was nervously interested in the question of chloroform. May laughed at her; she herself had never had even a whiff, with all her babies. Ella said mildly that Rob laughed at her, too, and reminded her that every baby in the world had been born—somewhere—of some woman. But she had been with her sister Lizzie when Grace was born—and she didn't see why she shouldn't have chloroform —of course a confinement was a perfectly natural thing—but after all, she was thirty-nine——

May was uninterested, in turn. Her thoughts wandered with great satisfaction to Esme.

". . .   but the doctor says he never will give it unless the husband agrees," Ella was saying, painfully, "and Bob says that he doesn't want to take the risk. I wish——"

May presently had to hurry for the boat, on which she was joined by Stephen and her older daughters. All four sat on the upper deck, to catch the breeze, the girls murmuring together. Esme seemed disappointingly quiet about her great day; she said that Roscoe had been "nice," and Lily "awfully nice," but that the boat had made her, Esme, feel a little sick— or her head ached or something. Questioned archly by her mother as to when she would see Roscoe again she responded rather subduedly and wearily that she did not know.

Victoria had the true story of the day, in undertones.

"Of course she was awfully nice, but she spoiled it all!"

"Did Roscoe hate her?"

"Well, yes, at first he did.   But then afterward——"

They exchanged a sympathetic glance. Then Victoria said: "She thinks men like that way she talks!"

"She just—piled it on," Esme said, very low.   "How she was

only nineteen when she married Elmer, and that they had horses—and—oh, I don't know, a lot of stuff! And then when I said my head ached, she kept saying 'But you're so quiet, Esme!' and the wind made the tears come into my eyes—and she was horrid—well, I know I never want to see her again! And then I sort of suggested that Roscoe come over for dinner to-night—but he said he couldn't. Well, maybe he couldn't—I don't know. But what's the difference, anyhow?" Esme finished, with desperate hardihood.

"Never mind, Es'," Victoria said, in an undertone rich with understanding and sympathy; "she's a flirt, Lily—but she's married, after all, and men don't like that sort of thing, except for a few minutes. He'll turn up on Sunday, you'll see. And anyway, you did have the lunch at the Spa, and the trip, you know!"

"Yes, I know!" Esme was comforted. To have fresh adventures with young men, to remember and discuss, was like adding to her bank account.

They fell to talking, in even lower tones, about Aunt Ella's expected baby. The boat careened gently in the tide from the Golden Gate, the blue water and the yellow hills tipped and shifted up and down; Saucelito's red roofs, rising above the curly tops of oaks and peppers, were before them. Stephen Brewer rose, and stuffed into his pockets the newspapers he and his wife had been reading.

"Well—finished your talk, girls?" he said, smiling sleepily. The girls followed him down the rubber-covered stairs, to the lower deck. When they were in the train Esme said cautiously, to Victoria.

"Did you see Bertie?"

"No. Was he on the boat?"

"With that Barbee girl!"

It was two nights later that Stephen Brewer brought home the expected news—and more than the expected news. The Robert Crabtrees had a son—Ella had been very ill, but she was all right now. They were going to name him Reuben, for his father's father. So much he told May in their bedroom, before dinner, when the girls were not within hearing.

"H'm!" May said with a pang. Ella's infant seemed somehow to displace Bertie. She looked at her husband expectantly. "Don't you think that's just a little affected, Stephen? She never saw Pa until a year ago."

Her husband was silent, but May knew him to be sympathetic.

"Much good may it do him—Papa's name!" she said lightly.

"It's done him this much good," Stephen said, bitterly, "your father is giving him this house!"

"This——" May's whole interior economy seemed to give a sick twist and plunge; she felt the shock in her very vitals. "This house?" she faltered.

"He said so. He was laughing about it, with Bob, and he said that he wondered how his namesake would like a country place."

There was a silence. They May said pleadingly.

"Stephen Brewer, are you going to sit by and stand *that?*"

"Be reasonable, dear, or I shall think I make a mistake in confiding in you. I was not consulted, you know."

"No, I know," May strangled; tears stood in her faded eyes. "Robert Crabtree is nothing but a *thief!*" she said passionately. "He was always like that—always getting more than his share, and Pa and Ma letting him do it! Steve, I *can't* leave this place," faltered May, "my home, my girls' home, for all these years. Why, I love every inch of it—every rose tree, my attic —where the old crib is, and the baby clothes—the laundry tubs that you put in, and paid for——"

"Why, May—May—May!" Stephen protested. "Now, now! He may not do it, my dear. In fact, he won't. You know your father."

May gulped, blew her nose, wiped her face on a towel, and spoke in a suddenly lifeless and moderate tone.

"No, of course he won't," she said, sensibly. She combed and brushed her thinning gray hair, put on her cashmere and plush dress, with a careful arrangement of pleats and bustle. "We will simply tell the girls that Ella has a little boy," she said. "But I do hope, Steve, I do hope," she finished, with a long breath of recovery, "that *this* time you will take a stand with your father. I'll ask Fanny if he has said anything about it. I'd much rather move to the city, outright, than go on paying a gardener and taxes and goodness knows what here, if that's the case!"

"I don't know what you mean by taking a stand, May,"

Stephen said, a little nettled. "Perhaps you'd like to come run my business for awhile; is that the idea?"

May closed the hall door that she had opened on her way downstairs. She saw that she had gone too far, and she experienced a sensation of panic. She could only listen silently while he continued.

"You girls—you and Fanny—can talk easily enough about my getting out of the firm, and showing your father this, and scaring him into that! My God——"

"Stephen!"

"Well——" his tone softened somewhat. "But what you never seem to realize, May," he said, "is that I *am* the firm— or part of it. Your brother Robert is *my employee*. You don't seem to see that your father could no more pass over the firm to somebody else, when he died, than I could—if I died to-morrow! No. About the house, of course, it's different! Your father said, when Tina was a baby, that he wanted you and your children to have a home——"

"I know!" May murmured submissively.

"And I have always felt that he would have given this place to you outright," Stephen said, easily bringing in an old grievance, "if your sister Fanny hadn't brought up the question, that Sunday, of saving a slice of it for her. Why Fanny thought she wanted—just at that moment—to specify that she might want to build a country house some day—confusing and upsetting your father and raising a perfectly new issue—however, that's over now!"

"I never shall forgive Fanny that," May interpolated firmly.

"As a result, she has probably done you both out of the house!" Stephen concluded gloomily. "However, we needn't go into that. I can always find a home for my family, and I have the satisfaction of knowing that I am virtually the backbone of the firm, whatever your father may or may not do! However, you might see Fanny in a day or two, May—I suppose you'll have to see the baby——"

May agreed thoughtfully. It was all very perplexing and annoying to a sweet good capable woman, the mother of four lovely girls, who only asked to be always in the position of the dispenser, the entertainer, the adviser, the stable and serene element in a mutable world.

She went down to the four girls, waiting for dinner, and se-

cretly electrified by the one sentence Victoria had overheard
from her in the upper hall, ten minutes before, and had lost no
time in repeating.   They might be going to move into the city
—Mama just said so!

After this thrilling thought, the announcement of Ella's baby's
arrival fell rather flat.   Lou was heard to murmur scornfully.

"What did you say, Lou?"

"Nothing, Mama."

"Don't say 'nothing' to your mother!"   Stephen said sharply.
"What did you say?"

"I said—that we knew it was coming, anyway," Lou stammered, frightened.   Stephen glanced with a sort of triumphant
accusation at his wife.   The girls were getting beyond him.

"Lou," her mother said, trembling, "I never want to hear
you speak on such a subject again; do you hear me?"

"Yes, Mama."

"And I am surprised at your sisters!" May said, taking her
napkin out of the old silver ring with the fat little birds upon
it.   Dinner commenced in a stricken silence.

Fanny, who came to San Rafael a day or two later to discuss
the latest addition to the family, was not reassuring.

It was a hot Saturday morning.   Tina was helping to decorate
the church for Sunday, but the other three girls were at home,
Esme and Lou sweeping tumbling masses of dried loose rose-
leaves from the porch, Victoria soaking the window boxes with
a long hose.   All three welcomed her gaily.

"But it's Mama I came to see!" Fanny, panting with the
heat, and with her bonnet-strings loosened, told them frankly.
Esme, blinking in the dim hallway, after the streaming sunshine
of the garden, piloted her indoors.   The whole house smelled
wholesomely of baking bread.   Mrs. Brewer was in the enormous pantry, busy with glasses of currant jelly, circles of white
paper, and a saucer of alcohol.

"Run back to your sweeping, Esme," her mother said pleasantly, after greeting the newcomer.   Esme, bursting with
curiosity, retired reluctantly.   The two elderly women murmured for an hour, and were noncommittal at luncheon.   Fanny
could only report that Pa was foolishly "tickled" about Bob's
son, and had at least threatened to leave the baby the family
homestead.

"After all, you've had it rent free a long time, May!" she said. "And what's new with my girls?" she added brightly, as luncheon was announced. Addie, who had been helping with the Saturday cleaning and baking, looked as if her face would burst with blood, as she moved about the table. Lottie was audibly furious, in the kitchen—company and clean napkins for Saturday lunch! She banged saucepans about noisily, and Mrs. Brewer, whose heart was heavy, frowned faintly as she heard them. Later when Fanny went into the kitchen with an armful of flowers and dropped rose leaves and odd bits of roots and stems on the floor, and spattered the clean sink with water, May was quite definitely afraid that Lottie would leave her on the spot. But if she did, the harassed householder decided exhaustedly, she would simply have to *go*. They must get another cook and laundress as good, that was all, if they had to pay thirty dollars a month for her!

Fanny did not fail to touch lightly upon the subject of Roscoe Beale, with the flushed and smiling Esme, and to rally Tina gaily, when she came in hot and headachy from church.

"Girls—girls—won't we have to behave ourselves beautifully, with a Reverend keeping his eye upon us! I shan't know how to act, for one! Does one kiss the creature?"

"Oh, at weddings and Christmas," Vick said, and the girls all laughed. Tina said, in great spirits, that she didn't propose to have everyone kissing *her* husband, if she ever had one. Victoria, everlastingly analyzing and segregating facts, reflected that Esme and Tina were both in a fair way to be married, now, Louisianna only nineteen, and she herself had dim plans for David, to say nothing of the preposterous attentions of the calf-like Ruy.

Mrs. Robert Crabtree did not recover from her confinement as rapidly as had been expected, and when her baby was four weeks old, had not yet left her bed. She told Robert, at about this time, that she did not want her sister, Mrs. Stewart of Boston, to have the Copley and the spoons, those were for the baby's wife, when he had one. "He's the oldest grandson of the oldest son in your family, after all," Ella said languidly, her cool hand in Rob's big warm one. "Don't let May Brewer—promise me, Rob—don't let her get everything—silver and chairs and all that. He—he has a right to his share, Rob. And you write my sister and tell her that I told you—my grandfather's cuff-links were always to be mine, and the smaller berry-bowl and the sugar-shell spoon. If she knows that you *know*——"

The voice trailed off weakly; she dozed.

She told Lucy, when Lucy came to sit beside her, that it had all been a good deal worse than she had anticipated, and when Lucy wholesomely assured her that it always was, but that there was no use in scaring people, and it was over now, anyway, she began weakly to cry. Lucy had to bend over to hear her whisper that she was afraid that there might some day be another baby, and she could not stand it.

A few days later she quietly died, seeming to care nothing for Robert's agitation, and very little for the baby's predicament. Lucy was closer to her than the other women, and Lucy boldly offered to take care of the tiny Reuben. But her claim was rapidly eclipsed by that of May, who suggested that the beautiful quiet country was the place for the child. Fanny, indifferent through these preliminaries, now stepped in and carried off not only the infant but his father, to the house in California Street, thus scoring a great strategic advantage. She now had father and brother and nephew, and from this day May was haunted by a sickening vision of Robert gaining influence with Papa and in the business, and of Papa really fulfilling his threat of leaving the San Rafael home to that ridiculous, heavy-headed baby, who, with Fanny to back him, would evict them all from their beloved establishment some day.

CHAPTER IX

"VICTORIA!"

"Yes, Papa!" Victoria holding floury hands free from his coat, stepped to his side and kissed him, as he came into the kitchen. "This is no place for you!" she said, affectionately. She and Tina were busy with dinner preparations, while their mother was, as usual, in the city, interviewing a dozen possible successors to Lottie. Lottie had been recently most impudent and ungrateful, and had supplied them all with tremendous feeling of virtue and magnanimity. As for poor Addie, the Brewer girls never would forget the unmentionable horrors of the final scene with Addie, a crying, frightened Addie, with a pulpy red face, and Mama magnificently rebuking, and themselves sent upstairs to talk about something else while Papa and Bertie packed her things, and harnessed the mare, and drove her beyond sight and sound of respectability forever.

Now for a few exciting days, the five females of the family had been scrambling through the housework somehow, employing makeshifts of all sorts, and yet always exhausted and late with everything. Butter went to the table in the round, two-pound roll, in these days, and crumbs remained on the dining-room floor, dead flowers grew slimy in their vases, and yet there was never an instant of idleness. Their girls' hands were scarred with soot and odorous of onions, their gowns were streaked with grease and wood-ashes, their feet ached and the backs were strained, yet that inexorable round of sheets and pails and brooms and dishes went on and on and on——

"Um—something smells good!" Stephen said, distracted in his mission. Tina offered him a cookie, from a pan into which underdone and overdone specimens had been segregated, before returning to the sink, in which bowls and egg-beaters and the great floury cutting-board were indiscriminately jumbled. Outside, the lifeless November day was quiet and dull, but the kitchen was hot.

"Your mother and I want you, Vick," her father said.

"What for?" the girl asked innocently. But she followed him into the library, expecting no immediate answer to her question.

Here was her mother, just back from town, agitated, mysterious. The room was shaded, and on the north side of the house, and through the thick, dry honeysuckle vines outside of the window only a cold dim light penetrated. Damp leather bindings, and musty pages, and the smell of unaired upholstery scented the air. Victoria felt strangely uneasy.

"Vicky, love," her mother said, tremulously. "Why have you never told Mama about encouraging this Tasheira boy?"

The solid ground failed beneath Victoria's feet, and her mouth felt dry. She looked down, swallowed hard, essayed a grin.

"I don't know, Mama," she said.

"Then you admit encouraging him?" her father said sharply.

"I—well, I have talked to him," the girl faltered uncomfortably.

"You have met him, you have written him, and you have allowed him to get idiotic notions about you!" her father summarized sternly.

"Well——" Victoria cleared her throat. "I do like him, Papa," she said bravely.

Both parents eyed her aghast. Her mother's look became almost as coldly unsympathetic as her father's was.

"Don't talk nonsense!" said the latter harshly. "You like this yokel," he said angrily, "you like this boor—whose boots smell of the stable—who can hardly read or write——"

"Oh, Papa—he had a grammar school education!"

"—who hasn't the faintest iota of an idea of what constitutes a gentleman," her father continued, "who very probably has no name——"

"Stephen, be careful!"

"I don't know what you mean by not having a name," Victoria said, in surprise; "his name is da Sã. Ruy Angelo Antonio da Sã. He's been baptized and confirmed—and as for having no name——"

"Never mind, dear, you'll understand what Papa means some day," said the mother.

"And this is the man my daughter chooses to marry!" Stephen groaned.

"But I haven't, Papa," Victoria cried, very much frightened and near tears. "I—I've just met him—places. And he brought me the lamb—you and Mama knew that! And—and—I know he likes me——"

"Listen, Vicky love," said her mother. "You trust Mama and Papa, don't you?"

"Of course I do!" Victoria was crying now.

"And you know that ever since you were a little, wee baby, Mama and Papa have tried to do everything to make their little girl's life bright, and to make her a good and useful and lovely woman, don't you?"

Victoria sniffed; even Stephen was moved and silent.

"Now, dearest, don't you think you can trust Mama and Papa now? Don't you think they deserve it, after all their planning and care? Of course she does, Papa! Now, Vicky, Mama tells you, and Papa, who is a good deal wiser and older than you are, Papa agrees with Mama in this, that in letting yourself think of this poor boy—my gracious!" May interrupted herself agitatedly, "I had no idea of it!—you only bring sorrow to yourself and perhaps pain to him. He may be good enough, dear, but he's not a gentleman, Vicky. He doesn't know anything about family, dear, manners and customs that we simply must have. You see that, don't you, dear?"

"Yes, ma'am," Victoria gulped, thoroughly ashamed of herself now.

"Well, then, we simply want you to go into the parlour and see him now," May said, triumphant and persuasive, "and tell him very kindly and gently that your father doesn't wish——"

"Is he here?" Victoria said, in consternation.

"Papa met him at the gate, dear, just now."

There was a short silence. Victoria looked down.

"I don't see why I can't be friends with him," she muttered sulkily.

"Because your father doesn't wish you to," Stephen said promptly and finally.

Victoria sniffed and pouted. Her father seized the moment for a brisk and masterly decision.

"Come with me now!" he said, extending his hand.

Still the girl hesitated. But he was her father, her unquestioned authority and oracle. May gave a great sigh of almost tearful admiration and relief as the two left the room.

Ruy was in the parlour. He was still a great, overgrown, awkward boy. He was only a year younger than Victoria; he looked no more than an enormous seventeen or eighteen. But he was changed from the day of their meeting; he wore his clothes more easily, his manner was less gauche, and his black hair was sleek above his burned, olive cheeks. He radiated utter rapture as the girl and her father entered the room.

Stephen responded to his silly ecstatic smile only with a brief, dry nod.

"No, I think we needn't sit down," Stephen said. "There seems to be a misunderstanding here, Mr. da Sã, and I think, for the happiness of all parties, the sooner we clear it up the better! I understand from my daughter here, that you have been annoying her with attentions——"

Ruy's face changed expression, darkened, lengthened. Victoria winced, and half-whispered a protestant "Papa!"

"You have been annoying my daughter with attentions that can lead to nothing," Stephen pursued firmly, "and I want my daughter to ask you, knowing that your feeling for her is only kindly and—and generous, to discontinue them."

There was the silence of consternation in the cold, orderly parlour. Ruy swallowed hard, and into his jocund, healthy brown face an angry colour crept.

"But Miss—Miss Brewer does not say thees," he said slowly and painfully, his eyes on her face.

"I think you will find she does, sir!" Stephen said, with warmth.

"What you say?" the young man asked, turning to her.

In the pause the nosegay of chrysanthemums and asters which he had been holding, slid to the floor. Victoria could smell the cold, wet, pungent chrysanthemums.

"Of course—I say what my father does," she said, almost inaudibly.

"She says that as a young lady with a social position—with —with a standard entirely different from yours," Stephen rounded it out, readily, "that attentions from you—however well meant! however well meant!—can only cause her—distress—and—and embarrassment. She asks me to ask you not to continue to annoy her. Am I not right, Vicky?"

Victoria's face was burning. She knew, if her father did not, that Ruy was remembering a score of deliberate acts on her

part, meetings, notes, messages, between herself and this—
she now saw—supremely undesirable boy.

"Of course you are, Papa," she murmured.

That was all. In another moment Ruy was gone, his horses'
galloping feet dying away into the cold, quiet winter day.
Victoria could accept her father's warm praise, his kiss, her
mother's tearful and grateful embrace, the flattering curiosity
of her sisters. Her blazing cheeks cooled, her whirling thoughts
quieted. Papa had felt no doubt about it, and a girl must
trust her father. He had never praised her so much in all
her life, and she delighted in his approval. He said that she
had acted like a little lady, she had carried off an extremely
difficult situation well. A young lady must expect these embarrassing attentions, but as long as she did nothing to encourage them, she could feel herself quite free to act honestly
and wisely when the crisis came.

All evening Victoria enjoyed the subdued self-satisfaction
of the martyr. It had been trying, but it had been indisputably
an adventure. A common girl, like Kitty Barbee, would have
no such sense of being protected and self-respecting.

But the next morning the reaction came. She remembered
then that Ruy, with all his defects, had been big, clean, strong,
brimming with young passion. She remembered then her
dim dreams of marrying him, being the idol of the old Señoritas
and the old colony of their dependents. She remembered
his big, brown, scarred hand, wonderfully sure with a horse's limp-
ing foot, a sheep's tangled fleeces, or a puppy's blindness.
Something new, something for which she had no thought, much
less a name, awakened in her, and cried out for that devotion,
that beaming grin, and that warm human nearness. Her
heart rebuked her day and night—she had betrayed her friend.
She had let him think she liked him, and then played him
false.

A girl's father knew best—a girl's father knew best. But
what if she had come boldly out, that day in the parlour, with
a confession that she had written Ruy, that she had admitted
to him, tacitly at least, that she liked him?

A sense of having failed him, and herself, and all that was
fine and true in her, haunted her. If he was not a gentleman,
she might have made him one. If he was not "in society," it
would matter nothing to her.

She deliberately mentioned his name to her mother.

"Vicky," her mother responded, in an unexpected tone, "I was speaking to Papa about poor Ruy last night. Did you ever understand, dear, that he is to have the old Señoritas' ranch some day?"

Victoria looked at her blankly.

"I never thought anything about it, Mama!"

"Well, I supposed that little Miss Espinoza, that little niece of theirs from Buenos Aires, was to inherit everything," Mrs. Brewer said. "But Bertie says her fortune comes from an uncle, a brother of her mother. It seems that the old Señoritas have really adopted this boy, whatever his exact relationship is——"

"I didn't know it," Victoria said, as her mother paused.

"You haven't seen him or written to him, Vicky?"

"Oh, no Mama! I promised you and Papa I wouldn't."

"That's a good girl!" But Victoria could have sworn that her mother was a little disappointed. "He surely admires my little girl with quite a Spanish intensity," she said urbanely.

Victoria was astounded. She pondered the matter for a few busy, tiring days, and then confided in Nelly, who had come to San Rafael for the Saturday after Thanksgiving, and seemed more intelligently sympathetic than any of Victoria's sisters.

"Well, I think if Ruy is going to have money, it would really make a difference to Uncle Steve and Aunt May," Nelly said sensibly. Victoria, a hot clean tumbler in one hand, a dish towel in the other, faced her with reddening cheeks.

"If I thought that—" she said, in a sick tone, "if I thought that—I'd write him to-night!" Tears sprang to her eyes. "Papa would have had *no right* to make that a reason!" she said, angrily.

"Oh, I think so, Vick," Nelly said, pacifically. "If he is going to have money, it means that he could take care of you—that he could give you the comforts that you have here, for instance——"

"I don't want comforts!" Suddenly Victoria knew how much she liked her big crude lover, how bitterly she had missed him. A panic of remorse shook her. They were young, he and she, they had everything in common, they loved the open, the sunshine, lambs and kittens and colts—it was not for Papa and Mama to dictate their lives!

Breathing hard, she went straight to her father. He and her mother were in conference in the dining room, and she remembered later that they looked at her with some consternation as she interrupted them.

"Papa, have you changed your mind about Ruy? Would you mind if I—I would like to see him, or to write him?"

Her father and mother glanced at each other.

"I have no objection, Vicky," her father said, mildly.

The utter injustice of it brought colour to her face.

"But you *did*, Papa!"

"Don't question what Papa does or doesn't do!" her mother said sharply. "Papa has a great many business worries that you don't know anything about."

"If you wish to write," her father said, hesitantly and heavily, "I will see that the letter is delivered."

Victoria fled, to compose, with Nelly's help, a dignified, yet unmistakably encouraging document. It was nothing to her that her father would read it; he and her mother had read every letter she had ever written, and with the exception of a few scrawled lines from Ruy, had ever received in her life. She gave him the letter on Sunday morning, and sang over the dishes, and thrilled as she swept the back porch, with a rush of high spirits that told their own story. Later in the same Sunday her mother told her that she had heard that Ruy was ill.

On Tuesday her father called her, with a very grave face, to say that young da Sã was dead. Victoria turned ashen under her healthy tan. Dead! Big, strong, brown Ruy dead! It made her feel giddy and weak for a moment and she was glad to catch at her father's hand.

"But what *was* it, Papa?"

"His heart failed, dear." Her father was watching her closely. "Mama and I had not felt particularly happy about your attachment to him, Vick," he said tenderly, "although we had softened toward him, as you know."

"Since you knew he might have money!" something inside the girl said clearly and bitterly. But she did not speak.

"We can only hope, dear, that you will find you did not care deeply, and that as the months go by, and other happinesses and pleasures come into your life, it will be less painful for you!" Stephen did not often use this grave, considerate tone with his girls, and Victoria was impressed by it. She had had a lover, and he had died, and she was not twenty-four yet! Poor Ruy! Poor little dream of youth and love in the setting of the old ranch!

She went soberly back to the making of rice-pudding, the egg-spattered and grease-stained pages of the cook-book propped open against the spice-boxes. Her sisters and Bertie were mysteriously gentle with her; her mother showed signs of actual tears. It was sad, and dramatic, and strangely gratifying.

Suddenly the dream broke and she was awakened. An undertone from Nelly to Esme, a blundered question from Bertie, and it was all clear. Ruy had killed himself.

He had brooded, he had been silent, he had waited—waited—waited. And on the Sunday of Thanksgiving week he had cut his own throat, dying on Monday, without ever having mentioned her name.

Victoria almost lost her reason, in the first few minutes of suffocating shock. He had waited to hear—he had waited for just a word—and he had never heard from her! Oh—oh——!

"Oh, Nelly—oh, Mama—Mama! You never told me—you never told me! Oh, Mama—he waited and waited to hear from me—oh, and I *wanted* to write him—I asked Papa—oh—! you wouldn't let me! And he never knew—he never knew—he lay there all those days—waiting—I could have gone to see him—I would have gone—I would have gone! He might at least have had that—! I could have gone in, just for a few minutes—just to say that it was because Papa advised me—Papa made me—give him up! Oh, you all didn't like him—but I did! You laughed at him, but I knew him better than you did—oh, my God, my God, my God!"

Thus poor Victoria, rushing from the kitchen, with several members of the distracted family rushing after her, sobbing and crying in desperate indifference to onlookers, to pride, to dignity. The girls were crying, and her mother, arms tight about her, was crying, too.

"Vicky, my lamb—my darling! You mustn't! Perhaps it was all for the best," sobbed and stammered May, distractedly. "Oh—if Papa was only home—what on earth shall we do? Vicky—Vicky dear——"

Presently Victoria was lying, silent and spent, on her mother's bed, her eyes absent, her voice an indifferent whisper. Esme and Nelly, quiet and frightened, sat near her, eagerly following any conversational lead that her infrequent murmurs suggested.

Of course it wasn't her fault—of course he must have been queer—of course these things happened, no matter what anybody did or didn't do. His mother had been queer, you know, and there had been some mystery about his father, and after all, his feeling for Vicky had been perhaps the happiest of his life—darling old ducky Vicky—she must drink her good hot tea and she would feel better——

Vicky drank her tea, and cried, and lay silent, and cried again. After supper she moved to her own bed and listened to Esme and Nelly and Tina when they came to bed and long after the house was all quiet she slept. But she would not let her father touch the sore spot, even at his most fatherly tenderest, and she rose up the next day a changed woman. Something was gone that would never come back to Victoria again. Papa and Mama had been wrong, although they did not say so.

It was not their objection to Ruy that scarred her growing soul so deeply. No, parents had objected to suitors since the world began. It was the fact that they had made her respect their objection, only to waive it the instant the suspicion of material advantage crept in.

Vicky did not go to the funeral; her name had not been associated with the tragedy, and her mother begged her to run no risk of scandal. Bertie went, and returned to report the Señoritas only apathetically grieved, and that Lola, the little imperious Argentinian, at home from her convent on a visit, was a "daisy." Ruy had vanished from the world as if he never had entered it, and the days began to go dreamily by again.

Esme's love affair had dissolved into thin air. Roscoe never came to San Rafael now, and her one or two efforts to bring him there were failures. Young Mrs. Duvalette was getting up some theatricals, and Roscoe was to be prominent in them. Tina persevered with her clergyman, quoting him, serving him humbly in guild and Sunday-school, dragging flowers and greens in and out of the little vestry. On Christmas Eve he gave her a gift copy of Mrs. Browning's "Geraldine" that had belonged to his mother, a present that fluttered Tina with greater happiness than if it had been the Cullinan diamond. She showed her sisters the yellowed end-paper on which was written, in flowing letters, "Esther from Mrs. Pope, Feb. 10, 1881," and commented a hundred times that it had—a sort of significance, it was a sweet, sweet thing for Vernon to think of.

The girls were looking at the old book on Christmas Eve, when, at about five o'clock in the afternoon, Bertie came home. The day had been soft and bright, but long ago the last sunshine had gone, and the mountain chill had fallen upon the bare garden and the roomy old house. They were all gathered about the dining-room coal fire, joking, reading, wasting time; a new "girl," named Mollie, was in the kitchen now, and Mrs. Buckey had come in to help her over Christmas Day, and a delightful sense of leisure had fallen upon the family.

Mollie came into the room at about the same time Bertie did, to light the gas with a long narrow brass tube through which a wax taper was pushed, and to draw the shades, and shut out the dimming yard with its shabby willows and tumbled chrysanthemums.

"Heard the news?" Bertie said.

His sisters showed a flattering excitement.

"Uncle Harry has lost his job, and little George hurt his foot," said Bertie, "and Nelly went off yesterday and was married to Rudy Sessions, and never told Aunt Lucy until it was all over!"

"Heavens!" said Tina, in the stupefied silence, "it seems as if something was happening every second!"

"But what will Aunt Lucy do, Bertie! Nelly—Nelly——" Victoria could hardly believe it. One of themselves married! Actually a wife! With a wedding ring and a new name—it was incredible. Married——!

There had been a little unusual stiffness in the Christmas plans. For years the entire family had gathered in the San Rafael house. But Fanny had pleaded for the gathering this year, and May, with bitter misgivings, had been obliged to see the family hub, as it were, shifted to the house in California Street. Fanny had Robert and his baby there, Papa was aging fast, and it was much nearer for Lucy. Carra and Maggie could manage perfectly well, especially if dear May would let the girlies bring over the china dessert plates and the other dozen teaspoons, which were Fanny's anyway, although they had long been part of the Brewer equipment. After all, there were only twelve of them to gather about the big table, for Nelly and her new husband were down in the country, at Rudy's ranch, and Harry stayed with George, who had lamed himself while skating.

Lucy was as usual gallant and undaunted. She wore a tight-fitting wine-coloured velvet that had been sponged and turned ever since the Brewer girls could remember ever noticing clothes at all, she took the centre of the group with her narrative, her pleasure in having news to impart almost eclipsing its unpleasant nature.

Yes, Nelly was married. She and Rudy had walked in just before supper last night, as calm as you please. "The children," as Lucy now called them, had decided it suddenly, because Rudy had "come into his inheritance." His uncle had died only two days before, so it must have been very quiet anyway, and he had gotten the license and carried Nelly off without any time for delays. Now they had gone down to the ranch, a beautiful place—from his description, anyway—in the Contra Costa region, the San Joachim valley. Rudy had had some flattering offers from various firms, but he and Nelly were wild to try fruit farming; he had been brought up to that.

About her husband, Lucy was brief, but mysterious. The Atlas people, through the obnoxious manager, Barrell, had indeed notified Harry, with a substantial Christmas gift in the shape of a twenty-dollar gold-piece, that his further services would not be needed. But, said Lucy darkly, she was pretty sure that wasn't the end of *that*. After fifteen years it was a pretty business if a firm could do that!

"My dear Lucy," Stephen said, almost horrified at the implied criticism of the sacred rights of corporations, "why shouldn't the firm dismiss an employee, if it wants to?"

"Good gracious, it's their money!" May added, reasonably.

"Well," Lucy said, retreating diplomatically, "a good rest won't hurt Harry, that's what I tell him!"

"Delightful, if he can afford it!" Fanny commented.

"Some years since *my* last vacation!" Stephen added good-naturedly.

"Oh, you—everyone knows what a snap you have!" Lucy said, lightly but annoyingly.

"Yes, indeed, a man who hasn't had a vacation for seven years has a great snap!" May responded, in the same tone, and with sudden colour.

"Dinner is served when you are!" Maggie announced suddenly, appearing flushed and breathless in the folding door that shut off the dining room. The girls, hungry and merry, streamed out beside their elders. The long white tablecloth was set with celery and glass dishes of scarlet cranberry sauce, there was a centre bowl of blue china, filled with variegated roses, and whenever conversation lulled someone said intently: "Aren't those roses just perfectly exquisite!"

There were oyster patties, and a new soup called "tomato bisque," and then the great turkey, with all the familiar accessories. Fanny asked Robert to carve, a distinct infringement of Stephen's rights. May, glancing at her husband, felt a rush of passionate admiration for the mild good-nature with which he bore this slight affront. The conversation was chiefly of the food, with an occasional outbreak of surprise over Nelly.

After the meal, the old man was helped upstairs to bed. The others sat about in heated discomfort for perhaps an hour, then the departures began. All the Brewers left in a body for San Rafael, the girls talking together in the fresh, cool breezes on the boat, their father silent, Bertie in low-toned conversation with his mother.

Any one of his sisters would have preferred to absorb Bertie. There was a good deal of jealousy over him, and to have Mama ignore them, and pay him so much attention, was vaguely irritating. It became evident, as the little *San Rafael* ploughed her slow way through the cold-looking tides, that Bertie wanted to do something his mother found unpalatable.

"But Mama wants her boy on Christmas Day," they heard her murmur; "she is a bad, selfish Mama, and she wants that day to be just a home day!"

"But Mama, they expect me——" Bertie protested.

"Then I don't know what sort of people they can be, dear, to ask an only boy to leave his family on Christmas Day!"

"They knew I was going to be in the city, Mama, and they thought if our dinner was over at—say, three, I could come to them at four or five, don't you see?"

"Yes, but, dearie, you're on the boat, now!"

"But I could turn 'round at Saucelito and go back," Bertie

said eagerly. May seemed to feel that she had lost a point, and answered with fond definiteness: "Oh, I think you had better stay with Papa and the girls, now, dear! I think that would be nicer, all 'round!"

"The Barbees!" Esme formed the word merely with her lips, and the other girls nodded. Bertie was darkly sulky and restless for the rest of the Christmas afternoon. Victoria saw that he was watching the clock, morbidly estimating just which train he was missing, just what possible connections he might have made.

CHAPTER X

RUDY SESSIONS had timed his last appeal to Nelly with an almost uncanny knowledge of her nature and her mood. She was exhausted, after the Christmas finale at the kindergarten. She was furious because the credit for the long sticky day of tree and presents and marching and singing had been calmly appropriated by Miss Caddle, her superior, and because Miss Caddle had told her complacently that she, Laura Caddle, had been made superintendent of the five kindergartens in the Mission, and hinted, with that air of authority that sits so unbecomingly upon certain women, that Miss Crabtree must please try to come back, after a good rest, with a little more real love for the children, and just a little pleasanter manner with everyone.

"Come back at New Year's ready to do your best," Miss Caddle said, enjoying herself; "make this work your first consideration—*that's* the important thing. Not how pretty you look, not what young man is waiting to walk home with you— no, that doesn't matter! But whether you're giving satisfaction *here*——"

There was much more in the same strain. Nelly had listened rebelliously, with murder in her heart. She had walked home brooding and despondent and tired, to find her father there, discharged, utterly despairing. Lucy had been brisk but bitter, Alice wide-eyed with awe. "But what will we *do*, Mama?" Alice kept whispering. "Where will we get money?"

"I don't know, I don't know!" Lucy would answer irritably. "Papa will get another position, that's all!" Later she told Nelly that Davy Dudley and his dreary aunt had gone to Napa, Miss Clay probably not to return. "They say she owes about four hundred dollars," said Lucy; "*that* poor boy's work is cut out for him!"

"*He* doesn't owe it!" Nelly said, contrarily. Christmas

167

would be in three days now; she told herself, with angry tears, that this was a *nice* Christmas prospect!

Then Rudy chanced to come in. His uncle was dead, and he told Lucy with becoming gravity of the lovely ranch where he had spent his boyhood, and of the crops and the team and the spring. It was all his, now. He had to go down to the funeral day after to-morrow, and he might stay there some time. There was a man on the place, Pete, and Rudy said he thought his own mother was there, although when she last wrote she was with his married sister in Portland.

"There'll be the deuce of a lot to settle," he said, "and I'm only working on commission where I am."

He and Nelly washed the supper dishes, and Rudy was helpful with suggestions to Harry; there were any amount of openings everywhere, according to him. In the evening he and Nelly sat before the little wood blaze in the dining room, and conferred in low tones. It was all arranged then. They would be married the next day.

"Everyone in the country knew Uncle Rip. Nelly, do you suppose—at the funeral, you know—that you have anything black to wear?"

Nelly thrilled. This was assuming a wifely position with satisfactory completeness. She would appear beside her husband, in proper mourning.

"My suit's black," she murmured, "and I'll get gloves and a veil and take the rose off my hat."

Somehow to figure in the public eye as Rudy Sessions' young wife, beside him at the grave, returning with him to the family farmhouse, was infinitely satisfying and exciting to Nelly. She and Rudy had been sweethearts for some time; he had kissed her more than once. Suddenly she knew that for better or worse this eye-glassed, quick-spoken young man was her fate, and she sighed.

The day of the funeral was bitterly cold; Rudy and Nelly reached Canfield too late to go up to the farmhouse, but met the cortège at the church, and went at once to the front pew. Here a muffled form was whisperingly introduced to Nelly as "Ma," and her lisle glove met a bony hand in a big cotton glove. Neighbours were creaking and whispering all about, and a wheezy organ was sending broken notes into the chill heavy air.

The graveyard was fortunately not far, the obsequies brief and cold. Nelly saw Rudy's own name upon the neighbouring stone, and presently his mother put back her stiff new veil, revealing a lined, hard, honest face, and knelt by this grave, tossing away the withered brown flowers that still hung in a round tin vase, and pulling at an obstinate weed or two.

It was all over. The raw dirt was heaped. It shone damply where it was slapped with spades. The steaming horses turned, Nelly and her mother-in-law climbed into the closed carriage, which smelt of wet leather and mouldy hay, the one other carriage and the half-dozen of surreys and phaetons rattled briskly down the hill after them.

"They say a funeral always brings a wedding," said the elder Mrs. Sessions with a sort of awkward and angular friendliness. Nelly, exquisitely pretty in her black, was deliberately essaying the conquest of this lanky, silent, alert woman. "I got home Thursday," continued Rudy's mother, "and lucky thing, too, because Pete couldn't do much for Uncle. He passed away Saturday afternoon, poor feller. Well, if there's a heaven, he's there—as Ida said. You don't know Ida Burns—she's Ida Larabee now," she said kindly to Nelly; "she was Rudy's baby sweetheart, years ago! She was up to the place this morning, Rudy, but I guess Joe come for her. Quite a few of the folks come up, but there's nobody there now. I didn't know as you'd get here, and I was going to stay with Mis' Pease if you didn't."

The road wound up and up, past vineyards, orchards, meadows, and belts of forest. They turned in at an open gate, rattled across a bridge, stopped under two fine oaks. Nelly, cramped and cold, stepped down.

The house was somehow oddly disappointing. It was a four-roomed white cottage, with a small front porch and an ornamental railing. It had a bay-window, showing draped lace curtains, and a glimpse of a pink china lamp. There were fruit trees in the yard, but only starved and straggling flowers, nasturtiums dying on yellowed stalks, marguerites overgrown with brown shrivelled blossoms. About the place the lines of orchard spread like the spokes of a wheel.

They went about to the back, and Mrs. Sessions took a key from under an empty milk-can, and unlocked the kitchen door.

Somehow the back of the place looked more inviting than the front, to Nelly. There was a porch, picking hens, a barrel of potatoes, a wood-pile. There was a summer kitchen built on, with a stove funnel wavering above it. There was a blinking mother cat with kittens.

In the cold, blank kitchen Mrs. Sessions briskly began dinner preparations. She told Rudy to take his wife into her room, remarking that she would take Uncle's room. Nelly found a lumpy double bed in one of the two bedrooms, a walnut bureau and a washstand with a damp, red-lined towel drying over a pitcher and basin. In the parlour was a patent rocker with a rep fringe, a centre-table, a large crayon portrait of Rudy's father, and a horse-hair sofa. The pink lamp stood on a cross-stitch mat with ball fringe; there was a rug with a Newfoundland dog design.

The house was bitterly cold and odorous. Nelly was glad to return to the kitchen, where a wood-fire was snapping and smelling pleasantly. Her mother-in-law was skimming milk with a bony, firm hand. She skimmed it by loosening the cream about the edges, and pushing it gently off in a great leathery fold with a stick. The kettle was already singing.

"I've got to make biscuit, there isn't any bread," said Mrs. Sessions, "look in that starch box, Nelly, and see if there's an egg there!"

Nelly stepped into the pantry, which released cold odours of food, old wood, and mice. She returned with a solemn look.

"Not one! But there's a pumpkin pie, and a bowl of something——"

"Yes, Milly Hicks brought me that pie," Mrs. Sessions said, "and that other stuff's tapioca—I sort of got hankering for it. Nelly, you yell to Rudy, and tell him to get me some eggs!"

Nelly looked blank. The village was five miles away. But presently she ran up to find Rudy at the barn, in a muddle of fences and gates and milking-sheds, great dim heights filled with hay, stalls showing the nervous hindquarters of horses, cobwebby tangles of feed-bins and meal sacks and paint cans, rough gates and doors and openings in every direction. The open spaces were cluttered with rusty and muddy machinery, chains and straps, tools and barrels and boxes.

Rudy was talking to Pete, whose dark forehead was pressed

against the flank of a red cow. Milk was hissing gently into the dirty foam in the pail, the cow turned her head, and eyed Nelly uneasily.

"Rudy—you've unharnessed? But your mother wants you to go for eggs!"

Rudy joined her with an ecstatic look; she was indeed exquisite in her black, with fire-flushed cheeks and rumpled pale-gold hair.

"And what does my wife want?" he murmured, an arm about her. The blue eyes flashed up at him happily, trustingly.

"Oh, you scare me to death when you call me that!" she whispered, dimpling.

"Nelly," Rudy whispered, "you're the most beautiful little thing God ever made—no, he can't hear anything but the milk!" he reassured her, of Pete. "Tell me, darling, do you like it—the farm?"

"Rudy, it's like a dream!"

"But you love me?"

She looked down, raised mischievous eyes.

"Well, what do you think?"

"But I want to hear you *say* it!"

His arm was close about her; the smell of his skin, the nearness and smoothness and warmth of his face, the heart beating against her tight-held breast, were confusing her senses again.

"Rudy—I came here on an *errand!*" she protested, prettily important.

He released her, laughing, her soft mouth burned and stinging from his kiss.

"Oh, is that *so*, Mrs. Sessions? Well, what is it?"

They had drawn somewhat away from the empty stall in which Pete was milking; now they went back. Rudy leisurely snapped shut the clasp-knife he was caressing, leisurely rested his foot upon an upturned tub and smiled expectantly at his wife. His whole manner had subtly changed even since yesterday; he was a farmer now.

"Eggs. Your mother wants eggs," Nelly said.

"And where do you think we get eggs?" he demanded, laughing.

From the hens, of course! Nelly laughed out merrily. She could help him hunt, in the cold ins and outs of the draughty space. Presently he whispered to her to say something decent to Pete, and Nelly obediently turned her pretty appealing eyes upon the swarthy Portuguese. She would have quite as gladly smiled at the pig, and much more readily at the cow, but Rudy had asked her, and that was enough.

There were other cows, horses, a hundred chickens of all types, wild barn cats who lived upon live meat, and, truly enough, pigs—giving off a quite hideous strong odour even upon this airless winter day.

The supper was good, with an abundance of eggs, cream, milk and sweet butter that Nelly found astonishing. The cream was almost too heavy, dropping in thick clots from the pitcher. They ate at the kitchen table, which was covered with dark red oilcloth. Afterwards she found herself stiff and weary as she and Mrs. Sessions busied themselves with the dark old tin pans and the black old pots and the thick china.

Night shut down chill and early, kerosene lamps were lighted. Rudy was delayed at the barns. Nelly felt weary and dirty; she did not know how to get clean; her trunk would not arrive for a day or two, but after that gay and confident little wedding she had put a few necessities into Rudy's leather satchel. She had not the energy to carry the lamp into their bedroom, to make trips for hot water, to undress far enough, in this biting cold, to take a sponge bath. She felt lost and forlorn, toiling about this strange kitchen in her best dress.

The days went by, but youth and love and laughter were ready for them all. Heavy rains fell, splashing and dripping under the bare orchard boughs. The chickens' three-pointed footprints marked the porch; Rudy brought in great clods of mud with the milk. Nelly huddled close to the kitchen fire; she was always cold; she laughed at herself, but she was cold, none the less.

Her thoughts were all of warmth. She thought of herself loitering home through the sunny Mission, on a September afternoon, between picket fences packed with marigolds and roses. She thought of burning Sundays in San Rafael, of herself and the Brewer girls all in white, and the banksia roses bursting with bloom. She remembered sleepy spring afternoons when she and Alice had helped their mother with the side garden.

The rain fell—fell. Mrs. Sessions cooked and washed dishes, her gaunt hands always marked with soot and grease. She was a silent, resigned sort of woman, beaten flat by life. But she liked Nelly, and Rudy did his best to amuse his wife. He never rattled down the hill in the old surrey without taking her along; they would buy gum-drops and oranges at the village store, and perhaps plan, as they splashed and struggled up the long grade, for future expeditions that would reach the city, and include books and new curtains and shoes. His own days were pleasantly filled with farm matters, questions of stock and implements; he was always warm, busy, interested. Nelly envied him.

Spring came early. By February the ranch was a paradise. Nelly could ramble forth in the heartening sunshine, gathering trillium and lilac in the woods, coming back to the house flushed and rosy and dishevelled. She kept flowers in the rooms; she would find herself out under a blossoming plum tree, almost dizzy with the beauty and brightness about her. When the cherries bloomed, bees gathered so thick about them that the breeze brought the zum-zumming to the ears of the two women, as they laughed over yellow chicks in the deep grass. There were buttercups, blue onion-flower, daisies, and clover waving in fragrant acres and acres, and silvery oats blew like the surface of a lake when the low winds touched them.

Nelly would lean her broom against an oak, run to the barn and waste blissful minutes over the calves, run to the spring, run up to the farrowing sheds to see the squirming baby pigs. She was always singing and always happy now, and Rudy was more madly in love with her than ever. She told him that as soon as his mother left, things were going to be very different. They would use the sacred parlour for a dining room then, and some day build a big sitting room right across the front of the house.

If they sold the fruit, Rudy told her, they would begin to build this summer, and this prospect so elated Nelly that she wrote her mother the first happy confidential letter of her married life. They were regular farmers now, wrote Nelly, and she was living on such cream and eggs as city people never saw. The place was small, but she and Rudy were going to build. She was writing out under the honeysuckle vine, and the valley, lying below her, was one stretch of pink apple-blossoms. She wanted Georgie and Alice to come up for vacation.

When the calves were sold, she knew Rudy got about a hundred dollars. But it had to go for seed, he said; seed, lime, cement, and the services of a neighbouring farmer for three days cultivating in the orchard. Also the bridge had to be repaired and the well cleaned; "the old man let the place run down," Rudy explained.

His mother left them in March, dispassionately warning Nelly "not to make work for herself," as she left. Nelly laughed buoyantly, and returned to the farmhouse brimming with planned changes. For several weeks she persevered with the pretty details of a big white spread on her bed, meals in the front room, flowers everywhere, and a little freshening of her own costume before she sat down at the table. But as the hot spring weather deepened and sweetened over the valley, Nelly gradually came to feel these touches unnecessary, and then impossible. Nobody saw them, anyway, she argued in secret disappointment. There were few callers at the ranch, and these few were country-women much better versed in house-keeping than she was. The youngest of them could tell her more than she had ever dreamed of hard water and soft soap, pig feed and chicken feed, starching and baking. She must make her pie shells by the dozen, soon, she was warned, and she must by no means accustom the hands to more than meat, potatoes, dessert, and coffee for their meals.

"Once begin 'em with asparagus and puddings, and they'll begin to complain the first time your oven goes back on you," said Pansy Billers, an overblown young matron, firmly. "Now and then a cherry or peach shortcake ain't so much fuss—but keep 'em down!"

Nelly told this to Rudy, with laughter, a few nights later. They had followed a favourite custom of theirs, and driven several miles to a mountain hotel, "French Eddy's," for the dinner of fried chicken and salad, French bread hot from the oven, and red wine.

These occasions were always happy ones. They followed delightfully upon the heat and burden of the day, and after the drive Nelly always had colour and appetite. The delicious hot food rested and refreshed them both, and the wine made Rudy tenderly sentimental, and Nelly contentedly acquiescent. They would sit long at the little garden table, looking down across the stretches of prosperous farming country, emptying their glasses, and crunching the brittle crust and the webby pulp of the famous bread. Eddy himself would come forth to talk to them, an immense old Frenchman, with a mud-coloured shirt soaked in perspiration, open at his dark throat.

"We won't have but about four or five men in fruit time," Rudy assured his wife. "And half of 'em will go down to Canfield every night for supper at home, anyway. If you leave plenty of bread in the box at night, and the coffee mixed, I'll see to the breakfast, and all you'll have is the washing up, and then of course dinner."

"I've got it all planned, Rudy. I'm going to do lots of cooking every morning, and have just piles of corn and tomatoes and peas. We'll start off always with a salad, then some good meat with at least three vegetables, and then some real summer dessert, gelatine or fruit custard, with cake. You may have to eat what's left for supper, you poor thing——"

"Oh, Lord, give me any old thing for supper! Say, Nelly, if you do that," Rudy said eagerly, "you'll have this whole valley talking about the board up at Sessions'!"

"Then when it's all cleaned up, at about three," Nelly pursued, "I'll take a good wash, and—will we have the saddle horse then?"

"Well, sure, if Pete finds one!"

"Well, then I'll go for a gallop, or if Alice is here, for a drive, and then back for a cool little supper, just ourselves, out under the grapevine."

They clasped hands and sat silent, in utter felicity.

Naturally their marriage had not reached its fifth month without an occasional squall. Nelly was sweet-tempered, and her husband idolized her, but their life was hard and lonely, and they were both young. It had been a real blow to Rudy to discover that his wife was not in truth a natural heir of old Reuben Crabtree. The fact had been elicited at an unfortunate moment, too, for it was when Nelly was aghast to learn, for the first time, that the ranch was held by them upon an extremely uncertain basis. Rudy's uncle had bought it in good faith, some twelve years ago, making a payment of twenty per cent. of the purchase price upon taking possession. Immediately afterward a defect in title had been discovered, and the bank, holding a heavy mortgage upon the farm, had stopped the sale where it stood. The original owner, dying at this inopportune moment, had complicated matters by leaving only two little girls, in a convent school in San Jose, whose interest in the farm had been but languidly and indifferently represented by first this relative and then that. The discovery of a splendid water-right upon the western boundary, and instant proceedings by the neighbour on that side to claim the entire spring, was one of the complicating details that the years had developed. Pending a decision the Sessions had lived along comfortably upon the place, faced, in some dim future, by the necessity of paying the balance of the price, amounting to several thousand dollars, or of allowing the bank to take over the property as it stood.

Nelly, to whom the word "mortgage" was fraught with everything terrible, had stammered out something of her utter consternation at this state of affairs.

"But, Rudy, what would we do? Just—lose it?"

"Oh, well, I could always get a city job!"

"Yes, I know——! But there's so much money in it, Rudy. All our pigs—you said you'd clear seven hundred dollars on pigs alone. And the prunes, and the bungalow we were going to build!"

"Well," Rudy had then said easily, "if your old grandfather dies, I suppose you'll come in for something, a few thousands anyway!"

"My grandfather? Oh, you mean Grandpa Crabtree? Well, he might, I suppose. But he'll probably leave it—you see, it isn't as if I was really his grandchild."

"How d'you mean really his grandchild?"

"Why, my father was Mama's first husband, Rudy, I told you that!"

Rudy looked astounded.

"Yes, you did—not!"

"I did, too! I told you the day—almost the first day we met. I said that—I'll tell you when it was! You and Papa and Georgie and I went to Oakland one Sunday just for the trip, don't you remember? And I showed you Carter's bakery, at Fourteenth Street, and said that that was my uncle."

Rudy had scowled.

"It said Ellen Crabtree on your marriage license," he said sourly. He hoped to scare her, but she was only anxiously placating.

"Well, I think Mama had my name changed—I know she did—before we went to England! But never mind, dear," said

Nelly courageously. "We'll save, and we'll raise pigs, and we'll pay it off ourselves, if the time comes!"

As a matter of fact she could have saved every penny that came in, or almost every penny. Except for coffee and sugar and flour they bought almost nothing for the kitchen, and Nelly could often get these in exchange at the village store for fresh eggs, baskets of new potatoes or greenings, or chickens she killed and plucked herself.

It fretted her to have Rudy spend money, spend big sums for machinery, for a new sulphur house, and for wire fences. She was accustomed by this time to all sorts of petty discomforts in the kitchen, saucepans mended with wisps of cloth, weary trips to the well for water, and the broken grate in the wood stove that would occasionally precipitate her good fire suddenly into the ash box. It was exasperating to see that Rudy could so instantly replace any bit of farm-gear that was worn or broken, while she struggled with a hundred ugly economies indoors.

She had been married six months, and hot June was upon them, when she first felt an impulse of something like hatred for Rudy. She had asked him and *asked* him, she told herself passionately, to get her a new soup kettle. To-day, with two strange men for lunch, and her head aching, and the possible sale of the peaches impending, the handle of the old pot, full of rich bean soup, broke between the stove and the sink, deluging Nelly, the floor, and the stove itself, with the cold pasty liquid.

She could get no heat into her oven to-day, the wind was wrong. She did not know whether the apple pie and the lamb would ever be done. The soup, and the new gingham dress it had ruined, had been her *pièces de résistance*. Nelly did not know it, but the hour was a milestone in her life.

Alice did not go up to the ranch that summer, and Georgie cried himself to sleep a dozen times because Nelly was where there were cows and chickens and a red bull, and had not even once written Mama to ask him to visit her. It was a hard summer in all their lives.

Nelly came down to visit her mother the very day after the fruit-pickers and harvesters left. She was very pale, as she left the Mission Street car, and walked slowly to the cottage, and on her somewhat drawn and colourless little face the big country freckles stood out plainly. Lucy meeting her at the gate, among dry geraniums and marigolds, saw that her wedding hat was carelessly placed upon her plainly brushed hair, and her wedding suit spotted and shapeless upon the distorted figure.

More grave than the physical changes was the mental attitude she presently discovered in her daughter, as they talked and talked and talked during that first day and evening. Nelly was curiously hardened and coarsened now, in ways that only a mother, and a clever mother, could see; even Lucy could not analyze them. The young wife displayed a certain stoic disillusionment; husbands were creatures to be discounted and endured, life was a drag, and Nelly commented upon her fast-approaching motherhood only with a philosophical "just my luck!"

By the time Alice came in, a quieter and shabbier Alice, the older sister had taken off her hat, brushed her hair, and had a drink of cold water, and she looked calmer. Alice was nearly eighteen now, and although her mother had never mentioned Nelly's condition, she had guessed it, and she recognized it at once, with a deep flush.

"And how's Papa?"

"Just the same."

"Is he—is he in anything now, Mama?"

Lucy lifted a stove lid, looked in, replaced it.

"No," she said briefly and quietly.

"He was working last week," Alice said timidly. "He was in a patent filter place, on Market Street, to show you the bugs, in water! But they closed on Saturday night."

"But, Mama," Nelly said in a worried undertone, "how do you get along?"

"I don't know, but we do!" Lucy said brightly and cheerfully. She stepped to the pantry, brought out a bowl of flour, and began to make biscuit. "They want this house, December first," she said, "they're going to put a store here."

"But, Mama, where will you go?"

"Well, we'll have to go somewhere!" said Lucy, courageously. "I wish to goodness I had taken that San Rafael house and rented rooms!" she added mildly.

"But, Mama, aren't you *worried*?"

"No," Lucy said, with a logical air, "I'm not. I shall get a position at once—I've decided on *that*. I may go in with Miss Donovan—millinery. She spoke to me about it some time ago.   I am really considering it, although it sounds crazy!   But you know me, I reach a point when I have to act—and I *act*."

Alice and Nelly were comforted, as they had always been, by her optimism.

"Seventy dollars in one month, that's what Mrs. Cullen made, selling 'Footsteps of Believers in the Holy Land,'" Lucy stated triumphantly.

"But, Mama—you couldn't peddle books!"

"I couldn't peddle books, no.   But if I did," said Lucy, "I certainly could earn more than Ida Cullen!"

"Don't put your milk in before your shortening, Mama!"

"Here!"   Lucy looked down suddenly at her hands.   "What am I doing?" she said.

Everything in the little kitchen looked pinched and shabby, to Nelly's eyes.   The battered dark tins, the almost empty jars and boxes, the thin slices of stale bread and the spoonful of apple sauce, carefully hoarded.   The table was chipped and discoloured, and Lucy's worn purse, lying on the sink, looked so shabby and flat.   Nelly knew just the pink milk-ticket and the dull half-dollar, and the coarse handkerchief that were inside. Poor Mama, who had to pay for every egg and every pint of milk!

They began to talk.   Nelly confessed that she had tried to do too much, all summer; she had cooked and washed dishes and skimmed milk and fed chickens all alone.

"Rudy wanted to get me a girl, but it's awfully hard, in summer, unless you want to pay twenty or thirty dollars—and of course that's ridiculous!   And when the hogs got sick, I was glad we hadn't wasted any money.   Every hog in the valley got summer cholera, so it was nothing *we* did—but of course it was discouraging!   And then Jummy and the gopher hole—the best horse we had!   However, Rudy knows the first trace of cholera now, and he can watch for it, and of course the other was just a pure accident!"

When Georgie came in, his sister was so much her old self that she could sit on the table beside him, and put her arms about him, and explain to him all about the past disappointment.

"Did you think I was the worst sister that ever was, darling? But I was so terribly busy, dear, and it was so hot!   And I was just *flying*—so much milk, you know, and I would have to rush out for eggs, and to the spring house, and for fire wood, and even dig a few potatoes——"

"But I could have done all that for you, Nelly," Georgie said.

"But I wouldn't want you just to work, Baby!"

"Yes, but Nelly, there'd have been such fun, in between times, and fruit—apricots and peaches, oo-oo, I'd love it!" the boy said eagerly.

"Yes, I used to feel that way about farms," Nelly said, thoughtfully, "and I kept saying to Rudy, 'Could you meet Georgie next week?' but you see, he couldn't spare the horses. And then *he* was so tired, and I was so tired—of course, I was sick——"

"What was the matter, Nelly?" Georgie was rubbing his head against her.

"Oh——" She glanced at her mother. "Headache, darling, and backache. And I got so thin—I couldn't eat anything, and the smell of the milk used to make me so ill! And then we had to save the currants—I didn't pick 'em, but I cooked them, and all the berries, and the clingstone peaches, three trees of 'em. I put up two hundred and eighty-seven glasses, Mama. I brought you down as many as I could. Ida Larabee always puts up eight hundred!"

"And what did you feed the men, Nelly, and how many were there?"

"Oh, pork—pork—pork! That's all they want. Pork, and pies, and cheese, and coffee. Sometimes I made cake, and once Rudy got a wonderful salmon, over at Martinez. There were four for awhile, and then seven. But all I ate was toast and cream."

"Imagine having all the eggs and cream you wanted!"

"Oh, and fruit, and chickens, too, only the smell of cleaning chickens made me faint, one day. But then I was sick; I tell Rudy it'll be very different next summer!"

"Nelly," said Alice, following some train of thought perhaps suggested by the allusion to illness, "I am going to be a trained nurse!"

"Oh, you aren't!"

"Yes, I am. You know Victoria wanted to be, but Aunt May wouldn't let her. But Mama says she'll let me, didn't you Mama?"

"But Mama, she'll be married in a year or two!"

"Well, I hope she will, and of course she knows that taking the training for a nurse will make men apt to think she's strong-minded," Lucy said, thoughtfully. "But it gives her a home, and eight dollars a month, and really—really, Nelly—Papa is so worried——"

"Ah," Nelly said, fondly kissing her sister, "I want her to have dances and pretty gowns, and then marry somebody! Don't let her go off and be a professional nurse, always having to work so hard, and half kill herself! It's only a few years, and then the right man will come along——!"

"I know," Lucy said, more than half convinced, "I feel that, too!"

"Maybe I'll marry the doctor!" Alice said, demurely.

"Yes, that's what they all say!" Lucy said. "But I notice the doctors want pretty, refined young ladies, when it comes to marrying!"

The subject was interrupted by Harry, who came quietly and wearily in at this moment. Nelly's heart stood still when she saw how worn and threadbare the smiling, tired little man looked.

"Well, Nell——?" he said, in the doorway. Nelly sprang to meet him.

"Papa—you darling you!"

"Well——" Harry said, with watering eyes, holding her tight. "Little Nelly back—eh? Seems pretty good, don't it, Mama? Well, Nelly—Nelly—Nelly!" he added tenderly, as the girl clung to him, ashamed of her own sudden tears. "Glad to see me, are you?"

Nelly laughed, and sniffled, and laughed again, gulping down the rest of her tears.

"I don't believe I knew how crazy I am about you all!" she said, "I can begin to realize now just how much you did for me!"

Harry's face was radiant. Whatever cares had dogged his homecoming feet were forgotten now. As they gathered about the meagre meal they gave Nelly all the news.

Rob's poor little baby was delicate, had convulsions and spasms and at least a suspicion of hip-disease. Fanny had had a hard time with him, and now he was in San Rafael, with the Brewers. Grandpa was failing fast, rarely left the house now. One of the Señoritas Tasheira had gotten smallpox, then almost an epidemic in San Francisco, and Aunt May had invited little

Miss Espinosa, their heiress niece from the Argentine, to come to them for the Thanksgiving holidays.

"So that Bertie'll fall in love with her and land that million dollars!" Alice said innocently, and they all laughed.

"Well, we're all well, and together again, and that's better than twenty million dollars," Harry said, contentedly. Nelly could respond honestly that in all her life she had never seen Georgie looking so well; the delicate blonde little brother was transformed, at fourteen, into a sturdy handsome brown boy. Her praise of him gave his father infinite satisfaction.

She stayed with her mother for ten days, happy days despite the overhanging worry at Lucy's house, and days that did Nelly much good. One day she and her mother left Alice in charge of the house, and went across the bay to see the Brewer family in San Rafael.

It was early October, a soft hazy day of yellowing woods, languid gardens, and sunshine veiled through brush fires. Leaves rustled under their feet as they walked from the train to the Brewer house, and Nelly felt breathless almost to pain as she sank into a chair on the porch. The little motherless Reuben, who was called Bobo, was asleep in Louisianna's old wicker baby-carriage, at the side of the house, under a mosquito net.

The girls gathered interestedly to meet their old companion, now so oddly altered in appearance and manner. Lou had washed her hair, and had been drying it on the tennis court, where Esme and Tina had been idly tossing balls back and forth. They said eagerly that Nelly had not interrupted their game— they were just killing time. Victoria came out blinking, with tumbled hair and warm cheeks; she was keeping a theatre book, she said, with programmes and advertisements and pictures of the actors and actresses she had seen, and she had almost gone to sleep over her lettering and pasting. Nelly took the floor with a buoyant account of affairs at the ranch.

Presently May came out, somewhat fluttered by the unexpected voices in their quiet garden, and delighted to talk. She had a new doctor for the baby, it appeared, a doctor who held the somewhat absurd theory that what the child ate affected its health.

"Steve and I had a good laugh at him," May said, "when he said he thought poor little Bobo had had too much mush! Mush——! The one thing in the world for a baby. He wants him fed at regular times, but I told him that he couldn't tell a mother anything about *that*.   I always fed my babies when they cried, and look at them—the dearest children a mother ever had!   I don't know what I would do without them—what I will do when they all follow Nelly's example!" she finished, with a little archness.

"Don't worry—the Brewer old maids are one of the sights of San Rafael!" Lou said, with a sort of laughing bitterness.   Her approaching twentieth birthday was making her feel anxious and old.   Esme laughed, too.

"You can't manage to get a husband for one of us, Mama, much less the four!" she said, with a sort of fond irritation.

"I don't want to!" their mother said, stoutly.   "I want my girls to take their time, and be sure of themselves before they make any change!"

"One of us will begin it, and the rest will go off like hot cakes," Victoria said, burying her head on her knees with a great yawn, as she sat on the top steps.

"You wish it!" Louisianna said, in a low voice.

"Don't be so disagreeable!" Victoria said quickly.   Their mother chose to take no notice of this little passage, but questioned Lucy about her affairs.   They all sat on idly content in the sweet, lengthening shadows of the autumn afternoon, while the air cooled, and in the long shafts of reddening sunlight, through oaks and eucalyptus, bees shot to and fro, and little clouds of black flies wove and circled.   The odours of tarweed, of grapes, of the gnarled, small dusty apples, came pleasantly across the dilapidated old garden.

"I ought to be watering!" Victoria said, and wrapped her head in her arms again, and yawned.   They all yawned, laughed, confessed to being mysteriously sleepy.

How was Bertie?   Oh, fine——!   Did he ever see the Barbee girl now?   Well, sometimes, but Mama was pretty sure that it was all over, in that direction.   How was Mr. Yelland?   There was hesitation; it was left to Tina to answer that he was fine, everything just the same.   And Uncle Rob?

May's face clouded.

"Stephen never says much," she said, "but it has been awfully hard for him, having Bob in the business, practically to educate, you may say!"

"Bertie's more use than Uncle Bob!" Esme added loyally.

"You don't know anything about it!" Tina observed, repressively.

"I know Aunt Fanny said so!" Esme returned with spirit.

"I thought Fanny and Bob were terribly intimate?" Lucy said interestedly. May shrugged.

"He's not living with Fanny and Pa, I know that!" she said.

"For pity's sake!" Lucy had unearthed gossip at last. "Since when?"

"Oh——" May scratched her full soft faded chin and stared at the sky. "Girls, when did Bobo come over here?" she asked.

"A week to-morrow, Mama!"

"Well, then, it was a week ago to-day that Pa and Bob had a terrible quarrel, and Fanny sent for Stephen. Bob said he'd leave the firm, and Stephen says that he has quite determined that Bob shall leave it, the minute—anything happens—to poor Pa! Fanny says that Pa has left poor little Bobo this house—well, of course, if he has, it only shows how pitiably Pa is breaking." May said sensibly, "and Steve says that he almost feels —he almost feels that it may be our duty to take out a guardianship for poor Pa——"

"Only Papa naturally feels that he ought to be the one to have it, and Aunt Fanny says that she is the one, and so——" Victoria was beginning candidly, when her mother interrupted her sharply:

"Never mind, Vicky—we needn't go into that!"

"But Mama——"

"Never *mind*, dear!"

Victoria subsided, and May resumed, in her comfortable, reasonable tone:

"Poor little Bobo—we're getting quite fond of him! After Bob and Pa quarrelled, Fanny was very anxious about him, for she has been so worried, and so busy she was almost beside herself! So I suggested that we take the little fellow for a visit and she was so relieved! He——" May dropped her voice, looked gravely at Lucy, and shook her head.

"Delicate?" Lucy asked, in the same tone.

"Can't live!" May almost whispered it. "No stamina!" she said.

Lucy perfectly understood the situation. Small as he was. Rob's baby was an important figure in the family situation. If he was with his Aunt May when old Reuben died, and if

Robert was really dropped from the family firm, what more natural than that the child, inheriting the San Rafael homestead, should continue to live there with May, for what remained of his poor little life?

"The minute we realize that Pa is near the end," May pursued, with solemn satisfaction, "I shall go straight over to Fanny, leaving the girls in charge here, and I shall not leave him again. Stephen thinks, with me, that my place, at that time, is there! I am to have Carra's room, and she will go upstairs."

"Aunt Fanny says she doesn't care how soon it comes, she is ready for anything, if only Grandpa will—will find the real happiness—the real truth, in—in God—at the end!" Tina said, her eyes watering with the effort of expressing herself. There was an embarrassed pause; of late months Tina had not infrequently touched upon subjects generally felt to be too sacred for open conversation, yet it was conceded that Tina, because of her church interests and her intimacy with Mr. Yelland, was becomingly interested in these matters.

"It's none of my business," Lucy said, feeling that it was very much her business, "but I should like to know just why that baby should be made such a fuss about!"

"Well, Pa was always a little partial to Rob, and then the baby's his grandson——"

"Georgie's his grandson!" Lucy said roundly.

"Oh, and Bertie, too!" May sighed, and fell into a musing wish that she had seen a little more of the Harry Crabtree children, years ago, had drawn Pa's attention to little George. Lucy and Harry were harmless rivals, very different from the buoyant Rob, with his breezy insincere laugh, and his annoying tendency to supplant worthier persons, and wedge himself and his interests into the very holy of holies.

The baby himself was waking now, with acid little wails, and Victoria brought him, rolled in wet blankets, to the steps, for a moment, before carrying him upstairs for bath and supper. He was a mottled, wrinkled infant, with claw-like little hands, abnormally thin legs, and a totally bald head. His relatives looked at him dispassionately, but Vicky hugged him toward her affectionately, as she carried him away.

Nelly went upstairs, too, and when Vicky had the baby on his back on her bed, Nelly said timidly:

"You know I'm going to have one, too?"

"Yes, I know!" Vicky said, with a conscious look, safety pins in her mouth. "Give me that cornstarch, Nelly! Yes, Alice told me. Are—are you glad?"

"Oh, of course!" Nelly said, rather lifelessly.

"I saw Davy, last week," Vicky said suddenly. She glanced at Nelly, a little afraid that the allusion might be unfortunate. But after ten months on the ranch, Nelly felt herself definitely removed from the old uncertain days of flirting and speculating, and she laughed naturally.

"Poor Davy! I did treat him horridly! Did he ask for me?"

"We talked about you. He's going to be a doctor, you know. He's in Doctor Hughes's office, mornings, and takes care of his horse. And he goes to the medical college. His aunt has rheumatism or something; she's at home with his mother, now. He looked awfully shabby. But I like Davy!" Vicky said.

Nelly looked thoughtful.

"I don't know why I was so mean to him!" she mused.

"You fell in love!" the other girl stated, with a laugh.

But Nelly only frowned faintly.

"Falling in love is different from what you think it is, Vick," she said slowly.

"It carries you off your feet, I know that!" Vicky said.

"No—that's exactly it! It doesn't!" Nelly answered quickly. "A few weeks after you are married you try to remember how you felt, and what made you act so—so positively, and you can't remember. You only know that you *did* this or did that, and you must have wanted to! And you look at your husband sometimes, and he doesn't seem to be the same person—oh, he's nice, and you love him, you know!—but he doesn't seem the same person that you used to meet accidentally in the street, and laugh and—and flirt with, and feel so strange about!"

Victoria, the warm, dry baby in her arms, listened in fascination, as dreamers of old might have listened to travelled Marco Polo. Both young women started, as May, stout, gray, a little breathless, came in with the baby's bottle.

"Vicky," said her mother that night, when Nelly and Lucy were long gone, "what were you and Nelly talking about to-day, dear?"

"When, Mama?"

"When I came upstairs, dear?"

"Why, I don't know.   Nothing, Mama!"

"You weren't saying anything that you wouldn't wish Mama to hear?"

"No, ma'am."   Victoria's face was scarlet.

"You will be careful about that, won't you, Vicky?"

"Yes, Mama."

CHAPTER XI

THE dreamy autumn days slipped by, the thinning sunlight made briefer and briefer stays in the Brewers' garden, and presently, on the dry pumpkin vines and crushed thistles near the stable there was the glitter of the first frosts on bright, chilly mornings, and in the shady paths down by the evergreen hedge the ground was slippery with dark films of moss. Great spiders' webs were sketched in gray upon the cedars, the pampas plumes were dirty yellowish brown, and in the rough dirt roads of the little country town pools of rain water reflected the pale blue, remote arch of the sky.

Somehow the Brewer girls kept themselves amused. There were occasional trips to town, occasional new gowns to discuss, occasional minute changes among their little affairs that interested and employed them. They altered their rooms, bringing this bookcase up from the parlour, sending that old chair to the attic, dusting, wiping walls, charmed with the novelty of the new arrangement. They took turns with the care of the baby, an alternate annoyance and pleasure. They walked, played euchre, cooked when Fricka had gone and Annie not yet arrived, and fussed with orris root and China silk for Christmas presents. Louisianna and Tina were flattered by an invitation to the coming-out dance of Miss Louisa Persons, in January; their mother took them to town with carefully packed "telescope" straw baskets neatly strapped, containing party gowns, and they stayed that night at Aunt Fanny's house. They came home flushed and confident with pleasure, the next day "everyone" had known Mama, and everyone had been lovely to them, and Lily Duvalette had told them to tell Esme to come see her baby boy, and Willy Barker and Bernardo Baker had said that they were coming to San Rafael Sunday. This social excitement carried all the girls through several weeks of complacence, especially as the young men did call, on a dripping Sunday, and were kept for supper amid much laughter and pleasantness.

Early in March Lucy came over to tell them that Nelly had a baby girl, born a few weeks early, and so before she, Lucy, could go to the ranch as she had planned, for the event.   Nelly was well, and had written herself, on the fifth day, to say that Hildegarde sent love and kiss to Grandma.

Fanny had chanced to be coming to San Rafael, too, on this warm, bright mid-week morning, and, finding May without a servant of any kind, the visitors felt the more free to remain to lunch, and there was informal enjoyment of the meal that the girls scrambled together with much waste of effort, and much running to and fro.

The baby, a pallid, good little creature, sitting apathetically in the sunny path, and firmly holding the spoon he apparently had no interest in using, cried and screamed in terror at the sight of the rattling jet ornaments upon Fanny's new, long-tabbed cape and high, narrow bonnet, and under her smiling displeasure was carried from sight.

"Bless us, what a little coward!" said Fanny, displeased.

"Poor little soul, I shall be almost glad when it's over—for his sake," Lucy said.

"I suppose Bob will feel it," May added.

"Oh, Bob!" Fanny said, vigorously.   "Nobody ever knows what he feels or doesn't feel!   You know how   he's treated Pa—walking out of the house, and going to the Southerlands— that boarding-house on Sutter and Taylor, you know, May? Well, that was October, and all this time he's been treating Pa as coolly as you please, going in and out of the office with just 'How are you, Steve!' or, if Pa was there—and he would go down once or twice!—'How do, Pa!'   And now—about a week ago, if he doesn't walk in, one evening, to see if Pa didn't want to play cribbage.   'Oh, no, Mister Rob,' I said to myself, 'that's a little *too* cool!"   But poor Pa had heard his voice, and—if you please, —Bob has been to dinner every night since, and he stays to help Carra get Pa upstairs, and of course poor Pa looks forward to the cribbage, so that really I don't know what to do!"

"Do!" May said, breathing hard.   "I wouldn't stand it! Steve says that we could get a guardianship of Pa *to-morrow*——"

"Yes, I know," Fanny said, with a cautious glance toward the kitchen, where the girls were washing lunch dishes, "but suppose Rob took Pa's part, and fought it?"

"Exactly," Lucy contributed softly.

"Bob Crabtree," May said angrily, "has been in California exactly three years—less than three years! Does he think—does he think that he can step in here, after we've put up with Pa for all these years, and be the one to champion and befriend Pa, and set him against all the rest of us, and defy Stephen and you and me, who have always done what we thought best for Pa——"

"That's exactly what he does think!" Fanny, high colour in her lined face, said grimly.

"Well, then, I think that's outrageous!" May said hotly.

"It is outrageous," Lucy said. The sisters glanced at her, simultaneously impressed with the impropriety of Pa's mere daughter-in-law expressing so intimate a criticism.

"I wish now, Fanny—but then I always did!—that you had not been in such a hurry to move Pa to town!" May said, gently.

"I don't see what that has to do with it!" Fanny countered, instantly tart, and beating her nose.

"Well, he would have been here, among the girls, where we could all have shown him how truly his happiness mattered to us, how perfectly—hypocritical Rob's ridiculous pretentions to being so—so devoted to him, are!" May said, finding the sentiment a little hard to define, but ending upon a triumphant conviction that she had mastered it.

"If it's hard for you, May," Fanny said, with a suddenly reddening nose and blinking eyes, "for me it's—it's simply terrible! You know how I have devoted myself to Pa—never married, practically gave him my whole life! Why, back in the old Powell Street house, before Tina was born, I remember telling poor Dick Folsom——"

"Who killed himself for the Fargo girl?" Lucy remembered interestedly.

"Well, that was years later!" Fanny said, annoyed. "But I have never failed Pa in the least particular," she went on firmly, blowing her nose, "and I won't put up with it, and I can't put up with it, having Rob preferred before me, and having to tell Maggie to set an extra place for Mr. Rob, and having him *ignore* me, at my own table——!"

"I remember telling dear old Stephen, coming home on the boat—let's see, it was a year ago Christmas—that I thought it was a great mistake for you to put Rob at the head of the family, as it were——" May said, with mild satisfaction.

"How do you mean?" Fanny snapped with a quick glance, beginning to beat the tip of her nose to and fro.

"Why, you had the dinner at your house, Fanny, and Rob carved——"

"Oh, nonsense!" Fanny said warmly, "that was because Papa was so ill. I certainly didn't do that for Bob. The idea of——"

"Why, Fanny, at poor Ella's funeral, I remember your crying, and telling Rob that he must brace up—he was the head of the family now——"

"I remember that, too," Lucy said, noncommittally.

"Oh, I remember it perfectly!" May echoed confidently, reinforced.

"I never heard such nonsense!" Fanny said with an angry laugh and a scarlet face. She tossed the bugled bonnet, and shrugged her shoulders in great disdain. "Dear me, it is interesting to know that one is being spied upon, even at a funeral!" she said, in a high, shaking voice. "I suppose, next thing——"

"Listen—! Listen, Fanny," May began pacifically. But Fanny was near to tears now, and would listen to nothing.

"Oh, no, May, you and Lucy have always been against me, and I've known it perfectly well!" she said, passionately. "Don't say one word—any one could see that! Whatever I do, whatever I say, however devoted I am to my own family, you and Lucy—and Stephen, too!—are only too pleased to spy and criticize me—and you set the girls against me—I see it! Don't think I don't! And you set Papa against me, too—I know it perfectly well—Papa, who is all I have left—since Mama died——"

May looked frightened and her eyes filled at this outburst; Lucy was sympathetic and uncomfortable if less disturbed. Fanny was given not infrequently to tirades filled with hysterical self-pity, and although she meant every word she said at the moment, she soon subsided into heavy tears and deep sobbing, followed by snifflings, proud apologies, and a much happier frame of mind. She rushed upstairs now, and, after a suitable interval, during which the girls came forth from the kitchen with scared faces and murmured with their elders in the lower hall, Esme was appointed to run up after her. Soon they were all upstairs, Fanny, on the spare-room bed, her face still tear-stained, quite gaily the centre of an easily amused and eagerly talkative group.

They had been getting Bertie's room in order when the visitors had interrupted them, and when Fanny and Lucy left they went back to the pleasant big apartment, which faced the south and west with bay-windows, and so was flooded now with spring sunlight. Curtains were down to-day, windows open, buckets of cooling suds and mops and brooms stood about. The paperers were gone, and Bertie would take possession to-night of totally transformed quarters.

While the girls, with infinite directing and changing, hung the stiff white Nottingham lace curtains, May sat in one of the windows, with the baby in her arms, and watched comfortably. Below, the yard was bright with new grass, there were pink blossoms on the old peach trees, and the syringa bushes were masses of fragrant, creamy bloom.

"It seems to me so important to keep the boy happy in his own home," May said sententiously. "I want him to feel that he has the most devoted Mama and sisters of any boy in the world! And that's why I tell you girls that it is your duty *not* to sit comfortably reading, in the evenings"— May was falling into her favourite moralizing tone—"but to do something that amuses Bertie—cards, some game that will make him associate pleasant times with his home! Esme and Tina have been sweet and dear about it——"

"And what about me, Mama?" Vicky said good-naturedly, as she ran a thin brass rod through the stiffened hem of a curtain. "Don't I play euchre with Papa and Bertie until I'm so sleepy I can't see?"

"You haven't been very nice about it, darling," her mother said gently, glad of the invitation to rebuke. "Two nights ago——"

"Two nights ago what happened?" Victoria took her up vivaciously. "Bertie was dying to go up to Neil Powers', and he said he was, and you and Papa perfectly well knew he was. And Papa told him to stay home and be satisfied with his sisters, and I *did* begin a game with him, but he was so sulky that he wouldn't even hold up his cards, and he kept squirming and sighing, and finally I said, 'Oh, for goodness sake, *go*! Get out! Anything's better than having you hanging about here if you don't want to——!'"

"Vicky, you interrupted Mama," May said, in disapproval, as the girl paused. And over Victoria's instant murmur of apology she resumed: "Boys are very, very different from girls. Their temptations are greater, they see more of the world, they get tired out in business——"

"Well, I'd like to see more of the world, and get tired out in business!" Louisianna said rebelliously, "and I agree with Vick that it's perfectly sickening to have to sit about and amuse and coax a great big husky boy who wants, all the time, to run off somewhere else! I say, let him go!"

Louisianna was the youngest and prettiest of the group, and so her mother was a little softer with her than with the older girls. Now May said reproachfully:

"Baby—Baby! Is that a nice way for a little sister to talk? We want our Bertie to grow to be a good, fine man, we want to save him from the dangers of life—of which," said the mother more firmly, "you girls have not the least idea—as you shouldn't have, of course."

"I suppose Kitty Barbee is one of them!" Vicky said, wickedly. "Well, Mama, I hope he jilts Kitty," she added, laughing, "and marries little Lola Espinosa, and that he finds he's made a fine bargain with that little Spanish spitfire, and never inherits one cent of her uncle's millions!"

"You ought to be ashamed of yourself, Vicky," her mother said warmly. "I don't think that's nice—even in joke. Sometimes you and Lou—and she gets it from you!—sometimes you and Lou talk as if you were actually strong-minded. And that isn't the sort of women men admire, my dear—you'll find that out!"

"Bertie may admire us, but he takes other girls out, I notice," Vicky said slyly, "and if ever you want him to take one of us, even to a dance here in San Rafael, you'd think he was going to be killed. He's never home on Sunday, any more, he never brings young men here——"

"That will do!" May said, now really displeased. "I am extremely sorry that my daughters cannot find anything kind to say about their brother!" she added with spirit, "nothing but criticism and recrimination! You girls live here in this beautiful home, protected and indulged in every way, and with never a moment's care or responsibility, and yet you cannot be generous to your poor brother, who must go out into the world and support himself—perhaps some day support us all! I call it very unkind of you—" said May, with watering eyes, "and very selfish——"

"Not me, Mama!" Tina said lovingly, on her knees beside her mother's lap.

"Not you, darling, and not Esme, who is always Mama's comfort!"

"You and I are popular, Vick," Louisianna said stoically, from the ladder.

May sniffed, wiped her eyes, and cast upon the rebels a resentful glance. She knew there was no hope of softening Vicky and Lou in this particular mood. In a few minutes she reproachfully enlisted Tina's offices, and they carried the baby away. The others discussed the matter over the last touches to Bertie's room.

"I notice our rooms get papered and cleaned, to keep us home evenings!" Louisianna said, bitterly.

"Oh, it makes me tired!" Victoria had made the bed, and was now crimping the great ruffled pillow-shams with impatient fingers. "Boys—and temptations and seeing the world! If they haven't character enough to keep straight——"

"I don't think you ought to talk like that, Vick!" Esme said, startled. "You don't know anything about boys' lives!"

"Vicky," Louisianna said, curiously, "how'd you feel if Bertie really did marry Lola Espinosa?"

"He won't," Victoria said, with some obscure satisfaction, "he's crazy about Kitty!"

"But imagine—Lola's uncle sends her three hundred dollars a month—pretty nice for Bertie!" Louisianna pursued, overawed at the mere thought.

"Doesn't that make you sick!" Victoria scowled. She had a brief vision of all that she could do with this sum—travel, far cities, plumed hats, and the glittering decks of ocean ships. "And she doesn't do one thing for it!" she added bitterly.

"You ought to be glad you have a good home and a father to take care of you!" Esme said, half-heartedly. "Mama says that some day we'll all look back on these days, and wonder why we weren't always on our knees, thanking God for protecting us from the world! Look at poor Aunt Lucy and Alice! Mama says that they hardly know which way to turn!"

"Yes, I know——" Victoria said, struck with her own ingratitude. They fell to discussing, in low and cautious tones, Nelly and the baby.

Bertie himself was far from being the care-free and debonair young social favourite that his sisters enviously fancied him. He was almost as unfitted as they to meet life, but the accident of his sex had placed him in a position to learn rapidly and painfully just how unimportant the son of the vice-president may be in an old family firm. He had begun his experience with Crabtree and Company full of buoyant, almost offensive, self-confidence. The salary seemed large to him, the freedom from schooling almost intoxicating, and the deference paid him by much older men, as his grandfather's and father's natural successor, had quite gone to his head.

To exchange a few family confidences with old "R. E." and to go to lunch daily with his father, had given Bertie a quite adventitious importance, for a few weeks, and during that time he had fatally affected the opinion of all his associates. When he began to suspect that he was disliked, avoided, and ridiculed by the entire staff of employees, and treated with quiet contempt by the heads of departments and the directors, it was too late. Bertie could not undo now the effect of weeks of arrogance and boasting, he could not efface the memory of snubs he had administered, and tales he had carried eagerly to his father, of this one's carelessness and that one's inefficiency.

Of his own mistakes, and they were many, he had to bear the full consequence.

"I think those are Mr. Albert Brewer's figures," Yeasley, the head bookkeeper, would say firmly, to Bertie's shame and Stephen's annoyance. "You left that message with Bertie," old Crane would state, more familiarly; "in the twenty-one years I've been here, I never let an order slip like that, yet!"

Bertie had times of feeling himself a martyr on the wheel of family ambition, tied in the rotten old office, with everyone acting so rottenly toward him, and with nothing but rotten old ledgers to work on. There were other times when the routine of life carried him along, comfortable and unprotesting, like a tide, and not infrequent intervals when theatres, plans with his friends, Sunday yachting trips and picnics with the enchanting Kitty blotted all unpleasantness from his mind and made him feel existence a pleasant hurry of enjoyment. Bertie knew himself quite captivating in his white duck trousers and straw hat, and with Kitty's uncritical crowd he passed for a flirt and a wit.

The contrast between Bertie's progress and that of his Uncle Robert, was a source of deep irritation to Stephen, and in lesser degree to Bertie himself. Robert Crabtree had returned to the firm with a glamour of eastern experience about him, and yet with a familiarity with San Francisco and western conditions that only a native son could possess. His breezy manner, friendly, eager, quick with praise and laughter, was delightfully welcome to the stale atmosphere of the old spice house. He remembered names, faces, characteristics, he met customers at trains or boats, lunched with them, sent flowers to their wives.

Stephen's attitude toward "the trade" had always been quite consciously superior; Crabtree and Company were the benefactors always, the great community convenience and blessing. The young markets of the state, tomato and corn canning, prune drying, jam and chutney making, would have been in a pretty fix, Stephen used to say, without Crabtree and Company! The bulky ingredients of the popular Painter's Catsup were no more important than the cloves and ginger and pepper that were measured into it, and where was there any other firm, from Seattle to Los Angeles, that could show forty years of experience in gathering together capers and carraway seed, peppercorns and bayleaves, for the convenience of Painter and Painter?

In the tea and coffee lines there were many rivals, yet conservative old firms in San Jose and Sacramento always dealt with Crabtree and Company, and there seemed to be no reason why the mail-order end of the business should not naturally expand with the rapidly expanding state.

"How long since you've been up over that Marysville and Napa region, Steve?" Rob said, one June morning, when he had been eighteen months with the business.

"How do you mean?" Stephen said, always uneasy under his brother-in-law's casual suggestions. Old Reuben was present this morning, half asleep in his revolving chair, but adding to Stephen's sensitiveness.

"I mean—who travels round, up there? To let 'em know that the firm's alive?"

Stephen smiled patiently.

"They know the firm's alive, Bob, never worry about that! I don't know half of them—never did———"

"I went up there myself, twelve years ago!" the old man piped unexpectedly. "Seen a lot of them fellers—went into their stores and set with 'em!"

His son-in-law glanced at him indulgently, but Bob nodded with approval.

"That's just what I mean, Steve! There's an awful lot in knowing those old birds—firms change, you know, and their line changes! The personal touch is damned important—if you ask me——"

"I *suppose* I asked you!" Stephen said good-naturedly.

"Well, you didn't, as a matter of fact. But that's the way to hold business, Steve!"

A clerk came in and presented Stephen with a telegram. He read it aloud before pigeonholing it in his desk.

"'Please double order of May ninth. Shipment arrived, everything satisfactory.'"

It was signed by the largest grocery firm in Los Angeles. Stephen glanced humorously at his father-in-law, straightened his amused mouth, and turned deferentially to Robert.

"Well, come on, Rob!" he said, in high feather; "tell me how to do more business, eh?"

"If you had a man," Rob persisted, a trifle daunted, but by no means silenced, "some fellow cruising about up there, say once a year, getting into personal touch, 'Hello, Mr. Brown, how's the baby?' 'Good-morning, Judge White, did you sell your trotter?'—that sort of thing!—you'd find it was a mighty good thing for the firm."

"Yes? Well, I have something else to do this morning than ask questions about grocers' babies in Oroville," Stephen said, unruffled. "It'd cost me—us—two or three hundred dollars, perhaps more, a month, and I don't see it coming back, myself! It'd be a mighty nice vacation, for somebody, but it's been a good many years since I had a vacation, and I think it'll be a good many more before I see the need of that sort of thing!"

Robert shrugged his shoulders and turned back to the third desk that had been put into the President's office. Stephen presently was called away, and then the old father and son were alone together.

"Steve's wrong," said the old man then, with a chuckle; "them little grocers don't stay little, forever. I used to know 'em all, myself. He's kinder high and mighty, Steve is."

"He ought to get out a little illustrated catalogue, at least," Rob said, frowning. "But he says he won't spend one cent on showing people what cans of cinnamon and packages of tea look like!"

They both laughed.

"He's sort of ruffled over young Houston," Robert confided.

"What's he been doing?" the President asked, with a spasmodic semblance of wideawakeness. "Wasn't there talk of raising him, last month?"

"He's going over to Finch—it's too bad, of course; he's a nice young fellow. But they've made him some sort of a proposition, and Steve got a little bit hot about it, and the upshot was that Houston got mad and he won't listen to anything, now! I told Stephen some weeks ago that I thought he was worth more—he's been getting one hundred and fifty a month. Bertie gets that now. I think it's a pity to let him go, myself. We need his kind!"

"Well—well—well—well!" the old man said, cackling; "Stephen is a remarkable man—in his way, Bob, in his way! Might make him that Marysville proposition again, some time, and suggest that he send Bertie! Ye might get another answer then!"

"Woolcock's the man to go!" Rob said quickly. "Bertie couldn't do anything!"

"*You're* the man to go, do a lot of talking and drinking, get 'em all interested," his father said. "But you won't get much chance! Well"— his tone reached its favourite level of genial reminiscence—"I made my own mistakes, Bob!" he said.

"Sure!" Bob said roundly, "everyone does!"

"But there's mistakes you find out about, and then there's the kind you never see, Robbit," said old Reuben, "and you ain't going to learn much from things you haven't got sense to see!"

Stephen returned abruptly, and saw that they had been talking about him. He settled to his work with a look of patient and kindly endurance.

A few weeks later Bertie went off for his three weeks' tour of the northern country towns, a real journey, to Bertie, and the cause of almost unbearable excitement and anxiety to his family. Victoria burned with ignoble jealousies, as the bag was packed, and the socks and handkerchiefs and clean shirts carefully counted and calculated. His salary was to go on, and he was to keep a careful account of his expenses—nothing to do but drink deep of life's delirious joy, in strange hotels, trains, new places!

The girl suddenly assumed a passionate affection for Bertie, grew sober when the last night before his departure came, kissed him good-bye even after his mother, with flashing tears in her dark eyes, and mourned and was restless until his first thrilling note arrived. It gave her tremendous pleasure to hear her father tell her mother, in an undertone, that this was dear little Vick's second taste of the sorrow of life—that da Sã affair had naturally saddened the girl—like any kind, sweet girl—and that he admired the child for her courage.

Then she went to see Ada Rehan, with Aunt Fanny, and wrote Miss Rehan a note, and had a signed picture of the great actress in return, so that midsummer was made thrilling, and Victoria had moments of feeling that she truly lived.

CHAPTER XII

IT WAS while Bertie was away that an important event occurred, to the great satisfaction of all concerned. Old Reuben not only altered his will but consulted his sons and daughters and son-in-law duly as to the disposition of his effects.

He had drowsily announced his intention of taking this step, to Fanny, who lost no time in quietly summoning the clan. They must come over, as it were, to a Sunday lunch; then Pa must have his nap, until about five o'clock. Then would come his brightest time when, rested and refreshed, with all the excitement of greetings well over, he could be delicately guided into the family talk for which they were all so anxious.

To be sure, Fanny, May, and Stephen felt that the boldness of this step might disguise dangers. Of poor Harry and Lucy, down at heels and meek, they indeed had no fear: Reuben disliked Lucy; but Bob was never to be calculated upon. Yet the sisters, and eventually Stephen, after much talk, decided that it would be infinitely better to face Bob's claims, whatever they were, openly, and perhaps by rational and friendly comment to bring Pa to his senses regarding them, than to have the usurper undermining their prospects without ever an opportunity to retaliate.

So they gathered at Fanny's on a dusty, blowy September Sunday, and Maggie strained and hurried without one instant's rest, from seven o'clock to two, that all might be fittingly prepared for them. May and Stephen came from San Rafael at about one o'clock, Lucy and Harry transferred from the Mission on the Polk Street car, Robert and Fanny were already on the scene. Lucy wore her hot old velvet, with yellowed, filmy lace about her strong, wrinkled throat; Fanny rustled in a new striped gray and black silk; May was matronly in gray figured sateen, with a black braided and corded wrap that hung down in front in elegant tabs.

Lunch successfully concluded, Carra engineered her old charge upstairs, and Fanny, tiptoeing down some fifteen minutes later, announced triumphantly that he was asleep.

They sat in the double parlours, whose white shades, with deep edges of ecru embroidery, had been drawn down against the afternoon glare. The wind was whistling and whining, and the fuchsias outside the window shook violently from time to time. Brown and yellow cable cars, with open seats front and back, jangled and throbbed by in the heat; there was a strange, unnatural silence out-of-doors, as if the city were dazed or stupefied, and the Crabtree family, heavy with rich food, uncomfortable in best clothes, felt dazed and stupefied, too.

Harry, nervous, shabby, eager for friendliness, engaged Rob in some discussion regarding Chinatown and the Chinese, leaving Stephen free to sink into light slumber in his father-in-law's old leather chair. The ladies occupied the front room; sewing was not for Sundays and their hands were idle. Fanny and Lucy sat on the horsehair sofa, Lucy with a red plush album of family photographs in her lap. May had the fringed patent rocker and rocked gently, her fingers clasped, her famous gold and jet hair bracelet showing upon a freckled, dry, stout arm.

"How are all the girls, May?" Lucy said.

"Sweet and lovely. Living for their brother's letters just now, of course. We've all been surprised at the way Vicky missed him—they've always been so devoted! But of course his Mama feels that she misses him most!" May smiled and sighed.

"Little——" Lucy lowered her voice. "How is little— what do you call him—Bobo?" she said. May quickly and gravely shook her head.

"The doctor says that I simply must not set my heart on his getting well," she said, "but I say that I would rather have him go now, than live to be crippled or to suffer!"

The ladies nodded.

"He's a pathetic little soul," May said; "Vick is devoted to him!"

"What I felt about to-day was," Fanny said, after an aimless silence and in a low tone, "that Pa would feel so much more— that's Mama's cousin, standing beside the swing, and that's her husband's sister, that died—I felt that Pa himself would feel so much happier, when this business matter was settled. Laws!" said Fanny brightly, "as far as I'm concerned, he could do—as he will do, anything he pleases! But I know— and I was telling him so—isn't that ridiculous, Lucy, that's May just before she was married—I said, 'Pa, if it would make you feel more comfortable just to have a talk about it, by all means do!'"

"He may not get round to business, after all," May said.

"Oh, I think he's asked Saunders to come in!" Fanny answered quickly.

This was important, and made them all look serious. Saunders was the old family lawyer, and the mere mention of his name gave the family meeting a real legal significance.

"Darling Pa!" May said, and sighed again with repletion, heat, and some genuine emotion.

Lucy reported Alice and Georgie as having a wonderful time in the country with Rudy and Nelly. Nelly's baby was surely the most exquisite little child that had ever been born, and this year Nelly had a hired girl and much more health and leisure. Alice was to enter the hospital, for training, early in September.

"And then we move," said Lucy bravely. Upon tactful questioning she admitted that she did not know where, exactly. "It's only Harry and Georgie and myself, now, and surely we can find some nice little place!" she said.

"Those flats that Ella was in were very attractive," Fanny said, thinking, with a hard hand clasping her hard jaw.

"I've no doubt, at forty-five dollars a month!" Lucy answered lightly.

"My dear Lucy, you have to pay big rents now!" Fanny answered, nettled at the slightest hint of opposition.

"My dear Fanny, nothing would be pleasanter, if I *could*. But there isn't much that you can tell me about rents!"

"Gracious—that's more than we used to pay for that immense house on Powell Street, where I was married!" May mused.

"You're going to have something of a surprise when you begin house hunting, Lucy," Fanny said, with her sharp little triumphant laugh. "*I* don't know where you can go, upon my word——"

Lucy was usually a resolutely serene woman under petty

irritations of all sorts. But to-day, and for weeks before to-day, she had been worried and burdened beyond her strength. Money, in all her hard life, had never been so scarce. She had come actually to hate the dingy quarters and half dollars that went so fast, and that were so hard to gain. Little persistent bills, just the thirty cents to the butcher, the five cents for bread, the milkman's wretched little memorandum of eighty cents, and two dollars for bill rendered, were eating out her soul. Poor Harry, quietly slipping in and out, always with the same story of effort and failure, sickened her spirit. She hated to have her lovely Alice committed to drudgery in a nurse's uniform, she was uneasy about Nelly, Rudy was—or had been—an unstable support. He had—once, at all events—frightened Nelly by returning to the ranch, one winter evening, hopelessly drunk. Nelly had written her mother anxiously about it, explaining that she knew men did that occasionally, and she had always known that Rudy liked it now and then, but was there anything a wife could do? That had been in January, and Lucy had heard nothing more of that sort of thing since, Nelly's springtime letters breathing only happiness, lilac-blooms, and the baby's beauty and goodness. Still, it was always there, in the background of Lucy's thoughts, and she had confided guardedly in Alice, and had asked Alice to bring her a report.

To-day, to see Fanny so crisp in new silk, so self-confident and smug, with Maggie and Carra to keep her comfortable, her old father further to protect her, and above all, Aunt Jenny Crabtree's legacy to make all life sure and serene, was almost too much for Lucy's equanimity.

"Fortunately I don't have to depend upon your decision, Fanny," she countered, sharply, "rich people have their own ideas about these things, but poor people can't waste much time on such pleasant theories!"

Fanny was furious, under a quick flush and smile. She beat the tip of her nose.

"Indeed, I'm glad to know that I'm *rich*," she said trembling. "But—I'm sorry to say that I don't think you'll find much *theory* in it."

"Well," Lucy said, almost humming, as she turned a page carelessly, "we shall see!"

"Luckily I am not entirely a theorist—poor me! when it

comes to new suits of clothes!" Fanny said, with a sort of shaking self-control, after a pause. "There's no theory about my putting my hand in my pocket and paying seven dollars for Georgie's school suit—oh, no! There's no talk of theories *then!*"

"Georgie's suit," Lucy said firmly, after a terrible pause, and still looking blindly at the old photographs, "I will send back to you *to-night*. That'll end *that*. If he has to go to school in——"

"Ah, girls—girls!" May intervened nervously. "Fanny didn't mean that, did you, Fanny? You mustn't take her up so, Lucy——"

"Perhaps I meant that I didn't intend to be insulted in my own house!" Fanny said, her breast heaving.

"Insulted! Why, Fanny dear, Lucy never dreamed——!" May said in a panic. "And here we all are having such a lovely family Sunday, all together! I'm sure it was lovely of you to give Georgie the little suit, and I know Lucy's been having a rather upset time——"

"My God, I'd give the child every stitch he ever put on!" Fanny said, violently, snatching out her handkerchief to wipe the moistened tip of her nose. "But to have it thrown up at me——"

"I threw nothing up at any one," Lucy said, with steely calm, looking up for the first time and meeting Fanny's glance firmly. "If you chose to make your brother's son a present, it seems to me you have a right. Perhaps I'm wrong. Perhaps I ought to say, 'No, Fanny, don't give it to him! No. Georgie, give it back!' Well, if I am, I'm sorry," Lucy continued, in a stern, proud voice. "I'm sorry! I'm sorry I didn't turn him against his aunt, and say, 'No, Georgie. Papa is having a hard time, Mama is worrying and working early and late!——'" Lucy's voice broke, but she controlled it and went on with the imaginary address to George. "'But you must refuse Aunt Fanny's gift, dear. You love her—you always like to go visit her——'"

"I thank God he does love me!" sobbed Fanny, deeply moved, and suddenly pressing her red fingers and her white handkerchief against her face. "I know he loves me! And I would stuff the new suit in the fire—burn it up—a thousand new suits——!"

The object of these heroic measures was not perhaps clear, but Fanny's breakdown preceded that of Lucy by only a few seconds, and May's faded eyes watered as she patted first one of her companions and then the other comfortingly on the shoulder. Presently they were all laughing shakily, noses and eyes were dried, handkerchiefs put away, and peace—and more than peace, returned.

"Lucy, I was wrong," Fanny said, in the luxury of self-abasement; "I'm hot-tempered, I know it!"

"My gracious, Fanny," Lucy returned, with equal generosity, "I realize that I'm as nervous as a witch, these days! It's a beautiful little suit——"

"Well, it wasn't much. But then, you know—for school——"

"Who's this, May? Is that Louisianna?"

"Oh, no—no!" May bent over the picture of a plump infant holding a hoople and stick. "No, that's Esme," she said, sentimentally interested at once, "wasn't she the dear little fatty? Look at the bare shoulders, Lucy, and the dear little scalloped dress. I remember that dress—Ma made it! It was a sort of browny-gray, with braid—black braid and pearl buttons. I used to wet her hair and make those little curls on a stick——!"

It was almost four o'clock when the old man tottered downstairs again. His family received him with fluttered attention, everyone getting up and moving about eagerly until he was settled. May kissed the dry, warm old forehead.

"Lovely to see you looking so *well*, Pa!" she said, enthusiastically.

"Yes, I'm well—I'm well, May!" Reuben Crabtree said, in his high cackle, as he sank into a chair and she settled herself at once beside him, "but I don't get much sleep!" he added, pathetically and anxiously, his eyes upon her.

"You don't sleep well!" May said, in a tone rich with pity and concern.

"I—wake!" Reuben added, piteously. Tears came into his eyes, and he patted her hand, gulping and shaking his head. "Gettin' to be old!" he faltered.

"We all must do that," May was beginning tenderly, when her brother interrupted her.

"You are not!" Rob interposed, with his easy confidence.

"Tell that to Joe Potter the next time he wants you to sell your Filmore Street lot!"

Old Reuben's face brightened and he chuckled, washed his bloodless old hands, and laughed heartily.

"He'll never git that fifty vara lot for fourteen hundred!" he announced triumphantly, bringing his jaw up with a convulsive snap.

"He knows it!" Rob said, sitting down on his father's other side and giving him a respectful yet comradely glance. "Why, that fellow just thought he could fool you——" May, who had been quite ready to melt into daughterly tears, looked a trifle foolish, and, swallowing hard, tossed her head in scorn for Robert's ubiquity. Fanny, sniffing sharply, seated herself with some stiff silken rustling, and Harry placed himself next to his wife on the sofa. Stephen supplied, as it were, the keystone of the half-circle, and there was a moment of expectant silence.

"Now, if you don't feel like talking, Pa dear, just you don't!" May said, all warm reassurance. "We don't want you to feel——"

"May." Stephen merely pronounced her name. May was silent.

"As I understand it," Stephen said, after a moment's pause, "we were going to have a little talk to-day about business— what your plans are for the business," he glanced at old Reuben, "and what we can all do to relieve your mind about the disposition of—well, what is it?" Stephen interrupted himself smilingly. "Property—bonds—I don't know! All I know about is the firm!"

"I want to satisfy ye all!" Reuben said, in tears, to May.

"Papa dear—as if you didn't—always!"

"I'm seventy-seven, Nelly!" said Reuben to Lucy. He often confused her name with that of her daughter.

"Well, I hope you'll live to be ninety-seven!" Lucy said, hearteningly.

"Now, about the business," Rob said. "Suppose we settle that, Pa, and then you'll feel happier. The stock of Crabtree and Company—and by the way, Fenderson and Yeasley have some stock, haven't they?"

"And Crane, too, Robbit, and of course Fan here has what her aunt put in years ago," the old man said, suddenly alert.

"Well, that makes——"

"Six stockholders," Stephen said. "You and Harry sold out," he added addressing his brother-in-law.

"I want May and Fanny to have the business, Rob," old Reuben said pleadingly. May's heart gave a great plunge of joy, and she smiled gratefully upon her father. Stephen controlled the muscles of his face, and looked gravely interested; he could only suppose this to be a painful surprise to Rob, but the oldest son gave no sign. Fanny wiped her nose with a sniff. "Yes, yes, I'll leave my girls p'vided for," Reuben pursued sentimentally. "And you'll watch their interests, Steve. You'll be president then, and it'll be your responsibility, unless Robbit decides to join you."

"That would be entirely for Rob to decide," Stephen said offhandedly and generously. He could afford to grant Rob this shadowy satisfaction in the overwhelming gratification of the moment.

"Don't speculate with your aunt's money, Fanny!" said her father, suddenly.

"Oh, for pity's sake!" Fanny said, with an intelligent laugh and a toss of her head.

"I've left ye the Santa Clara piece, Harry," the old man said. "It's rented for another three years, but it never paid me! Maybe you and your wife can git something out of it."

"Oh, thank you, Pa!" Harry said, in genuine surprise and satisfaction. "I—I didn't know you meant to do that! I knew I'd gotten my share years ago! I thought that old place was sold!"

"I sold it, but he didn't make his payments, and I got it back again," Reuben said, chuckling. Lucy's fine eyes gleamed with satisfaction.

"That would always be a home for us," she said thankfully. But Harry shook his head.

"I don't think there's a house on it," he said, "I think the house burned down. There's a barn, and sheds—it's an awfully bare, hot piece of country, you know, as flat as a table."

"There'll be enough cash beside to build ye a house," Reuben said. "Had to leave your boy something, Harry! Well— did ye make notes of all this Rob?" he said, turning to his son. "I think that's all! Oh, yes, I said somethin' about leavin' the San Rafael house to little Rube, May."

"To Bobo!" May said, still so wrapped in the enchanting knowledge that Robert's machinations were not to gain him a place in the firm, after all, that every other consideration was secondary.

"Well, we might have to live in the city anyway," Stephen said, in a quick aside, "but I'm sure the little fellow will always have a place in our home, and may it be a long time"— he turned smilingly to his father-in-law—"before he inherits his!"

"Ah, we all feel that!" said May.

"And we believe that!" Fanny added, lovingly.

"I don't want you to do Pa the injustice to think that he has cut me off," Robert said, quietly, over the pencilled notes he was studying. "He is giving me the Filmore Street property, and the bonds he has in the safe, and there are a certain number of bonds to be divided among the grandchildren."

"Just what are those bonds?" Stephen asked in a low tone, as the women began an affectionate exchange of thanks and congratulations about the old man. He had burned for many years to ask the question.

"I don't know!" Robert answered, with a glance up from his memoranda. "He merely—he spoke to me about this a week ago—you know!—he merely said that he would rather arrange it that way, since you were accustomed to the responsibility——"

"Well, that's true enough!" Stephen said, wondering what Rob really felt. He was divided between two natural fears: that Rob was receiving so little that he would some day dispute the will, and that Rob was receiving an undue proportion of the old man's estate. "Your father's been tucking them away for years, now," he said, speculatively. "But that San Rafael property is worth a good deal, Bob," he added, as his brother-in-law, looking pleasantly interested, said nothing, "even if you outlive the baby—which there's no reason to feel, but if you should! You'll inherit from your son."

"No, Pa made a note of that!" Rob said quickly. "That reverts to May, unless little Reuben reaches his majority. She's his trustee."

"My girls are very fond of him," Stephen said, with one more gnawing fear laid to rest.

"He's a nice little monkey," said Bobo's father, with a sigh. "I ran over to see him yesterday. But he's poorly, Steve. By George, I could put my thumb and first finger right round his little arm—I did it! I suppose he's all right, but I wish to the Lord he'd fatten a little!"

"He may," Stephen said, judicially. Fatherhood to him had come as a natural dignity, like his beard and his vice-presidency. He thought now for the first time that it would go hard with any man to lose his only child, and a faint pity for Bob stirred him—Bob who had no wife, no home, no real hold upon Crabtree and Company, and perhaps no son.

The conversation immediately became general, almost jocose. Everyone was pleased with the open frankness with which the vexed speculations of years had been settled. Fanny, who had mentally inherited the Filmore Street property, sandy lots in an almost uninhabited region, and who had mentally dipped into her precious capital for taxes and street improvements thereon, breathed the freer for knowing that her legacy was safe in the sacred fastnesses of the firm, and would take the form of just one comfortable dividend to deposit after another. She said to herself that she would be perfectly satisfied when her capital reached a certain even sum. It was now just a little short of this sum: she saw herself evening it. If there should be six thousand more, say—well, this house she was in was valued at eight thousand seven hundred and fifty dollars and Fanny wanted to buy it. Under cover of the droning family conversation in the stuffy parlours, Fanny had time to move her mental limit; the certain sum, and ten thousand over—she would never wish for more. The extra money was for papering, painting, a gas-stove, a handsome iron fence instead of the fat low wooden railings in front of the house, and a hundred dollars— or fifty at least, for the Ladies' Guild.

May, to whom Stephen found immediate opportunity to whisper the fact of her trusteeship and the reversion of the home property, shared her husband's gratification. Dear little Bobo —she hoped he would live to turn them all out some day, twenty years from now! It was of course the most fortunate thing in the world that he was actually with her, and that it would be natural for his father to leave him there. She had long felt herself the real owner of the country home, but it was pleasant to experience the first true thrill of possession. May, murmuring banalities, as the sun, dropping in the west, sent blazing rays against the windows and the crying and talking of the hot summer wind died away, had all the satisfaction due to the most important female figure in this important group, wife of the president presumptive of Crabtree and Company, and probable mistress forever of the beloved gardens and porches, the big high-ceiled rooms and the odorous dark halls of the San Rafael home.

As for Harry and Lucy, their position was truly too desperate to be affected by what might happen at Pa's death. What they needed was money now, for dinner to-night, for rent on the first of the month. They had been unfortunate, they had invested unwisely. "Hetty Green might do that," Lucy said. Some books, perhaps, some silver spoons to be divided between Georgie and Alice, and some of Ma's old yellowed linen, if any of it survived Fanny's dynasty—that was all that might naturally fall to the youngest son. Lucy, always imaginative, had indeed deluded herself for some years with the fond hope that Georgie, the only male Crabtree, might be specially remembered by his old grandfather. But now there was Bobo, who had stepped neatly into the place of the oldest son's oldest son, and who had the name, too, Reuben Elliot Crabtree. Lucy had often wondered of late why she had not given Georgie this name, and called him "Elliot." Elliot was a beautiful name. But somehow, when Georgie was born, she had been able to remember only an attractive Englishwoman on the steamer, whose appeals to her handsome blond son as "Georgie love" had impressed Lucy as most admirable. Anyway, reflected Lucy, all this fashion of family names and juniors had not reached California fourteen years ago, when Georgie was a baby. Ella had really introduced it to the family, and with it other aristocratic notions—of silver, and portraits, and china. Ella had seemed to unite these pioneer Crabtrees with other Crabtrees, judges and congressmen and writers, genealogy had mattered vitally to Ella, and she had made it seem important to them all.

To both herself and Harry, listening apathetically, heavy with the first full meal they had had for a long time, it was therefore sufficiently satisfying to know that the Santa Clara lot, and the vague "cash—something to build ye a house—something for Harry's boy" besides, were to come to them. To be sure, Santa Clara was a hot, remote region, in those days, given over to fruit growers and baked, six months a year, by merciless heat.

But it was something more than beggary—something more than starvation, and beggary and starvation had looked Lucy and Harry steadily in the eyes for weeks and weeks now. Pa was only seventy-seven, after all, he might live for a long time, but he could not live forever, and there was this certainty of something—*something* when he died. Lucy was comfortably drowsy with food and heat and idleness, her skin felt tight and hot; she was overcome with repressed yawns and sleepy blinking. She imagined herself borrowing the fare to Santa Clara from Fanny, packing for the move, finding a surprisingly decent house on the place, with a few great trees over it, settling down to thrift, production, prosperity. Her ever-active thoughts had taken a new turn, and she was refreshed by it.

What Rob thought nobody knew—nobody ever did know. They all might feel grateful to him for engineering this most satisfactory consultation, yet it was not natural to suppose Rob totally disinterested. He was taking the attitude now that this settlement of the family affairs was a mere casual detail in his enormous schemes—ease up Pa by all means, let the old man talk it over—it wasn't much of an inheritance, but it was just as well to have it straight!

Rob presently met the family solicitor, Saunders, at the front door, and carried him off to the dining room. Stephen, who had satisfied himself long ago that Saunders would protect the Brewers' interest, now said to May that they must go, and with many kisses and fond warnings they were gone, to catch the boat at quarter past five.

"It does seem to me to be so wonderful, dear," May said, in great felicity, on the boat, "I can't help believe but what it's my determination not to have differences among us all—I *can't* help believe that that has a great deal to do with it! Fanny is a dear, of course, but she's a always been odd, and Rob and Harry don't count. But I have"— May's tone became pathetic—"I *have* tried to be a good daughter and wife and sister," she continued, "raising my little family, praying for us all, gathering them together whenever I *could*—of course I don't mean now, for Pa's not really well enough to cross the bay now—but I *have* tried to fill my place—unworthily, I know, but yet, to have Pa show me, and show you, such confidence—you see you'll have Fanny's share, too, to manage—it makes—" her eyes watered—"it makes me feel that the sacrifices and the efforts that are—well, just second nature to me now, are really worth while.   Lucy asked me, years ago—or was it poor Ella?— I forget which—why I was so constantly thinking of other people.   Well, I laughed.   I said it was easier for me than anything else—always has been.   Ma used to say that.   He's gone to sleep," said May, half-aloud, as she glanced affectionately at Stephen, who was indeed in a heavy slumber, and even snoring. She settled her shoulder for his comfort, stared at the glaring light of late afternoon against the Gate, blinked and yawned herself as the little coppery waves dazzled in her eyes.

When he stumbled beside her to the train she came out of a reverie to ask him when he thought Pa would sign that new will.

"Saunders said he'd bring it in Wednesday morning," Stephen said, with a rending yawn that was like a silent shriek.

"I was thinking—wouldn't it be awful, Steve, if Pa should die to-night.   At his age—what with the effort and excitement and all——"

Stephen looked out at Saucelito, lovely terraced garden above garden, in clear shadow, and yawned again.   He was immediately asleep again, but May worried all the way home.

They walked through quiet autumn roads to the old gate, May vaguely satisfied as she raised her long skirts from the touch of dusty thistles and self-sown masses of marguerites beside the path.   It would be good to get back to the dear girls, good to get into loose old corsets and a scalloped calico sacque that she visualized as clean and stiff, in her middle bureau drawer.

"I suppose we'll have to offer Yeasley the vice-presidency," Stephen reflected aloud.   "But Crane's my own choice!"

May glanced at him alertly, answered with quiet readiness.

"Crane's been in the business longer than Yeasley, Steve, if he is younger!"

"By George, that's so," her husband responded slowly, struck.

"Oh, I'm positive of that!" May said eagerly.   "Why, I remember Hutton Crane coming to see us on Powell Street!"

"Sometimes," Stephen said, in deep relief, "you have a mind like a man's, my dear!" and this remark caused May almost unbearable happiness.   They had reached the gate now, and saw all the girls on the lawn, with Vernon Yelland laughing among them, flushed and heated in his heavy clerical black, and Bob's poor little baby staggering about in the new dress Esme had made him, of brown holland with diagonal line of big buttons fastening it from his little left shoulder to his pipe-stem of a little right knee.

Stephen and May had only time to decide that the girls must know nothing of this day's events. It might be well to tell Bertie, but was wiser not to upset the girls.

Fanny, buoyantly satisfied as to the outcome of Pa's talk with the family, and seeing herself as only increasingly rich and comfortable down the vista of the years, now found herself more and more seriously concerned for his spiritual state. As soon as— as soon as "anything happened," her path was clear. Simple but handsome mourning, an affectionate farewell to Carra, with perhaps some coloured gowns and a gold-piece as parting gifts to the old mulatto, the immediate purchase of the house, and a long, serious talk with Maggie, were among the first gratifying details she foresaw. Then some day she would go down to Crabtree and Company's office, inspect it floor by floor, and gain from Stephen a thorough knowledge of exactly what her own interest there was.

These things settled, there was no stumbling block in the way of well-dressed, independent, comfortable years, ruling Maggie, planning little treats for the girls, coming and going in a sheltered environment of admiration and envy. Some day she might take Esme—or Vicky—abroad, both perhaps. No, it would be better to have only one. What a flutter there would be among them when Aunt Fanny's glorious offer was first suggested!

Meanwhile it was shocking to think of her father's utterly godless condition. He never read the Bible, he never prayed, he never went to church. He had done all these things years ago, in Ma's day, as Fanny clearly remembered; perhaps he had done them somewhat lifelessly, but faith, she told herself, had been there. She determined to reawaken it, and for several weeks she read the Evangelists somewhat ostentatiously, and drew the conversation to holy things whenever it was possible.

Rob was a stumbling block; his laughing atheism was horrible to Fanny, and angered as well as shocked her. She could not keep her temper when Rob was in the room, if the question of religion arose.

"Plenty of people think what I think, Fan," he would remind her. "The ministers are in it for what they can get out of it!"

"Get out of it! Do you suppose a man like Phillips Brooks —one of the greatest scholars alive to-day—wouldn't have made much, much more money in the world?"

"Well, I don't know. They have it pretty comfortable, with a lot of women running to them with their secrets! They couldn't hold their own long on the Board of Trade."

"They're looking out for God's people—that's what they're doing! They're saving souls—laying away treasure——"

"Laying away real estate! The church is rich, all the churches are rich, whereas Jesus Christ—not that they care much about His ideas——!"

"Rob, I cannot and will not have you talk so about—religion!" Fanny always became passionate.

"You two can't agree because one of you's a woman and t'other's a man," Reuben might offer, with his old chuckle. "Leave the church to the wimmen, Robbit. The churches wouldn't git far without 'em! Ministers have always hed 'em fooled and always will!"

"Pa, it's wicked for you to talk as if religion was a matter entirely for ladies; you simply encourage Bob to display his ignorance and his—his coarseness! Prayer and salvation are for all—and I'm sure I never go into church without a sense of unworthiness that I—poor, wretched, unworthy me—should be saved!" Fanny's tears were always ready; from Bob's amused witness of them she usually withdrew in helpless fury.

The hour came, however, when old Reuben acquired a heavy cold, and the doctor's opinion was that the end could not now be long delayed. The doctor said that at Mr. Crabtree's age any heavy bronchial cold might run into pneumonia, and Fanny, in her agitated note to May, via Stephen, mentioned pneumonia as a settled fact. Stephen used the new telephone to his house, and May and Bertie started for the California Street house without a moment's delay.

Bertie had been at home with a cold, too, and upon the agitating arrival of the summons, Vicky's heart had leaped with hope. Mama would take her, of course, and she would share the thrilling hours at Grandpa's house, perhaps comfort and sustain them all if darling Grandpa died. But Bertie had most provokingly announced himself as ready to get up, and Mama, remarking tearfully that a man was really much more needed, had tremulously bespoken the support of her dear boy's arm for the trying trip. So the girls could only console themselves with awed speculations and settle down to a dark winter evening of wind and storm with the reflection that life was full of sorrow and change.

It was just after Christmas and bitterly cold. The bay looked bleak and steely, wind rattled at the windows of the boat, and howled across the ferry place. Fanny's nose was wet and cold as she kissed her sister, in the cold hallway. He was asleep, she whispered; he looked terrible! He had been quite well on Tuesday, but on Wednesday morning he hadn't gotten up, and Carra had made him tea. But then he had come down-stairs at about one—that was Wednesday, yes. Fanny had been going to the Guild Hall, but she had put it off, but Pa ate some supper, and even played solitaire—that was Wednesday. But Thursday—this was Friday, yes. Yesterday, then, he had complained of his chest, and she had felt terribly worried then. But Doctor de Zecchi had said it was only a cold, and he had had hot milk and had talked about dear Ma——

Fanny collapsed into tears, and May cried, too. Bertie found this crisis, which would have been so richly and dramatically satisfying to Victoria, profoundly boring. He yawned over *Harper's Magazine*, in the dining room. Later his mother went up to freshen her red eyes and creep into the sickroom, and Bertie spent that night upon the back parlour lounge.

His grandfather was surprisingly better the next day, and on Sunday his mother returned home, leaving her father playing solitaire in bed, Fanny somewhat cross in a natural revulsion of feeling after the strain, and old Carra moving like a shadow across the background of the strangely silent, strangely echoing musty rooms. The fresh cold country air felt delicious to May's jaded forehead, and to find her girls changing wet, muddy gar-ments after a walk, and resolved upon chocolate for supper, seemed soothing and right.

Fanny took this scare for a warning, and during this very evening, when her father asked her to read to him, plunged bravely into Revelation. Old Reuben listened with a thought-ful face, and Fanny's heart beat high as she went from line to line, hearing herself tell May that Pa had softened at last.

"Beautiful—beautiful!" said the sick man suddenly. Fanny looked up with passionate eagerness.

"Isn't it, Pa? Doesn't it just seem written for our times of weakness and need?"

"Your grandmother—your mother—Lulu, I mean," he said, irritated because he could not quite remember the relationships, "always was a great believer in the Word, Fanny."

"Oh, I know it, Pa!" Fanny felt that her heart was gushing a stream of hope and happiness.

"Don't ever let Bob laugh you out of your prayers, Fanny," the cracked old voice said, with emotion. Her father's face was back against the pillows; he now dropped his leaden lids over his eyes, and she saw a difficult tear or two slip down. Terror that this was the moment of passing shook her, and she fell on her knees beside him. "Say your prayers, Fanny!" he sobbed.

"Oh, Pa, I will!" Fanny said, crying heartily, "and you will, too, promise me, Pa! For Ma's sake——!"

"Yes, Fanny, she was always telling me to turn to the Lord!" and old Reuben cried again as he feebly patted her head. "I've done bad things, Fanny," he said anxiously, "but nothing your mother won't forgive me! Ask—ask your Dr. Jerome to come and see a sick old man—a failing, tired old man—to-morrow! Unless ye become as little children——"

He drifted off to sleep with Fanny holding his hand. But when she crept away it was to pin on her bonnet with trembling hands and run out herself to tell her pastor of the miracle. It was Sunday night; as Fanny hurried along Franklin Street women were moving about her through the wintry cold and dark, on their way to church; she smelt the Christmas evergreens as she went in, and heard the Christmas music again, and she told herself that Pa might keep his New Year in heaven.

Reverend Dr. Jerome, a fine, gray, well-built man, was robed for the service, but his sympathy was as ready as if Fanny had come at the most opportune time imaginable. He promised the excited caller that he would be at her house a little after ten, and Fanny dried her tears and fled home again. The doctor had come and gone; Pa had had his milk and was asleep, and Rob was before the back parlour fire. Fanny could triumphantly tell her brother the good news.

Bob took the surprising conversation rather quietly, with the remark that he was glad if it pleased her.

"Please me!" Fanny echoed, beginning to get her breath in the warmth and shelter. "It means his immortal soul—that's what pleases me! It means one more miracle of grace," Fanny stabbed the fire roughly, "and it reconciles me to his going as nothing else could do!" she said, with a wet sniff and a toss of her head.

"Fan," Rob said suddenly, "have you seen the baby lately?"

"Not since Thanksgiving. Why?"

"Oh, I don't know!" Rob tried to assume his usual careless manner. "I went over to-day, and it seemed to me he looked awfully weak and little. He's got a grip in his little fingers; it isn't that. But—I don't know! he kind of grinned at me, but he—Esme says he don't eat very well, never yells for food like a baby should. He just sat in my lap—the girls were all out but Esme, and I'd taken him a monkey, but he didn't like it much." Rob looked down at his book, his eyes brimmed, and he coughed. "I wish I had a God," he said gruffly, "a God that wouldn't take any satisfaction in hurting a baby like that!"

"A—what? I didn't hear you, Bob!" Fanny glanced at him suspiciously.

"Never mind! I suppose lots of children are delicate," he said, recovering his self-control.

"Lots! I remember the baby poor Mary Cutler lost, just kept losing weight and losing weight, we never did know what was the matter with poor little Gerald," Fanny said sympathetically. "I have never felt that Bobo was a well baby, Bob. But we can only hope, and realize that whatever happens it will be for the best. Better—far, far better, to have him go now than to live to suffering and helplessness——" Fanny listened. A bell echoed through the cold house. "There's Dr. Jerome!" she said, with animation. She went out immediately, and Rob heard her take the clergyman upstairs.

When she came down she was ecstatic with hope. Pa had providentially wakened, had welcomed his pastor. Fanny had left them together; everything was as it should be now, she said, taking her chair by the fire. Bob resumed his reading, but Fanny was too much excited to read. She fidgeted, sighed, fluttered and rustled unceasingly for twenty minutes, when the clergyman came downstairs again, his good face bright with a sort of sobered pleasure.

He came in to the fire, but had little to say.

"Impossible to say—impossible to say," he answered Bob's natural question gravely. "Age is weak—very weak. There is every evidence of—of a speedy—ah, trial—for those who love him. Our Heavenly Father alone knows, and He alone can temper the blow. Your father wishes to see me again," he said, turning to Fanny, "and I will be in at about ten o'clock to-morrow morning. He is much happier. I have every reason to believe that your prayers for him will be answered."

Bob insisted upon getting into his overcoat, to accompany the clergyman upon his way. Fanny, knowing Bob's hatred for the cloth, was touched by this evidence of filial feeling. The two men went out into the bitter still night together. The storm had blown itself out yesterday, the dark city lay under a high heaven blazing with cold winter stars, and seemed to ring faintly like an ice-bound dome of metal. Their feet echoed upon the pavements in the silence. Bob saw Christmas trees in draped bay-windows, the branching green touching the frosted glass, the gleam of red and gold amid the little candles, and he thought of his boy.

"I haven't thought of religion for twenty years," Bob said awkwardly but deliberately. The clergyman glanced at him aside.

"The death of an old man is a solemn thing," he said seriously and frankly.

"I am afraid I may lose my little boy; I lost the mother when he was born two years ago!" Bob could almost hear his own voice on the words, but he did not, and could not, utter them. He longed for sympathy, for advice, for something that would help him hold little Bobo here, with his crooked little grin, and his tightly grasping little claws. He wanted to cry out, to be brought into the fold where faith was sure, in either joy or grief. Just to know God was—and God cared——!

"Good-night!" he said heavily, at the door of the clergy-house.

"Good-night. Resign yourself to God's will. Most of us must outlive our parents," the older man said, in his ready pleasant voice. Bob was amazed at the ease with which he spoke of sacred and embarrassing things. He could feel no contempt for Doctor Jerome, as he hurried home in the dark.

Victoria came in the next day and she and Fanny had a satisfy-

ing talk instead.   Victoria was taking lessons in free-hand drawing from the draped model, this winter, in an old studio over
the California Street Market.   She loved the atmosphere of
crayons and chalk dust, the easels and skylights, the stale French
bread they used to erase, and the talk of the young men and girls
about her, who were all chiefly interested, as she was, in persuad-
ing themselves that the atmosphere of Hetheringtons was exactly
that of an *atelier* in the Latin quarter of Paris.   Vicky usually
took her luncheon to the studio and went home at quarter to
two, but to-day her mother had told her to go out and find out
exactly how Grandpa felt.

Fanny was delighted to see her, and after a little talk sent
Maggie down to Stephen for permission to keep the girl overnight.   The winter afternoon had closed in early and gloomy,
rain was slashing down, and California Street ran with streams
of muddy water.   The two women sat talking and brooding over
the fire, Fanny creeping upstairs now and then to see that her
father was still normally asleep.   Victoria did not exactly like
to suggest euchre, but at four o'clock the evening stretched long
before her; she filled her lap with the stereoscope pictures, and
looked at them while she talked, and before dinner she went all
through "The Bell" again, and looked at the cover of the big
Dante, but felt no inclination to open it.

Maggie banged things in the kitchen; Victoria would have
been glad to go out and help her, but she knew Aunt Fanny
would not like that.   The back parlour was warm and close,
rain dripped and dripped on the fuchsia bushes outside the window.   Victoria could smell upholstery, plaster, dust in carpets,
and the bindings of books, all vaguely unified by cold and damp
into one odour.

"The thankfulness!" said Fanny over and over, shaking her
crisp iron-gray braids with a sort of horror at the gulf from
which she had been delivered.   "Now—as I told de Zecchi—
now I am resigned to anything!   If Pa must go, and it is God's
will——   But the *thankfulness!*"

After dinner Victoria went into her grandfather's room for
a few minutes.   It was warm, orderly, lifeless: the medicine
bottles beside the bed, the glass covered with an envelope, the
shades drawn down at streaming window panes.   A green-
shaded gas lamp was glowing subduedly beside the grate, but
the bed was almost in darkness.   Victoria could see the thin

old wrappered shoulders, the bald head and ivory face in the gloom.

She essayed to speak, smiled unnaturally, cleared her throat.

"Hello, Grandpa," she managed, with the second attempt, "how are you?"

It was almost frightening to have the familiar voice issue from this mummy.

"Restin', Vicky. Well and comfortable, dear!"

"That's good!" Victoria said, swallowing with a dry throat and wondering, now that she had clasped his hand, how she could ever let it go.

"You better skip, Miss Vick!" Carra said, behind her, good-naturedly. Victoria gave her grandfather a parting smile, full of affection and encouragement. It was a great relief to her to go.

When she went downstairs again, it was to discover Aunt Fanny with two callers, women in mourning, whose thin kid shoes were modestly extended to the replenished fire. They were sisters, a widow and an unmarried woman, who lived together, renting rooms, and doing plain sewing.

Vicky knew this type, indeed almost all Aunt Fanny's friends were of this sort, and the girl liked them because they made her own life seem so young, so potentially rich and full. Poor little meagre shadows creeping among shadows, filling the back pews of churches, waiting their turn in bakery and butcher shop, debating the purchase of buttons and shoe polish, yet they took existence with a deadly seriousness. A tiny error in a bill, the non-delivery of a pint of milk, the loss of a shabby and almost empty pocketbook, these were their tragedies; they talked of death, sorrow, change, poverty, and illness.

"Indeed, you are blessed, Miss Fanny," said Miss Folsom, sadly. "It's a great grace. I remember my poor mother——"

"I was just going to speak of Ma," Mrs. Noonan said, smilingly shaking her crape-bonneted head.

"Oh, Ma was perfectly wonderful!" Annie Folsom exclaimed.

"Oh, the whole parish knew my mother!" Mrs. Noonan added. The two gray, drab women leaned forward in passionate acclaim of their mother. Ma had been almost a saint, Ma's house had been a regular headquarters for all the beggars and unfortunate of the parish, Father Cutler, who was a bishop now

—certainly, Bishop Cutler—oh, certainly—he knew Ma, depended upon her for everything, and came all the way from Arizona to be at her funeral service.

Fanny said she must have been a lovely woman, and Victoria added that it was wonderful ever to have had such a mother.

"Oh, you're right, darling!" Annie Noonan said, in quick affectionate sympathy for Victoria. Victoria glowed. "My mother was a saint, she prayed every day of her life for her father——"

The story of prayer and miracle went on, Vicky listening intently. Fanny, with her convert father, was the heroine of the moment.

Victoria went home in cold bright windy sunshine the following day, feeling, as usual, braced by the change, yet glad to go back to her own books and bed and place at the family table. Fanny saw her to the Washington Street car, and then went back to carry her mending into her father's room; Carra had been summoned to Oakland for the funeral of a small relative, and Fanny and the invalid were alone.

"There's something I want to consult ye about, Fanny," said old Reuben, out of a doze. "I was speaking to Doctor Jerome about it this morning."

Fanny arrested her needle and looked at him, expectantly smiling.

"I spoke to Jerome about it," Reuben said, musingly. He still had a startling habit of speaking of his clergyman familiarly, but Fanny was too well pleased with him just now to be critical. "He told me to speak to Carra," her father surprised her by adding, "but I thought maybe it'd be better to speak to you first."

"Well, I can hardly imagine that Carra's advice would be extremely valuable!" Fanny said, laughing, beating her nose, with her favourite bridling motion, a little indignant at good Doctor Jerome. "H'm! That seems rather funny!"

The old man was silent, and seemed dozing. Fanny subsided, shook her head, and resumed her sewing. He might be a little light-headed, she thought.

"I want to do what's right," her father said, presently. "I want to do what's right by Carra. She's been a faithful friend to me, Fanny, all these years!"

"Indeed she has, Pa. I was thinking of that—the real old family servant. Why don't you leave her a nice little sum that will make her feel that she can go to this niece in Oakland—furnish a room—live the rest of her life in comfort. If—if anything ever happens to you, I shan't need her—Maggie knows my ways now, and two servants would be ridiculous. Not but what I hope that you will be spared to me for many, many years!"

"How much do you think it ought to be, Fanny?"

"Well—let me see. Her room and board would cost her practically nothing—I suppose ten dollars a month would more than pay her niece, especially as Carra would be a real help with the children! She's quite old, you know—she says she's seventy-two. I should suppose a few hundreds—six hundred—five hundred—? Of course, May might want her—especially with Rob's boy there, that might be the solution," pursued Fanny, with energy. "If Rob paid her—I don't see why that wouldn't be a wonderful place for the dear old woman!"

"I said to your mother, 'Lou, I'll never live without ye!'" the old man said, with sudden tears. "And at the time, I never thought of marrying again. But a man's lonely, Fanny—no girl can understand that. I was lonely! And she's a fine woman, Carra, God-fearing, honest—she's a good woman. There's many a white woman would have felt different to what she did. 'No, sir,' she says, 'I'm not the right woman to be your wife, but I ain't going to be anything else!' Character, there, Fanny! Principle there, mulatto or no mulatto! About seven months after your mother died I took her up to Ukiah—you'll find it there if you look—but she'll never mention it. Not if you put it to her point-blank——"

Fanny sat actually frozen in her seat. The ugly, orderly room swam before her sick eyes. What was he saying—what was she hearing—what were these words that were echoing upon the still, close, heavy winter air? Her throat thickened, her heart seemed to have stopped beating.

Her father lay back, his eyes half-shut, he was lazily smiling.

"I felt different about it a week ago," he said. "But now I want everything to be done right, Fan. In God's sight that coloured woman is as good as any of us—better, perhaps. Yes, sir, Carra is a good woman. She reads her Bible, and she believes in her God. I've never heard an ugly or a mean word out of her——"

He drowsed. Fanny's head whirled. Her father was married to Carra—had been married for all the fifteen years since her mother died! The silent, uncomplaining, tireless old servant had had her unrecognized place in the family all this time!

No use to blame him, to agitate him with criticism and reproof. The fact remained, the humiliating, hideous fact that a gaunt old mulatto was Mrs. Reuben Crabtree——

Fanny felt herself suffocating. She had a murderous impulse toward her father. What *right* had he had to take this disgraceful step! Missing her mother, indeed, her handsome mother who, she and May had long ago decided, very probably had belonged to a branch of the distinguished Potts family of Virginia, and who had always been the model of virtue—and—and dignity—everything——!

He was serenely asleep. Fanny felt her heart bursting, and gathering her sewing, she escaped to her own room, where she wept passionately on her knees beside the bed.

Anger dried her tears. The situation was unbearable and she was infuriated by the realization that there was no escape. She rose, brushed her hair, washed her face, breathing hard all the while.

What would May say? Fanny's first impulse was to get hold of May, and she even got out her bonnet with the idea of crossing the bay. But a second thought prevailed. Rob had been in Stockton last night, but he would be at home to-night, and dine with her; she heard herself telling him the preposterous story.

But perhaps it wasn't true? Fanny snorted at her own weakness. Of course it was true.

She said to herself that she need not tell Bob, at once, anyway. She need not tell May—the fewer people that knew it the better. Dr. Jerome was safe.

If Pa went off quietly in his sleep this afternoon, for instance, and Carra had been taken suddenly ill at her niece's house, then nobody would ever know. Oh, surely silence was her only safety now!

"Mag' say if Mist' Rob goin' be here for his supper," said the mild soft voice of Carra in the doorway. Fanny felt a violent shock through her very vitals. Instant self-defence helped her. Carra did not know that she knew—nobody knew that she knew.

"He said so, Carra!"

"You want me to rip up that silk, Miss Fanny?"

"No. No, I'll do it. Thank you, Carra." Fanny was bathed in perspiration, she had to sit down to rest her trembling knees when Carra went away. All through the evening she found herself choking and absent-minded. Pa—married to Carra! Carra Pa's wife! Carra able to claim something—how much?—as Pa's widow?

Fanny was ready to think of illness, death, as crosses sent as guide-posts to perfection. But this disgusting matter appeared to her in no spiritual light. It was just disgraceful and awful and shameful, and she did not even think of praying about it. Prayer was for totally different "trials" than this, for conversions and happy deaths and temporal prosperity.

She shut it into her heart, but so dreadful was the confusion into which it had thrown her thoughts, that from this time on the thought of Pa's death was eclipsed by terror of what Carra's action would be when he died. Secrecy was the one vital thing, and either one of the old persons might betray the whole matter at any second. What could Carra claim? What would press and people say? How much would smoothly unscrupulous lawyers eat away from the estate before she, Fanny, would be free to enjoy that pleasant dream of an independent and free existence?

CHAPTER XIII

BOB'S baby was not well. The old San Rafael doctor, who had been extremely casual in his first treatment of the case, now spoke of it as baffling, and requested a consultation.

"Organically, the child is sound," said the doctor thoughtfully. "But there may be complications—of nutrition. There apparently is an incipient anæmia."

May, receiving this opinion, looked stricken. She tried to feel stricken as well; she did feel faintly sorry. The death of a small child, even an exacting and not prepossessing small child, was one of the events May classified as "too sad for words." But there were several considerations, and grief was only one of them. If Pa had really left Bobo the house, with a reversionary interest for May, then upon Bobo's death *that* troublesome point would be settled. Pa might not have done so, of course, or Pa might change his mind later, even if he had done so. While Bobo lived, May wanted the possession of him; if Pa died during his infancy then Bob might actually sell the house over their heads, or bring a second wife there——

It was confusing even to think of, and May instinctively hated thought. She went in and out of the baby's nursery telling herself that if it was God's will to take the poor little fellow she would not rebel. Time alone would tell. And meanwhile she honestly did her motherly best for him; anything less would have been quite impossible to her.

The girls shared with her the actual care of Bobo. It had seemed a little shocking to her ideas of protecting them, at first, that they should do so, and even now she would answer a serene "Never mind, dear!" when Lou asked why the baby was getting Dover's powders, or Vicky interrogated intelligently, "What is the peritoneum, Mama?"

"But I don't believe it will do them one bit of harm, Steve," May said more than once, courageously. "There is nothing *wrong* in their caring for a little child. And women are getting so bold, nowadays, and pushing into so many things, that perhaps it's just as well that the girls should know *something*——

"It's quite broken all their hearts, now that they realize it exactly," she told him, after the consultation. "He really doesn't think there's much chance, Steve. Well, we've certainly done all *we* could!"

On the day after the consultation Bob came over, a changed Bob, serious and silent. He went up at once to the big, airy chamber where his son was lying, languid and still, after a restless night. Bobo seemed most contented when in his father's arms, and Bob disposed his big body as best he might, and held the little fellow comfortably against him.

"What is it, old man?" Bob leaned over him, making his deep voice a mere gruff whisper.

"It's his fish," Lou interpreted, from where she was sitting beside the bed. "He calls that place on the ceiling, where the water-stain is, his fish!"

"Do you see your fish, dear?" Bob asked. Bobo gave him a shadow of his old, twisted grin, and shut his eyes. His dark lashes rested on a colourless cheek.

Vicky came in, looking anxious. She carried a cup holding the warm gruel, cream, and whey that was his food. Bobo refused the spoon fretfully, turning away his little silken head.

"He won't take it!" she said distressedly.

"Did you try the soup?" May, standing at the foot of the bed, whispered sympathetically.

The warm afternoon wore on, waned to sunset. Bob had a cup of tea; he sat on through the long hours, sometimes in the rocker, sometimes kneeling beside the motionless little form, always with his gaze fixed upon Bobo's face.

The child had a moment of strangling; they were all about him, propping, lifting, agonizing with him. When they laid him back on the pillows, breathing easily once more, Bob's hands were wet, and he saw the glisten of water on Lou's forehead.

They tried the warm food again; no use. Bobo would not even open his eyes.

The doctor came in at six; lack of vitality, he repeated. The child needed vitality. May, Esme, Stephen, looked gravely at Bob and Bobo, from behind him.

Then it was night, and a lamp made the warm room warmer.

Twilight lingered among the overgrown roses and pampas bushes of the garden, the air was sweet with the first dews. Tina and her parson were talking down in the currant bushes; Bob, standing at the window, saw the old wooden horse's head looking down over the stable door, and a pile of new planks beyond, where someone was putting a cottage in what had once been the pasture. An enormous moon floated up over the velvet black of the oaks. There were shadows like black lace under the old grape-arbour.

May sat and murmured with him for a long time; Stephen came in, gravely concerned. He shook his square beard.

"While there's life there's hope, Bob!"

Bob, for some reason angered, talked of the business. Eleven o'clock came, May said she would lie down; Stephen had gone to bed. Tina was to sit and keep Uncle Bob company for awhile.

He knew Bobo was very ill; for when Tina yawned and stumbled to bed, May came back, stupid with sleep at two o'clock, and after that, when it was nearly three, Vicky came in.

She looked rosy and dishevelled; her bright eyes were dark with sympathetic pain. In her hand she carried a cup of the warm food.

"The darling!" she said, kneeling beside the child. He jerked his head away from the spoon. Vicky looked at Bob's stricken face, at her mother's weary one, and sudden impatience possessed her. "Here now, Bobo, you stop being naughty!" she said sharply. The closed eyes opened in amazement; there was in them a certain surprised docility. The pallid little lips moved; there was a faint sucking sound.

"He's taking it!" she whispered, in a voice robbed of everything but amazement.

Bob had sunk upon his knees, his tired eyes were dark with hope.

"Dad's good little boy!" he whispered, trembling violently, one big hand covering Bobo's lifeless little hand; "he is taking it for his father!"

Victoria said no more, she had concentrated her whole being, as never in life before, upon the little face on the pillows and the spoon in her hand. Steadily, blind to everything else, she moved the life-giving fluid to and fro—five times, seven times, ten times.

"I'm afraid to give him any more!" she breathed. Bobo licked his little lips, turned upon his side with a satisfied sigh, slept. Bob broke into tears, hiding his face against the little hand on the bed.

"Ten spoonfuls!" Victoria said, eyes wide with utter astonishment.

Bob remained motionless; he had raised his head and was staring at her, but while the child slept he did not move.

Bobo had more nourishment at five o'clock, at seven he asked for his new bear. By noon the girls and the neighbours were spreading the news that the Crabtree baby was much better; yes, he had had quite a close call. May felt an irritated reaction, deep in her soul. She did not put it into words, perhaps hardly analyzed it, but she felt cross and weary all day. To Victoria's amazement, she recalled similar vigils with all her babies.

The girl walked in an aura of miracle. Death had been in that dark room; life had come back triumphant. She never forgot the slow gray dawn, raising the garden bushes from shadows into toneless shapes, from shapes into green beauty with the light tipping it. A red streak down toward the marsh, pink clouds sailing away like little galleons in a sea of trembling blue, and the windows of the Dufficy's house flashing like diamonds. And Bobo asleep with his bear, the cup empty on the stand beside him!

She gave him his breakfast at nine, and when the restored Bobo looked rebellious she said again sharply: "Now you be a good boy!" and he obeyed. Uncle Bob could leave comfortably for the office at noon; the doctor observed sapiently that he had known it was merely a question of restoring the child's vitality.

Bob put his arms about Vicky, in good-bye.

"I'll not forget what you did, Vick—what you all did. Just try me, by asking me a favour some day!"

"Resign from the firm!" was the daughterly thought that flashed into Vicky's mind. But she did not say it. Her lashes twinkled with tears as she smiled, and May kissed her in great felicity and approval, reflecting that this was an extremely satisfactory way in which to leave the matter. She did not see Bob dispossessing them now! she told Stephen triumphantly.

Tina was making herself a blue dimity gown. She had several delightful events in mind, as she made it, an autumn wedding to which she would wear it, and the lunch party Mama was going to give the sister Mr. Yelland expected soon from Boston. He might ask her to walk up past the convent, too, under the big maple trees, and she would surely wear it then.

Meanwhile it was a joy just to make it. The dimity was striped, dark blue on light blue; it was stiff, dainty, almost transparent, and was trimmed with some twenty yards of narrow cream-coloured lace. The sleeves were puffed fully at the top, each sleeve required four yards of the narrow material, and the skirt was belled and touched the ground all about Tina's new black oxfords. And she had a broad black-straw hat with several yards of mull wrapped around the low crown. Altogether Tina felt that she had never had a more pleasing costume.

Life had been a trifle flat through mid-summer after the gradual clearing of the clouds that hung over Grandpa and dear little Bobo. The latter had recovered lost ground steadily, but he had not stopped there. From deep sleeps and ravenous attention to meals, Bobo had progressed to roundness, rosiness, placidity; he sat in paths now, sifting dust upon faded calico aprons, and when Bob came to see him, he met his father with shouts, requests for more effalunts, and confidences regarding froggies and mousies.

Grandpa, more slowly, had also reached at least his former level of vitality. Presumably dying by inches through February, March, and April, he had turned some obscure corner, by nursing, resting and care, and by July he could reopen his desk in the office again, and make himself thoroughly obnoxious at the stockholders' meeting of Crabtree and Company.

Everyone felt the reaction from strong emotion, presumably even Rob, who so rarely displayed any sensitiveness. May sighed that it almost seemed that it would have been kinder, in some anonymous deity, to "take" dear Pa, rather than let him drag on in suffering and helplessness. Stephen grew grave, and there was more gray in his hair. He began a habitual nagging of Bertie that was infinitely distressing to May. At the tiny Bobo's triumphant rally from the actual chill of death, Stephen had merely remarked good-naturedly:

"We'll be paying you rent, yet, young man! Certainly," he had added, to May's surprised and displeased smile, "cer-

tainly. The minute your father dies we are this child's tenants
—you must realize that?"

Fanny's reaction was the most painful of all. She had
prayed for fifteen years that her father might not be snatched
from life without a complete reconciliation with his God, and
now, in the very instant of triumph, she must be sickened and
frightened by the revelation of his utter insensibility to decency
and propriety. She looked upon his complacent return to
health with impatient contempt. Oh, of course he would get
well, Fanny reflected bitterly. Of course Carra, having eaten
her way into the family like some pestiferous insect, would
fondly nurse and coddle him back to his old routine of milk-
toast and sunny windows, guarded airings and much reading
and solitaire.

He made no further allusion to his preposterous marriage;
Fanny was quite shrewd enough to suspect that he did not feel
quite sure he had ever betrayed himself. Carra wore her usual
mask of quiet attention, service, respect. What Mist' Crabtree
and Miss Fanny wanted was Carra's law, as she puttered to
and fro with trays and brooms, showing Dr. Jerome upstairs,
answering Bob's banter—Bob came in almost every evening—
with respectful yet appreciative laughter.

But her secret knowledge of Carra bit like acid into Fanny's
soul. It was all so humiliating—all such a farce. She herself
would continue Pa's dutiful and attentive daughter, until
such time as he really died, and then Carra would step in, and
claim everything that was Fanny's by right, disgracing and
shaming them all! And Fanny began to think that she would
like to go abroad now, right away. She wanted to see Italy.
The doctor had told her that her father might live five years or
more.

"H'm—a lot they know!" Fanny said, impatiently. "Make
you sick—doctors! Frightening the life out of you for nothing!
I believe Pa'll live to be ninety, myself!"

The Italian plan taking more and more hold upon her, she
went to San Rafael one day, to hint at it, and gratify herself
by witnessing the girls' ecstasies of excitement and interest.
She had thought it all over, and had determined to take Tina,
although she was really fonder of Vicky. But Vicky was too
uncertain, always plunging madly into absurdities, and then
Vicky had her art work. Esme was just a little bit prim and

old-maidy, and Fanny told herself with a jolly toss of her head that she didn't propose to be trammelled in any way on this particular spree.

It was Vicky's day at Hetherington's, this particular September afternoon that she chose to call, but the other girls were at home, grouped with their books and sewing on the lawn. The baby was toddling gravely about, making his white lamb bite various feet and hands in a most unlamblike manner, and causing Lou's cat to pull himself indignantly up, and move from one lazy position to another, over and over again. Lou looked extremely pretty in a faded old blue cotton, her soft hair had just been washed, and she kept pushing it about with impatient hands, and changing the pins. Esme was pale, and said she had had another neuralgic headache, was just getting over it. Tina was radiant, in her rather solid blonde fashion, in the new dimity; it immediately appeared that Mr. Yelland was going to call.

"You don't want me here, then!" Aunt Fanny rustled herself, but it was a mere pretense. She laughed gaily as Tina forcibly pressed her back into her chair.

"Tina may take a little walk with him, and then we'll all have tea here, with Vicky's new brass kettle," May said, serenely. Bits of gossip followed, Nelly had a new baby, a boy, born on the last day of August. She had named him Clifford. Esme said that Nelly had wanted another girl, to name Dorothy, but May, glancing at Lou, indicated with raised eyebrows that this hint of the unborn was not permissible, and Esme flushed and subsided. And poor Lily Duvalette was terribly ill—in the hospital. In the hospital! This meant a desperate situation indeed. Davy Dudley was in his second year of medical college, poor Davy. Bertie had met him, waiting on tables in a horrible cheap restaurant in Market Street. What Bertie himself was doing there she didn't know, May said, with a faint laugh of censure, but Davy had told him that he got his meals for six hours' service a day. Lucky Nelly, Esme said, that she didn't marry *him*.

Well——! Then it was time for Italy, and Fanny got all the gasps and raptures that she had anticipated. She did not mention any companion at first, but when Esme had carried Bobo in for his nap, and May and Lou had followed to make sandwiches for tea, Fanny found herself alone with the blue dimity ruffles, and then she could not quite resist the temptation.

"I know a very pretty girl that'll feel sorry if her old aunt gets lost among the catacombs!" she said, gaily.

"Oh, Aunt Fanny, even that would be fun!" Tina smiled, swiftly feather-stitching a little flannel sacque for the new Sessions baby. Her fair hair, still damp from brushing, her plump busy hands, her flushed, serene cheek all spoke alike the beloved and desired woman.

"Well, then—why don't you go with me?" It was Fanny's great moment; she looked up quizzical, daring, smiling.

"Oh, Aunt Fanny, you're joking!"

"If I am—" the gray head tossed— "the joke's on me, then!"

Tina grew red; but for Tina to-day there was no choice.

"There's only one thing that could keep me from accepting your wonderful, wonderful offer," she said breathlessly, after a a moment, "and that would be—because"— and Tina dimpled and looked down—"because someone—wanted me to stay here!"

This was unexpected, and Fanny's hard cheek grew red in turn. Her great treat, her unheard-of offer, had been quietly declined. Tina had other plans. Fanny's quick passionate temper rose and her laugh had an edge. She batted the end of her nose nervously.

"Indeed! I might have saved myself the trouble of annoying you with my invitation then!" she said, hardly believing her ears.

"Oh, Aunt Fanny——!" Tina was so much startled by the tone that she put her sewing aside, and dropped quickly on her knees on the dry grass, beside her aunt's chair. "Why, it was the loveliest thing—and I've always been dying to go—— But you see—you see—you know how it is, Aunt Fanny——!"

"I see that I'm not wanted, and so I had much better take myself away!" Fanny said, in a bright, hard voice. "Well, I'm surprised and delighted that any girl nowadays can decline to take a wonderful trip to Europe," she said loudly. "Italy, Paris, Venice—oh, just toss it off! 'No, thanks, I'd rather not!' Very well, dear—by all means do exactly as you like——"

"Aunt Fanny——"

"Oh, don't Aunt Fanny me! You may be sure that I won't

trouble you again, my dear! And now," said Fanny, on her feet and shaking her flounces, "I must go for that four o'clock train. I'll just stop and say good-bye to your mother and the girls. And some day, when you can spare the time, perhaps you'll deign to come and see me!"

Tina sat on, mechanically feather-stitching, a little dazed by the unpleasantness of it. Esme would have returned a fire of peppery remarks to Aunt Fanny's fire; Vicky would have rapturously accepted the invitation, even if she had been on the brink of an engagement, even if she had been on the brink of marriage, and trusted the future to settle everything harmoniously. Tina wished now that she had been a trifle more enthusiastic.

"But I can't help it!" she said, uncomfortably. "What could I do?"

And here, punctually, was Vernon Yelland, trim and brushed in his black, taking the chair near her, studying the flannel sacque with a smile, remarking that his mother, also a clergyman's wife, had had to make hundreds of *those*. Tina's heart sang again, and she saw a parsonage garden, and herself in another chair, and diminutive flannels again in her hands.

May and Vicky came out, Vicky just back from town. The time to suggest the walk up by the convent had come. But first Mr. Yelland had something to say.

"I've had another letter from my sister, and she gets here the eighteenth," he said beaming, "and now I want to tell you—my best friends here, a little piece of news. The young lady I am to marry, Miss Grace Fairchild, is coming with my sister, and I believe my old colleague, Harvey Masson, will come down from Sacramento to perform my wedding ceremony, as I did his some months ago."

"Well——!" May said bravely. And no mother sparrow ever drew the marauder's attention more gallantly from her young than did May hold his eyes from Tina now. "Well, what a surprise! So you are to be married!"

"When, Mr. Yelland? You must tell us all about it!" Victoria was a good second. "Miss Fairchild?" she said at random. "Is she a Californian?"

"No, she is a Bostonian, I served my first curacy under her father," Vernon Yelland said happily. "That was five—seven years ago, and I may say that ever since then——" He laughed, a dry little complacent laugh. "However, when I went back to Boston last year, for my vacation, the thing was practically settled, and a few letters arranged it all! Grace—" He took out a pocketbook, and from it a photograph of a virginal, plain young head. "That's Grace," he said simply; "she's very beautiful—one of the most beautiful faces I have ever seen! Yes. I wanted you to know—I told her that she would find a mother and sisters waiting to welcome her, in my dear friends the Brewers. We hope"— he was business-like—"to arrange for a Sunday wedding, possibly the twenty-fifth of September, possibly a week later. That will depend upon Masson's engagements, but I have no doubt he will arrange it. Most fortunately Miss Fairchild and Mrs. Masson were old friends, girl chums, in fact, so that will be very pleasant for Grace."

Victoria began to feel that she could not keep up the strain; Tina was pallid, but smiling fixedly, her sister could see her swallow now and then with blinking eyes and a convulsed throat.

"Well, I almost feel that I want to scold you for not taking us into your confidence before this!" May said, a little tartly.

"Mama——!" Tina articulated, suffocating with shame.

"Indeed, I should have done so!" Mr. Yelland assured them eagerly, "but Grace was unwilling that any one should know. I daresay that a penniless clergyman is not a brilliant match for a Bishop's daughter," he added, merrily, "but I must be duly humble, must I not? And now are we not to have tea? I have been waiting all day for my cup of tea!"

"I will——!" Vicky rose tumultuously. But May spoke quickly.

"You go, Tina, darling!" Tina flashed away in the blue dimity, and presently Lou came out with the tea, looking scared and bewildered, and then Esme with the fresh and dewy Bobo in diagonal buttons, and lastly Tina, pale and quiet but quite equal to the occasion.

When the gate had closed behind the clergyman, and the autumn sunset was streaming across the tumbled tea-things, May, looking timidly at Tina, said:

"Mama was proud of you, darling!"

The other girls looked constrained. Tina said, hurriedly and uncomfortably:

"Oh, that's all right, Mama! He had a perfect right to marry any one he pleases for all *me!*"

"I think he's got a gall," Lou said inelegantly. Tina laughed, became hysterical, and began to cry in Vicky's arms.

"I don't know what's the matter with me!" she choked, trying to laugh again. "Except that I ironed all those curtains this morning—and then they looked so horrid——"

"They looked perfectly lovely," May interpolated.

"And then Aunt Fanny was so disagreeable!" Tina pursued, looking at her handkerchief before she wiped eyes and nose with it. "You were awfully nice, Vick," she said, softly and thickly.

"Who cares what he does—the old stuck-up!" Lou said boldly.

"Lou—he is a clergyman, dear!"

"I know, Mama, but Tina'll have twenty better beaus than *he* is!"

"I hope she's a good manager," May said darkly, "but she doesn't sound so! He only gets nine hundred a year."

"She looks like a person who would recite poetry," Lou, the noncommittal, said scornfully, but Tina did not join in the general laughter.

"You had your fun with him, and now forget him!" Vicky summarized bracingly. This attitude was infinitely helpful to everyone except poor Tina.

"No, Vick, don't ever say she played with him!" May said, earnestly. "I hope my girls wouldn't flirt with any one!"

"No, Mama!" Vick said dutifully. They all had the cue now.

"But I think that a man in his position naturally would not aspire to a rich man's daughter," May went on, "and I think in your innocent sisterly friendliness, dear, you perhaps misled him a little. Mama knew that you were not serious, but perhaps Mr. Yelland did not quite understand!"

"Tina wouldn't have hurt him for the world!" said Esme, loyally.

"No, dear, Mama knows that. And no harm has been done. If he was hurt, as we know, he found consolation with this very plain, but sweet-looking girl—although she looks delicate— his old friend. He may have told her all about my Tina," May said, convinced from this second that it was so, "and while he was not in love with her then—for if he had been there was no reason in the world why he shouldn't have married her years ago—her sympathy was no doubt very pleasant to him, and now it's all settled, and we must try to befriend the poor little thing in her first struggles."

When May told her husband about it that night, she was entirely sure of her ground, and in subsequent recitals, to Fanny and Lucy, the story ran even more smoothly.

"Vernon Yelland told us of his engagement to-day, Steve—he is to marry quite a nice-looking girl, not pretty, but—well, and rather delicate, too, but pleasant-faced. He turned to her, when he couldn't get Tina, and this is the natural rebound. Oh, yes, Tina knows, and I think it's really a great relief to her, although perhaps she feels just a little bit sore now, dear child. She looked perfectly beautiful as she congratulated him. She *couldn't* marry him, Steve, and I can't blame her! He's not really in love now, you can see that, but it may turn out very well. Of course, like any girl, Tina was tempted for a little while, but I think she feels she's acted wisely, and I am glad he has consoled himself. Ministers' wives have such rafts of children, Steve, and while of course we could have helped out——"

And so on and on. But Tina was pale and quiet for a long time afterward, and the name of the fickle clergyman was quietly dropped from general discussion. A week later Tina told her mother something of Fanny's proposal.

"Mama, would there be any reason why I should not go to see Aunt Fanny, and just tell her frankly that I didn't feel like going away, then, but that I do now? I would so like to get away—there's next week, you know——"

Next week Mr. Yelland's promised bride was expected. May understood.

"Well, I think I would, dear. Go see Aunt Fanny. Talk about the wonderful trip she would have—Rob says she's given up the idea, lately, but never mind. Try to do what Vicky would do, Tina. Flatter her a little, nicely, you know."

"Oh, I can't chatter the way Vicky does!"

"I don't mean chatter. But there would be no harm in suggesting that you were so delighted with the idea of going with her that you rather—well, put off Mr. Yelland!"

"Mama—as if she didn't know he was going to be married right away!"

"I don't say tell her that definitely, Tina, but just suggest it!"

"But Mama—" Tina's honest blue eyes were perplexed—"wouldn't that be a lie?"

"You needn't make it a lie, Tina. Just please Aunt Fanny —you know she's a little cranky, dear!"

"Mama, I couldn't act a lie, for a thousand Aunt Fannies!"

"Well!" May sighed. "See what you can do, anyway!" she said, in conclusion.

"Isn't it a wonderful prospect that is opening before my little girl?" she could say pleasantly to Mr. Yelland after service the next day; "we think my sister—Miss Crabtree, you know, who has always been Tina's special fairy-godmother —may take her abroad."

Tina watched her chance, and one night on a visit to Grandpa, after she and Vicky and Aunt Fanny had been playing euchre with Uncle Rob, in the California Street back-parlour, and when Vicky and Rob were picking out "Tarara-boom-de-ay" on the piano, she bravely returned to the subject. Fanny had won the game, and was somewhat relaxed and mellowed, but she instantly saw her opportunity for a little retaliation.

"Do I ever think any more of Italy? Dear me, no—being snubbed once was enough!" Fanny said lightly.

"Aunt Fanny—as if I meant to snub you! *Imagine!*"

"I don't know what you *meant* to do, but dear me! I certainly put my foot in it that day—poor me! You almost frightened me out of my wits. I had *supposed* that being offered a trip to Italy might be considered pleasant, but it'll be a long time before I get my courage to offer anybody anything again!"

"Aunt Fanny, if only you knew how often I've thought of it since. It wasn't that I didn't mean that it was a perfectly wonderful opportunity——"

But it was too late. Fanny had the whip hand now, and never was a woman who enjoyed it more.

"Ah, well, you should have thought of that before, then. I don't go toiling way over to San Rafael just to have somebody say, 'Thank you, I'd rather not!' Oh, no, I have plenty of other things to do. It seemed to me you and I could have had lots of fun, poking about in London and Italy; you didn't think so. It's not my fault if you've changed your mind! It thought then that you were just a little bit too sure—but, laws! half the things you girls do is perfectly mystifying to me. If you wanted to come to Europe, all you had to say was yes. You didn't, and now my mind is full of other things!"

And Fanny, trembling a little, laid out a game of Canfield, and quite composedly hummed "Just a Bunch of Lilacs," against "Tarara-boom-de-ay!" as she shifted kings and tens. Poor Tina, with a murmur to the effect that she just wanted to thank Aunt Fanny, and knew perfectly well that the trip had been given up, assumed a sudden interest in the game.

CHAPTER XIV

FANNY was rasped just now because Harry, coming to see her with Georgie in mid-morning, had asked her outright for the loan of a few hundred dollars. It had always been an unwritten law in the family that Fanny hated to talk of money, and that her own was sacred, not to be touched, or even mentioned to her. It ruffled and angered her to be forced into refusing Harry, and yet, with all that she did in the way of Christmas presents, expensive books, for the girls, and teacups for May, and a money offering at Saint Mark's, and with her constant expenses at home, and the suit for Georgie, and the San Rafael tickets twice, when she chanced to meet Lucy at the ferry, it did seem hard that she should be approached so openly, and for so large a sum. She told Harry that she would have had a hard time to put her hand on that much money herself; it was a long time since she had had three hundred dollars to spend as she pleased, but of course if he felt he couldn't do without it, she would see what she could do. Pa was really the person to go to, or Stephen; men knew so much more about those things. But she would write Harry at once and let him know.

It had not been easy for Harry Crabtree to beg a favour from his sister, even though he was very fond of Fanny and they had never quarrelled. But it was harder for him to go back to the Mission and tell Lucy that while Fanny had been very nice, she had said that she did not have the money, and that if she could raise it she would write him. The mail came down Harry's street at about ten o'clock in the morning, and he reflected that even if Fanny wrote to-night, there would be another inevitable interval of worry.

It was a damp, foggy day, with whirls of cold, sudden wind. Harry walked all the way from California Street, down Van Ness, across Market, and out Mission. He felt tired and a little perplexed; a stupid sort of dullness seemed floating between reality and his brain. What was the matter with him? He had been a fairly confident, energetic sort of boy. He remembered yachting trips with young men friends, years ago, when he had been considered amusing and entertaining. But of late years he had felt so heavy, listening to other person's accounts of efforts and successes; so helplessly entangled in routine himself.

His father had told him several weeks ago that he would not lend him money. Stephen had his own responsibilities; Rob was not a likely help in time of trouble. It had been Lucy who had suggested Fanny.

He and Georgie entered the house quietly, going straight to the kitchen, as bare now as a schoolroom, where Lucy was cleaning the stove.

His wife saw, from his face, that the unbelievable had happened. Fanny had refused him. Lucy, her frog-like eyes fixed upon him, from the smearing of grease and the smooches of soot on her face, felt despair seize her, with a sort of nauseated impatience worse than despair. As she worked and planned for the last hours in this cottage, she had indulged in dreams of a future that Harry's despondent return rudely dashed to the earth. She had imagined that Harry might have been hurt in the street, and once more that solemn little scene had been enacted in her busy brain; the respectfully sympathetic strange men, the alarm, the hurry to a hospital. Lucy did not definitely wish this, she merely saw it all, with her mind's eye, and perhaps even then she saw nothing worse—nothing half as hard, for Harry, as this return to her empty-handed.

"Fanny——" she began, sitting on her heels.

"She was awfully nice," Harry said slowly. "I told her how we were, that we had to get out of this house to-morrow, and that—unfortunately, I had nothing in sight but that Elkins job——"

"Don't speak of that Elkins job!" Lucy said, venting a little of her soreness and disappointment and shame upon the words. Elkins was a plumber who had asked Harry to help him in his humble, cluttered, and odorous shop. Harry's sneaking fondness for machinery had leaped into life at this obscure prospect, and he had even eagerly defended, to Lucy, the salary of sixty-five dollars a month.

"So then she said she didn't have it, Lucy——"

Lucy swallowed, looked at the black rag in her grained and greasy hand, gave the stove door an angry touch.

"That's a lie!" she said bitterly.

"I mean she didn't have it now, Luce." Harry's big boy had come about the table now, and put his arms tight about him, and was doubled awkwardly into his lap.

"I'm sorry, Pa," Georgie said, for the hundredth time.

"Never mind," Harry said, hugging him. "Father's boy!"

"She said that she would let me know if she could get it, Luce," he added, timidly, to his wife.

"Let you know! Does she know that we have to move out of here to-morrow?"

"Well, yes, I told her that. She—you know Fanny, Luce. She said that she couldn't put her hand right on it, to-day."

"I told you to go to her last week!"

"I know you did. I know you did. I blame myself for that," Harry said wearily and anxiously.

Lucy brushed back a fallen lock of her graying hair, with a bent wrist. She came to take Georgie's chair, and sank into it with a slow movement and wincing face that indicated sore muscles. She had been angry with Harry before, she had been voluble only this morning. But now the situation was too serious for that. As well scold him if he and she and Georgie had been adrift on a raft in mid-ocean. Matters were desperate now, and the question of responsibility was a minor one. They had almost no food, no money, no prospect of food or money, no home. She was physically weary, and mentally exhausted with desperate and futile planning. Nothing of all her schemes had materialized; the last years had been a steadily descending scale of pinching, contriving, eliminating, self-denial. Lucy was too tired, too discouraged, to talk. She merely regarded her husband with dull eyes.

"Mama, did you go to see that lady at the kindergarden this morning?" Georgie questioned. Harry looked interested, but Lucy merely compressed her lips and shook her head. The thought of the young kindergarten teacher, happy, confident, busy, paid for her delightful work, made her feel bitter. She had thought there might be some branch of that work that would suit her, Lucy Crabtree, but pretty Miss Williams had smiled a negative. There was a course of training back of all this merry playing with sticks and paper mats. She could only give Lucy the address of the classes in which she had been trained herself. She knew that the classes were already crowded. Everybody, Miss Williams had concluded with a laugh, seemed to want to get into kindergarten work.

Lucy had walked back past the county hospital and had glanced at the old wrecks of humanity, sitting blinking in the mild September sunlight. They were past feeling, these bald, blinking old women in bundled woolens, these clean, lean, silent old men, past shame, past hope, even past love. They only hated cold, and meat too tough for old jaws, and the occasional epidemic that locked the visitors' door; they loved sunshine and tobacco and bread puddings.

Not one of them of her type, or Harry's, or within twenty years of their ages, Lucy's fevered thoughts had decided. Nelly was married: Alice lived in the training school for nurses. But what was going to happen to Harry and herself, and poor little defrauded Georgie, whose father had had his pony and his private teacher at Georgie's age? Would they starve to death? Would they beg in Market Street? What did happen to people when they came face to face with the last wall?

If Fanny tided them over this particular crisis, as Fanny of course would, Lucy's thoughts had travelled optimistically, then positively she would prevent any such happening again. Georgie must get a position, at fifteen, poor little chap, and Alice's nursing course would end some day, far away as that day now seemed.

These thoughts had buoyed her until Harry's return; now she felt the sudden fall to earth with doubled violence. There was nothing ahead—nothing. Everywhere was poverty, humiliation, need.

The day had been dark, silent; leaves in her garden had stirred restlessly in an occasional breath of air. At two o'clock there was an interval of dim sunlight, then clouds, and now a light irregular rain. The cold kitchen was gloomy.

"I could go to Pa again," Harry said, after awhile.

Lucy bit her lip, considering, then heaved a deep sigh.

"You know that's no use, Harry."

"I wish you would let me go into the grocery!" Georgie said, eagerly. "Driving Ludmann's horses down Howard Street—giddy-ap there!" He guided an imaginary team.

"Don't!" his mother said irritably. "Well, I suppose we

shan't starve!" she said thoughtfully. "I never heard of any one starving, right here in San Francisco!"

Harry and Georgie were hungrily eating bread and butter at the kitchen table, and Harry had poured himself a cup of tea. It was nearly three o'clock, and in spite of Harry's worry and apprehension he thought he had never tasted anything so heartening and delicious, after the long, wet walk. The mixture of hot tea and butter and spongy bread smelled delightful to him; Lucy apathetically pushed toward Georgie a handful of raisins and a half-bar of chocolate, unearthed by this morning's packing.

"There's some syrup there, Harry."

"Oh, no, thank you!" He was almost tremulously appreciative of her kindness; he and Georgie took care to clean table and sink scrupulously when the meal was over. Lucy, heartened by a sudden dream, and with her packing done, went out into the drizzle resolutely, leaving written directions for the preparation of dinner. She could write menus and formulas readily, although she did not cook well.

She had come to a rapid decision; she would go down to Merkle's Employment Agency, and register as a companion, or governess, for a young child. Two children, perhaps, but she would take no more. She could pay a Japanese boy to manage the house until she got home, at seven. Or she might get home at six. Harry and Georgie, who loved puttering, had a most delightful afternoon cooking, cleaning, and packing.

The next morning, a Saturday, brought no letter from Fanny, but Lucy awoke to fresh energy, and at eleven o'clock the little house was spotless, and Lucy surprisingly presentable herself in her brushed and cleaned old dress. Even this dismal doubtful change was an adventure, to Lucy. The grocer's wagon was to move their furniture, and Lucy's best walnut bed and bureau were to remain with the grocer's placid German wife as a return. The last meal in the cottage was not entirely depressed, for Mrs. Liedman had brought some fresh eggs as a little offering of farewell, perhaps hoping that this practical gift would soften Lucy's pang of parting from her handsomest bedroom pieces.

Harry had gone out, immediately after the meal, Georgie was making himself useful with all the joyous eagerness of a child out of school, Lucy found herself unexpectedly cheerful in the bright fresh sunshine. It was all uncertain and alarming, true, but at least something was happening, and Lucy hated routine. She thought what a strange thing it would be if Harry should be killed in some street accident this morning; his father must help them then, for a while at least.

It was almost noon when Rob, leading little Bobo by the hand, unexpectedly appeared at the gate. Bobo had been visiting his grandfather, it appeared, and his father was to return him to May that afternoon. But it was such nice weather, and Rob had understood that the Harrys were moving, and thought he might be of use——

"We *are* moving, this minute," Lucy said, welcoming him into the bare dining room. "Sit down on that box, Robert. Yes, they're packing the wagon now."

"So I see," Rob said. "Well, you've got a bright day. Where do you go?"

Lucy took him frankly into her confidence. She had looked at a lovely cottage just renovated in Valencia Street, but the rent had been twenty-five dollars—too much. So they were going, temporarily, to the Abbotsford Hotel, on Larkin Street. It was expensive, unfortunately, twelve dollars a week for the three, but it would be madness to take a house until Harry was working again, and his next job might be anywhere—in Oakland or in the North Beach district.

"Harry's unlucky," Rob said, reflectively.

"Oh—unlucky!" Lucy echoed. "You"—her frog-like eyes gleamed—"you haven't any idea!" she said.

"Pa knows how hard up you are?"

"Know it! Harry's been to him four times this year. At first he did help, a little. But the last time he told Harry that any man who had to borrow money for his living expenses hadn't common sense," Lucy said bitterly. "Easy to say!" she added, with scorn.

"The old man made his own way, and it's a sort of religion with him," Rob observed. "You couldn't go down to visit Nelly on her ranch for awhile, Lucy, and take it easy?"

She flushed, shut her lips.

"Nelly and Rudy haven't any too much," she admitted reluctantly.

"I see!" Rob mused. Georgie, who loved children, had taken his small cousin into the yard, and Bobo's shrieks of joy floated in to the adults as they talked. Rob listened to his sister-in-law, with a troubled face. He had had plenty of money responsibility, of uncertainty, himself, but not on this pinched and pitiful scale. He wondered vaguely what the matter was, with Harry. Too gentle—too unambitious. He and Lucy exchanged dubious syllables.

"But if you get all settled at the Abbotsford——"

"Oh, I shall hardly unpack! We have to go somewhere——"

"How much actual money has Harry, Lucy?"

"Actual money! Gracious goodness, we haven't one dollar—not *one*."

"But for heaven's sake—how do you propose to pay board?" Rob ejaculated.

Lucy looked at him with a sensible, frank smile.

"Tell me what you would advise, Rob," she said.

Rob was silenced; truly it was hard to say.

He was enjoying this talk surprisingly. His first impulse, upon seeing the sidewalk littered with chairs and boxes, had been to go quietly away again, without adding anything to the confusion of the scene. He had had no real idea of Harry's straits, merely imagining his brother's employment as something humble, and his pay as low. Harry had said, in some casual meeting, that he and Lucy had to move, he had explained none of the appalling difficulties of the move.

This hour of frank talk with a woman who was still attractive had a surprising interest for Rob. He and his sister Fanny had never been congenial; May had always exasperated and amused him in true older-sister fashion. But Lucy was clever, comfortable, full of friendly confidence, devoid of the affectations that made both May and Fanny so absurd. He had missed women, since Ella died, missed even her austere and chilly femininity. He thought now that Harry had at least been fortunate in his wife, this fine square capable creature ought to have made a man of him if any one could. There was gray in her crisp dark hair, and youth was gone from her healthy, pleasant face, but she radiated a strangely feminine appeal. Rob noticed the fineness of her strong wrist, the whiteness of the nape of her neck. He was so bewildered by his own sudden interest in her that he lost one of her brisk, definite remarks.

"I only said 'Here comes Harry, now!'" she repeated, when he asked her.

Harry came in flushed and radiant. He retailed his adventures boyishly. Elkins had repeated his offer, asking Harry to take care of the bicycle-mending end of the business. Everybody was beginning to ride "safeties," and Elkins sometimes had six or seven to mend in a day. Harry understood them perfectly, was confident that he could hold that job. And he would be interested, too, he'd bet "any money"—poor Harry, who had not a cent—that he could ride one of those low, two-wheeled ones the second time he tried.

Well——! And if he took this job, there was a big room right over Elkins' shop, a nice room, too, he had gone up to see it, and it was a daisy, sunny, and big, and with a back room where there was running water and a stove. How about it? How about it? Elkins would let them rent it for six dollars a month. If they furnished it, and sold what furniture it would not hold, and Elkins advanced them ten dollars on the first month's salary—how about it? He wished Luce had seen the place; it was in a little alley near Sixteenth Street, awfully nice.

"Look here, Harry," Rob said, as Lucy was silent, "that's all very well, helping a plumber, but it don't sound to me like a very good job for one of Pa's sons. You're a Crabtree, after all, and your wife's not the kind of woman to drag into an alley in Mission Street——"

Harry's face fell and he looked anxious and ashamed.

"How do you feel, Lucy?" he asked, after a silence.

"I feel as I have always felt, Harry," Lucy said slowly, "that you could get an office position if you wanted it badly enough!"

"I know," Harry said quickly, and was silent.

"What would your idea of Georgie be, in this delightful arrangement?" Lucy said, presently.

"Oh, he'd be with us!" Harry looked alarmed. "Wouldn't he?" he asked uneasily.

"Over a plumber's shop, in an alley off Sixteenth Street," Lucy said simply.

"Now look here, folks," Rob said, briskly, "that won't do—you see you can't do that! Why, Harry, an office is the only place for you, and we'll find you something—you'll see! When Pa dies, there'll be the Santa Clara place, and you and Lucy can buy a home—make a fresh start. Buck up——!"

There was an interruption; the two boys came in from the

garden. Bobo held a starch-box in his stretched little arms, and in the starch-box was a pink-eyed, lop-eared baby rabbit, with a busy, quivering little pink nose. A strong odour of decayed cabbage leaves hung about him.

"It's a raddit!" said Bobo, solemn with awe and utter rapture, "and yis boy gived him to me, and now he's mine, and he's my raddit, and I can have him all for my own, because he gived him to me!"

"Darling, your last rabbit!" Lucy said to her son. Rob read the faces quickly, Georgie's noble with generosity, Lucy hesitant, Harry proud of his boy.

"Look here, Bobo," Bob said, fondly, "you don't want to take Cousin George's last rabbit, do you?"

"Oh, yes—please, Uncle Bob!" Georgie said eagerly, "I want him to have it!"

Bob hesitated, looking at his young nephew.

"That's awfully nice of you, George," he said. And Harry added: "The two Crabtree boys, hey, Bob? Just as you and I used to be years ago?"

"You were always darned good to me, I know that," Bob said, smiling; "do you like that little feller of mine, George?" he asked. "Look here, Bobo, aren't you going to thank George for your rabbit? What are you going to call that rabbit, hey?"

"Sank you for dish raddit," Bobo said hastily and firmly.

"George——" his father prompted.

"Gorsh," little Bobo echoed, with a grin at his own limitations.

"Lucy," Rob said, taking out his purse. "I know you and Harry won't mind my helping you out—just for a few weeks. See here—that'll carry you for a couple of weeks anyway——"

Strangely feminine, strangely appealing for all her squarely built body and her graying hair, she looked at the gold pieces, flushed, took them into her small, workworn palm. There was no protest, no hysteria, no sham.

"I hope you'll want something we can do for you some day, Rob Crabtree!" she said quietly. The words stayed with him hearteningly all day. He felt that he had never invested money more wisely.

"But father," murmured Georgie into Harry's ear, as they jolted comfortably across Larkin and Polk Streets to their new home, "if Uncle Rob hadn't given Mama that money, would we have gone to live over Elkins', and would I have driven the grocery wagon?"

"A grocery wagon isn't a very good place for a boy your age, sonny," Harry said smiling. But he stifled a dream of their settling, so comfortably, so obscurely, into the big room and the little room, of his running out with Georgie to buy chops and bread and eggs, of his going down to work the next day, perfectly confident, for the first time in his fifty years, that he was equal to the demand that life would make upon him.

Their room at the Abbotsford, an immense wooden barrack of a building, occupying a whole enormous lot, was large, shabby, streaming with afternoon sunlight. It had a bed and a cot and a bureau and shabby worn upholstered chairs with gray-green tassels on them. The bay window was curtained in clean, darned Nottingham lace, they could look out toward Van Ness Avenue, rapidly filling with handsome homes, and see the little Polk Street cable car turn sharply into Pacific Avenue. Outside their rooms were long halls, numbered doors, an occasional door with "Bath" painted on it. Georgie had to guide his father and mother to the stairs; they were always confused by the passages and turnings.

Lucy loved the novelty, the luxury of having no cooking or dish-washing to do, the meals in the big barn-like dining room. They were all in good spirits over pork chops and cottage pudding, at half-past six, and Harry heard his wife telling a casual woman acquaintance in the hall that there was something about the place that reminded her of London.

A few days later Bob sent him with a letter to a wholesale stationery house in Market Street, and Harry was given a stool at a desk under a dropped gas light, three enormous ledgers, a sixth part of a small inside office, and seventy dollars a month.

They stayed on at the Abbotsford, Georgie travelling half across the city to the Polytechnic High School, Harry walking almost a mile home every night. Lucy said that she intended to find a little flat, but the weeks went by, and winter came, and they made no move.

Then calamity found them again, this time in a new form. Lucy had a terrifying bout with inflammatory rheumatism, and there was a doctor's bill; a terrible seventy-two dollars to find somewhere.

Dosing with salicylates recklessly, over-exerting and over-

eating, yet Lucy miraculously did recover in body, but in spirit
she was not the same. She had never been ill before, and it
frightened her to think how quickly ruin would be upon them,
should she become chronically crippled. This was the last
straw, this was too much for her courage. She had always
thought of herself as invincible, whatever the others might be.
She was suffering from the effect of pain, poison, and strong
medicines, although she did not know it. She only knew that
she had lain there, in that shabby hotel room, helpless, and
might some day lie there helpless again. It had come from
nowhere, this illness, it had gone with equal mysteriousness, it
was like an ugly and haunting dream to her. Lucy, like all the
women of her day, had more than one friend who was chained to
a bed for life. There were several types of illness that were
regretfully described as incurable; several men and women, even
among her own friends, were patient domestic burdens for the
term of all their days and nights. The thought, coupled with
her constant money worry, was utterly insufferable to her.

She limped back to health and life, began to walk abroad into
the wet spring sunshine, began to theorize again. Warmth and
green found out the Abbotsford garden, Lucy liked to sit on
a bench, wrapped in a crocheted shawl, and bask sleepily in
the sun.

April came, with twenty-five wet days in a row, and then
Harry had pneumonia. He had not been eating well, he had
had broken nights with Lucy, he had alternated wet car trips
with the close heat of the office, and when he collapsed it seemed
for several days that he would never be well.

Rob was away, but Fanny came, so moved by the thought of
her younger brother's desperate state that she told Lucy at the
door, in parting, that she must not hesitate to ask for anything
that Fanny could do.

"You know I had arranged to lend poor Harry some money,
just before you moved here," Fanny said, wiping her eyes and
nose violently; "but then Bob told me that you were all right,
and I knew that Harry wouldn't want to involve himself if it
wasn't necessary. But I had arranged it, went downtown twice
about it, and all that!"

"You're awfully good, Fanny," Lucy said, perforce, "and I'll
remember it! You see my doctor bill isn't paid, even, and
now there's this fresh expense!"

"Oh, well, doctors are accustomed to waiting!" Fanny said hardily.

"I know. But with the expenses here—you see we pay twelve dollars a week——"

"Well, with that I had nothing to do!" Fanny said crisply, flushing and laughing a little as she tossed her head; "you moved in here, Lucy, you must have known what it would cost you! Pa sent his love," she added, with a dexterous change of the subject, "and he said he would come, only it's so wet. Poor Pa, I'm afraid his going about is pretty well ended, now. He's"— Fanny unfurled her umbrella, shook her head—"he's failing fast!" she said. "Well, Pa's eighty, you know."

"Not quite, is he?"

"Seventy-nine!"

"Do you see the trouble poor old man Baker got into?" Lucy said, reminded suddenly of one of old Reuben's contemporaries. "That Pringle woman, you know, that housekeeper of his— didn't you see that she is suing him for breach of promise? They say that his children are perfectly frantic, and last night's *Post* said that there is another woman, from Humboldt county some- where, who says that she is his wife and has four children!"

Yes, Fanny had seen it, of course, characterized it as perfect nonsense. Lucy wondered why she seemed so pale and acted so strangely; hitting her nose violently as she dismissed the sub- ject. Watching her pick her way along the wet street, Lucy presently sighed, shut the door, and went upstairs. She had seen Fanny suddenly stop short in the rain, as if arrested by some paralyzing thought, and she mused about it, as she sat beside the only half-conscious Harry, in the drab, dilapidated room.

The rain fell—fell. Georgie was lying on the floor, reading about the great World's Fair. Alice had sent a message that she would come to spend her free afternoon and evening with them; Lucy wondered if the head nurse were being any more reasonable, if the lessons that Alice almost despaired of learning were less hard.

"Mama, would it disturb Father if I read you about this Ferris wheel?" Georgie said, over a "Chronicle World's Fair Album," purchased by himself for seven coupons cut from the week's newspapers and ten cents.

"I don't think I would, Georgie."

"Mama, will Father be able to get back to the office by the first?" The first of the following month had been the date generously set by Harry's employers as their limit in holding open his position.

"Sh-sh!" Lucy warned him, glancing apprehensively toward the bed. She suspected that it might be many weeks before Harry recovered sufficiently to make any effort again. But she knew that money was worrying him, even in his stupor. He muttered of bills, of Georgie's shoes and her laundry bill. They owed Rob a hundred dollars, and what to Lucy's idea was worse, she had descended to the humiliation of helping overworked Mrs. Saunders in the hotel, helping with marketing, marking linen, counting stores. It made that harassed and complaining woman lenient where overdue board was concerned, grateful instead of exacting. But how long could matters continue in this condition?

After this crisis Georgie must get a job. There was no help for it. One May night he danced home reporting that the man in the livery stable would pay him $30 a month for washing carriages and harnessing. Harry was sitting up now, but Lucy had not told him yet that the job with the stationery firm was filled by someone else long ago. She let the exultant Georgie kiss her over bitterly starting tears, and on closed eyes, and told herself that it would not be forever.

This same evening Bob came in, Lucy, shabby, quiet, hopeless, turned him over to Harry, who was sitting up in a rocker, weak and white, but beginning to be interested in life. Bob had been out of town for several weeks; he showed a somewhat awkward and puzzled sympathy: things, he said vaguely, ought never to have gotten to this state.

"I was thinking about something, Lucy—wish I'd thought of it before!" Bob said. Lucy, darning, hardly glanced at him with her passive smile. "Here's what I was thinking," Bob said. "You see, there's all Ella's stuff, in storage; I never shall marry again!"

Lucy was interested now, she looked at him keenly, with suspended needle.

"Then there's Bobo," Bob resumed, locking his big hands and watching them, hung loosely between his knees. "He's too far away from me, at May's—I never see him. And then, I want a home. I'm sick of drifting about: and if I tie up too tight with Fan, why then when Pa drops off she'll think I'm bound to stay on in that damn house——"

Lucy laughed out loud, and Harry's thin and colourless face suddenly brightened at the sound.

"Fan doesn't want Bobo in any case—said so," Bob continued. "So this is what I was thinking. You were speaking of a house you saw in Larkin Street to-day—twenty dollars. That's near Fan, and yet, if you and Harry and I took it, and you took Bobo in——" He hesitated, Lucy did not speak. "You think it over," Bob said, flushing a little uncomfortably, "maybe you'd rather not. Maybe you and Harry would rather see what else turns up——"

Lucy was sitting near him; now she stretched a firm, square hand out and laid it on his arm. The friendly touch thrilled Rob, who had been lonelier even than he realized.

"You mean you——" She stopped.

Harry was still weak; now the tears wet his face suddenly, and he tried to laugh at his brother, shaking his head.

"Oh, no, old boy!" he faltered. "We'll pull out of this somehow. It's too much——"

Bob was genuinely embarrassed; he had had no idea of their straits.

"It's a favour to *me*, I tell you!" he said.

"Oh, no, it's not!" Lucy said, quite frankly crying through her laughter. "No—no—no!" And with a breaking voice, she put her sewing suddenly aside, and pressing the fingers of one work-worn hand tight into her cheek, to control the trembling muscles of her face, she began to walk up and down the room. But Bob saw her suddenly raise both hands to her face, and saw the glitter of tears between her fingers. He got up; it was very sweet to him to stop her in her restless walk, and to feel her cling to him just a little in her break-down.

Presently she was business-like; stern and determined over new plans. Harry should go to Nelly for a holiday, she and Bob and Georgie should move into the wonderful Larkin Street house; Bobo should play in the sunny back yard all day long, and when Harry came back there would be time enough to talk of employment again.

Bob watched her, more pleased with the prospect than he had been with any, for a long time. He had been lonely, part of the time in Fanny's uncomfortable house, part of the time in boarding houses. He wanted his child near him. He wanted companionship for himself, a place at some table, the feeling that somebody missed him when he was away, cared to hear his opinion over the evening paper. This arrangement promised well for both Bobo and himself. The child would have the kindly older cousin to watch him, he would be among friends. And for Bob's self there would be his brother, and the friendship of this oddly discontented, powerful, strangely attractive woman. He believed her to be a remarkably capable person. She would talk with him sometimes, pouring coffee over a late breakfast table, she would keep him in touch with May and Fan with none of the present annoyances of association with them.

The next day he took her to see the Larkin Street house, and, almost bewildered with felicity, Lucy heard him actually rent it, actually bespeak the good offices of butcher and grocer, in Polk Street. To her the six rooms, sunshine lying in oblongs upon their dusty, empty floors, the closets, the pantry and bathroom, seemed a veritable kingdom. She took Alice over it, explaining, praising. Bob gave her the freedom of the storage room in which Ella's things were stored; they went there together, after seeing Harry off for Nelly and Canfield; life flowed gloriously in Lucy's veins again. She was happy, busy, with money in her purse and plans in her restless brain once more.

CHAPTER XV

NELLY met her father at the station, in a mud-spattered surrey, drawn by a lean bay mare. She was a little faded, eager-faced, but always pretty, only the fairy gold of her hair reminding him of the old butterfly Nelly. Beside her on the seat a slender, exquisite two-year-old girl, in a colourless apron and a shabby tight red coat, was wedged, and a fat, handsome baby boy was held by a strap.

"Kiss Grandpa, and get in the back, Hildegarde," Nelly said, leaning over for an affectionate kiss from herself to the beaming Harry. "Papa, will you take Brother on your lap? Don't cry, Brother! No—that's Grandpa. That's dear Grandpa come to see us!"

The horse started with a great jerking of loose straps and shafts; they splashed through puddles that caught pale sheets of the blue sky in their brown borders. The little village was bathed in heavenly warmth and sunshine, although such trees as the surrey-top touched, on the long road home, sent down heavy splashing of water upon its occupants. Harry gasped with pleasure and could only shake his head at the vistas through fresh green: the mustard tops and wild lilac, the fruit-blossoms below them.

If Nelly knew that life had changed her sadly, she showed no immediate consciousness of it. She talked along naturally and spontaneously, explaining that Rudy had driven three calves over to Martinez, and might have to go to Contra Costa for his tree spray before he returned.

Hildegarde was a friendly little soul, with blue eyes and flyaway gold hair, and a little upturned nose that needed constant attention and rarely got any. Brother was apathetic, heavy, silently terrified of his grandfather, silently letting great tears fall from the solemn eyes he fixed upon Harry. Hildegarde hung on the back of the seat, conversing sociably.

"Papa, you'll find us very shabby, we've been meaning to

paint for years," Nelly said, bustling about the surrey, when they stopped at the cottage. "But—let Mama wipe your nose, Hildegarde, and don't be so naughty! She hates any one to touch her," Nelly interrupted herself to apologize, as the child ducked her mustard-blossom head and emerged from the ordeal with reddened nose and suddenly tearful eyes, "but they always have colds all winter! Run along now, Hildegarde, Mama doesn't want those dirty shoes in the house. He goes in his coop," Nelly added, carrying the heavy boy around the house to an actual coop under a shabby willow, "get him his pacifier, Hildegarde, or he'll cry! Now come in, Pa, I'll take you the kitchen way, for I'm not going to make a stranger of you!— He'll stop crying in a minute," Nelly added, of her baby. "Sit down, Papa," and she laid her flushed, perspiring forehead against his cheek, and gave him a hug even before she got her breath, "and tell me how you feel. You were real sick, weren't you?"

Harry was amazed at the facility with which she managed the kitchen: lighting a wood fire in the cracked old stove, manipulating jars and bottles, flashing into the pantry for eggs and butter. The dingy, grease-stained kitchen reeked of stale food, the salty, oily smell of a churn, the spicy, soft odour of confined apples. It was not actually in disorder, although a red tablecloth and a big brown glaze sugar bowl were evidently fixtures on one of the tables, and the children's walnut high chairs, each decorated with a mush-spattered bib, kept their places at the board. Nelly's floor had not been scrubbed for years, nor her stove polished; her kettle and saucepans were thick with soot, yet there was no sign of neglected dishes, and a mush boiler, soaking on the range, was the only receptacle that was not empty and in its place.

"I keep my milk in here all summer," Nelly called from the parlour, "it's the only cool place in the house. Brother used to have his naps in here, too, but in winter I put him back in our room. I got a piece of meat in town, Pa, but we won't wait for it. You eat eggs, don't you?"

"Anything, darlin'," Harry said, conscious of being weak and tired.

She was uneasy because he ate so little; she kept jumping up to kiss him lovingly: they were both quite unconscious of the spotted tablecloth, the nearness of the odorous stove, the general slackness of the service. After lunch she dragged a rocker into the sunny sweetness of the yard, and he was glad to sink into it. The children were bundled down for naps with scant ceremony, in a dim bedroom, on an unmade bed, their little faces streaked with food, their small shoes thick with dooryard dust. Nelly whisked through the dishes, and rolled a churn out beside her father's chair.

"Usually I get through earlier than this," she said, smilingly, "but to-day I had to get them both cleaned up to meet you, and Rudy wasn't here to harness for me!"

"Hasn't Rudy got a man to help him?" Harry asked, a little anxious over her violent breathing.

"He has had always, of course. But this year everything has gone so badly he was glad enough to let Pete go; it seemed to me that that thirty dollars a month came round every other day! You know we had cholera with the hogs again—wasn't it a shame!" Nelly laughed philosophically. "After I'd nearly killed myself dragging food up there for the brutes! However, we did come out a little ahead. This is coming nicely," Nelly ran on, "and the reason that I'm doing it is that I have to feed the chickens to-night, since Rudy isn't back. Three hens came off this week—I want you to see the little chicks, Pa, you'll love them—and I hate that business of mixing them up meal and chopped stuff, it comes right at suppertime, and I want to get you a good supper! Rudy loves fresh butter with soda biscuit, and he hates me to let the cream spoil—as I just *had* to, three or four times last year, when Brother first came, and while the men were here. It just drives Rudy wild to buy butter! But Hildegarde was teething and as cross as two sticks, and my girl left me, and it was terribly hot!"

"It keeps you pretty busy, Nelly," Harry said.

"Oh, Pa, this is nothing! You ought to see us when the berries are ripe, and four or five men to feed every meal, and perhaps no girl, and your meat souring, and a child fretting and crying all day! Well, it almost drives you mad. One day Rudy had an ulcerated tooth, and he slapped Hildegarde— poor little tad, I thought he'd kill her, and let me tell you I went for him—the idea, you know, a big man to hit a little mite of a baby!" Nelly laughed without venom. "He was all heated up with pain, and so much work to be done," she added mildly. 'But I shan't mind anything as long as we can keep the place.

It's such a lovely home for the children, and we do get—that reminds me!"

She vanished into the house and returned carrying a glass of rich milk for Harry, the cream floating on it in blots and clinging to the glass. He could feel energy and calm spreading over him as he drank it.

"It's the way to live, Nelly," he said, breathing in the sweet summer air in gratitude, looking from the climbing rough grade under the orchard trees to the far blue line of the mountains. "That's Diablo, back there, isn't it? My Lordy—Lordy—Lordy—it's lovely! I don't know when I've had a holiday like this. I wish there was some little corner of the world like this where your mother and I could creep in. I'm planning a great lot of walking," he added, "over there beyond that barn, now, and up here backwards—where all that green is."

"That's the spring. Seems to me I dream of that spring nights," said Nelly; "the litigation is all about that spring, you know. Rudy'll tell you all about it. He can't talk much else. All is," she added, confidingly, using the common country phrase that had sounded as oddly colloquial to her a few years ago as it did to Harry now, "all is, Pa, that, in a way, I'd as soon farm somewheres else as here. There's a bunch of men here, well, they're all right, I guess, but they aren't good company for Rudy. The Bayliss boys, and Dick Billers, and Toady Cantrell—there's a regular crowd of them that gather at Brady's, nights—that's the saloon, you know—and it's awfully bad for Rudy—there's Brother! Wait a minute!"

She ran indoors, returned with the heavy baby, still dusty and now wet, rosy and damp with sleep, ready to cry with hunger.

"No, sir—you aren't going to have ninny!" Nelly laughed, refusing the determined little hands her flat breast, and substituting in Brother's fretting mouth the springy black nipple of a bottle of milk. "I had to wean him last week," she explained, "I couldn't satisfy him, and I was getting so run down! There he is—Mama's good sweet old boy——!"

The baby sucked and sputtered on the bottle, lying sprawled luxuriously in her lap, and she rested, relaxing her slender little body with enjoyment. Little Hildegarde stumbled out, crying vaguely, her face blotched with sleep. She ate the untouched cookies that Nelly had brought out with Harry's milk, and finished the ounce or two he could not drink, and settled happily down to play.

"I don't know where I got the name Hildegarde, nor this feller's name either," Nelly said, kissing the baby. "Clifford, we named him—I sort of wanted to call him Cecil, but Rudy didn't like it. But I always loved the name Hildegarde; I think it sounds pretty, don't you? Hildegarde and Clifford Sessions. Clifford Cecil, I called him, because I hope there aren't going to be any more!" She laughed and shook her head. "I tell Rudy two's *enough*," she said.

"You want to get your stren'th back, now, Nelly," Harry said, timid on this particular ground.

"Oh, yes—there's no sense in killing myself! I plan now to go straight ahead, get the farm paid for, then paint the house, or build, and maybe when they are both in school, get a riding horse and really begin to get some pleasure out of existence!"

"Nelly," Harry said hesitatingly, when she had bounced the baby into his coop again, carried churn and butter away, and was busily shelling early peas beside him, "Rudy don't drink, does he?"

She frowned, pushed a row of peas from the soft shell with a grimed and scarred little thumb.

"No, not exactly, Pa. You couldn't say that. But he wastes a lot of money treating, and he'll get himself mad and all worked up over nothing, and be late for meals, or maybe he won't come at all. It makes me mad, you know, winter nights, when I've been cooped up here with the children all day, and then dark'll come, and no Rudy! Now last winter, one day, when the black heifer calved—it was her first calf, and she ran way up into the hills, and I was afraid we'd lose the cow and the calf, too, and Rudy was downtown, I thought he'd had to go to court, maybe, about the case. Well, Ida Larabee went by—they're lovely people, own half the valley and she drove the children and me down, and they were playing poker—in Brady's; they'd been playing all night—and here they were, smoking, and their eyes bloodshot, and the place smelled like a pig-pen, and of course Rudy was just blazing. We lost the calf, too, the coyotes got it. Well, after he got over that, I told him I wasn't going to stand any more of it, and he was better for awhile. But in winter he hasn't got enough to do—especially if the pigs die off. I guess there isn't a woman in the valley that wouldn't burn Brady's down if she got the chance!" Nelly finished, with the hardy, bitter philosophy that sat so strangely on her slender figure and small, appealing face.

Harry watched her preparations for supper; those farm regulations so confusingly new to the city-dweller. The kerosene she slopped into the fire to make it burn, the quarts of skimmed milk she poured into a shapeless and discoloured bucket for the pigs and calves, the curious impression at once of waste and economy filled him with surprise.

There was small poetry now in Nelly's housework. These dingy rooms represented to her a sort of battlefield, where she met hunger, dirt, weariness, and defeat day after day. Nelly knew all the tricks of the enemy, now, the maddening hinge on the stove door, the grate that slipped, the ugly bump the sugar barrel loved to give her thigh, the bit of earth in the woodshed that was slippery from October to April. She had been happy in this dingy farm kitchen, she had been bitter, sad, sick, well, weary and energetic, languid and radiant. She had quarrelled with Rudy while she banged and clattered at this stove, she had had hours of utter felicity here, when he was cleaning his gun or mending his traps, and Hildegarde was making love to her father from her high chair, and she, Nelly, feeling blithe and capable, had been cutting cookies or rolling pie-crust.

Less analytical perhaps even than the average woman of her time, yet Nelly sometimes vaguely questioned her destiny. Women bore children, cooked, and were patient. Men had their pleasure, ate well, and worked off what tempers they would upon wives and babies. She did not understand it; it did not seem quite fair. She had wanted to marry, all girls did, whatever they said. But she had not understood what marriage meant. Was there no way—no nice way—in which girls might be told? Nelly's disillusioned smile would interrupt her musing here. Not much chance that they would marry at all if they knew!

Harry dissuaded her from using the beef for supper; he wanted only the rice and peas and the good hot tea, and more of that wonderful cream, he said. She promised him one of her own fryers in a day or two, and added home-made apricot jam and more cookies to the plain meal. She ate it with the baby in her lap, her body half turned toward Hildegarde's chair. Harry found the mushy gray rice delicious, and enjoyed the family gossip at the same time.

"So Tina's minister married an eastern girl, poor Tina! I know she liked him. They don't seem very lucky, those girls, do they, Pa? Esme was all worked up over that Beale boy, but nothing came of it! I'll bet you Vicky marries, although I know she felt terribly about the Tasheira boy—whatever his name was. And you know I think that was a shame —breaking that up. That's a wonderful ranch they've got; —Rudy says the cattle alone are worth thousands of dollars, and with all those Portuguese and Indians to help, Vick would never have had our troubles here!"

"Your aunt May never would have liked Vicky to marry a man like that—she feels that the family is above that," Harry observed.

"And Alice really studying—that seems so funny to me!" Nelly ran on. "She was wonderful here, last year. I had a girl, I couldn't do much, and she and Georgie and I had such fun! We used to make Rudy come down to the creek for picnics, and make coffee—he isn't much for picnics, farming people aren't. They have so much of the out-of-doors that they like to get in, and shut the windows, too! I remember, the first year, I used to make Rudy the nicest salads, but he never ate them. And cut-up fruit, peaches or berries—well, hired men wouldn't thank you for a ton of them! They want pies, and veal and pork; and even the best blackberries, with thick cream, they won't eat unless you make jam or pudding of them. Isn't it funny! Once I had just salad, and an omelette, and our own beans and corn, and Bavarian cream for dinner. Well, I haven't heard the last of that dinner yet!"

"That don't seem reasonable," Harry said absently. Hildegarde, with jam and rice hardening on her cheeks, had fallen asleep, a sour-sweet little burden, on his shoulder. The long afternoon was deepening swiftly to twilight; Nelly lighted an odorous kerosene lamp by the stove.

"You haven't the faintest idea how I love to have you here, Pa," she said.

Harry wakened refreshed and content. He was in the kitchen, grinning as he built a wood fire, when Nelly came yawning out at seven. When Rudy was away she slept as late as the children would, she said. They were very happy over their breakfast, and afterward had a felicitous hour with the baby children and baby chicks, and even the baby pigs, in the barnyard. Then Harry helped her harness, and they rattled down the sweet curving road to the village again, where Nelly traded new potatoes for staple groceries at the store and picked Rudy up at the train. Rudy was pleasantly cordial to his guest, kissed his wife, and embraced both his children with enthusiasm.

When they passed Brady's, a white saloon from which strong stale odours of intoxicants surged, Brady himself, clean, rosy, well-shaven, and aproned, came out.

"Do, Mrs. Sessions," said Brady. "Pleased to see you again Mr. Crabtree, hope you're going to make a long stay! Say, listen, Rudy—you was saying this morning——"

Rudy had taken the reins; Brady now placed a heavy foot on the muddy step of the surrey. They fell into low-toned conversation. Nelly, in the back seat, knew at once that Rudy had reached the village the day before.

"Well, sir!" Rudy said heartily to his father-in-law, as they rattled away; "Nelly making a farmer of you?"

"Rudy, why'd you stay with Cantrell over night?" Nelly demanded, directly.

"Who said I did?" Rudy countered, after a pause.

"Brady just said that you and he were talking this morning."

"Oh." He quite patently abandoned equivocation. "Well, where were *you* yesterday? I thought you were going to meet me yesterday?"

"Your train got in at half-past ten, and Pa's at eleven, and when you weren't in the surrey, of course I thought you hadn't come!"

"Well, there wasn't much to do, at home."

"You said last week you were going to get the Swede for the ploughing," Nelly said, "and here it is Thursday!"

"I didn't sell the calves, and maybe Brady will take 'em, that's how much I've been neglecting the place," Rudy said, not ill-temperedly. "I thought maybe your father had written that he wasn't coming until the afternoon train, so I did some trading, and by the time that train was in, it was too late! Cantrell and I and some of the boys had a talk, and I and he turned in early. I thought maybe I'd walk home, but my corn has been hurting me some."

"You couldn't drive up with Bud Larabee last night—oh, no!" Nelly said stingingly. But as Rudy did not answer, she presently cooled down, outwardly at least, and called her father's attention to the beauty of the blossoming valley in sunlight and cloud shadow. Rudy came to her side an hour later when she was busy among the delicious odours of the stove.

"Soda biscuit? You're awfully good-natured, Nell!" he said, putting his arm about her. "You aren't cross at me, are you?"

"It seems to me that you treat me awfully mean," Nelly said sulkily.

"But I don't mean to, Nelly!"

"Ah, that's what you always say—you never mean to! But I notice that doesn't stop you the next time!"

"How do you mean next time?"

"You know perfectly well what I mean; you know that you'll stay away playing poker with those boys just as soon as ever you want to, no matter what you say!" A tear fell, and sputtered in the frying pan.

"Now, look here," said Rudy, eagerly; "I was mean last night, I'll admit it. But on my honour, Nelly, I didn't realize just how you'd take it, just how mean it would seem. I wasn't sure you were coming down in the morning, and then when I missed you I thought, 'Oh, well, she has her father,' and, as I say, I was talking the sale of these three calves with Brady, and I just got into it! But now listen, I'll never do that again. You forgive me, don't you, darling? Ah, Nelly, I love you——"

They clasped arms about each other, and Rudy kissed her with a deep and passionate lover's kiss. He released her, and they smiled at each other, and kissed deeply again.

"You little devil!" Rudy said, laughing and confused with passion.

They started apart as Harry came in, and he joined in their laughter, well pleased to have them friendly again. Nelly turned back, smiling cryptically upon her pots and pans, and presently they all sat down to a happy meal.

But later, Nelly was not so happy. There was an eagerness, an affection and helpfulness about Rudy that filled her with unrest. She loved him and hated him at once, desired him, and yet plotted to evade him. Finding her happy and well, his return after two days' absence had renewed the greatest problem of her life. She did not know what to do, hardly knew what she wished to do.

Loving Rudy, it was life to her to have him friendly, conversational, admiring. But there was a price to pay for this happiness nowadays, and it was to be had only for that price. Men were like that, Nelly philosophized. Personally her passion would have been satisfied with kisses, with sleep as deep and sweet as a child's, in his arms. But men were different. And although poor little Nelly would have sacrificed her own finer instinct gladly and always, that Rudy might be satisfied, she could not—she *could* not—risk all the consequences and be content. Those dragging terrible months of struggle and helplessness, when milk and fruit and dishes and beds were one long nauseating nightmare to her;—no moment, no year of passion satisfied were worth that cost. Surely— surely that was not to be expected now.

While Brother had been nursing, her feeling for Rudy had been merely friendly indifference, but old fires were awake in them both now. Nelly foresaw difficulties, but she was determined. It was only sane to be temperate. Another summer was coming; they were shorthanded on the ranch; she was needed. Her house and her children would keep her busy, and she *must* be well, she *must* be hopeful and full of energy. It was so delicious to be well, to be equal to the long day! And it was so hard to be sick, pitied, and a burden to oneself and to everyone.

So Nelly steeled herself, and found small matters to delay her in the kitchen, when her father was snoring, and Rudy going to bed. And as she puttered about, mixing buckwheat and setting bread, she reminded herself of burning days last spring, before Brother came, of Rudy's glowing health and his impatient lack of sympathy, of the hearty meals he had eaten while she sat sick and despondent, of her maddened feeling that it was his will upon her that had placed her in his power, trembling with joy when he was kind, crying wretchedly when he scolded, filled always with apprehension and weakness and pain.

Well, that had given her her glorious boy, and she would bear it all over again for Brother, with his solemn fat face and watery smiles. But a woman couldn't be a work-horse and a mother, too; Nelly felt herself equal to one calling or the other —not both.

Rudy was awake when she went into the bedroom, he smiled at her from his comfortable position in bed.

"Why didn't you call me out there to help you?"

"Oh, that wasn't anything!" Nelly set her lamp on the bureau and began to undress, her face thoughtful and unsmiling.

"What's the matter?" Rudy asked, elaborately concerned.

"Nothing!" Nelly yawned a tearing yawn. "Except that I'm dead!"

"Well," he said affectionately, "you get in here with your old man and you'll be asleep in two seconds!"

She smiled reservedly, and when she did get into bed kissed him quickly and turned resolutely to her own side, curling herself up for sleep. There was a moment's silence, and Nelly's heart leaped with a wild hope that he was going to let her go to sleep in peace.

"Nelly," he said kindly. Nelly's spirit sickened. "What is it?"

"What is what?" she mumbled innocently, when he had repeated the question.

"Why do you treat me this way?"

"What way?"

"You know what I mean!"

Silence.

"Well, I suppose I'm tired, Rudy!"

"Tired! But my God, just because you're tired can't you be friendly—talk to me a little—what's the matter with you, anyway? I come home after being away two days——!" He had reared up in bed now; and was kissing her. "All I want is for you to kiss me good-night," he said.

She put a slender little arm about his neck.

"Good-night, dear!" she said finally.

"Now, look here," Rudy said roughly, "you make me mad when you act this way——"

"Well, you know perfectly well——"

"I don't know anything of the kind! All I wanted was just a little affection from you, just some proof that my wife loves me—that's all. I just want to talk—like we used to—lying here this way—that's right. You don't have to be afraid, Nelly, because I give you my word——!"

She would talk to him, but after a few minutes she returned courageously to her point and made him angry again.

"I know what the doctor said, when Brother was born; he said that he was positive that you would never have another child!"

"Yes, and he said that when Hildegarde was born, too! Doctors are men. They always say that."

"Well, listen—I want to tell you about what Miller said——"

"I think"—she sprang up a few minutes later, pattered barefoot to the kitchen—"I think that's the cat!"

When she came back she was ice-cold, but this time there was no protest as she curled up for sleep, and presently—music in her ears—Rudy snored. Nelly scored on this occasion, and danced through her housework next morning, feeling her father, her children, and her home, to be the best possible, and cooking fried chicken and rhubarb pie for a conciliatory lunch. But Rudy was not friendly.

She could have cried with helplessness and anger, when his irritation took the form of ugliness with the children, and coolness toward her father. The weather was so beautiful, everything was going so well, why couldn't he help instead of hindering the general happiness? She bribed him with a little hint of softening, and instantly the skies were clear again.

Rudy made a rocking-horse for Hildegarde, brought eggs, strained milk, led Harry into long talks. He tossed the baby in the air, and kissed him and kissed Nelly when he returned him. One heavenly day they all went, grandfather, mother, father, and children, into Martinez, a long forty miles away, where Rudy transacted some legal business at the court house and Nelly bought a great live fifty-pound salmon that was flapping amongst a thousand others on the pier. She had packed a wonderful lunch, and they built a fire by the marsh, and made coffee that added the last touch of deliciousness to it. The children were ecstatic, Brother sleeping in his mother's arms as they drove home in the summer moonlight, and Hildegarde's precious weight close against Harry's contented heart.

When they all stumbled into the close, warm, dark little house, and when Rudy came back whistling from the barn, to help her tumble the profoundly sleeping children into the disordered little beds they seemed to have left so long ago, Nelly smiled to herself resignedly. What did it matter, after all? Hers was a losing fight. And she did have her lovely home and a husband that truly loved her. For under all Rudy's innocent manœuvring for her favour, there was real love; he was not like some men, Nelly told herself, who followed other women. No, he loved her, as he had a perfect right to do, and for the rest, well, that was the way God had made women, and there was no help for it! Besides, there might never be another child, of course. Plenty of women had two, and no more.

Nelly recounted to herself, in the next few days, the many women she knew who had two children only. She laughed at her fears, regretted her previous coldness to poor old Rudy. Good heavens, weren't there thousands of women whose one hope and prayer was that their husbands would love them? And it was sweet to have him happy and devoted, sweet to have May sunshine waking the ranch to hundreds of half-forgotten beauties, sweet to feel so strong and confident and well over butter-making and chicken-farming and the packing of picnic baskets.

Harry stayed with them almost four weeks, memorable weeks for him and for Nelly. He was not only interested, admiring, and sympathetic with his wife's daughter, but he was genuinely helpful. To sit with a baby, to mend a chair or a wheel, was honour to Harry; he was like a woman where dishwashing and potato-peeling were concerned.

"Pa, if you didn't have to go back!"

"Well——?" Harry coughed his apologetic little cough. "I was just thinking that! I'll be glad to see your mother and the children again," he added dutifully.

"But do you suppose your next job will be in an office, Pa?"

"I guess so, Nelly."

"You couldn't get me into an office for any money," Rudy said, enjoying his after-dinner pipe. "I had three years of it—that's enough!"

They were in the kitchen, loitering after the midday meal. Both the children had been carried in for naps, the day was burning hot, and Rudy was in no hurry to return to the orchard he was cultivating.

The table was littered with plates and cups and food. A sucking pig that had been killed in a farm gate was the main dish, and Nelly had emphasized this unexpected treat with new potatoes and new asparagus and a deep cherry pie. Everybody had quite deliberately over-eaten, more pig, more tea, more tomato pickle, and more cream to finish the pie or more pie to finish the cream. There never had been such a feast; the kitchen reeked of it. Rudy had obligingly rigged a sort of awning outside the kitchen window, making it from the good portions of a rotted and creased old tent, found in the feed-house, and Nelly could not say enough of the added coolness and pleasantness at the window. She sat with her elbows on the table, playing with the pie spoon. Flies buzzed above the board, although she had shoo-ed them from the kitchen more than once this morning.

"If I had my life to live over, I'd take what I had and buy a farm," Harry said. "I was watching the blacksmith down in the village yesterday. It's living—that is. You feel that you're alive. But the minute I'm shut up I get a sort of dizziness in my head, like as if I couldn't understand what I'm trying to do!"

"And you've had so many years of it!" Nelly said, blinking the bright tears from her pretty eyes, as she looked at him. "You darling!" she added, laying her hand on his.

"Lots of men in my fix!" he said, sensibly.

"If I lost this farm to-morrow," Rudy said, "Cantrell would make me his farmer—he said so. That is, if it wasn't for Nelly and the kids. He won't have any women on his place!"

"Well, I hope Nelly and the kids make it up to you in other ways," Nelly herself said whimsically and appealingly, as she dropped her head on one side and smiled at him.

Rudy grinned back.

"There's lots of things a man could do if he wasn't tied down by his family," he said, dispassionately. "A feller's telling me the other day about going to Mexico; he's only going to be gone six weeks. He's going to get five hundred dollars for driving a bunch of cattle out, and he asked me to come along, share and share alike." Rudy half opened his mouth, emitted smoke, and gripped his pipe stem in his teeth again. "'Nope,' I said, 'Wife and kids!'"

Nelly pondered, her cheeks flushing deeper with excitement. Mama and Georgie here—Papa staying—she was more than equal to the demands of the early summer—and Rudy would be back for the heavy harvesting——!

"Rudy, why don't you go?" she began eagerly. "There's no earthly reason why you shouldn't! Oh, *go on!* My gracious, what a chance to travel and see something—don't you think so, Pa? We'll be perfectly all right here——"

"I see myself walking off!" Rudy smiled, indulgently.

"But why not? Old Roderiguez will come over every night and morning, and there's only the two cows now—oh, Rudy, why don't you?"

"Because I can't!" Rudy said, negligently. His calmness maddened her.

"Why do you say you can't?"

"Why do I? Because there's too much to do here, even if I could desert you and the children, that's why. You talk as if a ranch was nothing at all! Sometimes you don't talk as if you had good sense, Nelly!"

"But Rudy—it isn't fair for you to blame it on the children and me, if it's really the ranch!"

"Well, it *is* you and the children!"

"I'm perfectly capable of running myself and the children!"

"You think you are!" Rudy was superbly silent, sucking on his pipe. "You haven't any idea of the way some of these ranch hands act when a woman's alone!" he added, with inspiration.

Sex again. Nelly laughed.

"If you don't want to go to Mexico, Rudy, don't go, but for pity's sake don't pretend that it's on my account!"

"Well, I'm not going—and that's all there is about it!" Rudy got up, stuffed his pouch into his trouser pocket, jerked and shook himself generally after the lounging hour, clapped on his hat, and sauntered forth. Nelly, with a stoical smile for her father, which might quite as easily have been tears, began to pile and scrape dishes.

"Makes me so mad!" she excused herself, trying to laugh. The water in the kettle was cold now, everything coated with congealed pork fat, the kitchen baking hot in early afternoon. Besides that the children were waking, fretting and uncomfortable; Nelly risked a cold bottle for Brother, but poor little Brother paid for her hurry by being feverish all that afternoon and by crying all through the hot night.

Her thoughts were much with Rudy in the quiet days after her father left. She would follow him mentally through his comfortable, unhurried days, always able to handle his own affairs, to adjust his life to his own ideas. True, Rudy got up early, and brought the milk in at half-past six, but while he was moving through the sweet early morning to the dreamy silence and bigness of the barn, she was stumbling hurriedly between cribs and stove, catching her Mother Hubbard gown together, catching up her tumbling coil of hair, wondering desperately what had gotten into the old stove this morning, anyway. Milk, babies, kindling, matches, coffee-pot, Nelly snatched at one after the other; the possibilities of accident were limitless, and every morning had its share.

Rudy would stand smiling at her while she lifted the big pail of milk up to pour it into the pans. He might ask good-naturedly if the pans were clean, as he sat down to his hearty meal. A breakfast of potatoes and cereal, ham and eggs and hot bread was not enough for Rudy; there was always comment if the hot cakes were not forthcoming. He did not like toast, and to serve him plain bread was nothing short of a hostile overture.

"Ma used to keep her batter in a pitcher—there isn't much to a few hot cakes!"

"She didn't have two little babies to manage!"

"Lord—I don't care this morning. It isn't this morning! But the way you fuss you'd think nobody ever had to run a farm before. Look here, she's spilled this, Nelly—naughty, naughty girl!"

And Rudy would slap Hildegarde's little hand before he went out into the door yard. His oldest-born would follow him with piercing screams, and Nelly, mopping up the cereal, would feel nothing short of murderous.

"How about these currants?" he might say, returning to the door.

"Oh, for heaven's sake—go about your own affairs!" his wife would answer, in exasperation. "You've waked the baby up, with all this uproar! Now that means no more peace of me until his nap. I don't care about the currants—I can't make jelly unless Pepita comes up, and I don't believe she's coming!"

Rudy might whistle mildly.

"Well, they'll spoil here, my dear!" And he would wander across the door yard, eye the chickens thoughtfully, pinch a green apple without removing it from the tree, and so move on to the barn, where he and the assistant of the moment would have long, comfortable conversations regarding fertilizer or young pigs. True, he might harness the team before noon, drive into the village, to return with sacks of grain or tins of paint, or he even might plough furrows back and forth across the meadow or orchard, coming in to dinner at twelve genuinely tired or hot.

But if she asked him to take Hildegarde beside him into town, he never need give any reason for his careless, "I can't to-day!" And though he did occasionally put a child down for a nap, or change a wet apron, he would have thought her mad to expect this assistance. He worked, but it was simple, uncomplicated, straight-ahead work, subject to his own wishes.

She knew Rudy was convinced himself that he was the busiest and most responsible of men, driving a bull down to the barn, turning horses loose, mending a bit of harness, always whistling, unless he was angry, always unhurried and his own master. And from her watching of him she turned back to her own jumble of irreconcilable demands and conditions, to the burned fingers, the soured soup, the infantile croup or colic that shattered whole nights of rest at one blow.

Did she love her husband?—Nelly mused. Well, of course she ought to love him, and equally of course she might have done so. But she was fretted constantly by reminders of the unfairness of their division of their mutual cares. All the blame, all the hurry and worry, all the illness and helplessness and nervousness fell to her. He knew none of these things.

She had winced, years ago, when an outspoken neighbour had voiced the old country proverb: "If the men had to have every other one, there'd never be but two children to a family!" But now Nelly knew that it was true, and much less than the truth. Nine months of misery, followed by a year or two of nursery bondage—why, Rudy would not have faced that prospect for a million dollars! The mere hint of any sort of subjection infuriated him. When a steel sliver bedded itself in his eye, he had been nearly beside himself. He would kill himself rather than endure this pain, he had shouted. He would rather be dead than blind. The entire house had circled about his furious protests, until Nelly herself had deftly removed the hurtful splinter.

This had been on a Sunday morning, when they were all ready to drive over to spend the day with Pansy Billers. The children had been buttoned into clean dresses, Nelly herself was all but dressed for the treat. But Rudy, who no longer liked Pansy, because she had frankly told him that she thought he treated Nelly mean, had decided that he was too unwell for the exertion, and had gone to bed, nursing the convalescent eye, and faintly demanding darkness and poached eggs.

If only there was no question of "bossing" in it, Nelly would muse, no question of babies! If she had been as free to ordain the conditions of her own life as he was, then she would really love Rudy dearly. She would have her dining table out under the oak, which he hated, she would always have a cold supper in summer, another custom to which he violently objected, and she would dress for her work, as men did, in some radically different fashion—even in denim, perhaps. True, she might sew on his buttons and make his bed, but he would not feel it his right to remind her of these tasks. She would clean her kitchen once a day, right after breakfast, and she would sell every ounce of fruit that was not eaten fresh. After four years of farming, Nelly, like almost all farmers' wives, detested jams and preserves.

This was her dream. But in reality she had to do just what all farmers' wives have done since farms were. She cooked heavy, hot food three times a day, even when the thermometer stood at one hundred; she struggled with big pots and pans, with pyramids of dishes and great baskets of fruit. She skimmed milk, churned butter, washed children's clothes, her anxious eyes always finding fresh tasks even while she hurried through those in hand. The clocks raced, for Nelly. There was no beginning, no end. When she dropped into bed it was to remember that the dust was in curls under the parlour table, right near the milk, and that the kitchen door let the flies in where the children's little hands had pushed the netting free of the frame. She slept heavily, and her usual answer to Rudy's call of "six o'clock, Nelly!" was a deep, half-comprehending groan.

CHAPTER XVI

HARRY'S back from Nelly's," Stephen told his wife. May's mild, faded eyes flashed.

"About time!" she said drily. "Fanny was saying that she thought it was perfectly *outrageous!* Really—Steve!"

"Oh, nonsense, woman Lucy's age!" Stephen said, unsympathetically. There was a silence. "Bobo and Georgie there— nonsense!" he presently added.

"Well, I don't think there was anything *wrong*, Steve," May hastened to assure him; anxious to range herself with him rather than with Fanny. "I told Fan so. They're just getting settled, and Harry was too ill to help move in, and all that. But it *looks* so badly—why, imagine me, if you had had a brother—of course, you did have a brother, but I mean if your brother had lived, and then you had been ill and gone off to stay with one of the girls—if Tina, say, had married——"

"Harry was down at the office to-day," Stephen said, as unconscious of interrupting his wife as she was of being interrupted. "Looks badly. He was with Bob in the bookkeeper's room for quite a while."

"What doing?" May asked suspiciously.

"Helping Miss Foster, Bob said. I didn't pay much attention to them," Stephen said, yawning elaborately. "Come on, dear, let's go down."

"Helping Miss Foster!" May echoed, not stirring. "Is Bob going to work *him* in!"

"Oh, no—no—no, for heaven's sake, May!" Stephen said impatiently. He immediately joined Esme, who was loitering in the hall. "What has this girl been doing all day?" he asked.

"Nothing!" Esme said, yawning and smiling. Victoria and Lou came out into the hall, drowsy and stretching, they had been playing duets and pasting in their scrap-books and talking, all day. They admitted that the heat made them feel stupid. May was anxious and worried for a day or two, seeing a fresh menace to Stephen's power in poor Harry; but then Stephen told her that Harry, through Bob's good-natured intercession, had gotten a job with the firm of Finch & Houston. Thady Houston had been an office boy in R. E. Crabtree and Company's employ, years ago; he was head of a big coffee house now. Harry would get eighty-five dollars a month.

One Saturday night Bertie and Victoria stayed in town, at their grandfather's house, and Bertie took his sister to the Tivoli. It was one of the thrilling occasions of Victoria's life.

Grandpa had gone upstairs. Aunt Fanny had bustled off to a meeting, and Victoria was aimlessly and dully looking at the Doré "Inferno," when Bertie tossed the evening paper aside with a yawn, and said good-naturedly: "Want to go to the Tivoli?"

Want to go! Victoria's heart bounded with joy. Why not? This was the way things happened in books.

Trembling with excitement, she put on her hat. They went downtown on the Sacramento Street dummy, and Bertie remarked that she had a "keen" hat. They met a young man named Ross Hanna, a friend of Bertie's, and he looked as if he approved of the hat, and the face under it, too. He left them at Powell Street, but no matter—Victoria was radiant over the mere meeting. She told herself that he had admired her; Bertie laughed with pleasure in her company. He got two seats for "The Mikado" and Victoria thought Tilly Sallinger amazing, and the whole performance too wonderful for words.

She and Bertie were going home at eleven o'clock the next morning, when they met the Barbee crowd at the ferry. Victoria felt so happy, in the new hat, and in her comfortable blue sateen, that she quite warmed Kitty with her graciousness. Kitty hardly glanced at Bertie, a little coquetry which did not escape Victoria, but she clung to Bertie's sister with irresistible affection. Behind Kitty streamed members of her family, and intimate friends, perspiring in the unusual warmth of the day, carrying picnic boxes—big cardboard boxes that shirts had come in, shoe boxes, and even a corset box bound with shiny green paper—all filled with sandwiches of various kinds. There were also damp, mashed-looking circular packages containing cocoanut and chocolate cakes, bags of fruit through which mellow apricots and thin-skinned peaches were already oozing, and many supplementary boxes of candy and paper bags of rich, dark, sticky dates.

Kitty explained, as the group swarmed and straggled by, that a friend of her brother's was taking them all out on his yacht to-day; "she," the yacht, was way over beyond the Mission Street wharf, and they were going to El Campo, and going to get back about eight that night.

"And listen, you're coming along! Oh, nonsense, of course you are!" said Kitty's married sister, Mrs. Boyle.

"Oh, we couldn't!" Victoria said, amused at the enormity of the thought, and a little surprised to see Bertie's eager look. "Mama expects us home!"

"I could go!" Bertie said, with longing. But Kitty pounced upon him with a flash of protest as quick as Victoria's could have been.

"Yes, you could, you freshie," Kitty said gaily; "we don't want you, we want your sister! Aw, come along," she besought Victoria prettily, "we are going to have a grand day! Come on, it's a yacht, you know—brand new. It's just had its trial trip —never been used. And it's such grand hot weather to be on the water!"

Victoria, conscious of utter madness, actually considered it. The word yacht brought to her vision a wonderful picture of white sails ruffling in the breeze, brass and paint twinkling, a pennant bright in the sun. She had never been on a yacht, but yachts danced and dipped about the plodding ferry boats all summer long.

It was a hot day, very hot on the quiet ferry front, where the tar under her feet was softened in the heat. Only Sunday crowds moved, the streets were almost neglected, but the dummies that rattled down to the Market Street turn-table were packed with wilted pleasure-seekers, noisy children, perspiring men, and babies in arms. Appointments were being made, being missed, tired people were watching every arriving face anxiously, were springing forward with eager smiles as the expected forms appeared. The swarthy, bearded old molasses-candy vender, his pitted face dark above his golden wares, threaded the groups constantly. Every few moments the mellow blare of a departing or arriving ferry boat sounded above the voices and laughter, and the constant thin piping of a million circling gulls.

"All right, she's coming!" said a tall, blond, buoyant person named Teddy Green, as Victoria hesitated.

Victoria liked him already. A long, heavenly Sunday on a yacht, with this delightful person included——!

"Oh, but Bertie—Mama——" she faltered.

"I don't care, I'm going!" Bertie said airily.

"Well, I can't!" Victoria responded, suddenly cold. And it seemed to her for a second actually preferable to return virtuously to San Rafael, to be praised and applauded for her moral courage.

"Say, listen, I'll tell you what—listen, I'll tell you what!" said Mrs. Boyle eagerly. "You come with us, Miss Brewer, and we'll have the yacht put in at Saucelito, and you and Bertie can just take the next train home? Huh——? Isn't that an idea?"

"Even if we miss the noon train, we'll get the two o'clock!" Bertie reminded her, reassuringly.

In another moment she was running happily along among them all, her skirts gathered in her right hand, her left elbow grasped by the firm fingers of young Teddy Green. Everything was youth, sunshine, adventure. She was in love.

They ran on through heat and confusion, and over the yielding tar and the hot, rough cobblestones, and past wharves, fences, dock-offices, lumber, and all the heaped accumulations of the piers. There seemed to be imminent danger of being too late for the hour of sailing, and Victoria was conscious of passionate fear as she ran. Oh, if they missed it——!

About a last corner they dashed, and down a long wharf, and out through great grain-strewn doorways, and there they were. And there was the "yacht," a plain, big flat-bottomed vessel that looked more like a scow, except for the clean new sail with which several shouting young men were hilariously experimenting. Victoria was conscious of a first pang of disappointment; she looked singularly utilitarian, this craft, hardly rocking in the dirty rubbish-strewn water that eddied languidly through the chafed piles. Victoria saw orange peels floating, and cocoanut shells in their hairy husks, and chaff, and oil, and a box or two.

She liked the aspect of her fellow voyagers almost as little as she did the *J. and Dan McCloud*. They were disconcertingly numerous; there were perhaps forty young persons already on board, and it seemed to the girl that every flushed and noisy

couple who came running down the pier were also headed for
the new "yacht." Some girls and rather common-looking
young men, perched on the roof of the little cabin, were almost
embracing as they chewed gum and toyed with a concertina.
Two husky big men in their shirt-sleeves were wheeling a small
keg of beer on board.

The yacht had been scheduled to sail at eleven o'clock, but an
hour and a half later she was still secure at the dock.   The guests
were evidently all on board now, and one or two elderly women,
and one or two buxom young matrons, had established themselves on the shady side of the deck, where the luncheon boxes
were piled, and where a few babies and quite young children
could be managed safely.

The engaging Teddy Green still was faithful to Victoria, and
she knew the first thrill of mutual attraction.   He was one of
the handsomest men she had ever seen; he was conspicuously
well dressed, radiating good-nature, charm, wit, and a most
flattering devotion.   They sat on some lumber, on the pier, and
their conversation ran along in a manner only too familiar to
the popular Teddy, but full of breathless charm for Victoria.

"No, but tell me—who are you?"

"I've told you—Victoria Brewer, of San Rafael.   That's my
brother, over there with Miss Barbee!"

"I don't care who your brother is!"

"Well, you asked me——"

"I asked you who *you* were.   And I can see that we don't
need any incandescent lights where *you* are!   No, but seriously—what did you think when you first saw me?"

"Why, I don't know what I thought!"

"I know what you thought—but no woman ever will admit
it!"

"Admit what?"

"That she likes a fellow——"

"Do you mean that you liked me—right off like that?"

Mr. Green's voice dropped and his handsome head came a
little nearer.

"Don't you know I did?" he said, marking a rough plank with
a splinter and not looking up.   "Tell me you're a little glad I
did?"

"Well, of course I'm glad!"   Victoria gave a flirt's laugh.   "I
always like men to like me!"

"Ah, yes, but now you're not talking honestly! You're talking to impress me!"

His shrewdness almost embarrassed her.

"You're a funny boy!" she said.

"Why, my dear girl," Teddy said, with that thrilling easy familiarity that so oddly reached her innermost reserves, "you don't have to talk to impress me. I like you, don't you understand? And what's more," he added, as Kitty's loud hail took them in Kitty's direction again, "before this day is over I'm going to kiss you!"

Victoria's breath was taken away, but it was a delicious sort of fear, after all, that made life sing in her veins. She felt gay, fearless, confident, she was witty and she knew it. Teddy did not leave her side; other young men were attracted to her flashing repartee.

The hot, uproarious crowd moved noisily about them; there were signs of actual departure at last. The new sail was rattled up the mast by a score of shouting young men, it filled majestically, and the boom shifted. A little chuckle of disturbed water cut through the orange-peels and floating paper boxes, and crimped young women in sweeping organdies began to pass sandwiches.

Teddy had a pencil out, and was explaining a spinnaker sail. Vicky brought her bright face close to his, as if unconsciously. Suddenly he covered her hand with his own.

"You're a darling!" he said softly. And at his words her heart seemed to turn to water, and life was unbearably sweet. Immediately he went on with his diagram; Vicky watched, her colour rising, her heart thumping.

They walked along the crowded deck, and it was delicious to have him help her solicitously. He said that he had not intended to make this trip, until he saw her.

Vicky, cornered against the deck house, made the same confession. They murmured, looking down at the paper fan the girl's agitated hands were destroying. Suddenly Teddy put his arms about her, tipped up her laughing and protesting and scandalized face, and stopped her lips with a snatched kiss.

Victoria was honestly shocked, although the kiss was a boyish one, possessing none of the quality that she quite instinctively feared from such a familiarity. It was a boy-and-girl affair, fortunately lost in the general confusion about them. The *J. and Dan McCloud* was free of the piers now, and moving gallantly out upon the ruffled bay; the sail rattled briskly, and the new clean wood of the boom showed oily fingermarks upon its virgin surface.

Confused, the girl went to the rail and leaned upon it, watching the scudding water blindly. She felt hurt in some indefinable way; Teddy liked her the less for that kiss, and she knew he did. She had been unladylike, romping, a hoyden. The terrible words came to her instinctively; Mama would say them all if she knew. Vicky's face burned; she was frightened, she wanted to go home. Already the phrase throbbed in her heart, "Oh, if I only—*only* hadn't done it!"

Teddy had joined the navigating young men; he appeared to know a great deal about boats, as indeed he did about everything. Victoria busied herself with the older women, her heart a whirlpool of confused and ashamed thoughts. She cut sticky cakes and handled moist, rich sandwiches carefully, soothed by her companions' ready friendship and appreciation. They were common, she thought, but they were not vulgar.

However, there were two young women on board to whose correct class Victoria instantly consigned them although she had never seen them before, and had but hazy ideas of their pitiful calling. Their cheap, showy clothing, their painted faces and dyed hair made her uneasy, and as the yacht flapped her slow way past the docks, she saw the Saucelito boat coming slowly and majestically into her slip, and felt a wild pang of homesickness and regret.

There was little wind, until they had tacked past Alcatraz, and caught the unfailing breeze from the Golden Gate. Then the boom went about smartly, and girls screamed, and feet ran on deck, and there was sudden excitement and exhilaration everywhere. The blue water raced by, the white sail dipped, ropes rattled and spray splashed, and they were really under way. But so broad was the body of the *J. and Dan McCloud* that there was almost no motion, and to Victoria's disgust the more vulgar element among the guests began to dance to the music of the concertina.

She sat upon a square chest, her back against the sun-warmed wall of the deck house, and tried to make herself feel that the trip was the thing, the enchantment of sailing paramount in her thoughts. But it was in vain. She could only see the fascinating Teddy, who was completely absorbed among male companions, now, and could only feel, with hurt and helplessness, that that kiss had somehow committed him to her, as she indeed felt bound to him, and that he was deliberately ignoring and snubbing her.

Bertie and Kitty had disappeared; everything seemed stale, glaring, cheap, and disgusting to Victoria, and she began to wish passionately that she had not been so foolish as to come. They were tacking through the straits; she could not even see Saucelito, any more; they were in Richardson's Bay.

Presently Teddy returned to her side, but by this time she felt oddly heavy and self-conscious again; their friendship had too rapidly reached its climax; it could only recede. Victoria tried to be sprightly, tried to envelope herself once more in a veil of shyness and novelty. But that first violent romping had swept away this possibility, and in the glaring heat of early afternoon, in this environment of oily sandwiches, crushed fruit, and perspiring bodies, she was conscious only of a flushed face, a faint headache, and a hatred of everyone and everything, herself included.

The next two hours were wretched. Finally the boat was drawn in to an old dock near El Campo, and while almost all her passengers went up to the Casino to dance, Victoria helped with the beach fire and the preparations for a clam-bake. Teddy remained beside her, and at five o'clock, drinking delicious coffee from the same cup, they were deep in flirtation again, and Vick was happy, despite a gnawing terror of the parental attitude at home, and a guilty feeling that her conduct with Teddy was having a most demoralizing effect upon Kitty and Bertie, who were acting quite openly as betrothed lovers.

The feast was enjoyed on the beach, lovely now in the decline of the sun, and eaten by most of the revellers in a reclining position. While they ate and drank, they laughed, flirted, and sang, the "bad girls," as Victoria called them, resting comfortably against male shoulders, and twisting occasionally to kiss the nearest lips.

Five o'clock—and not a move made toward home. What time would they get home anyway? Mama and Papa would be furious, of course.

Another yacht, a small trim craft this time, put in to the

beach, and the four young men on board all knew Teddy Green.
Victoria's heart sank with a perfectly correct intuition when she
saw them. Of course they wanted him to go back with them,
and of course he would go.

He came to her with a murmured explanation; these fellows
were shorthanded, do you see? Victoria was deeply hurt, but
she could not show it. She must pretend that she did not care.
Of course he must go with his friends if they wanted him. Certainly she understood. Her brother was here.

"But I'm going to see you again," Teddy said earnestly, in
parting, "and damn soon, too!"

He jumped on the yacht, the sail went up, she dipped and
swerved smoothly upon her way. It remained for Victoria to
console herself with Kitty's enthusiastic comments upon Teddy's "crush," and Kitty did not spare words.

"But Bertie, it's nearly half-past five!" Victoria said, suddenly conscientious.

"Well, I told you I wanted to go home, before we ever
started!"

"Oh, you did not! You said you'd do what I did!"

"Well, I couldn't leave you and go, could I?"

"What's the diff?" Kitty asked, amused at the skirmish;
"we're going all the way to San Rafael, and we'll see you home,
if it's midnight!"

Midnight—Victoria turned cold. Papa—Mama——! She
looked helplessly about, at the bare beach, the rippling tide, the
littered camp fire. The *J. and Dan McCloud* lay as passive at
the weather-worn pier as if she had never moved in her life.
Suppose dark came, and there was no wind, and they drifted idly
about, hour after hour——

"How far is El Campo?" she asked. But Bertie and Kitty
were wandering away, and did not hear.

However, a shabby, tall young man who had just come down
to the shore, and who was standing looking idly about, did hear,
and touched his hat as he answered:

"About half a mile!" And then suddenly smiling, he added,
"Why, how do you do Miss Brewer—Victoria?" It was Davy
Dudley.

Victoria took his hand with a great lightening at her heart.
Sober old helpful Davy would get her out of this predicament.
They talked eagerly. Davy was driving, with a middle-aged

man who wanted to try a horse before he bought it. He took a time-table from his pocket; there was a six-seventeen train from El Campo, which would get her into San Rafael at about seven.

Home at seven—home at seven! Victoria could hardly believe it was possible. Safety, security, and her own book and bed at nine o'clock.

She flew to Bertie, and when Bertie turned restive, threatened to go home alone. But Bertie was too shrewd to permit this. This would at once acquit Victoria of all responsibility, and win for him a long sermon on the subject of protecting his sisters.

So Davy drove Bertie and Victoria, and Kitty, who decided to go home too, to the station, and Kitty sat in the front seat with the prospective horse buyer, and flirted with him as freshly as if she had just risen from a long and refreshing night's sleep, and Victoria was wedged between the two other men in the back seat, revolving just the grateful speech with which she too would take leave of Davy.

"Davy, you've been an angel to me—will you come and see me some day?" was what she finally chose, and Davy's happy flush and stammered response remained in her memory as the real moment of the day.

She and Bertie reached home just at seven, and joined the family for a Sunday night supper. They had gone off on a yacht, they explained, but it promised to be too much of a good thing, so they had persuaded "the people" to put them off near home, rather than alarm Papa and Mama.

May rather liked the sound of a yacht. Only rich and aristocratic persons had yachts. Whose was it?

"Well, I don't know," Victoria said, with an easy laugh. "There were quite a few people on board. It was fun, only we got tired of it!"

"You must be starving," Esme said.

"We are!" said Bertie, feeling that he never wanted to eat again.

"Be careful how you go off on yachts," Stephen said, vaguely. Tina only partially heard. Young Mrs. Yelland had told her this afternoon of an expected event at the parsonage; and Tina could still hear those thrilling and amazing words: "Vernon and I want you to be the first to know, Ernestine, that we hope for a dear little stranger here, about Thanksgiving——"

Tina's whole being throbbed in response to this news. She

was still a maid, and this gentle, mild woman had passed through courtship, and wifehood, and was now moving on to undreamed experience. Tina felt rich in being Grace's closest friend, the privileged confidante and sharer of all this richness. Nelly's mere motherhood had never meant anything to Tina, but there was something wonderful in the reverence and responsibility with which Vernon and Grace accepted life.

Victoria dropped wearily into bed at nine o'clock, sinking at once into the pages of "Wee Wifie." And as the big house became silent, and the voices of her parents rose and fell serenely in their bedroom, a great feeling of content and safety came over her, and she let her eyes wander about the shabby, comfortable room, and deliberately took out the events of the day for review.

Teddy—Davy—a trip about the bay. And the Tivoli last night, and art school Tuesday—life was certainly exciting. If only Mama never found out that to-day's outing had been connected with the objectionable Kitty——!

Victoria's heart began to beat fast. Mama never must find that out! She had a secret to hide. The offence began to look serious, now that the adventure was over. Bertie wouldn't tell. She wouldn't tell. Who could, then?

She opened the book again, banished all uneasiness. The crowd on the *J. and Dan McCloud* were probably still on the beach, but she was home, and the day successfully ended.

November was wet; it was long remembered as the rainiest season on record. The Brewer girls practised, read novels, sewed, and moped, their impatient eyes upon the beaten garden, the tumbled pungent chrysanthemums, the shabby evergreens and swaying, yellowed pampas grass. Their neat plaid mackintoshes hung in the entry, on hooks, their muddy rubbers were congregated on the balustraded front porch.

May had thought it well for Tina not to be too frequently at the parsonage just now; there was something indelicate in her sharing of the vigil before the great event. But one day Vernon Yelland appeared, white, and with wet, pink eyes, to say that dear Grace had a little girl, and then Tina could fly to her friend. Esme was sallow, restless over books and fancy-work. Lou had a great friend, the fascinating Lily Duvalette's sister, Daisy Baker, and while the lawsuit for old "Baked Potato's" money was being dragged through the papers, Lou and Daisy had been taken by the latter's aunt to a quiet country hotel at Congress Springs. Bertie came and went with his usual amiable reserve, and Victoria kept at her art.

Davy had indeed come to see her, but only to say good-bye. He was going to Germany, to do interne work in the hospitals there. Victoria asked him how his family could spare him.

"They can't," Davy had said ruefully. "Everything is as rotten as it can be, up at Napa. I think my sister 'Lizabeth may get married. My Aunt Lilly—Miss Clay, isn't very well, and they're all mad because old Doc' Boone up there asked me to go in with him—which of course would make ev'rything easier, all round!"

"Oh, but Davy——" She loved advising him. "Then I think you ought to!"

"No," he had said, with his earnest scowl. "I've thought it all out. I want to settle in some city—specialize. I feel this way, Victoria. If I go home, it means we never will get out of the hole. If I get some special training and make good, why, then I can help them all!"

"But meanwhile they may all starve!" the girl had suggested.

"Well"—his worried smile had not had much mirth in it— "well, they've all been starving, you may say, for ten years! Two or three more won't do much harm——"

So Davy, Doctor David Dudley now, had gone away, and the Brewer girls had blamed him heartily, and Nelly, coming down for a few days at Thanksgiving, had said that it showed how hard he was getting. Fanny had added that a piece of selfishness like that ought to be stopped by law.

Fanny was irritable and nervous anyway, just now. A recent trifling incident had worried her disproportionately, and she had suddenly decided once more to go to Europe and leave all domestic jars behind.

Carra had asked her, one afternoon, for a letter of reference for Carra's niece, one Queenie Rowsey, of Alameda.

"She want work on baids en some hotel place," Carra had said; "you knows Queenie, Miss Fanny."

Fanny really did not know Queenie, except by name, but she was exceedingly sensitive and apprehensive where Carra was concerned, and had silently seated herself at her desk, and dashed off a note to the effect that Queenie was known to her and she believed her to be honest, sober, and a good worker.

Having dismissed the incident completely from her mind, she was therefore disconcerted when a rather coarse man appeared in her parlour one afternoon, with a request that she tell him exactly what she did know of Queenie, who had disappeared from the Russ House with more than two hundred dollars from the till. Fanny tried to snub this man with an airy observation that she was not responsible for the negress, but the man had grown impudent, and Fanny flushed and trembling, and in the end he had departed with a most disquieting promise to call in the law.

"A lot he could do!" Fanny told herself a hundred times, with great tossing of her head. His last words, "Why, you'd never even *seen* the woman!" remained in her mind.

"That Queenie, she bad all thoo!" Carra commented, sagely.

"Well, upon my word—then, you might have given me a hint——!" But Fanny could not relieve herself, to Carra, not with Pa's shameful secret hanging over her. So she wanted to go to Italy and began to talk about it again.

This time she decided to take Esme, whose health was not very good.

Fanny went so far as to buy a trunk, and a green and blue fringed plaid, two objects that tremendously thrilled her nieces when they came to the California Street house. Victoria, wrapping herself in the plaid, assumed the airs of a person languidly reclining in a deck chair, and they all laughed. It suddenly occurred to Fanny that the girl would make a far more amusing travelling companion than Esme, and she excited Victoria almost to fever by telling her that she, Fanny, was coming to see Mama very soon, on a matter of great importance, and upon Victoria's asking her aunt's advice as to whether a new coat or another three months at art school would be the best investment, Fanny embraced her, and said with a mischievous and significant laugh:

"A little bird tells me that you'll need a heavy coat this fall!"

"Oh, Aunt *Fanny*——!" Victoria had said, ecstatically. And she went home upon air.

Fanny did indeed come to see May soon, on a January day when sheets of rain were sweeping across the old garden. The house was warm, except in the wide, bleak hallways, and Fanny found the whole family together, and extremely glad to have the dull day broken by a caller. Even Stephen was there, confined with a heavy cold, and Victoria was there, the weather having prevented her usual Tuesday lesson; Bertie alone was absent.

They were in the dining-room, the temporary absence of a servant explaining the informality of housework and meals. Victoria and Lou were flitting in and out of the kitchen, cooking luncheon, Esme had been reading to her father, Tina was trimming the raw edge from yards and yards of embroidery with a tiny, sharp scissors, the severed strip sliding down against her skirt of worn plum-coloured sateen. May had been at the entry door, letting in a wet draft of air as she negotiated with the old "vegetable Chinaman," who had lowered his big baskets on the porch, and lifted out their round trays to show sweet potatoes and red apples.

"Well, Fanny!" said May, in pleased welcome. "That's all, John," she said to the Chinese. "You tell me—I pay to-morrow."

And while the old fellow packed up his wares and balanced the long carrying-pole upon his blue ticking shoulder, May led her sister in.

"Mama—how much butter—about a lump like this?" Lou asked, from the kitchen door. "Oh, hello, Aunt Fanny! Vicky, here's Aunt Fanny!"

"Here's old bothersome Aunt Fanny come to make more work for you poor little girlies!" Fanny laughed, as her cold, hard, rosy face was kissed and her damp outer garments carried away by the gathering nieces. "Well, Steve, what does all this mean?"

"Oh, I've got an awful cold," Stephen said heavily, glad of fresh sympathy.

"Working too hard, eh?" Fanny said briskly, as she turned back her damp skirt, and exposed well-clad, sturdy feet to the fire. Her brother-in-law's face darkened.

"No," he said gloomily, and fell silent. Fanny raised surprised eyebrows and glanced expectantly at May. "They're doing things pretty much as they please, there," Stephen added, bitterly, after a pause, "and they'll run themselves on the rocks one of these days, I tell them!"

"Bob—and young Fenderson," May said lightly and in explanation.

"Young Fenderson—why, he's nothing but a boy!" Fanny protested.

"Thirty," Stephen said, drily.

"Well, but Stephen, I think it's your business to look out for things a little more," Fanny suggested, uneasily; "after all, there are stockholders to think of! It isn't conscientious—it's your business to protect them!"

"Imagine advertising—*spices!*" May said eagerly and readily; "things that everybody has to have *anyway*, imagine that Bob Crabtree put seven hundred dollars into advertising alone, last year! *Spices!*"

"That's only one detail," Stephen said sombrely and impatiently, with a half-indulgent, half-annoyed glance at his wife.

"I think Bob's crazy!" Fanny said, aghast. "Why do you let him do it?"

"You forget that I am only vice-president of the firm, Fanny," Stephen said, enjoying her consternation. "Talk to your father or Bob!"

"It's ridiculous for Pa to interfere as he does!" Fanny sputtered anxiously. "Rob, now—there's another drain on the firm! I'd like to know what board he pays Lucy! Lucy was in the White House, buying dress goods, last week—dear me, we are putting on airs! I asked her to come up to-day and sit with Pa, but she said she had Bobo on her hands, and that she had a Japanese boy cleaning on Wednesdays, anyway. 'All right,' I said, 'but all I ask is, don't come to *me* for favours, the next time things go wrong!'"

"Did she ever, Aunt Fanny?" Lou asked.

"Certainly she did, or Harry did, not a year ago," Fanny said, vexedly sniffing and beating the end of her nose. "Wanted five hundred dollars—I like the style!"

"I never knew that," May said, round-eyed. Stephen also looked interested.

"Well, they didn't get it." Fanny was too honest not to say. "I was arranging it, I had gone downtown about it, at least, to see what my balance was, when things brightened up, and this ridiculous arrangement with Bob began. So silly! All this domestic pose, 'Oh, she wants to make a home for Bobo, and for dear Bob!' Bob had a perfectly good home, and if—anything happens to Pa, I wouldn't have any objection to putting Bobo upstairs, he's getting older now——"

"I suppose Carra'd be glad enough to stay on, and look out for him!" May said. But this mysteriously seemed to annoy Fanny.

"I don't know what she'd do or wouldn't do!" she said, shortly. And to Vicky's deep disappointment there was no talk of Europe that day. The nearest approach that Fanny made to it was when she said nervously: "A body doesn't know what to do, with things in this state! It would be a nice thing for any one to get abroad, and then have their income cut in half!"

"Oh, *you*, Fan," May said, in good-humoured impatience, "with all Aunt Jenny's money!"

"Yes, of course," Fanny said, pale and trembling, and in a low tone. "Millions, of course—ha! Well, I just wish some of you good people—but we won't discuss it! Most of it's in the firm, anyway!"

"About a fifth," Stephen smiled, baiting her. "And you didn't put that in, your aunt did," he reminded her.

Vicky appeared providentially at the moment, with the changed subject of lunch.

Harry's simple happiness, at this time, was regarded by the various branches of the family with mingled annoyance, scorn, and even envy. Fanny, to be sure, had a more luxurious home; May had always had a servant, often two. But somehow Lucy's complacency, Bob's content, and Harry's utter felicity exasperated them all. They told each other things about the pretty cottage in Larkin Street; they added young Georgie's earnings to Harry's, estimated what his share of the mutual expenses cost Bob.

The room he awakened in every morning pleased Harry; it was a simple, sunny room. He liked to hear Georgie fussing with Bobo's buttons and strings in the adjoining room, to hear Lucy's bright voice among the pans and plates of the kitchen. They still babied him a little; he had not quite thrown off his cough. He went out to breakfast at eight, walked across Polk Street in balmy sunshine.

Everything would be fresh and attractive: damp sidewalks, daintily stepping women at the markets, awnings flapping coolly over the ranged fish and fruit. Sometimes he walked a few unnecessary blocks before taking the Sacramento Street car

He liked the friendship in the firm, too, the general smile and "Good morning, Harry!" as he came into the cluttered, over-crowded office that this miraculously clever and capable woman, Miss Blum, managed so well. Many of the clerks had begun in Crabtree and Company's office; the young firm was already the most serious rival old Reuben had. Harry's desk was on a sort of deck at the far back, above the cool, oiled, central floor where clerks were partitioned off into pens, and where Thady, his father's old office boy, walked and reigned. There was a dirty skylight overhead; the whole place was a jumble of temporary partitions, some painted white, some unpainted, bundles of old account books and papers roped together, odd desks of oak, and plain wooden tables. Addresses were pencilled upon smooth bits of plaster, calendars were tacked on the walls; and dust lay like plush upon the upper shelves of plain, built-in bookcases and lockers.

A smell of roasting coffee would ascend to this region every morning, at about twelve o'clock, just before whistles mellow and shrill announced the noon rest to the working city. Harry remembered this smell from babyhood; it had pleasant as-sociations. He worked hard and accurately at his ledger, but sometimes his simple pleasantries immensely amused the office, and Miss Blum liked to make him talk. Sometimes at noon he went over to Crabtree and Company's office—where he would see Stephen, Bob, and Bertie. Bertie was proving to be neither particularly useful nor particularly happy in the busi-ness; he still came and went dutifully, bored and indifferent, but he had not, in his father's phrase, "taken hold." Stephen sometimes wished that Victoria had been a boy; the girl showed so pleasant an interest in everything that touched Crabtree and Company, she had had to be told, indeed, that she must not come into the office on her art lesson days. It was no place for her, Stephen had said kindly, her mother could always find her plenty to do with her spare time, at home.

Stephen was fretted afresh every time anybody spoke to Rob as "Crabtree" or "Mr. Crabtree." If things had gone differ-ently, the firm might have been "Brewer and Son," now! And still the old man held on, and nothing definite could be decided or changed.

"How's Lucy?" he asked, perfunctorily, on a wet March even-ing when he and Harry happened to meet in the street. The warm, spring-like February was forgotten in a fresh onslaught of winter, but Harry looked happy enough in his old overcoat.

"Fine. And we have the little girl to-night," Harry beamed. "Alice—it's her free night. Lucy kind of likes to feed her up, when she gets a chance!"

Blameless enough; but Stephen, opening his umbrella, looked with dissatisfaction at the light sheets of rain that a spring gust was blowing into sudden whirls and hollows, along the sidewalks. It was twilight; the gas street lamps were pink in blurs of dull light.

"You're not afraid of that training breaking the girl down, Harry?" He looked to see the other's face cloud.

"Oh, she likes it!" Harry countered innocently.

"They don't know what they like!" Stephen said, vaguely discontented. "Vicky gets notions—wants to work. Run away from work, is what I call it. Well, good-night!"

"Good-night!" Harry's rather hoarse, happy voice called back cheerfully, as he ran for his packed and streaming car, in the dark. Stephen had a great many worries and fears, but Harry thought only of the warm kitchen, of Alice home and full of stories of the wards and the nurses, of Georgie and Rob playing cribbage while he admiringly watched, and of Lucy scratching her thick gray hair thoughtfully as she worked out a calculation regarding the successful culture and marketing of Belgian hares.

He had in his pocket a mica fish for Bobo, a fish that would curl up mysteriously upon the palm of Bobo's warm little hand. Harry loved the little boy; he often took Bobo to the Park on Sunday, as he had taken Nelly years ago, and then Alice and Georgie. There was a merry-go-round at the park now, and swings and see-saws, and a new band-stand; Harry, getting carefully off the Haight Street dummy, with Bobo, would feel his heart bursting with a joy as keen as the child's own.

Lucy had a scheme by which Bob and Harry were to board with Fanny, for the two summer months, while she and Bobo went down to stay with Nelly. As an equivalent for her board at the farm, she worked out a careful table of values, proving that her assistance to Nelly, in the care of Nelly's house and her three babies, would more than compensate for the slight additional expense. Meals for the hired men were estimated, and hours for the children's naps and play were planned.

It was somewhat disappointing to have Nelly write that Rudy's mother was there, managing everything, and that as Hildegarde and Clifford and the baby had all had whooping-cough, and were still coughing, it would be wiser not to bring Bobo. It seemed to Lucy that Bobo might as well risk the disease and get over it, and the thought of Rudy's mother in her place made her indignant. She went down for a week's visit, in April, and took Bobo with her as a matter of course. This was Lucy's first visit to her married daughter, and she went full of interest and enthusiasm.

It was not entirely her fault that the whole thing proved a failure; conditions were against them all from the start. The weather was real "fruit" weather, burning hot still sunshine all day long. Nelly's babies were still fretful and coughing convulsively. And Nelly's little house was crowded. When Bobo and Lucy came Rudy had to sleep in the parlour, on the floor, Lucy shared Nelly's small hot bedroom with the new baby and Bobo, and Mrs. Sessions had the two older children with her in what was still called "Uncle's room." They were all intensely uncomfortable.

Then Mrs. Sessions, while the most patient and efficient of household drudges, and simply indispensable to Nelly in this hot and busy time, was a dismal, silent soul, given to recitations concerning cancers and abortions, and none too nice in her speech. She liked, secretly, to make Nelly laugh with her homely country phrases, although her leathery, colourless, wrinkled, sun-and-wind-burned face never betrayed a sympathetic mirth.

"I guess this feller's got a holler leg," Mrs. Sessions would say of Clifford, when he was stuffing at the table; and once she made Nelly laugh by rebuking Rudy, who had scratched his head, with the words: "Leave 'em be, son. You hit something your own size!"

She was wonderful with the babies, had an instinct for the use of goose-grease or licorice powder, never worried about them, and seemed to have a quieting effect upon them. She was the old-fashioned type of woman who gets a wash out before breakfast on Monday morning, bakes pies by the dozen, and cakes by the yard, and yet who is seen in the early afternoon idle and ruminative in a chocolate or stone-gray percale and fresh apron, waiting for the arrival of supper time.

This made her invaluable to Nelly, and Nelly was always dreading a hint of "Ma's" departure. Rudy had a sister Mamie, much older than he, with a husband of whom "Ma" merely said, in description, that "he'd oughter be hung," and with eight children. Mrs. Sessions' heart was really with Mamie, in Oregon.

When Lucy came to the ranch, suddenly Rudy's mother began to seem the odd, cranky, common old woman she was. Nelly laughed at her no more: instead she felt constantly shocked and ashamed. She was always uncomfortable when the two older women were together, and scarcely happier when she and her mother wandered off for walks or long talks in the vegetable garden, leaving "Ma" plodding away in greasy gray dishwater at the sink in the hot kitchen.

"I don't know what she's doing!" Nelly would say uneasily. Lucy always answered heartily:

"Stop worrying about her, dear. She likes it!"

Lucy criticized Nelly's calling Rudy's mother "Ma," and Mrs. Sessions was scornful of the meat-chopper and soap-shaker that Lucy introduced. She continued to slop about with a rag in the dishwater, and she chopped meat with the old circular knife, in the round wooden bowl; the baby hunched on her hip even as she chopped and hashed.

Before Lucy had been there three days relations were strained all round; Lucy contemptuous of Mrs. Sessions, and Rudy's mother muttering about folks that had their heads full of fool notions. On the fourth day the latter openly hinted at her own departure for Mamie and Portland, and Nelly, heated and tired and nervous, burst into tears. "Ma" *couldn't* go until she got a girl!

"You've got your own Ma!" said Ma Sessions.

"Yes, but Mama doesn't know one *thing* about farm work!" Nelly cried, too anxious to be diplomatic.

It was at this point that Lucy magnificently decided to leave, giving no reason beyond the observation that she was merely Nelly's own mother, and consequently not as valuable as a hired girl, she knew. No, she must go, no, she must go, she persisted brightly. She had written Papa, she must get back.

She left, airily civil, the next day, and Nelly, seated beside Rudy in the surrey, cried all the way home. Against her own interests she upbraided him bitterly for real and imaginary differences in his treatment of her mother and his own, and Rudy was not wise enough to keep the peace. Their quarrel, and the cause of it, leaked out, and a week later Mrs. Sessions departed silently and apathetically to join Mamie, and Nelly faced the problem of children, house, kitchen, hired men, preserving time, chickens, and pigs alone.

CHAPTER XVII

W HO is it?" whispered Mrs. Brewer anxiously. The front-door bell, set with other bells on a line of great coiled springs high up on the kitchen wall, was still convulsedly shaking. Its ringing clanged through the house.

"Mama, I don't know!" Tina whispered, also peering through the closed upstairs shutter, at guests coming up the drive.

"Oh, heavens, where's Vicky?"

"Down there somewhere! Sh-h!" said Tina to Lou, who had come cautiously and silently into the bedroom; "it's somebody coming—we don't know who!"

"You look, Baby!" Mrs. Brewer, her face blotched, her thin gray hair in disorder from a heavy afternoon nap, gathered her combing sack about her, and creaked toward the washstand.

"I don't know who it is!" Lou rasped, in a loud whisper, "Listen, that's Vick opening the door—she'll see 'em, whoever they are!"

"They may be the Willy Murchisons, from the hotel," May said, hastily washing face and arms with a knitted wash-cloth, and always expectant of advances from "society." "You jump into something, Tina darling, and come down. Bertie was telling me that they are getting up dances there for next winter."

Esme, who had been lying down, arose at this mysterious hint when it was passed on by Lou, and, having "hooked" her younger sister, was hooked in turn. Mother and daughters, brushed and rosy and rustling, descended the stairs together fifteen minutes later, to find Vicky and the callers seated on the chipped and shabby balustraded front porch.

It was Kitty Barbee, and her stout, friendly, nervous mother. May's welcome congealed half-spoken, the girls dared not look at each other. The nerve! calling on Mama, ran all their thoughts.

"I've been trying to get here all summer," said Kitty, pleasantly but uncomfortably; "but somehow the time flies!"

Kitty, in pink challis, with a pink hat, looked positively beautiful. But she was far from happy.

"I've knew this place ever since we come to San Rafael," said Mrs. Barbee, having recourse to flattery; "it certainly is a grand place. Sometimes I'd say to Bertie—we're all awfully fond of him—I'd say that I was going to walk in, and he'd say 'Go ahead, Mrs. Barbee, my Mama'd be pleased to have you!' But I believe in waiting until you're asked—I've always said that to my children——"

Her strong, pleasant voice faltered; there was a faint murmur of response from the tense circle of the Brewers. Esme had recklessly put on her best dress, a pongee trimmed with rows of narrow brown velvet ribbon. Tina had sacrificed not only her fresh cross-barred muslin, but also the starched petticoat that held its full bell skirt so roundly. Lou, their real snob, was openly ungracious and impatient of this farce. The Barbees calling on Mama!

"Didn't we have a nice time that day on the yacht?" said Kitty desperately to Victoria. Victoria's heart turned to water, and her lips were dry.

"Yes, didn't we?" she said faintly, in an agony.

"I guess Bertie told you about our friend's yacht," said Kitty innocently, turning to May. May's eyes wandered to Victoria, and her cheeks flushed over their soft folds of flesh. She set her lips primly, with a vague motion of her head that might have been either negative or affirmative.

"I guess our young people made friends that day," Mrs. Barbee said, warming; "it seems a shame, with all the boys we have at our house, and you living so long here with all these girls!"

This appalling suggestion and overture visibly froze May, whose mouth looked as if the stiff automatic smile almost hurt it.

"You—you live down across the track, don't you?" Esme said, to say something. Mrs. Barbee agreeably explained exactly where they lived. Victoria's heart was lead. There was no talk of tea, no talk of further meetings. But poor Kitty, going, finally faltered out the real reason for their call. Where was Bertie these days? They hadn't seen him for ages. Tell him not to forget his old friends.

"Well, Lord, what have they got to be so stuck-up about!"

Mrs. Barbee said, hot with hurt pride, as she and Kitty picked their way homeward in the dust.

"I told you we oughtn't to go!" said Kitty, bitterly.

"She always did think she was too good for this earth!" her mother said, of May. They walked on for awhile in silence. Then the older woman added timidly: "We've got a right to call there, Kit. It didn't do them no hurt!"

"I'd like to kill them!" gritted Kitty, over the agony of shame and disappointment in her heart. "Ma," she faltered, breaking, "I—I don't think I'm going to get over it! And he never comes —now. He *never* comes!"

They were almost at their own gate now; Mrs. Barbee stood still in amazement. Kitty Barbee, great big girl that she was, crying like a baby, and running into the house!

For Victoria there was of course immediate judgment. The gate had barely slammed upon the Barbees when her mother, flushed and breathing stormily, said quietly:

"Vicky."

The other girls lingered, ostentatiously occupied.

"Sit down, Vick. Let me get the truth of this. That Sunday that you went off yachting—was it with the Barbees?"

Victoria was silent; looked down, looked up.

"Yes, Mama."

"You know how Mama feels about the Barbees, don't you?"

Victoria said to herself: "She can't touch me, she can't touch me! The Barbees are as good as we are!"

"Vick, did you hear Mama?"

"Yes, Mama. But Bertie——"

"Never mind your brother. You knew you were doing wrong, didn't you, Vick?"

Victoria was heard to murmur that she didn't see what was *wrong* about it——

"*What!*" said May, not believing her ears.

"Well, I'll tell you what was wrong about it," Esme said, sharply. "Letting dirt-common people like that come and call on us, and encouraging Bertie so that he'll probably marry Kitty Barbee, and ruin his life—and our chances—and making Mama even talk to a low, common woman——"

Vicky managed a scornful smile. Stephen, coming in weary, and pleased to find his womenkind together on the porch, was

regaled instantly with the whole disgraceful story.   His brow
grew dark as he looked at the sullen, flushed face of his second
daughter.

Some day, he said, when she remembered her lovely home, she
would wish that she had died before she brought such sorrow and
disappointment to her own family.   She was too big a girl to
whip, but what she should have had was a good whipping.   A
father and mother devoted to her, only anxious to see that she
grew to be a good and lovely woman——

At this point, to her rage and self-contempt, quite as if some
piece of machinery had set it in motion, Victoria's breast began
to heave and she knew she was going to cry.   They had come
into the dining room, and she was standing at the slide; the old
room was softened by drawn shutters, and the table was partly
laid for supper.   She knew that Lou and Mama and Tina were
listening in the kitchen.   She felt a deep wild hatred of father
and of all her family.

"Why, what can be expected of your younger sisters, if you
act this way, Vicky?" her father said sharply.   Victoria gave a
sort of snort, averted her face, choked, and fled blindly.   Stephen
went on upstairs to wash his hands for supper, and May, well
satisfied, told her other daughters that she thought Papa had
made some impression upon Vick—poor Vick.

Victoria went out through the big bare stable yard, where
neglected yellow grass was shining redly in the sunset, and up
past the currant bushes, and behind the barn.   For the past
year or two the Brewers had kept neither a man nor a cow, and
the place smelled sweet and dry, rust had grown thick over the
abandoned plough and the harrow.   Grandpa had sold the
pasture, and it had been divided into building lots, and was
ornamented with a real estate agent's sign, offering terms.   Papa
had put a three-plank fence in here, close to the old cowshed, and
Victoria leaned on the fence, and soothed herself with a con-
templation of the rapidly encroaching neighbourhood.

A pleasant, unpretentious little six-room cottage had been
built on one of the lots, and the girl liked to study at close range
the happiness of the young bride and groom who were so busy
with their new life there.   Their little dry rows of onions and
radishes, their amateurish clothesline that fell so often, their
short length of garden hose with which young Mr. Torrey tried
with manful stretching of his arm to reach the uttermost limits

of their domain—all this raw little study of poverty, love, and courage fascinated Victoria. Little Mrs. Torrey was very pretty, completely absorbed in the novelty and delight of being a wife and a housekeeper; she spent the hours that Eric was away in rapturous plans for his return, and her timid little essays in muffins and gelatines kept her for hours in her playhouse kitchen.

To-night they were climbing on a barrel to take turns peeping into a bird's nest that had been discovered wedged in next to the rain spout. The house was too new for vines, but next year there would be vines, as trembling tendrils carefully twisted about strings and faltering up from the dry soil, already attested.

Vick heard them laugh, and heard their murmurs. Eric Torrey boldly kissed his wife as they went up the three narrow steps to the microscopic back porch.

"You're too big a girl to whip, but you ought to have a good whipping!" her father had said. Her face burned angrily. She was indeed too big a girl to whip; no man ought ever to whip a girl! Her mother had often whipped her, years ago, when she was a child, and once when she was quite grown—thirteen, her father had. She remembered the last occasion; she was punished for being "saucy" to her mother. May, as not infrequently occurred, had threatened to tell Papa, and this once had kept her word, and had reserved judgment until Stephen came home.

Resentment and shame for this old outrage burned fresh in Victoria's heart to-night, and an actual physical thrill went through her body. She remembered her mother's triumphant silence all through the long afternoon. She had never supposed her father would whip a big girl of thirteen, especially as Bertie and Tina, if not equally impudent, had somewhat shared the offence. But her father had led her into his room, and had spanked her with a grieved deliberation and solemnity that she never remembered without shamed resentment.

Now she was too big to whip. But his words whipped her: his intimation that she was not to be trusted away from the parental judgment and care. She watched the silhouette of Eric Torrey lighting the kitchen lamp, and wondered, if Amy Torrey ever had a girl baby, if he would whip it. She suspected that there were great hopes in the little cottage, and was watching with deep attention for some confirmation of her suspicion.

When she went back to the house, supper was over, and everyone ignored her. Bertie was home, and merely reproached her, in a scornful aside, for "showing 'em that she cared." Victoria dried dishes, and afterward carried a plateful of dainties up to her room, established herself in bed, and lighted her lamp. She felt sulky, nervous, and apprehensive. Friendly relations had to be established with every separate member of the family, and she was in no mood for peace-making.

In the next few days her attitude of cold resentment troubled her mother, who kept up a constant little stream of allusions and explanations. Poor Papa, so worried about the business, poor Papa, who had tried so hard to wean Bertie away from this Barbee girl, poor Papa, practically carrying Grandpa and Uncle Rob and all the responsibility of the firm——

Victoria listened with a set, mutinous face. Suddenly they all bored her profoundly, these amiable young women who were her sisters, this stupid, fussing man and his wife who could control her actions, her thoughts almost, who could cripple and intimidate her very spirit. All very well as mere acquaintances, these Brewers, but why should a healthy, energetic, youthful human being be irrevocably tied to them?

The ready-made affections that had contented her from babyhood dropped now like dropping veils, and she eyed her family with a dispassionate coolness that would have horrified May, and that actually frightened Victoria herself.

Her father's smooth pink lower lip, showing above his beard; her mother's fluttering, loyal, ignorant criticism of Rob and young Fenderson; Tina, solemnly making a baked custard for her friend Grace and Grace's dear husband; Lou, furiously running the sewing-machine over the challis she meant to wear to Daisy Baker's engagement luncheon—these all filled her with utter *ennui*. As for Bertie, whose disgusting, selfish meanness to Kitty Barbee had caused all this trouble, and who was escaping scot-free, her old childish jealousy flamed up against him, and she felt that she hated him.

"Bertie, don't you like Kitty any more?"

"Sure I do. I always will. But Papa and Mama hated me to go there——"

"Yes, and a lot of difference that would make!"

Bertie had indeed entirely outgrown Kitty now, Kitty, whose nonsense never went beyond a kiss or a disputed embrace. He had passed into the hands of Mina Eisenwein, young Fenderson's stenographer, and his days were one long agony of apprehension as to just how strong a hold Mina had upon him. A few weeks of stolen and forbidden intimacy with Mina had passed lightly over his head, but now, when Mina met him in the office with red-rimmed, reproachful eyes, when Mina said that her sister said she was a fool not to go straight to Mr. Stephen Brewer, and tell him the whole story, poor Bertie began to spend feverish days and wakeful nights, and to wonder what else in his life had ever seemed to him worth worrying about.

Mina was a pale, homely little creature, with red, red lips. Bertie never would have seen her at all but for the necessity of carrying opened mail into Tom Fenderson's office every day. And somehow, seeing her every day, she grew to seem first interesting, then attractive, then irresistible, and there had been a few costly weeks when the thought of her, and the memory of her, had never been out of his head. But now the only desire Bertie had in connection with Mina was an ardent one that she might be painlessly and instantaneously killed by an accident of some sort.

She never was five minutes late at the office but what his heart rose on a great wave of hope. But she always came quietly and pleasantly in, hanging the black hat with the three yellow roses upon its usual nail, and straightening the wide "berthas" of her thick green serge waist. And Bertie worried and worried and worried, without knowing what to fear or what to hope.

Victoria's championship of Kitty infuriated him. He liked little Kitty, with whom his old flirtation had a misty purity and beauty, regarded in this new and sordid light. But he could no more turn back to Kitty than to the holland blouses and wooden horse of his babyhood. He could not even go to see Kitty, and May, seeing him thoughtful in the evenings, reading Scott at last, rejoiced that her darling only son was safe from the machinations of women, for awhile at least. She was triumphant, remembering Kitty's call.

"That sort of girl may have a temporary fascination for a boy," she told the listening girls, "but it is not of long duration!"

Victoria spent the autumn in brooding and planning. She

was twenty-six: she would never marry. But she must, she *would*, do something. She wrote to a business college for its folder; she went into a railroad office and priced a ticket to New York. On one of the new "vestibuled" trains. The clerk was polite; he pencilled lightly and adeptly: so much plus so much plus so much. It was not so great a sum!

Finally Victoria began to talk of a special course at the California University.

Her father forbid this dream sternly. Mixed colleges were "hotbeds of immorality," he said. If any girl anywhere in a certain house he knew about had any spare time, suppose she did some gardening? Things were beginning to look pretty shabby outside. And how about apple jelly? It seemed to him that he hadn't had any real good, old-fashioned apple jelly for a long time!

CHAPTER XVIII

ESME took the centre of the stage, immediately after Christmas, with a siege of typhoid fever. The mere word was enough to make May faint, and to send the other three girls whispering and awed about the silent house. Esme was moved to the third floor, feverish, uncomfortable, but amused at the excitement, and Alice, just graduated, came over to take Esme as her first case.

All this was thrilling and upsetting and interesting. Vicky did not see the justice of letting Alice run all the risk, if risk there were, but everyone else seemed to take it for granted that she should live upstairs, come to the table when meals were over, and take her airings on the cupola porch, or alone in the garden. For the first week, May quite frequently went upstairs for long visits with the invalid.

And then, as if *enough* hadn't happened, as Tina said, May broke her arm. Just a slip on the kitchen floor that Annie was washing, and down she went, and when she got up it was a queerly dangling left arm. Lou got great credit in the family councils for being the one to notice it.

"*I* was too much wrapped up in Mama's faintness," Tina said, a hundred times. "*I* didn't think of anything but the way she was laughing and crying! *Imagine!*"

"I daresay I was a little hysterical," May always supplied, smiling faintly, from the couch.

"Oh, I saw it instantly," Lou would say. "And I said, 'Oh, Mama, *your arm!*'"

May was able to move about a little, but the arm must not be strained; she spent a great deal of her time on the couch. And Vicky, to her almost unbearable gratification, was appointed to sickroom service in May's place. Vicky must wear her percale dresses, and somewhat keep away from the others——

Victoria did her part nobly. She would have liked a far more heroic isolation. She and Alice became close friends, talking

301

softly in the winter nights, while Esme muttered and tossed, and branches clicked coldly on the elm trees, outside in the dark. There were two coal-oil stoves, upstairs, and Victoria always associated their faint odour with Esme's illness; and with those nights in the dimly lighted, softly warmed sickroom, with the disks of golden glow from the lamp and stove shining on the low, mansard ceiling.

Esme was not very ill; presently she had reached the ravenous stage; windows were opened to a warm February, and Alice went home. But before she went she presented her Uncle Stephen with a neatly written bill: three weeks' professional services; seventy-five dollars.

Stephen was puzzled; he smiled, frowned faintly, looked with quizzical eyes at Alice, and folded the little bill carefully. That night he showed it to May.

"You don't suppose it's—serious?" he said.

"Well, I suppose so," May answered, uncertainly. "But it seems an outrageous sum for a girl that age to have, all her own! Our girls have never had anything like that."

"I don't mind showing Lucy's girl that I appreciate her devotion and her work," Stephen said, disapprovingly. "But she had her meals—everything. This is preposterous, it seems to me. What did we give Lucy, when your aunt died, May?"

"Twenty," May said instantly. But for once she was inclined to be progressive. "I think twenty-five a week's the regular rate, Steve," she said.

"Well," Stephen said, suddenly aware that he was helpless, "we'll see!" May heard no more of it, but she repeated this much to Vicky, and Vicky writhed to think that little Alice Crabtree had fitted herself so easily to earn so enormous a sum! Seventy-five dollars! What couldn't one do with it! If she, Vick, ever had it, she would go to New York and go on with her voice culture. She had sometimes sung to amuse Esme, in the long winter twilights, and everyone—even downstairs— had said that her voice sounded sweet.

Fanny, long before this, had come to see the invalids, but May was inclined to be a little critical on the subject of her tardiness; why, she had broken her arm nearly three weeks ago!

"I'm too much accustomed to sick calls, my dear, to push my

way in here before I'm wanted," Fanny countered lightly. "This isn't my first visit to an invalid!"

"Doesn't she look lovely, Fanny?"

"Why, she just looks wonderful!"

"Mama," said Esme happily, "this morning—to show you how well I am!—and Doctor Underwood just stood there at the foot of the bed—and he wagged his head, didn't he, Vick?—and he said, 'Well, young lady, I think you are fooling us all—there's nothing the matter with *you!*'"

"Used to go to school with his wife," said Fanny, hitting the end of her nose.

"I imagine his wife is rather—unsympathetic," Esme said.

"When I think—of all *times* for me to break my arm!" May mourned. "However, Vicky has been wonderful. I don't know what we should have done without her."

"Well, perhaps somebody will kidnap your wonderful Vicky, one of these days," Fanny said, fired to rather rash speech by May's complacent air of possession. "I know somebody who's beginning to get a sort of craving for travel again. I suppose that trip with Aunt Jenny, twenty years ago, sort of spoiled me! Well, if I go—I can't go alone, can I?" she ended, in innocent inquiry.

"Oh, Aunt Fanny!" Victoria said, giving her a little push.

"Well, can I?"

"Fanny, dear, you'll raise the child's hopes to fever pitch!" said May, with rich maternal protest.

"Poor little me, with no one to talk to!" Fanny said, with a whimsical face. "On the big liner—you've never seen a stateroom, Vicky, little white berths, and a port-hole——"

"Oh, wonderful!" exulted Vicky.

"And little white basins not so wonderful," Fanny suggested naughtily. Both the girls and May laughed outright. Victoria was in wild spirits for the rest of the day, and many days.

One April day, in an unusual mood of hope, she dashed off a note to Aunt Fanny. It was written at home, where Esme was sitting out in the sunshiny garden now, and all the family gathered about her in her convalescence. Victoria wrote:

DEAREST AUNT FANNY,

I have been thinking and thinking of what you said a week or two ago, and of course I am just wild about the idea. If I could once get even as far as New York, I believe that I would not much longer be a burden to you, as I have some plans that might keep me there: music, I mean. So that if you even got east and then Grandpa got ill, or your plans changed, I would certainly be no burden to you.

There was more in the same strain, but it was these fatal lines that brought Fanny flying over to San Rafael two days later, aghast at their possible meaning.

"Vicky," said her mother, patient, annoyed, still with a bandaged arm; "what possessed you to write such nonsense to your Aunt Fanny?"

"*What* nonsense?" asked Vicky, with a sick drop at her heart and a dry throat.

"Why——" May shooed out a few flies, shut the kitchen screen door, and sampled some rather tender and broken ginger cakes, as she indicated the garden by a backward gesture of her head. "Your aunt's out there," she said, "and she says you wrote her about going to New York, Vicky, and studying music, and I don't know what all. What on earth possessed you?"

"Oh, Mama, that was just nonsense!" said Vicky, scarlet-cheeked.

"Well, I wish you'd learn to outgrow your nonsense!" May said, with a sharp click of tongue and teeth. "Come out and talk to your aunt now, and try to act like a sensible girl! I don't know what Papa will say when he hears of these fine plans of yours! Where did these plums come from, Tina?"

"From the fruit Chinaman, Mama—I ran after him this morning, because you'd forgotten any fruit."

"I didn't forget, Tina. But they looked too green!"

"But we're going to cook them, Mama!"

"All right this time, then, and I'll pay old John for them. But I don't like you girls to act quite so independently, that's all! Come out, now, Vick," May led her second daughter out to the lawn, where Esme was the centre of a group in the shade. "Here's this silly girl!" she said, indulgently.

Fanny flashed a laughing look at her niece.

"Well, Vicky, I didn't know what to make of you!" said she, in elaborate alarm. "Poor innocent me, I make a mild suggestion about perhaps going abroad in a year or two, and here comes a hoity-toity letter about staying in New York and plans to leave home——"

"I don't know what got into me," said Victoria, grinning, and embarrassed by the general laugh.

"I should think you didn't!" Fanny was in high spirits. "And pray was I to telegraph your poor parents that you had walked off from me, in New York! Nice prospect for me! What did you propose to do in New York, Miss Rothschild?"

"Oh, I don't know——!" Victoria smiled, so that she need not cry.

"She's a perfect child, Fan," May said, half amused and half annoyed; "she hasn't the faintest idea of the perils and dangers of the world! She would leave her safe, happy home to-morrow, and plunge into any novelty—just because it was new!"

"Yes. Well, then I think her home is very much the best place for her!" said Miss Fanny, with a decided toss of her head. Vick presently went to set the luncheon table with a film of tears over her eyes, and hatred and despair in her heart. After lunch she deliberately neglected Aunt Fanny, and went up to the fence beyond the cowshed. There was no doubt about little Mrs. Torrey now; her pretty young face was strained and ugly, her figure, under the stretched little checked kitchen apron, showed a strange change. Victoria saw her often in the spring dusk, walking slowly along the level blocks on her husband's arm. For some reason not quite definable, or at least never defined by herself, the other young woman's situation held a fascination for Victoria; she was incessantly creeping out to the back fence to study her, to dream about her.

Fanny and May were glad to be left alone; they had several burning topics to discuss in low tones. May opened with the great and dawning hope concerning Bertie and Lola Espinoza. The Tasheiras' little niece was out of school now, staying with her aunts, and apparently inclined to great friendliness toward the Brewers. She had come to inquire for Esme, on a wet January Sunday, and had sat drying her plumed hat and riding skirt by the dining-room fire. Bertie had been—*undeniably*—impressed. He had gone up to see her twice, at May's suggestion, and she had spent another Sunday with the Brewers.

"It seems as if darling Esme were the means of bringing the greatest happiness of his life to Bertie!" May said.

Fanny pursed her hard lips, looked judicial.

"Pretty, May?"

"Well—sweet-looking. Very stylish. Spanishy."

"H'm!" Fanny sniffed.

"She'll be awfully rich, Fan!" May suggested. Fanny's eyes lighted.

"That old place will never sell for much—too far away!"

"Yes," May said, "but her uncle in Buenos Aires sends her three hundred a month—has scads of money!"

"Ridiculous!" Fanny said, her face growing red. "Girl that age—what can she *do* with it!"

Both sisters mused upon the prospect of Bertie wedded to this brilliant future; then May sighed.

"Bertie's Mama isn't any too ready to give her one boy up to anybody!" she murmured.

"Might be the best thing for him, May," Fanny said. "He's an innocent sort of boy——"

"Oh, he's like a girl. His sisters and I have done *that* for him!" May breathed thankfully. "And she's just a child too. Twelve years in different convents, you know!"

Then it was time to talk of Pa's possible retirement from the firm; May made him eighty-one, Fanny eighty-two. They agreed that it was time for him to think of retiring. And there was some talk of Bob getting out. This made May's heart leap, settle to a happier beat.

"A Sacramento wholesale grocery firm has made him an offer," Fanny said. "He'd be up there most of the time. They have a branch in the city—branches everywhere. I'd be just as pleased. Stephen says that he spends the firm's money like water; advertising, and I don't know what all! Steve would be boss, then, sure enough!"

"He *has* been faithful, Fanny!" May said emotionally, with watering eyes. Fanny made no comment.

"Harry," she changed the subject, "don't seem real well. Lucy was saying that he's been coughing ever since he had that bad attack last winter. Georgie was at the house when Lou was with me last week, and he said his father didn't look well. Bob said that he ought to get into a hot climate."

"Why, how could he?" May said sensibly. "He couldn't afford to go alone, and certainly Lucy couldn't leave Alice and Georgie, and go with him. Alice has to have a home, between cases. I don't see how he could go without a job.

They might go to Nelly's, but I hear Rudy Sessions is going to sell the ranch and go into a position. I guess they'll get a big price for it. Steve was saying that seven hundred acres there ought to bring in about three hundred——"

"That's not much!" Fanny, who had no idea of farm values, said promptly, in relief.

"An acre," May finished placidly. Fanny calculated quickly; scowled.

"There's one thing," she said firmly, "if Harry goes south, or anywhere, I hope—I do hope—I like Lucy, and I know there's nothing wrong, and all that! But I do hope she and Bob Crabtree won't consider keeping that Larkin Street place together, that's all. She's no relation——"

"I think it looks awful!" May agreed. "Of course there's Bobo and Georgie," she added with a noticeable lack of conviction.

"Bobo, a child of five!" Fanny said, harshly. "Georgie, who is away all day, and goes to night school most evenings, and Alice, off on cases all the time! May, it won't do. The papers are only too ready where prominent people are concerned. We shall have all sorts of talk—I spoke to Pa about it, but you know him: just laughed!"

"I'm surprised at Lucy!" May observed, sighing.

She held a cotton stocking high in air: the darning ball within it dropped duly to the toe. She wet her fingers before knotting the yarn in her needle.

"Pa's always been *scrupulous* about that sort of thing!" she mused. "Did it ever strike you as funny, Fan, that Pa never married again?"

Fanny tossed her head, her nostrils quivered, but she did not speak.

"Ma—she was his only love, the love of his life!" May said softly. "I think of her so often, now, Fan, with the girls growing up, and this prospect for Bertie—and I believe that he is the sort of man who can take care of money, Fan, spend it wisely and well, you know. His marrying will be of the greatest advantage to the girls, when they marry—and his selfish old Mama must think of that—and the girls will be only too generous, I know, in welcoming the dear little bride!"

This last was said to Tina and Lou, who came out flushed and weary from the hot kitchen, glad to settle in the delicious spring sunlight on the new emerald grass, and breathe the softer air. They were turning down their cuffs, and unpinning the skirts they had folded back across their hips, as they came.

Esme had had a sleep, and presently moved languidly out to the sweet new shade of the leafing willows, and established herself in pillows. Vicky, the girls said, seemed to have gone for a walk.

"Lola telephoned that she's coming down, Mama!" Lou said significantly.

"Everything seems to be Lola, now," Fanny observed drily. Lou looked up, with a superior sort of smile.

"It seems the greatest year for things *happening!*" she observed; "you know Lily Duvalette has taken a house over here, and Daisy is coming to stay with her—imagine the fun, for me! Daisy won't live with her father since he married that Mrs. Pringle——"

"Imagine him marrying his housekeeper—what possessed him?" May mused. "They think she'll get *everything!* I saw Bernardo the other day, and he says that if she doesn't the lawyers will! My, my, my," she continued contentedly, "we do seem so blessed, with nothing like that to worry about!"

Fanny longed to crash into her complacency with the dreadful truth, but she was afraid. No guilty secret of her own could have burdened her more than the disgusting facts about Pa. The fever to get away rose in her afresh. She rustled her silk gown, looked about the attentive but busy little group, and smiled with sudden intention.

"May," said Fanny, laying her hand upon Esme's, as Esme lay dreamily listening to the talk. "I want you to lend me this girl—for awhile, if the doctor thinks her naughty heart is quite strong again. I will go down to the office this week, and make my arrangements with Stephen, to be gone some time, and I think I'll get off about the first of August! How about it, Esme, do you think you can have some fun with your old aunt, for six or eight months? She thinks she can—good girl. Dear me," Fanny interrupted herself, smiling about the circle innocently; "what have I done to be hugged and kissed this way! Get back in your pillows, you little goose, and thank me, if you like, when we are going around Venice in a gondola, or riding on an omnibus in London—Lunnon, as I believe the dudes call it!"

"Fanny, what a fairy godmother you are to these lucky girls!"

"Oh, Aunt Fanny—Aunt Fanny——!"

"Esme, you lucky thing, you!" This from the quite frankly envious Lou, who was lying on her back in the grass. Tina smiled, artificially and fixedly.

"This is May," said Fanny, pleased, "so that gives us ten weeks to get ready, and for this girl to become entirely well! Ten *weeks!*"

"It will be just exactly what she needs, to rebuild her," May said, eyes full of love and happiness fixed upon the invalid.

"Mama—*Paris!*"

"Think of it——! What a piece of news for papa!"

"And won't Vick be surprised!"

"I don't know that she will," said Fanny. "Probably her important walk will seem far more interesting to Vicky than anything poor I could say or do. Let's hope *Esme* won't start any nonsense about studying music in New York! Well, I must get that four o'clock train. Who's going to walk with me?"

"No, Esme, you must rest, you remember what the doctor said about your heart," May said. "I will, Fanny! part of the way anyway. How about Lou?"

"Not if you want date pudding to-night," Lou yawned indifferently.

"Oh, I mustn't interfere with the date pudding!" Fanny exclaimed.

"She didn't mean that, Fanny! Tina, you come with Mama and Aunt Fanny!"

"All right, I want to stop and see Grace, anyhow!" Tina agreed, pulling herself up sleepily. "I don't know whether I told you, Aunt Fanny," said Tina, as they walked along toward the gate, "but I told Mama and the girls, I know, that Mr. Yelland wrote seven articles a few weeks ago, short editorials and book reviews, you know, and Grace and I, just for a lark, sent them to the *Coast Churchman*, and they took every one, *imagine*," Tina laughed joyously. "Wasn't that quite a compliment to him—I thought it was!" she resumed. "Grace was so funny with him—so cool, I mean. I was quite frightened when he came home with the paper, and his name among the contributors! 'Well, Galahad,' she said—she calls him Galahad

—'why did you write them if you didn't want them printed!'
Of course he hadn't one word to say. He says that he has always wanted to write, even since he was a little boy; always was
scribbling! So now of course he and Grace are planning that
he will write books, on religious topics, of course, and some day
take little Vera and go to England—Oxford, he's mad about
Oxford. And wouldn't it be a lovely life for him, just what he
loves! Of course the *Coast Churchman* doesn't pay anything, but lots of them do!"

A rider dashed up to the gate, as they went through it, and
Tina flushed with excitement as she introduced her aunt to
Miss Lola Espinosa. The girl gave her hand with a sort of
saucy readiness, her left hand gathering up the thick folds of
her habit, her dark eyes brilliant under a small riding hat.
She had flung the rein over the gatepost, as she dismounted,
and now she pushed the plastered, heavy black hair from her
forehead, her full high young breast still heaving from the
exercise.

Her speech was a rush of vowels, all consonants slurred or
ignored, the eloquent eye and mouth carrying her meaning
even when words failed.

"Well, my gracious, Tina, how many aunts you got?" she
laughed. "Aunts and aunts, and sisters and sisters—such big
family scares me most to death! I got so many aunts now—
how do you do—Miss Crabtree?—But the fat one last week was
also Miss Crabtree——?"

"That was Aunt Lucy, Lola, Mrs. Crabtree. But this is
Miss Crabtree!" Tina said, laughing, with an indulgent glance
at Aunt Fanny that invited her to smile, too, at this engaging
child. Fanny's expression, however, was one of cold scrutiny.
"The girls are up there under the willow," Tina added. "Go
right up. I'm coming straight back. Isn't she fascinating?
I think she is, perfectly fascinating," Tina went on, when the
girl had left them in the hot road.

"Very fascinating—extremely!" Fanny said grimly. "I
daresay she'll get sense as she gets older!"

May laughed merrily, and Tina also laughed reluctantly.

"You are a case, Fan!" said the older sister amusedly.
Fanny smiled, somewhat mollified, but still scornful.

"Why didn't Bertie pick out a Chinese, if an American girl
isn't good enough for him!" she said, her lips twitching to

smile. But before the others could share her smile, Tina uttered a pleased exclamation, and ran ahead of them to meet a sweet, plain young woman in a blue cotton dress, who was slowly walking along the road, leading a pale little staggering baby.

"There's Grace!" cried Tina, "and the baby! Hello, sweetheart," she said, on her knees beside the heavy-headed child. Vera twisted her head sideways and began to cry quietly. "See," said Tina eagerly, "Grace makes her these little aprons, Aunt Fanny, and then has these little embroidered collars ready to button right in and make the darling baby all dressed up. Yes, dat's what see is," Tina repeated affectionately to the child, who was now shyly smiling, "all dessed *up!*"

"With so much to do," said Mrs. Yelland, in a voice so low, pure, and sweet that it was almost startling, "a poor parson's wife must have recourse to many a little makeshift! No, not poor," she interrupted herself quickly, "but rich in everything that is truly worth while in life! You were coming to me, Ernestine? I knew Vernon wanted to speak to you about the crucifer's surplice. Did you get the book at the library? We are not sure," she added, turning with a smile to the older, "that the crucifer's surplice is *just* like the others, and in this, as in so many things, Ernestine and I can be of real use to a busy and a tired man!"

"Grace, you do half of everything!" Tina said impulsively.

"Ah, no, not everything!" Grace said reverently. "There are doors I dare not open. The ministry—that is his own!"

"He lives for his parish," May said kindly.

"Oh, Mrs. Brewer!" the young wife said, with shining eyes. "And if you knew him as I do! He is——" Grace's voice thickened, she blinked away a mist of tears, and smiled at herself. "He really is the most Christlike man I have ever known!" she said, seriously and bravely.

Victoria heard the great news of Europe from Esme.

"It's sickening that you shouldn't be the one, Vick," Esme said, fingers upon Vicky's wrist.

"Oh, nonsense! I—to tell you the truth, I loathe Aunt Fanny anyway! She gives me a pain!"

"Vicky!"

"Well, she does. I don't mean that I wouldn't go abroad

with her. I'd go abroad as a lion with a zoo, to get away from the fuss about Bertie, and Mama already talking about giving Lola all the silver, and the clock, and all that! But not with Aunt Fanny. I'm going to *get* away, too."

"But how?"

"Well, I don't know how, but you'll see! Esme, I'll miss you!"

"I've grown awfully fond of you, Vicky. I used to be so jealous of you. But now there's nothing good that I wouldn't be glad to have you have! And cheer up, Vick, things are changing all the time, now, and your turn will come."

"I've a good mind to ask Papa to send me as far as New York with you and Aunt Fanny, and let me take music lessons there while you are abroad, and then—if I didn't make good, come back with you whenever you come!"

"He wouldn't, though!"

"Well, look what he did for Bertie—his bicycle, and two months in the east, and all that!"

"Yes, but Bertie's a boy!"

"I know, but I'm going to ask him!"

"Well, ask him," Esme conceded half-heartedly.

But Victoria never got so far. For that very same evening Stephen spoke to her in no uncertain terms, when she came in to the evening lamp, after the supper dishes were put away.

"Now, look here, Vick," said her father, sensibly, looking up from his *Report*, "your mother tells me that you wrote some nonsense to your aunt Fanny, without consulting either of us, some high-school-girl rubbish about studying music in New York, or what not, and leaving her stranded there—I didn't quite understand it, and I doubt if you did! The result is that Fanny naturally turns to Esme when she wants a companion —your ideas don't inspire your aunt with any particular confidence, and I don't blame her! Now, Vick, you're a fine, dear, sweet, helpful girl. You've got high spirits—that's fine. You take an interest in music—in art—all that is very well. But how about your *family* getting some of the good of this? We'd like a little music, and a little of this cleverness of yours —right here in this family! Your place—and this is just what I want you to get through your head, Vick—your place is *here*, with your mother and sisters. You have a lovely home; all right, appreciate it. There are a thousand girls your age in New York to-night who would go down on their knees and thank God for a supper like this one, and Mama, and Tina, and all the rest of us to love and protect her! Just get *rid* of this foolishness about running off somewhere, to do some imaginary heroic thing that you can't do here. My dear child, if you want to *do* something, it would please me very much to have you make your father a batch of doughnuts that didn't trickle batter over his poor old hand——"

There was a titter from the listening girls and an audible chuckle from May. They were not unsympathetic with Vicky, and, standing dumb and rosy a few feet inside the doorway, she knew it. It was so rarely that Papa grew facetious in these days!

"There are a thousand and one things to do here, I don't have to tell a clever girl like you that," Stephen pursued, more mildly. "Cook—sew—go on long walks—cultivate the garden—water the lawn! We—we may have changes here, we may have a new sister for you to love—all that is the normal life of a well-to-do young woman. But this strong-minded stuff——!"

He turned back to his paper. But she knew he was not done.

"Pattern yourself upon your mother," he said, quietly. "You could not do better!"

Later May told him that she thought such a talk, coming from such a father, might influence a girl's whole life. Stephen, now in bed, bit at his full, smooth under lip, above the graying beard, and nodded thoughtfully.

"Vicky's a fine spirited girl and will make some man a magnificent wife, some day," he said, with a father's pride, "but she needs guidance!"

"Oh, Steve!—I forgot to tell you!" May said happily, suddenly reminded by some obscure train of thought of Rob. "Fanny told me to-day that Rob may resign from the business—isn't that remarkable? Says Pa said so—or almost said so!"

To her consternation her husband's face darkened to an expression almost apoplectic.

"Bob is going to get out!" he said, in a blank pause.

"Why, Steve—I thought you always—I thought—it was only Fanny anyway—but why—*why*——?" stammered May.

"Didn't you always—when Rob first came out—I certainly understood then——"

"*Exactly what* did Fanny say?" said Stephen, heavily.

"Why—why—let me see!" May recalled the conversation as well as she could; recalled it with unusual accuracy, indeed, for in her flurry she could not clearly decide what attitude Stephen wanted her to take.

"I'm not surprised," said Stephen slowly, "no—this doesn't surprise me. He wanted to be manager, he wanted five hundred a month, he wanted to advertise all over the state, and when he can't—he threatens to drop out!"

"Well, you—you hope he does, don't you?" May asked uncertainly.

"I certainly do not!" Stephen said, roundly.

"Why, but Steve——"

"May, you have not been following the developments of this thing as I have," her husband said, enlighteningly. "When Rob first came back he was entirely superfluous—yes. But that was six years ago! Now Rossi has dropped out, Crane is going over to Finch and Houston, and the idea was that Bob was to take up that stock and keep it in the family. Fenderson wants it, of course, and if what Fanny tells you is true, he may get it! *I* can't afford to buy it—your father can't! Bob was pretty outspoken in the last directors' meeting, said he was practically manager and wanted to be recognized as manager, wanted a big salary, and talked rather high-handedly then. I suppose this is what he meant!"

"But, Stephen, won't it mean a much freer hand for you if both Pa and Bob get out?" the wife asked anxiously.

"It will and it won't. There's young Fenderson, you know."

"Tom Fenderson! Why, he's a boy!"

"He's an awfully smart boy, then. Yes, Fenderson is extremely ambitious, and Yeasley, and of course old Fenderson, are right behind him!"

"Old Fenderson used to wash the windows, I remember that!"

"Well, young Fenderson doesn't. I wish—I wish your sister Fanny would talk a little less!"

May was frightened. Her heart was heavy with misgivings as she continued her preparations for bed. It was a satisfaction to her when she heard Stephen's even heavy breathing deepen to an actual snore.

She lay awake far into the night, thinking, or trying to think. It was all very puzzling: May wished she knew more about that great ocean that hemmed in her little island of life so completely. *Business.* It was mysterious; how much men knew about it, and how curiously it worked!

There was a hot bright summer moon shining down upon the country town; youth and laughter were abroad; May heard tinkling banjo strings, voices. The bedroom was black and close. Great summer moths batted at the screened windows, footsteps chipped up and down the wooden sidewalk, under the big trees. Now and then a warm puff of breeze brought in the clean, stiff curtains, and they streamed lazily in the dark. May could just see the shimmering mirror of the high wardrobe, the white glimmer of Stephen's underwear on a chair. She thought how terrible it would be if Pa died suddenly, and Stephen died the next day. Harry would be Bobo's only guardian, with Bob, and suppose he decided to take the San Rafael house right over May's head, and her children's heads! What could they do—*nothing.* What *could* they do!

If only one of the girls were married—if Vicky had tamed her crude Spanish lover, even. But too late to think of that!

"I daresay poor Bertie would have to take care of us all," May thought, twisting over once more in the living and thrilling darkness. "Heavens! What a moon! It must be twelve o'clock!"

"What—what!" Stephen half-mumbled, half-shouted, starting up. He hated to be waked from his first sleep; May lay motionless and tense beside him. She dared not turn again.

CHAPTER XIX

A FEW weeks later the Brewer family enjoyed a brief return of social favour with the announcement that the wedding of young Albert Edward Brewer and Miss Lola Espinosa was to be an event of the early fall. Miss Espinosa was beautiful and an heiress and, although not a Californian, had many friends among the younger set. Mr. Brewer was a son of the well-known San Rafael family; his mother had been the popular Miss May Crabtree before her marriage a few years ago. Miss Espinosa was at present visiting Miss Ernestine and Miss Louisianna Brewer.

There were a great many callers in the garden in the afternoons, and much flattery and pleasure for Bertie and Lola, and for the girls in a lesser degree. May did indeed bestow a disproportionate amount of the family treasures upon her prospective daughter-in-law, and engaged a good Chinese cook, at thirty dollars a month, to carry them over the wedding. The old friends were not apt to admire Bertie's affected, odd-mannered little sweetheart, and even the girls found it hard to understand Lola at all times. Her laughter and tears were altogether too easily aroused, and the Brewers witnessed more than one quarrel between the lovers as the summer wore on.

Bertie was unusually quiet; in truth he was a little bewildered. Mama had kept at him—and kept at him—for months, to go and see dear little Miss Espinosa, who had so few friends. Mama had manufactured all sorts of errands to take him to the Tasheiras, and now he had asked Lola to marry him, and they were going to be married; he supposed it would be all right. He could not fancy himself married to Lola; his eagerly chattering, impassioned little wife-to-be seemed curiously remote from his own inner heart and soul. There had been that Sunday walk, and lunch with her aunts; and then he and Lola had been laughing and eating chocolates over a fire, and then he had kissed her, murmured to her——

And then suddenly they had been rushing into the Señoritas sitting-room, with the smelly dogs and the big rocking-chairs, and they had all kissed Bertie and Lola. They were engaged!

Everything else had followed. Lola could not wait to tell his sisters; they had ridden into San Rafael that very afternoon and had supper with his family. Lola had laughed, exulted, run upstairs to talk with the girls; the whole house had rung with the excitement.

Nobody questioned it, nobody was surprised, nobody seemed in the least in doubt what to do, except Bertie. He was profoundly astonished and bewildered. He had not supposed himself proposing to Lola that afternoon—quite. He had not been quite "jollying" her, either. But to have the machinery so rapidly set in motion gave him grave disquiet.

She wanted from him only flattery and kisses; she strangled him with embraces. Bertie rather avoided being alone with her; she was not in the least like any other girl he had ever fancied, like joyous, healthy little Kitty, for instance, who had so many interests in life besides love-making. Kitty liked walks, and cooking, and even books, and babies, and church singing. Lola liked to be in his arms, laughing extravagantly, kissing him, and teasing him to praise her.

She was not mercenary; it mattered little to her that she had a splendid allowance from her uncle now, and would presumably inherit a great deal of money when Tio Pio, as she called him, died. It delighted her, quite frankly, that financial considerations need not delay their marriage. She was enchanted with all the details, congratulations from the Brewers' friends, presents, newspaper notices; Lola loved her rôle, and extracted every particle of joy from it. May admired her tremulously: dear little thing, not yet twenty, and with all that money, and yet such a merry, captivating, unspoiled child! Nobody discussed the engagement with Bertie: it simply *was;* like a birth.

This was a trying time for Bertie's sisters. They were all older than Lola, none had either so brilliant a present or so interesting a future. Lola not only possessed Bertie body and soul and was proud to display her possession of him, but there were other young men hovering about the little heiress, there were presents, there were long talks about the housekeeping of the young Brewers, there was Lola's amazing trousseau, any one item of which would have quite dizzied the Brewer sisters. And when all this was put aside, there was love, to confess, to accept, to possess. When Lola and Bertie wandered away into the early darkness of the garden, or were excused to go off on some small excursion together, as became betrothed youth, Vicky used to feel that life was too bitter to be borne. She didn't want Lola's lover, she didn't want any girl's lover—but was there none of the sweetness of life for her?

The painful question of the ceremony presently arose. Lola's aunts wanted a church wedding—this was impossible in Lola's church. May suggested Mr. Yelland and their dear little church, but this was forbidden to Lola, too. May had to have this explained to her seventeen times, by all members of the family, and even then showed an inclination to repeat, with a playful voice but in unmistakable annoyance:

"But surely, surely—even if they object to my poor Bertie in your church, dear, we have only the warmest welcome for you in ours! I should be quite vexed, myself, if Mr. Yelland dared to say that he objected! But of course he *doesn't* object —he and Grace and Tina and I should be only too happy to have the prettiest little wedding in the world——"

It was no use; it must be a house wedding, in the hideous old Tasheira ranch house. Lola grew quite peppery when somebody rather timidly suggested the Brewer home instead. It was so big, and the sitting-room and library could be thrown together, and the little reception-room at the end turned into a sort of little altar——

No use again, the Tasheira homestead and none other would do, so the Brewers must plan, as best they might, to share the first family wedding with the old Señoritas. May and Esme assured each other in despair that everything would surely go wrong. The oddly assorted servants at the ranch would make an utter botch of what should rightfully be a caterer's business. Caterers were an innovation in San Francisco; there had been for some years a general idea that they and their work were connected only with the "French weddings" that were so oddly celebrated with feasting, dancing, and tremendous family gatherings. But now the really prominent people were beginning to employ them, and May felt that her only son's wedding was a brilliant opportunity to show how correctly the Brewer family managed these affairs.

She could not resist just a little fling at her daughters, when the windy warm August afternoon of the great event actually arrived. Tina and Vicky were dutifully crowding their mother into her new gown, carriages waited at the gate for the allied families. May suffered in the rather stuffy heat of the day; she felt nothing but disgust at the way Miss Curry had ruined her striped brown silk; and she experienced all a mother's emotions at losing her only son. The upper sleeve was too tight; it drew her arms and her breast uncomfortably, and threatened to burst. She would not have an easy moment in it, that was clear. She thought her hair looked horrible, too.

"Well, lawks, what's the difference!" she said, hardily, watching her daughters in the mirror as they hooked her, "nobody's going to look at poor old me!"

"Breathe in, Mama!" Victoria was fully dressed, and looked charming. Her big hat was tipped over her eyes, her blue dimity dress, its ruffles edged with narrow blue ribbon, was most becoming. She laid new white gloves, with the tissue-paper floating gently from them to the littered floor, upon her mother's bed.

"Goodness, but you're all fine!" Lucy said, looking well herself in her new, water-stripe black silk. It was then May had her little revenge upon her daughters, who had just caught, in the hooks of her lined, high silk collar, some of the fine hairs at the nape of her hot, uncomfortable neck.

"I'm cross at these girls of mine, that don't give us a chance to show what a pretty wedding we could have here, in the dear old home!"

Victoria, and Lou, who was fitting on her gloves very carefully as she sat in the bay window couch, exchanged an eloquent glance. Tina laughed good-naturedly.

"You'd be the first one to object, Mama, if a son-in-law did come along!"

"I don't know," May said, archly, "I think I'd make a very nice mama-in-law!"

"You'd better ask Alice here about the next wedding," Lucy said. All eyes turned to Alice, who sat next to Lou on the couch, with Bobo, very clean and solemn, in her lap.

Alice laughed with amused scorn.

"Hear her!"

"Doctor Richards!" Esme said.

"Doctor Richards has got one wife, if you count that!"

"I know," Vicky exulted. "Dr. Babcock!"

"Not that old man!" protested May, quickly and protectively, looking from one face to another.

"Forty-two," Lucy stated drily.

"Heavens—with that beard! And hasn't he children by his first wife?"

"One girl—almost grown," supplied Lucy.

"Mama," Alice smiled, "don't be so silly!"

"I'm not saying anything," Lucy said innocently.

"No, but Alice, do you like him—but Alice, does he like you?" Vicky said, in excitement and interest. "What is he—a regular doctor?"

"Fine practice," Lucy said.

"But, Alice—ah, tell us!"

"I'll tell you nothing!" Alice said, laughing and flushed. "It's all nonsense! I like him, and so do Mama and Papa, but that's all! I'll tell you when there's anything to tell, fast enough!"

Stephen put his head in the door.

"Pretty nearly ready, Mama?"

"Just about, but I could cry," May answered, heated and cross, "when I think of the way she's botched this dress!"

"Looks kinder tight," Stephen commented, sitting beside his youngest daughter and putting his arm about her.

"Oh, *tight!* I'll never, never give her one single day's sewing again—a dollar a day for *this!*" May sputtered, revolving before the mirror and looking over her shoulder.

"Vicky, you're a picture!" said her father admiringly.

"Maxine Elliott!" Victoria said, making a deep bow.

"How do you suppose she parts her hair, Vick?" Alice murmured, among the girls.

"I don't know! Lou and I were trying it, just for ducks——"

"Listen," Tina contributed, in a cautious undertone, "last night Vick and I were drying our hair—did you tell her, Vick?—and back here, *imagine*, where the Torreys live, all of a sudden we heard——"

Their voices fell; they had all gathered in the bay-window and now and then they glanced toward the big shabby room and its other occupants, anxious not to be overheard.

"Oh, that's nothing—eight hours!" said Alice. She told

them a story that made Victoria shut her eyes and draw a quick breath.

"She was asleep this morning, when we went over to ask," Tina said, "but her mother showed us the baby. Alice, wouldn't you die of fright if you knew you were going to——?"

"You know Grace was so dear about that—about telling Vernon, I mean," Tina said. "She got one pink rosebud——"

"Oh, I wouldn't. That's why I will never marry!"

"I wouldn't mind it!" But Victoria said it to herself; for Bertie had come in, brave in his first frock coat, and his mother had raised her arms, tight in their brown silk sleeves, to put them about his neck and laugh and cry a little as she kissed him, and then all his sisters had to kiss him, and he kissed pretty demure-browed Alice, too, and after that there were no more delays. In a great deal of confusion, the rustle of new skirts, and uncertain laughter, they all fluttered downstairs. Aunt Fanny and young George were there; George was a big, innocent-eyed eighteen-year-old now, awed in the capable hands of his cousin Lou, who quite definitely annexed him. Also waiting was Bertie's best man, Neil Powers, who drove Victoria to the Tasheiras' in his own smart phaeton and told her on the way of his passionate devotion to Kitty and his hope that Kitty was softening toward him. Victoria, bumping along happily beside another girl's admirer, wondered what it would be like to have an admirer of her own.

The Tasheira house looked grimmer and shabbier than ever, in the autumn untidiness and dryness of grass and garden. A glare of merciless sunlight was striking across the world, and the wind whined and rattled in the phaeton's furled hood. Other phaetons, carriages, and surreys were gathering on the neglected and winding road, which took its own sagging course between the lipping waters of the bay, edged deep in bowing green tules and the yellow-brown rise of the fields.

Back of the distempered white house, which stood bold and stark in the harsh light, were farm fences that divided the parched garden from the old *casa*, and from the barns, corrals, and cow yard. Here there were assembled to-day perhaps a score of Mexican, Spanish, and Indian men, women, and children, laughing and nudging each other as they watched the scene.

The arrivals climbed out of their conveyances, shook themselves, eyed each other solemnly, and mounted the flight of peeled wooden steps to the hall door. Almost all the different groups were strange to all the others, but there was a general inclination to bow distantly and solemnly as their eyes met. Preceding them, Victoria saw rustling skirts, flowered hats, now and then a stiff frock-coat and silk hat mingling with the usual male attire of sack suit and derby. Esme and her mother whispered; they knew scarcely any one, they said. Fanny eyed the arrivals with distended nostril and scornful eye. Lou giggled with the enslaved Georgie.

"I suppose we go in here—I suppose we go in here——" the women murmured uncertainly, as they crossed the sill. The wide hall was bare and smelled of plaster; outside the wind rattled shutters and doors briskly. In the direction of the dining room there was the sound of voices.

"I think you go upstairs," said a descending guest, bravely but shyly. Her courtesy was acknowledged only by an embarrassed half-smile and averted eyes by the arriving women. But they all filed upstairs, May's breath coming a little hard as she mounted.

"They ought to have a maid there to direct people," Vicky murmured in her ear.

"Oh, my *goodness!*" said Bertie's mother in despair. "Where did Bertie go?" she asked anxiously.

"Off with Papa and Neil, I think."

"Poor boy!—Vick," her mother breathed, "let Mama suggest that perhaps it would be a little nicer not to call him Neil until you know him just a little better——!"

They moved into a large, bare, upstairs bedroom, principally furnished with an enormous bed draped with lace and pink ribbons, and a big coloured picture of the Blessed Virgin standing upon the globe, with a snake wriggling from under her foot. This room was full of solemnly circulating and vaguely murmuring women; those who were alone trying to look at ease, those who were with companions finding a great many unimportant things to talk about, under breath.

"Yes, we'll just lay these here, and then we can find them again—no, dear, your hair is very nice—I think I would wear my hat, Lou—I don't know— suppose now we go down again— I don't know—" murmured the Brewer party, circulating and uneasy with the rest. Irresolutely, exchanging questioning glances, they went out into the hall again, and descended to the lower hall, and were carried on the current to the rear room from whence they had heard voices.

Here were hostesses and guidance to spare; they were warmly welcomed into sudden dimness. It was dear Albert's family! there were kisses, received awkwardly enough by May from the laced and dressed and excited great-aunts of the bride. The Brewers were piloted through a confusion of aligned chairs, partly filled with twisting and staring and unfamiliar persons. They must come to the very front—here—and here was another chair—there were plenty of chairs—here and here——

A low undercurrent of chatter and subdued laughter surrounded them. It was a full minute before Victoria could throw off an overwhelming embarrassment and look furtively about her. She knew that they were temporarily the chief object of interest, in the long, darkened double parlours, whose shutters were split with shafts of sword-like light, in the mote-filled gloom, and she felt a spasmodic anger at Aunt Fanny, who audibly tittered: "Here are all of us old maids!"

"That's Victoria—isn't she handsome?" she heard somebody whisper, and she felt her heart jump with pleasure and thrill. A cracked clock somewhere struck five—they had nearly been late for Bertie's wedding.

Under all her impressions, under Esme's and Tina's and Lou's, was of course a profound and sickening jealousy of Bertie and Lola, of the mysterious ease with which everything desirable in life had come to them both. But Vicky's unconquerable optimism presently pushed this somewhat into the background. This was exciting and thrilling, anyway, and even when it was over she would still have the new gown and hat and she could still look forward to driving home with Mr. Powers.

Their seats were set at an angle to the long stretch of the room, and so they could see the crowd comfortably. Presently May could see her boy, waiting with Neil in the back hall, glancing grinningly out now and then to eye the room.

"Sweetest fellow in the world!" she said, trembling into tears and raising a folded handkerchief to bitterly shaking lips.

"Well, he isn't dead!" Fanny said, with her bright laugh.

"If they delay long enough, Harry may get here," Lucy whispered. "Only I'm afraid he'll never have the courage to come in!"

"Why do they darken it?" Georgie asked, leaning over various laps.

"Sh—sh——!" May whispered, "I suppose it's a Spanish idea!"

The old priest was led in by Miss Refugio; he had been driving and was blown and rosy; he looked interestedly and amiably about in the gloom, panted, wiped his forehead, and fell into an audible and deep-chested conversation in Spanish with his hostess.

"Hello, Vicky!" somebody whispered behind her. She whirled about to hang on the back of her chair. Her whole face brightened, and her heart gave a great spring of joy. Davy Dudley!

They whispered busily. Hadn't he planned to spend this midsummer working in Berlin? Well, he had been so tired, and he had had no conditions upon his fall work in the very largest and most important hospital of them all. So when he had met a Los Angeles man, old Tom Doran, who had had a leg amputated and couldn't come home alone, Davy had been glad to act as escort, just for the round trip. He had arrived only yesterday and was going to Napa on the boat to-night. He had met Bertie last night at the ferry, and Bertie had asked him to the wedding.

He looked shabby, lean, older. And when he asked him how things were with his family, he sighed and shook his head. Could he get away to Germany again? the girl asked. His face grew grim, weary. He nodded his head with bitter distaste.

"Next June I'll come home to stay and make it up to them," he said, sternly.

"Sh—sh!" May said, agitatedly. The wheezing strains of a little melodeon were threading the close air and silencing the murmuring and low laughter. Everyone waited expectantly for a few moments, then conversation gradually grew again, and after a while the melodeon stopped. Victoria did not hear the clock now, she was whispering with Davy. It struck the half-hour.

Bertie wondered a little, with the others. What was delaying Lola? He tried not to think of Mina and that wretched hour at Mina's house on Thursday. But the thought of her would come.

She had been in bed, a not-too-clean bed, and she had said she was sick, and looked sick. Her sister, a young wife enormous with child, had given him a dark and suspicious glance as she showed him in. He had sat awkwardly beside Mina, not knowing what to say or do.

She had held his hand, and patted it, and gulped—so small a woman, so deeply hurt. She had said, smiling almost with the effect of strangulation, that she hadn't meant him to come so soon, she had just written because she wanted to hear all about it—she was so—a rising tide of tears and sobs almost engulfed her at this point, but she had fought on bravely— she was so interested. If she had thought he was coming at once, she would have been up, and have tried to look pretty for him——

The memory of her smile made him wince, here in the Tasheira home, waiting for little confident, saucy Lola.

"I blame myself, Bertie," Mina had said, quickly, and with control, "I did what I knew was wrong, and I guess I've got myself to blame! But"— the shaking lips again, the eyes trying to smile over a sudden sob that widened her nostrils and made her mouth pitiful—"but I love you so!" Mina had faltered, breaking down, "you and me were so happy—'member that time we climbed up on the fence to get away from the dog, and that Sunday night we watched the stars——"

"I know!" Bertie had said, quickly and thickly.

"Bertie——" she had said, beginning to cry quite openly. And she had flung herself back on her pillow, and put one lean arm up against her face.

He had sat on, more wretched than he had ever been in his life. He had held her free hand, there in her sordid little bedroom, knowing that every fibre of her hurt body and scarred soul was hungry to have him slide to his knees, gather the limp little cheap nightgown and the convulsed face against his heart and kiss the wet and swollen and shaking mouth.

Gulping, sniffling wetly, swallowing, she had suddenly sat up, raised her disordered hair in business-like hands, dashed the tears from her eyes. He was going to be married Monday; she wanted to hear all about it.

But five minutes later the break-down had recurred, she had fallen back against the pillow again, her poor little colourless homely face once again wrinkled and distorted with weeping.

Where was the bride? What was the delay? At six o'clock there was general uneasiness and suspicion among the guests. But the Señoritas were smiling and calm; time figured little in their plans. Lou, a bridesmaid, was the only Brewer who had been invited upstairs to share the dressing, for Lola's room was packed with servants, obscure relatives from San Jose and San Francisco, and from Petaluma ranches, and school-friends from the convent.

At six o'clock these came down, and the melodeon began again, and exactly one hour and twenty minutes after the announced hour, there was the sound of laughter, tears, voices in the hall, the Señoritas and a few close relatives came leisurely in, Bertie and Neil walked somewhat uncertainly from their retreat, and stood embarrassedly buttoning and unbuttoning their white gloves. Bertie's ascot tie was crooked, the orange blossom in his buttonhole hung by a thread, he looked uncomfortable in the frock coat, and his gloves and Neil's looked large and stuffed with their fingers. The old priest rose, turning the pages of a limp little prayerbook and eyeing the gathering benevolently over his enormous spectacles.

The room was very hot; the wind was still audible outside. Suddenly a woman's trembling soprano clove the silence; she quavered nervously through "O Promise Me," the organ wandering at will and resting contentedly upon utter discord at the close of every phrase. It seemed to the Brewers, in their agonized consciousness of the few old family friends present who were unquestionably "in society," that the song lasted an hour.

Silence.

"Do we applaud?" Davy whispered to Victoria. Vicky emitted an unexpected and audible chuckle, which terrified her so that she looked down at the shabby Moquette carpet in dumb confusion for at least a full minute.

Tina told her afterward that at this moment a maid with a large tray of food had entered confidently from the rear of the house, under the impression that the ceremony was over, and the feast about to begin. She had been hustled out of sight.

Everyone was beginning to enjoy the absurdity of Bertie Brewer's wedding by this time, except his immediate relatives and himself. He and Neil looked doubtfully at the doorway from whose retreat they had prematurely issued, but decided to stand their ground.

The wedding march! Everybody rose. Nothing further happened except that a lean, brown, oily-faced old servant came in to whisper to Miss Lupita, who comfortably went out, taking with her the alert and willing, if surprised, Stephen.

Slowly, to the organ's vague meandering discords, and the turning of every crisp silk in the room, Stephen came solemnly and pleasantly forward, five minutes later, with a little dangling, lace-smothered burden upon his arm. Something had happened to delay Lola's old lawyer, who was to have performed this fatherly office, and Bertie's kind and willing father had been asked to take his place.

Lola's head hung, her little white-gloved hand looked very tiny upon his arm; and when her face finally could be seen, it was colourless, terrified, and staring blankly. May said later that even then, from that very moment, dear Bertie looked so big and tender and protecting, just as if wonderful new qualities had developed in him with this new great love and devotion.

"Just as sweet and pure as two children!" May said to Fanny, and Fanny, half angry at the tears in her eyes, nodded and tossed her head.

Immediately after the last word, Bertie turned to stoop and kiss his bride, the priest shook their hands, they became the centre of a whirlpool of kisses and congratulations. May, taking her boy to her bosom, looked as if she would burst with emotion, tight gown, and heat. The girls laughed through tears, as he gave them each a great embrace.

"Whew—that's over!" he said, and everyone laughed and quoted this spontaneous remark.

Lola was bright, voluble, laughing. She had gathered her satin train over her arm, and when her delicate veil caught upon a brooch or hat-brim she freed it with a happy toss of her elaborately curled little head.

"Don't you be so familiar, Mr. Albert Crabtree!" she said gaily, when Bertie straightened a twisted orange blossom in her wreath upon its wire, and that was quoted with laughter, too.

The tremendous meal that presently was served with much running to and fro, more than atoned in quantity for any irregularity in serving or choice of viands. The linen and the old silver were magnificent, the plates variegated. There were platters and platters of meats, hot and cold, and the conventional ice-cream, and great plates of cut layer-cakes, and there were also two great chased silver bowls—originally parts of a wash-stand set—filled with an ice-cold, rich, delicious cream punch, at which everyone smiled at first, but which everyone eventually respected. There were all sorts of wines, angelica and cognac, amazingly mellow red wine, and unlimited supplies of champagne, and with these the Señoritas kept pressing rich little cakes upon everyone, and grapes and great mellow peaches, yellow plums, and Mexican candies of honey and cactus gum.

Lola had time to grow pale with weariness again, Bertie looked flushed and tousled, everybody was hoarse with too much talk, too much laughing, too much eating and drinking. At about eight o'clock the bride and groom made a rush for the front door. By this time almost all the American guests had gone. But the others were evidently settling down for a night of revel.

"Bertie," said a shadow, coming up to take his hand, on the dark porch. Bertie started, but it was only Uncle Harry.

"Bertie, my boy," he said earnestly, "you must let me wish you joy. You have a—a mighty sweet wife!"

"Uncle Harry, I didn't know you were here!" Bertie, in his relief, had a moment of pity for Harry, so shabby and quiet and timid in the dark.

"It's my Uncle Harry," he said to Lola, who was peering down toward the expected carriage on the drive.

"I don't care if it is Saint Joseph!" Lola said, pettish and laughing.

"She—she—yes, she wants to get away!" Harry said hurriedly. "Of course—I understand—God bless you, Bertie! I was too late to see you married, my boy, but you understand. Trouble at the office—Good-bye!"

The crowd closed about them; they ran through showers of rice and tiny candies, carriage lamps flashed, spokes caught like fingers at the light, and they were gone. May sniffed; Stephen's arm was prompt and lover-like about her. Victoria, murmuring with Davy, was in seventh heaven, in the confused shadows of the big, half-emptying rooms, where nobody knew or cared what a pretty girl and an admiring man talked about, laughed about, murmured about. Lucy gathered her family with brisk complacency.

"Georgie, say good-night to your cousin Lou—maybe she'll let you kiss her. Bobo, love, keep my hand. Harry. Oh, Bob, see if that same man is waiting that drove us out!"

"How did you get here, Lucy?" Stephen asked, somewhat taken with her new silk and jet earrings.

"Drove from Saucelito, Steve. It was the easiest way. My dear," said Lucy, with flushed cheeks and sparkling eyes, and in a laughing, confidential undertone, "I am reaching—the *age* —when I can *not* drink champagne!"

Stephen, also warmed with good wine, was captivated.

"Sweet wedding, Lucy?" he said with a little emotion, kissing her.

"Lovely!" she said, pleased and flattered.

"This—this rig must be charged to me, Harry!" Stephen said seriously, to his brother.

"Nonsense!" Bob said. Harry was so touched and so thrilled by the occasion, his wife's beauty, Alice's wedding gown, the stinging and bubbling contents of the glass that one of the Señoritas had pressed into his hand, that he was wandering about almost aimlessly, ready to smile at any one and do anything. He had his beloved youngest daughter in the curve of his arm, all the long drive home down to Saucelito: Bob and Lucy had the centre seat. The double surrey rocked and rattled along in the warm night; the wind had died, lights in the bay were placidly doubled in the water. A pungent smell of dust and dew and tarweed, mingled with the strong odour of sweat-soaked harness and the sharp sulphurous breath of the marsh, smote his senses familiarly.

"They'll have about five hundred a month between them!" Lucy estimated. "Lucky Bertie!"

"They're welcome!" Alice whispered, in her father's ear, and they both laughed guiltily, like conspirators.

The boat trip was a glaring agony of heat and light. Lucy would not let her husband sit outside, because of his cough. They were all stiff and weary when they stumbled into the warm close hall of the Larkin Street cottage.

A card lay on the carpet; Alice twisted it in her fingers: Dr. Frank L. Babcock.

"Well, too bad to miss him!" Lucy said, anxiously bright. Alice said nothing; she kissed her father and went slowly into her room. Her mother followed her. "Think of his coming all the way from the Mission to see a certain young lady!" Lucy teased her smilingly.

"I wish he would stay in the Mission!" Alice said, busily hanging up hat and wraps.

"No, dear, don't say that, if the man is honestly in love with you. What have you against him?"

"I've nothing against him, Mama!" the girl answered impatiently. "But—well, I suppose the truth is, I don't love him."

Lucy was rolling a lace scarf thoughtfully, sitting in a low chair.

"I don't think most girls know what love is, until after they are married," she said slowly.

"But, Mama, then suppose they find it isn't love?"

"Ah, well—if the man is a fine man, and honest and true and intelligent, they don't," Lucy assured her.

Alice was silent, musing. She was twenty-two now, and she had her profession. But it was natural that the attentions of this man, twenty years her senior, this man of position, of some means and of so decided a character, should impress her.

"There's nothing I *don't* like about him," she admitted, after a pause. Alice had always been manageable, dutiful, inclined to take life and herself with conscientious earnestness. Her mother looked at her hopefully. "Would you really like me to get married, Mama?" she asked, smiling uncomfortably.

"Why, if it was for your happiness, dear!" Lucy answered, cautiously. "There isn't much else in life for a woman. Papa has a good deal of trouble, it would be a great comfort to him to have you settled in life. And Dr. Babcock is such a splendid fellow! You don't want to be an old maid, like poor Aunt May's girls!"

Alice was not imaginative; but the vague little dream of years seemed to be dissolving quite visibly before her eyes, as her mother spoke. She had never analyzed the dream; there was about it the fragrance of the forbidden country, of roses, laughter, a face close to her own, a joy that was half fear and a prayer for freedom lost in the exquisite sweetness of surrender.

"Many and many a girl has coquetted and trifled until it was too late!" Lucy said mildly. "Look at poor Aunt Fanny!"

"Yes, I know," Alice answered quickly. Horrible never to know life at all—to be superfluous among the busy and beloved women of the world! And Mama said—everyone said—that real love came after, not before marriage. "I'll—I'll *pray* about it, Mama!" she said seriously. Lucy laughed and kissed her fondly, for good-night.

Meanwhile the Brewers had reached home, and with tearing and exhausted yawns, were standing stupidly about the upper hall, leaning against each other and the walls, wearily discussing the wedding. When Tina described the maid, bursting into the room prematurely, with a tray, Vicky and Fanny laughed until they were almost crying; Esme had left the group and gone to bed, but at the sound of their shrieks she called them into her room, and then they sat upon the bed and went on talking for another hour.

The Señoritas had been perfectly awful of course—and that delay, what on earth had the Bakers and de Pinnas and the Murchisons thought of that! But never mind, everything went off pretty well, considering. Hadn't Lola been pretty—no, not pretty, but sweet. No, not sweet exactly, either, but anyway, it was awfully nice of them to ask Papa to take her in. And hadn't Bertie looked *darling!* Dear old Bertie, think of him with a wife and a separate home of his own! Lucky girl that Lola was, to get a boy like Bertie, instead of some fortune hunter. Hadn't Esme looked sweet—and Lou never had looked prettier. Tina had looked *lovely.* And Aunt Fanny, *always* have a bonnet that shape, the most becoming thing you ever had in your life!

Esme and Tina had always shared a room, Vicky doubling up with Lou—an arrangement that for obscure reasons was pleasing to all the sisters. Esme and Tina liked to feel that they could not share things comfortably with the other girls, and Lou and Vicky murmured their satisfaction over their independence whenever they really cleaned the room, moving the bureau and the bed.

Now Vicky, who had been removing the smaller articles of dress for some time, and held them—satin stock, silver-clasped satin belt, silver-tipped side-combs, silver chain bracelet—in her hand, dragged her yawning sister off to bed. But not before her dancing pulses and singing heart had received fresh fuel from almost every member of the circle.

Vicky and Davy Dudley, eh? Well, how about a poor country doctor for a son-in-law, Mama? Did you see them?

Did you notice that little affair? Well, wasn't Vicky the slyest thing you ever *saw*!

"D'you really like Davy Dudley, Vick?" Lou murmured, on a sort of yawning moan, as she fell into bed.

"No," Victoria answered softly, with something of the day's glory lingering in her eyes. "No. But I love him!"

And when Lou was sound asleep she slipped out of bed, and knelt down at the window, studying the familiar garden and the Torreys' neat little roof, and the willows and eucalyptus and locusts, and the lofty old stable with the wooden horse's head looking down, chipped and battered, from a chipped and battered wooden horse-shoe over the door. And for the first time in her life she really prayed.

"Oh, God, there *must* be something that gives you things, when they're not wrong—and you want them so!—and you —and you mean to be good. Please—*please* make it right with Davy and me—I love him so!"

She knelt for a long time, sometimes praying, sometimes studying the garden with dreamy eyes, sometimes hugging her bare arms, and yawning, and resting her dark head against the window casing. When she crawled in finally beside Lou, it was with the happiest and quietest heart that she had ever known.

CHAPTER XX

BERTIE'S marriage now became a quiet fact in a world of accepted facts. Discerning eyes would have seen, almost as soon as they returned from their ten days' honeymoon, that there was at present no tie between the young husband and wife but that of novelty, excitement, and physical desire. But there were no discerning eyes about them, and to every member of Bertie's family their youth, their devotion, their presents, their wealth, presented a delightful and satisfying whole. May said that they were just the sweetest and dearest little pair in the world, that Lola deferred to Bertie in *everything*, and that to see that dear boy—in his new responsibilities, so dignified and sensible—well——

May became incoherent, and wiped her smiling eyes. She began fresh plans for the settling in life of her darling girls, and the girls writhed anew. They hated to go, but they duly went to see Lola in a house in Sausalito—for Saucelito was Sausalito now, some purist having discovered the error in the old way of spelling it. Bertie and Lola had taken a somewhat more pretentious house than they had anticipated; it chanced to be for rent, partly furnished, and after seeing it they found everything else uninteresting. It was of dark brown shingles, with a dozen large rooms, porches, fireplaces, hardwood floors. Lola exulted in the thought of being mistress here, and Bertie felt that it was financially possible—anything was financially possible.

It proved to be cold and draughty, especially with only two persons occupying it. Breakfast in the big dark dining room alone was a dreary meal for Bertie, and he and Lola shivered at their dinner. There was an enormous amount of sweeping necessary, indoors and out; the porches were always coated with wet leaves. They had exclaimed, upon finding it, that it would be a wonderful place in which to entertain; but once in it, with one vigorous, ignorant maid, the entertaining somehow faded from their plans. Lola spent the first winter curled up anywhere that she could be warm, and their only guests were Bertie's family.

Vick and Tina and Esme and Lou, Steve and May, Fanny and Lucy, Alice and Georgie and Uncle Bob and Uncle Harry, all were invited to see the new establishment, and all exclaimed about the wedding silver and mahogany and glassware, the pictures and clocks. It seemed miraculous that everything fitted so wonderfully.

Grandpa Crabtree did not come, for he was not only feeble now, but decidedly childish, and the Señoritas did not come, because they never went anywhere. Usually they all got to church at Christmas and Easter, and occasionally one or two went to church during the year, on Sundays. But they only laughed unctuously when Bertie, somewhat hurt, coaxed them to come and see him and his wife, and told the young couple that they must come to the ranch instead.

Lola was not a good housekeeper, and loved to go to the ranch, where she had nothing to do but sleep. She had an amazing appetite for sleep, she liked to lie in bed almost all day, her rather thin dark hair in a braid, and her aunts, and countless women pensioners of the ranch—they could not be called servants— coming and going with trays, with fine lace-work, with babies and dogs.

Bertie was genuinely amazed, a little amused, a little shocked. She had long ago told him that she was as lazy as a lizard, but it had seemed to mean nothing then, whispered laughingly in the decent, orderly surroundings of his own home. He did not know exactly where he fitted in, on these Sunday visits to the ranch. If he rose early—and eight o'clock was early—he would meet a loosely robed, sleepy, protesting señorita in the big, airy upper hall.

What was the matter—he was not ill? He must go back to bed; there would be some breakfast presently; Lotta would bring it upstairs.

There was no morning newspaper at the ranch. Bertie might wander good-naturedly through the little adobe settlement behind the big house, surprising loud joyous shrieks from stalwart Mexican women, washing the upper parts of their brown bodies at wooden tubs, and grabbing covering, splashing and laughing at the intrusion. The slanting autumn sun would send lances through the eucalyptus, and over the high roofs of the sheds and barns. The world would smell pleasantly of cows and dry grass and sunwarmed earth, shot with whiffs of onions and oil frying together.

Or he might ride over and have breakfast with Mama and the girls; such a sweet, orderly breakfast, with Tina's lisle gloves and prayer book waiting, up next to the black marble clock on the mantel, and Vicky's fresh, firm neck smelling faintly of fine soap, where he kissed it.

Bertie would drink in the details of the fresh cloth, the old silver spoons erect in the silver mug, the glancing lights on Tina's muffins and on the steaming coffee urn. Lou would have put late sweet peas in the centre; Vick, if it was her turn to be cook, would bring in the omelette, a special welcome for Bertie under her usual vivacious nonsense. He loved them all so dearly, in these days.

He would go back, at eleven, to find Lola rested and vivacious over her coffee tray. He must have another cup, and then she would get out of bed and into his arms, as he sat in the wicker rocker at the window, and they would have an interval of kissing and murmuring. Aunts would begin to filter in, dressed and pomaded and armed with fans for the day; perhaps a rabble of dogs would waddle after; and Lola would spring back into bed, lazily interested in the time. One o'clock, was it? Gracious!

There was an enormous meal at two; but she did not come downstairs for it. She nibbled cakes in bed, all afternoon. She and the household's score of women chattered Spanish eternally; it distressed and annoyed Bertie, even though he knew that, as the man of the place, he was an important figure in their eyes, by no means to be scorned or disregarded.

At five o'clock Lola would be beautifully dressed, down in the odorous old parlour, rippling scales and operatic gems, *con variazione*, on the square piano. Then she would challenge Bertie to a ride, or, if it were a working day, and he in town, she would drive five miles to the station, to meet him. Dinner was supposedly at seven, but there was no time in Lola's scheme of life.

At home she always breakfasted in bed; Bertie did not mind. He dressed in cautious silence, before he left the bedroom he would stoop over to kiss her, and the soft olive arm would come up to catch him in a strangling embrace.

"Ah, he was her darling—her dove—the heart of her heart—the little drop of blood of Mary's Son!" she would murmur, in passionate Spanish.

After the first call, there seemed to be no special reason why Bertie's sisters should come frequently to Sausalito, and to May's great distress, they frankly expressed themselves as unwilling to do so. Lola was always in town, going to lunch with Bertie, or she had gone up to her aunts, they protested.

"I wish to-morrow," May said, at luncheon one day, "two of you girls would go over to the city, lunch with Aunt Fanny, get me some things at Michel Wand's and go and see Lola, coming home."

It was a dreamy, sunshiny day, in October; rendered even dreamier and more hazy than usual by distant mountain fires, whose drifts of pale blue smoke were plainly visible from the upper gate of the Brewers' back lot, to which the girls made frequent journeys of inspection.

"I thought Bertie and Lola were coming over here for lunch Sunday, Mama?" Lou said, adding more grape skins to the pyramid on her plate. "Are we to go on babying Bertie's wife, now that he has gone?"

"Lou, is that a nice way to speak to Mama?"

"Well, my gracious, Mama, why should we traipse——"

"Lou, I won't have that tone! I don't know what's got into you!—*I'm sorry, Mama!*"

"I'm sorry, Mama," Lou echoed dully, with impenitent scorn. She mumbled further protest into the hard, sweet, luscious heart of a large muscat.

"You and Vicky can go," May pursued, after a pause for recovery.

"Unless the fire gets worse, Mama; we don't want to miss the fun!" Vicky agreed obligingly.

"For pity's sake," her mother said, "don't even mention it! It makes me perfectly sick with nervousness just to hear the men going by the gate, and to smell it!"

"Grace and I walked up as far as the convent gate this morning," Tina said, "and Sister Mercedes told us that cinders were floating down, way up by their arbour. Grace is terribly scared, you know, Mama——"

She added the last three words with a significant look for her

mother.   May knew that Tina knew that Vera was to have a
dear little brother, in five or six months, and May and Tina had
had a solemn little talk about it.   Tina was to spend as much
time as she could with Grace, who was wretchedly ill and labour-
ing with financial troubles, as well as with a fractious and
teething baby, but May had stipulated that Tina and Grace
were not to discuss the coming event in any way.

"Oh, Mama, as if Grace would!" Tina had said eagerly, "why,
she told me that the other night she spoke of it to Vernon, even,
and he said so sweetly that if she would put it entirely out of
her mind, and just remember that it was perfectly natural, and
God's will, she wouldn't have all these blue, depressing moods!
She *never* mentions it to me!"

"That's right!" May had said, approvingly.   She knew she
could trust Tina, and rewarded her delicate little intimation
now with a motherly smile.   Vicky looked from one face to the
other with perfect comprehension; and a daring, and she knew
immodest, thought, thrilled her through and through.   Oh, it
must be exciting to have a baby!   And if she married Davy——

After luncheon she and Tina and Lou walked back of the
house to look at the fire again; the smoke was certainly denser,
and the girls' hearts quickened with excitement.   Little Mrs.
Torrey was sitting out in the yard, in the muffled shafts of the
sunlight; the nurse was still there.   She told them, after they
had duly inspected the sleeping, lumpy little baby, that Eric had
said that if it was worse, to-night, they must pack some things,
and go over to town on the nine o'clock.   Pale, and with the
anxious look of new motherhood in her proud and happy eyes,
she made a deep impression upon the Brewer sisters.

"We have no trunk, and just the telescope and the clothes-
basket," she smiled, "but Baby must be the first consideration,
of course.   We couldn't have anything happen——"

She had never known that look, two weeks ago, that protecting, alert, responsible look.   But her whole heart, so recently
carefree, was chained now to the terror of something happening
to the baby.

"How are you?" Victoria asked encouragingly, "you—you
were pretty sick, weren't you?"

The mother and nurse exchanged a cryptic, smiling look.

"No—o!" said Amy Torrey, who had died a thousand
agonized deaths two weeks ago to-day, and had told herself that

she would kill herself before risking another such event. "I'd do it all again for my little bunny!" she told them.

They climbed the hill. Fire brigades passed them, sweating men in dark shirts, shouting in the hot haze and dust. Women passed them, women who like themselves had come up to look at the fire. Victoria delighted in the common danger that made these women forget themselves completely, waive introductions, stand exchanging apprehensive words while they watched. Lily Duvalette was there, conspicuous in a striped yellow and red blazer, noisy in a mixed group from the hotel.

"Why don't you girls come over and have lunch with me?" she called.

"Yes, why don't we?" Lou murmured scornfully, as Victoria answered with only a false, mechanical smile. The memory of this smile made them laugh hysterically when they trooped home in the hot red afternoon light to report to their mother.

"Why don't we come to lunch!" Victoria repeated, "I like her style!" Lily's brazen monopoly of all men had long ago estranged all women. Lily cared, Lou and Vicky said, only for "*cases.*"

Their father was at home, and eagerly they led him out past the Torrey house, to see for himself. He secretly delighted them, in spite of their voluble protests and reiterated fears, by regarding the menace as extremely grave.

When they went back he reduced his wife to an utter misery of fear by saying that she had better get a few things together—if the thing once got over that hill, into the grass, the whole town was doomed! Wild with enthusiasm, the girls ran about busily and efficiently: this, Mama? and this, Mama? and where should they go—Grandpa's? To a hotel! They had never been to a hotel.

Stephen thoroughly soused the side gardens and the roof with water, the swish and drip inspiring the girls as they ransacked bureaus and closets. Their coats, here, where they could grab them, and all sorts of small treasures in the coat pockets. At half-past four Davy Dudley was suddenly perceived talking to their father beside the side faucet. Victoria felt that life was sweet and exciting enough, at last! As she made a demure errand out to greet the caller, her heart was brimming with bliss. What a dear good honest face his was, and what a look he gave her trim, aproned figure and mischievous, glowing face!

He had come over to see them, and had no further engagements; he proved a friend in need. For May was almost in tears over her best china, the precious half of the Canton set that had been in the dining-room closet almost since the closet was built. Davy suggested that they put it down the cellar, and the girls laughed and joked as they passed and repassed each other with loads of the sturdy thick pink-and-green platters and cups.

Victoria remained in the cellar, ranging the set upon the almost empty preserve shelves. When a moment came that found Davy and herself alone she said suddenly:

"I thought you might come over here before this, Davy."

"What?" David said, instantly embarrassed and red. "I—I really came to-day to say good-bye!" he stammered, clearing his throat.

"Oh, I see," Victoria said quietly.

"I ought to have gone back a month ago," David added, somewhat awkwardly. "I have my return ticket, you know, from old Doran. And of course I've been losing time! But my sister Mary was sick, and 'Lizabeth's married now and can't help, and Mother had a fire in her house, boarders all moved out. I had a chance to take old Boone's practise while he was East. I couldn't get away!"

"And when do you go?"

"To-morrow afternoon."

He could have sold his steamer ticket, and helped his mother. Probably he didn't have the ticket; just an order, or the money, the girl thought stubbornly. Well, she wasn't going to argue with him or to laugh as if it was all a joke. They had joked long enough. She dropped her head; she had no more to say.

He would have met any other mood bravely, but this hurt him and tugged oddly at his heart. He knew, long before this, that he liked her, that he judged other girls by what he remembered and knew of Vicky Brewer.

"The thing is, Vick," he said, all reason suddenly melting away and an odd hoarseness and eagerness taking possession of him. "The thing is, my mother hasn't any one but me, you know. I don't know when I'll be back, I've got to get all the interne work I can. I teach English every afternoon, in Berlin, to get through my hospital work. You see?"

The heavens had opened, down here in the cool cellar that

smelled of working preserves and cats and rotting apples and mouldy trunks. Victoria put her soft, dirty, friendly hand on his shoulder.

"Davy, I don't mind that!" she whispered, trembling.

"Last load!" Lou sang, coming cautiously down the narrow flight from the kitchen. Victoria turned back to her shelves; her heart singing; David sprang to lift the china from Lou. They had no other chance.

"Mama," Vicky whispered, a few minutes later, in the kitchen, "ask Davy to stay! He's been working so hard——"

"My dear, I don't see how we can! It's the lamb stew, and there's no lettuce. I really don't think he expects——"

"Oh, but please, Mama! And then we're going up to see how the fire is, afterward!" Victoria was briskly cutting yesterday's layer-cake, pouring canned peaches into a glass bowl.

"I'll go out!" May's motherly figure left the kitchen, and Victoria and Tina flew about with supper-getting, in glorious spirits.

But fifteen minutes later, when they announced the meal, Vicky was bitterly disappointed to see that Davy was gone. May appeared blandly unconcerned.

"No, dear, I didn't say anything to you about asking him. I said I would come out and see. And there appeared to be no reason why we should. I'm sure he didn't expect it; he talked to Papa for a few minutes and then went away."

"As far as I can see," Stephen observed, taking his place at the head of the table, "the young man has considerable money to waste upon travel!"

"He brought an invalid old man home from Germany, and Mr. Doran gives him the trip, Pa," Victoria said quietly, hating everybody and everything.

"No stew, Vick? No potatoes? What are you going to eat? I see," Stephen resumed gravely. "Well, his place is with his mother, in Napa. Wrong idea—totally false. At his age, I was supporting my wife and babies!"

"Very ordinary people, no family at all, but Davy is a sweet dear boy, and I hope we will always be friendly with him!" May summarized, with a brisk air of finality. Vicky knew that her mother was perfectly aware of the situation.

He had been hungry—he had worked and laughed and run up and downstairs—and he would have stayed if he had been asked! Victoria's heart boiled. No good-bye—no sequel to that thrilling moment in the dimness and dirt, down by the preserve shelves. And to-morrow he was going away!

She made her supper of tea and toast, enjoying the coolness with which she could parry Mama's and Papa's solicitude. She just wasn't *hungry*, she repeated with deep satisfaction. Afterward she helped with the dishes in a dignified, abstracted silence. May fell sufficiently into this little trap to ask just the questions for which Vicky had been hoping. The fire made the whole town hot to-night; the kitchen was insufferable.

"What makes our Vicky so thoughtful?" May hinted.

"Nothing, Mama!"

"Something Mama isn't to know?"

"Nothing at all."

May fidgeted and fussed, dissatisfied. And when, later, Tina and Lou and Vicky prepared to go up to the fire with their father, the anxious mother had more fears.

"Vicky dear, if ever a young man said anything to you that—made you—thoughtful, dear, that perhaps you couldn't quite answer, Mama would like to feel that you would tell her about it."

"Certainly, Mama!"

"That's your real protection, Vicky, your real safety, you know!"

"I know, Mama!"

May could say no more, she looked at the handsome, impassive face with a baffled sort of anger in her soul. Thank goodness, she said to herself, this impecunious, shabby, common country boy was leaving the country in a few hours!

Stephen and his girls walked up toward the hills, to the encroaching wall of smoke, again. Half the town was there; women in tears, children shouting shrilly, men's figures silhouetted against the dull pink glow. The air was thick and acrid with bitter smoke. The Brewer girls threaded the groups gaily, talking, exclaiming, lamenting, repeating sentences back and forth. Judge Dufficy, with a trio of his own little girls hanging on his arm, came over to Stephen. It looked bad, they agreed.

Red lights and lantern lights played over the shifting crowds against the background of trees. The foliage looked oddly artificial in the artificial light, figures came and went confusedly.

Victoria, standing alone in pitchy gloom, was absorbedly watching the thrilling scene, when suddenly something warm and smothering caught her, arms held her, and a face touched hers. Was it with a laugh or a sob that this breath-taking shadow in the deeper shadows pressed a warm cheek to hers, and touched her lips with a hard, half-savage kiss? She gasped, fighting for room to see who held her, although she knew, and knew Davy's whisper:

"Good-bye, dear! I—I waited for this! Good-bye, Vick!"

He was gone, and she had sent one frightened glance about her in the darkness. She was unseen. She was breathing like a runner, and now she leaned against a nearby stone wall and panted, feeling shaken and weak.

Through all her body the ecstasy of it ran like wine; she was thrilling like a harp smitten suddenly by a master hand.

"Oh—oh—oh! Davy!" she whispered. "Oh, he kissed me—that's what he did! He kissed me. He kissed me good-bye. Davy!"

After awhile she stumbled back among the others, carrying her secret like a concealed jewel of untold value. Above everything she said and did the knowledge of that stolen, enchanted second flamed like Northern Lights. The night was balmy with it, the moon shone among fast-moving inky clouds, just for that. Everything was sweet, thrilling, amusing.

"Vicky, were you talking to somebody, over there?"

"No, Papa!"

"I thought I saw somebody with you? Was it David?"

"No, Papa; it must have been somebody else!"

Stephen looked at her keenly in the gloom.

"It looked like your white hat over there!" Tina said, innocently.

"Not mine!" Victoria almost sang the words; she would never be afraid of anybody again! "When shall you be alarmed, Papa?" she asked cheerfully, of the still-encroaching fire. Stephen did not answer; he merely shrugged his shoulders. That *had* been Vicky and David under the oaks, he told himself. Had he kissed her? Would she dare deny it?

A great many buggies were rattling out of town, and the nine o'clock train for Sausalito was filled with refugees. But the Brewers remained, feeling heroic in their decision to do so. They would be sensible—they would not act upon terrified impulse.

Nobody went to bed, and as they went back and forth between the back lot and the hill, the late hours seemed filled with menace. The Torreys were gone, their little house was dark. Eric Torrey had indeed made an almost frantic appeal to Stephen, for help. "I don't ask it for myself, sir, but my wife is in a serious condition!" the young husband had said, agitatedly, coming to them at the fence.

Vernon Yelland was in the front rank of fire-watchers, offering a grave and logical opinion, based upon seasons, tides, air-currents, and atmospheric pressure, to any one who asked it. He told Tina that his idea had been that Grace should have hot coffee awaiting the fighters all night long, but he understood that the hotel people were doing that. Long afterward Tina and Grace used to tell each other of the townspeople's surprise when the parson tore off his coat and went after the flames like a madman, at about midnight. He gave his coat to a boy, and it was subsequently lost, but that did not detract from his wife's glowing reception of him when he came home at four. Everyone had gone home then, for a swift and merciful rain was falling. Grace had been wakened from deep, uneasy sleep by his return; she felt sick and stupid as she blundered about the gas-lighted kitchen, ministering to him. They both hoped to get off soundly to sleep again before the baby waked, but Vera turned and whimpered at five promptly, her fingers on her painful little gums, and Grace carried her into the kitchen, so that the weary fire-fighter could get his needed rest.

Victoria awakened to a new world. The fire was out, and in the quiet autumn day everything looked washed and fresh. Dust was laid by the rain, the air still held the strong acrid odour of soaked, burned wood and wet ashes. Everyone in the Brewer household slept late; there was a pleasant irregularity about the eleven-o'clock breakfast, with a white fog slowly rising over the toneless plumes of the peppers, and the dew glistening upon the tall, shaggy shafts and the hanging, motionless sickles of the eucalyptus.

Dishes were washed and beds made in a dreamy silence. Lou was going up to the hotel to see Daisy and Lily; Victoria walked there with her, and then walked on, wrapped in a thrilling golden haze of remembering. When she had passed the convent, and struck into the winding hills toward Sleepy Hollow, she stopped

under a great oak, and sat down, her enchanted eyes drinking
in the scene as if she had never looked upon it before.

The dry, aromatic-scented grasses stretched below her,
blotted, in the tender autumn sunlight, with the round shadows
of sprawling oaks. The burned area had crept down into a
cañon, which extended a charred finger into the duller grays and
browns. Below lay the muffling trees, and the slants and angles
of familiar homely roofs; and from them all the railway track
ran, a sharp straight line, through level stretches of marsh, to
the blue-gray blur far beyond that was more hills, and bays, and
sea. A glitter through the marshes showed the course of ca-
nals; and all about, like the circled sides of a bowl, were the faint
blue rises of hill chains, hardly a tone deeper, on this dreaming
blue day, than the faint sky.

Victoria walked home by the Torrey house; mother and
baby were placidly reëstablished on the front porch. Her nurse
had gone, called to another case this morning, said Mrs. Torrey
cheerfully. She had given the baby his bath all alone, and he
was just a little lamb.

Victoria sat on the upper step, flushed and smiling. And
presently Amy Torrey was telling her all about it: when the
doctor had been sent for, and what poor Eric said and did.
Victoria listened hungrily; all this seemed personal now.

"There is nothing in the world so sweet!" murmured Amy
Torrey.

"I hope—I shouldn't want to marry if I didn't hope for one of
my own!" Victoria said, with her bright daring smile.

"Is there—a Mr. Right—in the prospect?" the other woman
asked, eyes widening delightedly.

Victoria nodded, flushed afresh, and dimpled.

"My people aren't extremely enthusiastic about him; there
are money difficulties," she admitted. Amy was sympathetic, indignant; what right had any one to object? Why, she
and Eric only had a hundred a month, and it was nobody's
business but their own!

She pressed for more details, but Victoria was terrified with
her own boldness! She had carried the matter too far already.
She played with the great topic delicately for another twenty
minutes, and when she left, Amy Torrey kissed her good-bye. It
was with a glowing heart that she walked about the block;
Grandpa, through his agent, had been slicing off town lots from

the main property for the past several years, and now the
Brewer house had a scant two acres left of its original forty. The
Torreys, and a dozen other little home-owners, were making
monthly payments for their places.

Mama was introducing a new cook, a stout, elderly German
woman, to the ins and outs of the kitchen.

"Your salt and pepper, handy, right here," Victoria heard
her say. "We all like our eggs differently—breakfast will be at
half-past seven for Mr. Brewer, and my daughters and I come
down later. The garbage goes . . ."

Victoria slipped upstairs. The blessedness of having no
table to set, and no dishes to wash, while Frederika lasted, anyway! She had some delightful new writing paper: "Scotch
Heather," the box called it. She began her first letter to Davy.

"Davy dear——"

She hesitated; were they engaged? Her first sickening doubt
came into being. But she briskly dismissed it. They loved
each other, anyway. That was all that mattered.

"Davy dear, I have been thinking, and I know you have——"

"What is it, Mama?" asked Victoria, instinctively pushing
the nearest thing—it happened to be what was called a "picture-
card," soaked with Hoyt's German Cologne—across the writing,
and looking up innocently as her mother came in.

"Dearie," May began. "Writing letters?" she asked,
diverted.

"I thought I would. . . ." Victoria yawned.

"To Alice?"

"No-oo-oo!" Victoria carelessly tore into pieces the commenced epistle, closed her desk, dropped the fragments into the
waste-basket, and turned, smiling gallantly, to face her mother.
"It wasn't anything!" she said. "Just scribbling."

"I don't think I'd scribble on my beautiful birthday paper,"
May suggested. "Dearie, you will have to go to town on the
four-twenty. The telephone just rang, and when she said long
distance wanted me I had such a fright! I thought of course
your grandfather—however, it was Mrs. Pembroke, wanting
Lou to go over and have dinner with them, and go to the
Baldwin and stay the night——"

"Lou! Why Lou? Esme's their friend—at least she's
Jenny's friend——"

"Lou met Frank Pembroke at Daisy's last week, and I

imagine—" May stopped with a significant pressure of her lips, and arched brows. "Frank is younger than Esme—never has been attentive——" she reasoned.

"And where do I come in?" Victoria asked, her thoughts upon the scraps in the scrap basket.

"You'll have to go over with Lou, dear," May said, thinking of the same thing; "she can't go alone. Stay with Aunt Fanny and have a little visit with Grandpa. I want you to go to Quade and McKay's to-morrow, and Wangenheim, Sternheim's about the cups, I'll give you a list. And change the library books. You and Lou might have a soda at Maskey's, if you like. But don't miss the eleven-forty-five home, for Esme has that buzzing in her head again, and I think I'll take her in to Doctor Pawlicki."

Victoria nodded, well pleased. Things seemed to be always happening nowadays; it was very satisfactory. Yesterday, Davy and the fire; to-day, an unexpected trip into town and a prospective beau for Lou. When her mother left the room and Lou had come flying up, excited and radiant, they began the familiar, yet always thrilling, preparations for town. Stiff white petticoats, knitted worsted underskirts, heavy tucked corset-covers, new satin ribbon stocks, silk belts knowingly drawn into silver buckles, high buttoned kid shoes, lisle stockings with white heels and toes, white gloves odorous of benzine. They packed two telescope baskets; there was some running about to borrow Tina's and Mama's new straps.

But even before Lou came up, Vicky had found in the scrap-basket the tiny diagonal of paper that held the word "Davy," and had chewed it to harmless pulp. Mama mightn't, of course. But then again, Mama *might*.

"Don't you feel sorry for poor Lola—alone all day?" Lou asked contentedly, when they were floating on the placid blue bay a few hours later, and, from the deck of the turning *San Rafael* they could look up at the windows of Sausalito.

Vicky nodded, happily; it was delicious to pity Lola.

"Lou, do you like Frank Pembroke?" she asked, somewhat shyly.

Lou was different from her sisters; she was a mysteriously self-sufficient little person. Except for Victoria, she was the prettiest of the girls. Victoria's vivacious, spirited beauty made Lou look a little babyish and flat. But her buttonhole of a mouth was like a doll's, and since the age of twelve she had known exactly how to fix her hair.

"Yes, I like Frank," she admitted now, with a calm Vicky thought amazing. "But it's really Frank's friend, Howard Palmer," she continued thoughtfully.

Victoria rightly inferred that the word "it" indicated the person indirectly responsible for this flattering invitation.

"And do you like him, Lou?"

"He's stunning—plays polo and has horses. He's from the east. Yes, of course I'd marry him," said Lou, biting together the ripped tip of a glove-finger, "or I'd marry Frank, for that matter. But—you'll see. Mama'll queer it!"

"Oh, Lou, how do you mean?" Victoria gasped.

"And if she doesn't, Papa will!" Lou added, darkly. "How? Why, the way they always do! Look at Esme—what chance has she ever had! Somebody spying on her all the time——!"

"But, Lou," Victoria said dazedly, "they have to *watch* us!"

"Well," Lou said, indifferently, "I know that I'm going to marry the first man that asks me—that's all. Watch us! Why, no man is ever going to marry any one until he's kissed them!" Lou finished, ungrammatically but firmly. "I've watched Esme—poor old Es', she could have had men crazy about her— and I've watched Tina. Vernon Yelland makes me sick at my stomach, but she liked him—she might just as well have had him as Grace! And you, Vick, why, you're *stunning*——"

Victoria was drinking deep of a new and fearful wine. She laughed, flushed.

"I believe you!" she said.

"I know it," Lou resumed. "At the hotel dance the other night," said this terrible junior, warmly, "I was supposed to be chaperoned by Daisy's aunt. Daisy's aunt! She was playing euchre the whole time. I went out on the porch with this Howard Palmer—I had on my dimity—and we got talking—of kissing. I said that . . . well, anyway. . . ."

"Lou!" Victoria breathed, after an electric silence, "Did he kiss you?"

"Why, of course he did! And then I danced with other men, and he was wild until he got another dance with me, and then we went out on the porch again!"

"Oh, but Lou, you *knew* he'd kiss you again!"

"Well, of course I did! But we were talking, and telling each other about other crushes. . . ."

Lou smiled, cryptically. Victoria was silent, frowning, thinking.

"Mama would be wild, Lou!" she ventured.

"It's none of Mama's business!" Lou said serenely.

"Yes, I know," Victoria presently argued, "but last summer, I met an awfully nice fellow—on that yachting trip, Ted Green. College man, and all that. And he was awfully fresh—and he—yes, he did, he kissed me, in a sort of scrambling way, you know. . . ."

"I know!" Lou nodded, bright eyes on her sister.

"Well, but he didn't seem to like me so much, afterward!" Vicky confessed, her cheeks hot.

"Oh, well, that was just luck—the crowd—and it was a hot Sunday, and all that!" Lou, who before this had had the details of that dreadful day from Victoria, decided promptly. "But the truth is, men don't like ladylike, refined girls, Vick," she added, positively. "And Mama has no business to teach us that they do! If she wants us to marry, she has no business not to let men kiss us, and all that! I'm going to marry, but I'm going to take darn good care that Mama doesn't know anything about it. Howard asked to come to San Rafael, and I said no. I said 'Too much family!'"

"Lou, aren't you terrible!" Vicky gasped, in horror and delight. And presently she was telling Lou about |Davy, and a little mutual compact of silence and help was entered into between them.

"But, Lord, Vicky! You'll have to wait *years!*" said the practical Lou.

"I know. But I don't care!" Victoria answered happily.

"And then you'll let yourself in for poverty and everything," objected the younger sister. "Like Nelly!"

"Oh, I'll love it!"

Lou looked at her curiously.

"You're in love with him!" she marvelled.

Victoria laughed, bit her lip, looked out toward the Golden Gate. Tears were in her eyes.

Life was so exciting! She would not have changed places with any one, when she had carefully seen Lou to the Jackson Street car and was walking up the long block to California

Street.   She sat on the dummy, remembering resentfully, in this
new estimate of Mama and Papa, that they had never allowed
their daughters, as little girls, this privilege.   Bertie might sit
outside; he was a boy.   But little ladies were better inside.

Exciting to find Aunt Fanny just leaving for a marketing
round on Polk Street, and to accompany her into bakery and
candy store.   It appeared that Lucy and Alice and that doctor
of Alice's were calling to-night; and Fanny was going to have
layer-cake and lemonade and mottoes.

"Just a little bite for 'em, seemed pleasanter!" Fanny tossed
off casually.   But she was pleased with Vicky's enthusiasm:
why, it was going to be a real *party*!

"Aunt Fanny, do you suppose Alice is really *engaged*?"

"Looks like it!   Funny——" Miss Fanny said.   "He's got a
daughter almost's old as she is."

Exciting again.   Victoria walked on air.   She and her aunt
dined alone, Carra passing silently through the room once or
twice with the old man's tray.   Fanny hated this, and in freer
times she had once or twice suggested that Carra use the steep,
unlighted back stairway when a meal was in progress.   But of
late she had dared make no comment.

There was no dessert for dinner to-night, because there were
to be refreshments later.   Victoria tore upstairs and rearranged
her dark, rich hair, her eyes sparkled with excitement, and she
thought she looked rather pretty.   She and Fanny were restless
in spite of themselves, as they waited for the callers, Fanny
reading *The Church Visitor*, and Vick looking at the Doré illustrations of Dante's "Inferno."

The bell rang; Maggie lumbered through the hallway.   They
heard Lucy's rich, deep voice in a laugh, a strange man's voice.
Fanny went to the jingling bead portière at the front parlour
door that opened into the hall.

"Well, this is nice of you. . . ."

Alice's doctor looked old, Vicky thought instantly.   Well,
of course he *was* old: forty-two.   He was extremely dark, dark
hair, dark eyes, square beard.   He had a delightfully polished
manner, sending his bright smiling eyes from Aunt Fan to Lucy
and back again in an almost filial fashion.

They sat about the front room in a circle for awhile, and then
went into the dining-room, and had the cocoanut layer-cake,
fluffy, white, and sticky, and the lemonade, and the mottoes.

"Alice, tell me—you *are* engaged?" Victoria questioned her cousin, when they went up to Fanny's stuffy, orderly bedroom for a minute. Alice dimpled, looked down, and shrugged.

"What can you do," she asked, "when people won't take no for an answer?"

"But do you love him?" Victoria whispered, properly awed.

"Mama's crazy about him!' Alice answered, after thought. "It's all different from what you would think, Vick!" she confided suddenly. And with a puzzled frown and a momentary stare into space, she added: "How can you tell? I like him —he's fine, and all that. But I don't know how you *ought* to feel about a man when you marry him! I try to think it out, sometimes. But I guess it's just like anything else . . . the girls used to talk, at the hospital, sometimes. . . ." She flushed, scowled, and laughed suddenly. "I don't—I don't believe I'd ever be crazy about a man, Vick!" she finished, somewhat vaguely.

"You mean *like* to have his arms about you, and have him kissing you?" Victoria supplied, interestedly.

Alice turned scarlet.

"Oh, for heaven's sake!" she stammered, arresting fingers against her cousin's lips. "Vicky," she added suddenly, "I wish we knew more about it . . . marriage, I mean. Suppose one got into it, and didn't . . . didn't like it!"

"Do you suppose there's an awful lot of kissing?" Vick whispered.

Alice tried to laugh, but the subject was too vital to her ignorant hopes and fears.

"I don't know. That's just it!" she whispered back, suffocating. "I like the idea of a house, and friends in to dinner," she added, anxiously. "But I don't know—Frank's been married before, though. Maybe that would . . . make a difference!"

And both girls, confused by this touching upon a forbidden subject, nervous, excited, and hardly knowing what they thought or surmised, broke into almost hysterical giggling.

"You know I'm—Davy and I——" Victoria presently confided. Alice looked at her, horrified.

"Vicky Brewer! But he hasn't five cents!"

"I know he hasn't."

"But he's got his mother, all his family . . . and he's

working to pay his post-graduate expenses . . . Oh, Vicky," begged Alice, "does your mother approve?"

"Nobody even knows! But," said Vicky proudly, "when I think of . . . what we were just talking about . . . kissing, you know, and having children . . . then I *know* that I love him!"

Alice's disapproving expression did not abate.

"But, Vick, that's only part of it!" she protested eagerly. "Mama says that it's much safer for a girl to marry a man she respects, who has a profession, and a standing in the community, and let the rest of it follow. Why, Davy has *nothing* . . . you'd be like poor Nelly!"

And walking home between Mama and Frank, a few minutes later, Alice reflected for the first time with satisfaction upon the things that this man at her side could offer. His house, his comfortable income, his position, his well-established practice, his horse and buggy . . . these things *did* count. And as for the quick, authoritative flash in his smiling eye when he differed with anybody, and the dry, hairy odour of his face when he kissed her, and the fussy fashion he had of bothering her with the mention of rubbers and umbrella every time there was a cloud in the sky, why, these were mere trifles. Poor Nelly, and poor Vicky, and poor Mama who had struggled with pennies all her life! How much richer she was than these!

"You wouldn't be a real girl if you didn't have all sorts of little terrors and misgivings!" Lucy told her, when they were going to bed.

"But Mama—Papa doesn't like Frank!"

"Ah, my dear, did a father ever like the man that stole his little daughter away!"

Alice smiled foolishly; Mama was of course right again.

CHAPTER XXI

VICKY awakened in autumn sunshine, to a delicious sense of youth and health and content with life. She lay listening to the morning sounds of the house: Aunt Fanny was talking stridently, but far away behind closed doors, to Maggie; the canary was bursting his throat with song in the dining-room window, and Carra was crooning softly against an intermittent sound of running water. A faucet was roughly turned off, and the pipes thrummed and were still. The front-door bell rang stridently.

It was fun to be at Aunt Fanny's. Vicky thought she would get up; although one was never punctual at breakfast in this house, for Maggie was always agreeable about keeping the coffee hot, and Aunt Fanny rather liked her breakfast, with the paper and the letters, alone. There would be long slices of French bread cut in thin slants, and just enough cream.

The girl yawned, stretched, rolled out of bed, and went cautiously to the window. Sunshine was pouring over the city, but across the street below, the wooden houses threw gray shadows, and in the shadows sidewalks and gardens still glistened with dew. Vicky's room was at the back of the house; she could see a strip of blue bay, with the *McDowell* cutting a great silky fan across the water and sending up an occasional puff of steam from the whistle.

"Vick. . . ." The unexpected voice behind her brought her heart into her throat; she turned amazedly. Bertie was in the doorway, his face serious and tear-streaked; Aunt Fanny was behind him. "Vick," Bertie said gently, coming over to her as she sat down abruptly on the bed, in her nightgown, "you're to come right home. Esme—Mama sent me right over."

"Esme . . . .?" Victoria echoed stupidly and thickly. Bertie's eyes answered; the girl looked at her aunt.

"Oh, God help us all—oo—oo—oooo!" sobbed and moaned

Fanny, breaking down completely. She sank into a rocker. Victoria, very pale, whispered one word.

"Dead," Bertie repeated, beginning to cry quite simply, and without hiding his face. He gained control of himself, before Vicky's wide-eyed, awed silence.

"Bertie, in the night?"

Bertie swallowed, sniffed.

"Mama went in to wake her, this morning."

"Mama—did she faint?" The girl's keen, quick whisper seemed to cut through Fanny's weeping and the older woman straightened up, blew her nose, and looked almost resentfully at her niece. Bertie shook his head gravely.

"Well, she broke down, of course. Lucky Papa was there, and he stayed.—Poor Mama!—Tina telephoned me and I came right over, for you and Lou. Lola's going up home later, if they need her."

Vicky solemnly and tenderly kissed her brother, her cloud of soft hair on his shoulder, and he tightened his arm about the slender young figure in the thin gown.

"I knew you'd be wonderful, Vick!" he said, gratefully.

"I'll go right home! It's nine. I can get the nine-forty-five!"

"Vicky, if you could—! Of course they're all upset," Bertie said eagerly. "I've got to go to the office, and stop and tell Aunt Lucy. And of course Tina isn't much good, she fainted, and all that!"

"I declare, Vicky, I look at you in admiration," said Fanny, suddenly and harshly. "Dear me, you people who don't feel anything are to be envied! Calmly make your plans and arrange about boats, with your lovely sister—oo—oo—ooo!" Fanny wept again.

"Aunt Fanny," Vicky said unsteadily, "you know I was merely trying to get to *Mama*——"

"She and Esme have always been crazy about each other!" Bertie said, defensively. And at this championship, so infinitely dear in this strange and shaking hour, Victoria's eyes did brim, and for the first time the thought smote her in all its enormity. Esme *dead*. Esme!

She sank down on the bed again, fumbled for the loosened upper sheet, and put it to her eyes. Tears came in a flood; first with a pitiful crinkling of all her face muscles, then with a deep convulsion of her whole body. Fanny cried afresh, and Bertie stood, with wet eyes, uncomfortably watching them.

"Well, I *thought* this girl loved her dear, angelic big sister—too good for this world, and better out of it and all its mean, wicked sinful *dirtiness!*" sobbed Fanny, violently. "Just as we all would be, if we could only see it, safe with *God*—I *thought* she cared for our darling—you loved her, didn't you, Vicky? Poor Vicky, without her dear little confidante and chum——"

Vicky flung herself into the tumbled pillows; it seemed to her that she could not live, with Esme dead.

"But it's not *Esme* we must pity——" Fanny cried, strangling. "No, indeed, she's safe—she's *laughing* at us—safe forever, darling, darling angel that she was!"

She was a little annoyed again when Vicky suddenly sat up, wiped her face, and with a quiet nod and promise dismissed Bertie. She would get the nine-forty-five. Fanny sat on, rocking and sobbing, while the girl dressed, but Vicky did not break down again. Quietly and almost absent-mindedly she put on her flowered hat, went downstairs, drank her coffee. But though the red-eyed Maggie put eggs and French bread before her, Vicky drew away from food, and in less than twenty minutes from the time when Bertie had entered her room, was out in the strangely glaring, unfamiliar sunshine, going down to the boat. Her aunt of course accompanied her, and at the ferry they found Lou, crying uncontrollably, Lucy and Alice, serious, pale and constrained. The two older women talked together, and the girls were free for infinite murmurs and whispers—all about Esme. They talked of her as living, corrected themselves; spoke of her as dead and corrected themselves again. One of their number—*dead*. Not to hear Esme talking about the sort of man she meant to marry, any more!

Victoria began to tremble very much when they reached the home gate. The front door, up at the end of the curved, dry path between the shabby marguerites and the pampas grasses, stood wide. Window shutters upstairs were closed; the house was wrapped in a terrible silence.

The little party moved through the quiet, autumnal sunshine to the door. Victoria, in the lead, turned pale and put her hand to her heart as a low moan broke through the stillness of some unseen room. They could hear a little murmur of consoling and tearful voices.

Grace Yelland came quietly and lightly across the hall, and kissed Vicky and Lou, smiling seriously at the others, as she turned back with one hand lightly laid about Vicky's waist.

"Your mother and father are in the library, dear, so anxious to see their dear daughters—dearer than ever now, Victoria!"

The library door opened; Tina stood on the threshold. At the sight of Vicky her face broke again, despite her stern effort to control the shaking muscles, and the sisters ran together, and wept in each other's arms.

"Mama's wonderful!" sobbed Tina. "But—but come in to Papa! He's been asking for you!"

Victoria was not conscious of the general jumble of crying and kissing that broke out when May saw Lucy and Fanny. She went straight to the stricken figure in the shiny old brown leather armchair, and sank on her knees. With a great groan and sob Stephen caught her to his heart. Tears were in his eyes, and the marks of tears on his cheeks.

May was brave; marvellously, miraculously brave. She sat down in the chair opposite her husband, and Fanny and Lucy and Alice sat down, too. May wore her old gray cashmere with the purple plush strip down the front; her stout soft face was pale and strained, and she patted Fanny's hand incessantly as she quietly talked, quietly wept, and quietly talked again.

"She was our angel, Fanny. Always too good—always better than the other children! 'Mama,' she used to say to me, when she wasn't more than a baby—do you remember this, Steve? She had a doll. . . ."

"She never knew what sorrow and wickedness and suffering were, in all her beautiful, beautiful life!" Fanny said, violently and in tears.

"No, that's what we said!" May whispered, with an exalted look. "Steve and I kept everything away from her, except love and protection and happiness! Never did children have a home and love and protection as these children have . . . My first-born, Fanny," faltered May, suddenly pressing the folded handkerchief she held against her trembling lips. "Do you remember, in the old Powell Street house . . . Mama was with us then. . . ."

"Mama . . . Mama!" Victoria pleaded, turning, on her knees, to lay a restraining hand upon her mother's knee.

"A beautiful poem ended!" Stephen said gravely and thickly. Fannie heaved a sigh that lowered itself in jerky little stitches. Lucy, tearless but sympathetic, pressed her lips together, and shook her head. Alice's eyes were sorrowful, and she gripped Vicky's hand tightly, but she was thinking that this event might delay the marriage Frank Babcock wanted so promptly. Alice would have been glad of more time.

The girls, red-eyed but self-possessed, kept closely together in the sad, strange days that followed. Their subdued conversation was filled with new endearments, "dearest," "darling"; they looked slender and young in fresh, simple black. The household circled tenderly about Stephen, who sat, stricken and old, in the library.

Lucy came frequently, with Bobo; Fanny came, crisp and pious in her resignation. Vicky and Lou coaxed their father into country walks, listening to his every word, eagerly sympathetic. And often Bertie came, newly dear, tenderly consoling and affectionate. Shaken laughter was heard in the Brewer household again, when Bertie was there.

One day, some three weeks after the funeral, May came to the wide back porch, to find Vicky vigorously cleaning crabs.

"My precious," May said. "Uncle Rob has come home with Papa, to spend the night. Papa was speaking about Bobo yesterday, dear, and I want to speak to you darling girlies about our having Bobo here!"

"Does Uncle Bob want us to?" Vicky said, surprised.

"I am going to speak to him about it. The thing is," said May, "that I think dear little Bobo *ought* to be here! He's had that heavy cough ever since he got whooping-cough at Nelly's, more than a year ago, and this is the climate for him. And I think dear Papa would like it."

"But I thought Aunt Lucy—wouldn't she miss the money?" Tina asked interestedly.

May, with a vision of Lucy supreme in power the moment something happened to Pa, and Bobo inherited the house, narrowed her lips disapprovingly.

"I don't mean forever, Tina! I mean just for a few months, dear. And it seemed to me that Vicky is the one to ask Uncle Bob, he is so specially fond of her!"

Victoria's face brightened with pleasure, and she presently put the proposition to her Uncle Rob very prettily. They were all so fond of Bobo, and he really mustn't go into another winter with that cough. Couldn't they have him?

Bob, who was fond of her, considered this smilingly. He knew, what none of the others knew, that his resignation from Crabtree and Company was only a few weeks away. Things were not going well with the firm, and Bob could not control them. Stephen had opposed him steadily, in everything that concerned the family firm; he had come to believe it useless to attempt a harmonious coöperation with Stephen. Bob did not dislike his brother-in-law, but Steve's slow, deliberate, pompous opposition was exhausting and wasteful. He had agreed to enter a Sacramento wholesale grocery house on the first of the year.

He had been wondering just what arrangement to make for Bobo when he went to Sacramento to live, as he must, of course, do. Bob liked Lucy thoroughly, she amused and even somewhat allured him; but long before this he had come to an indulgent masculine realization that she was utterly impractical. Much better, he had thought, to have no business relations with Lucy, simply because, like most women, she didn't know what she was talking about. Her bright exculpating apologies for mismanagement impressed Bob no longer. When she and Harry moved from the Mission, some years ago, Lucy had handed over to Bob old bills for almost a hundred dollars, with an explanation that made her seem actually clever to be no deeper in debt. After the "Abbotsford" experience she had again asked him, in the most businesslike way, to "temporarily straighten her out." And now, following the harmonious Larkin Street experience, he knew that she was in fresh difficulties. Lucy was incurably a shopper; she bought a new mattress, garden tools, Italian oil, quite without reference to her money in hand. If she needed them, or fancied she did, she always reasoned that it was "economy" to buy them. Economy was a great word with her. Most women knew nothing about it, she said.

Only a day or two earlier she had frankly—it was always "frankly"—explained to him her need for two hundred and ten dollars. This she said, would represent his board, and Bobo's, in advance, for eighteen weeks at eleven dollars a week. But she would call it nineteen weeks, for interest. Bob hated to remind her that she had made a similar arrangement at Christmas time, covering a period of seven weeks, had accepted the seventy-five dollars he advanced, and had made no subsequent mention of it whatever, quietly accepting his weekly payment a few days later, as if no loan had ever been made. She and Alice had gone to his dentist, too; there was a charge of something more than forty dollars there, and her White House bill, presumably because of Bobo's necessities, was in his name.

So May's proposition came opportunely, and Bob was glad to kiss the glowing Vicky, and assure her that he hadn't forgotten that summer night of Bobo's desperate illness, and that whatever she asked him was already promised. And it was Vicky that May sent to get Bobo, very casually, at first, with just a telescope basket of little shirts and ribbed stockings. The Brewers were genuinely delighted to have the engaging, friendly little six-year-old back again and Lucy, with Alice's generous contributions added to her budget, was perfectly willing to part with him for a time. Later, when May's doctor was quoted as saying that the child needed the warmer air of the quiet, windless country town, Lucy was deep in a scheme for turning her back room into a hospital room for any case that Alice chose to bring there, and received the news indifferently.

The news of Rob's resignation followed, and as Bob and Stephen seemed entirely adjusted to the idea, and as the head of the firm was merely a cackling old child at this time, Fanny and May could exchange congratulations, unaffected by their own entire ignorance of causes and reasons for the change.

"Now, I shall feel that things are going *right!*" Fanny said thankfully, on a long breath.

"Well," May added, tremulously, "we trust Rob, of course. But we *know* Steve. There won't be any ridiculous waste on advertising, and that sort of nonsense."

"Rob wasn't spending his own money," Fanny contributed, in her most businesslike way. "Steve has stock there, you'll have some, some day, and of course I have! It makes all the difference in the world!"

"I wish I could understand business as you do, Fan," May said humbly, her soft, fat face and faded eyes expressing anxiety and admiration.

"Seems to me that sometimes I have more of Pa's business ability than either Bob or Harry!" Fanny conceded, tossing her head.

To the Brewers the winter was long and sad, and Christmas a day when Esme seemed more present with them than she had been even in the flesh. January rains blew and slashed across San Rafael and sluiced and tumbled down California Street in the gutters outside Grandpa's warm, orderly bedroom. At home, Vicky and Lou murmured in the hot dining room, roasting coffee, yawning over "No Gentlemen" and "On Both Sides." They filled the idle afternoons with walks, letters, duets, with idle dreaming. Tina had tea nearly every day with Grace; Vernon loved the informal little custom, the steaming kettle, the toast, and Tina and Grace eager to amuse and revive him.

Bobo was a real addition to the group; he went to school now, and wrote large "B's" on walls and books. Stephen was fond of him, and the girls petted and spoiled him; May said he was her comfort.

Lucy and Alice came over more than once, filled with wedding plans. Lucy was spending money recklessly on linens and laces, "the one time that one *must*," she explained. Alice, who showed the same odd combination of girlish complacency in her new plans, and most un-girlish hesitancy about furthering them, confided to Vicky that she did not really know, herself, why Mama was so wild to hasten this match.

"Mothers all are! Crazy to have their girls married!" Vicky suggested.

"But why, Vicky? I have my work, and I am perfectly willing—I mean I'd *rather* wait until fall," Alice answered seriously.

"Oh, your work!" Vicky laughed. "I don't suppose any girl counts her work, when it comes to getting married!" she said.

"Yes, but with Bobo gone, and now me gone, I don't know how Mama will manage!" Alice said, with her conscientious little frown. "Papa gives her everything, of course, but Georgie can't do much!"

"Oh, she'll manage. And it'll be a sort of relief to her to have you settled," Vicky said, briskly opening an oven door, and eyeing her baking muffins approvingly. Alice looked unsatisfied, opened her mouth as if to speak impetuously, decided not to speak, bit her lip, and scowled.

"May—it seems so *soon!*" she complained.

"Oh, Alice! Why, it'll be quite a long engagement. Look

at Bertie!" Vicky did not sympathize with her cousin's misgivings; her own affair with David was so much more vague and uncertain, and yet she was happy. If Alice wasn't happy, it must be that she was becoming fractious and exacting.

David had written her six or seven times since his return to Germany, friendly, temperate letters that might be quite simply handed to Mama, when they had been read. He described his work, his hospital, his boarding-house, the weather. Only eyes as romantic as Vicky's could have found food for dreams in these documents, but to her the arrival of each and every separate thin envelope, with its pale-pink stamps, was a delight.

Sometimes May, with the mournful air of pleasure that was her nearest approach to cheerfulness in these days, was reading the first silky, crinkled sheet before Vicky had reached the last. She would sigh, commenting upon Davy's handicaps; poor Davy. That mother in Napa, and poor Miss Clay, and everything! He would have to practise in Napa, with his mother and sister looking to him, in the next few years, to repay borrowed money, and house and feed them all. May disliked clumsy, pathetic, penniless Davy Dudley. She spoke of him as "audacious."

But there was no love-making in the letters; nothing remotely resembling it. May watched keenly for anything suspicious; it was never there. Vicky would be giddy and light-hearted for a day or two after one arrived, and would presently answer it. Her mother always saw the answers; Vicky wrote clever and witty letters, and since her actual childhood her mother had enjoyed them as much as any possible recipient could.

"You ridiculous girl!" she would comment, with an indulgent, sad smile. And sometimes she added: "I want to read this to Papa, Vick. It will make him laugh—I mean your description of Aunt Fanny!—and he has little enough to laugh at, nowadays."

This pleased rather than annoyed Victoria; she loved admiration, and she had no reason for secrecy with Davy. Until his letters assumed a lover's tone, hers certainly could not. She liked to think over what she had written him; the spirited little description of the day her hat blew into the bay, the latest baby story of little Bobo, her views of Alice's impeccable doctor.

But one dreaming day in early March a letter came for her in a slightly different vein. May and Lou were in town, calling on Aunt Fanny and Grandpa; the latter was far from well. Tina was drying her hair, on the upstairs back balcony; Bobo was at school. There was no servant in the Brewer house now, and Vicky had met the postman at the gate; it was time, more than time, for an answer to her last letter to Germany, and she never saw the gray uniform of the letter carrier without an expectant thrill.

Here it was; but she could never believe it! With a delicious thrill she tore it open, sitting in a flood of sunlight on the fat, low balustrade of the porch.

She read it; her heart pumped. She crumpled the thin sheets—four of them—hastily, and looked about for observing eyes. Everything was still; except far-away Tina singing "Marguerite" beyond closed doors.

Her hand shaking, the light that never was on land and sea shining in her eyes, Victoria read it again.

"Calhoun is here, and he has married his girl," Davy had written.

He has only his interne pay, but they live wonderfully on it. She cooks him little meals, and they go about seeing things. I tell you it gave me a kind of heartache, to see them so happy, and to think that the only girl I ever think about would have to wait years and years—even if I ever got up the nerve to ask her—which I won't. I'm thirty—gosh, it seems old!"

The next sentence was about his work: but before the letter ended he said something about affairs at home, in Napa. Mother had paid off her mortgage now, and Mary was working with the village millinery. They had thought Mary might teach, but her illness had ended her schooling. Well, he often thought of that day there was a forest fire in San Rafael. He had to go to the clinic now, kindest regards to all. He was hers sincerely.

Victoria hid the letter and made no mention of it. Her heart flew and floated like a bird; the whole world was metamorphosed into miraculous brightness. When her mother came home she had made rhubarb pies; two of them, criss-crossed and spilling candied juice. May was tired, sad. Pa was failing fast, and after dear Esme, it seemed as if she could *not* bear. . . .

They all fell at once to consoling her, a familiar process now. May sat in the kitchen, bonnet-strings loose, and her stout, discoloured feet in a bucket of hot water that Tina had suggested. Nothing like it for weariness and colds! These first untimely hot spring days were the dangerous times.

"Any letters, Vick?"

"Gas bill for Papa. And one from Nelly saying that she has a little boy, and they've named him Stuart."

"Yes, I know!" May said apathetically. "Lucy was at Aunt Fanny's—she told me. Poor Nelly had convulsions, she was terribly ill."

"Why should she have convulsions, Mama?"

"Because she was sick, dear!"

"But, Mama, why convulsions?"

May was pulling the tips of her black suede mourning gloves straight; now she compressed her lips.

"People do, sometimes, Vick. Never mind about that, now. Some day when you're married all this will seem different to you. Nelly's well again, and she has her dear little baby in her arms, and that's all we need to know! You made pies? Was Grace here?"

Victoria, rebuffed, reflected with deep and rebellious satisfaction that she would answer Davy's letter without telling Mama one word about it. She would wait her chance for privacy and the hour of inspiration.

It came sooner than she expected, for only a week later Fanny telephoned May in great agitation. Pa was sinking; May must come at once. May, who was just a little vexed with Vicky, over a slight difference of opinion regarding a salad, decided to take Tina with her on this interesting and mournful errand. Lou was again with the Pembrokes; even the unsuspicious Tina was surprised at the good-nature with which Victoria received the maternal dictum.

The whole family had felt May's little altercation with her daughter uncomfortably. Vicky, who was always wild for changes had read somewhere of a certain salad, and had eagerly offered to try it, for lunch. But May had decreed against wasting good food on experiments; who ever heard of apples and celery in a salad? It sounded all wrong to her. Vicky had sulked.

"Just now, when Mama has so much to bear, I wish you

could be a little more amiable, Vicky!" May had said, tremulously. But Victoria, hot with the kitchen-work of greasy dishes and sifting ashes, had answered sharply:

"I know, Mama. But we all feel badly about Esme, you're not the only one! And I don't see why we're not to try a new dish for the rest of our lives just because there's been sorrow in the family!"

"Vick!" Tina had gasped, aghast. And May had turned from the kitchen with her face actually pale from the shock. Vicky had remained, slamming oven doors and crashing dishes, and only a few minutes later the telephone had sounded, for Fanny's summons, and May and Tina had majestically deserted her, in an unforgiving silence.

They were barely out of sight when she flew to her desk. Davy's letter she knew by heart, but she spread its pages about her. When she went down to her lonely lunch of eggs and the cold bread-pudding, she carried these leaves to the kitchen, and burned them. And that afternoon she walked to the post-office and mailed a letter to Germany.

Phrases from it kept dancing in her excited brain as she went homeward.

"Why should 'the only girl you ever think about' have to wait years and years?" she had written. "Perhaps she would rather come on to you, and try managing on an interne's pay, than that. How shall I say it to you, Davy? A young lady is supposed to be silent, isn't she? She is never supposed to say that she loves a man, misses him—terribly. So I will only tell you that Bertie's wedding cost my father more than six hundred dollars. Is the fare to Germany as much as that?

"I shouldn't write this, I know. But I have never liked any other man, this way. Will you answer me honestly, and tell whether there was not something you wanted to say to me, that day of the fire? You see I don't know—I have no idea how you feel."

The last phrase had been heavily underscored. Remembering it, in the quiet autumn afternoon, Vick had a moment of panic. Suppose Davy had meant some other girl by the allusion to "the only girl I ever think about"? The letter was ashes now; she could not re-read it.

But she reassured herself; it must have been what she hoped. She had read it a hundred times without suspicion.

CHAPTER XXII

APRIL was long and wet; Harry had coughed all winter, now he began to cough again, convulsively and exhaustingly. Lucy kept him at home for two or three days, but after that he went back again to the office and struggled wearily with the usual details of bills and bookkeeping. His feet were always icy, his head always throbbing with pain and heat, and his throat sore. Sometimes he could think, all afternoon long, of nothing but the joy of getting home, of staggering to bed with every bone aching and every fibre shuddering with cold, of feeling the blankets over him, and the soft mattress beneath, and the hot-water bottle at his feet.

Three days at home, ten days at the office. It was on the tenth day, a Tuesday, that Harry knew that he could not stick it out. If it had been even Friday, with the prospect of the following half-day, he might have struggled on. But Tuesday—it was practically the beginning of the week! They were stock-taking, too, but he could bear no more. Every breath was an agony, his bones were racked and his legs were as weak as a baby's. He went to Miss Baum, his voice a mere wheezing shadow.

"I should think you *would* have to go home!" she said, good-naturedly. Harry, leaning on her desk, doubled up with hot, dry suffocation, managed a smile.

"So sorry, after last week!" he whispered. The trip home, the cold wet street, the racketing car, the stumbling steps to his own doorway, were so many agonies. He tumbled blindly to bed; Lucy was out, Alice on a case. Bob had been in Sacramento for several months.

Harry collapsed; great shudders shook him as the warmth of blankets and hot-water bottle began to penetrate deliciously to his aching bones.

"Whoo!" he kept whistling gratefully, "this is *good*. My Lordy! Whoo!"

When Lucy came in he was in an uneasy sleep; he wakened, began a crowing, hoarse explanation, coughed. He was glad to subside again, glad to be declared really ill.

The result of the five days' weakness and aching and fever was not fatal; but it was serious in other ways. By the time Harry, shaken and white, was moved out to the kitchen, Finch and Houston had filled his place in the office. Alice's wedding was now but a few weeks ahead; Bob was in Sacramento, Georgie ecstatic over the prospect of a good job, in San Jose. He would be employed in a little hardware shop, but would have entire charge of the bicycle-mending end of the business.

Harry sat listening, sometimes worried, sometimes only dreaming. All his dreams were of heat; the old burning heat of the San Rafael days, heat on deep grass, sunshine burning down upon dry piers above the hot flicker of water. He felt that he had never been really warm.

Resolutely, stubbornly, Lucy pushed on toward the wedding. She would not listen to Alice's mild protests. Certainly not! Nothing should be allowed to interfere with her happy time; every girl had a right to her wedding.

Alice had always been obedient, and with all her old simple earnestness and docility she obeyed now. Frank was sure; Mama was sure; and of course she wanted to be married; she did not want to be an old maid! When Frank was away from her, through her busy days, whether she was at home with Mama or on a case, she felt quite happy about it. But when they were together, and he quite naturally and quietly kissed her, and when he talked of their future, she did not feel so sure.

"Mama, it worries me, with Papa not working—you'll have all these bills!"

"My dear, we have bought very economically. It never pays to get poor stuff! And marrying off my last girl is something I shall never have to do again!"

She had evidently no misgivings; Alice tried to have none. Her grandfather, in one of his lucid moments, sent her a check for one hundred dollars; Alice eagerly applied it to the White House bill, although Lucy said it might be wiser to lay in some silver; silver was so cheap now. George sent her ten dollars; she was to get herself something nice. He was boarding with his employer, Fred Burgess, and it was dandy. San Jose was dandy. Everything was dandy.

The unexpected money, the general flutter, the wonderful new gowns and hats, were all exciting and delightful. Alice wore her wedding hat for a week or two, so that it would not look "bridey," and Vicky thrilled at the mere sight of the fated pink roses and blue ribbons. Actually to have a wedding hat!

A day or two before the wedding Lucy spoke to her of financial difficulties.

"I *calculated*, you see, upon your father. But his staying at home all these weeks has thrown me out completely. I *counted* on him—h'm. Now I find myself *exactly* correct, except that I have not gotten anything from him. I can get it, of course! I know Frank would be only too glad——"

"Oh, Mama, not Frank!" Alice was scarlet.

"No, no, of course not. But don't worry, dear, we're all *right*——"

Alice, sick with anxiety, had instant recourse to prayer. And that afternoon came a check from Uncle Bob, a hundred and fifty dollars. Radiantly, she took it to her mother, everything was all right now.

And on the twentieth of April, Vicky and Tina and Lou, in their black, came over to the little Larkin Street house, and witnessed the marriage of Doctor Frank Lawrence Babcock and Alice Madeleine Crabtree. Alice was exquisite in her solemnity and beauty; she wore a tailor-made dark green serge lined with scarlet; the belled skirt, edged with brush braid, swept the shabby carpet on all sides. The afternoon was bright and still. Drawn shades shut out the hot, bright spring day.

Dr. Babcock kissed her, the girls and her mother trooped forward gaily; she was kissed, confused, pulled this way and that. Lucy was eager with sandwiches, salad, coffee; Fanny made them all laugh. May had not come, explaining satisfactorily and mournfully that she "couldn't."

Alice ran to the side of her father's chair; Harry was still an invalid. She dropped to her knees, her young cheek, against his, was wet.

"Darling, you don't lose your little girl! I'll be right in the Mission; I'll be here every day!"

He rested his cool, bloodless face against hers wearily; he could not speak. Frank Babcock, showing his shining teeth in incessant smiles through his black beard, was talking to a group of women, was anxious to get away.   They went blindly, through a group of interested neighbours' children, to a carriage; they were married.

Now she should begin to feel confident and happy, Alice thought.   Now she would begin to love him.   She was terrified to feel that she hated him instead; his scented black moustache, his shining teeth.   His full, moderated voice, explaining things to her, in the train, filled her with fright.   She wanted to get away!

He was giving her his proof for the pronunciation of the word "advertisement," as opposed to her mother's chance pronunciation of the word.

He had asked her, "Shall I tell you some of your husband's terrible faults?   Well, he likes to be on time.   He doesn't like to waste his own or other people's precious minutes!"

Alice received this with a sickly smile.

"And then he likes the truth," continued Frank, smiling whimsically.   "Truth—is there anything more beautiful! Unless a thing is really awful, or killing, or tremendous, I do not think you will find him calling it so!"

She recognized three of her favourite words, legal tender, indeed, among all the girls she knew.

"Why, I hate him!" she thought, her heart in a whirl.   "I *loathe* him.   What am I doing, going down to Del Monte with him!"

When they came back five days later Frank was all her world. His tenderness, his wisdom, his devotion to her were her only topic.   She took possession of his furnished house in the Mission with a rapturous dedication of herself to its needs.   And when she and Frank went over for a Sunday dinner with Mama and Papa, Alice heard everything they said with nervous smiles, and watched Frank's face anxiously, to see how he received it. Frank's domestic comfort deeply concerned her; she must learn how to market, she must find out exactly how Frank liked his bureau kept.   She puttered about contentedly after her mother, all that long Sunday; wasn't it funny how Frank liked apple cake?   Wasn't it funny that he had said that if she read her book in the sunlight her head would ache, and it *did* ache!

To her old hospital associates, and to the Brewer girls, she felt a tremendous superiority. She wished they were all engaged to be married, she told them merrily, it was all so wonderful. But they would have to be married to her Frank to realize how lucky she was, and she didn't know how it could be managed! And to Lucy she said pityingly afterward that unmarried girls seemed awful fools, when one was married.

"He has such judgment, Mama," she would tell Lucy. "He sees into a thing so quickly! I often think he ought to be in politics—you know how he was talking about the business depression, last night; why, there'd not be any bank failures and all the rest of it, if everybody saw it as he does! And you *must* admit that he was sweet with Aunt Fanny—his dinner late, and all! But he's always like that—wise, you know. And I *do* think he's nice with Papa; Frank works so hard, you know, and of course Papa has nothing to do!"

She and Frank had happy Sundays at the Midwinter Fair; the great stretches of bright cheap buildings were full of fascination for them. They sauntered past Irish lace-makers and Turkish bazaars, smiled at the sad little Hawaiian babies, gasped on the scenic railway, and ate ravenously in the Viennese restaurant. Certain of the concessions seemed peculiarly their own by right of discovery, and they loved to meet less sophisticated visitors and tell them about the "Santa Barbara Amphibia" and the "Mirror Maze."

They sat over ice-cream, discussing the miracle of their first meeting in the Mission, of every step that had brought them together. They were destined for each other, from the beginning of time, of course. Even Josepha—Frank's first wife, did not much disturb Alice's dream. She had been a wonderful woman, a wonderful manager. But she was ten years dead, Alice had been but four years old when Frank was first married, and Frank's daughter, Josie, was now eighteen. Josie lived in Stockton with her mother's sister and had showed an unfortunately cold and unpleasant side to her father.

"Her aunts have spoiled her," Frank said, "they have made her impossible to control! However, some day we'll have her down for a visit, and perhaps things will go more smoothly. She had a quarrelsome tendency. . . ."

"Frank, as if any one could quarrel with *you!*"

"I'm not so sure, my dear! Perhaps you put too generous

an estimate upon a mere human man. But I think," Frank said, dropping his bantering tone, "I think that I am always *just*. I think out—it's natural to me to think out, to weigh a situation thoroughly. After that, I don't *think* I vacillate!"

The house in the Mission was one of a row: dark gray houses with bay-windows, flights of steps, balustraded porches over the front door. Everything inside was old, yet unworn; the dark-green carpets like iron, the horsehair chairs shining neatly in the dim parlour. Shutters let in a glimmer of light; all three bedrooms were in order, limp white spreads on wide, hard beds. Alice looked at it all appreciatively; the large china plates with a brown border in flowers, the blankly clean bathroom at the end of the long upper hall. Smells were everywhere; damp, clean smells of carbolic and yellow soap, and airless smells of horsehair and carpets and stale dust.

Anna was the servant; Anna did everything. She even dusted the two big parlours, where Frank saw his patients, in the way he liked. The front room upstairs was Alice's sitting room; she could look out at Mission Street, near Twelfth; people would be banging in and out of Young's Drug Store, at the corner, and the queer man opposite would have all his flags out on a rope. The warm summer winds blew yellow chaff and dirty papers against the curbs.

A few weeks after Alice's wedding Bob came down from Sacramento, to hear from Lucy with her usual bright decisiveness that she intended to give up the Larkin Street cottage.

"Oh, certainly!" Lucy said capably, "I've realized for some time that it was too big for Harry and me. Now that both Alice and Georgie have gone, we must make some other arrangement. Do you think I could have you paying rent here, for nothing? No, indeed. I have to think of these things, Bob, for Harry"— she smiled at him—"is a perfect infant! One of us has to have a head, and thank goodness I have had a hard schooling in money matters!"

Bob was pleased. His little boy was well and strong, and May pathetically determined to keep him. Bob himself was settled. He asked what Lucy proposed to do.

Lucy answered confidently that she was planning several things, but that Fanny needed her just at the moment; Fanny had a touch of Lucy's own old enemy rheumatism, and had hinted that she would be glad of an extra pair of hands about the house. Harry was to go off "for a little vacation."

"Where to?" Bob asked his brother. Lucy answered briskly that she did not quite know; but that Harry *must* get away. Against his own knowledge of her Bob found himself oddly convinced that this was a practical solution of their problem; Lucy, warmed by his tacit approval, laid a sheaf of bills in his hand.

"By some miracle," she said, "I've been able to keep these down—a wedding, imagine!—and you'll find that they don't total three hundred dollars. Frankly, I want your advice about them, Bob. I don't know myself how I did it, with Harry's illness, and all. Everyone supposes that even the simplest wedding costs *hundreds*. But, you see—ice-cream, salads—we didn't have any caterer; everyone does; I didn't! I wish May could see them, after the way money was thrown about for Bertie's wedding—and he a boy, too. But you know me, Bob. I can't be comfortable until these are paid. I'm made that way. Debt—ugh! I can't abide it."

"Bob, that isn't your business," Harry suggested, smiling from his chair.

"Harry wouldn't worry if the sheriff was at the door," Lucy said. "Unfortunately, I'm made differently!"

Bob looked thoughtful. But in the end he was able to offer a solution that immensely pleased the business-like Lucy. He would pay these bills now, and in three months, that is, on September first, he would send her one hundred dollars more, paying the same sum each quarter for four following quarters. In return, Harry signed an agreement that he would deed to him the Santa Clara property he would inherit from his father.

This prospect delighted Lucy. She liked the thought of telling Fanny that their affairs were in satisfactory shape.

Harry mildly acquiesced. He felt weak and confused and weary; he went to Fanny's house and sat in the back parlour, sometimes looking at the Doré Dante, sometimes going through the stereoscope pictures. Alice seemed as far away as if she had gone to China; poor Nelly, busy with four babies, never wrote now.

When the Larkin Street house was closed and empty, Lucy joined him, full of energy and satisfaction. She made herself extremely useful in his sister's house; the old man was a feeble, whimpering baby now, who lay for hours staring smilingly at nothing, or mumbled boiled rice with sloppy noises. He rarely recognized any one, but would invariably weep with emotion when some glimmer of remembrance was aroused by the sight of a familiar face.

Fanny, indignant and incredulous as the maddening stiffness in her knees and fingers remained, questioned her brother briskly.

"Well, Harry! Are you going off to see Nelly—is that the plan? How about Georgie—wouldn't San Jose be a splendid place to get rid of that cough? No use staying here, you know—worst place in the world for you! These fogs——"

Harry knew he was in the way, but he did not quite know where to go. He became extremely annoying to Lucy, in his very meekness and quiet. Pulling his chair out at the table, helping himself to more tomato salad, coughing in the still watches of the night; he troubled and exasperated her. Fanny fretted about expenses; here was a household of six people—everything going out, nothing coming in. Statements from the firm were extremely unsatisfactory, business was bad—poof! Fanny didn't believe 'em. There wasn't any talk of that in Pa's day.

After a few half-hearted efforts to find work in one of the Polk Street agencies, Harry announced one morning that he thought he would go south.

"Down San Mateo way, or in Los Gatos, I'll find work," he said. "Maybe I'll go up to Nelly. There's quite a lot I could do, with Hildegarde and Brother. And they felt real bad when I came away."

Lucy abetted him enthusiastically; she borrowed the money for his fare from Fanny; "I shall have my check in a few weeks now," she said confidently. Harry, with twenty dollars, went away on an August morning.

The day was windless, smothered in a soft, milky fog. There was a yellow sun burning behind the thick, still folds; the ferry boats were moving slowly, with constant honking of horns and ringing of bells. Harry had determined to begin in Oakland, and work his way on through Alameda, Haywards—somewhere there must be a place for him. Thin, coughing, still a little weak and bewildered, he disappeared into the all-enveloping, silent mists.

CHAPTER XXIII

IT WAS all wrong, May said. It was just the way modern girls did things. No nice girl's engagement had ever been announced in this reckless, haphazard fashion. She did not like it, and Papa did not like it. Mr. Palmer might be a very fine fellow, undoubtedly he was, that was not the point. What would people think of a girl who jumped headlong into an engagement that way?

Lou, breathless, and perhaps a little frightened at her own daring, listened in impudent silence.

The papers had simply had the statement, one morning. Miss Louisianna Brewer, youngest daughter of the well-known San Rafael family, was receiving the good wishes of her friends upon her engagement to Mr. Howard Palmer, of Philadelphia. No date had been set for the wedding.

Lou had informed her family—"condescended to inform them," May said—the night before.

"Mama and Papa," she had begun, with a somewhat artificial coolness. "I want you to know that Howard and I are going to be married. We settled the whole thing this afternoon!"

Vicky's heart had leaped with joy. This was definite, at least. She sent a look of admiration and fealty to her little sister. Poor May had not known quite what to do.

The man, handsome, assured, thirty years old, conspicuously well dressed, had come over to San Rafael a week or two before and had appeared, with a certain negligent good-nature, at the Brewer gate. No, he wouldn't come in, thanks awfully, he had his trap here, wanted Miss Louisianna, for a drive.

Lou had asked nobody, even though it was Sunday, and Papa was at home. She had tripped out to the shining, high cart, climbed in, and plunged into laughing badinage even before the amazed family lost sight of her. She took her admirer calmly, and gave her confidence to no one. Frequently, she went to Lily Duvalette for the night, in Lily's badly managed

noisy cottage at the hotel, or in town.   Two weeks of this ended
with the amazing fact of the announced engagement.

At the bottom of her heart May felt a secret elation and satisfaction.   No matter how it had been managed, it was a pleasing
thought.   One of her dear girls married to a rich man and living
in the east!   She treated Lou with a certain respect; Vicky and
Tina quite openly lionized the amazing junior who had taken
matters into her own hands so magnificently.

Lou was feverishly absorbed in her affair; incessantly away
with Howard, giving scant heed to their excitement and flutter.
She admitted that she was fortunate: money?   Oh, he was immensely rich, of course.   She told her father briefly and positively that she did not propose to have any such wedding as
Bertie's; Howard would much rather slip off some day and be
married, and she didn't mind.

"But it's a girl's pretty, happy time, dear!"   May suggested
tenderly.

"Mama," Lou answered, briskly and tensely, "any girl in
my position marrying a man as important as Howard can very
well afford to give in about the details!"

Fanny wrote a merry, teasing letter; Lou must run in to
lunch, or set a night upon which she could bring this Fairy Prince
to meet his old cranky, crippled relative.   She just couldn't
believe that little Lou was really going to outdistance all the
girls.   .   .   .

Lou tossed the letter aside, scowling.

"I see myself taking Howard there, with Aunt Lucy and Carra
and Grandpa."

"But my darling," May said, aghast, "Howard must meet
all your own people!"

"My own people!   With Grandpa in bed like a baby, and
Aunt Fanny talking about the year One!   I'm not going to live
here, Mama, I don't expect ever to come back, except for
visits!"

This attitude was intensely distressing to May, and even disturbing to Vicky and Tina.   The former felt old convictions
dying away; a girl's wedding wasn't always roses and tears and
smiles, then?   Lou was disquietingly business-like and practical.

Exactly eight days after the announcement, and before the
family were fairly used to the new idea and the new glory, Lou

came flying in, from town, one afternoon, and snatched the telephone receiver. Her face was pale, and she neither greeted her mother nor took off her hat. They heard her call Lily Duvalette. Evidently Lily was not satisfactory, but Frank Pembroke was there, and Lou imperatively demanded that Frank come to see her at once.

Her mother questioned her, simple curiosity getting the better of offended majesty, but Lou seemed not to hear her, and with a muttered excuse ran upstairs; they heard her door bang.

Frank Pembroke, with a serious face, came in the gate a few minutes later: May, determined not to be brushed aside again, met him at the door, and let him into the parlour, where Vicky and Tina were accidentally sitting.

"I guess Lou told you about Howard, Mrs. Brewer," said Frank, who looked pale and worried. "I only knew myself, to-day. I was telling Lily. He—I guess Lou went over to meet him for lunch, but he's gone east——"

There was a dry, dull taste in Vicky's mouth. She told herself that she had expected this, all along.

"I met him at the club, last winter," said Frank. "He seemed—he seemed a nice enough fellow, didn't he, Vick? Didn't you think so, Vick? But—but he's married, I guess. I guess the Philadelphia papers saw the announcement——"

May's fat soft face was deathly pale in the autumn heat. Vicky saw the beads on her upper lip. She swallowed convulsively.

"Well, he'll go to jail for this, Frank!" she said quietly, breathing hard.

"I hope he will, Mrs. Brewer!" Frank said, fervently. "I— I feel something terrible!" he added, forlornly. Mrs. Brewer did not seem to hear him; she was shaking her head, framing sentences with a dry mouth.

"It wasn't your fault, Frank!" Victoria said, her whole being still trembling under the blow.

"My poor little girl!" May whispered. "The *villain*. The *villain*. I suppose he can't be *hanged* for it—he ought to be. He ought to be hanged!"

"He ought to be tarred and feathered!" panted Victoria, fighting tears.

"He will be," May said grimly. "Your father will make him pay very dearly for every instant of unhappiness he has caused Lou. Yes, sir!" she said, as if to herself, in a tense undertone, "Yes, sir, we'll see! We will see, Mr. Howard Palmer," May went on, breathlessly and in a dry whisper, "exactly how well your wife likes the idea of having you in jail! People shall know of this——"

"There won't be a newspaper in the country that won't *mark* him for what he is!" Victoria cried passionately.

"Oh, he'll have to live somewhere else!" exclaimed Tina.

"He'll have to live his life out in some obscure, foreign country," May said, with a sort of raging, yet quiet, triumph. But after awhile her mood changed; the high-flown, indignant phrases failed her. "He's broken her heart!" she sobbed. Tina and Vicky cried too; Frank had gone sorrowfully and shamedly away.

"But, oh, Vick and Tina," breathed May, embracing them as they knelt tearfully before her, "this is just what Mama and Papa try to spare you! We fuss, we warn, we advise, we chaperon—only to save you from this! Oh, girls, you see it now, don't you—you see why Mama worries and watches, now, don't you? We are old-fashioned, we are laughed at——"

"No, you're not!" Tina interrupted loyally.

"—and it seems hard and dull and fussy, I know," May went on, breathing a deep sigh, and wiping her eyes, "but it is because we know how wicked the world is, how easy it is for a bad, unscrupulous man to wreck a girl's life!"

"Mama, is Lou's life wrecked?"

"I don't know—I don't know anything!" May said, weeping again. "When I think of it—the newspapers—and she did love him, poor misguided child! And I'll have to tell your father——"

Victoria went upstairs several hours later, ventured a tenth attempt; knocked on Lou's door.

"It's open!" Lou's voice said wearily, dully.

She was lying on her bed, in the warm autumn night that was still lighted with a reminiscent glow of sunset. She did not move as Vicky came over to kneel beside her and covered her languid hand with a warm hand. They stayed so for a long time.

"Papa saw it in the evening paper, just a really decent paragraph or two, Lou," Vicky said softly and gruffly, at length.

Lou merely sighed, in the gloom. "He was awfully nice about it," said Victoria.

"I knew yesterday," Lou presently announced indifferently. "I went to town to meet him to-day. I was going away with him anyway!"

This was awful. Vicky felt actually frightened.

"No, you weren't, Lou!" she said tenderly.

"Yes, I was. I think," further confided Lou, in an oddly detached and lifeless tone, "I think I always knew that there was something wrong. But I didn't care. He always seemed to be giving me so much—except the one thing. I knew he didn't love me."

"Lou—Lou!" Victoria pleaded, as the voice in the dusk was still, "will it—will it break your heart?"

"Oh, Lord," Lou said violently, sitting up and raising her hands to her disordered hair, "what's the difference if it does? Everything's rotten anyway—I've never had any real fun, like other girls! We don't—we're voodooed—as Carra says. What is Mama doing—but wishing that girls with such a wonderful father would *only* remember that all his rules are for the best——"

"Lou, don't!" Vicky said, shocked.

"I'll go down and have it over!" Lou lighted the gas. "It's all in the day's work!"

And to Vick's secret amazement and admiration she walked quietly out of the room, with her flushed face, tearless eyes and tumbled dark hair untouched, and her slender figure erect and proudly held.

The smoke of painful notoriety and criticism died away; life was what it had always been. Lola was ill, fretted by hopes of motherhood for the second time. Lou went to stay a night in her brother's house in Sausalito; ended by making a visit of many months. Lola spent almost all her time in bed; to her and to Bertie the presence of the helpful practical Lou was a godsend. Long before Bertie's delicate, Spanish-looking little girl was born, they felt that they could not manage at all without Lou.

One September morning, when life chanced to seem bright and entertaining to Vicky, her mother telephoned her from town. May had gone over to Fanny's house to be a few days with their father. Tina was with Grace, and Aunt Lucy was staying with Vicky and Bobo. Aunt and niece were having a delightful time, with dishes and gossip, and Victoria was secretly sorry that Mama was coming home to-night.

May was agitated; Papa was most anxious to know if Mr. Torrey had brought over an envelope yesterday. Vicky responded vivaciously in the affirmative. Did Vick know what was in it? May asked anxiously.

"Yes, Mama," the girl answered readily, "a hundred and seventeen dollars!"

"Sh-sh!" May said, in a panic of caution, "darling! A thief might be on the line. . . . Vick, you are to *pin* that envelope safely in your pocket and bring it *straight* to Papa. Bring your dress-suit case, and stay overnight with Aunt Fanny. Ask Aunt Lucy if she is going to have a bite ready for us poor travelers if we all come back on the five-fifteen?"

Lucy answered with alacrity; she would be only too glad to see to dinner. Vicky tore off her cotton gown, snatched satin stock and tailor suit, and ran for the one o'clock train.

This was very pleasant, she thought, sitting upstairs on the ferry-boat, watching the gentle tip of scrubbed decks and blue water, and feeling the autumn sunshine warm upon her polished black shoes and the neat flare of her long skirt. She clutched at her pocket now and then; the precious envelope was safe.

At the ferry, unexpectedly, she met her mother, looking harassed and grim.

"You have that money, Vicky? Take it straight to your father and then come directly home!" May said sternly. "And I ought to warn you," she added, "that he is extremely angry with you!"

Victoria paled. The bright day and the bright mood darkened together. Her heart jumped.

"Oh, Mama—*why?*"

"Why?" May echoed angrily. "Why, because a daughter of ours—a grown woman—writes to a common farmer's boy like Davy Dudley what is virtually an *offer* of marriage—that's all I can call it——!"

The girl felt her mouth grow dry and her throat thicken. Everything—the autumn sunshine on the long wooden ferry building, the moving crowds, the mellow sound of ferry-boat horns, was brassy and hideous to her sick eyes.

"Vicky, how can you explain what you wrote?" May asked

with ominous patience. "Fortunately, thank *God*—it never reached him!" she added passionately. "The postman handed it to Papa when he was leaving the house this morning—it had come all the way back! Evidently your friend David is no longer there and left no forwarding address.

"To a proud man like your father!" May went on, cuttingly, as Victoria, her face a deep red, made no answer, "Oh, how could you—how *could* you! As if Lou's affair wasn't enough! And you're not a child, Vick," May reproached her. "You know better!"

"I was only fooling!" Victoria stammered.

"Well, you go see your father, and you'll find out what he thinks of your *fooling*," May warned her significantly. "Fooling! I think it's about time you stopped fooling, then. He told me that he was going to—but you go see him. Perhaps a few days in your room, on bread and water, will make you feel differently about it! Papa spoke to me seriously about sending you away from home for awhile—away from your mother and sisters!"

"I wish to goodness he would!" Vicky said passionately.

May eyed her silently; pallid with heat and emotion.

"Some day you will wish that you had died, like our darling Esme, who never gave Mama one instant's sorrow in her life, before you said that, Vicky!" she said in a frightened whisper, trembling. "What happiness in life can come to a girl who—if that's right, I've got to hurry!" May interrupted herself, suddenly, in her natural voice, as she looked at the ferry clock. Grasping her bundles, she went on with a severe parting glance, and Vicky turned back from the ticket-gate with a bitter taste in her mouth.

Nothing for it but to go up and face Papa; and later to face them all. Nothing but to accept disgrace and punishment like a child. Her letter to Davy in their hands! It was too terrible to believe!

She turned toward the offices of Crabtree and Company, only a few blocks away from the ferry. Slowly, breathing deeply, and with her mind in a whirl, Victoria walked over the warm soft tar of the pavements, and up through the good smells of the warehouse district; smells of bananas and apples and coffee and onions and wet straw and horses, smells of clean citrus fruits and tarred new ropes and fresh pine boxes. It had always fascinated her, this region of sheds and tarpaulin awnings, of glinting sunlight on shaded sidewalks, of trampled peels and skins and cabbage leaves, of bursting barrels and crates and sacks. It fascinated her even to-day, and she loitered quite consciously there.

Bananas and pineapples from Hawaii, and coffee from Java. The very names were an inspiration, in these crowded streets that ran straight down to the masts of hundreds and hundreds of ships. The harbour was full of shipping, whistles blew, men with trucks ran to and fro. The world was full of stir and adventure.

Suddenly, miraculously, Vicky realized that she was not going to see Papa; she was not afraid of any of them. It was ridiculous—a grown woman of twenty-seven, trembling and fearing like a sick child! They could not harm her, they could not hold her. She was going to work!

Thrilled and exhilarated, she went back to the wharf; climbed upon a Market Street car, and went boldly up to the Palace Hotel. She had a hundred and seventeen dollars; and she was going away to find work.

The ticket offices were all up in the Palace Hotel. Just before she entered one, Vicky met Lily Duvalette, divorced now, and with a young man in tow. They took her to tea in the Palace Grill; Lily not too cordial, but Vicky her gayest self; so much so that Lily's escort turned the battery of his fatuous and inane remarks quite pointedly toward Miss Brewer. Vicky managed to give the angry Lily the impression that this was the way things always happened between men and Victoria Brewer.

Her mind was made up. She was going to Uncle Bob, in Sacramento. Uncle Bob had said that he would help her, if ever she needed him. She went briskly into the office; she must send him a telegram.

There was one real danger in the plan; she would have to risk it. Papa was always on the five-fifteen boat from the Sausalito ferry. The Sacramento train was reached by the Oakland boat at five-fifteen, only a few hundred feet away, from the same ferry building. He might see her. Well, he simply *mustn't* see her.

Half-past four o'clock now. Victoria bought herself a bunch of flowers at Lotta's fountain, and a bag of peanut taffy at Maskey's. Life flooded her deliciously; she was her own mistress for the first time in her life. She walked to the ferry down Mission Street; nobody one knew ever walked on Mission Street. A trembling excitement possessed her. Aloud she said, more than once:

"I'll show them! I'm not afraid of them!" And when a man coming toward her startled her suddenly with a resemblance to Bertie, she went past him breathing defiantly. "I wouldn't care if it was!" she said. "I wish it was!"

But she realized that she was frightened when she got to the ferry, which was surging now with the tides of returning country visitors, and commuters leaving offices and factories in the city. Hot shafts of sunlight streamed across the scene; cable cars clanged and clattered as the little turn-table reversed them, one by one, for the start uptown again. Victoria's heart beat fast; every man might be Papa, any chance encounter might betray her.

She sidled along the piers from Mission Street, past the little Post Office, into the Oakland line of the ferry sheds. Hay wagons, trucks full of thundering barrels, rumbled by her. Terror possessed her when she recognized the Kingwells, mother and sons from Mill Valley, running from the Howard Street car. Well—well—supposing they did see her, and did tell Papa on the boat that they had seen her, what could he do?

Five minutes past five. In ten minutes—in nine, she told herself, it would all be over. She would be on her boat, and Papa on his; after that every second would more and more part them.

She eyed the ticket-gate nervously. If it would only open and she might wait inside! But the Oakland boats were too crowded and too many; they never opened their gates until a few seconds before sailing.

Vicky stood in the protection of a post, nervously glancing to right and left. Her heart turned to water. Someone had come up. Aunt Fanny.

Victoria could hardly hear her. Everything was lost! She felt a faintness in her stomach, her legs trembled, and her voice was thick.

"Vicky! For heaven's sake!" exclaimed Fanny. "We've only five minutes. Where's your father?"

"Buying"— Vicky's throat was dry, but desperation lent her wit—"Buying a shine," she said. "You go ahead, Aunt Fanny. We'll—we'll meet you upstairs on the boat!"

"Yes, because I've got to get a ticket! Upstairs on the Gate side!" Fanny cried, hurrying away.

Victoria was alone again; but she felt shaken and weak. Her mouth was dry and her head confused. She felt the palms of her hands wet and cold. Suppose—suppose Aunt Fanny met Papa, in the Sausalito waiting room, suppose he asked—he was naturally anxious about both his money and his daughter—suppose he asked her if she had seen Vicky? Suppose he suspected and came flying over to the Oakland waiting-room—he would think nothing of missing his boat, to stop her in her flight!

If she could make the Howard Street car, disappear into the Mission——She dared not leave her post. She *must*. She picked up the dress-suit case at her feet——

Everything went black; her heart seemed to tear itself from her body. Everything was over. They had found her. She felt the muscles of her face stiffen into a terrified and sickly smile as she turned——

It was Davy Dudley who stood smiling beside her, his hat off and his hand held out. He had gotten home two days ago, he explained, with his first greeting, had seen them all at Napa, had come to the city yesterday, and was going home again now.

"Then we go on the same train; I'm going to Sacramento," Vicky said confusedly. All lesser emotions were lost in a deep flood of utter confidence and peace of spirit; here was Davy. She knew that she loved him more than ever, everything was all right now, nothing puzzled or frightened her, it would all be straightened out; here was Davy.

"You certainly didn't think I was going to leave you, no matter where you were going?" Davy said, meeting her mood in exactly her own spirit. He picked up her suit case. "Come on, we'll go on the boat," he said. He glanced sidewise at her, as she quietly and contentedly accompanied him; smiled with so deep and sweet and entirely happy a smile that Victoria needed no words. The miracle had happened; they were together again.

Streamers of sunset light poured over the city; their long shadows moved ahead of them. Everything, everyone looked delightful to Vicky, she was not excited, she was not agitated and doubtful, as she might have supposed herself to be, meeting David. Instead she felt only a fundamental joy and peace.

They were sitting on the upper deck of the *Encinal*, watching the traffic about the piers, and the circling gulls, when the *San*

Rafael, not three hundred feet away, whistled sharply; their own boat echoed the whistle, and both the clumsy vessels moved steadily from their docks. Every second now carried Papa and Aunt Fanny farther away over the shining sunset colours of the water; a deep content and confidence wrapped Victoria as in a garment.

She looked appraisingly at Davy, while they talked. He was taller, she thought, thinner certainly, and while still extremely shabby, he had improved enormously in appearance. His shoulders were better carried, his hair clipped shorter, and his big hands were covered by old gray gloves. In his face there was a remarkable change; it was older, and in some subtle way more grave, his mouth had definite lines, and Vicky liked the quick flash of response or question in his blue eyes.

He sat beside her, in the balmy late afternoon light, his hands thrust in his pockets, his ankles stretched before him and crossed, and his head turning to watch her whenever she spoke. Vicky questioned him about his work in Berlin, amused whenever a German word came inadvertently into his descriptions.

He was talking to her as he had never talked before; she realized that at once. He held her left hand firmly in his right, her elbow locked in his; he was telling her gravely and thoroughly just what difficulties he had encountered. His Aunt Lil's illness and death, last spring, had been expensive, and his mother had finished the rooms on the mansard floor of her house, that had never been completed. That was done now, and paid for, it was all paid for.

Vicky listening with an intent and serious face, said nothing aloud. In her heart she said over and over, "I love you. I love you. I love you."

"I told you last year I didn't want to practise in Napa; I want to specialize," Davy reminded her, with the new stern, firm movement of his mouth, on the words. "I went in to see Dr. Dunham yesterday. I thought that if I could work with one of those big fellows—— However, he's just asked Jack Chatterton. Gosh," Davy interrupted himself, shaking his head grimly, "That kid Chatterton is lucky! Well, I went to Newman and Newman wants me. But he's going abroad, moving his offices to get more space, and says he's got to have a vacation. He and his wife and boy are going around the world."

"I see," Vicky commented thoughtfully.

"Now, old Boone in Napa wants me," Davy said, dubiously. "It's good general practise, do you see? And of course my mother would be wild with joy to have me home. Everything's going better with them. 'Lizabeth's husband is making money, Mary has a job, and this would be the best thing—for her. But that means that I'm a Napa family doctor for the rest of my life. Otherwise——"

"Yes, I was going to ask, what otherwise?" Vicky interrupted, as he paused.

"Well, that means——" He tightened his arm about hers, and smiled down at her. "That means that I hang out a shingle in San Francisco, and *wait*," he said. And as Vicky sat thoughtfully staring down at the moving sheen of the bright water, and the riding and swooping gulls, he added, "It's for you to decide."

Vicky reflected; fear was gone from her, shame was gone from her, doubt was gone. For the first time in her twenty-eight years she was talking to a man honestly and simply.

"Davy," she said suddenly, all the womanly sweetness and tenderness she had always been afraid to show shining in her face. "I can't tell you what it means to me—meeting you this way, having you to help me—to stand back of me. I'm in trouble at home—I'm running away——"

She told him the whole story: David listening with an attentive frown that gradually relaxed into a smile.

"You poor girl, you! Do you call *that* trouble?" he asked, when she was done.

"Well, it doesn't seem so, now," Vicky admitted, with a laugh.

"Ah—h!" David breathed, on a long, relieved sigh. "The main thing—the important thing, is that—here we are."

"Yes, I know," Victoria assented, in satisfaction.

"We've got to settle it all to-night, right on this trip," Davy asserted further. "We may not have another chance. We've got to make our plans!"

"Yes, I know," Victoria said docilely again.

Davy sat staring straight ahead of him, for perhaps a full silent minute. Then he turned to her a smile that was a little surprised, under its quiet triumph.

"We're engaged, you know," he told her.

Victoria made a brief sound between "ha!" and "oh!" her bright eyes smiling into his.

"After all the worry, and the loneliness, over there in Berlin, here we are," Davy commented after a pause. "I can't believe it. I used to watch for your letters——"

"But, Davy, you didn't *write* very often!"

"Because I didn't dare—that's why. I wrote oftener than you did! You know what your father said, that day of the forest fire—he sat on me. Do you remember that day?"

"Lou and I were getting supper," Vicky nodded, "and hoping Mama'd ask you to stay."

"Well, your father asked me if I felt badly, leaving home again, and I said—Vicky, I had to!" Davy tightened her arm again. "I had to, dear!" he pleaded. "I was so down and out that day—I wanted so to ask you then, and have you writing me letters, you know!—to have something to *go* on. So I said that the thing I minded leaving most was right there in his house. He sat on me—I knew he would. He was sort of tut-tutty, he said it would be many years before I had the right to ask his daughter, or any man's daughter, that. Said he didn't want you upset——"

"Upset!" Victoria exclaimed resentfully. "When I was hungering—*hungering*—Oh, what *is* it?" she asked impatiently of an approaching deck-hand. "Oh, yes, we're in, Davy, we're the last!" she said with a confused laugh, getting to her feet. She followed David along the almost emptied deck, over the upstairs gangplank, down a long, rubber-coated runway, up the damp, dark, spacious passages between the trains. These were puffing and steaming restlessly under a high sooty roof; the ground underfoot was wet with cindery pools, and black with grime.

They did not speak, but every time David glanced down beside him he saw her eyes looking up, and into his own look, and into his own heart, there crept the first ecstasy of protection and companionship. Her beauty, her animation, her flowered hat, her soft glove, thrilled them alike; he watched her when she spoke in so confident and friendly a tone to the porter, when she settled herself in a red velvet seat in the hot train.

The long car was filled with pairs of these narrow, jointed seats; some passengers were stretched out in them as in deck chairs, others sat erect, with their heads held primly against the white towels of the head rests. The racks above the seats were filled with coats and telescope baskets, with here and there a smart new dress-suit case. It was dark in the car, under the shed, and the atmosphere smelled of steam and hot oil and thick dry dusty velvet.

David found two empty chairs, and stowed his bag and Victoria's above them. A train boy bumped through, and as they sat down, a steam valve below them was opened, the shrill strong gasp of escaping steam deafened them, and the white fumes poured by their window, and shut out the dark view of train hands and porters on the tracks.

They sat in darkness, their hands locked. And presently the train gave a violent jerk throughout its length, brakes screamed and chains jarred, and they were sliding smoothly out between the shining flat marshes, and the coal barges, and the duck blinds of the Oakland side. Vicky turned to see David watching her.

"Vicky," he said solemnly, "no man ever loved a woman as I love you. You are going to be the happiest woman in the world."

They looked out upon shabby little cottages and sheds, in the blaze of sunset light, upon back yards, empty lots, broken fences, and goats; and to them everything looked magically sweet and interesting. Their hands were still linked, Victoria leaned blissfully upon Davy's shoulder. Train boys went through with fruit and magazines; the sunset faded, the world was gray. And still they murmured unbrokenly, with their heads close together, reviewing, remembering, promising, exulting.

"Here's what we'll do," Davy finally decided. "You come home with me to Mother, to-night. You'll love her and she'll love you. We'll tell her we're engaged, we won't say anything more to-night, except that you had some trouble and left home. And to-morrow we'll be married!"

The magnificence of it took Victoria's breath away.

"But, Davy, your city practice?"

"I've thought it all out. This is what we'll do. I'll stay in Napa and practise awhile with old Boone. It won't hurt me, and it won't prevent me trying the city if we get a little ahead. You don't want to go back home; they'd only make you miserable—it's time you and I took matters into our own hands. You're not afraid, Vicky?"

"I'm afraid you don't know what a perfectly marvellous manager I am!" Vicky answered with spirit. "Afraid! What of?"

"Of poverty, darling!" Davy said, shaken with deep laughter. "Of work and worry—what did you say?"

She was suddenly grave, looking down.

"I'm only afraid of our being separated again, Davy, by Mama or Papa or somebody, or something," Vicky replied, very low. "I'm never afraid—with you," she said, smiling, but with wet eyelashes. Davy put his head back against the pinned towel and shut his eyes.

"Oh, my God!" she heard him whisper, breathlessly. And then for a long time they sat silent, with tight-clasped hands.

It was in a still-lingering dusk that they reached Napa. Victoria felt stiff and dirty and extremely hungry. Davy guided her in the lamp-lighted streets. Around this corner, across this bit of empty lot, and here they were—this was the house.

Victoria had an impression of a picket fence, looming dimly white in shadows, and of the front of a big square mansard house, surrounded by the lofty and gloomy shadows of trees. Davy pushed the gate, led her through, and up the front steps to the opened front door. Inside there was the unmistakable odour of old furniture and upholstery, at the end of a warm day.

Mrs. Dudley was merely a dim silhouette against the dull pane of a kitchen window. She was evidently dozing in the warm dusk; she started up in surprise; a match winked yellowly, and they blinked and smiled at each other.

"Well, good grief! Why in the land's name didn't you say you was going to bring Miss Brewer!" exclaimed Davy's mother, lighting the gas, kissing him, and after a second's scrutiny kissing Victoria as well. "I was reading the paper, and the light went," she explained apologetically. "Look at my dishes—Mary's gone to the rehearsal—and look at me in this old percale!"

"You look grand," Davy said, "but we're starving. You take Victoria upstairs, she's going to stay the night with us, and I'll start your fire up."

"If I'm not intruding," Vicky said nervously, on the stairs.

"No, my dear, it's not that," Mrs. Dudley said in an annoyed tone. Vicky's heart sank; it was something else, then. "But that boy!" the older woman said vexedly, introducing Vicky to a large dim bedroom—a girl's bedroom full of dance cards and souvenirs, a banjo and ship's ribbons and a red glass stein. "He walks you in here, and I looking like the wrath to come!" protested David's mother. "The bathroom's this way, dear, there's a step down. Don't it stay hot up here? Now, when you're ready, just come down, for I believe I'll run along and get you something to eat. You drink coffee, don't you?"

"Anything," Victoria said, wishing she was not too shy to explain that David's bringing her here to-night was an act of pure goodness. Feeling uncomfortable, but brushed and refreshed, she went slowly downstairs a few minutes later, and paused outside the kitchen door.

The sound of brisk frying was pleasantly audible inside, and above it Vicky could hear Davy's mother still grumbling and mildly accusatory. Vicky turned the knob.

"Oh, you're not going to set the dining-room table for us!" she protested, shyness instantly forgotten at the sight of the unfolded white cloth in her hostess's hand. "Oh, *please!* Do let us eat here—Davy, make her!"

And with practised hands she began to straighten the kitchen table, where it was evident some meal had recently taken place. Mrs. Dudley watched unfavourably. "The idea!" she kept murmuring. "Well, I declare!"

But when Vicky sat down with great appetite to omelette and fresh rolls and jam, and when Davy's eager laugh rang out, and when Mary, coming in with a high, protesting query, "Who left the gas burning up in the bathroom?" and joined them, and fell an instant victim to the charms of Davy's girl, Mrs. Dudley somewhat softened.

"Well, I declare, you're a wonder!" she conceded, as Vicky wielded a tea-towel with a practised hand, and refused to leave the kitchen until the last crumb was brushed away. And she came upstairs a few minutes later to find Mary and Vicky in friendly gales of laughter over the fresh sheets for the extra bed in Mary's room.

After that there was no more formality; they talked like old friends. Vicky heard a hundred details of family history that Davy would not have given her in a hundred years, and when he shouted from below that he wanted to take her for a walk, just around the block, both Mary and her mother protested. Vicky was in the middle of her own story; they were indignant and thrilled over it; Davy could wait five minutes, they said.

"Don't you stay out late now; you're dog-tired," Mrs. Dudley said, with a motherly kiss, before Vicky ran down. "You tell that boy he'll have plenty of time to talk to you, you're going to make a good long visit! I'll sit up for you, dear."

"I'll tell him!" Vicky called. But the man she found waiting for her downstairs was a Davy she had never seen; a man whose strong arm about her, whose passionate kisses upon her lips under the softly waving trees that had hidden hundreds of such strolling lovers upon summer evenings, and whose burning words, drove from her mind everything else in the world except that they loved each other, and were together at last.

The next day, at exactly eleven o'clock, he and she went into the telegraph office at the station, and worded a telegram. It was sent to Stephen Brewer, San Rafael.

"Safe and well, married to David Dudley this morning. Sending money. Love. Victoria," it read.

This done, they went home with David's mother and Mary, and there was great kissing and laughing. Mrs. Dudley was not the type that questioned anything her son did; Davy was perfection in her eyes. Vicky had had a fight with her folks, and she and Davy didn't see any use in waiting for fresh trouble to brew, was her explanation of the whole affair, to amazed and interested Napa. Davy Dudley's wedding was a nine-days' wonder.

Vicky and Davy were too utterly, exquisitely happy to care. Their only wedding trip was out to see a case in the asylum; they drove in Doc' Boone's old buggy, and lingered all the way. And Vicky's only establishment, as a bride, was the big front mansard room, into which Mary and 'Lizabeth and their mother, on the afternoon of the wedding, took flowers, and the best chairs, and the table, and the blue rug. That night, her wedding night, after a family dinner of chicken and ice-cream, Vicky and Davy took a long drive, again behind the old Boone horse, far up into the sweet silent hills. When they came back, at ten o'clock, the house was absolutely dark and still; Davy turned out the bead of gas in the lower hallway, and shut the front door, and guided Vicky up the still unfamiliar stairs, their hands clasped.

CHAPTER XXIV

DURING their entire occupation of the ranch, rent-free pending a court decision, for something like eight years, Nelly and Rudy had felt no permanent tie there. Their claim gradually weakened and weakened until, with no sense of surprise, they realized that they must either buy it outright from the heirs of the original owner, or move.

To move was their only course. They had no money saved; they revelled in a sense of bitter injustice, telling the few persons interested that the judge at Martinez had been bribed on account of the water right, and that they and their children were to be "kicked out." Nelly cried, as she went indifferently about the little greasy, smoked, dirty kitchen, and Hildegarde, watching her anxiously, acquired a life-long hatred for "banks" and "judges." There were three little boys in Nelly's nursery now besides her first-born girl, a red-eyed little baby named Stuart, with permanent sniffles, had displaced Lloyd as the baby.

But once the blow had fallen, Nelly found to her amazement that things had really taken a turn for the better. Rudy, to be sure, had lost the Canfield ranch, but he had sold his stock and machinery at a good price, and he was weaned, once and for all, from "Brady's gang" at the saloon. Then Royal Larabee, who had a brother-in-law in San Bruno, seven miles south of San Francisco in the real estate business, suggested that Rudy apply to him for a position, and Rudy went there at once, and wrote Nelly, full of enthusiasm for the place, and secure of the job.

Nelly was secretly a little astonished that he should do this; she had lost faith in Rudy, but she prepared herself and the children to move to San Bruno—wherever and whatever it was—with alacrity. Rudy was to have an office there, with Nels Pitcher, as agents for a San Francisco real estate firm, and he wrote Nelly that he had rented a dandy house.

Full of hope she dressed the children for the actual moving, jamming her trunks at the last minute with rubbish that they "might as well have." A load of furniture had preceded her: the rest was sold where it stood. Nelly was exhausted, and in a perspiration, by the time Hildegarde, Clifford, Lloyd, and the heavy, drowsy baby had been forced into best clothes that were too tight for them, and lifted into the train. Hildegarde was six now, Clifford five, Lloyd three, and the baby still nursing at ten months. It was a sharp winter day, sunshiny and bleak; the conductor was unpleasant about the one ticket upon which the mother and four babies were travelling. Nelly answered him angrily, and Hildegarde shrank nervously in her seat. Everyone was mean to ladies that had children with them, Hildegarde thought.

From the San Bruno station they walked four blocks; the children were smeared with bananas and molasses cookies now; they were all bewildered with sleepiness from the hot train. Nelly, dragging her telescope basket, looking anxiously about for Rudy, stopped, with little Stuart balanced on her hip, and took out his telegram. Had she made some mistake?

At that instant he came running up; business—the eternally adequate excuse—had delayed him. He shouldered Stuart, took the basket. Someone ought to have given her a lift!—he said. But they were almost there now—there, that was the house!

Nelly had not seen the new house until they arrived there, tired and dirty and hungry. It was a stark, bare place, standing harshly against the sunset, a tall, narrow, dirty-white house, with a flimsy foundation fenced with crossed laths, narrow steep steps to the parlor floor, and three barren bedrooms still higher up. It had no grace of line or proportion, everything about it was as ugly and cheap and as the economy of the German butcher who built it with his own hands could devise.

About it stood the straggling settlement; it was hardly a village. There were no trees, and the gardens were principally confined to tin pots on window-sills with corn and tomato labels still adhering to them. The houses were set at all angles on the muddy dipping roads, here a bit of tin-patched fencing staggered into a newly dug vegetable patch; this front doorway faced the primitive sanitary arrangements of that drear cottage, this tangle of rusting and fallen wires served as a barrier for a bleating goat.

The unfenced ground about the various buildings was strewn with all sorts of rubbish and filth. Nelly's nose discovered an ash dump before her eyes did; the unmistakable acrid smell floated toward her as she trailed her family to the back door, flung off little wraps and hats, and cut bread for the first meal. It was fresh "bakers'" bread, a great treat to farm children, and there was milk, and Rudy struggled with the fire so that coffee and a steak might follow.

But long before Nelly, with the whining baby at her breast, was discussing her first hot and heartening cup, Hildegarde, Clifford, and Lloyd were sound asleep on a mattress in what would be the dining room when the furniture was properly distributed; a dirty, weary, sour, and odorous heap of delicate human flesh and blood, worn out with all the excitement and novelty of the great day.

"The poor little things," Nelly yawned, stupid with weariness and food, "they haven't any sheets to-night. To-morrow I'll open some of the boxes; though I may have to wash before we can use 'em! God knows when we bought our last sheets! Are you going to be a good feller to-night?" she added, to the red-eyed, poor little baby. "You'll kill yourself," she added, gratefully, as Rudy, who had finished his meal, began a vigorous shifting and unpacking over his cigar.

"You bet your life he's going to sleep!" Rudy said good-naturedly, of little Stuart. He showed Nelly a now familiar bottle of soothing-syrup, one of the real blessings of their lives. All the young mothers that Nelly knew agreed that the baby got restful sleep enough to more than offset any harmful effects of the drugging, and some, like Nelly herself, could point to children as hardy and well as Hildegarde, as examples of the benefit of the system. By this time the syrup was quite a matter of course in Nelly's nursery, and Stuart, the most frail and fretful of all her babies, was dosed several times a day.

"Lord, I like this!" Rudy added presently, working away splendidly. He laid split boxes beside the rusty stove for her breakfast fire, came and went with bedding and plates, and even set up one bed. Nelly sat with the baby, cramped and stiff and blessedly warmed and fed, watching him.

"Well, we're in!" she said, with a great yawn. "It seems three days since I got up in the dark at the ranch! No more filling lamps!" And she looked gratefully at the hissing gas.

"Don't bother any more, Rudy, I'll fly round and get this all straightened out to-morrow! Lord, I could sleep right here!"

"You come along and sleep in your own comfortable bed," he said, with kindly authority. Settling the baby in the box that was his temporary crib and pulling off her clothes fully awakened Nelly, and she crept into bed chilly and weary and glad to get warm. Rudy was loving, cradled her head in his arm and kissed her hair. He asked her if she knew how much he loved her, but Nelly was honestly too warm and sleepy to answer coherently, and after a few more murmured affectionate questions, Rudy turned over and went to sleep.

Getting settled the next day was not a serious matter. The great drawback was that the china was so chipped and mis-matched, the children's clothes so shrunken and discoloured with washing, so torn and worn and patched and buttonless, that Nelly's great pile for mending, altering, and cleaning eclipsed in size the modest heap that was ready to put away. Every-thing looked much shabbier and uglier in this strange environ-ment than it had looked at the smoke-dimmed ranch-house, and there was little money to make a fresh, clean start.

Still, the new life had great compensations, gas and water and the blessed nearness to the grocery. Even Cliffy could be sent with a nickel for a loaf of bread, and Hildegarde was quite a clever little buyer of meat and potatoes. Then there were neighbours, too, other overworked, overburdened women, who sat on steps and hung on fences, and discussed with Nelly their husbands, their poverty, and their children. Nelly looked down upon them all, as a matter of course, but they entertained her, and the tragedies and comedies of their lives made her own days shorter and pleasanter.

Her blonde, fair-skinned children ran wild, poking like a little troop of foxes into holes and corners, swinging on gates, eating everything that was, or ever had been, food, shouting, fighting, screaming, and crying. She told Rudy that it was only for awhile, soon they would be in the city, and maybe have a girl, by which Nelly meant a maid, and put the oldest two children into school.

They were dirty, what was the use of cleaning them? Ten minutes in this place would have them filthy again, Nelly rea-soned. They had cookies from paper bags, apples in their hands, bread and sugar to carry away. What was the use of making a fuss setting the table, when it had to be undone, and done again, in so short a time! Nelly would wipe her sons' sore little noses on her limp checked apron, the children looking at her with tearful but affectionate eyes.

But now and then she gave them all a real treat: had chicken and talked about it for days beforehand, and had honey, or cake, or doughnuts, and made Hildegarde clean the boys for the meal. They had to remember that they came of respectable people, Nelly would say. Gracious, what would Grandma Crabtree say to this gipsy way of living! And Nelly would wash the boys' white coats, and force upon the thick gold of Hildegarde's lovely little head the baby cap that was now too small for her, and all the Sessions would walk forth in the summer Sunday afternoon, Rudy proudly carrying the baby, whose mottled unhappy little face was entirely eclipsed by a "French" bonnet, while Nelly and the other children walked decorously beside him. They would walk to Papa's office, and perhaps hear him talk readily and encouragingly to some timid prospective home buyer, with a nervous, apprehensive woman holding him back from reckless decision.

These days were the bright side of life. There were other days, when sad and noisy scenes darkened the kitchen. Papa was queer, the children knew, and he wouldn't give Mama any money. He had to lie down because his poor head was so sick, and his condition produced a reflective crossness and sharpness in Mama. Also when he stayed away on Saturday nights she was unreasonable and puzzling in her conduct, sitting moodily at the kitchen door, murmuring in undertones to Mrs. Hutchings or Mrs. Beebe, angrily indifferent to Hildegarde's report that the baby was awake, or to the fact that the tired heavy-headed little boys were stickily asleep on the kitchen floor.

"Don't yell at Mama that way!" Nelly would scream at the little monitor, "my gracious, I can hear you!"

But if Hildegarde went back, and began a futile tugging at the tumbled forms of her little brothers, Nelly was apt to follow and would call the child Mama's little comfort as she lighted the gas, and opened, or perhaps made, the beds.

Half-cooked makeshift meals, dirty rooms, souring food in spattered pans or smoky skillets, tight dresses that scratched her, shapeless shoes frayed in the toes, these were Hildegarde's first impressions of life. Her mother might tell her of a more glorious past, and her father prophesy a different future, but this was the only reality she knew.

Hildegarde was a beautiful child, with a creamy colourless skin, and a straight superb mop of tawny hair, heavy and bright. There was a refined charm about her full, cleft chin, an aristocratic fineness in the pencilled thick brows and heavy curled lashes, and a noble dignity about the set of the little head, even when the drab apron was dirty and full of holes, and the red lips were set in a frame of jelly and crumbs and breakfast egg. She was not only far lovelier than her mother had ever been, but there was a character and a poise about her, even in babyhood, that poor Nelly had never possessed.

She was a bad child, in certain moods a "holy terror," a "case," the neighbours said. She could be so bold, so "sassy," that better little girls looked at her aghast. At home she helped her mother, wiped dishes, ran errands, and saw that the little boys had their share of doughnuts or coffee cake. Abroad she thieved, lied, raided, defied law and order, wriggled her emaciated little form through fences and cellar windows, learned "swear words" from bad boys, threw rocks at policemen's backs, and led a gang of rebels only a little less daring than herself. Hunger and need were stern teachers. Hildegarde learned to extract food from apparently hopeless situations, and her shrill "Give us a watermelon, Mister!" "Give us an apple, Mister!" "Give us a cooky, lady!" were familiar to the fruit peddlers and the bakers' vans before she had lived six months in San Bruno.

Nelly only vaguely suspected her child's reputation. She was the sort of woman who loves her sons best, and imposes upon her daughters, but she was really grateful to the child for all the help she gave.

"Don't be bold, Hildegarde, remember you are a little lady," she would occasionally say, and the sky-blue eyes would look at her, from under the royal mane, and the scarlet lips stop chewing long enough for Hildegarde to say, "I ain't bold, Mama."

"Who says she's bold?" Rudy might demand belligerently, if he was sitting in the kitchen brooding over some situation that existed only in his own befuddled brain. "She's a good girl—she's Papa's girl, that's what she is!"

Hildegarde would escape from his sour and beery kiss, the

rough touch of his unshaved chin, out into the kingdom of the yard again.

She led her clan into every danger, and the clan followed shouting and admiring. A fire-wagon could not stop in that neighbourhood without risking the investigation of a swarm of tatterdemalion children. They gathered about "drunks" who spat and muttered in the empty lots; they surged into the trenches intended for sewers or water-pipes; they threw rocks, walked tracks and fence rails, tied ropes, chased runaways, dodged about fires, manufactured stilts and hoops, squabbled over buttons and marbles.

"My mama wants a bag of soda crackers and please to put it in the book!" Hildegarde's ready little voice would assure the suspicious grocer. Nelly had to tell him not to give the child any credit unless she brought a note. "No, Mis' Beebe, we haven't seen your tomatoes anywhere!" the child would say innocently, with perhaps two of the lost tomatoes in her little stomach at the moment. In any defeat she would mount a shed or windmill and repay her foes with insulting singsong. "Mary Curry, Mary Curry! Awful fat and eats in a hurry!" she would shrill. Or she would follow a harmless Chinese landryman with shrieks of "Chinee-mock-a-high-lo!" which was supposedly an oriental curse.

Her gang had a score of these slogans. "Mina, mina, the laughing hyena!" "Georgie Hersey, goes out with his nursey!" "Willy Shedd, wet-the-bed!" were some of them. Truth need play no part in the rhymes that Hildegarde improvised, and her friends chanted, to the confusion of the enemy.

When the season of heavy rains came, the dirt roads all about the house were turned into pools, and in these pools the children waded and splashed, floated crazy rafts, dug ditches and dams, and slopped contentedly for days at a time. Nelly's children always had nose colds from November to March, but nothing serious ever seemed to happen to them. In the spring, the little girls borrowed old dresses, and trailed about playing lady tirelessly, and often their conversation made the women look astonished at each other. Where did the little things pick it up? Nelly and Rudy were sometimes astonished at Hildegarde's precocity and shrewdness, but the child amused them more than she shocked them.

When they had been in San Bruno some ten weeks, Nelly

wrote her mother, and in March Lucy duly came down to see her grandchildren. Nelly had a Japanese boy for the day, for seventy-five cents, and the children were clean. About the corners of the rooms odd heaps of dirty clothing and broken toys still lingered, Lucy noted, if Nelly did not, and that if Hildegarde's apron was a dazzling new unwashed gingham, Hildegarde's visible underwear was a soggy slate-gray. Nelly made no apologies, however, not because she was proud, but because she was made blind to all this by long association.

The children fought and skirmished for the unwonted dainties, for banana layer-cake and fried potatoes and canned corn. The house was hot, on a balmy, unseasonable March day, flies swarmed in droves, sunshine streamed upon disorder, spots, and sticky plates.

But out of doors it was spring. Nelly's twisted plum tree was white with sweet bloom, grass was high in the littered back yard, and had washed like a wave against the fences. Everywhere was openness, space, drying roads, and crowing cocks; the afternoon shadows were soft and long.

Lucy and Nelly sat on the shady front steps, with the staggering Stuart, still pinched and fretful, with sore red eyes, at their feet.

"And Alice expects?" Nelly mused. "I'll bet she has it easy!"

"Oh, he does everything for her!"

"Got a girl now?"

"Oh, yes, the same one—Anna. Unpleasant sort of woman," Lucy frowned. "But I wish you could see her house," she resumed, "set tubs, and telephone, and gas-stove—everything!"

"Do you see her much, Mama?"

Lucy sniffed.

"Oh, my dear, they're not the old-fashioned kind that depends upon elders for anything!"

Nelly looked at her shrewdly.

"You don't like Frank?" she surmised.

"Certainly I like Frank!" Lucy answered, annoyed. "He's a good man, with a fine standing in the community, why shouldn't I like him? I used to say to Alice, 'Just be *sure*, dear. If you're sure you love him, then I'm satisfied!'"

"And she was crazy about him?" Nelly pursued.

"Well," Lucy protested, irritated, "she married him! Alice is old enough to know her own mind, I should hope!"

"I've only seen her once, you know," Nelly said. "And she didn't seem—well, happy. She didn't seem like herself!"

"I don't see why she shouldn't," Lucy answered, unsympathetically. "Frank's a determined sort of man, and I think he's jealous—well, that's all right, if he takes good care of her and loves her! He may be rude to me, *I* don't care. I didn't marry him. It entirely——"

"You advised her not to marry him, didn't you, Mama? A man so much older, and all that?"

"My goodness, Nelly, how foolishly you talk!" Lucy cried vexedly. "Why should I advise her against it! Vicky marries a country boy without a penny, and you married Rudy, and I don't see that it's gotten you very far. Frank Babcock has money, he has a fine house, Alice has a servant—I declare it makes me wild to have everyone——" She stopped short, exasperated.

"*Does* everyone think it's queer?" Nelly asked, innocently, as her mother paused.

"I don't know or care what everyone thinks!" Lucy said shortly.

Nelly was surprised. But she was accustomed to rather odd moods in Mama, and she presently opened a fresh subject.

"Vicky. Are they so poor? Has Aunt May forgiven her?"

"Oh, yes. She had to, I guess. We were all over there on Christmas night; Vick had on her old red dress, but she looked handsome, and she just carried everything along the way she always does, laughing and carrying-on!"

"But Mama—but Mama—" Nelly questioned eagerly, "tell me about them! Take that out of your mouth, Hilda," she added mildly, immediately screaming, "take that out of your *mouth*, when Mama tells you to! What on earth are they living on?" she questioned, in her natural voice.

"Well, Davy's working with some Doctor Boone, there in Napa—and I guess Vick works pretty hard. She cooks, I know, and there are chickens, and his mother isn't very strong. But they seem happy enough; she kind of carries things before her, the way she always does! Davy just seems crazy about her, I never saw a man so cracked!"

"And Vicky cooks and looks after chickens, in Napa," Nelly

mused, smiling in some obscure satisfaction. "How's Papa?" she asked.

Lucy sighed again.

"He was down Los Angeles way," she said. "He wrote me that he had a job, and his cough was better, and some day he hoped to send for me; there was twenty dollars in the letter. It came in handy, too, because I was having a nerve killed!"

"Poor Mama!" Nelly sighed. "You have certainly had your share!"

"Well," Lucy agreed thoughtfully, "when I think of the fact that I am naturally systematic, naturally a manager, I wonder where I'd be if I was like *most* women!"

"Oh, you'd be in the poor-house, Mama! Imagine where poor Papa would have been without you!"

"I know," Lucy mused. "But imagine where *I* would have been with half a chance!" she countered.

"It seems such a shame that you never had it, Mama," Nelly said loyally. "Shall you stay on with Aunt Fanny?"

"Not one minute after I can get a position that pays," Lucy returned firmly. "No, I shan't do that. Maggie's married, of course, but Fan has a Japanese boy who comes in after school. I went to see a man about handling an agency for the Waterproof Shoepolish people," she added. "Nothing now. 'But oh, Mrs. Crabtree,' he said to me, 'if I could get a lady, like yourself, to give little talks about it, up and down the state!' 'Oh, come,' I said, 'I'm not asking for anything special—' 'No,' he said, 'but I may be in a position very soon to make you a special offer.'"

"Mama, what's Georgie doing?" Nelly, who was not listening, asked suddenly.

"Oh, I don't know!" Lucy said disgustedly. "He sent me twenty-five dollars for Christmas, and ten for Easter. I guess he's making money enough. But I don't like what I hear of these Tates, this man he boards with. There's a niece, or a queer little thing they've adopted—I don't know exactly what she is to them, and when Georgie was up for Christmas he couldn't talk of any one else than this Tessy or Jessy or some such name. His hands looked terrible; he's lost the first joint of his middle-finger, you know. I'm going down there some day this summer, and find out for myself just what's going on. I don't propose to have Georgie marry any little foundling from

Santa Clara, or settle down there for the rest of his life, and I told him so!"

"Was he mad, Mama?"

"Oh, you know Georgie. His face got red. Lou was there and she began to laugh, and she said, 'You've got a better job than mine, anyway, Georgie!' I didn't have a minute with him alone, we were over at Aunt May's——"

"Lou lives with Bertie?" Nelly asked, diverted.

"Poor thing, she has to live somewhere. Terrible thing—that Eastern man!"

"Howard Palmer," Nelly supplied with relish, wiping Lloyd's sore little nose firmly. "Tootle-tootle-tootle-tootle!" she said loudly, over the child's protestant whimper. "It must be awful for Lou, I suppose she's nothing but a servant in Bertie's house. Give me that button, Cliffy," she added in a low tone, "give Mama that button. Pick it up, Hilda. Give it to Hilda, Cliffy. *Cliffy*——"

She caught the five-year-old boy dexterously, and manipulated him and his sodden little dirty garments upon her knee with a practised hand. Lucy tried to look blank as Cliffy's shrieks and Nelly's violent voice rose together.

"You naughty—*naughty*—boy!" Nelly said, her face growing red, her descending hand punctuating her words. "You do what Mama tells you—now! Now *howl!*" Nelly panted, jerking him to the floor. "Scream, yell all you want to! Next time you'll get worse! Take him out, Hilda. It seems a funny life for Lou," Nelly added, in a normal tone of voice, her high colour receding as suddenly as it had come.

"She looks terribly pulled down, poor girl," Lucy sighed. "May and Tina run the San Rafael house," she added, "and Bobo's there."

"Sit quiet and get your breath, Nelly! I hate to see you getting all pulled down, you don't look a bit well! I did hope you were going to marry a good manager—Rudy *is* a much smarter business man than Papa," Lucy hastily interpolated, "but then, of course, the drink comes in!—that's life, after all. Well, I've got to get back to town—Fanny gets all worked up if she's alone too long. She says that when your grandfather dies, she's got to let that house go—but I guess that's just talk. I guess Fanny's pretty well fixed. How's Rudy?"

It was the first time she had asked it; perhaps poor Nelly's forlorn and shabby surroundings were sufficient indication of Rudy's activities. Nelly was holding the baby on her shoulder, now; little Stuart was a sticky mass of dirt, food, and sodden clothing; he was weeping.

"Oh, pretty well," Nelly said indifferently. "Well enough to lose money, shooting craps last night—it made me crazy!" she added with a laugh. "I guess men have it pretty easy—if things go wrong at home they can walk right out. Hush *up*, Baby!" she said, not unkindly, to the fretting child. "Hilda, run get the baby's pacifier! Lloyd, you and Cliffy walk to the gate with Grandma. Hilda's got as much sense as a woman," she added, walking to the gate herself with her mother, as Hildegarde took her brother expertly into her thin little arms. "I don't know what I'd do without her. Rudy gets rough with her sometimes—he does with all of them—and it's usually poor Hilda that gets whipped." Nelly kissed her mother rather apathetically; she had been feeling wretched of late, and this long, enervating hot day had tired her. She had been up at six, cooking and cleaning and straightening, and had been tired enough to drop at ten o'clock. Nelly was beginning to think her stomach chronically troublesome: she thought now that her lunch had not agreed with her.

An ancient fear was heavy upon her as she went slowly back into the house.

CHAPTER XXV

FANNY was well again, and almost offensively brisk and capable once more. She began to talk, in May, of spring cleaning, and it was obvious, to Lucy, that it was her particular room that was destined for the first onslaught. Lucy ignored the matter as long as she decently could, and longer, but conversations between the sisters-in-law became strained, and with every warm, silent morning, and every windy, gritty afternoon, Lucy resolved afresh that she must make some move.

Harry was sending her a little money now, and she carefully hoarded the tens and twenties, without ever mentioning them to Fanny. She estimated the possibilities. To go to Nelly was out of the question; she would be simply an unpaid servant in that house. Alice—Lucy's pride was up in arms where Alice was concerned. She could take no favours there. Frank and his wife lived a full and prosperous life with no reference to her. Alice entertained her, when she called, in the parlour, that correct, carpeted parlour where patients came from two to four and seven to eight, and where the shutters were drawn against the westering sun. The upright piano, the oblong cherry table, the lamp with morning-glories painted on its china shade, the books and the stuffed chairs, were always speckless and in place. There was an artificial palm in the bay-window, its too-green leaves showing through fresh, clean, evenly looped lace curtains, from the street.

"Mama, you look so well," Alice always said.

"I don't know why. Fanny and I are going all the time."

"Frank and I saw Fanny and Uncle Bob downtown the other night."

"Yes. They said they saw you."

"Is he here now?"

"No. He's gone back."

"He's doing pretty well in Sacramento, isn't he?"

"Oh, I guess he's coining money."

A silence. Then Lucy might say:

"Do you see the girls from the hospital much?"

"Oh, never! Except that I had Mabel and Seppie here when I was first married."

"Do you feel pretty well?"

"Oh, finely, thank you, Mama!"

Lucy used to leave her daughter with profound dissatisfaction in her heart; it was hard exactly to analyze it, but it was always there.

She never suspected that Alice used to come to the clean bay-window, and look down through the fresh, looped curtains at her mother's sturdy figure going down the dirty Mission Street, with a feeling almost as troubled as Lucy's own.

Frank didn't like Mama, that was the trouble. He had said so, on that dreadful, amazing day when Alice had been so shaken as to cry, right on the Haight Street car; he had said so many times since. He wanted Alice always to be polite to her mother—Frank was so just. But he had said, and she believed him, that it would only distress her to have her mother lunching with her, getting the habit of running in, and that when the baby came he *positively* would not have her mother interfering.

"I make every possible allowance!" Frank had said. "But at that time my wish is *law*."

"Yes, I know, Frank! And I'm sure Mama wouldn't want to interfere."

"It's entirely up to you," he had said. "Much better a hint from you than a scene with me!"

"Oh, yes, indeed!" she had agreed thankfully. Frank was not too happy about the prospect, she knew. Alice told herself sensibly that it was not, of course, as if it were his first child.

This was being married, she reflected philosophically. One gave so much, one received so much more. She received all the dignity of Frank's name and position, the pleasure of being mistress of this house, of driving, dining downtown, going to lectures and concerts with Frank. She had plenty of pocket money; no grievances, really, unless this rather blank feeling of not belonging to herself, of not *being* herself, was a grievance, There were days when the clean, dark, orderly rooms, and the creaking of patients' feet into Frank's office, and the sudden clatter and stop of his horse's feet, when he came home for lunch,

seemed to reach her senses through a heavy veil of fogginess
and dullness.   There was a dreamy unreality, a baffling evasive-
ness, about it all.   Who was Alice Babcock any way?   Where
was the old, giggling Alice who had said her prayers so faithfully, and played Lotto with Papa and Georgie?

"And I have everything!" she would remind herself, struck
by her own ingratitude.   "What must it be for poor Nelly, or
Vick—marrying men who are actually poor!"

One day she had a letter from Vick.   It was a balmy, cloudless May day, a year after her marriage.   Alice had walked to
market; now she felt heated and headachy.   She went up to her
front room, and sat down, panting, with Vicky's letter in her hand.

"Dearest Alice," she read.   "You are not so smart with your September!
I have an engagement in December just as important, imagine—won't they be
adorable together.   You must have a boy to marry my daughter.   Davy and
I are terribly happy about it.   I'm writing you in the kitchen, chaperoning a
pot-roast.   Davy's mother is supposed to be the best cook in town, and her
popovers never pop, and mine do, so you may imagine the sinful pride of David
Dudley, M.D.   Davy cut a leg off last week—it was a Chinaman's, but he lived,
so score one for Davy.   I get so thrilled over cases, don't you?   Last Sunday
Mary Dudley and I saw Davy smile at someone in church, and we whispered to
him who was it?   He said, 'That's the tongue amputation!' and Mary and I
laughed so we had to go out.   He was furious!   This is really a jay place, but
I like it, we have pretty good times.   Of course we have to go to everything, to
show our public spirit.   . . ."

A strange expression came into Alice's madonna-like face as
she read this letter, and with a spasmodic movement of her
hands she destroyed it.   She put it into her scrapbasket, but
almost immediately took it out, patched it laboriously together,
and read it again.   About an hour later, she suddenly and in-
explicably began to cry.

"Woo—hoo!"   It was Aunt Fanny's strident voice, echoing
through the quiet halls of the San Rafael house.   Tina, putting
away breakfast-cups still warm from the dish-water, sighed and
frowned as she put her arms behind her to untie her kitchen
apron.   This meant luncheon, and Tina had promised to run
over to Grace's!   Mama could have taken care of Bobo very
comfortably; but it was too much to expect her to cook for Aunt
Fanny.

Tina had on her old blue dimity, daintily crisp from the irons.

Her fair, lifeless hair was arranged in the matronly braids she and Grace had affected years ago; they were meekly wound about Tina's head, and framed her rather full, square face. She smiled as she crossed the hall.

"Well, Aunt Fanny! Aren't you nice to do this! How's Grandpa?"

"Whew—ee!" gasped Fanny, returning her niece's kiss, her face scarlet. "Lawsy—it was warm in town, but nothing like this! Where's Mama? Old aunt going to be in the way for a bite of lunch?"

"In the way!" Tina echoed, affectionately reproachful. She thought that she could send Bobo with a note to Grace Yelland. May came to the head of the stairs cautiously; peering down sharply through her glasses.

"Oh, Fan!" she breathed in relief, descending. She wore a scalloped sacque, but Fanny was smart in one of the new shirt-waists that had been so quickly adopted by women everywhere. May admired this garment now. "I declare it's real cute, Fan," she said. "Vicky wrote me she had one. The cuffs come off, don't they?"

"The cuffs and collar come off," Fanny agreed. "Well! How are you? I just thought I'd come over——"

"I'm glad you did!" May said, leading the way into the cool dining room, where they sat down. "Bobo's playing round somewhere; he asked me for a nickel for a ball of string. My, isn't it hot?"

She looked with pathetic, faded eyes at her sister. May was gray now, and her stout figure stuck in and out clumsily at hips and bosom. Her recently brushed hair was damp on her forehead.

"We kind of thought Lou and the baby might run up to-day," she said; "Lola isn't well—it would be terrible if anything happened to her, with that young baby! Lou brought her up last week; she's a cute little thing—quite dark, you know. How's Pa?"

"He seemed real well last night," Fanny answered, unenthusiastically. "Lucy was reading to him. I asked him something about the business, but he just blinked at me. I believe," she added, beating her nose, "sometimes I believe he knows a lot more than we think. He'll go down to the Bank alone. And then you'll think he's dying, all of a sudden!"

"It would almost be a blessing——" May murmured.

"Oh, it would!" Fanny added, decidedly.

"Rob was in last week, Sunday, to see Bobo," May further confided. "Bobo looked nice; he'd been to church with Tina. Sometimes I think Rob'll have us all out of here, when anything happens to Pa!" she faltered, tears suddenly in her eyes.

"Looks like we'll all be living over here, at this rate!" Fanny answered bracingly. "I don't know *what's* going on, at the store. Steve say anything to you about it?"

"I know he's terribly worried," May said, sighing. "It seems so quiet now," she went on, "with just Tina. Vicky gone and Lou with Bertie, and Bertie—I don't see him hardly ever, unless they're all around—he used to be Mama's boy, you know——"

May began to cry. Fanny's sharp eyes watered, too, and she blew her nose.

"I get thinking of Esme," May faltered. "It's getting round to two years. . . ."

"I declare it doesn't look as if the next year was going to be much better," Fanny said, frankly and anxiously. "I went down to the office the other day, I don't like this business of no dividends! We've always had dividends in August, since Aunt Jenny's day——"

"Terrible hard times, Fan!" May suggested, in Stephen's defence.

"Oh, hard times—hard times! I've heard that until I'm sick of it!" Fanny ejaculated scornfully. "As things are now, I've a good mind to draw my money out—sell my stock!"

"Why don't you, Fan?" May said innocently, thinking only that Fan was a great annoyance to Stephen, and an interruption to his work when she went into the office. Fanny was secretly disappointed; she had hoped to cause May at least the uneasiness that this same suggestion had caused Stephen yesterday.

"Well, here's the boy that lost his tongue!" she said to Bobo, who sidled in smiling shyly. "Gracious, May, don't he ever speak?" she asked.

"Oh, he chatters all the time!" Tina assured her, gathering the odorous fringed cloth tablecover in a careless bunch, and flinging it on a chair, and ballooning a worn white tablecloth over the bare boards. "Awful the way flies get in here!" she said. "Mama tell you about Vicky? About December. Vicky's tickled to death!"

"Well, I hope Davy Dudley's tickled enough to earn some food and clothes for it!" Fanny said, rattling a hard finger violently in her own ear.

Tina laughed as she flung a handful of mixed knives and forks on the table; she began to put on the sugar-bowl and spoon mug with hard bumps.

"You folks aren't going to get much," she prophesied. "Bobo, be Auntie Tina's darling, and run over to Auntie Gracie with this note. We'll wait for you. I'll cut up the tomatoes, Mama."

"That's a good girl," May approved. "I don't know what I'll do when somebody steals this darling from me!" she said, tenderly.

"Know anybody who wants a cook, waitress, and chambermaid?" Tina laughed hardily. She put the meal on all at once—salad, tea, cake, sardines in the neatly opened tin, cornbread. "Whew—it's hot!" she gasped, the last one to sit down. "Use my butter plate, Mama. Poor Grace," she added, to her aunt, "she feels the heat terribly. Yes—" she nodded, to Fanny's questioning look. "Vera's only three, and Baby isn't walking yet! I usually have him here in the afternoons!"

"Too quick!" May said, shaking her head. Tina felt quite thrilled to be admitted to open talk on this delicate subject. She sugared her tea, nodding reflectively.

"I guess Vicky'll have a string of 'em!" Fanny commented, with relish. Vicky's mother shook her head again.

"Poor, headstrong, rebellious Vicky!" she sighed. "She looked shabby, last Christmas—her old suit. Doesn't seem to worry at all, walked right up to Stephen——"

Fanny and Tina had heard this before; they murmured in asides.

"This wonderful woman has come into his parish," Tina was saying, "Mrs. Lundeen. She lives at the hotel—they say she's worth half a million—*imagine*. She's taken a great fancy to Vernon, isn't it wonderful? She gave him the chancel windows as a memorial to her husband——"

"She may die and leave him money," Fanny suggested.

"Oh, Aunt Fanny, aren't you awful! She's only twenty-six, *imagine*," Tina said. "She doesn't like Grace—she says that she doesn't like any women, and that made Vernon quite angry with her. So then she sent Grace a lovely coat from the Woman's Exchange, for little Vernon. Vernon says that she *wants* to be saved, yet the grace is lacking; he said an extraordinary struggle between the flesh and the spirit. Grace is wonderful! She says that she knows that's a churchman's life, that he belongs to his parishioners more than to his wife——"

Fanny listened, nodding. Presently May urged Tina to run off to Grace; she and Bobo would clean the kitchen. Fanny and she sat on, almost silently, in the heat. Bobo was picking the raisins from his cake, May in a dream over her teacup. The table was littered with cups and plates; the cloth rumpled. The burning midday heat lay heavily over the old wooden house and the dry garden, and the sleepy town. Carpenters' hammers were noisy from the lots beyond the back garden. The new Torrey baby was acidly wailing—wailing. A wagon rattled by.

Stephen. He had come quietly through the front door, and stood watching them, in the hallway. May exclaimed and bustled; Bobo ran to meet him.

"Not sick, dear?" May asked, alarmed.

He felt the heat, he admitted, sitting down and wiping his forehead slowly, with a big, crumpled handkerchief. His curly gray hair was getting very thin, he looked heavy and oddly aged.

"No cake!" he said, to the plate Fanny proffered. "Well!" he added, on a deep breath, but with no particular concern, as he looked about. "Well—the jig's up!"

"What do you mean, Steve?" May asked, instantly anxious.

"Uncle Steve," Bobo confided, in his ear, "I fixed an elevator, and it works! I tried it on a chicken——"

"I mean that Crabtree and Company went into the hands of a trustee at eleven o'clock this morning!" Stephen said mildly, wiping his forehead again, and looking thoughtfully at his handkerchief before he bunched it and put it in his pocket. "Yes, sir," he added, "at eleven o'clock this morning——"

May and Fanny had been speechless for a moment; Fanny's face growing red as May's paled. Now both spoke together:

"*What!*" And May added, pleadingly: "What is it, Steve? Is it bad? What is a trustee? I don't understand!"

"Yes, it's bad. It's been bad for some time and now—now, I guess it's all over!" Stephen told her unemotionally. "Yesterday we had a meeting of creditors. I didn't say anything last night, May; I thought perhaps they'd let me continue. But they met again this morning, and—and they want to liquidate. Crane's over with Finch and Houston; they want us closed up. They own a majority of stock in the Pacific Importation Company and they are our heaviest creditors. It's all a conspiracy; it's all Crane's doing."

"I don't understand what you're talking about!" Fanny said sharply. She was breathing hard and white dints showed in her quivering nostrils and about her mouth. "Is Crabtree and Company in any real financial difficulty?"

"There won't be any Crabtree and Company, Fanny, after they get through. They've put in young Tom Fenderson as Trustee, and he's managing the business, now; he's going to close everything up and divide the assets among the creditors."

"Well, I wasn't one bit too soon—you know I told you this very day that I meant to withdraw my money, May!" Fanny said, tossing her head. "And that's what I shall do, the first thing in the morning! I'm sorry, Steve; I daresay it wasn't your fault, nor anybody's fault. But I've got my own interests to look out for——"

Stephen frowned, shaking his head.

"I'm afraid you don't understand, Fanny. The creditors are going to close Crabtree and Company up—shut its doors. Your stock, my stock, even your father's stock, is worth nothing—unless by some miracle there should be something left, and you can bet Tom Fenderson will see that there isn't."

Fanny laughed heartily but briefly.

"Ha! That's all very well for *talk*, Steve," she said, trembling. "But there's nobody in this world can convince me that —sitting back and not doing one thing!—I have lost all that money! All the money that Aunt Jenny put into Crabtree and Company and left to me! You've been saying 'No dividends— no dividends,' for I don't know how long, now, and I was willing to believe that perhaps the firm wasn't making as much money as it had; but you can't take my share of ownership in the firm away from me, just like that—without so much as 'by your leave'!"

Stephen mopped his forehead again, but he made no retort. Fanny, watching him with a sort of anxious triumph and scorn, breathed hard.

"Steve, what about Bertie?" May asked instantly.

Her husband shrugged his shoulders and shook his head.

"Can't say, May. They may keep him on there for a few weeks; they may let him go right away. Tom Fenderson's got it in for the boy; he'll probably fire him as he did me."

"Steve!"

"That's what old Fenderson's boy did to me the minute he was made General Manager," Stephen said slowly, paying no attention to the women's agitation. "He told me he could get along better if I wasn't around; said Yeasley and Woolcock could give him all the information he needed! Old Fenderson's boy whose father begged me to give him a chance a few years ago!"

"But how can they? *We're* the business!" May said stupidly. "After all you've done for them Steve! It's base—it's the *wickedest* ingratitude!"

Tina came in with little Vernon Yelland in her arms.

"Oh, Tina—Tina," May faltered, suddenly pressing fingers to lips that had begun to tremble, "Papa—your poor Papa—has come home with some very bad news."

"Oh, what?" Tina gasped, sinking into a chair at the littered table over which the flies were now rioting unchallenged.

"The firm's failed!" May stated baldly, bursting out crying. "Papa's ruined! Everything's gone—just at your happy time, when you ought to be having nothing but pleasure! And Bertie——"

"Mama," Tina asked intently, "nothing dishonourable?"

She could tell Grace afterward that this was her *first* thought, and that when dear old Papa said, with tears in his eyes, that it had been nobody's fault, she had gone to him, kneeling, and kissing and comforting him.

"What a blessed consoler you must have been, dear!" Grace said, from her couch. She was resting, in the long summer twilight, after the flurry of getting the babies to bed. Vernon was dining with his spiritual charge at the hotel, Tina and Grace could loiter deliciously over a late tea. "*Dear*," Grace added earnestly, "can we doubt that the way will be found, for all of you?"

May was by this time comforted, too. Fanny, after writhing in her chair in most unhappy and unwilling silence for some time, had snorted, tossed her head, turned over the little watch that was pinned with a silver bow to her stiff new shirtwaist, and had departed for the three-o'clock train. Then Stephen seriously

and kindly had told May and Tina all that they could understand, and May had stopped wiping the dishes to assure him
passionately that she and Tina would manage—they would
take boarders—he would see.　And as long as Pa lived they had
their home, May had reminded him in an undertone, glancing
out at Bobo, who was solemnly elevating the Torrey hens in his
improvised elevator.

So that by six o'clock, when the loveliest hour of the long sweet
day arrived, he found himself bodily weary, but with a soul almost at peace, placidly watering the plumbago and heliotrope
by the side door, with May cheerfully clattering dishes in the
kitchen, and conversation going back and forth between them
pleasantly.　If Stephen didn't have to go in to-morrow, he and
she would go down and see Bertie's wife and baby.

Poor Steve, after all these years, slaving and working, and
carrying the whole load for everyone; if he didn't deserve a little
vacation, who did?　By nightfall they were laughing most dis-
loyally at Fanny; poor old Fan, hadn't she been wild?

"She has all Aunt Jenny's money left!" May said, "and we
lose *everything*.　I declare I don't feel one bit sorry for Fan!"

And after some three or four days had passed, a strange peace
fell upon the more-than-ever united family.　Bankruptcy
sounded frightful; but there was nothing frightful to May in
having dear Steve so contentedly at home, puttering with Bobo
among the varied activities of yard and garden, snipping marguerites, watering the flowers.　Rob had long ago offered to
pay board for Bobo, now he began to do so.　Tina got a ticket
for the Woman's Exchange, and took over glasses of jelly, and
armsful of chrysanthemums.　And in October Fanny proposed
that she and Pa and Carra should come over; there was plenty of
room, and they would be much better off paying board to May
than paying a Japanese servant and rent and everything else at
the California Street house.　This made May feel useful and
satisfied; she expressed herself as only afraid that Pa could not
stand the strain of the move.

The calamity seemed to have softened everyone; even Fanny
was unwontedly pacific.　She held tenaciously to her untouched thousands, never mentioning them or business at all.
Saunders cut her coupons and put her checks in the bank.　She
watched her father dutifully, when Carra was at meals, helped
Tina with dishwashing, and gossiped with May in comfortable

old-lady fashion. About twice a week Fanny flashed into town feeling quite rich with no household bills to pay, lunching at Swains', changing a library book, stepping into the Woman's Exchange to see how Tina's cup-cakes were selling. She talked with other women on the boat, tilting up and down gently on the blue water of the bay, the sweet fresh air reddening her harsh face, her decent buttoned boots showing under her brush-edged long skirt, and her hands encased in worn, shiny black kid gloves. She knew everybody.

"Who is it, Mama?" a little girl, nicely dressed for town, might whisper.

"That's Miss Fanny Crabtree—don't you know nice Miss Tina Brewer's aunt?" the mother would answer abstractedly, settling string bag, book, umbrella and wilting nosegay of country flowers beside her seat. "They're old San Franciscans— pioneers, I think."

And if, streaming slowly off the boat, she saw Fanny again, she would ask, pleasantly: "All well in San Rafael, Miss Fanny? That's good!" before hurrying across the ferry place, and anxiously manœuvring for dummy seats on the Market Street car.

Old Reuben Crabtree was almost, if not quite, childish. He did not seem to realize much of the firm's failure, but he was well enough now and then to go into town and see Saunders. For the most part he was delighted with Bobo's society. If any one ever spoke to him sharply, even in kindly warning, he wept, sometimes also he wept for love, and wanted to kiss Lou or Tina over and over again. May, Stephen, and Fanny all felt that he was utterly unfit to manage what remained of his affairs, but they had no choice. He consulted none of them.

Stephen seemed a tower of youthful strength beside him— Stephen, who could climb step-ladders and prune roses and walk briskly into town to send a telegram. And Stephen liked the rôle of powerful, gentle guardian; May often said that Steve's being home just now was a perfect godsend. He and Carra followed the old man about, and when his knee was bad wheeled his chair; old Reuben would gabble and sputter over his meals like a duck, he had to have his napkin tied about his neck, to Bobo's surprise and awed pity. It could not be long now, May and Fanny said.

Before the autumn came, it was as natural for May to call out into the garden a warning to Steve to bring Pa in, and for

Tina to set "Aunt Fan's place" at the table, as had ever been any other order in the old house.

Lucy, entirely counted out in this new arrangement, had adjusted herself to it with her customary suavity. Fanny was eaten with curiosity as to where Lucy's money came from; she always had it; Fanny would see a gold piece or a silver dollar or two whenever her purse happened to be open. Lucy went to the Misses Grandet; decayed and forlorn and black-clad French sisters who managed a languishing boarding-house in Hyde Street, took possession of a small hall bedroom, and spoke placidly of Harry's getting a little more "settled" before she joined him.

Occasionally she came over to San Rafael, the pleasantly interested but unconcerned visitor. Once she mentioned having been to Sacramento: Fanny's eyes shot to May's, and her jaw snapped. No reason in the world why Lucy shouldn't go to Sacramento, of course.

"Did you see Bob, Lucy?"

"Oh, yes, indeed. He took me to dinner!"

Fanny laughed sardonically.

"Well, I hope the good Sacramentans think it quite natural for a lady to go to Sacramento to see her brother-in-law!" she said lightly and playfully. Lucy widened her frog-like eyes.

"My dear Fanny, I am fifty-three!" she said good-naturedly. Fanny turned a resentful brick-red and said no more.

CHAPTER XXVI

VICTORIA came down to breakfast, quite as usual. She preceded Davy by several minutes, going out into the kitchen at once, and sitting, panting, on a chair. Davy's mother was at the stove, his sister Mary cutting bread at the table. Both smiled at her, and Mrs. Dudley said affectionately: "Good night?"

"Too good!" Victoria answered ruefully. "He's going to be late for all his engagements; he gets it from me!" she added. All three women laughed together.

"Boo! This is a cold day!" Mary Dudley breathed of the icy out-of-doors, as she came in with the milk and paper. "What did you get up for, Vick?" she added, reproachfully.

"I've got to do *something!*" Victoria protested. "I think I'll ride horseback!" she went on rebelliously.

"I declare I'm never going to try another baking powder!" Mrs. Dudley said suddenly. "Now look there, Mary. I done just exactly what I done before, and they come out splendid!"

Victoria, her coffee cup steaming with the delicious hot drink, the baking-powder biscuit split in her fingers, looked about the kitchen and sighed. It would be good to be lithe and brisk, like Mary and Mother again. She felt as if last winter were ages ago; those cold, sharp days before Christmas, when she and David had walked and gathered red berries on the hills.

It had been in that first winter of her marriage that she and Davy had won forgiveness from the family in San Rafael. For a few weeks after their marriage there had been no word; then Vicky wrote as charming and winning a letter as she could manage, and sent it to her father with the money that had been through so unexpected an experience with her. She was sorry, she said simply, she wanted Mama and Papa to forgive her, and love her again, because she was so happy.

May answered immediately, luxuriating in reproaches and tears, sure that dear, dear Esme never would have treated the best father in the world, "and a Mama who at least *tries* to be a real chum and confidante of her girls," in so cruel a fashion. May, however, was not sorry to have a daughter married, and Vicky suspected the truth that lay back of the wavy underlining and the crossing at the tops of the pages. Her mother longed as much as she for a reconciliation. So, learning from Lou that there was to be a family gathering on Christmas night, Vicky and Davy went boldly to San Rafael, and in five minutes everything was right again. Stephen talked confidentially and appreciatively to Davy, and Vicky buttoned on an apron and set the table and made the gravy; she was married at last, with her husband like a son in the old home, and there was more laughter and warmth and harmony in the Brewer household than there had been for months.

That was last year. But Vicky would not go down this year; she would have a "young baby." Women didn't go abroad when they had young babies. Her heart thumped furiously. "It might come any day now," she said to herself, with awe and trembling.

Mary flashed down cellar; the odour of spicy apples came in with the cooler air. Mrs. Dudley climbed on a chair to reach jam. Victoria's baby was two weeks late; she felt as if she had been dragging about in this state of indefinite expectation for years instead of months.

Davy came in, ready for breakfast; the clock struck seven. It was pleasant in the shabby, worn kitchen, when all four of them were discussing biscuits and omelette, and the desultory talk of the day was under way. Mary wanted Vicky to come with her to the meeting at church; just women, she pleaded, and the walk would do Vicky good! Victoria laughed; all right, if Mary would take the chances.

There was a table outside the kitchen window upon which the morning sun slanted coldly. A bright pumpkin and some sweet potatoes were on the table in an old pan; the cat leaped up there, and licked them tentatively. Out-of-doors was bleak; a chill wind rattled the bare whips of the willows. But here in the kitchen everything was hearteningly warm.

"I'm going to stay in and get quite a lot of things out of the way," Mrs. Dudley announced. "The Graysons may be in to-morrow, and I ain't got a taste of cake on the place. I thought maybe I'd marble one, and have the other plain, with orange frosting. Folks get kinder foundered on cocoanut, this cold weather!"

"Don't like cake—never touch it—prefer you to do something else!" David said, amiably. His mother, a lean, tall woman with oily gray hair and a long, hard-working hand, eyed him scornfully.

"It's too bad about you!" she observed. Mary resumed one of those endless small-town ruminations that are always on tap.

"Speaking of Jen Hooper—as' Lizabeth says, if she had really meant to give it up, she would have done it that night, but her waiting until Jo Harper got here—and as far as that goes, Jo said she never wrote her about it, not one word—says *she* heard of it from Minnie Kane. 'Why,' she said, 'is it likely I would have sat there like a bump on a log——?'"

Victoria listened to them all; indeed was deeply interested in what she heard. She had not lived fifteen months in a small town without falling captive to the fascination of small-town gossip. Mrs. Dudley, who was "Mother Dudley" to everyone, was no lover of scandal. Reputations were never destroyed in the old kitchen, but they were dissected, analyzed, inspected, compared endlessly, and with undying relish. Small things when seen close enough are great, and these things were larger than the largest scrap of restricted, curtailed, divided life that can ever be lived in a big city. These were chronicles of birth and death, of love and hate, all the interplay and complication of feuds, intermarriages, inheritances and prejudices that had been growing undisturbed for fifty years, in this simple and spacious environment.

To go to the theatre in San Francisco with Bertie had been amusing; a delightful evening's entertainment. But to go to a concert here in Napa, with David and Mary, and have all one's intimates about one, all the hereditary enemies of the house also in the hall, all the "talent" either to be scorned or abetted, every little encounter of eyes or voices deeply significant; this was life. Mary would be managing two swains at once; Minnie or Dora or Anita would come to whisper some delicious development in Vicky's ear, Davy would murmur her the history of the famous Unger murder case, when Dolly Unger got up to sing, and everyone would be free to observe that Nat Perry was with the Hudson girl again.

The days were full of events, significant hurryings to and fro.

And the evenings—especially the summer evenings—when all the young people of the place loitered up and down River Street in the warm dark under the big trees, and ordered ice-cream sodas, and bought writing-tablets or toilet soap or pencils in Terry's, were something for which to wait all day.

It had been great fun, last June, to answer a whispered "yes!" to all the eager insinuating and questioning; everything had been fun until these last dragging weeks, when Vicky had felt so tired all the time, and so stupidly useless. And now here was another cold day; the third, and so the last, of the "snap," but somehow to be got through with books and sewing——

She listened, smiled, even commented. But under it all ran undisturbed the great river of doubt, fear, hope, ignorance, upon which her life had been floating for nine long months. Would her hour be bad? Would it be wonderfully good? What would it be? What was it all about? The unrealness of speaking of "after the baby comes," of making definite little flannelly garments for this mythical little person, wrapped her in dreams. It was suffering; she had never known suffering. She listened to the older women anxiously, when they spoke of her "ordeal," of her "trouble," of "labour." She would be brave. But would she be brave?

"Would you chance driving up to the Springs with me, if I have to go?" Davy asked, with his parting kiss. She drew his hard, firm cheek against her soft one.

"My dear, I'd chance a trip to the north pole!"

He laughed tenderly at her fretfulness and spirit.

"Never mind, you poor old darling——!" he was beginning, when Victoria, who had gotten to her feet, clutched his arm sharply, and sat down again.

Something happening at last! It was so welcome, after the long delay! Mary ran over to 'Lizabeth's house, next door. Mother, gravely and cheerfully efficient, kept Vicky in the kitchen rocker while she carried the oil-stove upstairs. Davy rushed off to hurry through morning rounds, and be back again. The telephone rang; Miss Gussy was on her way, Doctor Boone would stop in about ten o'clock.

Now was the time when she was to be brave. Victoria rallied her courage heroically, she would be brave. She felt rather cold, vague, and frightened. Chills ran over her, her face burned with fever; tiny tendrils of pain seized her momentarily and were gone.   She sat in the rocker, useless, while Mary and 'Lizabeth and Miss Gussy flew about with sheets and towels.

They all came down to the kitchen; it was warmer there. Victoria was conscious of a hope that this discomfort she was so gaily enduring might turn out to be the worst of the whole thing. Other women *were* cowards about pain——

The doctor came; she and the nurse went upstairs with him, came down again.   Everything splendid—he would come back.

"When, Doctor?"   She hated herself for faltering it.

"Long before you need me, Missy!"   He went out into the cold front hall, and was heard talking with Miss Gussy—talking about some entirely indifferent matter, Victoria discovered, with a pang.   She was not really into it, yet, then!

"That's the time old Tom got what was coming to him!" the doctor said, chuckling.   "I don't know as Tom's wife felt any too bad about it," Miss Gussy answered laconically.   "He's the kind that don't often get his come-uppance!"

Miss Gussy came back to the kitchen; it was still the warmest room in the house, although a great fire was going in the "air-tight" in Mrs. Dudley's room now, and the door into Vicky's room, adjoining, was open.   'Lizabeth and Mary came and went cheerfully; their mother reminded them that things must be warm and comfortable for "company unexpected."   Victoria wished that something would happen; she seemed to be the only person not involved in this excitement.

She stood at the window, studying the cold yard, and the wind ruffling the bare willow whips.   'Lizabeth ran home across the back lot to her own babies, both girls.   She had told Vicky that if her child was a boy, she—Aunt 'Lizabeth—was going to pack hers off to orphanages.   Vicky tried to smile, remembering the jest, but she felt too frightened and solemn to smile.

Mary had put on her coat and the geranium hat, and gone off to market, to the Post Office, to excuse Mother to Mrs. Bean, who was ill—on a thousand alert, happy errands.   Victoria hoped that Miss Gussy and Mother realized that she was in pain.

They chatted comfortably.   Miss Gussy, who was really Mrs. Thomas Petters, was a big, broad, softly padded woman of about fifty, the mother herself of several grown children.   Vicky did not like her much, on second view.   She had happened to see her nurse only once before.

Davy's mother evidently liked her, though, and Vicky had great faith in her judgment. "Mother" was the idol of the house. To her gaunt homeliness her children were blind; she simply existed in perfection like an ocean or a mountain. Vicky, during the first months of her marriage, had watched her wistfully; it would be so nice to have everyone love one!

Mrs. Dudley deeply loved her son's wife; she and Mary thought Vicky the prettiest, wittiest, most charming person they knew. They had welcomed her into the family warmly, they boasted of her to the neighbours. She had been a special favourite from the moment she had arrived, shy and smiling, beside the radiant David, on a soft September evening now more than a year ago. The miracle of the girl's passionate devotion to David never grew old in the mother's thankful heart. And when Vicky tied on a kitchen apron, and brought, with new laughter and new life into the house, a practised, practical knowledge of housekeeping, the last barrier went down before her.

To Vicky, hungering all her life for just such appreciation and just such an opportunity to serve, this domestic harmony threw an added glamour over the glorious happiness of being beloved by David, of being "Mrs. Dave" in River Street and in the Post Office, of all the new delights and dignities of married life. There was a delicious sense of being established, when Mary chattered of her beaus, or Tina wrote about being chaperoned to a concert. She, Vicky Dudley, might sit back and listen to all the different girls complacently; there was a gold ring on her finger and a man waiting for her.

And now the first newness of that was over, and the long months of wondering, hoping, fearing about just one thing were over, and it was a cold, clear still December morning, with frost on the chrysanthemums, and the great hour had come.

"Finally, I up and asked her," Miss Gussy was saying comfortably, over a late cup of coffee. Vicky turned and glanced at the two talking women. The kitchen was almost too warm now; steam was on the windows, bright in the winter sunshine. There was a little ruff of dried grounds about the spout of the stained blue coffee pot. Miss Gussy had on a stiff gray percale; she had worn a warm shawl, but she had taken that off now. Mother wore her faded chocolate calico with the big brooch at her throat.

"I up and asked her," said Miss Gussy, chuckling. "I says 'Mamie, there's ben considerable talk this way and that, but all is,' I says, 'all is, if your father didn't rent Judd House's lot——'"

"I hope," Victoria said, laughing uncomfortably and trying to be humorous, "that you don't think—just because I'm behaving so well!—that I'm happy!"

"Poor child!" Davy's mother smiled with infinite tenderness as she went to the sink. Miss Gussy gave her a shrewd glance through glasses.

"I'm watchin' you like a cat, dear!" she answered. "It's the sickness that gets worse before it gets well, as the little girl said. Well, she give me a look . . ." she resumed, of Mamie. Victoria set her teeth and picked up a dishtowel.

"Now we are beginnin' to get somewhere!" Miss Gussy decided, when the patient, some fifteen minutes later, grasped the back of a chair, and panted with dropped head and shut teeth. "Suppose we go up?" she added, to Mrs. Dudley.

They went upstairs; Victoria reached her room spent by another spasm of pain on the stairs, and glad to see the neatly turned bed, and to feel the warmth of the clear, fresh air. Mrs. Dudley, anxiety in her eyes, took the rocking chair; Miss Gussy fussed with the contents of the blue basket with the dotted swiss ruffles, pins, scissors, cornstarch pad. Little blue bootees with tasselled ends—who had given her those? Who had given her those? Oh—oh—oh—it didn't matter——

"Keep walking, lovey!" Davy's mother urged. Victoria moved restlessly. 'Lizabeth came in, a plain woman of thirty, with none of the bloom of youth left in her bright, sensible face. Mary peeped in the door—lunch was ready!

"We're takin' our time," said Miss Gussy cheerfully. "I don't know why you shouldn't come down and have some lunch!" she added. "This feller may keep us all waitin' dear knows how long!"

Victoria's heart sank; nothing had happened yet. She went down to drink some tea, crumble hateful bread.—Davy came in, anxious and loving; she could not smile at him. She had his strong arm upon which to get upstairs again. He said he would stay 'round now; get in some wood. That was *something*. Davy wasn't going away again. Writhing—grinding—writhing—grinding—Nelly had had this four times, poor Nelly!

Poor—but this was not *right*. This couldn't be right—they couldn't know how bad——

"I'm going down to the kitchen for a few minutes!" Miss Gussy was actually leaving her! Mother was talking to her pleasantly; only she could not hear. Mary came to the door with a message: Doctor Boone would be at the hospital until half-past four. If they wanted him they were to telephone.

Half-past four! Victoria sent a sick glance at the clock. It was quarter to three——

Five minutes to three. "I can't stand this!" she stammered to 'Lizabeth, in tears. 'Lizabeth's face was pale with comprehending sympathy.

"Don't stand it!" she said sturdily. "Raise the roof—that's what I do!"

Victoria managed a twisted laugh.

"I had to laugh at Winny Tafts, with her last one," remarked Miss Gussy. "She says, 'If I had anything to do with it folks'd be made different!' She had it real easy, though—I don't b'leeve you're going to have much more of this, Mrs. Dave. Seems like you're helping real good, now."

"I think we ought to get this girl to bed!" Victoria could have kissed her husband's mother for the words.

"I'd keep walkin'," Miss Gussy answered, amiably. "Dave," she said, to David, who came in with an armful of wood, ten minutes later, "step to the telephone and tell Doc' Boone that I'd be real obliged if he'd sagatiate his corporosity round here just as soon as it's handy. Now I b'leeve we'd better get you into bed, dear," she added, to Victoria, as Davy rushed from the room.

Writhing—grinding—writhing—grinding. Victoria got into the warmed sheets. She was panting now, her breath coming short, her palms wet, and the dark curls stuck to her temples. She looked intense, frightened, grim.

"This is the very worst, dear. There isn't much of this!" Mrs. Dudley said, holding her slippery, desperate fingers.

"Ow—ow—ow—" the groans were dragged from her, one by one. Davy heard them, as he and Doctor Boone came in downstairs. Then there was a silence. Victoria whispered some indistinct words, broke into hard groans again.

They were all about her; but there was no world, no David, no heroism, and no future. It was all one blind whirl of agonies seething into deeper agonies. She was screaming—she was panting again in a moment's respite—she was screaming, high and hard, again——

Davy was kneeling beside her, busily greasing her face. She tossed her head away from him, away from the little strainer he was holding over her mouth. Far off—among the burning, shrieking stars—the hideous relentless pinprick was beginning again, it was coming nearer—it was growing——

"Just breathe deep, my darling—it will help you!" Davy's voice said, in the dark. But she could not breathe deep—she could do nothing, in this bath of flame——

She did breathe deep. She heard her own scream indifferently; as she went brokenly, blindly, into velvety blackness and space.

Something was alive. Walled all about by darkness, yet it was alive. It was breathing; it was hot, wet, exhausted. It could, with infinite weariness, open its eyes and see.

The window, the ruffled gray sky of the December day outside—Mary's graduation picture—Davy's face.

Victoria could not smile, she could not speak; she closed her eyes again.

Water was running; people were stepping softly. Someone was holding her hand; her head ached. She was Victoria Brewer Dudley, long, long ago she had been screaming——

"Yes, she did. She looked at me, Doc." That was Davy.

Peace. No more pain. Her head cleared. Delicious rest and peace.

"I think we can make her more comfortable! Just hold that aside, Davy——"

How kind they were! Hands were raising her, settling her, easing her on to pillows. She began to cry; opened her eyes.

"My sweetheart!" Davy's tear-wet face was not six inches from her own. Victoria's lashes fell, bitter tears squeezed between them. "What is it, darling?" he breathed.

"You're all so kind to me!" she whispered, pitifully.

She heard him laugh brokenly and repeat this. She whispered a question of the time.

"Quarter to four!" Victoria turned this over in her mind; it must be some other day, then. She dozed heavily, briefly, her head against her husband's arm.

Then suddenly her eyes were open; the lamp was lighted. She smiled, roused herself, almost raised herself in bed.

"Davy! Was I asleep?"

Miss Gussy was smiling at her.

"Well, how do you feel?"

"Oh, wonderfully! But starving!"

"You've got a little boy, Vicky!" David said, kissing her. Victoria kept her eyes faithfully, expectantly, upon him. But now they filled with tears, and her lips trembled. Ignorant, repressed, deceived. Somehow she had come through her thirty years of hunger and bewilderment, to the glorious reality of this hour. Miraculously, the boy was here, snuffling busily in fragrant blankets. The miracle of a tiny mottled fist gave way to the miracle of a dark, tiny, soft, and angry face.

Victoria's eyes were shining with immortal glory. She moved a weak hand, smiled.

"You cross little baby, you!"

"He's a beautiful child—perfect!" Davy's mother said. "I never saw such a child—he's like a three-months' baby!"

Victoria looked at him, her heart swelling with a profoundly new and marvellous emotion. Thought came to her; Davy's arm about her, Davy's mother sitting here in the low rocker, with her baby.

"Isn't he—little—and innocent?" she marvelled; feeling for new words for the great new discovery. They put him beside her.

It was over: the earthquake and fire. Now came the still small voice of the Lord, with infinite peace, infinite joy. What a transformed room this plain bedroom was, what a transformed life lay beyond this great hour, what a transformed woman little Davy Dudley's mother must be! Miss Gussy, with a cup of hot tea, seemed to Victoria everything that represented domestic beauty, hearth-side warmth in bleak winter twilights, comfort, rest, triumph.

She was a little hot and headachy in the night; worried by Miss Gussy's indifference to the baby's crying. He must be crying for *something*——

But she did sleep, and was patient for the nine days in bed, beautiful as she had never been in her life, newly poised and sweet. She leaned on a crooked arm, laughing at the busy little ineffectual lips at her breast; she braided down to a single hair the end of her long, soft braid.

On the tenth day she was sitting up, congratulatory neighbours and friends could peep in. None of the flurries and anxieties of first motherhood were hers, for Davy's mother handled the baby as calmly and as expertly as if he had been no more than a little cabbage, and 'Lizabeth was always accessible for consultations.

Her own mother wrote her, tremulously glad. May said that she wished Vicky had seen dear Papa's pleasure in the news of a grandson. He had said at once that some day Vick must bring the boy home for a visit. Grandpa was well, Bobo was well. Aunt Fanny was very busy over the gingerbread fête for the hospital. "Life and death seem strangely mingled—" May's indeterminate handwriting ran on—"poor dear Tina has had another sorrow to bear, in the death of our dear Grace Yelland. There was another little one coming, and a fall upon what we *think* was an old piece of wire fencing caused her a premature confinement. The poor little baby, a girl, is living, Grace wished her named Alma. Tina is crushed. A Mrs. Lundeen, one of Vernon's new parishioners, has the baby with her and her maid, at the hotel. We help with the others as best we can. What a sad, sad Christmas!"

Victoria lay warm and snug, in the terrific storm that brought in the holidays, and thought of the other young woman whose life had ended just as her own seemed so gloriously in flower. Poor Grace, lying in her rain-swept new grave, and poor Tina grieving. And poor Lou, working in Bertie's household for Bertie's wife. Poor everybody, indeed, who did not have a place in this shabby, warm old mansarded house under locust trees, a share in the joy and the responsibility of Taffy.

She looked at Taffy, who was asleep in a well-lined clothes basket beside her bed. He was on his side, his small body superbly curved and plump, his fine, round little head dark against the white pillow. While she looked, he sighed profoundly, whimpered perfunctorily, and rolled on his back.

"Davy!" Victoria whispered, startled, as David came in and took the rocker. "I wish you could have seen him roll over! All by himself!"

Davy clasped her hand. He was tired, but he smiled.

"How's the day gone, dear?"

"Oh, beautifully! Miss Gussy's gone—did mother tell you? I was down for lunch. I just came back to bed to be good."

"Want the lights?" He looked at a window slashed with raindrops that were black against the gray twilight.

"Oh, no; I love this!" He moved the rocker so that he could hold her comfortably braced against his shoulder. They fell into wonderful talk, of themselves, of their lives and plans, all to be readjusted now to fit the sleeping occupant of the clothes basket. They remembered their wedding eve, the ferry place hot in autumn sunshine, the long memorable talk in the train. They remembered wonderful winter evenings, wonderful February walks in nipping winds and past chirping frogs, Easter with roses and bridal wreath, and the hot summer nights under River Street's lights and heavy branches.

And to Victoria, the breezy, confident Vicky of all these times seemed the ignorant little sister, seemed but the child, indeed, of the tempered, tender, grateful woman who was lying here, her husband's arm about her, speaking of all these things. Would she want ice-cream sodas downtown and Welsh rarebits at Anita's—after Taffy? It was hard to believe it. She was possessed only by a passionate desire not to fail them—her husband, her son, Davy's sister, Davy's mother.

"I heard from Dr. Dunham again to-day, Vick."

"What about?" She was instantly alert. "I suppose Dr. Chatterton hasn't died suddenly?"

"No, but he's not well. Asthmatic. And Dunham says he may have to move to Southern California——"

"Oh, Davy, and that nice little wife! Just as they were settled in the new house!" Vicky mused for a minute. Then she said steadily, "He wants you!"

"I don't know," said Davy, and was still.

The twilight was almost darkness now; the window a dull gray square in solid shadow. Victoria tightened her fingers.

"When? Immediately?"

"No. Not until June."

She twisted the knife in her heart.

"Definitely, Davy?"

"Well, he said nothing of terms. And it was terms we couldn't arrange before, when he took Chatterton."

"Then you must go," Victoria said.

The baby was suddenly wide awake, with an enraged scream. His mother gathered him to her heart; warmth, dewy sweetness, faint flannelly odours, sodden little unresponsive weight and muffled roars. She fed him, her face bent down to watch him as she lay in pillows.

"I don't see how you—and the baby—could make it," Davy said slowly. "I could batch it, with old Dunham—you couldn't. And Mother does so much—we'd have to have a servant, probably two."

For awhile Victoria did not answer.

"I was thinking of that, Davy," she said presently. "But for awhile Taffy and I would stay here!"

"Oh, nonsense!" he said finally. Victoria watched in silence as he put the baby back.

"Is Dunham as good as Newman?" she asked, suddenly.

"Dunham? Oh, he's the finest in the business—in the world, I guess. He took his intern work at Johns Hopkins—he could have had the surgery in the Berlin Hospital, on that sort of case——"

"And that's your specialty, Davy?"

"Well, it was. But I'm darned glad to get this general practice, with Boone. Nothing like it!"

He sat silent, and Victoria was silent. Mary came upstairs; lighted the gas in the adjoining room; hummed as she changed her street clothes to a cotton gown. A shaft of light struck across the clothes basket. Rain streamed steadily down the window panes, and drummed on the low tin roof. Davy leaned toward the basket, and put his big finger into the boy's grasping palm.

"I noticed this morning that his skin seems to be peeling off his palms," he said, mildly curious.

"Your mother says they all do that—that's just lint, from his blankets!"

"Lord, it'll be good to have you around again, Vick, coming into the office, and walking home with me!" said Davy.

"Vick!" Mary called, "coming down to supper?"

"Oh, certainly! I'll slide into my wrapper." She pulled Davy's face down for a kiss. "My smart old San Francisco specialist!" she said.

"Vick. Don't think of it again. It's utterly out of the question. I wouldn't give up the kid's first year for forty San Franciscoes!" David got up, lighted the gas, fumbled among wrappers and shawls. "Which is the top of it?" he asked.

"This is December," Vicky thought. "Six months—it's only twenty-four weeks. But it's his chance. He's got to go!"

And tucked up on the sitting-room lounge, watching him in the family group that evening, the pattern all seemed plain to her. The irresponsible joy of the honeymoon days, the soberer summer with its approaching responsibilities, the winter, with Taffy, and now the new hard step—parting. Life couldn't be just ice-cream sodas, and Anita's parties, and Sunday walks, for David. He was too big for what he was doing now; he would hunger, sooner or later, for a wider life. Next summer wouldn't be like last summer, like that first free summer of their marriage. Everything would change—Taffy, and Taffy's father, and she must change, too.

Presently in low undertones, she began to place the plan before his mother.

CHAPTER XXVII

BERTIE'S little daughter had been a very tiny baby, as alert and pathetic and wizened as a little monkey. Lola had elected to have her baptized Maria Anita Dolores; she was never called anything but Nita. She had been prematurely born, Lola refusing even to get out of bed for some weeks before the event, and spending the time in sleep, reading, and long conversations with her aunts. She had gone back to the old ranch-house before Christmas; Nita was born in February.

Meanwhile Lou, sternly quiet and unresponsive, kept house for Bertie in Sausalito; Bertie going to Lola and the baby on Saturday, and Lou joining the family in San Rafael. Bertie had never before really loved his youngest sister; Lou had always been too cold and too self-centred, but he came to love her now, when disillusionment had so oddly touched them both.

In April, when Lola returned to Sausalito, Lou assumed practical charge of the household. Bertie gave her what money he could, certain bills she presented to Lola, who loved to scribble checks. A village girl came in for the heavier housework; the rest Lou managed. Lola did nothing.

The baby was fortunately quiet and manageable, and if Lou, in this dark time of humiliation and readjustment, loved anything, she loved the tiny Nita. Nita would lie for hours with her dark little emaciated fist clenched under her dark little pointed chin; she never finished a bottle, never fretted for food, never cried. But sometimes over her olive face a toothless shadow of a smile would break, when Aunt Lou picked her up.

The crash in the family fortunes came, when Bertie had to find a new position. He finally placed himself with Le Breton, the big paper house in Sansom Street, his salary little more than half its former size, his life strangely altered from what it had been as the grandson and heir of old Reuben Crabtree. Lola, who had always indifferently handed her checks to Bertie, went on serenely charging and wasting, she took almost no interest in the change.

But Lou showed a certain silent sympathy with her brother, and often led him into discussion of the new work and the new environment. She would place the lean little olive-skinned baby in his arms, at night, or call him upstairs to see Nita mothering her rag baby.

She wrote Vicky, briefly, that she wished she was dead. "But what's the difference?" added Lou, drearily. "Life doesn't last forever!" Her days were tiresome rounds of domestic drudgery, endless dusting and washing of dishes, making of beds, marketing, care of the baby. A deep and an intense dislike of Lola darkened and made even less endurable everything she did.

However, it was better than home; and Lou, at twenty-six, knew herself to be an old maid without means, and therefore specially blessed in having a living at all. She lived with Lola without friction, only by heroically effacing herself in every possible way. She had no position here, the very slattern in the kitchen was more independent, but she did not know what else to do. Papa and Mama were having trouble enough to keep themselves afloat now.

So Lou silently worked and brooded, wheeling Nita out into the side garden to sleep in the shade, pouring kettlefuls of hot water over the pink cups and the green dishes, whipping up beds and wiping down chair-legs. Sometimes there was a maid, sometimes none; to Lola it made no difference whatever, to Lou it was the vital fact of life.

The house was too large, cold, and sunless: they all hated it. Lou lived with the baby in the kitchen: the only bright room in the house. Down the steep, hilly slopes to the bay, she could look through gnarled and sprawling oaks to blue water; she could look up from darning or reading, and see the ferry-boats going to and fro past Alcatraz.

She got up early, had her coffee with Bertie at half-past-seven; Nita, in the high chair, would suck solemnly on a crust. Bertie departed; Lou gathered up breakfast china, and carried it into the kitchen. The maid of the moment would have started to furnish Lola's tray; Lou would finish the job, and carry it in to Bertie's wife. Lola would roll over, perhaps peevish and sallow, perhaps good-natured, with colour in her dark cheeks.

"What do you think of my dreaming again about that same place, on a beach, and that same man that was riding a white horse?" Lola might begin. The price of her good-nature was that Lou should sit leisurely at the foot of the bed and listen to dreams, to imaginary tales of Lola's prowess and conquests, for the better part of an hour. Nita would wail from the dining room, hammering with a napkin ring. "Let her cry," her mother would say with an impish grin; "it's good for babies that they cry!"

A mischievous, elfish naughtiness was Lola's favourite pose; she always wanted an audience. If Lou would sit there, interpolating half-shocked, half-amused, and wholly admiring comments of "Lola, how could you! Good gracious, what a gipsy you were! I never *heard* of such a flirt!" then Lola was happy. She would sit up in bed, hugging her knees, her narrow, rather plain face glowing, her gaiety almost wild.

But if Lou was practical, in a hurry, with a hundred things to do, then Lola sulked, sniffed, and too often vented her mood upon Bertie or the innocent Nita. She would slap the baby angrily, and when Nita shrieked, slap her again. They had hideous battles, for Lola's rages were battles, in which Bertie and Lou were helpless, and these rages were things to be avoided at any cost. At the slightest provocation she was enraged. Lola screaming that she would *make* the baby mind her, was a Lola that Bertie and Lou wished never to see.

So Lou drilled herself to be amused, indulgent, interested in seeming, at least. And frequently she won Lola to sweet and merry humours, in which Lola wanted to give the baby a taste of cognac, or dress the little creature in floods of fine Spanish lace and rosettes of bright blue baby ribbon, with a too large embroidered cap coasting over the indifferent little face.

Bertie's wife was an egotist, but one thing in the world interested her. She never read a paper or anything but the frothiest of novels; she made no friends. But she liked to go to her aunts, because they and the servants spoiled her and talked incessantly about her, and she loved to enter such shops in the city as bore the sign: *Habla Aqui Español*, and delight and amaze the swarthy clerks with her liquid Spanish.

Once or twice, when Lou had superintended a carefully planned company dinner for Bertie's men friends, with "Tipo" wine and finger bowls, she and Bertie had had oddly embarrassing experiences with the mistress of the house.   Bertie's men friends, warmed by wine and good food, had been inclined to find Lola rather fascinating; her chatter, her pretty groping for English words, and the knowledge that she was an heiress.   And Lola had taken the centre of the stage confidently, laughing, flirting a big fan, adding extravagance to extravagance in her conversation.

Bertie had asked Lou to play "El Capitan" for them: he loved—all the world loved, the new Sousa marches.   But before Lou could move, Lola had flashed to the piano, to rattle through one convent "exhibition piece" after another; until, indeed, everyone was bored and satiated with music.   Then she had sung, with tremendous rolling of eyes and with bursts of significant laughter.   And finally, on one uncomfortable evening, she had danced to her own humming, snapping her fingers, whirling her body dizzily, and seriously disarranging her clothes, so that the exposure of brown breast and lace petticoat highly discomfited Lou and Bertie.

The men had clapped, of course.   But they had not come again; the pleasant little American-English colony of Sausalito did not assimilate Mrs. Albert Brewer, although the grave and dignified Lou was always welcome to reading classes and mothers' meetings.

"I can't understand why the men aren't after you!" Lola would say to Lou, teasingly.   "Me—if I wasn't married, they would be like the bees after the honey!   In Buenos Aires—do you think a girl can get to be as old as you are and not marry? She must enter the convent if she is to do like that!"

"I'll surprise you, one of these days," Lou would answer smiling, with the patience she would have shown to a child of four. She tried to remind herself of Lola's good points; she was generous, she was absolutely indifferent to money, she adored Bertie. And she was amazingly inexacting; if the morning came when Lou simply could not force herself to carry in the breakfast tray, Lola did not complain; meals could be at any hour, any food was satisfying.

Not long after Nita's first birthday, on a warm, balmy Saturday morning in Holy Week, they all went up to the ranch.   Two of the old Señoritas had died and been buried a few weeks before; Lola had grieved passionately and violently, but she was in great spirits to-day, and little Nita very engaging in white stockings and caped coat. Lou and Bertie were later to drive to their mother's house for Sunday supper; they were accompanying Lola and the baby merely as escort to-day.

Lola's uncle, the generous source of her large income, had come to California for the first visit in twenty years, just in time to see his aunts again, and was lingering on at the ranch; a dark-skinned, gray-moustached old cavalier who looked much more than his fifty years. He murmured Spanish with the surviving Señoritas, picked his teeth with a beautifully chased ivory and silver pick, smoked without ceasing, ate and drank heartily, and in three weeks had not been a hundred feet from the house.

The arriving Brewers had the usual welcome: tears, laughter, shrieked blessings. Refugio and 'Ception rarely moved from their chairs now; the old dogs, or their descendants, waddled lazily about, the room smelled of them.

Señor Pio Tasheira seemed pleased to see his niece, and played amiably with the baby. Lola as usual collapsed; she changed her clothes for a loose wrapper, and sank into a deep chair, in the midst of her relatives. Bertie and Lou, when the exemplary baby was asleep, walked over the ranch in the sweet spring afternoon. Green fresh grass was high, the fruit trees were in leaf. Ascension lilies were blooming in the neglected garden. Bertie and Lou poked over the sheds and outhouses, peeped into the old *casa*, stepped cautiously past chicken yards and pig pens, and skirted once more the stiff, churned black mud of the cow corral. They could look down, hanging on the rail fence in the shade of the peppers, to the file of gaunt eucalyptus marching to the bay. The marshes were green to-day, the water beyond them a hazy blue. Back of all were the smooth curves of the hills. To the south, beyond the bay, San Francisco lay in a tangle of smoke and of sun dazzle, on roof-covered hills.

"Funny, isn't it?" Bertie mused; "I remember coming here to Ruy da Sã's funeral——"

"I remember coming here for a walk with Rudy and Nelly and Vick and Davy, before any of them were married," Lou said.

For a few minutes they were silent; then Bertie said again:

"It's funny. I mean the way life goes," he added hastily. "I remember seeing Lola that day. But I was in love with somebody else then."

"Kitty!" Lou supplied.

"Yes, Kitty. She married Neil, you know. She has two kids. I saw her the other day—she's awfully nice——"

"But why didn't you marry her, Bertie?"

"Oh, Mama, I guess. Mama made me promise once not to see her for two months. And Papa talked to me about it, on the boat, and said I would always regret it." Bertie flung away his cigarette. "I used to go to sleep at night," he confessed, "thinking how nice it'd be if Mama met her somewhere by accident, and Kitty did her some favour—don't you know?"

"I know . . ." Lou said thoughtfully.

"Lola—she's all right," Bertie said suddenly. "She has been a little spoiled, I guess; she's young. And then having a baby is a good deal of a strain."

"Having *hers* wasn't," Lou countered flatly. "Poor little Nita didn't weigh four pounds. And Vick's boy weighed eleven!"

"Lou, were you ever in love?" Bertie asked, half-laughing.

"No. And never will be!" his sister answered promptly and unemotionally.

"Not even with Palmer?"

"Heavens, no!"

They hung on the rail fence, staring down at the bay and the hills, past the file of eucalyptus.

"It's funny," Bertie said again, after a pause.

Señor Tasheira was on the porch as they came in; Lou sat down on a gaunt old wicker rocker; Bertie went in to his wife.

"Don't you ever walk, Señor Tasheira?"

"My dear young lady, no. Sometimes I ride, yes. But not the walks!"

"You've been to our beautiful park and the seal rocks, in San Francisco?" Lou asked.

"Not since I was the child. They do not interest me."

"Oh, come!" protested Lou. "We cannot let you go back to South America without at least showing you how many beauties we have. Some day I shall take you for a day's trip."

"You couldn't get him to go with you for money!" Lola said, coming out. Her uncle gave her his chair, and kissed her finger-tips. Lou's face grew red.

"Sometimes when the beautiful young lady take me on a trip

it is the money she make love to, and not me!" remarked the Argentinian, laughing.

"Oh, what a terribly ungallant thing to say!" Lou exclaimed lightly. "Lola, why don't you scold him?"

"The old man does not make to be always polite," Pio said, pleased with his English.

"Don't call yourself old!" Lou protested. "You are not more than forty!"

"More than that!" he said, smiling in gratification.

Lola, with a scornful look at Lou, jabbered to him in Spanish.

"I told him that you knew perfectly well he was fifty-one," she said to Lou. "We were speaking of it in the train!"

"You *aren't*," Lou said to the man. Señor Tasheira smiled, shrugged, and lighted a cigarette. Conversation died, and after a few minutes, Lou, humming lightly, went into the house to change her dress for dinner.

At dinner he sat between Miss Refugio and Lola, but Lou was opposite, and she watched him with bright, sympathetic eyes. As the meal warmed, with wine and talk, she seemed to hear everything he had to say. And finally, leaning across Bertie, she said:

"Don't forget that you said we were to go to the Cliff House some day, Señor Tasheira!"

"Oh, no, Señorita, it was you who said that!" he countered quickly, his shrewd eyes dancing. And he turned to his aunt with some words in Spanish. Bertie glanced quickly at Lou, but decided that he must be mistaken as to the exact purport of the words, for Lou was placidly continuing her *tamale*. But later, when Lou was at the piano, Pio sauntered over to it. Lou went through the long window to the narrow porch, and Pio followed her.

"I don't like to see a man as handsome as you are, all alone," Lou said to him immediately, in a low tone. "You are too young and too good looking not to have a wife and a home!"

"And my money, he is good looking, too, is that it?" Pio laughed, excited with wine, and enjoying this fencing with Bertie's pretty sister.

"Someone to travel with—to talk to; someone to whom you would be the whole world!" Lou murmured, standing at the rail, with the man close behind her. "What good does your money do you? You need someone to entertain your friends, someone to make you a home——"

"You are trying to make flirtation with me, and I don't like that you should do that!" Pio interrupted, uneasily.

"Why should I flirt with you?" Lou asked, glancing over a bare shoulder, below which her round, firm arm disappeared into an enormous puff of stiffened silk. Her dark eyes glinted in the spring dusk.

"I don't know why you shall, for I do not wish that I shall ever marry, me. I am the bachelor!" Pio exclaimed.

"Not me, but some other woman," Lou conceded negligently. "There must be a great many pretty women in the Argentine!"

"Because they marry the money, not me!" he said, angrily.

"A wife, a home, someone to talk to, someone to buy pretty things for, and have other men admire——" Lou persisted.

"Tio Pio!" Lola laughed, coming out the hall door, suspicious eyes on Lou. He caught at her arm with a little breath of relief, and did not leave her again that evening.

But the next day, when Bertie and Lou were going off in the phaeton, for supper with their mother, Señor Tasheira was on the porch, even though it was the hour of the sacred siesta, to say a parting word.

"Me—I shall bring Lola and the baby home on the Tuesday," he said.

"Thank you, Uncle Pio!" Bertie said. Lou laughed.

"'Uncle' sounds too old!" she said. "Shall I see you to-morrow?"

"No, because I shall send Carlotta up from the train," he answered. "I shall wait at the station. I am too old for climbing hills!"

"And what about our little day in the city?" Lou asked, pleasantly persuasive. "There's Chinatown—and then we might have a little bite of lunch, and then drive out to the cliff!"

"Thank you so much, Señorita, but I see him long ago, and I do not wish that I shall see him again!"

"Well, I'll say Friday, just in case you change your mind!" said Lou. "Friday on the ten o'clock boat. And this is my day, you know—you will be my guest!"

"I am afraid I cannot come!"

"Lou!" Bertie shouted, from the phaeton seat.

"I'm coming!—I'll be on the ten o'clock boat, anyway!" Lou murmured, running down the steps.

"Do you like him, Lou?" Bertie asked curiously, as the mare lurched on her way. Lou laughed heartily, with sudden colour. But she made no other answer.

They reached the Brewer house at five o'clock, and were duly kissed and welcomed. Tina, in a trailing gray challis, was setting the supper table; May and Fanny were on the side porch; Stephen was whittling a "Fifteen Puzzle" for little Bobo. Old Reuben, it appeared, had just been taken upstairs, and it would be better not to disturb him. He sometimes slept through all the dark hours unbrokenly.

"Carra has a cot in his room; dear, devoted old woman, I don't think she'll long survive him!" said May. "Think of it, Lou, eighty-four this year!"

"Can't we start a scandal between him and Carra?" Bertie said, with his boyish laugh. Fanny shot him a sudden glance, but nobody else paid any attention; it was a recognized fact now that Bertie was always light-hearted on these visits at home.

"And how's Lola, dear?" May pursued dutifully. "And the dear little baby?"

"Lovely! Lola's always saying that she's coming to see you, Mama, but you know how hard it is. She's busy——" Bertie's eye met Lou's quiet, reflective look, and he amended it quickly, "or she thinks she is!"

"Some talk of Davy Dudley coming down to practise with that Doctor Dunham!" Fanny said, beating her nose. "I tell May that Vicky'd be crazy to let him. What does he know about operations, anyway! He's much better off in a small town, if you ask me!"

"I wrote her that they must use their own judgment," May said, mildly, "but that on *no* account ought a man leave his wife and baby, even for a time! Her baby is a fine-looking child—Tina's got the picture in the dining room, I guess!"

Lou went in to find her sister, busy among the familiar chairs and plates; the old spoon mug, the old napkin rings.

"Tina—the table looks sweet! Vernon coming?"

"Well, he is, as it happens," Tina said, with a toss of her head. "But I didn't put the flowers on for that!"

"I hope that if he asks you, you'll be sensible, Tina," Lou suggested, seated, and nibbling cheese.

"Oh, my dear! He's not apt to ask *me*," Tina said airily. "I assure you that I don't count—any more! It's Florence, and dear Aunt Florrie—and presents—I wish you could see the White House boxes of clothes for Alma!"

"Mrs. Lundeen?" Lou said reflectively. "Is she rich, Teen?"

"Oh, rich! She has one of the hotel cottages, and everything. When I think of Grace," Tina added, beginning to throw knives about recklessly, and with a sort of harsh brightness that somehow suggested Fanny, "it just makes me *sick*! She's there, at the Parsonage, *all* the time, and of course she has the baby—idolizes her. I notice she wasn't so awfully nice to Grace, though! There wasn't so much talk of presents and Aunt Florrie *then*! I suppose Vernon thinks that if he could land a rich widow it would all be smooth sailing—well, all I can say is, I hope he *does*! I just hope he does! He'll see—shh-shh—that's the gate!"

Lou had not seen the clergyman since his bereavement in January. She went out to say a few sympathetic words to him.

"He has set us all an example in bravery!" May said, motherly and smiling.

"No, no," Vernon Yelland quickly disclaimed it. "No, but I was the closest friend and companion of a brave and noble heart for five years, Lou," he added, simply and gravely, "and what can I be but brave?"

And he went in, with the intimacy of an old friend, to have a few minutes with Tina before supper began.

Tina bloomed into her prettiest aspect as she took her place beside him.

"Vernon, I was thinking——" she began, over the salad.

"Well, that's edifying!" he commented, with a grave smile. Everybody laughed.

"No, but I was thinking I might come in to see you about the reredos to-morrow," the girl suggested, flushing happily.

"To-morrow—Monday, h'm!" he mused. "I believe my little people have a plan afoot for a picnic to-morrow," he remembered, his eyes narrowed smilingly on space. "I try to be with them—now. And I heard a great deal to-day about basket-luncheons—I don't know quite what. But how is Tuesday?"

Tina, limp, lifeless, agreed to Tuesday.

Louisianna Brewer walked on to the ten o'clock boat on Friday morning without a backward glance. It was an unusually warm morning, and the girl was charming in a flaring skirt of white duck, trimly drawn in to the white satin belt that neatly finished her pink shirtwaist. Her hat was a dashing, rough-edged sailor, with a pink band, and a black chatelaine bag was secured to her belt by its metal clasp. In the bag was her usual shopping list. "Shoes, Nolan and Descalso, paper, Coopers, library book."

She opened a book: "The Duchess," by "The Duchess," and selecting a seat in the shade, against the cabin wall, composed herself quietly to read.

Groups passed her, shopping women, men whose hours were those of ease and leisure. A man alone——

"Good morning, Señorita!"

Lou closed the book; smiled a wise smile. She slightly shifted the white duck skirt so that he might sit beside her.

They wandered through noisy, crowded, odorous, fascinating Chinatown, they lunched in the Palace Grill. And in the afternoon they drove out through the Park.

Lou did not have much to say; she asked an occasional question, smiled an occasional rebuke. Parting with her companion in Sausalito, in the mellow lights and shadows of five o'clock, she made no further attempt at an engagement.

She knew it was not necessary. She knew that the memory of this day's companionship would accompany Pio Tasheira to the lonely ranch, that the picture of a fresh, erect young figure in duck and pink gingham would contrast itself over and over again with the bulgy old figures and oily old faces of Refugio and 'Ception.

Lola was furious with her when she reached home.

"That girl didn't come back, and there's not one bit of butter in this whole house——"

"I brought the butter!" Lou was rapidly divesting herself of best clothes. "You sweet lamb!" she murmured, catching up Nita's wiry and agile little form. "I'll manage all this, Lolita.

You set the table—if you want to. Whatever became of Carrie? How have you done your hair?"

"That's the real Spanish fashion!" Lolita, instantly pacified, stated laughingly. "Well, what do you think of me?" she asked, catching up a fan, and giving Lou a flirtatious glance over it. "Oh, what a devil I was in school! Those poor nuns! I used to dress up like this——"

Lou lifted a stove-lid, began to pick out smoking charred kindling and half-burned paper. The wretched thing was drawing badly again——

A night or two later Pio Tasheira came to dinner, driving one of the Señorita's old horses down from the ranch. Lola was in a contrary mood this evening, would not be gracious, and went early to bed. Bertie, worried by her temper, followed her. But Lou and Pio murmured over the piano for half an hour longer, and then sat talking on the porch for a full hour after that. Lola was awakened by the clatter and rattle of the departing phaeton, and next morning was curious and cross.

"What on earth were you and Uncle Pio talking about?" she queried.

"Oh, I don't know!" Lou's tone was indifferent. But when Pio arrived for supper again on the following Friday night, tired from a day in town exactly as Lou was tired from a day in town, Lola's dark and incredulous suspicions were suddenly aroused. Had they met in town? she asked.

Uncle Pio pursed his lips, shook his head.

"We meet on the boat!" he presently announced, with every sign of secret mischief.

"Coming or going?" Lola further inquired, too cross to be diplomatic. Again Pio looked mysterious, but he did not answer her.

"Look here, this some of the Spanish Inquisition now!" he commented chuckling.

Lola determined to take a hand in this matter herself. The next time she had her uncle to herself, which was more than a fortnight later, she casually took occasion to tell him of Lou's unfortunate experience with Howard Palmer, and of her own impression that Lou was anxious to get married, and would not mind making a fool of any old man she could find.

But Lou had long before this confidentially informed Pio of the Palmer episode, and had learned in return of a beautiful married woman in Rosarios, who had tried to involve Pio in some wretched implications, and had more than partially succeeded. So that he listened to his alarmed and anxious niece only with his cryptic and Latin smile; deeply offended by her use of the word "old" but showing no trace of anything but his usual insouciant calm.

Lou, with her soft, light-brown hair, her pink cheeks, her serene smile, looked more attractive than ever to him, as she came in with Nita, interrupting this conversation, and leaving the darkly flushed and trembling Lola no course but to retire from the field.

Lou kept her own counsel, as she always had, receiving Pio's flowers with no comment for the frantically curious Lola, destroying the Argentinian's letters as soon as they were read. She went to town, as always, on Fridays, and, as always, had nothing to say at the supper table of her day's employment. Lou began to speed the plans for her uncle's return to South America. It could not be—it could not be—that there was anything serious in this ridiculous business! He was just playing with Lou, as Howard Palmer had played!

One brilliant June morning, when Lou brought Bertie the morning paper, to enjoy with his coffee, she pointed out a glaring headline that occupied a conspicuous place on the first page.

"Young Grass Widow—Childless—Kidnaps Clergyman's Babe—" he skimmed hastily. "Florence Lundeen Asserts Her Love for Yelland Child. Wanted Merely Something to Play With, Father's Love-making Unwelcome, Asserts Pretty Ex-wife of Harry Lundeen."

"For Heaven's sake!" ejaculated Bertie laughing.

"No, but read it, Bertie!"

"'Residents of San Rafael are deeply interested in the alleged abduction of Baby Alma Yelland by pretty Florence Underwood Lundeen,'" Bertie read. "'Mrs. Lundeen's devotion, to the child has dated since its birth, and the mother's death, last January. Baby Alma has made her home with the wealthy young widow, at the Hotel, until last Wednesday, when Mrs. Lundeen, according to assertions made by the child's father, on her own initiative removed the baby to her summer cottage at Fallen Leaf Lake. The father, the Reverend Vernon Yelland, immediately placed the case before the authorities, who sent for the child.'

"'Mrs. Lundeen, upon being approached last evening by Deputy Sheriff George T. Bonnet, of Marin County, admitted that she had carried away Baby Alma without the father's consent.

"'"I love the child," she asserted, "but I was not interested in the father's love-making, and was practically driven away from San Rafael by his attentions."

"'Baby Alma is to be restored to her father to-day.'

"Well, *that*—" began Bertie, with deep relish, "that will about cook our dear Vernon as far as Tina's concerned! What possesses women to fall for those clergymen——"

"Poor old Teen!" Lou smiled. "That's the last straw! But she'll have some excuse ready—you'll see!"

And she expressed no surprise when a busy, important ecstatic letter arrived from Tina, three or four days later.

"Lou darling," Tina wrote, "you will have seen the terrible behaviour of Mrs. Lundeen described in the papers; our darling Alma was safely returned to us on Saturday afternoon, Vernon and I meeting the boat and bringing her straight to Mama, where the other dear children were awaiting. What a meeting, as their devoted father gathered them together again! Vernon is splendid about Florence's lies and insinuations; he says he cannot imagine what he ever said or did to give her any impression except that his first thought was for the children's good.

"And now, dear, for my happy news, happiness strangely mingled with sorrow, for the memory of Grace must always be one of the precious things of life. It is only six months since our angel left us, yet, as Vernon[1] says, in the case of small children there must be special laws, and this last disgraceful experience has taught him how difficult his pathway is—alone. Lou, dear, after next Monday, it is not to be alone. I have always loved him as a brother, and now that love is something deeper and truer than life itself. We feel that the right and dignified thing to do is to stand before the world in all truth and honour as man and wife, and then unscrupulous adventuresses like Mrs. L. cannot touch him. To the curious press he will give this announcement, hushing up the Mrs. L. affair once and for all.

"My wedding is to be a very simple one, under the trees of the old home, with Papa to give me away, and the white gown that I was already making, my wedding dress. And my wedding trip will be only to the dear new home that has been like a second home to me for so many years!

"Vernon is—not happy, he says, but deeply, and holily, content. Grace would have wished this, we both feel. And to Papa and Mama he says that they do not so much lose a daughter as gain a son. Dear Reverend Harvey Manson, who married Grace and Vernon, will come down from Sacramento to marry us."

Lou read the letter aloud to Bertie and Lola, half-laughing, half-sympathetic.

"I ought to go home to help them out," she said, smiling.

"I'd like to!" Bertie had a sudden pang of homesickness for Mama and the girls, for the old days of spoiling and freedom.

Lola seized upon this pretext eagerly. She wanted to go to the ranch anyway; Tia Refugio was seriously ill, and Uncle Pio—she shot a glance at Lou—would soon be going away again. Bertie and Lou could spend a week or ten days at home, and she would visit her aunts.

CHAPTER XXVIII

SO LOU and Bertie, in unwonted holiday spirits, took Nita to her grandfather's house, to share the excitements of Aunt Tina's wedding. The summer sun was shining warmly down upon the shabby old mansion when they came in at the peeled and weather-worn gate.

It was late afternoon, slanting shafts of light came down through willow and pepper trees, the air was sweet with roses, dust, and watered grass. Bobo and Stephen were watering and raking busily; they called and waved a welcome, and little Nita's grandfather led her about admiringly from one garden sight to another, his big figure stooped sideways to accommodate her fairy-like smallness. Nita looked solemnly down at Bobo's bantam hen and up at the wooden horse's head over the old stable door. Bobo pushed open the old entrance and she peeped into bare gloom sweetly scented with dry grain and mysterious with the scurry of rats. After awhile she whispered that she wanted "Doo-doo!" and her dark little face twisted with agonized tears.

"I know, Uncle Steve!" Bobo said eagerly. "She calls Lou 'Doo-doo'!" And he bundled her into his awkward, short little arms, her brief skirts twisted about her bare little brown knees, and carried her, panting manfully, in to Lou.

Lou was in the very centre of delicious womanly conference. Mis' Underwood was there, fitting Tina to a blue sateen; her cold scissors touching the warm smooth flesh of Tina's arm. Fanny was idle at the sewing machine; May in a rocker with a lapful of white sewing. They were upstairs, in the room Vick and Lou had shared for so many years; it was a scene of utter confusion now. On the bed, in a jumble of new table linen, and new night-gowns, and new hat box, were two or three small green boxes and dark-red baize bags, from Shreves, holding the Wesley's pie knife, and the Baker's carvers, and the lovely spoons from Fanny and Frank Pembroke. Tina, looking over a bare shoulder, called Lou's attention to the Persons' chocolate set and the tongs from Alice and Frank Babcock.

The bride elect was radiant, with a sort of solemn and intense radiance sacred to this time alone. She must remember everything; she must think for everyone; she must always be serene and sweet. Arriving friends kissed her, and the admiring family gathered about in deep interest whenever a present or a letter arrived. Tina's look was brightly dutiful. "Yes, Mama dear? What is it, Papa darling?" her sweet voice echoed all day. She tripped happily to and fro, and always ready with a smile that was close to tears, or the hint of tears that a smile made sweet, when the approaching change was mentioned.

"I've written Nelly, at San Bruno, and Alice, and I do hope Vick can come down!" she told Lou. "It's such a poor little wedding, as far as money and style go, that I want it rich in love!"

"Who but my Tina would say that?" May said, fondly. Tina, freed from the dressmaker, ran to kneel beside her, with a little emotion.

"Mama dearest, you praise me too much!"

"Ah, no, I don't!" May said, sighing heavily, as she pushed back the fair, rather lifeless hair. "Well, you're not going very far from poor Mama!" she added, smiling through tears.

"And you already love my Vernon, don't you?" Tina asked coquettishly. "She flirts with him!" she told Lou.

"I kind of think he likes his poor old mother-in-law," May confessed, smiling. "Hold that up against yourself, dear. Lou, is that long enough?"

"There, that's your wedding nighty!" Fanny exclaimed suddenly, adding a beribboned garment to a snowy heap. "Far and away the prettiest of the lot!" Lou's eyes went to Tina's, and then to her mother's; all three looked conscious. But May saved the moment by saying affectionately:

"Not many girls are as lucky as Tina, with an aunty to give them so many pretty things!"

"Do let's go over this list, Mama!" Tina urged, the scarlet colour ebbing slowly from her face.

"Think of me, with only one girl left!" May mused, for the hundredth time. "I think I must be a managing mama!"

The shabby old thready carpet of the room was littered with bits of ribbon, material, and cotton, but it was to be all cleaned to-morrow, for guests would be put in here in a day or two. Everyone was busy; women, passing each other in halls, laughingly explained their errands.

"I'm just taking this rubbish down—I'm just after the ladder to straighten that curtain—I'm just going to the door—someone's ringing!"

May could rattle off any list almost automatically.

"The sandwiches, four kinds, oyster patties, the cakes, the ice-cream—we don't have to worry about that!—coffee, chocolate, lemonade—there was something else—there was something else—oh, yes, salad. And Fanny suggested olives and mottoes—Bertie said he would get them. And I've got it on my list to count the napkins——"

Or, if the query was different, she could say just as readily, in an abstracted voice:

"Bobo in our room, with Papa and me, Bertie on the hall lounge, Vicky in Esme's room, if she comes, Lou and Tina in Tina's room—dear Tina, her last night in the old home!—Rob in the sewing-room, and Lucy in Bertie's old room—if she comes. Then I have the double mattress from Pa's room for Nelly, in the playroom, and Carra will go upstairs——"

Too quickly the bright days fled, and it was only three days to Tina's wedding—only two—it was "to-morrow"! Tina continued "wonderful;" here she was, in her simple little cotton frock, arranging ferns and roses in the parlour, with no other helper than Vernon Yelland!

"Tina!" her mother said, happily scandalized, one arm about her. "Why, what would people think of a bride and groom doing their own decorating! Don't you know that you two aren't supposed to see each other at all until to-morrow?"

"That will do for fashionable weddings, Mama," Tina said, lovingly, "but Vernon isn't getting a fashionable wife!"

"He's satisfied," Vernon said for himself, blinking through glasses and brushing wet rose-leaves from his hands. He was radiantly the expectant husband; Tina laughed in confidence to Lou that he was *already* saving her fatigue and strain.

"He says he doesn't want a tired-out little wife!" she quoted merrily.

Vera and little Vernon were playing with Bobo and Nita. The Yelland baby had been hospitably taken off their hands by a kindly parish matron. Everything was fragrant of roses, everything was thrilling and wonderful. All doors were open, all windows, and in every room laughing persons were busy at delightful things. They admired each other's handiwork; the cake frosting, the arrangement of roses and ferns, the lovely spaciousness of the old parlour when the piano was pushed back and the lounge taken upstairs.

There were shrieks at the front door, laughter, and the noise of kisses. Nelly——! The girls welcomed her with embraces and exclamations. And this beautiful thing with her must be Hildegarde!

Nelly was stouter, but she looked pale from the hot walk. Her hair had lost its fly-away golden shine: she seemed oddly shabby and slipshod; her hat was not so much old as badly worn and cheap, her shirtwaist pulled away from the heavy serge skirt that sagged to the ground in back. She had lost a front tooth, which made her a little self-conscious; she kept twisting her face involuntarily to show the complete side of her mouth, and her fingers went to the gap whenever any one looked at her directly.

Hildegarde was exquisite: slender, solemn and fairy-like at seven, with deep violet eyes in fainter rings of violet shadow, a skin of amber, a proud aristocratic mouth, not too small, teeth that were white and square between scarlet lips, and a glorious mane of deep gold hair waving in a mass off her soft forehead and curling into bright tips on her shoulders. Her cleft chin was clean cut and well raised, her figure erect and beautifully modelled; for the first half-hour she was like an awed and silent little princess. Bobo reported that she did not talk at all when he took her out to play.

"She's a queer one," Nelly laughed. "Deep. Even Rudy can't do much with her when she gets mad. He gave her an awful whipping last night; she was sassy to him, and Rudy won't stand that! She was sorter fooling, I guess, and she called him a 'sucker.' I don't think she meant anything, but he begun licking her, and then she'd yell it all the more. Do you think he could stop her? There's nobody could when she gets started. But Yetta—she's the girl I have now, only pay her fifteen a month—she's a little crazy—she began to yell at him that there was a man outside wanted to see him, and then she sneaked Hilda out the back way. But she's a good child, Hilda is," Nelly went on, to correct a possible misrepresentation, "she's lots of help with the others. And she's crazy about the baby——"

"My land, I don't see how you can keep track of the babies!" Fanny said, with her harsh, bright laugh. "How many are there now?"

"Just the four, besides her," Nelly said, surprised. "There's the three boys, Cliffy, Lloydy, and Stuart, and then Maybelle. They're all well, except Lloydy—he has sore eyes all the time. It makes him stupid, the poor little fellow. I don't have much trouble with them. I thought Mama might come to me, when Georgie acted so terrible to her, last fall, but she says she has friends in Sacramento."

Fanny sniffed, looked expectantly at May. But Lou quite innocently interrupted.

"What did Georgie do, Nelly?"

"Oh, didn't they tell you?" Nelly wiped Hildegarde's nose, hard. "Why, since Papa seems to be so unsettled in Los Angeles, or wherever he is," she said, "and Georgie was doing so well—he's bought his hardware shop!—Mama went down to visit him. And—this neighbouring lady told her, first, that he was married to a girl—well, I guess she wasn't straight. Wasn't that it, Aunt May? A girl named Dessy Tate. Mama walked about a mile to find his new shop, and it was one of the hottest days of the year, and when she got there Georgie wasn't there— or else he was, I forget how it was, and poor Mama was almost fainting, and she wanted to come in and sit down—no, that's how it was, Georgie wasn't there, but this girl was, and she said —it seems—to Mama, that she was Mrs. Crabtree and Mama said something, Georgie says that she insulted his wife, and said that she was no better than she should be, or something like that—anyway when Georgie came back she had locked the door——"

"I heard she called out of the window all sorts of lies about your mother!" Fanny supplemented.

"Well, anyway," Nelly said, "Mama had to go into a neighbour's house, and they gave her water, she was almost fainting by that time, and they told her a lot about this Dessy—that she was pretty bad, I guess. And after awhile Georgie came over, and Mama wouldn't see him—and I think this girl—she is his wife all right—came after him—I forget just how it was. I know it was before my Maybelle was born, because Vicky and Georgie's wife and I were all that way. But her baby died, we heard. Look at my stocking!" interrupted Nelly, pulling the black web up over her leg. "I gave Cliffy my garter when we were getting dressed this morning. My land, I didn't think we could get away at all!"

"Rubber neck!" Hildegarde shrilled from the window, to Bobo, outside. The unexpected sound made all the women laugh.

"She's a terror to pick things up!" Nelly admitted. "That's the latest—she'll yell that at everyone. That's not ladylike, Hilda," she chided the child. "Why don't you go out and play with the nice little boy? And button your shoe. Rudy was wild at my leaving," she admitted further, "but I hadn't been anywhere for so long I just had to come! If he doesn't like it he can lump it."

"If your mother's in Sacramento she probably won't come," Fanny suggested, expectantly.

"I don't know just where Mama is," Nelly answered innocently. "Well—let's talk about Tina. Getting married tomorrow, huh? I like the style! And starting in with three children—that beats me!"

"We think that dear Mrs. Manson may take little Alma for awhile; they have no children," Tina said, in a motherly tone; "that would leave me only the older two, and little Vernon is nearly four now, so that there really isn't so much to do. I am going to teach them both, and Vernon says he will help——" Tina broke off for a playful laugh. "I can't do much these days without the offer of an assistant!" she complained happily. "But I really thought that I might teach other children," she added, "because, with four of us, a hundred and ten dollars a month isn't one bit too much! And besides that, in that way I would keep in close touch with the little unfolding souls and minds—what are you laughing at?" she broke off to ask Nelly.

"Nothing—except that you're so killing!" Nelly answered good-naturedly.

"Here's a little girl that has lost her tongue!" May said, to the silently staring Hildegarde. "Tell me how many little brothers and sisters you've got?" she coaxed.

"I have Cliffy and Lloydy 'cept he's got sore eyes and Stuart and my baby Maybill!" Hildegarde answered suddenly and unexpectedly, marking with a dirty little finger the pattern of

May's old sateen. "And Mama said she would have had six children 'cept that the time the horse ran away—back when I lived on a ranch—and she had a miss! And the day Maybill was born a man came after Papa and Yetta yelled at him he ought to be ashamed of hisself!"

She finished this extraordinary recital triumphantly, and again subsided into an admiring silence. May cleared her throat; she hardly knew what to say. Tina looked distinctly embarrassed and Fanny scandalized, but Lou merely laughed.

"Isn't she a holy terror?" Nelly said, with something also triumphant in her mild deprecation. "Run along, Hilda," she added, "see what a pretty house Aunt May's got!"

Hilda departed on a tour of investigation. It seemed a palace to her. The rods on the old stairway, holding the worn brown strings of the original "body Brussels" in place, were alone a source of delight. The wooden slide between the dining room and kitchen she opened and shut forty times, sometimes running out into the kitchen to peep through it into the dining room, sometimes running back to peep into the kitchen again. And when she discovered that there was a back stairway, ascending into obscure upper hallways where the laundry basket and the bedroom broom and the carpet-sweeper and the rag-bag were huddled together with stacks of folded newspapers and empty cardboard boxes, she spent an ecstatic hour going solemnly up one stairway, discovering the other with a cry of delight, and going seriously down to rediscover the first again.

In the wedding excitement she and Bobo, with the blonde and tearful Vera, whom they both despised, had an exhilarating share. They tasted crushed "bouchettes," licked spoons and scraped bowls; Hilda had her first olive, and because the dashing and fascinating Lou had said carelessly, "Oh, olives! Delicious!" she knew that she ought to like the hard, bitter thing, and made a point of eating Bobo's, too, with firm scrapes of her white, square little teeth. Aunt Tina, who was going to be married to the man in the eyeglasses who was Vera's papa, said "eyethere" for "eether," and that he would "telegrarf Vick." Hildegarde altered her own vocabulary correspondingly; she was learning something every instant.

"Grammer," whom these people called "Lucy" and "Aunt Lucy," arrived with a large, dark, laughing man who was to be known as "Uncle Bob." Hildegarde was inclined to cling to her mother and grandmother, when darkness came, and she found herself still in this unfamiliar big place, among so many strange faces. After dinner she felt very hot and stuffed; she had eaten too many queer things; her clothes felt tight. She sat squeezed into a big armchair with Bobo, and Uncle Bob said he would show them how a regular Indian war-cry went.

But Bobo's rough little sleeve, behind her, was pulling against the fine floss of her hair, and his sturdy little body had coasted against her in a most uncomfortable way. Lights blazed in her eyes; she was dropping with fatigue. And a brown old woman— or was it a monkey in a red shawl and chocolate-coloured apron? —suddenly appeared, chattering something Hildegarde could not understand, but that Aunt May immediately interpreted by saying that they must make less noise, that dear Grandpa had been wakened up by the war-cry, and was talking about the Apaches.

She roused out of a sort of stupor, her little mouth sour from too much candy, her heavy eyes drooping. Someone with a baby had come flying in out of the hot summer dusk: another aunt. Aunt Vicky.

Everyone was making a great fuss over this aunt, who was dark and quick-mannered, with a laughing face. Everyone grabbed her serene, sleepy little boy, who was wearing the whitest coat and socks and bonnet Hildegarde had ever seen. There was great laughing and kissing——

Somebody was wiping Hildegarde's face with a wet, warm towel, somebody was raising her aching little arms to take off her dress. Vera was asleep in a nice, wide, low bed on the floor; Hilda was beside her, deliciously stretched; lights blazed, and were out. The last dreamy reality was Aunt Vicky's voice:

"He'll do beautifully there, Mama, the darling. He'd sleep if you hung him up on a hook! It's so wonderful to see you all! And think of to-morrow—and old Teen——"

There was a high fog the next morning, but by nine o'clock it was gone, and the old house stirred sunnily with happy events. The kitchen was very important, for everyone ate a casual breakfast there, and then everyone fell to making sandwiches. And after the kitchen there were last flowers and last touches, and then the final glory of dressing.

By this time superlatives were exhausted. Stephen was an

angel—Lou was just a darling—the dining-room looked simply gorgeous, the children were too utterly sweet!

The children, first dressed, sat primly on the front steps. Distracted elders rushed to and fro. Tina had disappeared into her bedroom, where most of the women were. Stephen with a broom mildly brushed a few leaves from the front path.

Lou had arranged Tina's hair; Vicky sat holding her baby and chattering; Tina was pale except for a blazing spot on each cheek; she looked oddly pretty with her faintly crimped hair. Fanny, in water-striped black silk rustled and sniffed. Lucy was self-possessed in a new plum-coloured sateen; May tremulous in gray silk.

"Bertie and Lola—" somebody announced from the window. May put the plain white muslin in a stiff ring over Tina's virginally bowed head; Tina's bare arms vanished; the effect for which Mis' Underwood had striven so gallantly was there, in all its beauty. The bretelles were straight, after all!

"Teen—you're going to be simply adorable!" the girls said, when the veil floated over the crimps.

"Am I?" Tina asked fixedly, faintly anxious, and not moving eyes or lips or head while the delicate business of adjustment was under way. Solemnly she revolved; and solemnly they chorused their admiration. Vicky, on the floor to straighten the bell-like flare of the hem, sat back on her heels, her eyes shining. She was so charming, now, this married Vicky, leaner, graver, more definite somehow; no longer the old restless egotistic Vicky; all the absorbed wife, daughter, and mother.

"Isn't she lovely, Mama? Proud of your bride?"

But May was in tears. It was time to go down, and down they all fluttered; a few friends—"just the precious few who *count*," Tina said—were waiting in the lower hall and the decorated parlour. Alice Babcock was there, looking oddly pale and strained; Lola's uncle was there, and walked with Lou.

"Just between Mama and Papa, as I've walked to church since my little baby days!" Tina said, emotionally. And between her mother and father she walked, a little white glove in Stephen's fatherly arm, May gathering her gray ruffles from the dust, beside her.

The others all preceded them: Lou talking quietly with Lola's funny Spanish uncle, Lola and Bertie on each side of Aunt Lucy. Fanny walked with Bob, finding nothing to say; the children boiled over the paths like weeds. Vicky and Alice murmured, Vicky apprehensive that her rioting baby would disgrace her in church.

Here they were; the little churchyard was full of loyal parishioners, the Hardisty girls were audibly admiring, summer gowns fluttered, and happy voices murmured a blessing on the bride. The strains of music wheezed through the warm, flower-scented air; dear Dora Manson was at the organ. And here were the altar-boys all in white, to lead the little procession, and form an aisle to the door.

Solemnly, sweetly, her head beautifully erect, her eyes exalted, Tina went through them all, was somehow in the dark, neat aisle, with Papa's shoes creaking decorously as he led her on. She knelt down in the front pew with Mama and Papa—it hadn't been arranged so, she thought, but no matter—she should have been the last one in, everyone should have been in place. She could hear them creaking and rustling in—it was ridiculous to have the bride already in full view, she murmured to her hammering heart. Never mind. Now what—did she stand up, or what? They had somehow mismanaged the whole thing! She should have come in on Papa's arm, and been handed straight over to Vernon—no matter.

She saw Vernon, murmuring to Lyn Hodges, his best man; Lyn was only twenty-two, and he had been three years in San Quentin Prison. Vernon was reforming him, and he had asked Tina if she would mind his showing Lyn his trust and affection by this great distinction. Tina did not like Lyn; there was something sly and loose and clammy and coarse about him, but she loved Vernon for the thought. Darling Vernon, she was going to be married to him——

He was coming toward her; she rose. And all through the rest of that happy, bewildering, memorable day the others told her how charming it was; that simple, graceful rising, that shy step toward him, that surrender of the little lisle glove. It was different from every other wedding that ever was; it was just too touching and wonderful, they said.

Seething like a boiling pot, the old house rang with laughter, tears, blessings, good wishes. Pretty gowns crushed pretty gowns, voices rose and fell. The happy hours flew by; it was afternoon, the guests melted away. Lucy was gone, and Bob was gone, and Nelly was gone with beautiful little Hildegarde.

Lola and her uncle and Bertie had disappeared, quiet began to fall upon the tired household. Alice had gone first of all. Tina took her husband's arm; she had taken off her veil and wore a hat wreathed with daisies, and her wedding gown. They would walk home for supper, beginning their married life, she said, as they meant to live it, simply and unostentatiously.

"Hasn't it," gasped Vicky and Fan and May and Lou, then collapsing into chairs, "been simply *perfect!*"

Weary in their finery, they reviewed every detail. Wasn't the weather, the music, the children, the late luncheon—wasn't everything perfection? Hadn't papa been lovely? How sweet Tina had been when she said—how lucky that just as the sandwiches—how pleasant little Mrs. Manson was! And Lola's uncle—extremely nice of him to come—he was really very nice——

"Oh, don't begin to clear things up, Lou darling," Vicky yawned, "let's eat sandwiches for dinner—if any one's hungry—I don't feel that I'll ever eat again! Wasn't my baby pretty good—he did let out one little yelp, bless his heart, but he always shouts that way when he hears any one talking."

"Too bad Davy couldn't come," May said, yawning too.

"He comes down next month, to stay," Vicky said, her bright face suddenly serious. "Darn the old dollar-eighty, anyway! It does seem such a lot to put into a ticket! I don't suppose he'll ever get home!"

"Will somebody have the extreme goodness to tell me," asked Lou suddenly, after an inspection of a ripped ruffle, "what is the matter with Alice?"

"I'm afraid she isn't very happy, poor Alice," May said amiably.

"She cried right through the service," Victoria contributed, frowning thoughtfully. "What's the matter with Frank?"

"Tight!" Lou said laconically.

"He won't let Aunt Lucy live with her, and I guess the poor child is a good deal cooped up, out there alone in the Mission," May contributed. "We never see them—I was surprised that she came to-day. She didn't seem one bit like herself."

"But where does Aunt Lucy live?" demanded Victoria.

There was a momentary silence, and then Fanny answered stiffly:

"She says she has friends in Sacramento."

"Who?" Vicky pursued, surprised.

"She says she has a position in the Post Office," May admitted noncommittally. Vicky, in some bewilderment, looked from one to the other, and laughed.

"Mama, why did you say it so funnily?"

Fanny pursed her hard mouth in a hard smile.

"I suppose there is such a thing as working in a Post Office," she said, primly. And suddenly they all laughed violently and long, May trying to restrain herself, Lou at first with a scornful smile, but in the end all heartily and together.

"Yes, and there are other jobs!" Vicky tried to get it said just before the gale, but it was no use, she was choked off by laughter, and could only faintly gasp, "Yes, and there—there—t—t—t—!" over and over again. "I was going to say that there are other jobs in Sacramento," she said weakly, wiping her eyes. This sent the others off again.

"I declare we ought to be ashamed of ourselves," May began roundly. But her voice faded mysteriously, and her bulky form in the gray silk began to quiver. "I don't know what's got into us all!" she sobbed, in a full flood of uncontrollable hilarity.

"Vic—Vic—Vic——" Fanny panted, suffocated, and buried a loud "Ha—ha—ha!" in her handkerchief. "I can't say what——" she whined, in a high tone that utterly convulsed Vicky and Lou. They buried their faces frankly in their hands with a sound like crying.

As suddenly as it had risen, the storm passed.

"I declare we ought to be ashamed of ourselves," May said again, huskily and almost steadily, drying her eyes.

"Well, I thought then that I was going to *die;* I don't know what came over me!" Fanny, similarly busy, added with a long breath of relief. Vicky, still with reminiscent breezes of laughter, went to get her baby, Lou trailing after. Fanny and May fell into a good-natured discussion of Nelly: how slatternly she was, how pathetic, how cheerful.

"It seems a pity that so many nice young fellows drink; it makes it so hard for their wives!" May commented mildly, of Rudy.

"Vick, tell me what you do all day long," Lou said, on the foot of the bed. Vicky, in the low, armless rocker that had crept so many miles over shabby carpets, with its freight of mother and baby, looked down at her child's head with a thoughtful smile. She had a vision of the dreaming, pleasant country town, of bridal wreath in the garden, of fish horns sounding lazily through Friday morning calms, of Minnie or Anita stopping at the gate to coax her into wheeling Taffy downtown, to buy a spool of pink cotton or a bottle of witch-hazel. At the Post Office, at the pharmacy, all the way down River Street, there would be news, friends, gossip. She might even see Davy, filling his old medicine case in the drug store or hurrying out to the Martinelli baby.

She thought of the kitchen, firelight, and lamplight, herself busy with coffee pot and kindling in the sharp winter mornings; Davy adoring and content over his second cup, Taffy riotous in the shabby high chair. She remembered the delicious sense of thawing in her cold fingers, the delicious beginning of sunshine across the frosted backyard and the steaming manure pile out by the stable, the delicious sweetness of Taffy, curly-headed and rosy from deep sleep.

But she could not tell Lou of these things, and so she only smiled, and shifted Taffy, and said vaguely that there was not much to tell, but that she liked it.

"And Davy?" asked Lou.

"I wish you knew how wonderful Davy is!" Vicky said quite seriously. "Lou, what about you and Mr. Tasheira?" she asked in turn, as Lou fell silent, and Taffy, refreshed and alert, sat up strongly, and gazed about the disordered room with starry eyes.

Lou smiled her inscrutable smile.

"Did you notice anything?"

"I did. I don't know that any one else did!"

Lou dimpled, looked into space, shrugged.

"Lou, do you like him?"

"In a way. Do you?"

"Well, I don't know him. He looks rather dark and small and foreign," Vicky said slowly, feeling her way. "I can't imagine him as a brother-in-law!" she confessed smilingly.

Lou got up and shut the door. Then, studying herself in the mirror, she said quietly:

"Well, you might just as well begin!"

Vicky stared at her in silence; her mouth opening for a word that failed her, her eyes wide.

"Two weeks ago yesterday," Lou stated cryptically, her eyes meeting Vicky's, in the mirror.

Her sister got to her feet, set the baby in the centre of the bed with a bracelet to rattle in an old silver mug, her eyes not moving from Lou.

"What!" she said, in a sharp whisper, coming to the bureau. Lou maintained her half-amused, half-indifferent, superior smile.

"Certainly!" she affirmed airily. "In the vestry of the old Spanish church on Broadway!"

"But—but good *heavens!* Didn't any one see it in the paper?"

"Apparently not."

"My heavens!" Vicky gasped, utterly at a loss. One could not take this self-possessed creature into one's arms for kisses and tears like Tina's. "Lou—why did you keep it a secret?" she asked.

"Well, I'll tell you. But come here and sit down, Vick." Lou drew her sister to the old bed, where they had sat together for confidences many years before, and where Vicky could keep a hand on Taffy's skirts. "In the first place," Lou confessed, in a low tone, "I didn't know it was going to happen. He's very odd, Señor Tasheira, and in a way he was—well, not exactly afraid, but he didn't want all the talk and fuss—Lola would have been furious, and the old Señoritas are sick, do you see? Well, on Fridays we have been having all sorts of little trips, he and I—did you know that?"

"Know it!" Vicky echoed, holding her sister's hands tight, her eyes eager with sympathy and interest. "I didn't know you even knew each other!"

"We've been to the Cliff, and the Park, and the Mint, and over to Fruitvale, and everywhere," continued Lou. "I think Lola knows that—suspects it, anyway. Last Friday we were in Chinatown, and he asked me if I had ever been in the old Spanish church. I said no. He said, 'You and I will walk in there and be married some day, and then they can say what they like!'

"Just then a carriage passed; he hates walking, and he stopped the man. And at that instant he looked at me and said, 'Why not to-day? We can drive to the City Hall.'

"I had no time to think. I thought he'd change his mind long before we got there, but it occurred to me that it wouldn't matter much if he did. Mama and Papa weren't along to queer everything——"

"Lou!" Victoria said, with a shocked laugh.

"Well, they always do, you know!" But Lou's look was apologetic. "I'm awfully glad to talk to you about this, Vick!" she said, with a sudden break in her voice.

"Go on!"

"Well, we went to the City Hall. He—there was no love-making, you know. I didn't—expect it, in a way. I know what he wants, companionship—anyway, I know. We went back to Guadaloupe church and were married. He took me down town and we had lunch, and he gave me—look!"

And on the palm of her hand she showed Vicky a splendid brooch of diamonds and silver.

"Lou Brewer!"

"Isn't it superb? I went home," Lou continued. "But that Sunday—last Sunday, I told Bertie I was going to be here with Mama, and Señor Tasheira told Lola that he had to go to San Jose. And we did, we went to San Jose."

"I see!" Vicky murmured, meeting her sister's significant look gravely. And buoyantly within her rose the old exultation: things were happening at last! Lou—Tina—good gracious, all the Brewer girls were married!

"Now we're getting everything in order for going away, and then—if there is much fuss—we can simply—depart!" Lou finished.

"To—where is it, Zanzibar?"

"To Buenos Aires."

"And Lou, are you thrilled?" For Vicky was sparkling and glowing with excitement.

"Well, I suppose I am, in a way. But the truth is, Vick, I'm like a person picked up at sea. I just know—that I'm rescued," Lou said, whimsically but unsmilingly. "There was nothing for me, except marriage, and there was nobody to help me! Papa and Mama mean well, but they have no sense. This is—I know what I'm doing! He'll never regret it."

"My darling! If you won't——?" Vicky whispered lovingly, a little uneasy at Lou's manner.

"Oh, I never will. The person who'll regret it," said Lou, with a sudden vicious closing of her handsome mouth, "is Lola!"

Victoria burst into a relieved laugh; she had not thought of Lola.

"Lou, isn't he very rich?"

"Yes, I believe he is. Anyway, when I spoke of Mama and Papa, he told me that I must help them, regularly, you know, now that Bertie isn't doing so well and Tina's gone. He'll do anything for me!" said Lou, simply and almost scornfully.

Victoria's heart soared; Lou married to a rich man! Arrogant little confident Lola so neatly foiled in this totally unexpected manner! The situation was not entirely ideal, but then what situation was? She carried her baby downstairs with a singing heart; life, at thirty, was lots of fun.

Stephen, with Bobo's eager help, and that of the two servants hired for the day, had actually put the entire kitchen in applepie order. They had scraped pyramids of plates, consolidated foods, carried away rubbish, and put napkins into the wash basket; washed and wiped and put away every cup and spoon, and brushed the floor.

Dear old Papa, with his apron on, and his mild beaming smile, and his curly gray head! No wonder the neighbours all thought old Mr. Brewer such a dear. Vicky would not eat. But she would sip scalding tea, and nibble nut wafers, as Lou and Fanny and May and Stephen and Bobo all talked together, similarly toying with the salad and the sandwiches and the reheated chocolate.

"Our darling girl will be in, in the morning!" May mused, happily. "Papa was saying that we must send some of the cake back to our bride and groom!"

"We go at ten-ten," Vicky said in a hushed voice, her ear toward the hall. Was that Taffy? No, it was a cat somewhere. "But I'll surely see Teen first!" she said, aloud. May eyed her speculatively. She wanted to give Vicky a little advice before she left. She must speak to Lou, too, about a little matter.

The chance with Lou came later, when Fanny and Vick, with Stephen, were out in the side yard in the lingering twilight.

"Lou, love——"

"Yes, Mama?"

"There was just one thing that rather troubled Mama, dear. About Lola's uncle—Mr. Tasheira. You didn't know it, Lou, but you rather monopolized him, it was quite noticeable, dear. Now he is an odd man, elderly and a little eccentric, and we don't want to make any feeling of ugliness between him and Lola, do we? You see, it's our Bertie's happiness as well, and

Lola was quite angry to-day—you were with him in the church and walked back with him—you didn't know how that would *look*, I know. But Lola will inherit all his money——"

"But Mama," Lou said mildly, slipping a handful of hot clean teaspoons into the mug that held them. "He's only fifty. He may live twenty years!"

"I know, dear, but he may not. Down south there—bull-fights and fevers and things," May said vaguely. "And as Lola said to-day, he is a man who never has married and never will, and who is more like her father than her uncle!"

"I see——" Lou conceded, with her mysterious half-smile.

"And you won't anger Lola about it, Lou? Because after all, she and Bertie give you your home, you know."

"I'll remember!"

"I have to take special good care of the one girlie I have left!" May said, playfully, following Lou to join the others in the yard. And almost immediately she found her chance for a little serious talk with Vicky. She did not like this plan of Davy's coming down to San Francisco, leaving his wife and baby with his mother. It *never* worked, May said. Members of a man's family always made trouble between him and his wife. Besides, so much liberty was a very bad thing for a young man in a strange city.

"Davy's mother may be a very excellent old woman," said May, "but she is only a farmer's wife, after all. There is no family, there, Vick, no *blood*, dear. You must remember that the Crabtree and Brewer families are the finest in the state, Vick; you could be a Daughter of the Revolution a dozen times over! You mustn't allow Davy to bury you in a little country town——"

Victoria's colour rose in a smooth, thin cheek; she looked patiently at Lou.

"I see, Mama. Well, but we hope Davy'll only be down here a few months, alone. Our plan is that I come down next summer—a year from this fall, anyway!"

"Don't separate at all, and don't have any member of his family with you!" May summarized finally and firmly "Promise me, Vick!"

"I can't exactly promise, Mama——" Victoria's mild glance met Lou's again.

"Then Mama doesn't know what is for your happiness—

Mama has had no experience?" May asked, hurt and annoyed.

"It isn't that.   But——"

"But Mama is advising you selfishly, for her own pleasure; is that it?"

"No, Mama.   But——"

May smiled, shaking her head gently to and fro.

"Oh, Vicky—Vicky—Vicky!   Always stubborn, always head-strong!" she sighed.   "Some day——"

Vicky kissed the creased, soft old forehead, between the worried, faded gray eyes.   Mama would be sixty next year; it seemed old to Vick.

"I'll talk it all over with Davy, Mama, and let you know!" she soothed her, amiably.   But to Lou, when they were walking to the gate, for a neighbourly word with Judge Dufficy and Edwina, she sent an oddly compounded expression of hopeless indulgence and exasperation, accompanied with a great released breath and a flinging motion of both her hands.

"Whew—!" said Vicky.   "What can you do?"

"What we have done, I suppose," Lou suggested in a demure murmur, meeting the callers.

CHAPTER XXIX

DESSY CRABTREE watched him coming along the highway: a bent, quiet little man, oddly hesitating in manner. She was not an especially observing person, at nineteen, but she was pleased with the world this morning, and perhaps a trifle more inclined than usual to notice it.

There had been long and violent rains, for weeks and weeks. But yesterday had had a wet and yellow sunset, embellished by the sudden note of a lark, and to-day was warm, cloudless, sweet, with balmy odours of saturated earth and green things floating lazily about. The grass had somehow found time, between deluges, to get a start; it spread an emerald film everywhere, and the locusts were in thin, new, unfolded leafage, and there was mustard bright against the old fence. Dessy sat on the steps at the side door of the building; George's repair shop was in front, their four little living rooms at the back.

The sunshine baked her slender childish shoulders; she could be lazy without self-blame. Next month the new baby would be here—the first baby; for the shadowy coming and going of her hopes a year ago had not made, at the time, a deep impression on poor little ashamed, confused Dessy. But she and George were exulting in this new prospect with a joy that was tremendously augmented, although they did not fully realize it, by what they had lost.

The man came nearer and nearer; stopped. He quavered a question; was this George Crabtree's place?

"Ain't he there?" Dessy gathered up her skirts and came about to the shop. It was open, but empty. She knew every oily nut and length of chain, every hammer and end of pipe and plane and clipper within it; she knew the dark, stained tables littered with bits of leather and nails, and the calendar with the rosy fruit, on the wall, and the flat-sided pencils, and the disorderly papers and bills on a file, and the chipped, discoloured stools, and the frail new cobweb on the window she tried to keep clean.

George was nowhere in sight.

"That's right; he had to go to Santa Clara! Did you want something done to a wheel?" asked Dessy, smiling sympathetically at the tired little friendly stranger.

"No. I guess I'll just wait," he said, rather timidly.

"Wait round here, then!" Dessy said hospitably, leading him to the side door, under the great trees. He sat down, looking she thought, rather ill.

"I'm his father," the stranger said. Dessy did not answer: she looked frightened.

"It's kind of sweet here," Harry said, after a silence, a little frightened himself.

"We think we're fixed real nice," Dessy answered timidly. "George bought this place. He's doing real good."

They were silent, like bashful children. When the noon whistles shrilled at the fruit cannery, Dessy got up and went into the kitchen. Presently she came out to find Harry dreaming; she surprised him with a plate of food.

"Say, I wouldn't have had you do that for anything!" he protested, overwhelmed at her kindness. "You certainly are awfully kind!"

Dessy said nothing, but she felt less fearful.

He ate the fried egg and the stewed potatoes eagerly.

"You've no idea what home cooking tastes like," he said, gratefully. "I guess you're a real good cook!"

Dessy was pleased. She had not a great many friends in the neighbourhood, because she had so recently been the "Tate girl, who got into trouble with George Crabtree." And it was agreeable to her to have this mild, kind little old man helping her with the dishes and putting things in order.

They had just finished when there was a rattle of wheels in the yard, and George came in, amazed to find her in such company. He stood, tall and strong, shutting out the bright spring sunlight, in the kitchen doorway. Beyond him was blueness, gold, greenness; the full soft glory of the exquisite day. Chickens picked in the yard; the old horse turned in the shafts to look after his driver.

"Hello, Dess! Say——" And suddenly his puzzled look changed, and a sweet, boyish smile that Dessy had never seen, came over his dark, strong face. "Hello, Pa!" he said.

"Hello, dear!" Harry answered, smiling and trembling.

"I was near here, Georgie!" he faltered anxiously, "and I thought I'd come in and see how you were!"

Georgie kissed him in the old nursery fashion; Harry and Dessy watched him sympathetically while he ate. They did not talk much, George was not interested in family news, if Harry had had it. The eyes of the son, however, were fixed keenly upon the father when Harry told his own story. He had had a position in Los Angeles in a school, giving out books and pencils, he said, and then he had been ill, in the city and county hospital, and then he had worked in a restaurant.

"You've had it kind of tough, Pa," Georgie commented, finishing his coffee.

"Well, I got through it," Harry answered, smiling with wet eyes. His son's sympathy was sweet to him.

"How about having my father here with us for awhile?" George asked Dessy. "Could you stay, Pa?"

"I'd love it, George," his wife answered shyly.

"I'd—I'd be real pleased," Harry said, clearing his throat. The busy spring afternoon, the lingering twilight that followed, the chickens, the dishes, the talk with his son, seemed to Harry the happiest time he had ever known in his life.

"Mama write you about coming down here and finding out I was married?" George asked him abruptly the next morning, when they were busy over bicycle repairs in the shop. Harry nodded, looking uneasy.

"You mustn't blame your mother," he answered placatingly. "She had been kind of calculating on coming down to live with you; she was planning on opening a cake shop——"

"*Cake* shop!" Georgie repeated, astounded.

"Well, you know your mother, son. She hadn't heard you were married, and it was a hot day—" Harry gave his son an appealing and anxious smile. "She kind of started off wrong with Dessy," he pleaded. George looked at his father, small, eager, shabby, and his face softened.

"Dessy's good enough for *you!*" he said gruffly. "Now, I'll tell you about Mama," he resumed belligerently. "She came here, and nothing was good enough for her, and she called Dessy names! All right, if my mother can't get along with my wife, she can get out. I don't want to see her, and I don't want to write to her. I'm *done*. Dessy got crying and everything, and she was sick. If she had died that night, I would have—

well, that's all right. But I never want to see Mama *here* again!"

Harry nodded, sick at heart. He felt that he did not quite belong here, either, and when his visit had lasted for almost a week, he began to fear that any day might be the last.

Eagerly, he made himself useful, sweeping, raking, burning rubbish, watching the shop.   He fed the chickens, he knew every one of the twenty-seven individually now.   He held long talks with Dessy, who said that he knew more than a book.   And every time George said "Pa" with any particular intonation, he felt a sick pang of premonition.

One night, when languid springtime twilight was in the kitchen, and when the three were sitting long over asparagus and rhubarb and other springtime fare, Harry cleared his throat and approached the dread subject.

"I don't know but what I ought to be getting on," he began.

George, pulling on his pipe in the shadows, his wife on his knee, listened quietly. If Pa felt that way about it, that was all there was to it, he said. He and Dessy had noticed that Pa was kind of quiet——

"It isn't that, Georgie," Harry said wretchedly.   "But you and your wife might feel like you'd rather be alone——"

He hesitated, laughed nervously.

"Well, we *don't!*" Dessy burst out suddenly. And to his amazement, to his incredulity and joy, Harry realized that she was crying bitterly.   "You've—you've been to London and New York and all like that!" she sobbed, strangling, "but— but you *did* say you liked the chickens, and you *did* say that I and you would go to San Jose and get some roses! And—and George and I never had a ba-ba-baby!" hiccoughed Dessy, "and I can't—I can't——"

"See here, honey, see here, honey," George laughed, with shaking lips, as he took out his handkerchief.

Harry took out his cotton handkerchief, too, and wiped his eyes.   There was a silence, and then Harry spoke:

"Why, Georgie," he faltered, smiling, "why, Dessy! I should be real pleased to stay. I don't know as I ever saw a place I liked so much!"

"Thank you, Pa," Georgie said simply.   Dessy came over to kiss him, and laughed and cried, and Harry laughed a little and cried a little, too, and they were all deeply content.

Dessy's baby chicks were handsome young broilers, and her baby son almost four months old, on a burning July day, when Harry came in from the yard with a telegram in his hand. The kitchen, on the northwest, was cool until noon, and Dessy had watered the orderly dooryard, in the shade of the trees. But the scorching day lay brilliantly on the dusty roads, and the chain of eastern mountains quivered in a blue haze. The very shadow of orchard trees diffused a hot light. The village scarcely stirred; the baby slumbered in his crib in the yard, beads of perspiration shining upon his rosy little face and flattening his downy red-gold hair.

Harry, who had on oily overalls, tiptoed past the crib with a look of fatuous adoration in his face, and came to sit upon the step.

"Georgie gone?" he asked.

"He just stepped up the road with a fellow that had bust his wheel," Dessy answered simply. "Sit still, Pa, and I'll get you some root-beer off the ice!"

"I've got to dress and go up to the city," Harry explained. He put into her hands the telegram. Dessy read:

"Dearest Pa sinking, end very near. Be brave as Fanny and I are trying to be brave. Love. May."

The train was hot, and littered with papers and cracker crumbs and orange peel by travelling children. But Harry was possessed by a sense of well-being, and enjoyed the trip; he had not seen his native city for some time, and he felt the blowing hot gritty winds and looked at the gray, dingy streets of wooden houses with appreciative eyes. He had money in his purse to-day, and in a few days he would be going back to Dessy and the baby and Georgie. Thinking that he would go into Will and Finck's and get them all little gifts, he looked with deep interest at the shops, and the people, and the cable-cars, the blaze of midsummer flowers at Lotta's Fountain, the awnings so pleasantly lowered over Kearney Street. It was getting to be a big city, thought Harry, rattling along in a Valencia Street car to the Mission, and Alice. He had determined upon a brief glimpse of her before going to San Rafael.

He found her house with no trouble, although he had seen it only once before: a grim, gray, bay-windowed house in a row, with shades drawn against the afternoon sun, and papers and chaff blowing in a lazy eddy about the area door. He mounted the wooden outside steps; Alice's grim servant, Anna, opened the door. Mis' Babcock was in, she said. Would he step in?

Harry stepped into the dark parlour, with its iron carpets and horsehair furniture. There was a clean rodded grate, photographs on plush and wooden frames, trembling grass in a blue vase between two pink vases on the mantel. A scalloped cover of fine plum-coloured cashmere covered the mantel; a similar cover was upon the upright closed piano. Two patients, stern-looking women, in cotton gloves, were waiting for the doctor.

After a full five minutes, in which flies buzzed on the windows, and cable cars droned by in the street, Anna reappeared, and said that he was please to come upstairs. To his surprise and concern Harry then learned for the first time that Alice was not well; she was lying in her clean, flat, white bed in a dreary room over the front parlour. She wore a nightgown with a tucked yoke and long sleeves; her hair was in a long braid.

"Hello, Papa!" she said, trying to smile. But immediately she burst into tears; Harry sat beside her on the bed and wiped them away. But he could not express the distress and uneasiness her appearance and manner caused him, and Alice evidently had no intention of expressing anything but happiness in seeing him again.

"Well, dearie—dearie—" he said, over and over again, and over and over again she kissed him, with gradually lessening emotion. But even when she was comparatively calm, she clung to him still, and avoided certain too-tender queries with a quickly shaken head and a resolute stiffening of her lips.

They talked somewhat vaguely; Alice always with a nervous air of listening for some interruption from without.

Harry asked for his grandson.

"Artie—he's lovely," she answered, with a faint cloud following the smile in her eyes. "He's not very strong, Papa, and when I was taken sick last week, Frank took him to his cousin, in Berkeley. I—he's never been away from me before," she added quickly, with moistening eyes, beginning to beat lightly on Harry's hand, and fighting for control of her throat muscles, "and I felt very badly about letting him go—and about l-l-losing my other dear little baby, too!" she burst out suddenly, turning about to hide her face in the pillows and beginning to cry bitterly. "I—I want Artie so! He always comes toddling in here, in the mornings, over to me——"

Harry looked wildly about; this was terrible. She must not cry so! He patted her shoulder, crammed his handkerchief into the white, bloodless hand.

"Here," he said, in his desperation hitting upon the one thing that would reach her, "shall I see if Frank's come—shall I call Anna?"

"No, no, don't do that!" she stammered, instantly controlling herself, but with an effort he found it painful to see. "I'm—I'm all right!"

And she began to talk again of indifferent things, and did not cry again, even when he left her.

Harry walked away from the house in a rather depressed mood. He did not like her pallid, cool face, her nervous manner. Her very parting words—"Please don't worry about me, Papa darling! And please don't tell Mama anything that will make her feel she ought to come out here"—had anything but an assuring ring.

He pondered sadly on the change in her, as he rode downtown on the Valencia Street car; it was her illness, he thought, natural enough! She was nervous and unstrung. Harry thought that in the event of his father's death, or indeed in any case, he would see Alice again before he left the city.

At the ferry his memory was pleasantly stirred; he had made this trip many times, seen these hurrying commuters, the circling gulls, these jarring and jangling cable cars. The old candy man nodded to him, with a smile upon his pitted dark face, and one or two old friends stopped to speak to him.

Harry told them seriously that his father was low—dying, he supposed. He was on his way home now. He liked their concerned, grave faces, their nodding "Is that so?"

Presently, in the waiting room, Bertie joined him. Bertie looked older, Harry thought, his mouth was lined, there was gray in the thinning hair at his temples: he seemed genuinely pleased to see his uncle. He gave Harry the news; Grandpa had died at just noon, Mama had telephoned Bertie at the office. Harry looked impressed. "Is that so?" he said heavily, as the other men had said.

They walked on the boat together and sat talking of the old man. "He was quite a figure here, in the early days, Bertie,"

Harry said reminiscently, and Bertie said thoughtfully: "Yes, I guess he was!"

The very last persons to rush on the boat, almost missing it, were Lucy and Bob. Bertie met them at the head of the stairs, and all four sat together. Lucy looked florid, and was as usual somewhat oddly dressed; she was badly out of breath.

"Heard how the old man is?" Bob asked, and Bertie answered simply:

"He died to-day at noon, Uncle Bob."

"Is that so?" Bob said profoundly, after a pause. "You don't tell me!"

Lucy looked stricken. She had given Harry a kiss before seating herself, now they all began to talk of the dead man, of pioneer days, the stock market, of odd and fantastic and shrewd things Reuben had said and done, of the stories men told of him.

The boat careened mildly in the breeze from the Golden Gate; windows in Alcatraz flashed in the sun, the painted white rope of the rail moved gently up and down over blue water and over San Francisco's hills.

"Harry, it does me good to see you looking so well," Lucy said cordially, after awhile.

"I feel well, too," Harry responded. "You'll have to be coming down our way, Looce, to see how nicely we're fixed," he added dutifully.

"You see Georgie almost every day, don't you?" Lucy asked suddenly.

"Well, yes, I do, Looce," Harry answered mildly.

"Ever see his wife?"

"Sometimes. She's a nice little thing."

"She's pretty," Lucy said briefly, "and that's enough for a man. However," she added, "the climate seems to agree with you, and that's the great thing. No, I don't see how I could get down there. I'm helping Mrs. Hatch in the Post Office, you know, and I live with her. It seems to me best, just now, until you're able to live in San Francisco again, to leave things as they are," finished Lucy with her judicial, capable air. "Your health is the great consideration, you know!"

"Well, I suppose so," Harry conceded, sighing over a great wave of relief. He trembled for fear she should change her mind; reopen the subject.

But instead they were all silent, each thinking his own thoughts, and Harry was free to return in spirit to the little repair shop with the oily dirty bicycles leaning against the door, and the sunshine and shadow falling upon Dessy and the baby, under the elms. The mid-morning crowing of the cocks, far and near, the sound of Georgie's hammer and plane, the rise and fall of Dessy's half-articulated little song in the kitchen, all these came to him in a pleasant dream; his soul was flooded with content.

Bertie was in a deep study, too, but it was with stern, brooding eyes, and with a set mouth. Look where he would nowadays, there was small comfort for him. With Lola he had long ago come to realize that he had nothing in common; she contributed only one problem after another to his life. There was no companionship, no congeniality between them; they lived in the same house, but Lola went her way and Bertie his, and there were no more discussions and quarrels. Lola was incapable of consideration or tact; Bertie never spoke to her nowadays without carefully estimating first exactly what the effect of his words would be.

Bertie was a book-keeper in the catsup manufactory of Painter and Painter. He despised his work, it held no future for him. He wandered about the piers during his luncheon hour every day, and looked longingly at the busy traffic of the bay; the big liners, the coffee ships, the freighters that went to Guam and Lima and Astoria and Sydney.

"Grandpa's business was a wonderful chance, Uncle Harry," he said suddenly. "I wish I'd been older! There's no reason why Houston should have sapped it, as he did—we could have built up a magnificent trade! But Grandpa was pretty old, and Papa forced Houston out, and Uncle Bob out—just as he did you, for that matter! He liked the feeling of being the head, I guess. Poor Papa! It makes me sort of blue," Bertie added, "to see him puttering around at home and taking Mr. Tasheira's check every month!"

Harry withdrew his gaze from the rising roofs and trees of Sausalito, the shining stretch of marshes to the foot of the mountain. He was suddenly smitten with a sensation of real pity and affection for this subdued, quiet boy; even for Stephen, who had never been a good friend to the Harry Crabtrees.

Bertie, now that there was only one of the old Señoritas left, had sometimes thought longingly of the rancho; it must come to Lola, and what happier solution of their problem could be found than that he should live there and manage it? But Lola's utter contrariety had circumvented this; she had persuaded the aged Miss 'Cension to put in charge a handsome callow Mexican youth called Antone, and Antone, Bertie knew well, was mismanaging things in every way. Lola flirted with him, in her wild way, ignoring a pale Spanish girl who was Mrs. Antone, and the two Antone babies. The whole matter sickened Bertie; he hated to think about it.

"I guess he never meant any harm, Bertie," Harry said mildly. "Lou's husband has considerable money, hasn't he?" he asked.

"Millions," Bertie answered, sighing.

"Your wife gets her allowance?" Lucy asked interestedly.

"Oh, my, yes. He's very generous. He told Lola, when he and Lou told us that they were married, that there wouldn't be any difference about *that*."

"Did Lola resent Lou's marrying him?" Lucy questioned.

Bertie smiled his wise and weary smile.

"Oh, no!" he answered quietly, with a look of mild surprise. He remembered the scene still, with a shudder. Lola had never spoken to Lou since, nor been to his mother's house. Uncle Pio had come alone to the rancho to say good-bye to his family, Lou preferring to avoid the issue. Oh, well, Bertie thought tiredly, what was the difference?

They were at Sausalito, where his maid met them with Bertie's solemn little monkey-faced girl in her arms. Mrs. Bertie had gone to the rancho, Mr. Crabtree was please to take Nita to his mother. Bertie took the child eagerly, kissing her brown little face; she pawed his face with her brown soft hands.

When they got into the train he saw Kitty Barbee Powers with a fat, heavy-headed baby boy in her arms. Bertie joined her eagerly; the Powers did not live in San Rafael, and Bertie had not seen her for years.

Kitty, pretty, matronly, a little stout, admired his baby while he made friends with her silver-headed, tearful boy. She had an older child, she said, a girl. She was well. Neil was well. How were all Bertie's folks?

She seemed to Bertie everything that was gentle, womanly, and sweet; he liked her kindly, soft manner with Nita, he liked her voice. His solicitude hovered about her vaguely; he wanted to be sure life was kind to her.

"You look well, Kitty. I'm glad Neil's doing well. You certainly have a nice little boy," Bertie stumbled. "You—you're happy. I'm awfully glad——"

Kitty looked at him fully; they were nearing the station now, Bertie had told her all his news; they were at ease again. And they might not meet again for years.

"You know I left Neil," she said quietly. "I had to. Yes," she added, laughing at his expression, "I had to. He was drinking; you know he always drank. But after awhile I went back; I'd gone to his mother, and he came after me. Yes, I'm happy, Bertie. I have the loveliest children a woman ever had. I'm as happy as most people are, I guess!"

She was forcing on the baby's velvet coat. She kept looking up at Bertie with a philosophic and hardy smile, and looking down at the limp arms of the whimpering baby.

"Now give Uncle Bertie a nice kiss—no, a *nice* one, Neely," she admonished the child, "Give Aunt Kitty a nice kiss, Nita. Ah, that's a lovely kiss! and a bi-i-ig hug! Good-bye, Bertie. Give my love to your sisters, and tell your mother I sent my sympathy."

"Good-bye, Kitty!" Bertie went back to his own people, his old serious look returning to his face, his spirit sobering itself to meet Mama's first onslaught of grief.

Tina was at the doorway as her uncles, and Lucy and Bertie, came up the path. The shabby hallway behind her was full of summer-time gloom. Her face was radiant, solemn, sweet.

"Gone from us here, for a little while," she said, with her welcoming kisses, "but safe—safe above."

"Dead," Bob said, with a grave nod.

Tina shut her lips, nodded in turn.

"At twelve o'clock. Just like a weary child. Come and see Mama; she's being so *wonderful!*" she said.

May was in the back sitting room, panting, in a deep chair. Fanny stood at the window, looking out into the dry willows and peppers. At the sight of her brothers, May's fat, soft old face wrinkled into tears.

"It's just we four, now!" she sobbed. "Oh, Papa—Papa—Papa!"

"He went just like a baby, at about noon," Fanny stated, a

little huskily, beating her nose nervously. May hugged Bertie convulsively, her wet face against his.

"Go find Papa, darling," she charged him. "He's been so marvellous! I think he and Bobo are in the kitchen—my boy! Did Lola mind your coming up to Mama, darling?"

"Nope," Bertie answered good-naturedly and briefly.

"Lola doesn't let him come see me any more!" May said tearfully, to the others.

"She'll get over it!" Bertie assured her, with a faint impatience. He went to find his father, and May padded her eyes with a folded handkerchief, and proceeded to give her brothers an account of the event.

"He hasn't known any of us since last January, you know. Except that he would smile at us sometimes—and I think he knew Carra. Fanny, don't you think Pa knew Carra?"

"I'm sure I don't know," Fanny said with brisk firmness, from her chair, her heart hammering at the mere mention of Carra.

"But yesterday," May resumed, "yesterday he seemed to sink into a sort of *sleep*—he was eighty-five, Bob," she sobbed suddenly, "and now I'm the oldest—I'm the next one to go-o! And I can remember Ma and Aunt Jenny—when I was just a little bit of a girl, at Crabtree's Crossing——!"

"Ah, no, no, no, Mama!" Tina said tenderly, on her knees beside her mother's chair. "We're all here about you, dear, and Vernon was saying only this morning that we all looked to you for courage and help. *Please*, Mama——"

May grew quieter with an obvious effort.

"I hate to think of changes, Harry," she said plaintively, to her younger brother. "I've been here—this has been my home so long! I suppose I think of Esme," sobbed May, "all the associations!"

This, addressed to Harry, was nevertheless directed at Bob. Bob knew that Bobo was supposedly to inherit the house, and that May naturally feared that he, as Bobo's guardian, would rent it or sell it. He had not made up his mind what to do in the matter, and he would not commit himself now. But he felt sorry for May.

"Now—now—now, don't you worry!" he said, patting her heaving, stout shoulders. "Things aren't as bad as you think!"

May sniffed, dried her eyes, and tried desperately to catch

up with an undertoned conversation between Lucy and Fanny.

"Might as well be there as in San Francisco, which I've always hated," May heard. "Until Georgie's wife apologizes —climate, anyway—that's the main thing, with poor Harry——"

Under all her grief, May felt vexed. If Lucy was justifying herself for her perfectly extraordinary conduct in living in Sacramento, while her own husband lived in the same state, then May desired to add a word or two to that conversation, and give Lucy Crabtree a "piece of her mind." It was maddening to hear Lucy ending smoothly with a warning not to discuss it before poor Harry because he was a little sensitive about it, and to see Fanny, who hadn't the backbone of a mouse, nodding abstractedly in consent.

Fanny was abstracted because there was an interruption. Carra, weazened, trembling, half-witted old servant that she was, was the most important figure in this little drama, to Fanny. She felt herself shaking, when at this moment Carra came into the room.

"You Pa's dead!" the old mulatto wheezed, to Bob. "You's always his favourite, Mist' Bob. You step up and see whar he a-layin'!"

She ended with an eldritch chuckle. Bob put one arm about her affectionately.

"Yes, I know, Carra," he said kindly. "We're going right up."

"One thing you-all don't know——!" Carra shrilled, with her brown claws clutching spasmodically at her flat breast. "You-all think you smart, but Queenie Rowsey——"

Fanny felt the solid ground falling beneath her feet. Harry, Bob, May, and Tina all would hear! The next words would be Pa's secret marriage to this dreadful old creature——

"Never mind now, we don't want to hear about Queenie Rowsey," Fanny interrupted her harshly and hastily. "You told me an hour ago that you were going to lie down, Carra, and you've been in the kitchen with Queenie all this time—don't you believe one word of it, Harry!" she added agitatedly. "It's ridiculous! The poor old creature doesn't know what she's saying, anyway," Fanny went on a little more quietly, as Carra wavered away, "and listening to her's an utter waste of time!"

"Well, but—good Lord, Fanny!—you shut the poor old girl

up fast enough," Bob said, between surprise and amusement. "What on earth had she done to get herself hustled off that way?"

"Nothing at all!" Fanny answered, somewhat heatedly, and batting her nose. "But I get tired listening to her, that's all! Lawsy, I don't suppose we have to stand upon our p's and q's with Pa lying dead in the house!"

"Oh, hush!" May whimpered softly. Immediately they all went upstairs, and into old Reuben's room.

The oldest son of Annie Ballard and George William Crabtree had reached the end of his long pilgrimage. His chamber— that chamber that had been so oddly peopled with ghosts, for the past days of feeble struggle with breath—was silent now, and in stilly order. He had been seeing odd snatches of the eighty-five years come and go dreamily: San Francisco harbour filled with neglected ships, Lulu Potts in hoopskirts, with brown ringlets on her firm neck, fat babies in scalloped, sleeveless little frocks, dark men raging in the wake of the Vigilante Committee, ferry boats cutting their way across the bay for the first time. He had remembered prairie schooners, rumbling on in blowing winds and slashing rains; he had remembered a quarrel with the builder of the San Rafael mansion.

And finally he had seemed to see the smoke-seasoned main room in the cabin at Crabtree's Crossing, snow in a blue whirl outside, and laughing, perspiring young men and women busy with an odorous "molasses stew." A little boy had been lying in the gay calico folds of one woman's lap, looking at the flaming fire, drowsing and waking, and now and then his mother had put her young face down to kiss his little bandaged thumb.

How had he burned his thumb—cut his thumb? Or was it a bee sting? Reuben Crabtree, dying, more than eighty years later, could not remember. But he remembered the loving, plain young face, the drooping curls of dark-brown hair, the smile that bent above him in the warm firelight. And from this dream he roused to the last agonized need of breath—breath— air——

Now he lay still, an insignificant little figure under a straight white sheet. And Harry and Bob stood still, watching him with uncomfortable faces, not quite sure of what they ought to say, if anything—to feel, in any case. May sniffed audibly;

she was quite at home here already. Fanny had gone to lie down.

Bob thought, "I wonder how long we stand here? He was pretty small—Lord, how his face has sunk in! Teeth, maybe. No sense in standing here this way——"

Harry felt confused and a little sorry, but he thought suddenly of a bowl of cold mush that he had stuck almost out of sight under the porch, on a beam. It had been intended for the chickens. It would sour, this weather, and Dessy would need the bowl——

"Poor Pa!" he murmured aloud. And Bob echoed in relief: "Poor Pa!"

"I wonder if he doesn't know that we're all standing here!" Tina, who had come noiselessly in, said softly.

Bob and Harry sighed, and shook their heads, and for a few moments more they remained standing, looking very grave.

Sunshine battered at the drawn shades; the shabby old room was full of luminously swelling and receding lights. A few flies circled in the soft gloom, alighting now and then on the sheet. Life moved even in the motes that danced in the forbidden tiny shafts of sunlight. But Reuben Crabtree did not move, and Bob felt the muscles of his own face stiffen as he watched that immobile mask of sleep.

About Reuben were his household gods: a crayon enlargement from a photograph of his wife, her mouth firm over false teeth, her broad bosom ornamented with velvet scallops and ball buttons; the purple plush rocker; the walnut table with a marble top; the fringed receptable for newspapers; the china lamp with butterflies and pink daisies on the shade; the colourless dark carpet, and fringed window curtains of maroon rep. Among these had he moved for years, bending them to his comfort. Now any one of them seemed to hold more life than he.

"We must all come to it," sighed May, on a long, hitching breath.

"I suppose so!" Bob found that his dry throat made only a confused sound. "I suppose so!" he said louder, clearing his throat.

Awkwardly and mournfully they filed from the room.

Fanny was dutifully lying down, but her thoughts were in an agony of hurry and confusion. No bodily rest was possible while they raced and tumbled so maddeningly. It was six o'clock; she had had little to eat, all day, and her head ached. Terrifying visions possessed her.

She had known Pa's secret all these years. Could they arrest her for that? Well, if they did, she would simply serve her term and come out again. A lot she cared what people thought! She would have Aunt Jenny's money—anyway——

A disturbing thought came to her; where had she heard the expression "lawyer's fees and costs"? Might they force her to pay these?

And the newspaper headlines! "Death Bares Secret Marriage." There would be a Crabtree scandal, like the Baker scandal. Poor Lily and Daisy Baker had inherited nothing, after all, and Lily, people said, had gotten her divorce because Elmer Duvalette acted so disgracefully about it. A mulatto—Mrs. Reuben Crabtree! It wasn't bearable——

Of Queenie Rowsey, Fanny thought with something like hatred. The stupid, big young negress had somehow gravitated to San Rafael, in the past year, and was doing day's work. She had been employed in May's kitchen since yesterday. Fanny felt herself hideously responsible for her extravagances and vagaries. Queenie was a beggar, a thief, an idler, a malingerer already; what would she be when she learned of the actual hold she had upon the decency of the family? Queenie inhabited a tumbledown two-room shack a few hundred feet away; it had been a builder's tool house, and why the Fosters left it standing, Fanny irritably wondered.

Pa dead—it seemed so strange! If Bobo remained here, and May and Stephen continued to live in the old house, Fanny saw no reason why she herself should not stay. She and Pa had been paying eighty dollars a month; half that would not be so much. Bob paid board for Bobo—but that would stop now——

She sat up, her heart thundering. There was a knock at the door, the round and shining black face of Queenie appeared. Fanny felt sick with apprehension.

"I ain' goin' to git nobody no dinner, Miss Fan," Queenie stated, entering. Fanny could only eye her in wild surmise. "I got to step back," announced Queenie importantly. "My aunt Carra she jus' lay on her baid, and pass out like she a baby—Yes'm, she daid. I walk home with her, en she sayin'

'Queenie, seem lak my haid hu't!'—en she lay down—frow her se'f down lak——"

There was more, but Fanny did not hear it. She sat staring at Queenie in an agony of apprehension.

"Mah husban' dat I ain' lef' yet," Queenie was saying, "he got a letter f'um Aunt Carra, en she say—yes'm, en she sign hit, too, she sign it 'Carra Normaysey'—dat's her name, Miss Fan, Carra Normaysey—en she say she want dat I should have her money and her furmcher en her clo'es, yes'm."

"When did she write that letter, Queenie?" Fanny asked with dry lips.

"She write hit on Sunday, when her haid feelin' queer, en she say hit's a las' willum tesmunt," Queenie supplied garrulously. "She a widow, Miss Fan. She ma'ied fifty yeahs ago, mo'less, en her husban' die inna *mines*," the mulatto added, chewing gum mournfully as she talked. "He name 'Quincer Normaysey,' cause Aunt Carra she have his Bible——"

She knew nothing. She knew nothing! Nobody knew now but Fanny, and Fanny felt the warm blood coming back into her heart. She put her feet to the floor, reached for her slippers.

"Our dear old Carra gone!" she said in a shocked and sympathetic voice. "Well, well, well. This will be a real loss to us all, Queenie, on top of the greater loss. Certainly, I will see that somebody gets dinner—you'd like your money now, wouldn't you? No, don't bother about the change—that's all right. Keep it. And let us know, of course—Mr. and Mrs. Brewer will feel so badly about this——"

"Albut goin' to see 'bout her fumeral 'surance," Queenie said, soothed and gratified, preceding Fanny downstairs, "en I reck'n we lay her with mah firs' husban'. Albut say she got some money in bank. So I guess I ain't come back to wuk for you, Miss Fan."

"That's all *right*, Queenie," Fanny assured her, with kindly heartiness. "Tina," she added, waylaying her niece in the lower hallway, "go tell your mother, dear. Queenie tells me that dear old Carra walked to her cottage, and lay down, and died almost immediately!"

"For Heaven's sake!" Tina ejaculated, wide-eyed. And immediately the elated Queenie was the centre of a sympathetic group.

"You know that you have our heartiest condolences,

Queenie," Stephen said, with his pleasant old blue eyes shining above his gray beard. "There was a time when we might have made you a more substantial offering, but——"

"It's the spirit that really counts," May said tenderly, and Stephen showed his full lower lip in a dreamy smile, as he nodded his head in assent.

Queenie departed, and over their quiet cup of tea a little later May told Fanny that she must have gotten some good sleep, she looked like a different woman.

Davy Dudley came in, serious and shabby, anxious to be helpful. Vicky was well when she had written, a few days ago, he said. The boy was splendid. Yes, he missed them both; he was busy, but it was a little slow. He sat between Vernon and Bertie, and May eyed them all with pride: three rather tired, somewhat uninteresting young men in the eyes of the world, but to her fond optimism three splendid sons. To see Tina fluttering over Vernon's cocoa shells—she would not let him drink tea at night—to have Davy's report on her grandson, and to speak of Lou as being at sea—dear child, she would get this sad news when thousands of miles away from home and family! —was soothing, even now, to May. Bobo sat next to her, and she mothered him tenderly; she meant to hold Bobo and Bobo's house, if she could. She was not hungry, but she ate something under Stephen's kindly sternness.

After all, there was not an adequate representation of the family at the funeral. Stephen was there to take May into church, Fanny was on Bob's arm. Harry walked with Tina and Lucy. Bertie was there for a few minutes, but could not even come to attend the interment or come back to the house; neither Alice nor Frank Babcock came, although—as May said apathetically— "it was in the paper."

Of the others, Lou and Pio were on the high seas, Georgie and his wife did not come from San Jose, nor Vicky from Napa, nor Lola from the ranch. Davy, who had said that he would make it if he could, but that he was busiest in the mornings, was considered to have an honourable alibi. From Nelly, in San Bruno, no word at all was received. Vernon of course officiated in the church.

A few of the old friends came; not many. Old Tom Wesley, who had been nursed through scurvy by Pa in 1863, and old Mrs.

Pembroke, and the Rossis and Fendersons and Cranes. But none of them followed to the graveyard; May assumed later that they all sensed that the family would rather be alone there.

And of this shrunken family there were even fewer present at the reading of the will, three days later. Harry, apologetic but firm, had gone back to San Jose on the very evening of the funeral. His heart yearned for his grandson, for his chickens, for Georgie's serious voice and Dessy's babyish affection. To miss three suppers, two breakfasts, three luncheons, was a real loss to Harry. He wanted his old clothes, his delicious freedom and usefulness. In San Francisco, he did try to see Alice. But the servant told him coldly that Mis' Babcock was drivin' with the doctor, she was well again, and the little boy was comin' home to-morrow, and with that brighter intelligence of Alice, Harry was only too glad to hurry to Fourth and Townsend Street, and leave the grime and winds of the city behind him again.

Bertie could not get away from business, and Davy's interest in the will of his wife's grandfather was so slight that there was no question of his coming. Vernon pleaded a sermon; he was represented by Tina, who brought the children, and occasionally interrupted proceedings by going to the door and whispering to them to be quiet—Mama was coming right out. Bobo was choo-choo-ing up and down the side porch audibly, as Mr. Saunders dispassionately proceeded through legal terms and repetitions.

The family, comfortably grouped, listened gravely. Stephen was in a large chair beside May, their hands clasped. Fanny, looking alert and suspicious, occupied an armchair, and continually adjusted a large cushion at her back. Lucy sat with her full firm arm resting on the table, her frog-like eyes attentive, her head judicially tipped to one side; Bob sat on the old sofa, listening, nodding, not too seriously concerned, but intelligent. Saunders, the old lawyer, was at the table opposite Lucy. What he read became less and less comprehensible to his audience; his words droned in the warm, shaded room.

" . . . in the event of the decease of the said Lulu Potts Crabtree previously to . . . hereby decreed and granted in compliance with the conditions of Article Four . . . not to exceed the sum heretofore mentioned. . . ."

"Signed: Reuben Elliott Crabtree Witnessed by Jerome E. Saunders, and Samuel L. Doggett."

"And there is an envelope here," said Saunders quietly, when he finished reading. "It is marked 'For Carra.' I presume we may open this. . . ."

He did open it: it was full of greenbacks. Saunders counted them quietly, in a dead silence. Everyone looked steadily at him, no eyes wavered.

"Two thousand dollars," he announced, with a great sigh. "Well, I think—since the old servant is dead, and no mention of her name occurs in the will," he added, thoughtfully, "that this will naturally lapse to the estate. I will deposit it with the other securities this afternoon. Yes. I can attend to that. . . ."

Everyone felt that this was a satisfactory disposition of this detail: Bob immediately possessed himself of the envelope and tore it into fine scraps; it was never mentioned again.

But the expectant tension in the room was not appreciably lightened. May and Fanny exchanged grave yet interrogative glances, even Bob looked a trifle nonplussed, and Lucy spoke boldly.

"But there's another will—that's terribly old. Don't you remember the will we all talked about—in the California Street house, that Sunday?"

Everyone felt grateful to Lucy for voicing this question; its propriety was debatable, but they all were thinking it.

"What is the date of this document?" Stephen asked.

May felt that wisdom had spoken, and said, "Exactly!"

"February 12th, 1871," old Saunders said. "Your father never signed the will I drew up for him in 1889. I reminded him of it more than once. 'Come now, Rube,' I used to say— he was considerably older than I was, four or five years, but we were young men together—'Come now, Rube, let's finish up this little bit of business.' No, sir; wouldn't do it."

"But that will is twenty-five years old; Ma was living then," Fanny protested. "I don't understand it——"

"I get the house!" May added, anxious but sure.

"Yes, you get the house, May," Bob assured her soothingly. Stephen, intensely puzzled, was merely looking profound.

"Bob, you get the Santa Clara piece!" Lucy exclaimed. She did not know whether to laugh or look apologetic; Bob had paid seven hundred dollars for Harry's presumptive interest in that property.

"Let's go over this," suggested Bob. "Just what did my father leave? The will is too old to be much use. You see he leaves his interests in the firm to my brother Harry and me—we were both with him then. Now, of course, he *has* no interests in the firm. He leaves the Filmore Street property to Fan——"

"But I understand that he no longer owns that property?" questioned old Saunders, who was rustling and glancing at papers in a business-like fashion.

"No," Bob answered frankly. "I own it. There were some old sheds on it that my father rented for stables, and he mortgaged the piece as heavily as it would carry. Some years ago, when he was going to let the whole thing slip, I assumed the mortgage, and he gave me a deed of gift. I've put some flats and stores, there," finished Bob.

"And now do those belong to me?" Fanny asked, with an eager glint in her eye.

Only May paid any attention to this remark. May looked interestedly and alertly at Bob and the lawyer, less hopefully at Stephen, and then with mild pity at Fanny.

"I get *this* house," she said softly.

"Your father managed his own affairs, very often against my advice, until almost the end," old Saunders said. "He had invested pretty heavily in the 'Three Toms' mine, some years ago, I don't think he ever lost faith in it, and I imagine that certain large sums, which he acquired from time to time, he paid into that for various assessments. He sold some of the property about this house—sometimes he had me invest it in bonds, sometimes he made no mention of it to me whatever——"

"Then there *are* some bonds!" cried Fanny. She felt herself an authority on bonds.

"There are eighteen bonds," Saunders said. "Those were left to your late mother," he told Bob, "I presume they will be divided among her natural heirs." He turned to Fanny.

"And I think some bonds belonging to you, under the will of the aunt deceased in 1876, are in your late father's safe-deposit box at the Bank, Miss Crabtree?" he said. "Did you wish them to remain there? Will you communicate with the Bank? Some of them are practically valueless, still——"

"Practically valueless!" gasped Fanny, turning brick-colour.

"You must be aware that several of those companies have been paying no interest for several years?" the lawyer asked mildly. "I have made a note here. The California Sugar Refining Company—sixes; January and July. Bought at 75; now worth 26. The San Joachim Fruit Company—fives. Bought at 71; now worth nothing. I don't believe that company will ever get on its feet again. The Pacific Light and Power is in pretty good shape—*fairly* good shape, and I don't think the Contra Costa Transit Company's bonds will go any lower. They've been at 62 for a long while—your aunt bought them at 95, if I remember correctly. Yes."

And Saunders took off his glasses and wiped them negligently with gentle little motions of a thumb and middle-finger.

Fanny sat dazed and terrified, as a general conversation went on. What was this hideous earthquake that threatened the solid structure of her world? How dared they say that Aunt Jenny's bonds—that precious inheritance that had coloured all her life—were questionable? She, Fanny, had done nothing to deserve this! She had not speculated, like other foolish women, she had never risked one penny!

True, when her half-yearly check had come in, of late years, it had been smaller than formerly. But then it had always come, and Fanny was thrifty, and had always managed to have a comfortable balance to draw against, at the Bank. Once or twice she had complained, years ago, to her father. "Hard times, Fan!" he had told her, chuckling. She had never had any further explanation. She had resigned herself to these unpleasant hard times, rejoicing in every item of her personal expenses that might be put upon her father's bills, and pleased when their return to San Rafael resulted in definite economies for herself.

But that anything could ever menace her capital was unbelievable! What was it to be rich, if this sort of thing might spring at one out of the void?

"Then I suppose I'm a pauper?" she suddenly interrupted the murmuring of the men to ask bitterly.

"No, no, no!" Bob reassured her, smiling. "You're just where you were, Fan. You'll go on getting your coupons cashed, just the same—your income's no less. It's just that a lot of those bonds have depreciated. See?"

"The house is mine," May murmured, to nobody in particular. The oftener she said it, the more secure she felt.

"This house, yes," Saunders took her up. "There is a mortgage upon it, I believe?"

"Oh, no!" May protested, aghast.

"There's a four thousand dollar mortgage; the place would be valued at about ten," Bob said.

"About *ten!*" May stammered. "Bob Crabtree—you know what this place cost? Why, it's a *show* place. It's worth forty thousand if it's worth a *nickel!*"

"No, no, May," Stephen corrected her mildly, "your father's been selling these lots for fourteen and fifteen hundred. We have two lots——"

"But the house, Steve, with the electric lights and the hardwood floor in the hall! And eighteen rooms not counting the cupola——"

"The house isn't worth much, May," Rob said. "It's pretty much of an old barn, you know. These wooden houses——"

"I never heard such nonsense!" May said indignantly. "A barn—your own beautiful home that your father built! And a mortgage—I never heard anything about a mortgage and I don't believe Pa——"

"You can pay that off with your share of the money," Lucy suggested soothingly. Her frog-like eyes were keen with interest and pleasure. Harry would have a slice of that legacy, too. As for the Santa Clara piece, for which they had received several hundreds from Bob—well, Bob was prospering, he was a well-to-do man. Lucy began to think about catching the five-fifteen train.

She and Bob left San Rafael together, quite openly, at half-past three. The lawyer had already gone. May and Fanny watched them go, Lucy stocky and dowdy, and yet somehow with her baffling air of alertness and young energy; Bob tall and lean, grizzled, and, as usual, utterly indifferent to appearances. Lucy was going back to Sacramento? Good, so was he. He kissed Bobo, Lucy kissed his sisters; they were gone.

"Well, I never saw anything as calm as *that!*" Fanny commented to May briefly. May merely raised her eyebrows. Tina, with murmurs and embraces, led the Yelland babies homeward. The sun, hotly descending, sent blazing shafts of light through the shabby old willows and eucalyptus trees; the carpenters on the little new house that stood where the old vegetable garden used to be packed up their tools and disappeared; the old house settled into afternoon peace.

Stephen, Fanny, and May sat down in shabby old wicker rockers, on the side porch. Now and then a wagon rattled unseen down the street, or voices and footsteps approached, grew audible, and faded away, from the direction of the sidewalk. Stephen was weary: he dozed.

Fanny was thinking hard, her eyes alert, her hard chin cupped in a hard hand. She would certainly meet Mr. Saunders in town to-morrow—nobody was going to get the better of her just because she was a woman! In any case, from now on she would handle her money herself, every precious dollar. Pa's death had always seemed to her as an indefinite point from which to date very definite changes. But these changes seemed oddly unlikely to materialize. Pa was dead, and Carra was dead; the exquisite relief brought by the latter event still possessed Fanny. In short, she reflected, as she grew rested and more calm, there was nothing really to worry about. Still, she seemed to miss some expected sensation.

"Don't get your feet wet, dearie!" she said crisply to Bobo, who was drenching the garden. Bobo looked impressed, and with his dragging hose, moved discreetly out of sight.

May mused also, with a surprising amount of content. It had always been a landmark ahead for her, too, Pa's death, attended by various apprehensions, hopes, questions. Now it was all over. There was no fortune to inherit, as there had been when first May's thought had begun to speculate upon the day when "something would happen" to Pa. That part of it had been alarmingly changed; May had expected the house, and Stephen the business. But the business was gone, and even the house anything but the proud inheritance she had thought it. A mortgaged old barn, indeed! It was preposterous!

Still, Mr. Saunders had certainly been extremely sensible about that envelope marked for Carra, and he would probably be equally considerate in the little matter of clearing up May's inheritance before she received it. There would be *some* money; Pa's illness had cost almost nothing, and his interment had been simple. He himself had erected the stone that now stood over both himself and Ma; it had been standing now for—May sighed—twenty-three years. How short they seemed, looking back; yet Ma had died a comparatively young woman, and Pa was old when he went.

"My goodness, Ma was only my age!" May reflected uncomfortably. She herself felt quite young, in her heart; a conviction of years was always most reluctantly forced upon her. "I'm a grandmother, too!" she reminded herself, suddenly struck with the familiar fact.

Pa dead—and yet the world was not changed! Things would go on just as usual to-morrow; Fanny would cut some roses for the Woman's Exchange, and whisk about in increasing excitement until she departed for the ten o'clock train. Stephen would read the paper thoroughly and edify his womenkind for the rest of the day with a hundred interesting items that had escaped them. Dear Tina would come over to wield a brisk glass-towel on breakfast plates and cups, while Vernon and Vera played with Bobo under the willows. There would be pleasant family discussion in connection with poor Pa's shrunken estate; there would be moments of debate over expenses. The mail man would come, and the fruit-Chinaman with his dangling baskets of figs and tomatoes and corn.

There might be one of Vicky's giddy spirited letters; or even a line from Lou. Now and then Alice and her husband and the little boy came to San Rafael for a Sunday outing, and they always stopped for a call.

And then there was always darling Bertie; so much more Mama's boy now than ever, when Lola had proved so—well, such a child. After all, he *had* been saved from Kitty Barbee's clutches, and Lola's uncle had generously taken for granted the continuance of her splendid allowance, even after his marriage. Bertie's problems, his mother was sure, would all "turn out right."

When all was said and done, she, sitting here wearily and comfortably dreaming, was May Crabtree Brewer, the head now of one of the oldest of the California First Families, and she had married off her three girls and her son; no old maids in her family! None, that is, except Fan, whose fortune was a pleasant thought, just now. Fanny might easily have been a burden, lots of unmarried sisters were! As it was, she would leave something to Tina's children—Vicky's children—or even to May——

"We'd be just lone women if it wasn't for Stephen being

here, so wonderfully good and helpful!" May thought. "I wish people appreciated him more; he seems to me *wiser* and *better* every day that I live!"

Bob would go on paying board for Bobo, that was settled. And the check would come from Lou. Fanny would more than pay her share, and May could pay off the mortgage and thus be rent-free. It would work out well; their expenses here were extremely small. Maybe some day dear Tina and Vernon would come and occupy some of the empty rooms; May was struck with this thought, and looked from Steve to Fanny for audience. But Fanny was deep in study, a somewhat contented expression upon her florid, harsh face, and Steve was lightly asleep, his parted red lips showing through his beard.

Silence. The last yellow rays of sunset dropped from the dusty rose bushes, and the dirty plumes of pampas, and the fallen bright-red berries of the peppers.

"Gracious, Fan, don't time bring changes!" May said. "It seems only yesterday that we had all the children here, and Esme's room and Pa's room just like all the rest, and ice-cream and layer-cakes on Sundays! And now they're all gone, Vick and Lou and Bertie—of course they'll come back, but there were so many years when it didn't seem as if we'd ever be separated! I can remember when we just heard of San Rafael, a place across the bay, where people picnicked. There was only one boat a day then, it used to take the buggies and trucks that were going up Napa and Point Reyes way! Don't you remember the day that you and I and the boys and Ma and Pa came over here with a picnic, and Pa said he'd like to have a home here! But that was more than thirty-five years ago!"

"Lawks!" said Fanny, tired, thoughtful, rocking in her chair.

"They don't seem to care much," lamented May mildly; "Vicky seems to think of nothing but Davy and the baby—Lou's just lost, and dear old Bertie almost never comes. And yet we've launched them all into lives of their own, Fan! Stephen and I never let our own plans interfere with their happiness!"

Bright day still lingered in the garden, but the sunlight was gone. Bobo was on the windmill ladder, dangling a tied paper that blew idly in the fitful breeze. The day had been warm, but there was peace and quiet and coolness now.

"I remember the day Esme was seven," May said, slowly. "Bertie was five, and Vick four, and Tina was such a lovely baby.

It was the day before Lou was born—their birthdays came to-gether. And I remember Ma——"

"Don't cry, May," Fanny said kindly, as her sister's voice thickened and was still. "You're still all shaken up from Pa's going."

"It isn't that," May said, after a silence. "But I've always felt that everything would be different when Pa died. But what with all of them in Napa and Buenos Aires and Sausalito and dear knows where, and Alice and Nelly not coming, and Bertie not here—it doesn't seem to make any difference at all!"

"I was thinking that," Fanny mused. "But I suppose it'll be like this to their children when—well, when you and I die, May!" she added.

May looked struck.

"Yes, I suppose it'll be like that!" she agreed.

"Do you remember leaving Saint Joe, Fanny? The oxen we used to call Pete and Lady? Remember the time Pa said he'd tan us if we didn't quit scraping the sugar—the night the Indians were after us?"

"Lawks!" Fanny murmured thoughtfully, with a remembering face. "Can you remember Ma greasing Pa's and Uncle Lem's boots with mutton tallow, back in Polo?"

"For the land's sake!" said May, softly, shaking her head.

They sat on in silence. The garden grew gradually dark, and little Reuben Crabtree the second came up to the porch and roused Uncle Steve, who was dozing there, with a whispered suggestion of French toast for supper. Fanny and May presently saw the yellow streak of gaslight flash out from the kitchen, and mingle under the willows and peppers with the soft brilliance of the early summer moon.

THE END